PRAISE FOR JOHN J. DWYER'S *STONEWALL*

"In this remarkable novel, John Dwyer brings the character of Stonewall Jackson to life. The colorful and paradoxical man who was both an ardent opponent of Southern slavery and a loyal defender of Southern liberty, who was both a gentle teacher of the Scriptures and a fierce master of artillery, and who was both a forthright gentleman and a wily field commander vividly comes to the fore.

"Dwyer has a knack for dialogue, for action, and for presenting the paradoxes of both that great age of conflict and that great man who so dominated it. He has simultaneously painted with broad brush strokes and with an eye for intricate detail.

"This is a sumptuous, sprawling, and scintillating historical novel that you'll want to curl up with for many hours."

—George Grant
Author of *The Blood of the Moon* and
Grand Illusions

"In his novel *Stonewall*, John J. Dwyer makes one of the great heroes of American history accessible to modern readers."

—*The Daily Oklahoman*

"*Stonewall* put me to thinking about what it takes to lead a moral life . . . The world is a dangerous place for souls, and as we make our way in it, we could do worse than take advice from a Christian soldier."

—H. W. Crocker III
Conservative Book Club

"In John Dwyer's *Stonewall*, you'll find a riveting story of war, an absorbing history, and a tender love story. But, above all, *Stonewall* is the story of a man who could truly lead . . . because he was a man of character."

—Penna Dexter
Point of View Radio Talk Show

"I have rarely read a more compelling biographical novel. Dwyer's writing keeps the reader coming back for more."

—Howard G. Hendricks

Robert E. Lee

HEROES IN TIME

Robert E. Lee

A NOVEL

JOHN J. DWYER

BROADMAN
& HOLMAN
PUBLISHERS

Nashville, Tennessee

Published by Broadman & Holman Publishers,
Nashville, Tennessee

Dewey Decimal Classification: 813
Subject Heading: HISTORICAL FICTION

All Scripture citation is from the
King James Version of the Bible.

2 3 4 5 6 7 8 9 10 06 05 04 03 02

For my darling daughter Katie

That is the land of lost content,
I see it shining plain,
The happy highways where I went
And cannot come again.
—A. E. Housman

PROLOGUE

AS IN THE BEGINNING, SO IN THE END AGNES'S THOUGHTS RAN TO Arlington. Always Arlington, her home. The remembrances were at once jumbled together and immortally painted across the valleys and ascents of her memory as separate, self-sufficient worlds of color and sweetness and love.

The fragrance of the juniper and jasmine drifting past the grazing sheep and up the hill from the river merged with the cameos of Annie's beautiful face—the most beautiful of all the Lee girls—yet stood strong and distinct on its own.

So did the chill that marched, sometimes when least expected, up from the river that ran along the foot of the hill and that would forever separate her and hers from all on earth they had ever known or wanted.

Mama's renowned rose garden, with its reds, pinks, and yellows—Annie's favorite—merged with and yet stood apart from the glint of Orton's steel grey eyes, his long easy gait, the sudden surprising power with which he could sweep Agnes, or the strongest thoroughbreds in northern Virginia, into his orbit.

And how dangerous that orbit could be. How unyielding and unrelenting and never-letting-go.

Just as the love of her father never let go. Too rarely did Arlington gaze upon his manly countenance. Yet he towered over all and any that would ever come near it.

She remembered his goodness and greatness and how he stood for all that was ever true and honest and just, all that proved pure and lovely and of good report. All that had virtue.

But the treasured pearls of one remembrance alone came always together—inseparable, indivisible, unconquerable, immortal. The day he returned home, in the year of revolution, after the long, long fight against the

1

dreaded Santa Anna in Mexico. It was the first time she had ever seen white in her father's hair. But then, she had been barely five when he left for the war.

That day's reunion would constitute her final conscious thoughts at her life's end. She and gentle Annie were picking apricots when he came riding up the hill—great rows of oaks and chestnuts and elms his towering escorts right and left, and ornery little flop-eared Spec the herald of his return—and dismounted his huge frame from his magnificent charger.

Orton's sister Markie, visiting from Washington upon hearing of the hero's imminent return, and Mama sat in the front downstairs foyer. Mama tended a cut on little Rob's cheek earned while fighting Santa Anna himself among the expertly formed battalions of trees crosshatching Arlington's apple orchard. When they heard the little girls' screams and Rooney's hollers, Mama looked up and cousin Markie sprang from the bench where she sat. Their eyes met, Mama's knowing and placid, twenty-two-year-old Markie's dazzling silver reflections of the lighted chandelier above.

Without speaking, Mama remained seated, conveying her permission, and Markie rushed toward the front door, opened on cue by Nathan the butler. Mama saw her beautiful cousin's tall comely figure silhouetted in the open doorway—tense, anticipating, without breath, and looking out toward him as was forever her place, as the younger woman watched her uncle offer Sam the reins of the rented gelding.

And then he picked Annie and Agnes both up, one in each hard thick arm, and he kissed them and told them they were *his* girls. Annie giggled and Agnes's eyes closed as his two daughters clutched him. He offered silent benediction to his heavenly Father as he felt their little hearts beating against his barrel chest and as the knot grew tight and climbed up his throat.

And then all was right. All was safe.

His name was Robert E. Lee, and he was their father.

PART ONE

"How are the mighty fallen in the midst of the
battle! O Jonathan, thou wast slain in thine high places.
I am distressed for thee, my brother Jonathan:
very pleasant hast thou been unto me: thy love to
me was wonderful, passing the love of women.
How are the mighty fallen, and the weapons
of war perished!"—2 Samuel 1:25–27

CHAPTER ONE

AGNES UTTERED SILENT THANKS THAT MAMA HAD STAYED HOME. Never could she remember a hotter day. But of course the day was oppressive in many ways.

Finally the black-plumed hearse, pulled by eight shining white stallions, appeared through the capitol gates. Agnes, and every other woman in sight on the capitol driveway where she stood and below, lowered their tattered fans and stared as the muffled drums continued the Death March. The marching brass bands had given up trying to play "Psalm 30" several blocks back down Grace Street because of the shrill sour cacophony the weeping of so many of their members had produced from their instruments.

What is that? Agnes thought, glancing around at the sudden sound. *No, the sudden—silence.* Thousands spread to the limit of her vision, down the capitol drive, out the gate, and back along the funeral route. *Grace Street, indeed,* she thought with sadness, *and how much grace have we seen since this war began?* Before the thought even completed itself, she chided herself for it, thinking of her poor dear father, with his still-hurt hands, both broken in the fall during the Sharpsburg campaign last year, the persistent labored breathing and chest pains. Why, so heavy was his responsibility, he could not even leave his post up on the Rappahannock for a few hours to attend this, the most important event in the history of Richmond.

How can it be so quiet with so many? she wondered. Even the drums had stopped.

Then she noticed the assembled leaders of her Confederate nation. The soldiers—Longstreet, the peg-legged Ewell, the ring-curled Pickett. The statesmen—grave sallow-faced President Davis, frail, sickly Vice President Stephens, the entire Cabinet and Congress. And the people—*oh, the people!* She wanted to weep as she observed the crowd, among them many of Richmond's—and

4

Virginia's—greatest, with nary a new dress or frock coat, nor even an old one not worn or frayed or faded.

Now the strapping Longstreet and the other pallbearers were lifting the flag-draped coffin from the hearse. *The new Confederate national standard,* Agnes realized. The Stainless Banner, brilliant white save for the Southern Cross in the upper left corner. *How appropriate that the Stainless Banner should grace the coffin of what the Washington papers call the Confederacy's "bravest, noblest, and purest defender,"* she thought.

She did not know that the President of the United States, Abraham Lincoln, had promptly written that Washington editor and thanked him "for the excellent and manly article . . ." Nor did she know that the flag had been intended to fly above the Confederate capitol building and was the *first* of the new design ever produced.

Finally Agnes was inside the Confederate House of Representatives building, the old Virginia Senate Chamber, following the long procession up to his open casket. She gasped upon actually seeing the sturdy, bearded face. Only then did the enormity of his loss strike her, and she would have fallen to the floor had not a one-eyed Confederate veteran in worn, patched—but clean—butternut caught her and steadied her.

Oh, Lord Jesus, she thought, the terrible understanding for the first time breaking through her tired mind, *he, our greatest—and our best—gone, gone from us forever. He, our hope, our destiny—oh, whatever shall our destiny now be?* Now the terrors multiplied, and she could not stem their assault upon her tender heart. *Brother Rooney, Brother Rob, and Papa in constant danger in the field. Even the most basic of food and other supplies exorbitant in price and hard even to come by. Not a word in weeks to anyone from my beloved Orton. And Arlington— oh, when will any of us see Arlington again?*

She saw then the bright mayflowers filling the general's coffin to overflowing, covering all the adjacent legislative furniture, and carpeting the floor in every direction. She gazed around at the endless procession of mourners, with their drooping shoulders, shuffling feet, gaunt countenances, and shattered hopes. *How much we loved him, our defender, our protector, our champion!* she marveled. *Truly, he was the people's hero—all the people, rich and poor, great and small.*

And then she dropped her mayflower into the coffin.

By day's end, twenty thousand people would file solemnly and tearfully by the flower-strewn bier. The earlier quiet would give way to such demonstrations of wrenching corporate sobbing that as Agnes returned to her home it seemed as though all of Virginia were weeping forlorn tears onto those sad, scalding city streets.

At last, at dusk, Governor Letcher ordered the doors closed. Minutes later the furious sound of a fist pounding on the front door and an aggrieved voice screaming at fever pitch outside resounded through the building. When neither government officials, military guards, nor anything else could be done to assuage the tardy, importunate intruder, the weary and sweat-stained governor himself stalked angrily to the door.

The visage before him would last with Letcher until his dying day. There stood a grizzled, dysentery-ridden, one-armed Confederate veteran, wearing rags and soleless shoes. Tears streamed down the dark leathery face and he raged, "By this arm, which I lost for my country, I demand the privilege of seeing my general once more!"

Letcher's own eyes now blinded with stinging, unwanted liquid. He who had stood up to Abe Lincoln's demand that Virginia furnish thousands of her sons to aid in the suppression of angry South Carolina in 1861 put a gentle arm around the soldier's narrow shaking shoulders and escorted to the open coffin the last, but certainly not the least, person who would ever look upon the earthly face of the fallen warrior.

"Thus God teaches how good, how strong a thing His fear is," the famed Virginia theologian, the Rev. Dr. Robert L. Dabney, the general's former chief of staff, would preach a few weeks later to another host of twenty thousand at a memorial service for him. "He makes all men see and acknowledge that in this man Christianity was the source of those virtues which they so rapturously applauded; that it was the fear of God which made him so fearless of all else; that it was the love of God which animated his energies.

"Even the profane admit, in their hearts, this explanation of his power, and are prompt to declare that it was his religion that made him what he was," Dabney concluded. "His life is God's lesson, teaching that 'Righteousness exalteth a nation.'"

General Robert E. Lee was fresh from his greatest victory of the war and preparing for a second invasion of the North when he received the news. As was his way, his outer demeanor remained sure and steady until he was alone in his tent with his old West Point comrade and now artillery chief, the Reverend and General William Nelson Pendleton.

"I am grateful to God for having given us such a man," Lee said, his stricken voice no more than a jagged whisper. "Such a good and great man." He wanted to speak again; his mouth attempted to form the words, and Pendleton leaned forward, straining to hear.

But no more words came. Instead the granite exterior of the commander of the fabled Army of Northern Virginia cracked and he burst into loud, long, weeping tears.

The world's most renowned newspaper, the London *Times,* wrote, "That mixture of daring and judgment, which is the mark of 'Heaven-born' generals, distinguished him beyond any man of his time. Assuredly the most fatal shot of the war to the Confederates, whether fired by friend or foe, was that which struck down the life of 'Stonewall' Jackson."

CHAPTER 2

THE BURLY MAN BEFORE HIM HAD PROVIDED THE PERFECT TWIN barrel to Stonewall Jackson's in the Army of Northern Virginia shotgun that had shattered a string of Federal commanders and armies in the Eastern theater of the War for Separation, now in its third blood-soaked year, and branded that Southern army as the fiercest fighting machine in the world. And James Longstreet carried with him confidence, long experience—including combat in the Mexican War of the 1840s—and a tenacious ability, once entrenched, to withstand Federal assaults of any magnitude. Fredericksburg, five months earlier, had been the latest example of that.

But now Lee had Longstreet and two new corps commanders. One, Ambrose Powell Hill, had the distinction of being arrested by both Longstreet and Stonewall, respectively, while serving under them. He had never commanded more than a division at one time. The other, one-legged Richard Ewell, had served Stonewall well as division commander but was chosen by Lee largely on the testimony of others. Lee barely knew the man.

Then there was Longstreet, who had never exhibited Stonewall's aptitude—or inclination—toward aggressive offensive movements. Now known affectionately as the "Old War Horse," the stubborn Dutchman was campaigning Lee that he, Longstreet, should be dispatched to Tennessee to aid the commander of the Confederacy's Army of Tennessee, Braxton Bragg, in dealing with the forces of Federal General William Rosecrans.

He was also campaigning, unbeknownst to Lee, with one of his new division commanders, Lafayette McLaws, to leave the Army of Northern Virginia. Longstreet chafed at the close proximity of Lee's headquarters to him in camp—though the Dutchman had just completed an ineffective stint when given independent command around Suffolk County—and he was not pleased at being left in command of roughly one-third of Lee's army, rather than the better-than-half he had formerly had.

Longstreet also seethed at what he viewed as Lee's continued predilection toward placing fellow Virginians in positions of high command. Both A. P. Hill and Ewell hailed from the Old Dominion. McLaws, a Georgian like Longstreet, and North Carolinian Daniel Harvey Hill, who had been Stonewall's brother-in-law, both ranked A. P. Hill but were passed over by Lee for him.

"I fear the current situation around Vicksburg must demonstrate the danger inherent to a splitting of one's forces before a superior enemy," Lee said benignly, hoping to assuage the big man's temper, which simmered like the steaming June 1863 day. "General Pemberton is all bottled up, and Joe Johnston cannot reach him with the succor he needs."

The thought occurred to Longstreet to cite Lee's spectacular splitting of his own forces at Chancellorsville, but he demurred, remembering his own view that many more such spectacular victories as that would leave the Army of Northern Virginia with a deathless record of triumph—and with no troops left to continue the fight for Southern independence.

"General," Longstreet countered, struggling to demonstrate the respect he truly held for his superior, "our only hope to hold Vicksburg, and thus escape the sundering of the Confederacy by Union forces, is to reinforce Bragg in Tennessee, defeat Rosecrans, and march my corps with Bragg and Johnston down to Mississippi to break Sam Grant's hold on our last Mississippi River outpost. That would, sir, allow you to maintain a strong defensive position and continue to retool the Army of Northern Virginia."

"While, I fear, that army starves for lack of provisions—and General Hooker continues to replenish his forces until they are even greater than before Chancellorsville," Lee replied softly.

Longstreet flinched as if struck. His great bearded head blushed crimson. His mouth tightening, he knew this battle was lost.

"We need not only food for our men and horses," Lee said, in the manner the apostle Paul might say, *Come let us reason together,* "but we need those people out of Virginia—and away from Richmond—so that our farmers may bring in their crops, and so that our people may escape the terror and vandalous depredations of our invading foe."

The gentle brown eyes kindled as Lee leaned his hulking upper body across the maps table toward Longstreet. "And thence the enemy's entire summer campaign will be thwarted and perhaps his troublesome forces far to our south recalled home."

Now the eyes blazed and the color rose on Lee's bronzed cheekbones. "And, God willing, our day of peace might be accelerated, as the peace movement that now seems burgeoning in the United States might be accelerated when those people witness our arms marching across Maryland, foraging in the rich granaries of western Pennsylvania, and, perhaps, threatening Washington City itself."

This last was freighted with passion and implication, marked by Lee's reducing his voice to barely more than a whisper.

For a moment even Longstreet was given pause by the audacity of the vision. Only a bugle from somewhere outside broke the deathly silence that enveloped the tent. Straightening himself, Lee's Old War Horse at length said, as though to a co-commander rather than his superior and elder, "I would consent to the Pennsylvania strategy, if with a view toward establishing a defensive position against which on the day of battle the enemy will again be drawn to spend his manhood in futility against our impregnable forces."

The point of his statement did not connect with Lee, whose agile mind already raced north to Pennsylvania. Had that connection been made, for good or ill, the destiny of the Southern nation might have proven quite different.

Poor fellow, thirty-two-year-old United States Cavalry Captain Wayne Marley thought with remorse upon gaining his wits after screaming awoke him yet again in the small hours of the morning. The shouts, pleadings, groanings, and screams of the wounded and dying rang from one end of the day to the other, each day, every day, in the enormous Federal hospital near the banks of the Rappahannock in north central Virginia. Usually some respite occurred sometime after midnight when the exhausted surgeons collapsed for a couple of hours of sleep.

How many did we lose? he wondered. Over twelve thousand killed, wounded, and missing, he had heard. He pondered the nightmare of Chancellorsville. The incessant throbbing of his shattered nose, the rawness of the throat through which he now had to breathe, and the limp arm that had barely escaped amputation—and the death that so often accompanied it—all bound him indelibly to that hellish deathscape of more than a month ago.

An endless series of horrific slaughters stretched back nearly two years to another day Marley wished to blot from his tortured memory—the First Battle of Bull Run, the day on which "Stonewall" Jackson was born—and now this, the most devastating defeat so far.

The loudest, longest shriek yet pierced the night air. Marley turned his head to the side, blind with tears. *When, oh when will I ever get home?* he cried silently. He thought of his friend and commanding general, Oliver Howard. Old Prayer Book. Routed twice now by Stonewall Jackson, the latest because he wouldn't listen to counsel. Marley remembered that Stonewall, too, had ignored the admonitions of subordinates when he pressed so far forward on the Chancellorsville battlefield at dusk.

Stonewall, who had been his friend and mentor since the two of them shouldered the cannon up onto the road and helped turn the day at Chapultepec—the day seventeen-year-old Marley lost his left eye—which helped win the Mexican War.

Stonewall, whose counterattack turned the day at Bull Run and killed Marley's beloved, betrothed cousin Joe Freiburger, and turned the Confederate war chief into Marley's implacable foe. For nearly two years, Marley had cursed Stonewall and prayed for his demise and death, even an opportunity to get a shot at him himself.

It had all come together at Chancellorsville. As Stonewall and Lee's outnumbered, underfed troops roared through the flanked, stunned Federal lines, Marley had twice been nearly killed himself. And then as the sun set on the smoking, flaming Wilderness inferno, Wayne Marley had looked up to see Stonewall Jackson squarely in his rifle sights. All the hate, all the confusion, all the mixed feelings, and even the old respect and love had boiled over in that instant as Marley lowered his long gun and let his old friend ride away.

Within minutes Stonewall's own men had accidentally riddled him with bullets. Eight days later, "Old Jack" was dead of pneumonia, brought about not by his bullet wounds but by a lung punctured when soldiers dropped him from a litter.

Old Jack, Marley mused to himself, thinking back through the years, the years when Stonewall had taught him to be a soldier, had paved the way for his acceptance to the Virginia Military Institute where he taught, had exhorted him to stand against the "demon rum" that had nearly wrecked Marley's life. When he heard the snores of the man in the next bed over, he remembered the other thing Stonewall had done for him. He had taught him the gospel of Christ, though Marley admitted, with a twinge, that his history of following it was checkered.

That snoring man, a Puritan sort from Connecticut—*that's a dwindling breed,* he thought wryly—had invited Marley to join his officers' Bible study tomorrow morning. Marley nearly had to remind himself that he had found Christ again—rather, Christ had found him again—of all places, out in that horrid Wilderness.

Yes, I need to be there, he thought, his eyes drying. *And I'll be there with the Bible Stonewall Jackson gave me long years ago.*

Agnes offered silent prayers of gratitude to God that her brother Rooney had survived the wound, and that so many of the family were now gathered in one place as mid-June approached. Soft sobs wafted down the hall to her as she prepared to descend the wide staircase of Hickory Hill, plantation home of her uncle Williams Wickham, north of Richmond in Hanover County. She looked back toward the room where she had moments before left beautiful, sweet, frail Charlotte tending Rooney.

How much she has suffered, Agnes thought, feeling a tiny stab in her heart. *I have lost Annie—but so has she.* Agnes remembered how gentle Annie, more than anyone else in the Lee family, had enveloped the shy, sensitive Charlotte with love and acceptance from the day Rooney introduced her. *And she has lost two children in the last six months, and had her husband nearly killed at Brandy Station by one of those ghastly new Yankee Spencer repeater carbines their cavalry uses and whose cartridges splinter and stay in the wound and work their wicked slow death.*

Now she heard voices from downstairs. Her mother and old Uncle Williams. Agnes canted her head to listen. *Yes, just as I thought,* she mused, *he is complaining anew about how little sugar she put in his favorite pudding last Christmas. Sugar. Whoever has sugar now?*

When she arrived at the bottom of the stairs, where the carpet was just as frayed as it had been all the way down, she discerned that the discussion was coming from the parlor. As she entered it, an eerie sensation overtook her. She felt acutely the awareness of the last time she saw Orton, in this very room. And something else . . . but what, she could not say.

Oh, Orton, she thought to herself, lighting upon a wing chair, her beautiful face betraying nothing of her ruminations. *Dear Orton, what have I done to you?* She grimaced as her venerable companion, the pain of her neuralgia, slashed through her cheeks, jaws, and neck. Neither her arthritis-ridden mother, herself now unable even to move from one room to the next without a rolling chair, nor old Uncle Williams noticed Agnes's expression. They were enmeshed in a passionate debate on the merits of peanut coffee versus the chicory variety.

That last night, in this very room, Agnes remembered. Oh, the night had started so well, with Orton so gallant, his old self. He had swept her off her feet and into the barouche. *From where had he procured that,* she yet wondered, *halfway through the second year of war, and way out at Hickory Hill?* Off Charles the driver had taken them, through the lovely banks of soft clean Virginia snow, to the Christmas party at the Woodwards. True, it was a "Poverty Party"—the guests giving gifts to the war cause rather than consuming refreshments—but the music and dancing and visiting had lasted till long past midnight. And never had Orton looked so dashing, so manly! Even the hardness that had overtaken his square-jawed face during the war seemed to have melted away. Not a trace of alcohol appeared on his breath any day of his visit, and his clear blue eyes betrayed no bloodshotedness.

Towering several inches over six feet, he nonetheless fairly glided across the dance floor, with Agnes in tow. She saw ladies, young and old, whispering to one another while following him with their gaze. Even the men wondered aloud at the lean, light-footed, tall blond captain with the handsomely cut, gray, broadcloth hussar jacket; red sash; and Wellington boots. The whispers told of his awe-inspiring heroism at Shiloh.

But then they had come back to this room.

Odd that it is how he was that I remember best, Agnes thought to herself. *How he was* . . . so much of life had she learned from young Orton in those years that he had practically lived at Arlington. She fondly remembered that dearest of places on earth and her play with Orton about its fields, her walks with him, and her long rides with him on horseback through its forests, along its streams, and across its pastures. Her sisters and the neighbors had all marveled that she—skinny, shy Aggie—would catch the fancy of the most dashing young man any of them had ever seen.

The pleasant visage painted across her flawless features turned, almost imperceptibly, as she recollected her father's ambivalent feelings about the brilliant reckless youth. "Yes, he is exciting and somewhat dangerous," she had admitted to Papa, "but he is brave and true and has a deep and tender heart too."

Her countenance grew solemn as she remembered how Papa's—*wise old Papa*—divinings had proven increasingly omniscient. Orton's darker edges had not come into focus until well into the war. Yes, she had always known that side was there—*that is the side for which he needs me,* she always reasoned—but when she learned that the gay cavalier energy could give way to dark inebriated brutality, when his generous and forgiving spirit had been lost to one who had murdered one of his own subordinates for defying him, and finally when his kind, compassionate conscience toward all things great and small had evidenced an irretrievable searing that had broken her heart to witness amid his shiny saber, jingling spurs, and martial airs . . . then had they come back to this room.

She remembered the letter from cousin Markie, who had remained in the North when war came, that she still clutched in her hand. "I long to see you all," the flowing words spoke, conjuring up visions of past pleasant remembrances at Arlington. "Have you heard from my dear, dear brother, Agnes? Do you know how and where he is? Do tell me everything you know of him. It has been more than a year since I have heard from him," the plaintive lines went on. "I wonder sometimes if he ever thinks of or cares for me. Please give much love to him and tell him I have written until I am exhausted of writing."

Nearly six months had it been since Agnes had heard from him, not since they had come back to this room and he had left angry and hurt and confirming of all the hesitations Papa had always harbored about him. *Not even misgivings,* she thought, *just . . . hesitations.*

Agnes's finely sculpted lips and mouth snuck upward again as she realized for the first time how often Papa had written her since the night Orton and she had come back to this room, ever so much more often than he had written before, though he had written often enough even before, considering he was commanding the Army of Northern Virginia in history's greatest American war. How sensitive and kind had Papa been in his letters to her these past months, how encouraging and affirming, how . . . how *Papa*-like had he been. Yet never once, she realized now as if struck, had her father even mentioned Orton's name in any of the dozens of missives he had sent.

Wise, loving old Papa, she thought to herself with a smile that contrasted curiously with the sorrow that beat in her lonely heart.

━◇ ━◇ ━◇

Lee leaned back against the wooden camp chair and watched Walter Taylor, his fine young adjutant general, leave the tent. The young man carried the letter the general had penned for President Davis. Even after poring over it for hours, writing and rewriting, Lee fretted that he had not adequately or persuasively conveyed his thoughts.

Despite the Army of Northern Virginia's stunning parade of triumph, Lee warned Davis that as the Confederacy's human resources dwindled, those of the North, despite huge losses, only grew as wave upon wave of new soldiers came into the fray. Only "such deliverance as the mercy of Heaven may accord to the courage of our soldiers, the justice of our cause, and the constancy and prayers of our people" could conceivably deliver the South from the inevitable consequences of its foe's advantages. And that, Lee did not expect.

Thus he exhorted Davis to make every effort toward a peaceful reconciliation with the United States, one which the Virginian maintained would be supported by a healthy percentage of Northerners. At length he concluded he had put forth his contentions as well as he could. They would, at least, receive a fair consideration.

As Lee's mind moved on to the litany of other issues pressing in on him, the dull hard pain in his chest returned. Breathing deeply, he thought, *And why should it not return?* "Fightin' Joe" Hooker, thrashed by Lee and Stonewall at Chancellorsville, still threatened Richmond, capitol of the Confederacy, from at least a couple of directions. This last was itself an additional source of concern. Lee no longer knew just how significant was the Federal threat anywhere. For the first time, because of the improving Federal cavalry and Hooker's near-paranoid commitment to the security of his own forces, Lee suspected, correctly, that the enemy knew more about his own operations than he did of theirs. Lee additionally feared that if he did not drive on into Pennsylvania, Hooker might fall upon Richmond in such force that the Army of Northern Virginia would be forced to turn back and defend its capitol, thus abandoning the invasion he now felt must be made for the continued survival of the Confederacy. Moreover President Davis tenaciously refused Lee thousands of his most seasoned troops, insisting they be dispersed for "guard duty" at remote locations. Finally, Lee must make his invasion with too many generals in too many positions of too much authority with too little experience to attack their powerful enemy on its own ground. But he had not the luxury to do anything else. He no longer had Stonewall Jackson.

Then there was the news he had received just days before. The Federal government had refused his cousin's tax payment—with interest—on Arlington. He now understood *those people* had no intention other than to take his home, which had belonged to the family of his wife's great-grandmother and her husband—President and Mrs. George Washington.

Taylor returned with a copy of the *Daily Richmond Examiner,* his smooth face pregnant with gloom. As Lee read the lead story, the dull pain grew sharp. Colonel Orton Williams had been arrested by Federal authorities in occupied Franklin, Tennessee, charged as a spy—which he swore he was not in a final letter to his sister Markie—and hanged within hours, on order of that faithful Christian general, James A. Garfield.

CHAPTER 3

ALL THAT COULD BE RIGHT WITH THE WORLD SEEMED TO BE so to Brigadier General James Ewell Brown "Jeb" Stuart as he rode out of Salem just after midnight on June 25, 1863, astride the great bay Virginia he had ridden since the loss of his beloved Superior at Chancellorsville. *The most that could be right, that is, with dear little Flora having been called home to her heavenly Father eight months ago,* Jeb thought with a wince.

Yet summer fields filled his nostrils with sweetness. He commanded the cavalry for the Army of Northern Virginia, the greatest fighting force in the world; he was heading straight north into the teeth of the invader; and he knew, as always, that his Savior was with him, "even unto the end of the world." And even after the near-calamity at Brandy Station a couple of weeks before. The largest cavalry battle in history they were calling it. Ten thousand Federal troopers under Pleasanton had ambushed Jeb's ninety-five hundred. It happened the day after Jeb paraded his largest-ever contingent of cavalry, and it jolted the whole South into realizing that new horses—well-fed new horses—and an endless supply of men, equipped to the gills and now experienced too, had achieved near-parity with the Southern cavalry. The South's fabled "Black Horse" had incited panic at the Battle of First Manassas and a host of other battlefields, but were now, in the third year of war, tired, hungry, and dependent on captured Northern stores for most any clothes, supplies, or weapons they received.

Jeb Stuart had those attributes so detested by lesser men—fame, success, adoration, and good fortune. So the struggle at Brandy Station had prompted for the first time a torrent of criticism that Stuart had "got too big fer his britches," "had one too many colors of sashes in his wardrobe," and "had started reading too many of his own press clippings." Most of the critics, Jeb reminded himself, either disliked him to begin with or had no idea what had really happened at Brandy Station. What had happened was a brutal, daylong fight, ended when the Confederates finally beat off Pleasanton—a West Point classmate of Jeb's—and his thousands.

The fight didn't end only when Pleasanton decided his reconnaissance was completed and withdrew. Also Lee never sent infantry to support Jeb's horse soldiers, the Virginian reminded himself. Those rumors were flying about among Jeb's detractors on both sides of the Potomac.

Brandy Station had been a jarring surprise nonetheless, and Jeb was itching to atone for any perceived diminishing of his leadership ability. He had not attained worldwide renown as perhaps the greatest commander of cavalry of the age by *not* setting out to prove something. Wise old King Solomon's words from Ecclesiastes, in the Old Book, were his constant companions in time of war or peace: "Whatsoever thy hand findeth to do, do it with thy might."

In line with Lee's orders, Jeb had dispersed the largest two of his five brigades to screen the Blue Ridge Mountain passes for the divisions of Longstreet, Richard "Old Baldy" Ewell, and A. P. Hill as they left Virginia, crossed Maryland, and marched into Pennsylvania. Also in keeping with Lee's written directives, as penned by Taylor, Jeb would lead the rest of his men northeasterly around and behind Fightin' Joe Hooker's northward-moving Army of the Potomac—which Jeb, Lee, and Stonewall had thrashed only the preceding month back at Chancellorsville—toward a rendezvous with Ewell's Second Corps on the Susquehanna River up in Pennsylvania. In further accordance with Lee's commands, Jeb would collect what information he could as he went—he received no orders from Lee to report the enemy's movements to him—disrupt Federal communication lines as able, and, especially, glean the rich granary that was southern Pennsylvania to provide for the thousands of hungry Southern soldiers.

Jeb had already sent one of his most dependable couriers toward Lee, immediately upon learning that Fightin' Joe Hooker had wheeled around and, with alacrity, headed north. But that courier was shot dead by a Federal sharpshooter. As he had carried his message only in his head, no one on either side ever received it. Lee did not know it had been sent, and Jeb did not know it had not been delivered.

Full of purpose and belief in his cause and devoid of fear, Jeb began to whistle a tune from Scott. Then he began to sing it.

> *Sound, sound the clarion, fill the fife!*
> *To all the sensual world proclaim,*

One crowded hour of glorious life
Is worth an age without a name.

●◇ ●◇ ●◇

How charmed had life been thus far for twenty-year-old Federal Captain Ulric Dahlgren. Even he reflected from time to time upon the amazing path that had arisen to meet him.

A man he seems of cheerful yesterdays
and confident tomorrows.

Six feet, seven inches tall, handsome, and blond he was, with what one Confederate acquaintance called "manners soft as a cat's." Ulric was also the son of one of America's most famous military chiefs, Admiral John Dahlgren, whose renowned Dahlgren gun was such a favorite of the U.S. Navy. The same admiral whose close personal friend Abraham Lincoln had hosted both Dahlgren men as his guests in the White House. And the president weekly visited the admiral at the Navy Yard, normally for nothing more significant than to share coffee, cigars, and opinions on military strategy and war news—and because the rough-hewn shellback provided an enthusiastic and trusted audience for the president's bawdy jokes.

Well Ulric remembered the day last May when he arrived in Washington City to find his father and Lincoln visiting in the office of Secretary of War Edwin Stanton. For nearly a year he had helped establish naval artillery in defensive positions around the capitol. Those duties ended with his visit to Stanton's office. The admiral had lobbied Lincoln to have his son appointed lieutenant in the army. The president had brought the request to Stanton moments before Ulric's appearance.

Stanton refused to grant the request. Instead he appointed the young man, who had been studying for the law in Philadelphia when war broke out and who had no prewar military training or experience, an aide-de-camp—with the rank of captain.

Ulric had validated the good fortune visited upon him by proving himself a stalwart soldier. His lanky frame rode with the German general Sigel as that man helped play the foil for Stonewall Jackson's legendary Shenandoah Valley campaign. He served in numerous other adventures as well, including the

Second Battle of Bull Run, or Manassas. Everywhere he went his coolness and wise judgment left their mark on his superiors.

The laurels began to gather about his name one frosty day last November after Sigel had assigned him to lead a contingent of cavalry into Fredericksburg, on the Rappahannock in eastern Virginia. Ulric rode his men nearly fifty miles through a curtain of snow, then charged them down Main Street in Fredericksburg, guns blazing and sabers flashing. The bluecoats temporarily scattered the sizable Rebel horse, gathered thirty prisoners along with information on Confederate troop dispositions, and returned home to Washington, covered with glory and national acclaim.

A few weeks later Ulric was in the front rank of Federals who crossed the river and forced the graybacks out of Fredericksburg, prior to the great battle on Marye's Heights, December 13.

Chancellorsville, like Fredericksburg, was a bloody dark day in the history of the Union—but not in the favored life of Ulric Dahlgren. So rough and ready was his mounted presence on the fields of Stonewall Jackson's last and greatest battle that he garnered a reputation among the Northern forces for volunteering for dangerous missions. He raced, saber gleaming, in a charge that brought his horse down, thrice shot, and nearly saw Ulric captured; earned plaudits in the nation's greatest newspaper, the *New York Times,* for his "cool and dauntless bravery"; and was applauded by his superiors, in the losing cause, all the way up to the commanding general, Hooker. That man singled out Ulric for his "zeal, efficiency, and gallantry."

Now June was ending as Lee and his near-mythic Army of Northern Virginia thundered north into Pennsylvania. Ulric, the energy of his keen mind cracking like a whipcord, purposed, as he was wont to do, to go beyond the norm, to accomplish that which no one else had thought to do. He sought and received permission to lead a detachment of Federal cavalry around to Lee's rear in a harassing action.

The steaming hot summer day had stained black the shirt of every man in the detail. Every man, that is, except their steady leader. Ulric had strung the couple of hundred men comprising his two troops out in a net across an area where they had reports of traffic from miscellaneous Confederate outriders.

"Captain, sir," the Irishman Connelly shouted, racing up, his horse skidding to a halt on his hocks. "We've caught us a Reb courier sure, sir."

The prey was snagged.

Ulric's clear-skinned countenance beamed. Without a word, he spurred his mount after Connelly. When they found the captured Southron, Ulric had Connelly shake him down. From inside a secret liner in one of his boots came the reward.

President Davis regretted to inform General Lee—in final and certain terms—that neither General Beauregard nor any further Confederate forces were available to support the move on Pennsylvania. Lee was on his own.

Ulric knew the significance. Union commander George Meade, for whom Lincoln had sacked Hooker, was known to be verging on apoplexy, not only over the invasion, but on the potential size of Lee's retooled invasion force. Thanks to Davis, Ulric knew Meade would be much relieved that the force would not exceed sixty-five thousand. Meade's was one hundred twenty thousand.

When the Northern newspapers caught wind of Ulric's capture of what would prove historic information, his national renown would mushroom in a Union thirsty for dashing young heroes, or heroes of any stripe.

A relieved Meade would now be able to form his plan of battle for the inevitable clash accordingly.

She would not think of Orton now, she told herself. She would think of him tomorrow and concentrate on today. That was what Agnes told herself each day, day after day, as the temperature rose and June ran down. Her mother's glances were few and her words on the matter fewer, but Agnes knew her heart was crushed as well. Mary saw more in Orton than had her husband, and the drawn look on her already-pained face, along with her decreasing movement, spoke more than words.

Truth be known, Mary had always loved the orphaned boy, seeing so much of her own beau in him, even if he was not made of quite the same stuff—or did not have Anne Carter as his mother—and even if he came to a different end.

But now Agnes had no time to think of her own feelings, her own hopes and dreams—*When will I understand the vanity and despair of placing expectations on this world?* she thought, hating herself even for thinking this close to the matter—for her brother Rooney had nearly died from the three jagged holes the shots at Brandy Station had left, entering and leaving his upper thigh. Nursing him back to health had exhausted everyone in the house.

Rooney's emaciated, bedridden form, illumined by the brilliant sun of a clean central Virginia summer morning, jolted Agnes anew as she brought him breakfast the morning of June 26. As Charlotte, her delicately featured face a ghostly white, cleared a spot for Rooney's breakfast tray, Agnes came closer to crying than she had at any time since the war began, including when—she caught herself—*anyone* had died. Could this be her big brother Rooney, raucous, reckless Rooney, about whom it was said that he was too big to be a man but not big enough to be a horse?

He had nearly died. So it was really no secret, then, why he should appear a mere shadow of his hulking former self. She would think of it no more, and she would not look at him, other than in the face. She would not consider it again today.

Even though the gunfire was hundreds of yards away, in the woods that stretched out from the Wickham place, Charlotte unleashed a strangled staccato scream of fright and buried her head in Rooney's now board-flat chest. More shots sounded, then Agnes's little brother Rob—detached from his Confederate infantry service to help with Rooney—bounded up the stairs, three at a time.

"Yanks, Rooney!" the nineteen-year-old's voice resounded even before he got to the room.

Rooney made a brief abortive attempt to rise but shook his head and wrapped his arms back around Charlotte's quaking body as she trembled and sobbed into his chest.

"Make a run for it, Robby," Rooney gasped. "It's no use for me. I can't even sit up." Charlotte's sobs grew louder, and Rooney stroked her lovely, thick chestnut hair, which ran to her pencil-thin waist. His focus was all on his wife. "It'll be all right, darlin'," he said soothingly. "They'll do nothing barbaric here. Not even *those* people would start a rumpus with women and children on the premises, and us Lees to boot, sugar."

Now Agnes could hear the pounding of horses, a lot of horses. She still held the tray. Through glorious beams that filled the entire room with their golden wonder, she saw blue-coated cavalry emerging from the woods. It looked like no more than a dozen. When she turned to put down the tray, something caught her eye. It seemed as though the woods had been lifted high and shaken, expelling dozens and dozens more riders.

"Run, Robby," Rooney blurted.

22

The boy turned, sprinted out, and flew down the sweeping tall staircase, his feet touching the ground no more than half a dozen times before he hit the main floor, caught a squirrel gun and cartridge pouch on the fly from one of the servants, and disappeared out the back door.

A few more shots resounded across the front lawn, and the earth itself seemed to tremble as two full regiments of Federal horse thundered around the Wickham big house and outbuildings, surrounding them all.

Uncle Williams, thick hickory cane in hand, rose from his rocking chair on the front portico as Agnes's sixteen-year-old sister Mildred rolled her wheelchair-bound mother back into the house. The old man walked to the edge of the porch and pointed his stick at the face of the Federal cavalry commander. All around him troopers flew from their horses, surrounding the house and rushing up the front steps past Uncle Williams and through the wide front entryway.

"There is a great arbiter of justice who weighs in the balance the deeds of men and nations," Uncle Williams spoke, his ancient voice spreading forceful and clear over the assembled host. "And He shall have a day of reckoning, and all those whose ways are violent shall go down into the innermost parts of the earth."

So forceful was the old man's proclamation that the Federals for a moment paused as one. Then their commander offered some silent signal and the commotion resumed.

Twenty to thirty troopers rushed up the stairs, their spurs cutting the carpets and chipping the polished walnut banister and the baseboards.

When they burst into Rooney's room, Charlotte let forth such an unearthly howl that the hardened soldiers, armed to the teeth, stopped, unnerved, in their tracks. Agnes stepped between them and the bed. Charlotte's sobs now took on more the tenor of eerie, cadenced growls as she clung so hard to Rooney that her nails drew blood out of both his arms.

"If you men are gentlemen, you will leave this wounded soldier, who can do you no harm, in the care of his grieving wife, who has lost both of her infant children and her home in recent months," Agnes said, her quiet spirit exuding a portrait of calm strength amid the chaotic scene unfolding about her.

The eyebrows of the lead Federal soldier, a blond captain, arched. Then his blue eyes narrowed. "Ma'am, that wounded *general* commands a brigade of Jeb Stuart's cavalry. Jeb Stuart is this minute moving north through United States territory, perhaps toward Washington City itself. Now I may not be able to stop that, but I can for sure keep this killer from joining them. Gather him up, boys."

"Killer!" The captain's tough countenance blanched. "You Yankees are the killers!" Charlotte shrieked, rising from the bed and flailing her tiny fists at the soldiers who surrounded the bed. "You've taken my babies, nearly killed my husband, and—"

A burly sergeant with a copper beard gently lifted Charlotte out of the way as the volume of her screams rose.

"Darlin', it'll be all right," Rooney said soothingly. Silent tears ran down Agnes's face as a half dozen Yankees lifted the mattress upon which Rooney lay off the bed and carried it toward the door. Agnes went to the semidelirious Charlotte.

"Let her go and leave this house now," Agnes said, looking up at the towering sergeant, her eyes aflame and her chin quaking. Her words at once arrested Charlotte's shrieks and unsettled the Yankee. He released the again-sobbing woman, who collapsed into Agnes's arms.

Down the stairs came Rooney and his mattress. The Federals marched him past his mother, whose face remained impassive as granite, only her eyes belying the grief and terror filling her bent arthritic body.

Out onto the porch they came toward Uncle Williams, who whipped around, cane in hand. He swung it like a battle axe and dropped the closest Yankee like a sack of bricks. He reared back to swing again when another soldier clubbed him from behind with his musket. Then as Rooney and the mattress passed and went down the steps to be loaded onto a waiting wagon, two other soldiers hauled the semiconscious old man up, dragged him around the side of the house and beat him until a sergeant pulled them off the still, bleeding form.

Uncle Williams would regain consciousness, but not for nearly three days. By then the one hundred or so Federal horse soldiers it took to overcome his hickory stick and capture Rooney Lee on his mattress were long gone.

◦◦ ◦◦ ◦◦

The effects of Rooney's wound and his devastating removal from the arms of his distraught wife had rendered in him a state of near shock. One image alone remained with him of his trip to the Pamunkey River landing dock where he would be loaded onto a ship headed for a Northern prison. That image was of the blackened chimneys he passed that stood as lonely sentinels amid the ash heap that before the Yankee torches came had been his beautiful White House plantation home.

Now Agnes rocked Charlotte like a baby on the one chair left in the room where Rooney had lain. She would not think of what happened today, of how her wounded brother had been taken away to a Federal prison camp and perhaps his death. Of how the best friend she ever had, gentle Annie, had been taken from her a few months ago down in North Carolina before she could even say good-bye. She would not even think of how she had broken the heart of the only man she ever loved or would ever love as a woman loves a man. And she would certainly not think of how she had never again seen that man before he rode to his death on a fruitless and suicidal mission far away from Virginia and Arlington.

No, she would not think of any of these things today or tomorrow either.

CHAPTER 4

MRS. ELLEN MCLELLAN CAME TO LEE'S TENT OUTSIDE THE southern Pennsylvania farming community of Chambersburg on June 28 because all the men in town were in hiding. They had no intention of coming into the clutches of the Rebels as retribution was meted out on them and their properties for the desolation wrought across the South by Federal troops.

Ellen herself, of vigorous Dutch stock, feared little on earth. But she did fear what was coming for her community now that the vanguard of the Army of Northern Virginia had arrived. And she feared what response might await her, a woman, from the greatest traitor the American Republic had ever known. And a savage at that, who not only had trounced army after army sent by the United States, but who was even now invading *Northern* soil for the second time!

For just an instant, she resented her husband. Yes, she had suggested—and insisted—that he hide with the other town leaders while she came before General Lee. But now, as Walter Taylor opened the tent flap—she noticed the letters *U.S.* stenciled on it—she was suddenly incredulous that Mr. McLellan could have allowed her to come here. *How could he?* she wondered. Then she was uttering a silent petition to God and following Taylor into Lee's tent. Her inner panic subsided a bit as the tall, barrel-chested man with the white hair, lantern jaw, and full downy beard stood, bowed, and offered his hand. Caught up in the sudden old-worldliness of the scene—and the stunning brown-eyed handsomeness of the fearsome Rebel—she found herself curtsying in spite of herself.

"Mrs. McLellan, is it?" Lee asked, the kind eyes seeming almost to sparkle at her. She barely had time to blush before he was asking, his brow suddenly furrowed, "I pray hope your visit, refreshing as it is for leathery old soldiers, is not occasioned by any misbehavior on the part of our men."

Ellen winced as if struck. This was not the greeting she had expected, and she hadn't the foggiest notion what to say, now that her stern, laboriously prepared inquiry—er, lecture—had been preempted.

"Please, sit down, ma'am," Lee said, motioning to the nicest of the three rude camp stools resident in his tent.

With no earlier intention of sitting on a scuffed old Rebel camp stool, she found herself seated—and receiving a mug of tea!

"Cream or sugar, ma'am?" Taylor asked.

When she looked to Lee in mute surprise, he smiled. "A notable benefit of leaving our dear Virginia is that one is able to offer a beautiful woman tea, if only in a mug."

"Sugar," she stammered to Taylor. "Two teaspoonsful?"

"Ma'am," Taylor answered, spooning the precious snowy powder into her cup.

Ellen had her camp stool, her tea, her sugar, and Lee's attention. Now she must have her wits about her.

"Thank you for your kindness, General," she said after two sips and another moment passed. "But I must bring to your attention that the confiscation of provisions by your men—courteous and restrained as they have admittedly been— has rendered no small number of our citizens in danger of starvation. I must ask what, as a humanitarian, if not a Christian, you plan to do to rectify this unfortunate predicament."

Lee's mouth dropped open. "I . . . I'm so sorry, Miz McLellan. We have all been marveling at the bountiful beauty of this fertile, untarnished country. I had no idea any such suffering could be afoot."

Ellen paused. She handed her tea mug back to Taylor. "General Lee," she said, "being a Virginian, no doubt you have recognized that harvest time is yet weeks away. Your General Ewell, polite as he and his subordinates were, has already acutely levied us. And now all the mills around are in Confederate hands." To her own surprise and embarrassment, Ellen's eyes watered, and her voice cracked as she said, "Might our people at least have a distribution of flour, sir?"

The speed with which Lee's large muscular body flew up from his own camp stool amazed Ellen. "They certainly shall, Miz McLellan, and more besides. Colonel Taylor, call for our quartermaster."

By the time the Chambersburg miller Ellen had summoned had completed his own requisition from the Army of Northern Virginia—and she had completed another mug of sugared tea—a host of questions were vying with one another to be asked of the traitor, General Robert E. Lee. He perceived her confusion and reached for a worn leather volume on his desk.

"Miz McLellan, our catechism teaches us that it is God who ordains civil authority, and that it is the Christian's duty to honor and obey that civil authority—even in 'enemy' territory," he concluded, a twinkle brightening his eyes. "Sadly, I command an army that itself verges on a state of wholesale starvation. We requisitioned in order to provide food for our troops so that they could be kept from coming into your houses. God help you if I permitted them to enter your houses."

Ellen gasped at the very specter of hardened killers, far from their own homes, running amok in quiet civilian dwellings. She did not know how common that very scenario had become in nearly every state of the Confederacy.

"A major reason for our coming north was to obtain food for these men," said Lee. His countenance grew somber. "And to remove them from our homeland so that their parents, wives, and children would have enough to eat."

Lee noticed Ellen's perplexed expression. "The hunger of our own families was most greatly exacerbated by our being nearby and consuming the food they needed."

Ellen had not read of that in the Pennsylvania newspapers.

Lee grabbed a sheet of paper off his desk. "I have ordered, Miz McLellan, that the Army of Northern Virginia shall only requisition items necessary to its operations and the physical survival of its men. Even these are to be formally requisitioned from legitimate local authorities or purchased and paid for in Confederate money."

He went on to explain that where Confederate notes were refused, receipts were to be issued, promising reimbursement to the property owner.

"I have reiterated my intentions with this order," Lee said, bringing the sheet before his eyes, then remembering to retrieve his spectacles from the desk and put them on.

"I cannot hope," he read, "that heaven will prosper our cause when we are violating its laws. I shall, therefore, carry on the war in Pennsylvania without offending the sanctions of a high civilization and of Christianity."

Lee then startled Ellen by handing her the document. "You may read it for yourself," he said simply.

She did. "The duties exacted of us by civilization and Christianity are not less obligatory in the country of the enemy than in our own. . . . The commanding general considers that no greater disgrace could befall the army, and through it our whole people, than the perpetration of the barbarous outrages upon the unarmed and defenseless and the wanton destruction of private property that have marked the course of the enemy in our own country."

When Ellen glanced at Lee, his eyes stared into space. He seemed to be somewhere else. In fact, anxious foreboding had swelled within him. *How have I arrived at Chambersburg without having heard a peep from General Stuart in nearly a week—and with not one regiment of cavalry present?* he thought. *Where are my eyes?*

With a jolt, she remembered having read somewhere that Lee's own home, a beautiful plantation owned by his wife's family—*something to do with George Washington?*—and the birthplace of all but one of his children, had been confiscated by the United States.

"It must be remembered that we make war only upon armed men," the order continued, "and that we cannot take vengeance for the wrongs our people have suffered without offending against Him to whom vengeance belongeth."

Mute, Ellen held the document out to Lee. Still lost in thought, he did not detect her movement. She stood and placed the sheet gently on his desk. She glanced at Taylor and at Charles Marshall, another young aide who had entered the tent some moments before. Then she turned back toward Lee and considered him. Her eyes narrowed, and her face twisted into an expression that suggested actual physical discomfort. *Such sorrow fills this man,* she realized, as if in a revelation. *And such strength.*

Suddenly she blurted out, "General Lee, may I have your autograph, sir?"

Lee snapped out of his fog. Shaking his head in wonder, he asked, "Do you want the autograph of a Rebel?"

After an instant, she noticed the twinkle had returned to his eyes. Her handsome chin thrust forward, she proclaimed, "General Lee, I am a true Union woman, and yet I ask for bread and your autograph."

Scribbling "R. E. Lee" for her, he said, "It is to your interest to be for the Union, and I hope you will be as firm in your principles as I am in mine."

A couple of days later, after Lee had headed east across South Mountain toward another little village where the Army of the Potomac and its new commander, Meade, awaited him, Ellen's fourteen-year-old son raced up on horseback and told her of having spied the Confederate chieftain from a rise outside of town.

"He stopped, Mother," the youngster said, marveling, "in the road, in the middle of the entire column, got off his big gray, and walked over to some bars, opening to a pasture, that his men had knocked down. He—himself—put them back up, then remounted and rode on."

"Perhaps, sir, we finally have the men we need in place," General in Chief of the United States Army Henry Halleck, relief washing over his perspiring face for the first time in weeks, said to President Abraham Lincoln.

Lincoln glanced at Secretary of War Stanton, sitting across the president's desk a few feet from Halleck in the sweltering Oval Office. The secretary offered only a half nod. But Lincoln knew such an indication from that hard, fierce Democrat was tantamount to a flowery speech from most of his Republican cabinet members. And it calmed the tall Kentucky-born head of state.

"With Grant and that rough-hewn band of lieutenants of his—Sherman, Sheridan, and the others—carrying the fight out west and George Meade now heading the Army of the Potomac, we shall soon see how long Bobby Lee and his Army of Northern Virginia can play out their string," Halleck continued brightly. "Especially without Stonewall Jackson."

The mere mention of that fearsome name drew the glance of Lincoln and Stanton. How well the president remembered long nights spent in this very room, on that old couch right over there, his brain aching and his stomach churning from the menace of pious old Stonewall Jackson as he rampaged through the Shenandoah Valley and elsewhere. As he flung shattered Federal armies out of Virginia and back into Maryland. How many times had Lincoln received reports of "Old Blue Light" crossing the Potomac *en masse,* headed for the capital itself? Thank God it had never happened—no thanks to Jackson,

Lincoln was sure—but the president would never again feel that Washington was completely safe from Rebel forces.

And somehow Bobby Lee had snuck tens of thousands of Rebels right past the main Federal army and invaded the North again! Fightin' Joe Hooker had done a solid job getting the Army of the Potomac out of Virginia and all the way north to Pennsylvania, where reports indicated Lee's corps were converging, but Hooker had now made the best contribution of which he was capable to the Federal war effort; he had submitted his resignation. With the Army of Northern Virginia churning through Maryland and Pennsylvania farmland well north of where Lincoln himself sat; hundreds of thousands of American soldiers already killed in this horrific two-year-plus conflict; his wife, Mary Todd, increasingly troubled over what all he knew not; and his dear son Willie dead these several months, which still felt like the jabbing of a sharp knife into his very heart, Lincoln found little solace in the changing of an army commander, but he did find some.

Even that melted into the steamy furnace of a midsummer Washington day when an aide entered the room with a report regarding Jeb Stuart and his Black Horse cavalry. Operating in apparent independence from the main Army of Northern Virginia forces, they had chased down and captured an enormous Federal supply train headed out of the capital for Meade's army, while cutting Washington City completely off from the main Federal army.

"And sir," the aide sputtered, attempting to maintain his composure before such an august audience, "one of our teamsters who escaped said he saw Jeb Stuart himself, only two hours ago, sitting astride his horse—in full view of our capitol dome—ready to ride straight for us, sir."

CHAPTER 5

COLE CULPEPER DID NOT UNDERSTAND GENERAL LEE AT ALL. How could such a great general fuss so much about religion? Culpeper had expected that this second Confederate invasion of the North would yield more success than the previous year's that had resulted in the bloodiest day in American history—and the drawn battle of Sharpsburg. But he also hoped that it would provide rich opportunity to exact retribution on the scurrilous Yankees for their rampage of destruction through the Confederacy and their multiplied terrors visited upon the defenseless civilian Southern populace.

Instead Lee arrested men if they so much as stole a goose that was not properly requisitioned from a Dutch farm or vandalized *any* property not deemed necessary to the Federal war effort! As he marched back and forth along the darkened picket line on the outer perimeter of A. P. Hill's position east of Cashtown, swallowing from his last chaw of tobacco—he never spat—and swatting at the invisible tormentors who buzzed around him and bit at the exposed flesh of his neck and cheeks, Culpeper seethed at the remembrance of the order itself. "The Commanding General, therefore, earnestly exhorts the troops to abstain, with most scrupulous care, from unnecessary or wanton injury to private property; and he enjoins upon all officers to arrest and bring to summary punishment all who shall in any way offend against the orders on this subject."

Lee's words to sixty-year-old Confederate General Isaac Trimble had cast the issue into more majestic relief: "I cannot hope that Heaven will prosper our cause when we are violating its laws. I shall, therefore, carry on the war in Pennsylvania without offending the sanctions of a high civilization and of Christianity."

Swatting at another flying pest, the rusty-haired Culpeper cursed and swallowed another gulp of tobacco juice. *At times like this,* he thought to himself, *it's*

*tempting to refer to Marse Robert by his old name of Granny Lee. How has he won
so many victories? Only because of Old Jack. How can we even hope to beat the
Yankees if'n we don't fight down and dirty like they does? That Lord Walter Raleigh
or whoever him and Jeb Stuart reads may be pretty words, but it don't win wars. If
he don't change his ways, we'll lose this war, sure.*

Before he could swear further oaths to himself and to whatever God or
gods had ordained this miserable world, Culpeper's ears, grown keen from a
lifetime of hunting and feeding off the land around his native Rockbridge
County in the Upper Shenandoah Valley, came to full alert. *Someone's approaching the bridge over the stream,* he realized.

"Halt! Who comes there?" Culpeper shouted, cocking the hammer on his
loaded musket and aiming by sound alone at the man's heart, all in a fraction of
a second.

Culpeper's sudden challenge startled Captain Ben Dancer, inspecting the
area pickets. Dancer had long amazed both subordinates and superiors at his
innate ability to string the most basic of profanities and oaths into the most
majestic of epithets. Now the unnerved officer stumbled and fell toward the
water, cursing and roaring the Lord's name.

With nary a pause, Culpeper turned and, swallowing, called toward his
mates, "Guess who's comin', boys!"

Thus far Jeb and his three brigades of cavalry had ridden nearly completely around the Army of Potomac; seized one of the largest supply stores of
the war, one hundred twenty-five wagons; captured hundreds of Federal prisoners; torn up miles of valuable Baltimore & Ohio railroad track crossing the
heart of the North from Washington City to the west; cut off the main Federal
army from communication with its capital (and vice versa), thus leaving its new
commander Meade in a daze of confusion as multiple Confederate forces
churned through Maryland and Pennsylvania; and drawn enormous attention
to themselves from both the Federal government and military that would otherwise have been locked onto Lee's infantry corps of Longstreet, Hill, and
Ewell.

With Lee's powerful force stretching from the Maryland border northeast
through the Cumberland Valley nearly to the Pennsylvania capital of
Harrisburg, Meade directed his main force toward Jeb Stuart.

"I can now only say that it appears to me I must move towards the Susquehanna, keeping Washington and Baltimore well-covered, and if the enemy is checked in his attempt, to cross the Susquehanna, or if he turn towards Baltimore, to give him battle," Meade, with difficulty, couriered to Halleck in Washington.

But Jeb was only beginning. Calling for one of his mounted harmonica-blowing troopers to strike up "Bonny Dundee"—

Come fill up my cup,
Come fill up my can
Saddle my horses
And call out my men . . .

—through sheer force of will, his own powerhouse physical constitution, and frequent petitions to God for strength and protection, Jeb drove his exhausted men northward toward his ordered rendezvous with Ewell's corps at York, twenty-odd miles into Pennsylvania.

A few miles north of the Maryland-Pennsylvania border, another of Jeb's accomplishments exhibited itself in an unwelcome fashion. Two entire divisions of Federal cavalry had been dispatched by Meade eastward to deal with Jeb, leaving only one with the main Federal force. One of these divisions, led by the swashbuckling, headline-hunting Judson "Kilcavalry" Kilpatrick, attacked Jeb at Hanover.

The fight was a rough one in unfamiliar territory. Jeb rode with his staff officers and couriers to an open field to watch. He grew nervous, knowing that many of his best men were not on the field. *Wade Hampton and his men are guarding the wagons, and Fitz Lee is off covering our left flank, toward the main enemy force,* he thought to himself. Just then two Federal squadrons—over a hundred men each—stampeded out of the smoky, swirling battle and thundered straight at Jeb. He and his men drew their pistols and began to fire, Jeb emptying his nine-shot LeMat revolver within seconds. The front rank of bluecoats and their horses tumbled down in a screaming, sprawling heap. But the men behind them were not deterred, and they stormed on. Jeb swung his carbine out of its saddle holster as bullets began to sing on all sides of him, and his men began to fall from their horses. He leveled the short-barreled gun at one Yank flying out front of the rest and knocked him cleanly from his saddle. Then the Federals were within thirty or forty yards, and the Confederates were tearing out in all directions. Only when all his men had fled did Jeb wheel and spur the long-shanked Virginia. She exploded ahead, quickly putting distance between him and his pursuers. But on they came, twenty of them straight for Jeb, firing revolvers and repeating rifles. Somewhere in the back of his mind Jeb thought, *Those boys are finally worth doing battle with.*

Just when he thought he was away, a wide gully appeared across his path, embraced on either side by impenetrable woods. *Deep it is,* he thought, *a running stream, and fifteen feet across.*

But Jeb Stuart hailed from Patrick County, southwest Virginia horse country, and he could know only one course of action. As bullets whizzed past him, he called to Virginia for her best, leaned low over her blowing mane, and uttered a quick silent prayer to his Lord, the sole source of his strength and courage.

William Blackford and several others of Jeb's staff sat silently astride their horses on a rise a couple of hundred yards away, now out of harm's way. A knot climbed up Blackford's throat. *Oh God, if the fall doesn't kill him, the Yanks will,* he thought, near tears.

Then Jeb and Virginia, to the amazement of all looking on, blue and gray, took to the air, bullets burning all around them, two clipping his saddle and one the long purple plume of his hat, and with a high, long Rebel yell, they soared over the gully. Virginia's legs hit hard on the other side, flexed but did not buckle, then she bounced up, and horse and rider raced away.

The Federal horsemen, suddenly at the gully themselves, two of them nearly sliding down the embankment, lowered their weapons for a critical instant, stunned at what they had just witnessed. When they regained their wits and again raised their guns, Jeb had disappeared into a grove.

Blackford and his men witnessed this as well as many other deeds of valor, chivalry, and derring-do by their captain. And for them all, and most of all because they knew he loved them, they loved him as much as brave men can love other brave men.

"I shall never forget the sight of this beautiful animal away up in midair over the chasm and Stuart's fine figure sitting erect and firm in the saddle," Blackford wrote his wife.

●◇ ●◇ ●◇

Before the war Wade Hampton was one of the richest and most powerful plantation owners in South Carolina—indeed in all the South. Like Rooney Lee, he possessed enormous physical size and strength. In his youth, he wove himself into the enduring folklore of the Palmetto State by his legendary sojourns into thick, dark woods, armed with a knife, looking for bears to fight. With no military training or experience but immense natural gifts of leadership and cool judgment, especially under hot fire, he had distinguished himself at a host of the current war's most fiercely contested battles, from First Manassas onward.

Now commanding a brigade and a formidable reputation as a leader of cavalry, he brought his men into the Hanover fray and slashed the Yankees back. The fiery Kilpatrick lost two hundred men, most of them belonging to the brigade of another horse soldier with a mounting reputation of success, the dashing George Armstrong Custer of Michigan and West Point, whose renown had already begun to gather about him as his long shiny golden curls clustered around his broad shoulders.

On his way back to the van of his force, Jeb came upon an orchard of cherry trees. The sweet fragrance filled his head and soul with joy. *He hath done all things well,* Jeb reminded himself. Then he spotted the twisting, climbing forms of his own lean men strewn throughout the trees, cramming their hats and haversacks with the precious fruit. He let out a delighted cry of laughter. Then gunfire cracked from behind him. A bold troop of dismounted Yankee horse.

Jeb could scarcely extricate himself from the predicament, so filled with mirth was he at the sight of his boys clambering, shimmying, tumbling, and leaping down from the prized trees. As minié balls whizzed all around, Jeb's laughter echoed off the surrounding hills.

"What's the matter, boys?" he called. "Those cherries sour?"

Kilpatrick, stung by the ferocity of Hampton's response, backed off, following Jeb's long train at a safe distance but not contesting him further.

Jeb had other problems than "Kilcavalry," however. He and his men had been in their saddles nearly continuously for a week. Even Jeb, whose stamina could carry him through days of vigorous exertion with little sleep while strong men around him dropped in their tracks, felt a dark aching shadow descending upon him. The merry cavalier lived his life in the light of the future and the opportunities for accomplishing good that it held. Now, though, as darkness descended on the night of June 30, the memories and brotherhood of his mighty men now gone washed over him like the final poignant bathing of autumn splendor on his native Piedmont before winter.

Sweeney, the peerless banjo player who had brought joy to the entire Army of Northern Virginia before he fell . . . jolly stout-hearted Prussian giant Heros Von Borcke, invalided out after being shot in the throat . . . handsome young adjutant Channing Price, killed while helping Jeb retrieve a cannon for Stonewall Jackson at Chancellorsville . . . and gallant John Pelham, the teenaged artillery chief whose valorous death had brought tears even from General Lee.

How I miss them all, Jeb, tired in body and spirit, thought to himself. Then, as he passed a burning Federal wagon, he pulled out the worn little photograph. Her likeness might fade, especially in the flickering light of the flames, but her memory grew only grander and more perfect, and along with it every precious moment he had ever spent with her. *I shall only see you again in the next world, the better world,* he thought, holding the little picture to his broad chest, *but you are with me always, little darling,* he thought, his throat tightening.

Then his best scout, in fact the greatest scout he had ever known, including Turner Ashby and himself, was next to him, calm yet alert, cool yet bursting force and energy simmering just beneath the surface. John Singleton Mosby was a small man in stature but so large in ability that he had become Jeb's chief scout, and whispers already abounded in the corps referring to him as the Gray Ghost.

In a flash the photo was hidden, along with the melancholy, and Jeb had a smile and a salutation for Mosby.

The Gray Ghost was sending men ahead to make sure all was well in York, the expected point of gathering with Ewell's men. But Mosby may have been the only alert man besides Jeb in the entire cavalry division. Rankers rode along dead asleep, some with their eyes wide open. Officers had to be shaken from slumber to receive reports. Men fell from their horses all night long, some not awakening even when they hit the ground. Jeb stared in amazement as one rider fell from his gaunt mount onto a rail fence and remained sprawled there, face up, snoring toward the heavens.

My men are on their last leg, the horses are half-starved and with no grain for days, the wagon mules are wearing out, and everyone is thirsty, Jeb thought, wincing, after Mosby had left. *But even if we ride into our graves in these lonely Dutch fields, I shall rendezvous with Ewell as ordered, and I shall deliver General Lee's men these fantastic provisions.* The remembrance of the one hundred twenty-five Federal wagons returned a smile to Jeb's face, and he vowed anew, *Never shall I let down the general.*

●◇ ●◇ ●◇

Even the Gray Ghost could not prevent the darkness that came with the dawn of July 1. "Sir," he told Jeb, saluting. "General Early has quit York for Gettysburg."

Exhausted and sleeping staff officers all around him, Jeb sat for a moment, stunned, as Virginia snorted, her belly empty. Looking around at them, he thought of how mightily he had striven to accomplish all that Lee had asked of him, of the steep price his men and horses had paid toward that objective. The troops were spent, officers the more so for having, with just as little sleep and rest, to push the troops to keep moving.

"But why were we not informed?" Jeb asked. "We couriered General Lee some days ago that we were swinging wide around Hooker, and they knew we were moving to meet with General Ewell's men at York." But he found reassurance in the steady, undaunted gray eyes of the Gray Ghost. *With men like this, we shall always overcome any obstacle before us,* Jeb thought, new energy and hope swelling his breast.

Then something caught Jeb's still-sharp blue eyes. "Captain Mosby, two of our men appear to be ransacking civilian property."

The keen-eyed Mosby, turning and squinting, could barely make out the scene, a couple of hundred yards distant.

"Sir," Mosby saluted, the mere flick of a rein conveying to his trusty mount to wheel and go. The Gray Ghost knew the men were to be arrested, like the others who had pilfered or otherwise affronted Northern civilians or their property. He had heard Jeb's words on the subject more than once.

"Any army who wars on defenseless civilians, no matter its excuse, is no army at all, but barbarians unworthy of the name Christian."

●◇ ●◇ ●◇

Robert E. Lee awoke hours before gentle breezes ushered in that fresh bright morning. As he did every morning, he put on his spectacles and read from the worn old volume whose embossed lettering could no longer be seen. Once it had read *Holy Bible.*

As in so many of the psalms of King David that Lee revered, the initial moments of his devotions and petitions were fraught with anxiety. Only hours before he had learned of Orton's demise. Newspapers North and South were sullen and suspicious over the brutal treatment of the young Virginian and his Confederate companion. A reporter for the *Detroit Free Press* who had interviewed Orton commented that he was one of the most handsome, intellectual, and accomplished men the journalist had ever known.

But Lee's heart pangs were for the living. *Oh Markie, oh poor Markie!* The grief had tumbled over him, bringing him awake and straight up in his cot as her comely feminine image faded into the shadows of his tent. "No," he whispered, wanting to reach out to her, "come back." But she was gone again. As had happened so many times, his sorrows drove him to the Good Book and the heavenly Father of him whose earthly father had left Lee and his mother when the boy was six years old, never to return.

How long since he had seen her? Or even received a letter from her? His correspondence with his cousin dated back to 1844, when Markie was barely eighteen. But he had not seen nor heard from her in over two years, since before the war began. The decision to stay with the majority of her remaining family in Federal territory was the most wrenching of her life. *How are you, my Markie?* Lee wondered, smiling at the memory of her and of the man she thought him to be.

Other concerns crowded in. *Where can Stuart be?* He had not heard from the "eyes" of the Army of Northern Virginia since he crossed the Potomac. *What of old George Meade's exact location—he could be anywhere between here and Middletown, Maryland—and how strong is he? I have always thought we would encounter those people in the vicinity of Gettysburg, and today we shall ride that way; if old George still hasn't found me, we'll go find him. And dear suffering Mary. Such a difficult road has been hers to traverse, and so often without me there to support her.*

But as with "the man after God's own heart," the unsettled sensibilities, just as they seemed certain to overwhelm him, bowed out of the path of an onrushing tide of calm serenity and the trust of a beloved son for the Father who has long walked both with him and before him.

He remembered the glorious sweep of religious revival that had spread through the Army of Northern Virginia, due in large part to the influence of Stonewall Jackson. *How valuable was he to us in so many ways,* Lee thought.

Somehow it seemed as though Stonewall was still present with him, even in the camp. *Certainly his influence and his example are,* Lee thought, smiling at the memory of the stern-visaged, kindhearted man who would slaughter thousands in the most powerful army the world had ever known, never batting his ice-blue eyes, then collapse in tears at the suffering of one of the many little boys or girls he had befriended.

So many more have yet to forsake their wicked ways, Lee thought with sadness. *Perhaps out of the horror and waste of this evil conflict a greater good shall emerge—the eternal deliverance of many whose temporal destinies shall find no escape.*

Then he was thanking God for the many saved souls in his suffering army *(Oh, for more men like the towering Presbyterians Dabney and Thornwell, Lacy and Palmer, the Baptist firebrand John William Jones, and our own gospel-preaching Episcopalian stalwarts!)* and that of "those people," and the memories of his beloveds, and that somehow he, who was so undeserving, had been spared the dark fate he should have received, and instead, perhaps, in some small way, was actually being used in God's service.

Within moments, he was taking a cup of steaming, but weak, coffee from Taylor and calling for Longstreet to ride east with him toward Gettysburg.

CHAPTER 6

HOW WONDERFUL TO BE BACK AT ARLINGTON! AGNES THOUGHT with glee as she dashed around the garden fence, the air redolent with the fragrance of Mama's roses. *Oh, will I get there first?* she wondered, calling upon her slender firm legs for more power. Glancing out of the corner of her eyes, she wondered, *Will I beat Annie—Annie?*

Then her mother was calling to her, or to someone. "Arlington—what have they done to Arlington?" Agnes shuddered upon realizing that distress filled Mama's voice, in the next room, speaking to her sister Mildred, "Precious Life," as Papa called her. Arlington was not in full spring bloom; it was covered with Yankee tents. And the ancient oaks and pines did not bless earth's most treasured acres with their cooling grace; they were now cut down by Yankee axes.

With a jolt, Agnes came straight up in bed. *No, I am not at Arlington at all; I am at the Wickhams. The Yankees are at Arlington, and Mary Custis is trapped behind Federal lines, and Precious Life is leaving again for school at St. Mary's, and Papa is away up north somewhere*—at this she felt a piercing pain in her chest—*my darling Orton is*—*No, I shall not think about that now*—*and Mama is weeping because the Yankees are getting ready to steal Arlington from us permanently because they won't accept the tax payment from my cousin.*

As she drifted to sleep the night before, Agnes had been remembering the joy of her spiritual conversion at age sixteen. Such a long pilgrimage it had been. For so long her life, so full in every other way, had been beset with a hollowness at its core that had rent her prostrate in despair at the insupportable weight of her sin. And then the sweet peace that finally stole over her, making her so very happy, calming her angry passions, and stilling her complaining tongue. The feeling of deep gratitude to her Father in heaven who had made her so wretched for so long to make her turn to Him, and to her Savior whose blessed promises of pardon and mercy to all who seek Him had raised her to hope and strive while before she was in despair at the awfulness of her sins.

Oh, she cried out to God, tears filling her eyes, where now was that joy, with all around her crashing to earth? Did other Christians, at first and for quite some time radiant with the confidence and joy of Christ's presence and leading, later sorrow, even to the point where their feelings seemed no different than those that possessed them before Christ's calling them to Himself? *Christ—yes, He sorrowed too, did He not, at the garden . . . sweating great drops of blood . . . was it truly blood?* She must remember to ask Papa when next she saw him . . .

But now a name she had never before heard was being uttered in the next room, the name of a small town in Pennsylvania where the combined legions of the two greatest armies in history appeared to be crashing straight into one another.

Just one more great victory, Papa had said before going north, and England and France will come in, the Northern people will have had enough, and we shall be free on earth as we are in heaven.

Her head lowered and her bottom lip began to quiver. *I miss you, Papa.*

Culpeper hurried back into camp, swallowing the juice of his favorite leaf as he went. Another July now set to work to melt away the cool sweetness that had marked the night and the advent of the day. The Virginian possessed the lean sinew and nervous energy for picket duty, and a country boy's keen eyes and ears for the night watches, but that didn't make him like it any the more, even considering that his division sat near Chambersburg, miles to the west of and across the Cashtown mountain pass from the front of the Army of Northern Virginia, posted by Lee in the stead of Imboden's cavalry, who had not yet arrived to secure the town. He almost would prefer being closer to where the action was, just to help pass the time of day some.

He scowled when Luke Gunter announced the luncheon menu to have returned to coffee—or whatever they called the unholy greenish-brown brew—and hardtack. What had happened to the fine victuals upon which they had been feeding during their northern sojourn? He watched Gunter gnawing at the quarter-inch-thick cracker of unleavened flour.

"There's a easier way to git that chawed, Lukey boy," Culpeper said, mischief sparking his emerald-green eyes. "Bite down hard with your gob and put your chin on that there stump, then I'll thump the top of your bean with a mallet."

The boys standing nearby laughed out loud, but Culpeper was already swearing a silent oath at Granny Lee for not letting him and the boys loose to forage for themselves. He was known to be one of the best foragers in George Pickett's division. For that matter, in the whole First Corps. Him and some of that Hood's Texans. *Why we oughter be able to burn the whole country right down to the ground up here if'n we like,* he thought, chasing hardtack down with the warm acidic liquid, *the way they laid waste to the Southland.* He was thankful the Yankees hadn't yet gotten to Rockbridge County. *Course, what'd they want with my little shack nohow?* he thought with a scowl. *Curse these rich generals and their kind that got us into this mess. And curse them bluebellies what started it all. I'm missing a lot of good fishing back home right about now. Home,* he thought, slinging his tin cup to the ground and wiping his stubbled chin with the back of a dirty butternut sleeve. *Heck, back home our houses ain't as fine as their barns are in these parts. And these Yank fences!* Cole Culpeper would never trust people who put up as many fences as these Pennsylvanians did.

Then he saw General Pickett ride by, surrounded by staff officers. At first he hadn't liked Pickett, with the slick way he heard he had of talking and his long dark curls that fell all the way to his shoulders. And those mustaches! Culpeper had heard tell Pickett actually put wax on them to make them curl. The only wax Culpeper had ever seen was from the occasional stubby little candle his Ma had had back home before she passed on. He sure hadn't seen nobody put none on their face, least of all a *man,* even counting some of the dandies back in Rockbridge County he heard lived over in Lexington.

Still he thought he sort of liked George Pickett now, after hearing the man had got himself shot to pieces planting the American flag someplace important in the Mexican War, and when he heard Gunter and the other boys talk about how word had it that Pickett worked like the dickens to get them extra food and good water and the like. Plus the whisper had it that Fancy Pants George had him a choice belle half his age stashed in Richmond he wrote poems and the like to. At this Culpeper chuckled right out loud. Man of nearly forty that had that tucked away fer himself couldn't be all bad. Now he found himself actually sort of almost admiring Pickett, even if he was a general.

But he didn't believe in no Granny Lee nor a God who created the world, church talk and preacher man or no. He thought that soon he would go forage anyhows, Granny's orders be blasted, and soon after that he might just head home for a spell to fish and bring in some summer crops for his cousin Emma and her children, his niece and nephew. *Besides, our Shenandoah girls are lots prettier and better shaped than most of the ones around here.* The last one he had seen had a face he thought looked like a doorknocker.

●◇ ●◇ ●◇

"Some barns they got in this country, General," were Longstreet's first words since Lee rode out of Chambersburg with him a couple of hours before. "And stone too."

Lee glanced at his Old War Horse. He suspected Longstreet had a different vision of how this campaign should be waged, that philosophically, though he shared Lee's comfort with offensive strategy, the big bear of a Georgian preferred defensive tactics. Still, there wasn't a general on either side in the current unpleasantness with whom he would prefer to be riding into war.

Unless, of course, you counted Old Jack.

He would pitch camp in Cashtown tonight and consolidate his troops. The Third Corps of A. P. Hill, Stonewall's old nemesis, was already there, "Old Baldy" Ewell's Second Corps was heading in (either to Cashtown or Gettysburg, eight miles to the east, Ewell's choice) from Carlisle to the northeast, and Longstreet's First Corps stretched from Cashtown west all the way back to Chambersburg.

Lee knew the day before from Hill that the Federals were in Gettysburg, at least cavalry. And the bang of infantry drums beyond that, to the east. But he did not know how many, did not know where they all lay. He had just opened his mouth to continue a theological discussion of the day before with the Rev. General Pendleton, whose Episcopal parish previously encompassed Stonewall's hometown of Lexington, when a ripple of cannon fire from the east began to echo across South Mountain, which they were ascending since the pass beneath was clogged with Confederate troops.

Longstreet, Pendleton, and Taylor all noted the animation that blossomed in Lee's tanned, chiseled face. *It must be a brush with those people's cavalry,* Lee thought. As he neared the peak of the mountain, the volley to the east grew more contentious. His color deepening, he excused himself, removed his broad-brimmed black hat, and swatted Traveller on the flanks, urging him over the crest and down the mountain.

In Cashtown, Lee had found Hill, one of the army's fiercest and most successful warriors. He wore his "bloody red fighting shirt" but appeared emaciated and ashen-faced. One of his divisions had headed into Gettysburg that morning to raid for shoes. "But I gave them strict orders not to force any engagement with the enemy until the rest of the army comes up," Hill said. Lee noticed perspiration dotting the small man's forehead and upper lip.

Hill, barely able to walk for his pain and fever, brushed aside the proffered arm of an aide and left to reconnoiter Gettysburg himself. Now Lee, anxious, his chest aching, called for Richard Anderson, one of Longstreet's division commanders. The thunder of guns grew heavier as it carried over the hills. "I cannot think what has become of Stuart," Lee said softly, pain piercing the interior of his left breast. "I ought to have heard from him long before now." Anderson stood in silence. "I am in ignorance as to what we have in front of us here. It may be the whole Federal army; it may be only a detachment."

It was the Iron Brigade—tough farm boys from Wisconsin and Michigan. The fabled, black-hatted brigade's baptism of fire had occurred in a toe-to-toe, three-hour shootout with the Stonewall Brigade during the Second Manassas, or Bull Run, campaign the year before. Neither brigade would ever face a tougher foe. Fearless and immovable to the death, neither would exist as a recognizable unit by war's end.

One of Hill's brigades found not shoes but the Iron Brigade west of Gettysburg. The outnumbered Confederates shoved the enemy back but then were outflanked by reserve units of the Iron Brigade and themselves driven back, the Southern brigadier taken prisoner. The thought flashed across Lee's mind when he learned of this that no Army of Northern Virginia general had ever been taken prisoner while Stonewall Jackson rode in the saddle with him.

As the gunfire ahead of him intensified, Lee peered through his field glasses toward Gettysburg, three miles to the east. *That's Willoughby Run at the bottom of this hill,* he thought. *And at the top of the ridge across from us—that must be the Lutheran Seminary. Beyond the ridge, that's Gettysburg.* Then the engineer's eyes, keen even at fifty-six years of age, swung their gaze rightward where rose up, south and southeast of the town, a long series of irregular and generally formidable hills, woods, and ridges.

As Lee rode forward with Taylor, Pendleton, and other staff officers, burgeoning drifts of gun smoke wrenched tears from his eyes. He fretted having a larger fight than he had desired being thrust upon him before the rest of his army was up or before he knew the size of the foe that faced him. *Of course,* he thought with a twinge of sardonic pride, *when have those people been anything but two to three times as numerous as we? Still, I believe we may yet extricate ourselves from this action before—* Now he heard more sound, more distant but quite heavy and insistent, from the northeast. *Were I closer,* he thought with a grimace, *I believe I should feel I was in the presence of Thor himself. Why? Has all of this come upon us because of our impatience to find shoes?* His lips parted slightly and he noticed the stream of wounded filing past on either side of him. Bloody, limping, staggering, carried in wagons, on carts, and across their comrades' sweat-blackened shoulders, more of them than not still attempted to shout, speak, raise a hat, salute, or in some cases just smile at him.

"We give 'em what for, General Lee."

"I'll go back and give 'em my other arm if you want me to, sir."

"We love you, Marse Robert."

He removed his hat and nodded, his throat tight and shame sweeping over him.

My boys, he thought, as the memories returned of Fredericksburg's crystal white snow drenched scarlet by the tracks of hundreds of bloody bare footprints—his boys' footprints, for *those* people certainly had no shortage of shoes or food or medicine or anything else. His own wife, Mary, wheelchair-bound, bent, and crippled by arthritis, spent every waking moment that she was not praying or reading her Bible or prayer book, knitting socks with her ruined wrists and fingers for his boys and gently bullying every woman who came into sight to do the same.

Yes, my boys do need shoes, he nodded, tenderness and love for them flooding his heart.

Then his boys, under Ewell and Hill, from Alabama and Maryland, and North Carolina, Mississippi, and Virginia, and all across the Southland, charged into the main army of the United States of America like God stretching forth his hand against Egypt. They drove back the Federal cavalry and its spanking-new, seven-shot repeating carbines. They killed perhaps the greatest general in the Army of the Potomac, John Reynolds. They left the lifeless forms of the cream of the Iron Brigade piled in neat rows across a cornfield. And they drove the

Federal army in headlong retreat through the shell-shocked little town of Gettysburg and into those formidable hills a mile south and east of it, capturing five thousand of them and killing or wounding nearly as many more while doing so.

As Lee again surveyed the unfolding tableau through his field glasses, this time from atop Seminary Ridge, half a mile west of Gettysburg, he saw through the billowing mountains of smoke the Federal thousands fleeing toward a tall hill just south of the town. From that hill extended southward and, it appeared, eastward, the line of hills and ridges he had seen with less clarity earlier in the afternoon. Now he recognized the significance of the tall hill, Cemetery Hill, and the ridge and other heights that proceeded from it.

If we take Cemetery Hill this evening, he thought, *we shall command the entire line of rises, south and east, before those people can get more than their reserves and artillery entrenched and fortified. Then they must be forced to shatter themselves against us on those high ramparts or flee in our wake—as we choose whether to gobble them up or invest Washington City, or both.*

Perhaps, he concluded, the enormity of the specter rendering him momentarily light-headed, *we may by this time of the morrow have earned ourselves the right to an honorable peace.*

But Richard Ewell with one leg and no Stonewall Jackson to command him was not the Richard Ewell of two legs and Old Jack. He worried and he considered and he pontificated and he let the sun go down, and then rise again, without even attempting to take the heights of Cemetery Hill that old Isaac Trimble vowed himself to engage and take with just one regiment: "Because Old Jack would have taken them as sure as the turning of the earth!"

A bit later in the afternoon, Longstreet joined Lee on Seminary Ridge, named for that nearby Lutheran seminary. The hulking Georgian's stolid exterior melted away after he surveyed the terrain before him through his field glasses.

"If we could have chosen a point to meet our plans of operation, I do not think we could have found a better one than that upon which they are now concentrating," Longstreet exclaimed, referencing the campaign strategy to which he thought Lee had assented prior to leaving Virginia. "All we have to do is throw our army around by their left, and we shall interpose between the Federal army and Washington."

As Lee stared at him, Old Pete grew more animated. "We can get a strong position and wait, and if they fail to attack us, we shall have everything in condition to move back tomorrow night in the direction of Washington, selecting beforehand a good position into which we can place our troops to receive battle next day. Finding our object is Washington or that army, the Federals will be sure to attack us."

Now Longstreet's face lit up as Lee had never seen it. "When they attack, we shall beat them, as we proposed to do before we left Fredericksburg, and the probabilities are that the fruits of our success will be great."

Lee had not thundered through two entire Federal corps to hand the momentum back to General Meade. Plus he knew not the Federals' composite strength or their positions. And following Longstreet's suggestion presented him with the terrible specter of an outnumbered invading army, surrounded, finding itself either unable to establish a strong defensive position because of the constant motion required to garner the requisite food and supplies for itself, or, if making such a stand, hemmed in and unable to feed itself or its horses and mules off the land, as its foe watches it starve to death.

"No," he said with force, thrusting his gauntleted fist straight at Cemetery Hill. "The enemy is there, and I am going to attack him there."

Has he forgotten his agreement to attain a strong defensive position on this campaign upon which the enemy will again futilely throw himself? Longstreet thought with alarm as he fired back, "If he is there, it will be because he is anxious that we should attack him—a good reason, in my judgment, for not doing so."

Lee took quiet note of Longstreet's unusual outburst but assumed his refusal to countenance the plan would end the matter.

Longstreet gathered his thoughts and determined to revisit the important issue. *This evening, if possible,* he thought.

●◇ ●◇ ●◇

Meanwhile, Winfield Hancock, the vaunted Federal general born less than one hundred miles from the spot he now sat his horse, just assigned command of the field by Meade, shook his head. Fewer than seven thousand men, including reserves—less than one division—could be mustered from those two devastated Federal corps to make a stand on Cemetery Hill against Lee's rampaging veterans.

But thanks to Ulric Dahlgren, Hancock knew exactly how many of those veterans there were and that no more were coming. He would prepare to defend Cemetery Hill while his own reinforcements came up. For he knew they were coming, and far more of them than the numbers of men that now comprised the Army of Northern Virginia.

A gentle breeze bearing a sweetness birthed by recent showers awoke Lee at 3 A.M. the morning of July 2. As he dressed in the silent early watch, his mind returned to the military strategies it had left less than three hours previous. A chill of dread rippled through him as the incipient, small churning stirred anew deep inside his bowels. *Not again,* he thought, a brief pang of terror striking him. His responsibilities would have long since broken most men, especially his recurrent chest pains and the sense of leaden lethargy they imported through his body he tried so vigorously to fight through. If the debilitating effects of multiplied hours of diarrhetic attacks now returned, on the sweltering field of battle . . .

But he could not help fret the reticence of his corps commanders to press the previous day's smashing victory to a conclusion that could prove monumental in its import. Ewell, who did not—and would not—attack Cemetery Hill on the Federal right, would not agree to Lee's idea to bring his corps round to go in with Longstreet on the Federal right, only then suggesting he could, after all, attack Culp's Hill on the far Federal left.

Hill, ever game, feisty, and loyal, was ill to the point where a lesser man would not even be on the field.

And Longstreet. The evening before, Old Pete had returned to his refrain that the army move around the far U.S. left and interpose itself between the Federals and Washington, awaiting their attack. *Have I not made my rejection of such a dangerous plan manifest?* Lee wondered to himself. *To say more, I would risk injuring the man's pride and dignity. At least he knows I wish the Federal left attacked and that such attack will trigger Ewell's movement against Culp's Hill. Old Pete may not possess the offensive brilliance of Jackson, but he has never yet failed me, and he certainly understands the opportunity before us, the importance of bringing his men up quickly this morning, and the urgency of pressing the attack with alacrity, before those people are further strengthened in their position.*

Lee's summary statement to his exhausted staff around midnight, just after Longstreet had departed, was "Gentlemen, we will attack the enemy as early in the morning as practicable."

He emitted a sigh of relief as he realized that he had prepared his subordinates and they would prepare their men, and if it pleased God, the heights those people held would be in his possession before night.

The words of his mother as she held him upon her lap and taught him the catechism half a century before rebuked such ill-timed meanderings of his mind. He found that his thoughts ran increasingly toward the past and often toward his mother. The older he grew, the more humbled his increased understanding of her saintly suffering and sweet piety rendered him. How frail and ill she had always been, how fretful she must have been over the family's declining fortunes . . . and as tragedy engulfed his father . . . having to leave failing, once-great Stratford . . . the years passing one after another, she never to see her betrothed again in this world . . .

It had been an honor to become the man of the household at age ten, in their small, borrowed Alexandria quarters, his older brothers having already departed. To nurture and care for his mother as she had for him. Yes, well he knew as he opened his Bible and prayer book in what low esteem Ann Carter Lee would suffer the estate of a man going directly to war before morning devotion and prayers.

"Ah, yes," he said quietly, smiling as though at the return of a familiar valued friend, as he saw that the prayer book—for the Thursday of the second Sunday after Trinity—directed him to Psalm 63. Like David who had written it, Lee knew well the psalm before he returned to it. Yet he knew as well the power—and the necessity—of a passage to restore his faith and hope, no matter how many times he returned to it; in fact, ever more so, the *more* he returned to it.

Yes, I believe I understand how the shepherd boy felt, Lee thought with a nod, recalling that David penned the psalm as he fled in fear and confusion from King Saul, God's anointed, who had been as a father to him but now sought his very life. Tears filled Lee's eyes as he realized the nation which had been a father to himself, she who had been a father to his fathers, General Washington and Light-Horse Harry Lee, now sought his life and those of the three sons he had brought into the world and who had grown to splendid manhood amid the fair plains and forests of her precious, bled-for earth.

"O God, thou art my God; early will I seek thee: my soul thirsteth for thee, my flesh longeth for thee in a dry and thirsty land where no water is," the psalm read. *Yes,* Lee thought, nodding, understanding to the depths of his heart.

Then David's ancient pen reflected the loving intervention and deliverance of the living God of Israel, as the verses turned. "To see thy power and thy glory, so as I have seen thee in the sanctuary. Because thy lovingkindness is better than life, . . . My soul shall be satisfied . . . and my mouth shall praise thee with joyful lips: . . . But those that seek my soul, to destroy it, shall go into the lower parts of the earth. They shall fall by the sword: they shall be a portion for foxes."

Now a smile washed across Lee's bronzed face, his heart swelled, and even his aching hands, broken more than a year ago on a fall from Traveller, provided cause for joy and gratitude.

"But the king shall rejoice in God; every one that sweareth by him shall glory: but the mouth of them that speak lies shall be stopped."

Now, he thought, bowing his head in thankful prayer, *frail and wretched a creature as I am, I believe I can bear whatever the day shall bring.*

CHAPTER 7

LEE REMINDED HIMSELF A FEW HOURS LATER, AS HE RODE
back toward the center of the line after issuing Ewell updated orders, that lack
of sleep over many days, the strength-sapping pain inside his left breast, and the
debilitating effects of the feared diarrhea that had revisited him regularly
through the morning, would cause even normal situations to seem formidable.
But this Gettysburg affair was proving no normal situation. Even so his mind
barreled forth across the entire American continent in its anxious meditations.
He recalled the ordeal to wrest permission from President Davis and his cabinet even to come north, then the struggle to secure a force sizable enough to
present a promising scenario for victory. He winced as he thought how valuable
those two big veteran brigades of Pickett's would be, had not the president
insisted on keeping them much farther south for defensive purposes. Lee chas-
tised himself. *I must accord him the same consideration I should myself desire.
Indeed he carries responsibilities upon his shoulders none of us can gauge.*

And how stood Vicksburg? He trembled as he recalled the tales of women
and children, huddled in underground caves to escape Federal shells screaming into the civilian-filled town itself, forced to eat rats to survive Ulysses S.
Grant's relentless siege. Was it true? Briefly, he pictured his beloved Agnes . . .
"Precious Life" Mildred . . . and his crippled, pain-racked wife. . . . *What if it
were Richmond?* he thought, his blood running cold. *What if it* becomes
Richmond?

Finally, with the reluctance of a child opening wide his mouth for the dentist to yank a bad tooth, his mind returned to Longstreet. Perhaps most discon-
certing of all was Longstreet. Instead of having at least Hood's and McLaws's
divisions in place to attack by dawn or shortly thereafter—he resisted the urge
to give way to the thought of *as Jackson would have with his divisions*—Old Pete
had arrived with only a portion of his men, and those arrayed for marching, not
fighting. The rest were strung out for miles toward the rear. *He must have begun*

the march no sooner than it should have been ending, Lee thought with a frown. And Longstreet had proceeded to renew his vigorous counsel to pull around those people and get between them and their capitol. At the remembrance of his having simply to walk away from the Old War Horse's insistent protestations, Lee felt his bowels begin again to churn. He hoped he could ward off this latest urgent inclination, but after a moment, he realized he was about to be greatly embarrassed. He hurried for nearby cover, noting Taylor, Pendleton, and a few other officers observing him from a short distance away. Already the incidents were taking their toll. A leaden sensation had enveloped his powerful legs, and his head felt light as he struggled to keep in mind the multiple components at play on this field like opposing pieces on a chessboard.

The good news was that the Federals had appeared at first light to have extended their line neither west, into the valley between them and Lee, nor south, into the area of the rises Round Top and Little Round Top, which constituted the southern terminus of the high ground that the Federals held. But Lee's bowels began again to swirl, and his chest to knot up, as he recalled the lines of dark blue that started to stream toward those areas before his very eyes even as Longstreet had continued to plead his heartfelt case.

He glanced at his gold timepiece. After ten o'clock! He jerked the field glasses back up to his eyes. Masses of Federals continued to appear at the fence bounding Cemetery Ridge, then pour into fields and woods that had been empty when Lee felt Longstreet should have been sending his men hurtling toward them. *Not a Confederate soldier in sight,* he thought, *nor the sound of a drum, bugle, or gun.* "What *can* detain Longstreet?" Lee virtually shouted as the field glasses released from his still-stiff hands and dropped to the lower reach of their leather straps.

Ignoring his bowels, his hands, his tightening chest, and his many cares, he urged Traveller into a canter, to find the man who was to lead his army into what he still hoped would be the climactic battle of the war.

●◇ ●◇ ●◇

When he found Longstreet around 11 A.M., the sun having now abandoned all pretenses of midsummer moderation, Lee was stunned to see that while Meade had continued to reinforce Cemetery Ridge, Old Pete's First Corps not only had not moved into action but was scarcely more ready to do so than it had been two hours before.

"General, you will commence your attack at once, with whatever forces you now have on the field," Lee said, the normally gentle brown eyes burning like lasers into Longstreet's, and all the considerable force of his rank, fame, and moral character gathered into a voice now as stern and immovable as the low stone fences that ran everywhere through the Pennsylvania fields surrounding them. So extraordinary was the direct order—the only one he ever issued Longstreet—that the officers within earshot, despite themselves, sat breathless and transfixed.

Longstreet did obey the order, and he did hurtle his men into battle—five hours later. This after fierce, towering Division Commander John Bell Hood of Texas thrice petitioned—all but begged—Old Pete, without success, to allow him to flank the Federals around the southern tip of their position.

Only this once in Hood's entire military career did he suggest to a commanding officer that an order be changed.

Fearless, blond Hood gazed up at the sinister heights of Devil's Den and Little Round Top, now bristling with the bright reflections of Federal steel. *Never in my life have I been ordered to attack up anything approaching such a grade,* he thought, *and with rocks, boulders, hidden positions of all sorts, and everywhere the enemy dug in deeper than an armadillo on a Texas prairie.* He told Longstreet's staff officer, "The enemy's position is strong—it is impregnable."

Then Hood motioned down the extended Federal line, full of juts, nooks, and crannies. "We shall be caught in a hot enfilade. Regardless of that, the grade is so steep, all they need do is throw or roll stones down the mountainside as we approach. Tell General Longstreet the situation is much changed from when General Lee issued his orders early this morning; still, a flanking move will yet allow us to wrest from the Yankees the southern heights of their line."

Hood's blood grew cold as yet a fourth rebuff came from Longstreet. "We must obey the orders of General Lee."

●◇ ●◇ ●◇

Never had Longstreet's aides seen a gloomier cloud settle over him. He viewed Lee's plan as so far inferior to his own that he still could not believe his commander intended to follow through with it. And so Old Pete gave Lee every opportunity to reconsider. Grim and sullen, he marched and countermarched the thirsty, sweat-drenched First Corps back and forth, over and around, and he refused to countenance any variance from Lee's original orders, even though

Hood and other subordinates reported the significantly altered Federal troop dispositions.

Then, hewing to the letter of those orders in a manner unlike that exhibited by the previous actions of himself and other Army of Northern Virginia commanders that had won the army its fabled name, he sent his men against a position he himself had never believed could be taken and which he had indeed assured could not be by allowing tens of thousands of additional Federals time to dig themselves in over the past eight hours.

But no one remembered to mention that to the men of Texas, Mississippi, Arkansas, Alabama, Georgia, and Virginia who roared up the Emmittsburg Road and into the Wheatfield, the Peach Orchard, Devil's Den, the Round Tops, and even onto the crest of Cemetery Ridge itself. For five hours the best men of two nations fought one another with rifle, musket, pistol, sword, Bowie knife, stones, and, finally, fists, knees, elbows, and teeth.

Hood's division, Lone Star flags of Texas and other banners waving, even when riddled by minié balls, mowed through the Federal line in the Peach Orchard; shot, clubbed, and slashed through the smoky blood-curdling deathscape of Devil's Den; rousted the enemy from Round Top and took its heights; then fought two-thirds of the way up the steep, open face of Little Round Top, five regiments uphill against eight and artillery, a galling hail of bullets and canister raining straight down into their faces from the Federal soldiers entrenched above.

At length, when charge after charge had left the blood from hundreds of broken bodies gathering in puddles and running in rivulets down the tortured hill, the call came to retreat, followed by a downhill countercharge led by Twentieth Maine Colonel Joshua Chamberlain, a former minister, who would win the Congressional Medal of Honor for his exploits that day.

And so it was that time after time, from one end of the line to the other, the Army of Northern Virginia, hampered by a haphazard tactical plan, less-than-inspired corps command, uncoordinated attacks, and a disadvantage in men, guns, and ground, charged furiously toward their assigned objectives and still made it almost to the summit before falling just short.

Longstreet's First Corps under Hood—who was nearly killed by a shell fragment—and McLaws alone took on six entire divisions and portions of three others, twenty-two brigades with their eight. The Southerners nearly all the while were on the attack, and that uphill.

Just north up the line, one of A. P. Hill's brigades actually took a central section of Cemetery Ridge itself but could not hold it because troops were not coordinated to support it.

And farther north "Old Baldy" Ewell's division under the rough-and-ready Jubal Early fought all the way to the top of Cemetery Hill but, again, had to fall back because the necessary support, though on the field, was not directed toward its aid.

Perhaps on this day of blood and valor, when success failed to crown its exploits, the actions of nineteen-year-old Texas cavalryman Will Barbee were representative of the Army of Northern Virginia.

Barbee, itching to get knee-deep in the fight, had been constrained to serve as a courier for Hood. When the big Texan went down, the youngster, weighing barely one hundred thirty pounds when soaking wet, was temporarily without orders or direct commander. He seized the opportunity to race toward the Devil's Den melee. A Federal sharpshooter shot his horse out from under him. The little Texan hit the ground running. He climbed atop a boulder, and a cluster of wounded Confederates below passed loaded muskets and rifles up to him. A crack shot whose father had taught him before he was ten years old how to use his first gun to pick off sage hens around their homestead on the barren Texas prairie, he fired as fast as his compatriots could shuttle long guns up to him. He cut down one bluecoat after another in the swirling desperate fracas, like so many tenpins. Then, in clear view of the enemy, he took a minié ball in the leg. The blow almost knocked him off the boulder, but he clambered back up and resumed firing. Now more Federals drew down on the murderous little one-man firing machine. Another ball tore into his other leg. He crawled back to the top of the boulder, took a rifle, and nailed a Yankee officer who had rushed toward the boulder, blasting away with his Colt revolver.

Then a third ball tore through his rib cage and sent him sprawling and his rifle clattering down onto the heads of the wounded Confederates below. As blood poured from his wounds and the other soldiers attempted to tend him, Barbee screamed at them to help him back up onto the boulder.

◆ ◆ ◆

As night fell, Longstreet told one aide, "I do not hesitate to pronounce this the best three hours' fighting ever done by any troops on any battlefield."

Lee, who spent the afternoon on a stump on Seminary Ridge, gazing across the valley at the distant action through his field glasses and roiling billows of gun smoke, realized that though he had not captured the high ground he sought, he very nearly had. He believed the shaken Federals were ripe for the death blow he now decided he would deliver the next day with his fresh brigades, notably those of the dashing George Pickett's division.

As the battle grew hot, a visitor had galloped up to Lee. The commander's eyes widened in joy upon sight of the rider, though he could not at first discern who was the more exhausted—the heaving, foaming great bay or the strapping young horseman who had not slept in nearly two days. After Lee's initial silent euphoria at witnessing the dismounting young man to be safe and well, a scarlet cloud passed over his bronzed face. He stood, took a step toward Jeb and raised his arm. Jeb winced. *Oh, no, he is going to strike him!* Jeb's assistant adjutant general, Henry McClellan, standing nearby, thought with horror.

But he did not.

"Well, General Stuart, you are here at last," Lee said, frost tinging his voice in a manner Jeb had never before witnessed.

"But . . . sir," Jeb began, his heart swelling with alarm and foreboding. Nothing on earth would be more unbearable than to disappoint Marse Robert.

"I have not heard a word from you for days, and you the eyes and ears of my army," said Lee, lowering his arm, his fist clenched.

Jeb stood stupefied. His accomplishments over the past grueling week flashed through his keen mind like so many fluttering quail flushed from the thicket. *But from the beginning I did as ordered,* he thought, agony of disappointing General Lee creeping over him. *I crossed the Potomac to the east of the Blue Ridge as General Longstreet approved. I broke up the Federal supply line, drew after me two entire Yankee cavalry divisions, forced them to place a whole corps of infantry to secure their line of communications as we tore up railroad track and tore down telegraph wires, captured nearly one thousand prisoners, threatened and put the fear of the Almighty into Washington, beat Kilpatrick's cavalry, kept thousands more Yankee infantry near Carlisle and away from General Ewell—and left two brigades of cavalry, under Jones and Robertson, with General Lee, not to mention Brigadier General Imboden's force. And Yankee prisoners tell me their new commander, Meade, is near apoplectic, not about General Lee, but about me!* So shook was he, however, that out of his mouth came only, "I have brought you one hundred twenty-five wagons and their teams, General."

"Yes," said Lee, "and they are an impediment to me now."

Then by the mere wave of the arm that a moment before had been raised, Lee at once dismissed any charges and declared Jeb not guilty. The fatherly gentleness the younger man had so often seen fill his eyes, all the way back to those jolly afternoon teas with the Lees at West Point when the general was superintendent, and Jeb and the boys would serenade the Lee girls, returned. *Yes, he does still believe in me—he does still approve!* Jeb realized, relief and joy filling his heart.

See how he loves him, Henry McClellan thought, Lee seeming unlike any military commander he had ever before seen.

"Let me ask your help now. We shall say no more on the matter," Lee said simply. Then his wounded hand was patting Jeb's shoulder like a proud father receiving his beloved prodigal back from the far country, and the commander was saying, "Help me fight these people."

In that moment Jeb Stuart could no sooner believe that if he had not trespassed, Robert E. Lee would ever hold aught against him than that if he had so erred, he would not be deserving of the General's just chastening—or that his precious daughter Flora was not now in the presence of her Savior.

About blasted time, Cole Culpeper, cleaning his rifle to a sheen bright as a full moon on the Shenandoah at midnight, thought to himself when the order came down that he and the rest of Pickett's division would attack the Yankees the next morning. "Why in blazes did we come all the way to this Yankee land with their big barns, little fields, and ugly women, if not to fight, for pity's sake?" he asked ole Luke Gunter.

CHAPTER 8

I SHALL LEAVE NOTHING TO CHANCE TODAY, LEE THOUGHT AS HE emerged from his tent, dressed for battle, shortly after 3 A.M. *How close we came yesterday,* he thought, wincing. *Had we but attacked when I thought we would, those people would not even have been in position to receive our assault.*

He ate a spare breakfast, then set out with Taylor to find Longstreet. He would not lay the burden on Old Pete's beefy shoulders this time. His instructions would be more direct, and he would remain with his lieutenant long enough to make certain they were carried out. Longstreet's gloomy sullen countenance had saddened Lee yesterday. Losing nearly a third of his attacking force and failing to carry the heights that he believed would end this grievous and unnecessary war saddened him more.

The absence of pain in Lee's chest, shoulders, and arms heartened him as he rode along the crest of Seminary Ridge and glanced upward at the host of pale stars veiled somewhat by a light fog. But a chill of dread ran through him as he realized that already the churning had begun in his lower abdominal region. *Above all other days,* he thought, in part reflection and part petition, *I must have my strength and all my faculties.*

Just as a brilliant array of rose, pink, and gold streaks arched across the low eastern horizon, he spotted Longstreet. *Yes, he appears his old bluff, confident self,* Lee thought, joy filling him. He needed his warhorse in peak form today.

Before a single word could emerge from Lee's mouth, Longstreet spoke, his big head alight with mirth and his trademark log of a cigar jutting from his mouth amid his bushy brown beard. "General, I have had my scouts out all night, and I find that you still have an excellent opportunity to move around to the right of Meade's army and maneuver him into attacking us."

As Longstreet churned on, the realization seeped over Lee that his colleague had in fact already issued orders directing his troops to swing south, around the Round Tops and the Federals, and move to a position between them and the capital.

Stonewall Jackson would have this man arrested where he stands, and Napoleon would have him shot, Taylor seethed to himself.

When the lengthy monologue swirled to a close, Lee raised a yellow-gauntleted hand, pointed northeast toward Cemetery Ridge, and said evenly, "The enemy is there, and I am going to strike him."

Longstreet's demeanor could not have plummeted more precipitously had he learned that one of his children had died, as three already had. At first, Lee thought Old Pete's cigar might fall from his mouth. Then it appeared as though the burly soldier might bite it in half. When Longstreet spoke, the words rang with somber conviction. "General, I have been a soldier all my life. I have been with soldiers engaged in fights by couples, by squads, companies, regiments, divisions, and armies, and should know as well as anyone what soldiers can do." At this Longstreet pulled the cigar from his mouth. "It is my opinion that no fifteen thousand men ever arrayed for battle can take that position."

Lee regretted the umbrage Longstreet took with the plan, particularly since the Georgian would be in overall command, but his subordinate's words no more moved him than a blanket of winter snow would move the Blue Ridge Mountains. Longstreet did offer what both men considered sound reasons that persuaded Lee to change the target of attack to the Federal center rather than the left, as had been tried yesterday.

The center was precisely where Federal General Meade expected the Confederates to concentrate the new day's attack.

Leaving nothing to chance, Lee rode the length of the miles-long Southern line twice with Longstreet, then once more by himself.

Just after noon an eerie silence spread over the entire field. Culpeper, long since moved up to the front with the rest of General Richard Garnett's brigade of Pickett's Virginia division, his throat dry and what remained of his thick, sweat-soaked wool uniform stuck to his skin, heard a stir. His sharp eyes spotted, a distance away, Longstreet and Pickett and a few members of their staffs riding past.

What a study in contrasts were the two generals, friends since the Mexican War, where both had won fame for their exploits. Everything about the suavely tailored Pickett seemed to shine or sparkle—his knee-high black riding boots, his golden spurs, the double row of fire-gilt buttons fronting his coat, even the handsome English riding crop he sported whether mounted or afoot. All about Longstreet appeared mundane and unassuming. His slender body erect and poised, Pickett rode as a Virginian who had spent his entire life astride the finest horses the Southland could bring forth, which he was and had. Longstreet slouched atop an animal whose only purpose was manifest—a beast of burden to transport its rider's bearlike body from one place to another.

Pickett's goatee curled forth from a face so handsome it drew admiring glances from men and women alike, the immaculate growth enveloped by the long drooping mustaches whose ends he waxed upward, while his auburn-tinted dark hair fell long, ringleted, and perfumed onto his shoulders. Longstreet's bushy beard and stolid face, overhung by a stained slouch hat, resembled rough-hewn boulders from Devil's Den that time had ravaged.

How happy is that Pickett, Culpeper thought bitterly. *He looks like one of them kings such as Ivanhoe or Arthur—or Arnold or whoever—off for war, with us peasants readied to bleed and die for their lands and glory. General Longstreet looks like a man being led to the guillotine. Are these men old friends? Are they even in the same army?*

Culpeper grimaced up at the sun, blazing for a moment through a break in the woods where Garnett's division had stood, sat, laid, and dozed for hours. The blasted hellish ball only seemed to burn hotter as the day wore on. *Must be near one o'clock,* he gauged from the orb's position. Gazing at the sweat-drenched, vermin-infested men about him, he lifted silent curses against Pickett and Longstreet, all generals, and rich men of any stripe. *We been penned up here for hours,* he thought with venom. *These woods be gettin' hotter and steamier with every minute that passes.* He started to comment to Luke Gunter on the day's foolishness and the fools orchestrating it, but now Yankee shells began to drop among the Confederates.

Blast all powerful men, he thought, hatred filling him. *Blast all men who take other men's lives and use 'em for their own ends. Blast them all to perdition.* His fury mounted as he saw chaplains moving among the men, even as shot and shell rained death and horror upon them. *And blast them most of all,* he thought, beside himself with anger. He hated them, and he hated it when the ranks began to pour forth with General Lee's favorite church hymn, "How Firm a Foundation," while on the march.

61

When a Yankee missile screamed through the trees and exploded, obliterating one wounded man and decapitating the chaplain who knelt beside him,
cradling the soldier with one hand and holding a Bible with the other, Culpeper
secretly cheered for joy.

More shells flew in. More men screamed and bled and died. To his amazement, Culpeper realized that he could spot the high-arching shells as they
cleared the crest of Seminary Ridge behind which the Confederates crouched,
and could observe them all the way in. Many of the men around him attempted
to sleep, as soldiers always have when awaiting battle, but the suffocating
woods, sulphurous fumes, and thunder of opposing walls of artillery that
stretched a full two miles in length allowed few that luxury.

On and on it went.

"Leastways you'd think they'd let a man stand up and have a chance if'n he's
gonna die anyhow," Gunter said when splinters from a shattered pine tree tore
a nearby seventeen-year-old's throat from his shoulders.

Culpeper said nothing. *Least we ain't boiling in the sun and out in the open
like them poor devils in Kemper's brigade,* he thought, glimpsing those regiments
spread in a field below and to the right of the woods.

As the scene grew more desperate and the stinking, choking darkness
descended on the woods like one huge ghastly funeral pall, the chorus of spoken prayers rising from the anxious vast company of planters and farmers, merchants and mountain men and schoolboys, grew into a small roar of its own.
*These fools will lead us straight into hell, shoutin' all the while they have heaven's
blessing to do it,* Culpeper thought bitterly. *God A—— I'm thirsty,* he thought,
cracking his parched lips as he tried to lick them.

Then they were on their feet and moving forward. Ahead he saw Garnett,
shivering and ashen-faced with sickness, barely able to climb into the saddle of
his great black stallion, even with the help of two men, his uniform buttoned to
his neck and a huge blue woolen greatcoat wrapped tightly around him on the
hottest day Cole Culpeper could ever remember living through. *Still he tries to
prove that fanatic Old Jack wrong,* Culpeper thought.

Stonewall Jackson had removed Garnett from command of the Stonewall
Brigade at Kernstown and court-martialed him after Garnett, his outnumbered
men out of ammunition and in danger of being exterminated, had ordered a
retreat without consulting with Stonewall. With that retreat the rally Stonewall
was orchestrating came to naught, and for the first and only time he lost a battle.

Now Richard Garnett, from one of the best families in Virginia, would lead his brigade into battle and into history against the waiting massed soldiery and artillery of the Army of the Potomac.

Lee watched again from an observation post atop Seminary Ridge, silently petitioning the protection of Almighty God for his men. He did not know that through a series of miscues, the Confederate artillery barrage designed to soften the Federal defenses for this final audacious confrontation had been crippled by a lack of ordnance. Thus both the Federal army and its enormous array of field guns not only survived the epic artillery duel—the most titanic in the history of the North American continent—but were now fastened like a huge set of vise grips into their sturdy, high-ground positions along the summit of Cemetery Ridge.

Had Lee known the extent of this pivotal turn of events, he would have called off the entire attack.

"Oh, may God in His mercy help me as He has never helped before," George Pickett scrawled to his beloved fiancée Sallie, who was twenty years his junior and would for the remainder of her long life call him "My Soldier." "Remember always that I love you with all my heart and soul," Pickett wrote, tears welling up in his eyes, "that now and forever I am yours."

Then he sealed the note, handed it to his adjutant, and rode out before his men. "Up, men, and to your posts!" he shouted. "Don't forget today that you are from Old Virginia."

And now a gray-and-butternut wall comprised of the flower of the Southern race—of Virginia, North Carolina, South Carolina, Georgia, Florida, Tennessee, Alabama, and Mississippi; of men whose forefathers had founded the great Republic these men had learned they revered less than the invaded sovereign countries that had borne and succored and loved them—moved down into the valley of death between Seminary Ridge and Cemetery Ridge.

For on this day out of men would be birthed myth, from deeds would be begotten legends, and the earth would stand still and tremble and wonder at the majesty and horror of this vast new American nation. And for a few moments the arrayed Federal host would, in spite of themselves, grow very quiet, and stop and stare at the awe-inspiring sight spreading before them.

"Why, they're gonna do it, sure, sir, they're actually gonna do it," red-headed cavalry sergeant Patrick Flanagan of County Kildare uttered in amazement to his captain.

That commander, viewing the unearthly specter through his field glasses high atop Cemetery Ridge, an unfamiliar blend of detestation and grudging admiration vying for his affections, whispered softly Tennyson's now-fabled refrain:

> *Cannon to right of them,*
> *Cannon to left of them,*
> *Cannon in front of them*
>   *Volley'd and thunder'd*
> *Into the mouth of Hell*
>   *Rode the six hundred.*

For the great and terrible events of July 3, 1863, would not leave Ulric Dahlgren the same man he had been before that day arrived.

CHAPTER 9

FOR THE FIRST FEW MINUTES, IT WAS NOT BAD AT ALL. WHILE A. P. Hill's wing, six divisions, which actually comprised the majority of the attack force, moved immediately down from Seminary Ridge into open country a few hundred yards north, Pickett's three divisions descended into a ravine, then back up it. The thought actually crossed Culpeper's mind that perhaps the Yanks had lit out again. *We been kickin' their tails so long, they may just have finally had enough,* he thought, the clinking of thousands of canteens, knives, belt buckles, and eating utensils against one another sounding as he and nearly twelve thousand other men marched east, their arms shouldered as if on parade. Oh, some fool bands had struck up "The Bonnie Blue Flag" and "Dixie" and the like back somewhere behind the crest of the hill, but he could hardly hear that now.

Culpeper didn't know for sure if the Yanks were still there because great choking clouds of gun smoke and sulphur had enveloped the entire field as far in every direction as he could see. As Pickett's men cleared the forward crest of the ravine and came into full view of the Federals half a mile to the east of them, he heard the screams of men before he even heard the report of the cannons that had resumed their fire along the Yankee line. Irritation more than disappointment marked him at this occurrence. He was bone-tired of walking into walls of flame and fire for "honor" and "virtue" and "principle." Such notions were only the ancient airs put on by rich planters and merchants so they could stay on top. He didn't give a lick one way or t'other about the darkies, even though he had heard the Yankees said he did. He had never owned no slaves and wouldn't if he could. Most of the blacks he knew were spoiled and lazy, kept on by masters that most times of the year did not have enough for them to do. He and all the Culpepers he knew could farm their own little spreads themselves just fine. In fact he did not know of more than a half dozen men in his entire company who had ever owned even one slave. As far as he was concerned, he wished they would all go north. *Course, I heard most of them Yankee states won't even take 'em in,* he thought. *Lincoln frees all the slaves he don't have no say over and leaves those alone that he does, in the border states and what-not. That's a politician for you,* he thought. *That's a man with power and a career he's thinkin' about at the workin' man's expense.*

Then, even as the mounting fire began tearing holes in the Confederate ranks, came the officers' calm orders to dress the line.

In full view of the Army of the Potomac, the left arms of Pickett's entire division shot forth, and their heads turned right to form a straight alignment. The man to Culpeper's right was blown down even before the alignment was consummated, so Culpeper and the next man to the right closed together.

"Jesus, Mary, and Joseph—er, sir," Sergeant Flanagan, watching gape-mouthed through the field glasses, called to Dahlgren. "They're dressing the line."

Dahlgren grabbed the field glasses and stared. *Lord in heaven,* he thought to himself, his stomach beginning to churn, *surely they can't actually reach our lines.*

At first Culpeper paid little heed to the cannons. He had long since grown inured to the fearsome thunder and concussion they blasted forth, which could make a man feel as though he were being blown to shreds even when the explosion struck nowhere near him. After a few minutes though, his ears ringing, he realized this was no ordinary bombardment. Men were beginning to go down, too many men. The regimental colors, the roster of battles they had fought the past two years stitched into the red cloth in white by the wives of the officers, went down. They reappeared a moment later, carried by stout new arms, then fell again, only to rise anew. *Holy Moses,* he thought, his eyes widening and his mouth tightening as if he were stumbling finally onto the revelation of what was happening—and what was about to happen. *We're marchin' straight into the whole bloody Yank army, with no cover a'tall, like we was headin' for a Sunday picnic, and they won't even let us shoot our guns.* He glanced to his left at Gunter. *Yep, ole Lukey boy's ready as ever to die for his country,* he thought with disdain;

the rest of the line beyond Gunter, too, as far down as Culpeper could make out their grimy determined faces.

Suddenly a shell burst overhead and a whole cluster of men to his right went down, screams and blood and bone filling the air. Something spattered across Culpeper's cheek and neck. He wiped it off. *What an odd color,* he thought. Realizing what it was, he retched. But his throat and stomach were too dry to vomit. For the first time in the war, true fear filled him. He was tired and thirsty and angry and nauseous, and he had had enough of it all. Whether the Federal flag or the Stars and Bars flew over the Rockbridge County Courthouse didn't make one whit of difference to how the Culpepers ran their farms. *What am I doing here?* he thought, desperation beginning to creep in.

Ahead Garnett, looking for all the world straight and strong in the saddle, rode on, men falling around him like ducks shot down at dawn over Culpeper's back ponds in February. Culpeper's eagle eye observed the Emmittsburg Road, the low meeting point of the facing hills just beyond Garnett, creased with a rail fence. Blue-coated skirmishers stood firing from behind the fence. *That's mighty contrary for the Yanks to stick so long to a skirmish line,* Culpeper thought. Down the fenceline to the right, fire and smoke leaped from some buildings, perhaps a house and barn. The very sight of it through the dark roiling haze seemed further to heat up Culpeper's broiling skin and head.

Them preachers preach hell from their Book, Culpeper thought, *but they's wrong. This is hell.*

On he marched, for nearly a mile in full view of the assembled might of the Federal army. Never before had either army attacked across so long a stretch sans cover. At Fredericksburg, half a year before, fourteen Federal assaults up Marye's Heights had less than five hundred open yards to compass. Not one man did.

Just ahead Culpeper saw seventeen-year-old Billy Peacock limping along with no shoes, like many in the regiment. But blood pumped forth from one of Billy's bare feet, where a shell fragment had torn it, and he used his musket as a crutch. Another explosion sent white-hot metal flying through the ranks. Billy went sprawling. Culpeper helped him up. When the youngster saw that the ankle of his other foot was lanced and bleeding, he looked around, found the nearby musket of a dead man, and positioned it as a crutch under one arm, and his own under the other, then began to lurch forward.

Fury filled Culpeper. This boy, even if he lived, was probably going to be legless. "Just what in tarnation are you doing, Billy boy?" Culpeper shouted. "How you plan to fight them bluebellies even if you make it to that clump of trees we're s'posed to take?"

Tears streaking his smoke- and dirt-smeared face, and his beardless chin quivering, Billy said defiantly, "I'll fight 'em good," then staggered past Culpeper.

"You hold it there, Billy boy," Culpeper said, grabbing the boy's shoulder. "Now you git back to the lines before I drag you back there myself by the nap o' your scrawny neck."

Billy hung his head, then turned slowly around, burst into tears, and hobbled back.

Culpeper resumed his place in line next to Gunter and glanced around, pondering the chances of a solo escape in a direction other than back to Seminary Ridge. Then another shell was tearing another hole in the men and an officer was shouting again, "Close ranks! Close up, men!" And he was glancing to make sure Gunter was still there, which he was, and moving to the left to form on Lukey boy. Before he knew it, he was in a mass of men stalled down at Emmitsburg Road, the Yankee artillery unleashing volley after volley on them.

"Get those fences down, boys," an officer ordered from somewhere, no more urgency in his voice—probably less, in fact—than in that of a judge announcing the winner of the turkey shoot at the county fair. A few of the veteran rankers, with no assurance a minié ball, shot, or shell would not bring to a close their earthly life in mid-sentence, began to crack wry jokes. One unlettered private from the Blue Ridge Mountains felt certain he could put at least one chunk of post to better use than it was now employed by using it to "beat the daylights out of that there baboon Abe Linkin what started this here set-to."

Men fell in droves along the fences on both sides of the road as far as Culpeper's burning eyes could see in either direction. Still, starting up Cemetery Ridge, the roar now deafening, the black smoke strangling both sight and smell, and Garnett still astride the splendid black, they closed ranks. Culpeper marched upward as if he were a machine. For an instant the smoke broke and he glimpsed, perhaps two hundreds yards ahead, the low stone fence over which fired the Yankee first line! "Jumpin' Jehosophat," he uttered audibly, "is it possible we might actually git to that fence?"

The clump of trees Lee had targeted for all twelve thousand in his assault force rested immediately behind the stone fence.

But now the fire, coming from three sides, grew overwhelming. The death melody of whizzing minié balls sang all around him. Still more men fell, some screaming, some falling with not a sound. When a group of soldiers just in front of Culpeper dissolved into a red mist, Culpeper thought, *They've brought out the canister*—coffee cans full of lead pellets, similar to gargantuan shotgun shells.

He glanced again at Gunter. Still there. Amazingly the jaws of every man around Culpeper now appeared set like flint. *These fools actually think they can reach that blasted stone wall,* he thought to himself, cringing and hating generals and politicians and rich men in smooth shiny coats and shiny carriages drawn by shiny horses more than ever. Then fear and anger returned. *By gobs, they ain't stopping.* His heart sank. *Guess I'll have to go on the whole way.*

He had been hoping that long before now the assault would wilt under the furious Yankee fire and he could hustle back to the lines—maybe even back to the farm in time for summer harvest—perhaps with his sticky, sweaty hide intact. He could not believe they—he—were still moving forward—*closing ranks in perfect order all the while, no less!*—into this nightmare. *When in blazes will those fools let us shoot back? Much longer and they won't be any of us left to shoot back.* Suddenly the man in front of Culpeper was blown back into him, nearly knocking him down. When the man hit the ground, Culpeper, smeared with his blood, counted four bullet holes ranging from the soldier's forehead down to his private parts. *My life is over,* a voice somewhere back in his mind told him, *any second now I'll be heading on a one-way trip straight to—*

Then he heard Garnett coolly shouting orders, and Culpeper and all who still stood swung their long guns down from their shoulders, pointed them straight ahead, gleaming bayonets charting the way, and sprung ahead, double time, unleashing the screeching, blood-curdling Rebel yell they had not yet sounded on this blood-soaked day of perdition. Yet maintaining their order, the decimated Confederate lines charged straight up the hill. As all the Federal army could muster rained down on them, from straight ahead, from above on the crest of Cemetery Ridge, from the left atop Cemetery Hill, and from the right on the Round Tops, and with nearly half his brigade already down, Culpeper forgot the wall of fire and steel into which he ran. He forgot his anger and resentment and even his fear, and he screamed and ran as fast as his rope-muscled legs would carry him, not noticing that the final shreds clinging around his feet fell away. And when Garnett at long last barked that fateful word, "Fire!" Culpeper drew a bead, and he blew the top off the head of a Yankee who was at that instant drawing down on him.

Despite the heat, the thirst, the exhaustion, and the gauntlet they had run, the sharp-shooting Virginians hammered the stone wall from length to length, blue-hatted heads exploding and falling away all along it.

Finally committed to the action, Culpeper, even as a geyser of sod showered him from the explosion of a nearby shell, pulled a paper-wrapped load of ball and powder from his cartridge box. He tore it open with his teeth as he ran and poured the contents down his rifle barrel, then shoved it home with his ramrod. Still running, he pinched a percussion charge from its pouch and placed it where the hammer would strike it when he pulled the trigger. Then he halted just long enough to sight through his tortured tear-streaming eyes another Yankee head behind the stone wall. *No, look at those gunners, runnin' away from us like a bunch o' kicked yard dogs now that we can shoot back at 'em.* Cursing them and their mothers with an oath, he shot one squarely through the back as the man fled.

Gunners and their horse teams fell like Pharaoh's army before the smiting hand of God, while a whole other row of Federals behind the stone wall were shot down at a range of twenty-five yards.

Out of the corner of his eye, Culpeper saw Garnett, waving his men on with his hat, fall dead from his saddle. Another voice shouted, "Give them the cold steel!" and Culpeper was leaping up onto the stone wall. One fleeting thought danced through the back paths of his mind: *We have come all the way across that mile-long hell on earth, and we have taken this high place.* A blond Yankee on his back on the ground aimed a revolver up at Culpeper and fired. Ducking, he felt the shot take his hat off. Then he was hurtling through the air, landing on the man, tearing the pistol from his hands, and shooting him in the face with it. Quick as he could spring to his bare feet, he was up and shooting down one bluecoat after another, until he had emptied the revolver on them. The combat that swirled around him was hand-to-hand, and it was savage. A Yankee officer drove his sword through a Confederate up to the hilt, just as another grayback cracked the Yank's skull open like a split cantaloupe with the stock of his musket. Culpeper saw two men, grunting, squealing, and cursing, fighting over a Confederate battle flag that had a bayonet strapped to it and had thus been converted into a lance. Before either could get the advantage, a blast of grapeshot shredded both of them and everyone around them, Federal and Confederate. Culpeper stood in stunned stupor. One of the cannon in the battery to the rear of the stone wall was still firing into the raging melee that contained its own comrades.

"Curs," he uttered, grabbing the "lance," which had survived the blast, and running for the gun that was belching canister. "Aiiiiiyh!!" he screamed, holding forth the weapon and leaping over bodies, minié balls and their deadly missives flying all around him, as the Federals frantically rushed to reload the cannon. Culpeper ran straight for them, realizing the Confederates were now over-running the second Federal line. His vocal chords were held captive by the Rebel yell. Twenty feet from the gun, the barrel yawning directly at him, he saw a cannoneer grab the lanyard to fire. *Valhalla, here I come,* he thought, never slowing, screeching only louder as a hail of rifle fire off to his left splintered the cannon, its entire crew, and all their horses. *Lukey and the boys,* he thought with glee, glancing in their direction and seeing a cluster of them converting their smoking guns to clubs against the enemy that retreated before them.

Oh no, Culpeper thought, seeing a Federal had emerged from nowhere, grabbed the ramrod of the silent cannon, charged forward, and was swinging it like one of those Yankee baseball bats at him. Culpeper ducked away, felt the hefty piece graze his skull, then stood and ran his foe through with the lance. The next thing he knew, he and Gunter and a whole pack of Southerners were chasing the Federals on foot. Culpeper lunged at one and tackled him by the legs. Now the action was so wild and furious, he did not know what happened next, only that he was beating somebody with his fists, felt a knife blade skim along the exterior of his own ribs, then heard someone shout that the Yankees were massing for a countercharge.

He looked up. *General Armistead,* he realized with a jolt, seeing that brigadier a few yards back from him—but still forty yards past the stone wall—mortally wounded on the ground next to the same cannon, which had been turned partway around toward the Yankees. Armistead lay unconscious, one hand on the cannon and the other on his sword.

Bodies—blue, gray, and butternut—covered the ground in piles all around Culpeper. Many pairs and clumps of men continued to fight, desperately, with all the strength of their beings, sweating, wheezing, groaning. He realized he and the other Confederates were gradually being overwhelmed and sur-rounded by the sheer weight of numbers reinforcing the broken Federal lines.

But where are our *reserves?* he thought, anger filling him. *We have done our part.*

He saw one of the regiment's captains, an older man named Spessard, cradling the lifeless, bloody head of the man's own son—who was to be married upon his return to Virginia—in his lap. Then he saw Gunter dive into a cluster of three Yankees, taking them all to the ground with him. Culpeper and two more bluecoats leapt into the pile. Culpeper pulled his hunting knife from the back of his belt and slashed it as wild and low and fast and dirty as he could. Screams filled the air around him. Moments later he was on his feet, his forehead and nose bleeding from heavy blows. All the Yankees he had fought—and Gunter—lay in a dead crimson heap.

"Lukey boy!" Culpeper screamed as gun smoke billowed over the hellish scene and up into his burning nostrils. Hardly a Confederate still stood, but those who had fallen—dozens within a few yards, and a host of battle flags with them—were ringed by an enormous circle of dead Yankees.

Now several Federals, sporting all manner of bleeding wounds, moved in on Culpeper, some with bayonets, some holding splintered portions of rifles, some with just their bare fists and the grimness of death written across their dirty faces. Over their shoulders, Culpeper saw appear from the roiling smoky clouds entire massed columns of Federal reinforcements, closing in on three sides. *Where are our reserves?* his mind screamed.

Unlike some who stayed and fought, and were beaten and shot down until they had no life left in them, Culpeper turned and ran as fast as he could back toward his own lines. Fearless valor vanishing in an instant into horrific fear, he knocked down more than one Confederate on his way, and was cursed by others who fell back in order, some still firing their rifles, as they observed his loss of nerve.

"Slow down, you yellow coward!" one Southerner shouted after him.

Just then, the thought impressed Culpeper that were he to die with a bullet to the back while fleeing the field at Gettysburg, all the Culpepers would be ashamed for the good family name. So he slowed and turned back toward the Federal lines and began to walk, rapidly and backwards, toward his own camp, so that any bullet that might find him would be an honorable one and not one that brandished the name of a coward.

❧ ❧ ❧

With his field glasses, Lee had seen fragments of the attack through the smoke and dust. How his heart had pounded with excitement as those dozens of deep red battle flags swarmed up Cemetery Ridge! *Yes,* he thought, nearly overcome with the awesome implications of it, *they are indeed . . . invincible.*

Now his heart pounded, but in a different way. And pain became its unwelcome companion. A dull ache, growing sharper, spread across his chest, shoulders, and upper arms as his shredded legions spread their flower across and atop Cemetery Ridge.

The king is the land and the land is the king.

Fleetingly the thought flashed through his mind that the war would not after all be won this afternoon. And with it a question: *Where were the reserves General Longstreet should have supplied to support the first wave of attackers, who appeared to have accomplished their mission of rolling over the first Federal lines?* But just as quickly a different pain pierced his heart. *My boys . . . I must go to comfort my dear boys.* He mounted Traveller and rode forward to where already they streamed in—bloody, battered, blackfaced, and gone through as much as a man's two legs could carry him.

Pity and compassion swelled his aching heart. He grabbed at it, could feel a tearing sensation in it, could feel it pulsing against the breast of his tunic. Tears formed in his eyes at the ravaging of these men who so often had proved their willingness to do anything and more asked of them for their country.

Yet he must now ask them to do even more for that suffering, besieged country. The Federals were massing for a counterattack. His men must turn and fight again, to stave off total annihilation.

"All this will come out right in the end," he said, kindness filling his words, as he rode among them. "We'll talk it over afterwards. In the meantime all good men must rally. We want all good and true men just now."

There is Pickett, Lee thought. *Oh, he is overcome with grief. . . .* "Come, General Pickett," he said, "this has been my fight and upon my shoulders rests the blame. The men and officers of your command have written the name of Virginia as high today as it has ever been written before. Your men have done all that men could do; the fault is entirely my own."

When the staggered survivors of regiments whose fame had reached the length of the world looked up and saw the source of the gentle words, their eyes lit up, white smiles painted their filthy faces, and many, even among the wounded, cheered their love for him.

One dying, gut-shot North Carolina private was the eighth consecutive soldier shot down heading up Cemetery Ridge carrying the colors of the Old North State's 11th Regiment. His older brother was cut down on his right and his younger on his left. He called out for the men carrying him to stop. Burbling through the blood that trickled from his mouth, tears running down his powder- and smoke-blackened face, he choked, "I love you, General Lee. I love you, sir. It's not your fault."

Now Lee's head drooped to his chest, his heart beat even harder, and tears blinded his eyes. *I must not let the men see me like this,* he thought. When he looked up, his eyes were dry and another mounted officer was beating his own horse because it would not move where he wanted it to go. "Don't whip him, Captain," Lee called, pitying the animal. "Don't whip him. I've got just such another foolish horse myself, and whipping does no good."

Then General Cadmus Wilcox, whose brigade, belatedly attempting to support the attacking units, had been savaged, was before him. He attempted to give a report but was so distraught over the condition of his men that he burst into tears in front of everyone. Lee shook his hand and patted his shoulder as the battle-hardened veteran wept. "Never mind, General," he said, like a father encouraging a son who has squandered, in an earnest, worthy endeavor, the family fortune hard-won by the father. "All this has been my fault—it is *I* who have lost this fight, and you must help me out of it the best way you can."

"No!" bloodied soldiers nearby, some of them on all fours, having crawled all the way back from the battle, cried. "No, it's not your fault, sir!"

"We'll fight them till Hades freezes over, sir, then we'll fight them on the ice!"

●◇ ●◇ ●◇

After Culpeper had neared Seminary Ridge, he faced again toward the west. The farther from the shooting he moved, the more his blood boiled with anger. Now something caught his eye—on the ground, face down. He could tell without even rolling him over that it was the lifeless body of Billy Peacock, both legs ruined and a bloody, large-caliber hole squarely in the center of his back.

Culpeper stared at him. *Billy Peacock. The Spessard boy. Lukey Gunter.* His keen eyes swung up toward the summit of Seminary Ridge. *I am done with this cursed war and I am done with Robert Lee,* he thought to himself, the venom of pure undistilled hate overflowing within him.

His barefooted uphill steps took on new purpose. He was going to find Lee. He did not know what he would do when he found him, but if a gun was handy that might be a part of it. *That old man will not ruin any more of my life. There he is! Talking to the men. Telling them to fight more, as he plans, like all generals do, like all officers and rich men always do, how he may shift his own blame to others. Well, not this time,* Culpeper thought as he cursed Lee, his lean hard legs gaining new life, their strides lengthening. *This time, for once, a guilty general will answer for his sins. Yes! Listen to the men shouting! They are shouting him down, they are finished with it like I am, and they want no more excuses, no more lies.* His heart jumped when he spotted an officer's Navy Colt lying nearby. He scooped it up. *Yes—four bullets!* Now he was shoving his way through the men massed around Lee, cocking the hammer back, reaching the front of the group, looking up at Lee, and hearing him . . .

"It is my fault, men."

"No! No, General!" they shouted, they screamed.

Culpeper, pistol in hand, stood stunned. *What did the old man say?*

"Yes, it is all my fault."

For an instant Lee's eyes met Culpeper's, and the younger one was pierced straight through. Being at this point an ignorant and angry man and full of sin and blind hate, he could not interpret the look in those eyes. Rather they interpreted him. Guilt rushed through him as the men around him continued to shout, more of them now breaking into sobs as they pled Lee's own innocence before him. Culpeper lowered the gun and his head, then turned and walked back through the growing crowd.

He would continue to walk, south, until he found a loose horse, a Federal one, whose rider had been shot off it as Hood's Confederates slaughtered a late, ill-fated Federal cavalry countercharge. Then he would ride south, out of Pennsylvania, through Maryland, and back across the Potomac into Virginia. He would go home, and he would curse this infernal war and the men who led it, curse them into the outer darkness, except that he did not believe there was any darkness greater than that which he had witnessed on the other side of the stone wall.

CHAPTER 10

SLEEP, BLESSED SLEEP. IT HAD FINALLY RETURNED TO AGNES as the train lumbered lazily through the rolling Piedmont toward Hot Springs, the verdant morning sweetness wafting in through the open sliding doors. Then, like a fiery dart from the chambers of hell, the neuralgia knifed back through the nerves in her face and neck.

"Oh!" she cried, grabbing herself. Even as she shuddered at the sudden attack, guilt coursed through her. Her poor mother, who could no longer move at all without crutches, did not need this. Her eldest sister, Mary Custis, had returned finally from behind Federal lines in northern Virginia, but anxious and ill at ease in a manner unlike Agnes had ever seen her. And poor, poor Charlotte, Rooney's frail sweet wife, seemed intent on descending down the long dark tunnel to madness if not death. How could she impose on any of them for aid? Yet they swarmed over her within seconds, even Mama, who dragged herself over from her nearby seat, encouraging Agnes, hugging her, placing a cold compress on her tortured face.

She caught a glimpse out the window. Across a narrow valley an emerald forest blanketed a chain of hills. *Oh, how it reminds me of . . . dear old Arlington,* she thought with a twinge. But Arlington was now long ago. And it was before— *Gettysburg.* Twenty thousand Confederates had been killed, wounded, or captured in three days. Could such numbers be true? Then she remembered the roll of the dead that she knew. How many there were! Other figures that had been trickling into Richmond before she and the Lee women left for Hot Springs tumbled through her aching head. She could barely contemplate horror on such a scale. Of the nearly five thousand men in George Pickett's division who marched into the might of the Federal army on the third and final day of the titanic battle, only around *one thousand* answered the muster for duty the next day.

Her father had written that the Army of Northern Virginia might still have been destroyed, even after the three days of slaughter, as it retreated toward the Potomac. But torrential rains and enormous casualties of their own bade Federal commander George Meade to offer only a moderate thrust at the retreating Southerners.

The Yankees had lost even more men at Gettysburg than the Confederates, over twenty-three thousand. Some of their best generals had gone down. Reynolds, killed. Hancock, seriously wounded. Meade himself narrowly escaped death when a Confederate cannonball sailed through his headquarters house, missing him by only a few feet and blowing up in the very room where he stood.

Agnes thought of how well the words of Lee's letter to his mother while Meade's legions bore down on the Army of Northern Virginia as they retreated back into Virginia summed up the situation as well as her father: "I trust that a merciful God, our only hope and refuge, will not desert us in this hour of need and will deliver us by His almighty hand, that the whole world may recognize His power and all hearts be lifted up in adoration and praise of His unbounded lovingkindness."

And she remembered the final sentence of the missive: "We must, however, submit to His almighty will, whatever that may be."

His almighty will, she reflected soberly as the neuralgia finally relented. *I fear that proves a more burdensome load to bear as the terrors and tragedies multiply.*

While even Meade himself would not claim it as a victory—the most the Federal commander would say was that Lee was defeated in his efforts to destroy the Army of the Potomac—the results of the epic Gettysburg conflagration were much better than almost anything heretofore for the Northern Army. Everyone who wore blue and was still standing had regained hope that not only might the destruction of Washington and the North be averted but that the war might actually, someday, be won!

The many weeks Marley had convalesced had given him opportunity to contemplate the blessedness of that reality as well as many others his careworn, sometimes downright desperate, life in the field had not allowed him occasion to do. For one, the contribution of Tom "Stonewall" Jackson to his life. Only now, after some time had passed since Stonewall's death and with it the bitterness Marley had held toward him, was the full import of that contribution becoming manifest to him. The day Stonewall had demanded that Marley be a man and do his duty at Chapultepec—*I lost an eye but gained my manhood and became what folks called a hero.* The example Stonewall set by founding and doggedly nurturing the first successful black Sunday school class in the history of Lexington, Virginia—*against stern opposition, and me, a Northerner from an abolitionist family, caring not one whit for the Negroes, other than that they might remain in the South and not migrate northward into my homeland.* The huge religious revival in the Army of Northern Virginia Stonewall had led, which Federal intelligence reported continued to grow—*whilst I carried only hate for the man who led it, his people, and, yes, too many of my own.*

Marley's thoughts turned toward Stonewall's widow, Mary Anna. *So devoted she was toward Tom, and so sweet toward me, when I had shown her nothing but disdain in my drunken un-Christian arrogance,* he thought. He recalled the origin of the very Bible he held in his hand as he stood to walk toward the officers' Bible study. He opened to the front flyleaf.

> To the finest young man I know, with my fervent prayers that your bright future shall soon be illumined as will that holy city of which the sainted apostle wrote, "had no need of the sun, neither of the moon, to shine in it: for the glory of God did lighten it, and the Lamb is the light thereof."
>
> Your ardent friend and supporter,
> Thomas J. Jackson

Marley stared at the inscription and swallowed. He closed the book and ran his hand along the smooth leather. *Not smooth enough,* he thought with a twinge of guilt. *These gilt embossed letters are still far too visible. And the pages inside are crisp and clean as if I had just purchased this volume.*

Stonewall Jackson had given Marley the Bible as a gift before the war started.

Perhaps I might continue to read and meditate on this book as I have these past weeks, and doing so begin to understand God's mercy toward and purpose for me in them, and how I might more effectively be an instrument in pouring out that blessing on others as He has poured it out on me, Marley thought. He glanced at the gold timepiece his parents had sent him from Pennsylvania. *Oh—I'm going to be late.*

He walked quickly through the rows of hospitalized Federal troops, hundreds and hundreds of them. *How many must there be up in Pennsylvania since Gettysburg?* he wondered. Finally, up ahead, in a tent outside the main makeshift building, gathered the men for the officers' Bible study. *Looks like the number is still growing,* he was glad to see. But when he arrived at the tent, the faces all around him were stricken with gloom and despair.

"What is it?" Marley asked. "What is wrong?" Now heads had dropped and he heard a smattering of sniffles.

"It's McCreery," handsome, blond Kurt Schumacher, one of Old Prayer Book Howard's German cavalry captains answered, his eyes red. The Puritan-sort from Connecticut who snored had "gone up."

The news stunned Marley. *Every time I find someone to help me, something happens,* he thought. The war had taken him away from Stonewall, his wounds at Chancellorsville had separated him from Old Prayer Book, and now this.

"But . . ." Marley stammered. "He was better, he was due to go home tomor—"

"They don't know what happened," a Vermont officer, hard-shelled as the rocky heights of his Granite State, answered. "He took a fever during the night, and by sunup, he was . . ." The man's voice trailed off, and before the tears welling in his eyes evidenced themselves too clearly, he lowered his head.

"Well, what do we do now?" Marley asked, like a suddenly orphaned child.

Around the tent men began to trade glances. Marley catalogued in his mind who might be best to take over as the Bible study teacher. *Probably that tall red-headed major from Indiana,* he thought.

"I say we elect Marley to teach us." The unmistakable hard Yankee brogue of the Vermonter.

In an instant a chorus of voices chimed their assent. This shook Marley as much as the news of the Connecticut man's death. "No," he fumbled, "not me. I'm not qualified. I'm still learning."

"That you'd say that cinches it for me," the Vermonter growled. "Anybody say different?" he half-asked, half-warned the group.

No one, least of all God Almighty Himself, had any intentions of suggesting anyone else.

ROBERT E. LEE

⊷ ⊷ ⊷

"C'est les magnifiques!"

Dahlgren had learned his French as well as he had learned his fencing as he grew into a man, and well he had learned that utterance from the French commander who watched the charge of the famed British Light Brigade into the massed infantry, artillery, and cavalry of the Russian army at Balaklava nearly a decade before.

The words had returned to him over and over again since he witnessed the epochal event the newspapers were now calling "Pickett's Charge."

Epochal, perhaps, for the Rebels, hopefully for the Federals, certainly for Captain Ulric Dahlgren. At once infuriated and inspired by the singular effort of so many thousands wading into what they must have suspected was certain death, Dahlgren swore that history would never write how any bunch of bare-footed, raggedy-britches Rebels took the measure of him in bravery, zeal, or commitment to cause. Why, how could those in the right but hang their heads in shame if they were to be outshone in valor by the misguided ignorant hordes they were sworn to defeat?

And that, Dahlgren realized, a shiver running down his spine, was very nearly what he witnessed on the slopes of Cemetery Ridge a few days before. He had stood in stunned bewilderment as the Rebels, having marched across more than a mile of wide-open fields straight into the massed power of the United States Army, shot, slashed, and slugged their way through two lines of Federal troops; and for several chilling moments, seemed on the verge of putting the whole Northern army to flight.

Had they but received reinforcements as we did, how differently might history have written the day—and the war? he wondered to himself, shuddering at the thought before consigning it to the perdition of his subconscious.

We must purpose to vanquish them with the superior ardor of a superior cause, he vowed as he led his small detachment of horse soldiers south into the little Maryland town of Boonsboro. *And I must determine to play a keener role in that vanquishing by catching Bobby Lee, or whatever of his force I can, before the whole lot of them have escaped across the Potomac.*

He knew at least one man who would answer that challenge. "Kilcavalry" Kilpatrick rode next to Dahlgren. The two had crossed paths as they fought Jeb Stuart's plucky horse soldiers the last few days. Kilpatrick impressed him as one of the few Federals as singlemindedly devoted to the utter destruction of the Rebels as Dahlgren himself. They presented some pair, the odd-featured, rusty-bearded Kilpatrick better than a foot shorter than the fair, handsome Dahlgren.

The younger man found himself amused by the bandy-legged little Jersey native who strutted around as cocksure as a twenty-eight-year-old general who planned nothing less than one day to be the President of the United States, which he did.

Kilpatrick, for his part, quickly perceived the similarly well-connected Dahlgren as the sort around whom action and the opportunity for laurels would festoon themselves, and decided to ride with him a ways.

"Understand you and your father are fast friends with the president," Kilpatrick opined as they neared the center of the village. Dahlgren, curious as to why two scouts he'd sent ahead had not yet returned, turned toward Kilpatrick in surprise. *Such chatter for a time as this,* he thought.

"I should say Father more than myself," Dahlgren said, his countenance genial, "though I have been graced with the president's—"

Before he could speak further, gunfire resounded through the main street of the town. Three blocks ahead, Dahlgren saw one of his scouts and the rider-less horse of the other round a corner and charge toward him. Mere yards behind them were—

"Rebel horse!" Dahlgren shouted, whipping his saber from its scabbard. He glanced at Kilpatrick, who, his own revolver drawn, nodded his assent to Dahlgren's lead.

"Death or glory," Kilpatrick said, a wry grin parting his beard, which Dahlgren realized for the first time was quite curly and not awfully thick.

Then bullets were flying and Dahlgren was shouting orders and leading his men—who were outnumbered and to a man would not have engaged the Confederates if the decision had been left to them—straight into the enemy. It took only seconds for the two forces to collide, men screaming, horses tumbling, guns cracking, and bullets singing in every direction, shattering store windows, thudding into other horses, and knocking men from their saddles. As Dahlgren hacked away with his sword in the swirling melee, sight becoming precious as the air filled with thin blue-white gun smoke, he realized a Reb trooper had aimed a pistol point-blank at his head. Dahlgren scarcely had time to be scared before he heard the Reb gun's hammer go *click*. An instant later one of Dahlgren's men blew the Southerner out of his saddle. Then another Confederate came at that Federal, slashing with his sword. He was driving the man back when Dahlgren raised his own blade high and swung it down like the scythe of the Grim Reaper himself, nearly decapitating the man.

Then, amid the ear-ringing din of the battle, which had grown brutal and desperate, as Dahlgren refused to relent and the Rebs, for once with superior numbers in a fray, weren't about to turn tail, Dahlgren winced at the deafening sound of gunshots close by. He turned to see a Reb shoot a Yank a few feet away out of the saddle. Then the Reb turned his long-barreled Colt toward Dahlgren and fired. Ulric ducked and turned away, but the man kept shooting. Dahlgren felt one bullet singe his ear, then another tear into his foot. He spurred on his mount across the street and away from the shooter as bullets, screams, and curses continued to fly through the smoke. Some yards away he squinted to make out— *Could that be Paul, the newspaper reporter?* he asked himself in amazement. *By Jove, it is!*

E. A. Paul, correspondent for the *New York Times,* had chased after Dahlgren and his men when he heard the shooting break out. Dahlgren and the tenacious journalist had shared wine, cigars, and more than a few laughs during the war.

"I say, Paul!" Dahlgren hollered, as pain began to course through his foot and up his leg. "I think I got it this time!"

Paul looked up from the pad upon which he was scribbling. The fat stump of a Cuban cigar blazed from his mouth. *That man is a better horseman than I gave him credit for,* Dahlgren thought, admiring how still Paul's horse remained under him.

"Dahlgren!" Paul shouted. "I say, you'd best be gettin' out of here. You've too many men down!"

Dahlgren glanced around. Wooziness began to overtake him. "Think so?" he asked, turning back to Paul, of whom he now saw two.

Then Paul's horse began to wobble, and the scribe managed to hop off it just before it crashed to the dusty ground. *Well, no wonder that ride was so steady,* Dahlgren thought, *he had four bullets in him—or was it two?*

"Come on, let's get out of here!" Paul shouted, running toward Dahlgren and taking his proffered arm to swing up onto the soldier's horse.

Dahlgren managed to solicit the call to retreat from his bugler just before that man was shot dead from his horse. Then they were riding away from Boonsboro fast, Rebel bullets helping them on their way.

Dahlgren had thought he would be the first one out of town, but he was surprised to find Kilpatrick waiting up on a ridge they had crossed a couple of miles back.

"Shot but not dead," Kilpatrick grinned. "You'll be more of a hero now than you were before, boyo."

The ground was spinning under Dahlgren.

"Ulric, you're going to be drained dry if you don't get down," he heard Paul say.

"The Rebs," Dahlgren gasped, shoving his saber back into its scabbard and pulling out his revolver. "We've got to form a line to fight off the Rebs. They'll be coming; they always come."

"Not this time, boyo," Kilpatrick said, laughing. "They're trying to get out of Maryland, not in."

They were the last words Dahlgren heard before he slid from the saddle.

CHAPTER 11

ONE EVENING A FEW WEEKS LATER, AS THE ARMY OF Northern Virginia, unpursued by the bloodied Federals, licked its own wounds in quiet camp near the northern Virginia town of Orange Courthouse, Lee dispatched Taylor on a final errand. All his aides having been so dispatched or dismissed for the night, the Southern commander sat alone in the soft kerosene light of his tent. Outposts of crickets chirped their evening lullabies to the encamped Confederate hosts as the clammy heat melted into the gentler warmth of the night watches.

So often his thoughts ran at times such as these to Arlington. *Ah, dear Arlington,* he would think, recalling the splash of bright colors; the intoxication of rapturous aromas; the contented bliss of treasured children, happy acres, and forests; and the love of a good woman.

Almost at the end had come those fateful days in April 1861 when one of President Lincoln's closest friends, Francis P. Blair Sr., and the commander of the American army, Winfield Scott, a fellow Virginian, both petitioned Lee—on behalf of Lincoln himself—to take command of the *Federal* army. The offer constituted all that Lee had toiled an entire, often thankless, career to attain. Thirty years of dreary army posts mostly without his family, without the woman a man needs. Desolate dusty frontier duty where the loneliness and regrets of mistakes past and missed experiences present could burn out a man's brain more certainly than the scalding sun above. A tense, bloody war to the death with the savage Comanche Indians as two peoples fought for possession of one land—Texas.

He had refused the honor, one of the highest his nation could bestow. He felt as though drawn in twain by a great broadsword, two parts of him, for how could not part of him ever reside with the Union his forefathers had carved out of wilderness with blood, steel, and tears?

Then, the guns of Fort Sumter and Lincoln's call to all the states, including Virginia, to supply their share of seventy-five thousand troops to "suppress insurrection" in the South. War.

The night pro-Union Virginia's legislators refused to supply their levy for the killing of their Southern brothers and cousins, instead voting to join the infant Confederate States of America—the night they knew for sure their fate was cast in stone—Lee completed the family prayers after supper and went to his room upstairs. For hours he paced the floor as Mary sat knitting downstairs. *A Union that can only be maintained by swords and bayonets, and in which strife and civil war are to take the place of brotherly love and kindness, has no charm for me,* he thought, *agitated by Cotton Belt hotheads and myopic, self-righteous Northern abolitionists alike.*

The bewitching fragrance of new life birthed during springtime at Arlington from God's eternal cycle of creation, growth, death, and resurrection had filled his nostrils as a breeze drifting up from the river kissed Mary's lace curtains back from an open window. His still-sharp eyes could just make out the dome of the Federal capitol building across the Potomac as it loomed into the clear evening sky above dimly lit Washington City. *That beautiful feature of our landscape has ceased to charm me as much as formerly,* he thought with much regret. *I fear the mischief that is brewing there.*

For some moments he stood, staring and remembering. *How?* he wondered. *How can I leave my country and all that it means?* His mind roamed back through the many years of his own service to it, of Washington his hero—and his own wife's step-great-grandfather—and of his own father, the famed Light-Horse Harry Lee, Washington's cavalry commander. *Just as young Jeb is mine,* Lee realized.

And he thought of Arlington, forever a lush gateway to the squalid dirty capital, and stately Georgetown, both directly across the river from it. Were its high hills, its massive white columns, and enormous, forest-flanked structure now to become a defiant and foreboding sentinel of the land at whose head it stood and which spread thousands of miles behind it? Was the Potomac the now-severed chord of its union with the Old Republic?

The Republic bought for me and mine by the blood of my fathers, he thought in agony. *And what is more, I do not believe in secession as a constitutional right or that there is sufficient cause for revolution.*

Still he paced back and forth, the hard oaken floor creaking beneath him. Finally he dropped to his knees before his open Bible and prayed for more hours in much agony of soul, as so often had Washington who had forged the union Lee might now destroy. Downstairs, when Mary heard the familiar sound of his massive frame going to the floor, she joined her own silent prayers to his, praying wisdom and understanding and courage for him.

And yet, with all my devotion to the Union, and the feeling of loyalty and duty of an American citizen, how can I raise my hand against my relatives, my children, my home? he thought, resolution crashing home to him as the waves birthed by a hurricane roaring over a defenseless Tidewater beach. *Had Virginia stood by the old Union, so would have I. But now that she has seceded, I must follow my native state—she who has succored me from my birth,* he realized as renewed gratitude and emotion for that incalculable gift flooded over him. *With my sword and, if need be, with my life.*

All these remembrances in mind, it seemed strange that Providence had brought Lee to his current plight as the summer of 1863 faded. Still he had thought it through from every conceivable angle. All pointed in the same direction. Of course, cynics and enemies would assign motivations of cunning and calculation to him. *My resignation, they will say, is intended only to wrench from President Davis a public show of support and confidence for my continued leadership. Ah, how easy to appear brave and wise from behind the politician's stump, the publisher's printing press, and the academician's lectern,* he thought with gentle mirth. Sighing, he dipped his quill in the inkwell and began to write. He knew nearly all his lieutenants had erred at Gettysburg, some of them grievously. And yet, since the fall of Stonewall and others, were many of them not new to their elevated positions of responsibility in the reorganized Army of Northern Virginia? And had not they all done their very best? His eyes grew wet as he recalled the toll taken on those of field rank, colonels or higher, in Pickett's division. Only one of thirteen colonels lived through the debacle—and that man had lost an arm. None of Pickett's generals would ever again take the field.

Knowing full well that Davis might release part or all of this correspondence to the world, Lee wrote nonetheless, "No blame can be attached to the army for its failure to accomplish what was projected by me, nor should it be censured for the unreasonable expectations of the public—I am alone to blame in perhaps expecting too much of its prowess and valour." *Yes, it is all my fault. I indeed thought they were invincible.*

He stopped for a moment and drew a deep breath, reflecting upon all he had sacrificed to arrive at this sad day. *But God disposes, and that should be enough for us.* He reinked the pen and wrote, with resolution. "I therefore, in all sincerity, request Your Excellency to take measures to supply my place. I do this with the more earnestness because no one is more aware than myself of my inability for the duties of my position. I cannot even accomplish what I myself desire. How can I fulfill the expectations of others?"

As frustration welled up in him, he paused before continuing. "Everything, therefore, points to the advantages to be derived from a new commander, and I the more anxiously urge that matter upon Your Excellency from my belief that a younger and abler man than myself can readily be obtained. I know that he will have as gallant and brave an army as ever existed to second his efforts, and it would be the happiest day of my life to see at its head a worthy leader—one that would accomplish more than I could perform and all that I have wished. I hope Your Excellency will attribute my request to the true reason, the desire to serve my country, and to do all in my power to insure the success of her righteous cause."

He signed the document and sat quietly for a moment. *God's will ought to be our aim, and I am quite contented that His designs should be accomplished and not mine.* Yes, that was enough.

"General Lee, sir?"

Lee looked up to see the revered Presbyterian clergyman Beverly Tucker Lacy. Even before the war, Lacy was regarded as one of the greatest preachers in the South. Stonewall handpicked him to oversee the religious organization and instruction of the entire Second Corps of the Army of Northern Virginia, from where spiritual revival had blossomed and spread throughout the army, now even to the West. The two men prayed and conferred with one another virtually every day. Lacy, who had lived in the Chancellorsville area, directed Stonewall to the route by which he outflanked the Federal army and won the greatest victory of the war for the Confederacy. And Stonewall chose Lacy as his bedside chaplain the final days of his life.

With Lacy was a young Baptist pastor, John William Jones. When Lee expressed familiarity with Jones and his work, the diminutive little man blushed scarlet and seemed about to topple over.

Lacy addressed the chaplains' business. "General Lee, a growing desire is evidenced by many faithful men, officers—many of them at the highest levels—

as well as those in the ranks, that effort be imparted by the army to hold the Sabbath Day in better observance. Our old friend General Jackson"—at this, Lee's eyes flickered—"retained, by his own stainless example, the high and holy observance admonished to us by the written revelation."

Lacy cleared his throat and glanced at Jones before continuing. "Regrettably, sir, of late, sans the leadership of Stone . . . er . . . General Jackson, certain high-ranking officers have not deemed fit to continue such observances. Indeed a growing tendency seems evidenced toward converting the Sabbath into a grand gala day for inspections, reviews, and the like."

Now Lacy looked Lee full in the eye. "It is proving in some commands, sir, a serious obstacle to the efficient work of the chaplain."

Lee pondered the comments, the fact he would no longer be commanding this army momentarily forgotten. For was not the war for men's immortal souls the true and final conflict? A kindly smile crept out from behind his thick beard—a beard nearly black at the war's start and now, two years later, nearly white—and his eyes seemed focused on an object not within the tent where the three men sat. "I can remember General Jackson stating that his greatest military desire was to lead a 'converted army,'" Lee said.

A broad smile replaced the solemn set of Lacy's features as that man spoke. "He told me the only thing that gave him any apprehension about his country's cause was the sin of the army and people."

Jones drank this in as though he were a field mouse snuck in under Lee's tent flap to watch history—and Christian history at that—being authored in his presence. For over fifteen thousand men just in the Confederacy's Army of Northern Virginia would profess salvation through Christ during the winter of 1863–64 alone. *I should like to have made the acquaintance of Stonewall Jackson,* Jones thought, his admiration laced with a bittersweet tinge.

"The good and great Jackson," Lee mumbled, now staring into his flickering lantern. Then his attention swung back to the chaplains. "Yes, by all means, I shall issue a written address, by tomorrow, reminding the army of the blessed duty of all people of faith, and certainly of those who would comprise a Christian army, to honor faithfully the fourth commandment. Men, it seems as though every brigade in the Army of Northern Virginia by now has its own log chapel, and some more than one. I understand they all host meetings every night of the week. As our sorrows and losses mount, the spiritual interests of the army seem to do so concurrently."

While Lacy elucidated the profound transformation sweeping so many through every division and regiment of the army, Lee's countenance grew radiant, his eyes glowing with joy as he nodded his large head.

At length, Lacy's expression again turned serious. "General Lee, sir, I must inform you of the deep interest which all of our chaplains feel for your welfare. I daresay that not a moment passes day or night in which at least one is not invoking the blessing of Almighty God on your behalf, sir."

Lee's eyes, so happy an instant before, now filled with tears. "I sincerely thank you for that," he said. Jones seemed surprised at Lee's depth of emotion, as well as the difficulty the words seemed to have in squirming out through the general's choking voice. "I can only say that I am a poor sinner, trusting in Christ alone, and that I need all the prayers you can offer for me."

A few days later, Cole Culpeper reigned in his mount, still boasting Federal saddle and accoutrements, at an unkempt little inn sitting astride a crossroads several miles shy of his family's farm. It had taken him weeks to traverse the Old Dominion. Deserters had streamed home after Gettysburg. A host of reasons compelled them to do so, many of them legitimate, such as getting wounds nursed, bringing in summer crops, visiting long-missed loved ones, and performing reparations around run-down, often Yankee-ravaged homes, outbuildings, and fields.

When victory did not visit itself upon an army, however, the inevitable dividends included the exodus of malcontents like Culpeper who had tired, albeit some of them only temporarily, of the sacrifice they might find bearable with victory.

As it was, Lee and President Davis held secret meetings in Richmond to discuss a strategy for dealing with the Confederate military's manpower shortage in general and its desertion problem in particular. That strategy took several forms, including the issuance of furloughs and amnesties. It also took the form of an aggressive home guard assigned with the "recovery" of soldiers absent without leave.

Culpeper, his beard grown long, full, and nearly orange in color, and his face burnished dark brown, had twice come within an eyelash of encounters with mounted home guard units. Both times he had eluded detection, but the narrow escapes had forced him to back roads, most of them unfamiliar to him.

His constant fear, coupled with the toll taken on his mind and body by Gettysburg, provoked him to long and frequent bouts of sleep, which further delayed his progress.

Now as he sat down to a bowl of bacon fat and hard bread—*I might as well be back in the danged army,* he thought, *at least I don't have to pay for bacon fat and wormy bread there, and sure not at these crazy prices*—he faced another jolt. The gaunt woman who served him seemed intent on staring a hole through him. *She looks near fifty, but how could she have all these little urchins if'n she was near that?* Culpeper wondered.

"Why you lookin' at me like that?" he growled, shoveling the food down. He had not eaten in two days. The war and the Yankees had not left much in Virginia even by August 1863.

"Guess General Lee's revival ain't took holt o' you, yet," she said, her voice hard and flat.

He stopped, wooden fork halfway to his mouth.

"You're a deserter, ain't cha?"

Culpeper didn't know what to say.

"My Horace deserted once, then he went back, got hisself religion, and died o' dysentery." She turned away from Culpeper and scooped up one of the several dirty young children that scurried about the splintered wood floor. "This here's Horace Junior, but little Leah over there favors Horace more'n he do."

She sized Culpeper up some more.

"You didn't git religion yet, did you?" Culpeper stared at her, cursing God— or the gods—that he should have come all this way to have a half-crazed woman swarmed over by children quiz him about religion. "Didn't think so," she answered herself. "Then you prob'ly won't like this." She shooed another of her children off a nearby stool and retrieved a newspaper from it. She shoved it at Culpeper, jamming a rock-hard chunk of bread into his nose.

"Lady, be careful with that!" he blurted. "Your bread's sure to kill me one way or t'other, if'n I stay 'round here long enough."

Culpeper wasn't long on education, but one of the Lexington ministers had taught him and all his brothers and sisters how to read and cipher. *Richmond Daily Examiner.* The headline read, "President Davis Calls Nation to Day of Fasting, Humiliation, and Prayer." A subhead read, "General Lee's Address to Troops."

Culpeper's eyes shot to the Lee story. "Soldiers! We have sinned against Almighty God. We have forgotten His signal mercies, and have cultivated a revengeful, haughty, and boastful spirit. We have not remembered that the defenders of a just cause should be pure, in His eyes; that our times are in His hands, and we have relied too much on our own arms for the achievement of our independence."

Culpeper's eyes narrowed.

Lee directed special attention toward the Sabbath. He renewed earlier orders calling for its strict observance and ordered that nothing should be done on the Lord's Day not critical to the maintenance or safety of the army. He also called for all the army's facilities and resources to be devoted to religious services on Sunday. Finally he exhorted officers and men alike to regular attendance at those services.

Culpeper slammed the paper shut and slung it into a corner. His green eyes glinting with fury, he crushed the remainder of the stonelike bread to powder in the palm of one hand.

"Don't say whether them Sabbath rules apply to deserters or not," his hostess intoned.

One communication to which Culpeper did not have access was President Davis's prompt response to Lee's resignation: "To ask me to substitute you by someone in my judgment more fit to command, or who would possess more of the confidence of the army, or of the reflecting men of the country, is to demand an impossibility . . ."

As one hard-bitten Confederate soldier would say, "The army would have arisen in revolt if it had been called upon to give up General Lee."

CHAPTER 12

MARLEY STARED AT THE CHILLING HEADLINES. EAGER anticipation of his return to active cavalry duty the next day had until moments before filled him. *Can this be true?* he wondered, a chill spreading through his chest and abdomen. *Have we not enough enemies already that we seek to destroy? Must we turn our guns—our cannon!—on our own populace? And who are the supposed oppressors of the Negroes?*

Yet there it was, screaming across the front page of one of America's greatest newspapers, the *New York Times*. While America destroyed the best men it had in war with itself, all of the North seemed to be smoldering with fury back home. *Especially New York City,* Marley thought, shaking his head in astonishment.

The *Times* offered numerous explanations for the riots, including Democratic accusations that Lincoln's Republican administration was drafting too many Democrats and not enough Republicans. Also that Republican soldier votes brought in from the battlefields filled Democrat-dominated New York City's ballot boxes. And that giving blacks the vote—and perhaps even shipping them in from the South to work—intentionally threatened local white political power, as well as the jobs of whites, especially the Irish.

Regardless of the reasons, a mob that mounted in size and fury as it went destroyed a local draft office, cleaned out an armory, and, now armed to the teeth, proceeded on a rampage of destruction and theft that included, but was by no means limited to, jewelry stores and liquor establishments. Marley's blood began to boil as he read how "many, many" incidents had been reported of mob members running down blacks "as hounds would chase a fox," beating them, and hanging them from street lamps.

For three days the mob, now numbering in the thousands, pillaged and ransacked its own city. They torched a black children's orphanage and roared their approval of the blaze.

"This whole bloody war's the darkies' fault sure," one young hellion-shouted, swigging rotgut and firing a revolver into the air. "Let them feel the bite of war their own selves!"

Marley shook his head in disbelief as he read how the mob eventually cleared out the law and gained control of the entire city! *I cannot fathom it,* he thought with rue, *the largest and greatest city in the history of America, taken over by street scum, wharf riffraff, and the flotsam and jetsam of Europe's immigrant castoffs.*

Of course, it was not quite that simple, but nothing less than the Army of the Potomac could end it. Thousands of Meade's men swarmed into the city. The Northern rebels and the bluecoats crashed together with a fury rarely exceeded on the bloody fields of Virginia. It took a pitched battle, house-to-house fighting, Federal bayonets and sharpshooters, and massed volleys of grapeshot and canister from the mouths of smoking Federal batteries to finally put down the insurrection.

Hundreds were killed, many thrown—some dead, some dying—shot, stabbed, riddled with grape by their fellow United States citizens, into the middle of the street by the battle-hardened, combat-frenzied Federal soldiers. Secretary of War Stanton declared that the draft, in every Northern state, would be enforced, "even should there be a riot and mob in every ward of every city."

Sleep came very slowly to Marley that night. Over and over the horrific scenes roiled through his head. At length he slept, but only after realizing that for the duration of this long American nightmare the United States would need men, many men, determined to persevere to the end, and to do so without forgetting the humanity and civilization they so often cited as the genesis of their "Manifest Destiny."

Else a darkness beyond the ability of any of us to comprehend may, God please forbid, descend upon this once-fair land, he thought with much foreboding.

Ulric felt badly before the surgeons examined him. He felt worse afterwards. "That foot had better come off," they had said. Over and over the dread proclamation marched through his head. *"If the infection gets into your bloodstream . . ."* Already they had cut several chunks of bone out of his foot. At first he had felt quite well. But now . . . rather than gaining strength, each day seemed further to drain him of energy. His body grew hotter. The soft pulsing discomfort grew to a pounding, tearing pain. *"That foot had better come off."* *But how can I possibly cover the Dahlgren name in glory riding a wooden desk in filthy Washington City?* he thought, desperation creeping in amid the fever. *And what will Father think?*

He could not know that Admiral Dahlgren, commanding the Federals' South Atlantic Blockade Fleet, was writing to him, "There is nothing good that could happen to me which by any possibility could compensate for a serious evil to any of my children."

He heard his mother's voice as she greeted someone at the front door of his parents' home, where he had resided the past several days since arriving on a stretcher from Maryland. *Dear Mother,* he thought, his eyes misting with tears, *what must her heart now be bearing? Me lying here shot up, maybe about to lose a foot. Father in combat out at sea, hundreds of miles away. And my older brother in the next room, near death from the malaria he brought home from Vicksburg.* Dahlgren began to sink into a funk. Next thing he knew, his mother was at the bedroom door.

"Ully?" she said, as if afraid that if her words were spoken too loudly they would knock her son's foot right off his leg. "You have a very special visitor, dear."

Now Dahlgren discerned the joy and pride painted across the face that still, in her mid-forties, drew stares of admiration from the men who walked the nation's most potent corridors of power.

Into the room stepped Abraham Lincoln.

"Hello, son," Lincoln said, crossing to the bed and sitting on it next to Dahlgren, then shaking the weak hand the younger man proffered. Lincoln could barely mask his shock at Dahlgren's loss of weight and color. He had no idea the boy's condition had so deteriorated.

"Hel . . ." Dahlgren started, his voice weak and raspy, ". . . hello, Mr. President."

"I don't know which to bring you up on charges for first," Lincoln said, the deep-set eyes dull with sorrow, "the uncharitable way you been dealing with these Rebels, or havin' the audacity to call your old friend Abe 'Mr. President.'"

Only then did he who was bedridden divine the merriment that lit up Lincoln's eyes. Mrs. Dahlgren saw the first smile crease her son's perspiring face she had seen in two days. *Such a good fine boy he is,* she thought, holding her hand to her mouth lest a sob connive its way out, *even the president sees it.*

"Now I want you and your brother to rest easy," Lincoln said, patting Dahlgren's forearm. "You may consider it a direct order from me that you obey with alacrity the instructions imparted to you both by your mother and by the doctors. I realize that for warriors and men of action such as yourselves, that ofttimes proves difficult. That is why I am giving you the straight medicine myself."

Mrs. Dahlgren swelled with pride as Lincoln continued.

"We've much too important work for the both of you. You must mend up and return to the field in as timely a fashion as is possible," Lincoln said, patting Dahlgren's arm again as the younger man tried to speak. "But with your strength and faculties intact, Captain." Lincoln glanced around at Mrs. Dahlgren, the hint of a smile curling his beard-wreathed lips upward. "Though I daresay that particular rank may fail even to outlast your present indisposition."

Dahlgren stared up at the president, discerning the sparkle that returned to his eyes, but not the portent of his statement. Mrs. Dahlgren, tears filling her eyes, did understand.

"You rest easy, young man," Lincoln said, patting Dahlgren's arm anew. "The United States of America will wage this war whilst you heal, then cheer your soon return to the ranks of her protectors."

Outside the room, retrieving his stovepipe hat from an aide, Lincoln looked Mrs. Dahlgren square in the eye. His face had regained its normal solemn countenance. "How can words evince my gratitude to you for the sacrifice your family is making?" he said. "I know only that a nation comprised of such brave men as your husband and sons—and of valorous women the like of yourself, madam—is a nation whose history is not finished being written."

Marley's first orders were to report to Fightin' Joe Hooker in Washington. The Federal scout's importunings to his friend and corps commander Major General Oliver "Old Prayer Book" Howard to buttress his vulnerable right flank at Chancellorsville had been remembered to Fightin' Joe by more than one officer who had witnessed the heated exchange. Especially after Stonewall Jackson had proceeded to hurl his entire Confederate Second Corps, in a lightninglike shock attack that drove everyone and everything before it for three full miles, against the precise spot Marley had pled with Howard to fortify.

Though Lincoln had sacked Hooker as commander of the Army of the Potomac—his army thrashed and himself nearly killed by Lee and Jackson at Chancellorsville—Hooker still possessed a solid reputation in knowing military circles. He knew a new and important assignment awaited him, and he planned to be ready for it. Investigating Wayne Marley and his sterling record of service, Hooker suspected he had found a man who might prove invaluable to him when that assignment came.

"This Pinkerton outfit," Hooker fairly spat out to Marley as their barouche turned into one of Washington's most stately neighborhoods, "may yet win the war. The issue in question is whether they shall win it for us or the d— Rebels."

For most of the sweltering ride over from Stanton's office, Fightin' Joe had regaled Marley regarding the incompetency of the private security firm that Lincoln had employed at the war's outset to supply intelligence to the Federals on Southern plans and movements. "Those—people," Hooker thundered, tossing his handsome blond head back in the direction of the capitol building and White House, "have blamed each succeeding commander of the Army of the Potomac for timidity, ineptitude, and sloth, when, truth be known, these Pinkerton fools have consistently led us to believe Lee's armies, which I am beginning to suspect possess only a fraction of the number of our troops, actually outmatch us in men, guns, horses, and equipment!"

Now Hooker's eyes narrowed and darkness covered his face. "I intend, if I can keep Stanton's and Halleck's—and Lincoln's—mitts off the reins of this army long enough, to find out from where this traitorous, mercenary stench that fills and shames Washington emanates."

Marley did not know whether he or Hooker was more startled by the outburst. When Hooker's driver swung open the door, the general shot a sheepish glance at Marley, saying, "I know enough of you and your . . . character not even to have to tell you how confidential are all my conversations with you."

Then Hooker realized the carriage had been stopped at the end of the street, which was blocked off. "What is this?" he asked a provost guard.

"Orders, sir. From the president himself," the man replied. "No vehicles of any sort allowed down this street."

Hooker canted his head, then motioned for Marley to follow as he moved past two other soldiers manning the street barricade. Another stood posted outside the house Marley followed Hooker into and where lay maimed another of those bold, capable men that Hooker, underrated and slandered because of his

Chancellorsville defeat, recognized through a military career that included distinguished service in both this war and the Mexican War of the forties, that the United States desperately needed.

As he stepped into the large, marble-floored foyer, Marley noticed the doorbell had been taped over. A chill ran through him as he sensed that presence whose visitations had become so familiar to him. The quiet, the medicinal aromas, the aura of something amiss, something missing—they all pointed toward the presence of death.

The grave middle-aged woman whose eyes shone with the bright light borne of that unholy intercourse of fatigue and terror struck Marley nonetheless as one of the most beautiful females of her age, perhaps of any age, that he had ever seen. The tones of her brief exchange with Hooker were hushed.

"I am so sorry, madam . . ."

"He is not even aware Secretary Stanton has made him the youngest colonel in the Union army . . ."

"Is there any service that we may render?"

"He is not able to receive any visitors at all now, General. The doctors have taken his leg and still they do not believe he will emerge from the coma he has been in for three days. They say he will be taken from us at any moment. And his brother lies dying of malaria in the very next room—"

At this she broke, and a black servant and an elegantly attired, fiftiesh white man who appeared to be a family member or close friend, escorted her, sobbing, back into the interior of her home.

Marley noticed that Hooker's gait had slowed as they retraced their steps up the street.

"Willard's," Hooker ordered the driver as he and Marley climbed back into the carriage. "I can tolerate the death and destruction and dismemberment, and I can be sober, but I cannot do both at all times," he said to Marley, his countenance absent of mirth. "Not when men the caliber of Ulric Dahlgren are lost to me."

Agnes, Mildred, Mary, and feeble, failing Charlotte returned to Richmond in October. The Confederate capitol scarcely resembled the refined prewar Southern city of forty thousand people. It burst at the seams with people, people everywhere, of every stripe. Blockade runners, spies, army deserters.

Speculators from all corners of the globe, along with refugees, often widowed and orphaned, from every corner of Virginia, especially those where battles and marauding Yankees had visited their wrath. Many others had simply migrated to Richmond for safety, to join loved ones, or to find work.

Then there were those like vultures hovering over a vulnerable carcass, some building fortunes off the misfortunes of others, some taking with blade or gun what they wanted under the cover of darkness.

With few able-bodied men present to defend the populace, the Lee women determined the streets of Richmond were no place to be at night, even in the respectable neighborhood where Mary had managed to rent a home.

Only the barest essentials could be afforded by nearly everyone, and those at exorbitant prices, many times what they had cost only twelve months previous. Everything else simply could not be had at any price, other than by those who placed their own comfort and interests above those of others, those of the Confederacy. The Lees knew too many of those sorts existed, when sacrifice was what was so desperately needed.

Agnes realized, as she knitted a pair of socks that might render one less Confederate soldier barefoot, that one sort of folk did not constitute part of the city's teeming masses. Rarely did she see a white man between the ages of sixteen and fifty who had two arms and two legs. *They are all away from us,* she reflected, *some forever . . . like . . . him.*

She gazed out the window, where the leaves were turning. *They are already gold and red and orange at Arlington,* she thought, smiling at the remembrance. *And there are so many of them.* Her attention turned to the house around her. The rented house. Someone else's house. *But how fortunate we are even to have a house, and not a bad little house at that,* she thought, knowing the crowds in Richmond that had no permanent shelter; the many who were crammed, several to each room; and others, their income ruined by war's devastations, who now shared their homes with boarders, ofttimes boarders they did not know, and who were selling their furniture off piece by piece.

Yes, we are indeed blessed, she thought, *and though we have little enough furniture, we indeed have enough glasses to go around, even when company comes to sup!* True, the glasses belonged to others, as did the modest supply of china. And yes, even the knives, forks, and spoons. Nearly everything had been left at Arlington, and what hadn't was stored at the Wickhams.

A stab of neuralgia sharp enough to cause her to release her knitting and put her hand to her face occurred simultaneously with her recollection of the sad letter her mother had received the day before. Yes, Arlington had been confiscated by the Federal government. Yes, the Congressional law mandating a direct—and large—tax on real estate "in the insurrectionary districts within the United States" applied to Arlington. Yes, that levy must be paid by the owner in person! And Mary Lee had learned with the reading of the letter that the United States government did not care for the tax money as much as they cared for the appearance of the landowner in Washington City. Government officials refused to accept payment of the extortionary tax in full by one of her cousins. Federal commissioners intended to issue a tax title to the U.S. government.

Mary, stiff and ashen-faced, rose from her wheelchair with the aid of Agnes and laid her pained little body down to rest the night before, realizing for the first time that she might never even see Arlington again.

How she has kept us all going through this nightmare, Agnes thought, tears filling her brown eyes, *and now, after a lifetime of service to humanity and kindness to everyone she ever met, she is left homeless and with hardly a possession in the world!* She began quietly to weep. *Just as Father now appears to be keeping the whole Confederacy going through the nightmare.* The public and the newspapers alike grew ever more venomous in their criticism of President Davis. Many cried for Lee to be named commander-in-chief of all Southern armies—a position Davis had indeed finally relinquished to close friend and supporter Braxton Bragg, whom the public had virtually demanded be recalled from his overall command in the Western theater because of his inability to convert opportunities into victories. This, so the uproar went, while Lee created victories in the east where no opportunity had even existed.

Moreover, word had spread that the South's greatest fighting force, the Army of Northern Virginia, now fought for Robert E. Lee as much as it fought for freedom or family or the Confederacy. A smile gradually took form across Agnes's flawless face. The Richmond City Council, amid all the want and woe of the ceaseless conflict, was actually in the process of buying a beautiful home in one of the city's loveliest neighborhoods and giving it to the Lee family as a gift. *And Papa—only Papa could have refused them, saying far too much want and suffering existed for him even to consider such a thing!* she thought, shaming herself that her pride was mitigated by a tinge of covetous disappointment.

Papa . . . an unexpected knock on the front door interrupted her musings. With all the Lees' servants freed or left back at Arlington, Agnes answered the door herself. A lovely, familiar face framed in a stylish bonnet greeted her, flanked by two blacks, and a carriage beyond the front gate. That face, bejeweled with a dazzling pair of sea-colored eyes, broke into a delighted smile. The eyes, which seemed to change not only with mood but with lighting and time of day, recalled the name of Agnes's Virginia Female Institute schoolmate to her lips.

"Rachel Anne McDowell!" she exclaimed, hugging the visitor and kissing her cheek. The two had not been close at school, but a smiling face from happier times, times associated with Arlington, filled Agnes with joy.

"Eleanor Agnes Lee, dear, such a woman you've become!" Rachel Anne said, her finely sculpted face luminous with mirth. For a moment she stared at Agnes in wonder. "You have grown only more beautiful with time."

"And you," Agnes said without guile, "such a lovely dress—my, can it be satin? So rare I see so beautiful a dress in these times."

"With Father and all my brothers off at war, I just can't resist galavanting over here to ole Richmond whenever I can shake the dust off ole blue-stockinged Rockbridge County to do some shopping," Rachel Anne said, "but one cannot go far at these horrid prices." She looked Agnes over from top to bottom. Failing to find a dress meritorious of a compliment, she returned to Agnes's personal beauty. "So tell me, Aggie, do the boys still trip and stumble over themselves to earn just a little ole speck of your attention, dear?"

Agnes's eyes dropped to the ground as if she were struck.

"Why, Aggie," Rachel Anne said, alarmed. "Did I say something imprudent? Is your family well?"

Agnes looked up again, her eyes wet. Her words came forth cushioned with softness. "Come inside, Rachel Anne, so that I may enjoy the blessing of your presence. Have you lodging?"

"Yes, dear," Rachel said, wary. "Father, though somewhere north with your father—how famous *he* now is!—arranged my stay at the apartments of one of our Rockbridge legislators. One of his wife's tea friends mentioned having heard that you and your family had rented these quarters, so, not wishing to bankrupt Valiant—our plantation near Lexington—with the purchase of another dress at these extortionist, blockade-running prices, I determined to come see you instead. Your company is infinitely more edifying and not nearly so painful to one's purse!"

In the course of the next two hours, over the weakest tea Rachel Anne could ever remember tasting, she learned of the loss of Annie, the wounding and imprisonment of Rooney, the death of his two children, and the illness of Charlotte. She neither learned nor knew anything of Orton.

Agnes learned that Rachel Anne's father, one of the richest planters in the Upper Shenandoah Valley, had equipped an entire company of Confederate cavalry from his own considerable holdings, appointed two of his three sons as officers under him (the third joined Wade Hampton's horse from school in Maryland), and left his Yankee overseer in charge of Valiant, the McDowells' thirty-thousand-acre plantation. Rachel Anne expressed regret and some embarrassment that nearly a dozen of Valiant's sixty-one slaves had vanished north since the beginning of the war, and she evidenced a degree of irritation with "this foolish ole war" continuing to interrupt the life she was attempting to live. The latter sentiment struck a chord with Agnes, though being the daughter of Robert E. Lee she declined to acknowledge so. Still, Rachel Anne praised God that the McDowell men had thus far dealt out a wagonload of misery to the Yankees with no more recompense from their actions than a few scratches and bruises.

"How lucky you and I are to have such brave and gallant fathers and brothers, Aggie!" Rachel Anne concluded, her radiant skin aglow.

She is charming and pretty as she always was, Agnes thought to herself as she watched Rachel Anne and her servants climb into the carriage and depart. *And she still has all of her kin, all of her possessions, even new dresses, and her Valiant.*

After the Gettysburg campaign, Meade had brought the Federals back down into Virginia. As autumn progressed, the two bloodied armies stared sullenly across the Rapidan at each other, in virtually the same places they had stood in June.

"Sir," Taylor said to Lee one bright midday in early October. "More has arrived."

Lee peered up at him from the makeshift desk in his tent. "More?" he said. Taylor had been after the general for months to accept the various offers of lodging that inevitably came when the army was in the field. *Now,* Taylor thought, *in his condition, he simply* must *start paying heed to such opportunities.*

Lee stepped outside. Nearby stood nearly an entire wagonload of food and supplies.

"The usual, sir," Taylor said. "Turkeys, wine, cheeses, cream, duck, preserves, pastries with frosting, horehound candy, woolen greatcoats, new leather boots, spurs, hats—even real coffee, sir." This last, Lee thought, seemed to carve more of an impression on Taylor than all the others.

Lee glanced at Taylor as he returned to the tent. "Then dispose of it in the usual manner," the older man said simply.

"But sir, surely something for your meal—" Taylor attempted as the tent flap closed.

Lee gazed at the maps spread before him. In a maneuver only slightly less audacious than that he had employed with Stonewall Jackson two years before that resulted in the smashing victory at Second Manassas—and the removal from the Eastern theater of the civilian-terrorizing Federal General John Pope—he would send the corps of A. P. Hill and Richard Ewell to the west and around Meade's right flank and attempt to sever him from Washington, thus forcing another pitched battle.

Now, however, travails mental and physical intruded upon Lee. Since Chancellorsville, he had lost his two previous—and best—corps commanders. Stonewall had died and Longstreet had been sent west by Davis to lend aid to the befuddled Bragg in Tennessee. If not for perhaps his most impassioned and persuasive presentation of the entire war to Davis, Lee himself would have been heading west to take command. He shuddered to think how close had been that call.

More of his troops had been sent by Davis to defensive positions along the Atlantic Coast, more still to other positions farther south, in the interior. Thousands more had been lost at Gettysburg and to a subsequent wave of desertions, many of the latter men answering the pleadings of their families to bring in what they could of the season's crops.

All tolled, Lee calculated he now commanded only forty-six thousand men. Meade had nearly eighty thousand, and his ranks were expanding every day.

Rooney, wounded, lay rotting in a Federal prison somewhere up north. Charlotte slipped bit by bit away from her once-promising life with each passing day. Mary, Agnes, and Mildred lived in rented quarters with virtually no possessions of their own in a Richmond Lee now felt too dangerous for them to live. He had urged Mary as such, stopping short of ordering her to leave, for fear such a move might exacerbate her deteriorating physical condition.

Now more darkness appeared on the horizon. With mounting frequency, reports were finding their way to Lee from Jeb's spies and scouts suggesting a Federal raid on Richmond to free their thousands of cold, hungry, disease-ridden prisoners held in Libby and Belle Isle.

Summoning the collected wisdom of four decades of soldiering, his knowledge of his native Virginia, and an unusual ability to peer into the workings of his adversaries' minds, Lee called together his entire staff—Taylor, Venable, Marshall, military secretary Armistead Long, and two others—spartan as it was, and pointed to an obscure spot on the map whose name did not even appear.

"That is Ely's Ford, gentleman, and that is where Meade shall cross the Rapidan," he said. "I want pickets and at least two of Hampton's scouts posted around that ford without cessation until this attack comes."

Taylor, marveling that Lee could be so certain even that an attack would occur, much less of its launching point, noticed a cloud pass across his commander's face. The younger man did not know its origin was the specter dawning on Lee of thousands of heavily armed horse crashing down on a war-exhausted, refugee-loaded city possessed of scant military defenses, except tens of thousands of hungry, frightened women, children, and elderly. *What manner of war is that?* Lee wondered, his face ashen.

Remembrance of his own clay frame returned as an unwelcome intruder to Lee. "Rheumatism," one doctor had said. "Lumbago," diagnosed another. "Sciatica," a third announced. And these, the best doctors in the South.

All Lee knew was that since Gettysburg, the third day of Gettysburg—since seeing his slaughtered regiments limping, crawling, and bleeding back to him from Cemetery Ridge—his chest, arms, back, and in particular his left side had ached, and he had not felt well.

The steaming aroma of Lee's dinner mercifully terminated this anxiety-borne train of thought.

"Your usual, sir," the young aide said, placing the food before his commander. "Boiled cabbage."

Lee eyed Taylor's disapproving expression across the tent.

"Captain Taylor, have you any idea how many women, children, and aged Virginians, many with not even a roof over their heads, would treasure a dish of bowled cabbage for their lunch today?"

Taylor blushed crimson and thought of many things to say, knowing the wagonload of booty was even now being distributed among the troops and any civilians remaining in the area. Had he said anything, it would have been *Robert E. Lee is not like other men.*

"Not feeling well" meant for Lee not being able to mount his own horse, Traveller. It meant having to be transported in a wagon for the first two days of the campaign, his barrel-chested upper body throbbing more with pain with each and every bump and jolt of the springless vehicle.

His sound plan fell victim to an uncharacteristically brash attack by A. P. Hill at Bristoe Station that a Federal ambush chewed to pieces, along with nearly fourteen hundred Confederate soldiers.

News of the setback gave Lee the sensation someone had kicked the air out of his lungs. He had held high expectations for the offensive move, and he wanted the Yankees out of Virginia for Christmas. He still held secret hope that a devastating-enough defeat might elevate the public and political pressure on Lincoln to the level that he would have no choice but to negotiate an honorable peace.

With plenty on his mind to say to Hill as they rode over the carnage-strewn field the next morning, and fully aware that the press and national and world opinion would assign the blot to his own record rather than his subordinate's, Lee perceived the anguish racking Hill over the losses and said simply, "Well, well, General, bury these poor men and let us say no more about it."

Jeb Stuart's cavalry, however, ran roughshod over the Northern horse, chasing Kilpatrick's forces on a five-mile gallop that history bequeathed the name the "Buckland Races." The battle-hardened Army of Northern Virginia held Meade's growing forces at bay for the rest of the year.

Still, as Thanksgiving Day neared, and the ever-expanding Federal armies contrasted with the South's irretrievable battle losses; bloody, barefooted, and malnourished soldiers; starving horses; and Lincoln's blockade stranglehold, Lee felt the weight of the world on his aching broad shoulders, and well could he empathize with King Solomon's words:

"O Lord my God, thou hast made thy servant king . . . I am but a little child: I know not how to go out or come in. And thy servant is in the midst of thy people which thou hast chosen, a great people, that cannot be numbered nor counted for multitude.

"Give therefore thy servant an understanding heart to judge thy people, that I may discern between good and bad: for who is able to judge this thy so great a people?"

Culpeper's first inkling of trouble came when none of his dogs greeted him as he neared the family farm. Riding closer he saw fields overgrown with weeds and secondary growth brush, jackrabbits and other small animals flitting among them. A cold surge mixed of equal parts shock and fear rushed into his chest. *These fields have not even been worked this year,* he thought, his mind struck dumb with confusion.

His eyes caught hold of the source of a persistent slapping sound, a quarter mile down the road—the front door of the Culpeper home, flying back and forth, open and shut. He rode on, a greater fear lurking deep inside him than he had known as he marched up Cemetery Ridge.

When he reached the little family graveyard in the oak grove behind the house, he saw the new crosses. His grandfather, 1861. His sister, 1862. His mother, three months ago. Staggered, he realized that left only his sister's eight-year-old son, and evidence of him, dead or alive, was nowhere to be seen. Nor was anyone else—the Culpepers had never owned slaves on their modest land. Most of the family's furniture still remained in the house, along with a racoon and a cluster of field mice.

Where can he be? he thought. He had seen the empty farmhouses of the only neighbors within five miles on his ride in. *I'll go to Emma in Lexington. Maybe he's with her and her own two little ones.* He had wanted to see Cousin Emma first anyway.

He had left the army and traveled across a war, home guards, and three states to come home. Only there was no more home. For a moment he thought he might fall to his knees and cry. But he was a hard man and he grew harder. As he mounted up to leave, he began to consider upon whom he might wreak vengeance for all his sufferings, and now those of his family.

CHAPTER 13

MEADE, LIKE LEE WISHING FOR DECISIVE RESULTS BEFORE winter spread its eiderdown blanket over Virginia, parlayed surprise and the cover of night to swipe a key bridge fortification of Lee's across the Rappahannock. The move pressured the Confederate chieftain to pull his forces back to the Rapidan.

But Meade wanted more, and so did his Washington masters. The year shortly to close had seen the most terrific campaigns of slaughter America had ever known. It had seen widespread discontent and bloody riots. It had seen, Meade knew, a United States citizenry stunned both by the personal and corporate depth of its losses, impatient for a termination of such horror, and cognizant of the presidential election in twelve months that was shaping up as a referendum on Lincoln and, as more and more were whispering if not shouting, "his war." That emancipation of the slaves, in the South at least, now figured into the mix, generated more anger than enthusiasm among Northerners.

So Meade, winner of the biggest victory yet for the North at Gettysburg, but possessed of at best lukewarm support from Lincoln and Stanton, swung his forces across the Rapidan and around Lee's right flank, intending to split the corps of Hill and Ewell, then gobble them up one at a time.

But the "Gray Fox," as a grudgingly admiring Northern press now called Lee, anticipated the action. Shifting his own men into a north-south line to meet the now-westward movement of Meade, he honed the practice of trenches and earthworks he had pioneered as far back as Second Manassas, and which would prove the linchpin in history's greatest wars for better than the next half century. With a force barely more than half the size of Meade's,—the old engineer dug his raggedy soldiers in with such pluck that Meade found no way even to attempt an attack.

Many thoughts coursed through Lee's mind as he rode on an inspection of Hill's positions one Sunday morning, the musket cracks of skirmishers not far away garnished with a gathering chorus of artillery fire. *One of the miseries of war is that there is no Sabbath,* he thought, regret filling him. The illness of Hill and that man's failure as a corps commander to match his slashing, sometimes dramatic, success as a division chief presented itself next for Lee's meditation. And poor Ewell—Lee flinched at the specter of a metaphor in the exertions of "Old Baldy" to mount his horse and stay astride it with aplomb—what was to be done about that valorous man whose physical and leadership prowess, like Hill's, had both plummeted since his ascent to corps command?

Or am I guilty of holding them to the standard of our great Stonewall? he wondered to himself. *How can any of us—how can I—attain to that? We have not been the same since he—* The remembrance of that devastating loss was too painful to complete.

I cannot understand why God would place me in a position of such importance when I am so unworthy—and so incapable. If only we had a better man—a younger man, another man like Jackson—to lead us, our independence would be assured! All I have done is lead so many brave men and boys to their death, prolong the inevitable—at least inevitable as long as I am leading—and slowly kill this magnificent army. Why, God, why will Thou not place a better man than me at the head of—

Then he saw them, more of them. It was at least the tenth such group he had spotted this morning on his tour. The others were all too distant to visit, but not this one.

Before Taylor, Marshall, Venable, and the others knew what was happening, Lee was off his horse, his hat was off his head, and without a word he was on one knee at the rear of a semicircle of perhaps twenty soldiers, kneeling and bowing as one of their fellows—not even a chaplain—led them in prayer.

"I am full of infirmities, wants, sin," the soldier, his own head bowed and his eyes closed, said. "I confess my sin, my willful sin. A fountain of pollution is deep within my nature."

Yes, Father, yes, Lee thought, gripped anew at the realization.

"I have gone from one odious room to another," the praying man continued, "walked in a no-man's-land of dangerous imaginations, pried into the secrets of my fallen nature. Lord, dost Thou have mercy on me?"

Please, Father, please do, Sir.

"Thou hast struck a heavy blow at my pride, at the false god of self, and I lie in pieces before Thee."

And that is why my burdens are so heavy.

"Thou hast given me another Master and Lord, Thy Son, Jesus, and now my heart is turned towards holiness; my life speeds as an arrow from a bow toward complete obedience to Thee."

Oh yes, thank God, yes. Thou has not yet forsaken me or given up on me!

On the prayer went, as in a psalm, life, succor, and fruit breathed into the barren ashes and waste of depravity by the knowledge of one's sin, and the hating of and repenting from it. By the time the prayer had ended, Lee felt as though his body and soul alike had received a fresh gust of life. He rose, stronger, his fear gone. He turned away and grabbed the reins to remount, as a whisper rippled through the assembly, the men only then recognizing his presence among them.

"You have seen them," Taylor said quietly to him. "They are everywhere, sir. They are dying, they are losing arms and legs, they are far from their loved ones. But the whole army, or at least most of it, seems to be in a revival." Taylor bit his lip and tears filled his eyes, the first Lee had ever seen from the steady young man. "They want to be like you, sir."

Smelling out Meade's surmisal of Lee's stout position, the Gray Fox went on the offensive himself, only to find the Federals lit out back across the Rapidan.

While disappointed at being outmaneuvered by Lee's smaller force, the Federals considered themselves fortunate to reach safe ground for the winter. Lee's lieutenants marveled at the craftiness of their superior as they stood among thousands of still-smoking Federal campfires.

The response of the commander of the Army of Northern Virginia? "I am too old to command this army. We should never have permitted those people to get away."

Davis remained convinced the only man who could win for him in the West was the one who had done so in the East. Lee would go to Richmond to discuss the matter, fearful he could no longer forestall the president's desire for him to take the reins of the Army of Tennessee, which, while outnumbered, was numerically more the equal of its foe than was Lee's Army of Northern Virginia, but which had fared far worse through two-and-a-half years of war.

"I am called to Richmond this morning by the president," he told Jeb as he prepared to leave camp. "I expect to be back but only long enough to gather my staff and depart to join the army in Georgia, to where General Grant has pushed them."

"If Bragg had flanked the Yankees at Chattanooga after his victory at Chickamauga, as you suggested, instead of dallying in front of the town, they and not he would have been cleared from Tennessee," Jeb said, his gray eyes flashing.

Lee blushed, uncomfortable at criticism of anyone, in particular a fellow officer. But conviction filled Jeb. "When *will* President Davis do what every reasonable-minded man believes he should do and appoint you commander in chief of all the Southern armies? Should he do that, these excursions and exertions of effort and thought about who should command what and where will disappear like the mist in the morning."

Lee canted his head and glanced down. He looked back up and placed his hand on Jeb's shoulder, suddenly filled with gratitude for the younger man's guileless valor and devotion. "You are one of the greatest men in the South, General, and the future of our country will go with none more than you. But let us remain charitable toward our fellows, especially those fallen upon difficult times."

Those last words came hard for Lee, as he agreed *in toto* with Jeb's heartfelt comments. But he would say so to no man.

As Lee mounted Traveller to ride to the Virginia Central Railroad depot, Taylor handed a letter up to him that had fallen out of the bag when the mail was delivered earlier in the day. The letter evidenced having plunged into a mud puddle, and the ink smeared across its front was barely legible. One word shone clearly, however—Minnegerode, the surname of the pastor of St. Paul's Episcopal Church in Richmond, where Lee attended when in the capital. The small letters appeared, however, to have been written with the hand either of a person very early or quite advanced in years.

Lee glanced down at Taylor. *He'll have brought it especially to me because of the name Minnegerode,* Lee thought, reminded anew of how valuable the boy was to him, carrying a load no three normal men could shoulder, and filling a role no sane man would want.

Lee peered again at the name Minnegerode, the tiny letters, their form clear and careful. *I believe it is the writing of a child,* he thought. Thus he must open the missive without delay.

> We the undersigned write this little note to you our beloved General to ask a little favor of you which if it is in your power to grant we trust you will. We want Private Cary Robinson of Company G, 6th Regiment, V. Mahone's Brigade, to spend his Christmas with us, and if you will grant him a furlough for this purpose we will pay you back in thanks and love and kisses.
>
> Your two little friends,
> Lucy Minnegerode
> Lou Haxall

Lee had never proven himself invulnerable to the innocent thanks and love and kisses of the fairer sex—particularly to two nine-year-olds. Thus his first order of business upon the train's departure on the rickety rails to Richmond involved the writing of a letter:

> Dear Misses Minnegerode and Haxall,
> I received your joint request for permission to Mr. Cary Robinson to visit you Christmas, and gave authority for his doing so, provided circumstances permitted. Deeply sympathizing with him in his recent affliction, it gave me great pleasure to extend to him the opportunity of seeing you, but I fear I was influenced by the bribe held out to me, and will punish myself by not going to claim the thanks and love and kisses promised me. You know the self-denial this will cost me. I fear too I shall be obliged to submit your letter to Congress, that our legislators may know the temptations to which poor soldiers are exposed, and in their wisdom devise some means of counteracting its influence. They may know that bribery and corruption is stalking boldly over the land, but may not be aware the fairest and sweetest are engaged in its practice.
>
> Respectfully yours,
> R. E. Lee

Lee's joy upon arriving in Richmond because of his imminent reunion with Mary, Agnes, and Mildred melted away as he rode from the train station toward the uptown Lehigh Street quarters they had rented. Some of the streets bore little resemblance to the quiescent, tree-shaded prewar lanes that had marked Richmond as such a distinctively Southern town.

I do not believe many of these people hail from Richmond, or even Virginia, he thought to himself as he rode down one street ominous with the portent of postdaylight mischief and trickery. He witnessed an actual fistfight on another street, complete with a small cluster of cheering onlookers, one of whom appeared to be taking bets on the donnybrook. *Can this indeed be Richmond?* he wondered, remembering a town whose streets could never have been darkened by such behavior, and if they had, would have seen to the quick incarceration of participant, and spectator, alike. *Oh no,* he thought, *two of the observers are female!* That jolting realization brought his own women to mind. Before the thought had even coalesced completely in his mind, a sharp paroxysm shook his left side. He feared for a moment that he could not remain in the saddle. Straightening himself, he rode on. *I cannot let the people see me in such a state,* he thought, glancing back over his shoulder once more. *No, there are* three *females in that crowd,* he thought with regret.

Two blocks farther on he saw two more women, engaged in a heated argument over a loaf of bread. *How can I have let them move here alone?* he asked himself. *I am a worse husband and father than I am a general.* A hard cold shiver ran through him as he recalled the infamous Richmond "bread riot" the previous April, wherein a mob hundreds strong had stormed first through the government commissary, then a series of shops, smashing windows and stealing food and supplies. Some of the rioters were emaciated women of the lower, and in some cases, middle classes. More ominously, some were not citizens of Richmond at all, and some had clearly missed no meals. Nonetheless, it had taken the threat of a home-guard fusillade and an impassioned plea from President Davis himself, offering to share his own last loaf of bread and throwing all the money he had into the crowd, to disperse them.

When finally Lee arrived at his destination, he stared at its inauspicious wooden structure. But he saw the fields and forests of Arlington. And the aroma permeating his nostrils was that of apples and jasmine and fresh apricots, not the garbage pile that lay rotting near the street in front of the next house over. Tears filled his eyes as he glimpsed Mary's hunched form silhouetted in a front window. *Dear Father, forgive me for failing them. I am the reason that they—that she—is huddled in this unassuming little house instead of glorying at our treasured Arlington. But what else could I have done, Sir?*

Then, thankfully, he saw Agnes's face in the window, lighting up, an instant before she was coming out the front door, Mildred a step behind her. *It is not Arlington, but it is those I love most,* he thought, climbing down from the gaunt horse he had been loaned at the train station.

Mary's condition filled him with foreboding. Not just her bent tortured wheelchair-bound body. *War has hardened her,* he thought, remembering for an instant the elegant daughter of Martha Custis Washington's grandson, and how every man in Virginia, and some from farther away, had set their cap for her. One, he recalled, had recently passed away, the first president of the Republic of Texas and the first governor of the state of Texas, Rockbridge County-native General Sam Houston.

At first reticent in his presence, Mary evidenced increasing irritation and sullenness as the days passed. She complained about Richmond, about President Davis, about the war in general, about the Yankee depredations against the people and property of Virginia, about the difficulty of obtaining even the most basic foods and supplies, about the unnatural lives her daughters were pressed into living, and about their eldest son Custis's unhappiness at being kept from a field command for his position as a high aide to Davis.

Day after day Lee sat in meetings with Davis, with Confederate congressmen, with railroad executives, and with War Department officials. Night after night he observed the rueful quiet of Agnes and the edgy cynicism of his wife.

Yet all the while Mary constructed a virtual manufactory on the first floor of the two-story dwelling. Family members as well as many other women labored for hours every day knitting and darning socks, longhandles, trousers, mittens, and scarves for the Army of Northern Virginia.

"Don't know how long a pair of socks can last on a man when he has no shoes on over them," Mary said one evening after all but family members had left and she struggled on a scarf with needle and thread and hands that a grim and unrelenting rheumatoid arthritis had long since purposed to ruin. As Lee read the copy of Hugo's *Les Miserables* that Agnes had loaned him (she called it "Lee's Miserables," in reference to his army, most of which shivered through another frigid winter in the cold, hard open fields of central Virginia), the room grew silent except for the crackling of the one small log in the fireplace. But he knew his wife, even in this reduced condition, and he knew her mind was churning.

"And how infrequent are your letters to me from the field!" she blurted. "An old woman would think nothing in the world was becoming of her husband, but then if that were so, why would he not care to write to her on a reasonably frequent basis?"

He had heard it all before, too often, usually in her letters. He closed the book and spoke, his words soft as leaves falling on autumn grass. "But do you not forget how much writing, talking, and thinking I have to do when you complain of the interval between my letters? You lose sight also of the letters you receive."

He thought to stop there, but remembrance of the energy he did exert toward writing to her, despite the inevitable fatigue and pain that accompanied the late-evening, even early-morning, efforts, provoked him forward. "I fear you are relapsing into your old error, supposing that I have a superabundance of time and have only my own pleasures to attend to. You do not recollect that, after an absence of some days, matters accumulate formidably, and that my attention is entirely engrossed in public business, rendering me unable to write you as often as I should like."

She struggled on with her knitting, not looking at him. Enough time passed that he thought to reopen the book when her quavering voice sounded again.

"Never know day to day what friend or loved one will be next to fall," she said. Now she glanced over at him. "And look at you. This dastardly war has aged you by twenty years and left you hurting every minute of every day. And I pay no heed that you have not once mentioned such in the nearly two weeks you've been here, for I know you and I tell you, your body is racked with pain."

Lumbago, the doctors were calling the latest addition to Lee's growing collection of maladies. All he knew was that a throbbing ache had come to his lower back since the onset of winter. The irritating aspect to it was the difficulty he had in locating just where to apply the pressure that would in some small way alleviate the pain. And as Mary had pointed out, spending hours a day in the saddle, as he often did, possessed few equals in its pathological effect on the disease.

"It is necessary we should be humbled and taught to be less boastful, less selfish, and more devoted to right and justice to all the world," Lee said, his voice not devoid of tenderness.

At this Mary began to tremble, and sobs fought to exit her broken frame. Lee laid aside the book, crossed the wooden floor, bent down, and wrapped his strong arms around her, pulling her to himself. He felt her body relax and soften.

"I am the proudest husband in Virginia," he said, his voice smooth and soothing as a dripping ladle of molasses. Then he looked her in the eyes. There she softened, finally, as well. "Has Mr. Lee told Mrs. Lee of late how much he loves her?" She pleasured in the twinkle finally returning to his eyes.

"*General* Lee," she said, on the verge of a giggle, as his lips pressed urgently against hers.

The grave pallor that had further imbued Davis's countenance since Lee's last visit with him jolted the Virginian as he entered the president's office. The president was careworn and widely despised, even hated, by his own people. *What cause have I for repining my condition when faced with the hard way endured by this man?* Lee thought. Respect for Davis filled him as he gazed around the spartan accommodations of the man's modest office; respect, not necessarily affection, and not respect for the man's abilities as much as for his honesty, integrity, and commitment to a cause that from its outset Lee had believed to be a long shot to win. Few people in all the South outside of the president's own family knew how hardscrabble an existence Varina and Jefferson Davis eked out. Noble was the career of service the Mississippian had offered to the United States, as West Point-graduated soldier, congressman, and even Secretary of War. Yet he and his wife were not personally wealthy, and a Southland governed by wealthy men had considered no provisions for an unwealthy man who chanced to inhabit its highest office.

Lee, like few others, knew that when the cake appeared—especially if it was coated with sweet frosting—for affairs of state, none enjoyed it more than President and Mrs. Davis. For because of his inability to provide an income due to his presidential duties, the diet of Davis and his wife was as plain as that of a farm family without husband, father, or the year's crops.

Serving with Davis, whom Lee had known since their West Point days thirty years before, had proved challenging, even exhausting, for the general. Those whom the president trusted and believed faithful to him, he would go to the ends of the earth for, however ill-advised such devotion, as in the case of Braxton Bragg. But earning and keeping that trust presented its own campaign of strategy, perseverance, and, mostly, either agreeing with Davis or so supporting him as to make disagreement appear only another devoted avenue to support of and loyalty to him.

Still Lee had never seen even one man more committed to the freedom of the Southern Confederacy nor one more willing to sacrifice all he was and had for that beleaguered cause. *How few who cast stones at him have or would even consider offering the sacrifices he and Varina have,* Lee thought, with some anger.

Lee took his seat around a scuffed table in Davis's cramped office with the most powerful men in the Confederacy—among them the president himself, Secretary of War James Seddon, the Jewish Secretary of State Judah Benjamin, and Postmaster General John Reagan of Texas.

Davis turned his considerable powers of persuasion on Lee.

"We face dire straits in the west, General," he said, the gray eyes open and without guile. "I cannot seem to find a commander of your . . . capabilities . . . to lead. Will you take command of the Army of Tennessee, General Lee?"

Lee breathed an inward sigh of relief. It was indeed a *question* Davis had put to him, not an order. Now, how to answer with effect, and with respect for his honest, beleaguered president, who, Lee realized with a wave of compassion, came now to him as needfully (and only slightly less frequently) as did Traveller for his oats.

"Your Excellency, I am again humbled and honored to be considered for such an important post," he said, gentleness imbuing the deep voice as did a summer shower the hard dusty road of an afternoon march through central Virginia in August. "We are all aware of the unfortunate conflicts resident within the high command of the Army of Tennessee. I fear an inability on my part to assuage such inclinations or even to be permitted by commanders on the corps or division level legitimate opportunity to do so. Withal, I doubt my temporary presence in that army would effect fruitful results."

When a pause yielded neither response, movement, nor sound, Lee continued. "I would submit the need for a younger, permanent commander acquainted with the officers and possessed of more vitality with which to harness the troublesome nature of their energies and shepherd them in a more edifying direction. And were I to leave the Army of Northern Virginia, we should find ourselves searching for yet another commander, as Generals Ewell and Hill are both too physically unwell to lead that army."

Lee thought at this point to stop, but when the other men around the table remained mute and still, his snowy brows furrowed and he glanced downward, a slight blush charging his features. "The hard truth is that I do not feel able to summon the physical strength concomitant for the meeting of so arduous a task." As if on cue, a painful spasm racked his left side. He barely managed to conceal the episode from the other men.

After a moment he looked back up at Davis, his jaw set. "I have no ambition but to serve the Confederacy and do all I can to win our independence, Excellency." His back already ramrod straight, Lee seemed to draw himself even a bit more upright before the hushed group. "Please understand that I am willing to serve in any capacity to which the authorities may assign me, sir."

Davis vetoed Lee's suggestion of General Pierre Beauregard, hero of Fort Sumter and First Manassas, but he reluctantly assented to a second choice— Joe Johnston, who had preceded Lee as commander of the Army of Northern Virginia before being shot in the throat. Of late, Johnston had commanded the Army of Mississippi and had been unable to relieve the besieged Confederate forces fallen at Vicksburg.

Davis liked neither Beauregard nor Johnston, but he had no more Stonewall Jacksons and only one Robert E. Lee.

Richmond—the old Richmond, not the dangerous, mercenary flotsam and jetsam of the world that had filled a new Richmond—offered the best it had to give to Lee. The Confederate House of Representatives passed a resolution granting him a seat on its floor. Gifts of all sizes and values—from people who were now selling their most prized possessions merely to survive—found their way to the Lees' rented house. And at Saint Paul's Church, when Lee stood at the close of the Sunday morning service, the congregation stood with him; but as he walked up the aisle to the church entrance, they stood motionless in his honor, gazing upon him as he bowed and nodded to scores of them.

Forty-year-old Mary Chesnut stood in that company. Wife of Confederate general James Chesnut, her *A Diary from Dixie* would become the most famed journal of the war. A portrait of Tidewater beauty and sophistication, and a close friend of President Davis's wife, her soirees were graced by the most powerful men and women in the Confederacy. When Lee saw her, he bowed low, and she gleaned a hearty smile of recognition.

Mary Chesnut, in her own words, "blushed like a schoolgirl" at being recognized so in front of all Richmond.

Agnes and "Little Robert," as adoring Richmond referred to Lee's youngest son, returned home from a visit to Mary Chesnut's the evening of the twenty-first to find their father, amid the year's spare Christmas decorations, preparing to return to the battle lines.

"But Papa," a stunned Agnes uttered, tears filling her eyes in spite of herself. "Christmas is only four days hence. I thought for sure . . ." Her chin began to quiver, and her words trailed off as her head drooped. *Four years it has been since Papa has spent Christmas with us,* she thought, sadness and recognition of the swift passage of time sweeping over her like a tidal wave.

Lee blanched at the first clear demonstration of emotion from Agnes he had witnessed since before the loss of Orton. He did not know what to say. He had thought his own heart would be the only one battered by his early departure.

At that very moment back at camp, Taylor wrote to his sweetheart, "It will be more in accordance with General Lee's peculiar character if he leaves Richmond for the army just before the great anniversary of the Savior's birth; he is so very apt to suppress or deny his personal desire when it conflicts with the performance of his duty."

A few moments later, as Lee himself saddled the horse General Chesnut had loaned him for the cold evening ride to the train station, his eyes were drawn to a window through which he saw Mary in the sitting room, hunched over in her wheelchair, her twisted hands knitting a pair of socks for someone else's shivering soldier boy. For an instant the hands were no longer bent and arthritic; they were the strong sure hands of black seamstresses. And no longer were they knitting socks but the most splendid trousseau he had ever seen, the stitches so fine they could not be discerned by the human eye.

Then Mary Anna Randolph Custis was descending the wide sweeping candlelit stairs of Arlington with her father; Mary Custis, who had been courted by the flower of the young American nation with their names and their fortunes. She had chosen none of the great and famous. She had chosen the quiet boy she had loved from girlhood, the financially broke boy her father had taken so long to approve, the steady West Point-graduated boy from a once-great line fallen on hard times, even shameful times that came when you had brothers with sobriquets like "Black Horse."

Rain had soaked the clothing of the towering Episcopal minister, and he performed the service with the borrowed clothes of Mary's father, the coat sleeves barely eclipsing the minister's elbow and the trousers fitting more snugly than Robert Lee would hold his bride in his arms before that golden night had died. Then for an entire week the wedding party, remaining at Arlington, would mount and ride along the country roads by day and dance the Virginia reel to banjo and fiddle by night.

Looking down upon it all were the silent but watchful family portraits. No ordinary family portraits these, they were the patriots of the Revolution, the man they called the "Father of His Country," and further back, Mary's great-great-grandfather, Virginia-born Colonel Daniel Parke, aide-de-camp to the great Duke of Marlborough at the battle of Blenheim and the man entrusted by Marlborough to ride night and day and cross a stormy English Channel in a fishing skiff in order to deliver into the hands of Queen Anne the message of the earth-shaking victory.

They were all witnesses that night, more than thirty-two years before; they were all witnesses at Arlington. And so was the bride whose clay tenement was now crumpled, broken, in a wheelchair, and preparing to spend yet another Christmas without that husband she had loved the best.

CHAPTER 14

CULPEPER RODE SEETHING ACROSS THE MAURY RIVER BRIDGE and out of Lexington. His search for Cousin Emma and her children and his sister's son had proven fruitless. His status as a deserter had rendered it all the more difficult, as it forced him to keep virtually out of sight and refrain from seeking information through traditional channels such as the town marshal or even most of his own acquaintances.

He did learn that Emma, still weak from an old case of diphtheria, and with three young mouths to feed, had left town. But he did not know her destination, only that she had once mentioned to a neighbor many folks had refugeed to Richmond and she might have to some day as well. Her other neighbors had never liked him and would report him to the home guards sure if they saw him, so he did not talk to them.

He raged against everyone and everything, especially the war and God, as he headed east into the black night toward the Blue Ridge. Fortunately he had found a couple of empty houses in Emma's neighborhood—down the hill a couple of blocks behind Sheridan's Livery and Hotel—from which, by cover of night, he had filled the saddlebags he retrieved from his own barn. Even after two and a half years of war and constant rumors of Yankee raiders threatening the area, valley folks still never contemplated locking up their homes. Truth be known, most would prefer that the hungry traveler or refugee take their fill of food and supplies even in the homeowner's absence, rather than be kept from such sustenance by lock and key.

The fools, Culpeper thought with scorn as he spurred his stolen mount past the low fields of the McDowell plantation toward Buena Vista, along one of the very trails he and Ethan McDowell used to travel to hunt squirrels, rabbits, turkeys, and deer. Ethan was the only rich boy that had ever given Culpeper the time of day. The fleeting realization struck Culpeper that Ethan was the only *friend,* outside of family—and precious few of them—he had ever had. And that little belle Rachel Anne— "Huzzah!" he shouted into the dark, a large white puff of air attacking the hard cold, upon the fond remembrance of the spirited young beauty. *She must be twenty-one by now,* Culpeper thought, a smile traversing his chiseled face for the first time in weeks. *Wonder where she is,* he thought. *Probably hitched to some Tidewater colonel. Nothing less for the daughter of the richest planter in Rockbridge County, right?* He swore a silent oath. *Rich men got us all into this stinking war.* A speck of light from the McDowells' big house, nearly a mile distant, caught his eye. He peered toward it. Only two, perhaps three twinkles greeted him. He remembered seeing Christmas decorations in Lexington. Emma's neighbor had mentioned that today was Christmas Day. *Humbug,* he thought, rehearsing his own favorite greeting of Christmas cheer. He remembered one year actually feasting at Christmas with Ethan and the whole McDowell clan, including Ethan's father, Sam. Culpeper and Ethan had been out hunting when a sudden blizzard blew in and dropped nearly a foot of snow on them in one evening. They had let Culpeper stay with them—in the big house, no less—for two days, till he could get out and return home. *Guess I had me a good Christmas that year,* Culpeper thought, fighting off a twinge of emotion.

Culpeper glanced back once more at the tiny twinkles, one of which had gone out. *Don't figure it to be much of a celebration for the McDowells this go-round,* he thought, pulling the collar of his frayed coat against the thick beard that had forested his jaw in the better than five months he had ridden, hidden, drank, stolen, and hated since Gettysburg. For he remembered overhearing Mr. Brown, the blacksmith in Lexington, say that Ethan's older brother, Horace, was rotting away in Fort Douglas, a Yankee prison camp out of which terrible tales of disease, freezing, shootings, and even starvation were emerging.

On his way back into camp, Lee rode past a stream of women and children refugees walking along the open road, bitter winter winds laced with sleet whipping their sullen faces. The sufferers included both black and white. Lee knew that many slaves had escaped to the Federals, though some would return when the stern dictates of self-responsibility exerted themselves. But the vast majority remained in the South they considered their homeland too. When the Federals burned down houses, these blacks—some free, some slave—shivered too. When the food was stolen and the crops destroyed, their stomachs also growled. And when even the rudiments of living proved impossible, they also sought refuge on the open road.

Why must they war against our innocents? Lee wondered. *Whence comes such villainy? Is it possible the authorities in Washington know of such acts?* He canted his head and observed, across the road, a stringy white girl of thirteen or so pulling a cart in which was loaded her family's possessions, and a wheezing, ashen-faced boy of maybe eight, covered in blankets. Just behind the cart was a woman Lee gauged to be the girl's mother, carrying a bawling infant in her arms. The woman's shoeless feet were swathed against the Arctic-like cold in strips of torn, filthy cloth. *They cease not their harassment, their plundering, their burning, even though this country is so barren our soldiers can not possibly draw supplies from it,* Lee thought, his anger kindled.

He spent a somber Christmas in his tent with his lumbago, catching up on reports of the autumn's actions. At one point, sentimental thoughts tided over him as he perused photos and daguerreotypes of his beloveds (all but Annie, who never consented for her likeness to be done because of her childhood eye accident), and he opened his Bible back up.

A short time later, heartened, he called for Taylor.

"Have we any sort of coffee at all, Major?" Lee asked, rubbing his hands, which still ached in the cold from their pre-Sharpsburg breakings, "even if made from acorns?"

But he knew in an instant that Taylor possessed something else, not nearly as warm or welcome as even acorn-flavored coffee. The younger man handed Lee the telegram without comment, then left the tent. He would not return until Lee emerged, for he had come back the year before, when he brought his commander the correspondence announcing Annie's death. Lee had read it without reaction. In fact he had placed it to the side and continued working through his stack of administrative papers. Thinking all was well, Taylor left on an errand. When he returned, Lee, alone and still at his desk, sat sobbing, quietly enough so as to not draw attention from outside the tent, but in such agony and intensity that tears poured down his face and his entire body shook.

Taylor had not known what was in that communication, but he somehow suspected what was in this one. He vowed not to again witness what he had seen before.

Charlotte had joined her two little children in the upper sanctuary. How piercing the sorrow for Lee as he recalled the Federals' refusal to exchange

Rooney in the manner they had with such zeal pursued the exchange of their own captured general officers. They refused out-of-hand even a temporary exchange of Rooney—for his own brother Custis, who offered to take his place in prison while the younger brother visited his dying wife. And so Charlotte Wickham Lee, by nature sweet but frail, and all the more, having become bereaved from the deaths of her tiny children and the terror of her husband's rough capture before her eyes and his potentially permanent imprisonment, had died of war, death, and a broken heart.

Lee put down the telegram, uttered a deep sigh, and inked his pen, attempting to ignore a painful new wave of spasms shooting up his left side into his chest. *How much I shall miss her sweet gentle spirit,* he thought, his throat tightening, as he began to write to Mary.

"It has pleased God to take from us one exceedingly dear to us, and we must be resigned to His holy will. She, I trust, will enjoy peace and happiness forever, while we must patiently struggle on under all the ills that may be in store for us. What a glorious thought it is that she has joined her little cherubs and our angel Annie in heaven. Thus is link by link the strong chain broken that binds us to earth, and our passage soothed to another world."

Lee paused for a moment, the sweet remembrance of other Christmases filling his heart, Christmases made the more precious because he had so often been apart from his loved ones till just before the Advent Day. He inked the pen and continued. "Oh, that we may be at last united in that heaven of rest, where trouble and sorrow never enter, to join in an everlasting chorus of praise to our Lord and Savior! I grieve for our lost darling as a father only can grieve for a daughter, and my sorrow is heightened by the thought of the anguish her death will cause our dear son and the poignancy it will give to the bars of his prison. May God in His mercy enable him to bear the blow He has so suddenly dealt, and sanctify it to his everlasting happiness."

Agnes smiled as Mary Chesnut raved on about what she termed Mary Lee's "Industrial School." Agnes knew that the move of herself, her mother, and younger sister Mildred into a handsome house on Franklin Street had pleased Mary Lee. Now they could walk to both Capitol Square and Saint Paul's Church within a few moments. They lived with brother Custis, still a key aide to President Davis, who had been renting the home with a couple of other young officers. And the wide halls, large rooms, big windows, and spacious porches all rendered the abode much more comfortable for Mrs. Lee than their previous quarters.

Rather than serving to provide a nest of comfort amid which Mary could repose with her physical afflictions, these improvements served only to fire her ardor for supporting the Army of Northern Virginia. She had transformed her rented quarters into a beehive of activity. She, her daughters, and a parade of other women knitted night and day for an army where one division alone had four hundred barefooted soldiers and one thousand without blankets in the midst of the coldest winter any Virginian could ever remember. Each morning Agnes had to crack the ice out of her own washbasin. The gas lamps were often incapacitated by the cold. Not with any thanks to Mary Lee's Industrial School, however. As Mary Chesnut piled compliment upon compliment about Mrs. Lee, Agnes marveled at her mother, the center of the entire enterprise while unable even to rise from her rolling chair.

"How the Lees spend their time," Chesnut continued. "What a rebuke to taffy parties!"

As Agnes resumed her place and her sewing of a pair of gloves, she realized that she had smiled more in the few days since arriving on Franklin Street than she had in the last six months. A bit later, Mildred brought her a letter from Cousin Markie Williams, residing within Yankee lines with her family in Georgetown. Agnes's heart leapt at the sight of Markie's name. Her own long affection for her older cousin—*she must now be thirty-six, no, thirty-seven, and never married,* Agnes thought—meshed with the ravenous inexorable thirst she could never escape for anything, anyone remotely connected to *him.*

With as much haste as she could summon and not draw attention, she hurried to the room she shared with Mildred. She tore open the missive and read, her pounding heart breaking anew as she consumed Markie's staggering announcements. Markie had met a "deranged" woman who claimed she had been engaged to Orton just before his death! Markie had seen a letter penned to the woman by Orton in his final hours as he awaited the gallows. His words told the tale: he still hoped to reunite with the woman and marry her. Such dreams he harbored for a woman already married to another Confederate soldier—who himself soon died a bloody and heroic death in battle against the Yankees.

Agnes felt faint. Her head rang like the tocsin bell over at Capitol Square. She slumped over on the bed, the half-read letter fluttering to the knotless pine floor. For some minutes she lay there, staring into space. Only later would she be able to summon the fortitude to finish the letter. Only then would Markie's sweet prose, bathed in poignant remembrance, scald out whatever tender life remained in her battered heart. "In my mind's eye I can see you now as children," Markie wrote. "You and our darling Annie and he, sitting around the nursery fender telling fairy tales. But then when you had grown up, we all were always asking, 'Where are Agnes and Orton?' Those forest shades could tell . . ."

Now was she walking through the brittle brown-limbed backyard of her new rented house in the city and remembering forest shades and the fragrance of juniper and jasmine wafting up from the river. *Oh, how I hate that river and all that it means!* she thought desperately, clenching her fists, *and*—she could not yet even think his name—him *and his smile on his horse . . . and all of it wrapped safely within the loving protective wings of old Arlington.*

Had her heart been still alive, she could not have continued reading, but her heart was now dead, killed by what the river stood for, so she just read right on. "You are very dear to me dear Agnes—and ever will be. You seem like my little sister. Our beautiful home!"—for truly it was Markie's home as well— "What sorrow the memory of it brings to my heart. I have never been to Georgetown or Washington since my great grief. I feel as if I never could go again. Every place there is associated with him—especially dear A."

Yes, dear A. Agnes knew quite well what was dear A. Who was dear A. *How close we were,* Agnes thought, returning the letter to its envelope. *For she has written the very words carved upon my own heart before it died, before it was killed by the river. The river killed him, the river killed Charlotte, the river killed Annie, and the river has killed my heart. How strange that it should suddenly become so clear.* Having one's heart killed so that one can no longer feel pain had distinct advantages, she realized.

When she heard her mother shrieking and sobbing from inside, from the middle of the crowded Industrial School, because the river had now killed A. also—the Yankees had officially confiscated it, were chopping down the forest shades, and converting it to a Federal cemetery—she for the first time began to wonder if all she had known had not after all been true.

If what Papa lived was not true.

What, withal, did it all matter, if they were all to be taken from her, one after another in a long endless procession down into the gray gloomy dooryard of death? If not even Arlington could be saved?

She noticed with surprise that no tears came. Then she remembered that her heart was dead.

CHAPTER 15

LINCOLN HAD COME TO DESPISE THE LONG WALK DOWN THE threadbare burgundy-carpeted hallway from his White House living quarters to his office. It had evolved into a virtual gauntlet of Northern citizens in various states of distress. Waiting for him for minutes, for hours, sometimes all night—he would not allow the public to be kept from what he called "the People's House," most of which was open to them—they would bring their pitiful petitions directly to their president.

"Please, sir, our boy Lance . . . since the Battle of Chickamauga . . . no record of his whereabouts . . ."

"He's all I have left in the world, Mr. President, my husband and all my other sons have been killed . . ."

"The last letter we received said dysentery . . . his handwriting was so weak we could barely recognize it . . . not a word from him in six months."

They whispered, they asked, they begged, they sobbed, they shrieked, touching him, grabbing him, tripping and stumbling before him.

When finally the door to his office closed behind him, he felt as though he had been ransomed from a firing squad. *A firing squad,* he thought. Perhaps that would prove preferable to this long, agonizing, never-ceasing death.

For he had his own burdens, not the least of them whole Confederate prisons full of captured Federal soldiers in Richmond for whom he could do nothing. "Vermin . . . filth . . . excrement . . . he was shot merely for looking out the window . . . no glass in the windows from top to bottom of the prison building, nothing to slow the howling winter winds . . . fleas . . . lice . . . bedbugs . . . hundreds and hundreds have died of chronic diarrhea . . . dysentery . . . typhoid . . . pneumonia . . . rats, big rats, unintimidated, spreading disease through the men like wildfire." These and countless others were the reports returning north with released, and occasionally escaped, Federal prisoners.

Now his appointments would begin. And the petitions, beseechings, and importunings would resume. Following a relentless string of them one day in early February 1864, the last appointment was with a Midwestern congressman warning Lincoln that the folks back home were fed up and were going to back a "peace candidate" in the November presidential election, one who would negotiate a truce with the Confederacy.

After the congressman left, Lincoln sighed and pulled out the latest correspondence from Federal spy Elizabeth Van Lew, whose Northern family had moved South a few decades before and had since left her as one of Richmond's wealthiest heiresses.

"Richmond is still only lightly defended and in fact could be taken easier now than at any other time since the war began," she wrote, urging his consideration of a lightning cavalry raid to free the thousands of Federal officers held in Libby Prison near the James River in southeast Richmond, and the even larger number of Federal enlisted men kept in the prison on Belle Island, out in the James to the southwest of the town center.

Lincoln leaned into his high-backed chair and swiveled to look out the window behind his desk. Charcoal clouds hung like gloomy streamers in perverse celebration of another in an unending processional of national death days. The comments of a Federal prisoner exchanged out of Libby returned to him. Captured the previous summer in Kilpatrick's cavalry attack that nearly reached Richmond during the Chancellorsville campaign, the man's words constituted a haunting reprise Lincoln could neither forget nor draw solace from: "There is not a sound pair of legs in Richmond, sir. Our men, had they known it, could have safely gone in and burnt everything and brought us Jeff Davis."

He uttered a small silent prayer that the raid the militarily inept but endlessly innovative General Ben Butler had launched on Richmond from Federal-held Williamsburg forty-five miles to the southeast might accomplish its mission. Meanwhile a servant arrived to shave Lincoln. As the black man lathered his face, an aide announced the arrival of "the tallest officer I have ever laid eyes on, sir, half a foot at least over six feet, young and dashing and blond, and walking on crutches."

Lincoln gained a brief reprieve from his sallow-faced, baggy-eyed countenance of doom when his entire visage lit up like a crackling winter fireplace upon seeing his old young friend.

"Ully Dahlgren!" the president shouted. "You have been spared!"

●◇ ●◇ ●◇

Before the gray sky turned black, Lincoln would receive another blow. Alert Confederate infantry had stopped Butler's raid cold, and Lee's men had pummeled a diversionary force of Federal infantry to the north to the tune of nearly three hundred casualties.

Had Lincoln any reservoir of emotional or physical strength to draw upon, he would have wept where he sat. Having none, he stared back out the now-darkened window and wondered how men such as Lee and Stuart, Hampton and Longstreet, Forrest and Johnston, would ever be defeated. And how he would ever gain reelection in nine months if they were not. How, indeed, the war-weary Union, riotous in the East, on the verge of refusing to furnish troops in many places in the West, needy of martial law across the border states from one end of the country to the other, could be held together long enough to win this blasted war, especially if Bobby Lee pulled one more rabbit out of his slaughter-filled hat. Then he remembered recent reports that the Rebels were constructing a new prison way down south somewhere, where the Richmond prisoners would soon be transferred. *We shall never be able to rescue them then,* he thought, a sullenness thick and dark as pitch pouring over him.

That is when he received a confidential message relating a new and even more ambitious plan to raid Richmond. The plan originated with the bold, young womanizer Judson Kilpatrick, whose wife and only child had recently died. The outline for its execution took Lincoln's breath away. Finally someone had the audacity to propose the sort of plan Lincoln himself had secretly harbored for months but had not had the gumption to voice.

How, indeed, will history adjudge such an undertaking? Lincoln wondered to himself. He turned to his aide. "Send immediately for General Kilpatrick."

●◇ ●◇ ●◇

Dahlgren was now twenty-one, the youngest colonel in the Federal army, a decorated war hero of national fame, and a quick and eager learner. He had learned, for instance, that two central repositories of power and influence existed in pig-rooting, water-polluted, brothel-infested Washington City. One claimed residency at the White House. The other resided at Willard's Hotel. Having well established himself at the one, he set about doing so at the other.

128

And that is how he happened to learn, while supping with a notable coterie of congressmen, newspapermen, and government contract hunters on steaming oyster soup, turkey, roast duck, and a chandelier-lit tableful of other culinary delights, including orange marmalade, plum pudding, and Madeira, that his acquaintance and comrade-in-arms Judson Kilpatrick was about to embark on a rapacious feat of mounted daring-do, of some sort, in Old Virginny. Under the direct sponsorship of President Lincoln.

Rumors swirled thicker than the cigar smoke in the main dining room of Willard's that the little banty rooster "Kill-cavalry" had concocted the whole enterprise himself and had actually consulted directly with Lincoln and Secretary of War Stanton over the heads of his military superiors.

Dahlgren had regained most of his strength, learning he could ride just fine with his spanking new, custom-designed wooden leg, and itched to leap back into the war, despite his father's desire that he find himself a safe job in Washington, or at least as a staff officer. Within forty-eight hours, Dahlgren was dining with Kilpatrick, in that officer's own rented Washington apartment. Dahlgren knew where the track lay to further action and glory. Kilpatrick determined to hitch himself and his audacious enterprise to one of the most golden boys in the entire Federal army—and one of Abe Lincoln's favorites.

"Such a desperate enterprise begs only for those men who crave that challenge before which the normal man, even the brave man, must only cower," Kilpatrick announced, as one of the lovely black females who served him in many more ways than at the table, poured steaming coffee into his Wedgwood cup from a crystal decanter.

Dahlgren, remembering that neither spirits, tobacco, nor cards were counted among this strange man's vices, could barely stifle the pounding of his thrilled heart.

"It is that man who would accomplish the unusual, that man who would pursue the undoable"—now Kilpatrick leaned so far forward that Dahlgren thought he must come across the china-covered walnut table at him—"that valorous man who demands success from any venture to which he sets his hand, to which our needy nation has now turned its face."

Kilpatrick, noting the glint firing Dahlgren's eyes, let that sink in. "The Union has bestowed upon you its richest laurels," he rolled on. "I myself have been a very witness to your gallantry, under fire and while having been bloodied nearly unto death. I have seen in you, Ulric Dahlgren, that new man upon which the future of our great Republic rests—if we are to have a future, which, by all the thunder heaven can send down, we shall not be denied!" With this, Kilpatrick's own small fist came crashing down onto the table, shattering a saucer.

That so odd looking and morally retarded a man could engender such a grip on Dahlgren's imagination electrified the younger man, but there it was. Kilpatrick and Stanton and Lincoln would have it, and the nation would, once it knew what was to be accomplished, and Dahlgren would as well.

The actual mission came virtually as an afterthought.

"The president wants our brave, starving, freezing, and illness-racked thousands redeemed from those filthy Secesh prisons in Richmond," Kilpatrick said. "He wants the Rebs' interior supply and communications lines destroyed. And he wants amnesty flyers by the thousands broadcast to every corner of Virginia, so that those good men who wish to be welcomed back by their mother, America, would have the opportunity to forsake their prodigal ways."

Dahlgren sipped his own coffee, while noting that Kilpatrick's was untouched. "Noble and worthy aims all," said the colonel.

Kilpatrick nodded, then telegraphed to his lovely servant a silent message to depart the room. When she had done so, the general lowered his voice. "No doubt you are aware of the president's endorsement of General Butler's design, during his own recent aborted raid on Richmond, to seize Jefferson Davis."

Dahlgren attempted mightily to conceal his excitement. Only the slightest brief flicker of his eye conveyed to Kilpatrick the expected confirmation that the younger man was mightily in support of the project, that he would no doubt be mightily in support of virtually *anything* encompassed by it.

And so twenty-seven-year-old Brigadier General Judson Kilpatrick plunged forward, even as bodacious a man as he unable to prevent his voice from quavering a bit at what he would say over the course of the next few moments: "And I should add that Secretary Stanton has authored an exciting postscript of his own to the enterprise."

●◇ ●◇ ●◇

One of the many strange ironies of the War for Southern Independence was how a baby-faced, ninety-four-pound blond not yet twenty-one years of age, initially refused entry as a volunteer into Jeb Stuart's manpower-needy Army of

Northern Virginia cavalry due to his diminutive appearance, had become "Stringfellow, the infamous spy and murderer," one of the most feared men in the United States.

Benjamin Franklin Stringfellow, the Confederate scout Jeb trusted perhaps most of any of his men. The prewar Greek and Latin teacher who had spent more time behind Yankee lines than Confederate, who through stealth, intelligence, quick wits, sure riding, eagle shooting eye, and sheer physical courage had single-handedly established a complex spy network that spread across northern Virginia, through Alexandria, across the Potomac, into Washington, and up into some of the highest echelons of the Federal military-governmental establishment.

The near-legendary Frank Stringfellow had been hunted, shot, imprisoned, near-drowned, announced as killed in action. He had seen his beloved Virginia farm devastated by the war and his own mother shot and nearly killed as battle raged across the precious acres his forefathers had fought, bled, and died to win from the American Indians who had brought forth neither the bounty of God's earth from its acres or the bounty of men's souls from His gospel.

This same Stringfellow, this frigid February sunset in 1864, now had another bounty leveled on his own handsome head—the enormous and unheard-of amount of seventy-five hundred dollars, far more than the annual income of President Abraham Lincoln.

As young Ulric Dahlgren did not hate the Rebels against whom he flung his whole strength time and again, neither did young Frank Stringfellow harbor weightier antipathy against his Yankee adversaries than that they be driven forever from the Virginia they had invaded and continued to despoil.

None of this now entered Stringfellow's mind as he emerged from darkened woods to confront a lone Federal cavalry captain making his way south along the hard frozen road. Stringfellow's appearance particularly surprised the Yankee because the unwelcome intrusion occurred midway between two Federal cavalry camps near Culpeper Courthouse and no more than one hundred yards from either of them.

The Federal wheeled his horse around only to have a second Confederate rider snag his bridle. Then the bluecoat reached for his revolver. Just as his yellow-gauntleted hand clasped the stock, the gloomy barrel of Stringfellow's carbine appeared in the gathering darkness. Six-chambered pistols poked out right and left from the Southerner's belt.

"Good evening, Captain," Stringfellow spoke, a genial smile accompanying his words. "You seem to be heading south. Allow us to act as your escort."

●❖ ●❖ ●❖

Their journey south toward the Rapidan River and Confederate lines presented Stringfellow and the other two grayback scouts with bitter cold, stinging winds, sleet that slashed their faces, and Federal scouts and patrols so numerous they seemed to spring from behind every tree and from around every ominous bend in the road. At one point, Stringfellow heard the crackling of Yankee saddle leather. Twice he made out the conversations of passing Federal troopers. And Yankee bullets chased after them the next day even as they forded the Rapidan and melted into the woods.

That evening, Stringfellow sat at a Confederate picket station, wreathed in a wool blanket and relishing the crackling fireplace before him, whose warmth penetrated to the marrow of his icy damp bones.

The authorized pass through Federal lines that lay before him, however, was a mystery. For it bore the name of Sally Marsten, one of the loveliest young ladies in Culpeper County and a good friend of Stringfellow's. *Why would Sally Marsten, who has had two brothers killed by the Yankees, desire a pass through their lines?* he wondered.

He sent one of his men for their prisoner.

The young officer was not inclined toward solving Stringfellow's mystery for him.

"Oh, come now, Captain," Stringfellow said, "you're not aiding your own plight by adopting such an attitude. We'll find out one way or another. You know the young lady, of course?"

"Y . . . yes, I know her."

"Did you know her before the war?"

"No, only just a week ago. She came into our lines, seeking to learn news of her brother, who has been missing in action for some time. She thought perhaps he had been captured."

At this the Federal canted his head and looked downward. "I . . . I tried to help her, but I fear I wasn't very successful."

"And this?" Stringfellow asked, lifting the pass.

"I . . . er . . . well . . . I sort of felt sorry for her," the captain answered. "What with losing two brothers—she's had a hard road. I had thought I might help divert her mind to happier things, at least for a spell."

Stringfellow's arched brows posed the question *How?*

"Well, my regiment, a bunch of regiments—" At this, he caught himself. "—my regiment is having a ball tomorrow night, and, well, I hoped she might come."

Stringfellow smiled. "You must have held her in high esteem to try making it through our lines—with this."

The captain bit his lower lip. "If I send a postal for her with you, will you make certain she receives it?"

Stringfellow stood and offered his hand. "Of course," he said. Sympathy tinged his voice, but already a plan was taking shape in his mind. *"My regiment, a bunch of regiments."*

Sally Marsten had no business being at that ball tomorrow night, but what critical intelligence might be wafting about amid the whiskey, cigar smoke, and vaingloriousness of a large gathering of Federal troops, which Stringfellow suspected just might be the arrayed host of the Army of the Potomac's officer corps?

Returning to the blessed warmth of the fireplace, he determined he would be there to find out.

As 1863 froze into 1864, drink, illness, and the darkness of his soul carried Culpeper far from his pursuit of Emma and his niece and nephews. He gambled, smoked, drank, and fought in Richmond as much as he dared stay in the glutted city.

The brutality of General John Henry Winder's home-guard forces had grown in approximate correlation to the violence and lawlessness besetting what had been one of the antebellum South's most genteel cities. Culpeper had several close calls with the home guards, once physically thrashing two of their grim ranks who had drawn down on him in an alley behind a wharf-side saloon. They had mistaken him for another deserter wanted around Richmond. That misidentification proved fortunate for Culpeper, since he brained one of the men with a piece of firewood and shot the other five times with the guard's own revolver.

Both men lived, and their tale of terror tripled the bounty on the deserter they thought they had found, which man happened rather to be headed for the West Indies on a blockade runner ready to be repacked with every manner of delicacy and luxury for that elite Richmond class, most of them not Richmonders or even Virginians, who grew the wealthier the longer the casualty lists and the greater the suffering of North and South.

So Culpeper melted into the countryside to hunt, drink, and sleep when he sensed danger from the home guards.

One frigid mid-February evening so cold that even the cheap rotgut that flowed in Ramsey's Tavern, Yankee blockade or no, seemed unable to thaw a man's insides, Culpeper let loose with his one of the few Rebel yells he had ever screeched. Two-headed drunk or not, he could not mistake coming through the front door Ethan McDowell and the unmanageable shock of white-blond hair that crowned his forage-capped head, even though a newly acquired gimp from a Mine Run bullet now accompanied his lanky frame.

To the extent that the cold preserved Culpeper's senses to recognize Ethan and renew their friendship, it could be counted good fortune. But it would also open the way for overwhelming news.

Ethan, while convalescing in Richmond's sprawling Chimborazo Hospital, had witnessed that not even the personal ministrations of the famed volunteer Jewish nurse Phoebe Pember herself could rescue from typhoid fever—fostered by cold, exposure, and hunger—Emma, her little boy and girl, and the son of Culpeper's dead sister.

Culpeper, who loved hardly anyone or anything, including himself, had loved all these from birth as if they were his own.

CHAPTER 16

MARLEY COULD DIVINE NOTHING ATTRACTIVE ABOUT THE SOIREE other than the man for which the George Washington Birthday Ball was name-saked. Fightin' Joe Hooker, "Old Prayer Book" Howard, and other Third Corps leadership who best knew of his exploits had been relieved of command and transferred to assignments in the Western armies after the drubbings they received at Chancellorsville and Gettysburg. So Marley knew not the origin of his orders to be in attendance. He knew only that its genesis was *very* high.

How I now detest such inane vanity, he thought, surveying the sweeping scene before him. Federal axes had cut down yet more Virginia forest to construct the enormous ballroom filled this night with the dress blue, medals, and ribbons of Meade's Second Corps, and the swirling, waltzing skirts of the most coveted ladies in the Republic. Marinated with the lilting strains of the choicest musicians from the Corps' regimental bands, the most glittering assemblage of the Union's elite since the "picnic" on the bluffs overlooking Bull Run nearly three years before flirted, danced, intrigued, drank, and seemed almost to forget that a war and a bloody new campaign awaited them on the morrow.

The Confederate minié Marley had taken in the shoulder the day of that picnic still stiffened and pained him in cold like this frigid February evening. And he was not now inclined toward flirting, dancing, intriguing, or drinking, any of them. He could only ponder how many of the gay souls before him would within days lose their lives or their loved ones—to someday stand before the judgment seat of Christ, to be consigned to an eternity without the love of God. He shuddered at the dullness and darkness of men's imaginations and of, he realized with regret, his own hard spirit. He thought he must step outside or risk losing what little sanity still resided in his brain.

As he neared the wide, open doors, a stir wafted in from outside. When he reached the entrance, he observed the object of the growing tumult. One of the handsomest young men he had ever witnessed—tall, blond, and goateed—reined one of the most magnificent coal-black stallions he had ever seen. But when the man dismounted, he had to be helped down. One of his legs seemed stiff and unresponsive.

"Is that really Ulric Dahlgren?" came the hushed, thrilled whisper of a nearby Northern belle, her beauty so striking that Marley caught himself staring involuntarily at her.

"It is he—hero of Boonsboro, Chancellorsville, and Gettysburg, and performer of a cadre of other exploits," a colonel replied in a scarcely less reverential tone.

Even Marley was impressed. *But he was on his death bed,* he thought, marveling. And now, he looks so—

"Commanding."

"Majestic."

Now the titters ran into the ballroom, and that gathering of the North's greatest and most powerful—Vice President Andrew Johnson, the governor of Rhode Island, a Supreme Court justice, senators and congressmen, and powerful representatives from nearly every power in Europe—raised a thunderous applause for the twenty-one-year-old warrior whom the president himself adored.

Even now, the words of his father's letter from months before echoed in Dahlgren's ears. *It is not so much what we have in the world as the use we put our means to. You can do a great deal more minus a foot than most young men who have two. It's no small matter to have fought your way to a colonelcy at twenty-one, and that must lead to more.*

Dahlgren had not earlier realized—he wondered if his father did—how profound could be the impact of a father's encouragement and belief in a son. With his father's belief buoying him, he felt as though no task were too formidable for him.

Buoyed by compliments, backslaps, and offers of food, drink, and more, Dahlgren took up his crutches and hobbled through the admiring crowd, the haunting strains of "Annie Laurie" weeping forth from the band.

Few were the pleasures greater for Kilpatrick on this evening of pleasures and pomp than the sight of Dahlgren, whose heroic appearance replete with crutches and wooden leg Kilpatrick suspected had now boosted him in the Northern public's eye close to entry into the pantheon of Greek gods. *Such a warrior, such an idol—such a favorite of the president's,* Kilpatrick thought to himself with a smile—*shall contribute mightily to the fame of our noble endeavor.*

For Kilpatrick had only one career goal in mind for himself. The elite of Northern society which now surrounded him, the proposed raid on Richmond, the fiery oration he had delivered in Culpeper before the ball—the likes of which had earned him acclaim as the Demosthenes of his day—and nearly every other deed, word, or thought he performed worked toward one end. That end would not arrive this year or this decade, and maybe not the next decade. But even those suffering, soon-to-be-liberated Federal prisoners in Libby and Belle Isle would dutifully perform their roles in the attainment of Judson Kilpatrick's destiny.

That was the job currently held by Abraham Lincoln.

The appearance of such a lovely and diminutive Southern belle at the grandest ball of the year surprised the Federal sentry at the river. He felt obliged to escort her to his lieutenant. That man wondered that a Rebel girl, who would normally have been expected not to "dirty your shoes on the likes of us" would come across the hellish northern Virginia winter warscape to fraternize with the enemies of her people.

Sally Marsten's explanation that the brave young captain at whose invitation she had come had helped her search for her missing Confederate soldier and then ridden at the risk of his own neck through Southern lines to deliver the message, impressed the lieutenant.

"I'll provide one of my men as an escort for you to the party, Miss Marsten," he said. Then, touching Sally lightly on her lace-stoled arm, he added, "Perhaps a bit later the captain might suffer me a dance with you."

"I cannot imagine why he would not, chivalrous as you have been," Sally said, her eyelids fluttering then dropping as she curtsied.

But then again, she thought to herself, bracing against the winter chill outside, *if the lieutenant calls the turn too boldly, he will learn I have more under my skirts than hoops and crinoline.*

Indeed Miss Sally Marsten's petticoats included an extra inside layer: trousers with the legs rolled up—and twin derringers stuffed in the pockets.

For slim, handsome, ninety-four-pound Frank Stringfellow, alias Sally Marsten, tended to spend a lot of time incognito around the Yankees but never without sufficient firepower to remove himself when necessary. In this case, amid a building full of the mightiest names in the Union, firepower in addition to Sally's face powder and dress, her mother's hair switches, and coaching from the both of them on the finer points of feminine posture, walking, and speaking.

All this, and that seventy-five-hundred-dollar Yankee bounty.

Another man stood with Kilpatrick when Dahlgren ducked his head and entered the small windowless room illumined by a single oil lamp and tucked into a corner of the large ballroom building. A lean, hard man with hard, gray eyes and grim mustaches black as midnight and as foreboding. His presence conveyed more a sense of some*thing* to Dahlgren than some*one*—though an air of silent competence hung about him—and the younger man relished Kilpatrick's affable salutation.

"Ah, yes, our wounded, gallant knight," Kilpatrick said, a pearly smile lighting the incongruous terrain of his bearded face, as he stepped around the room's lone piece of furniture, a small new pine table, and hugged Dahlgren.

Kilpatrick detected the quizzical look etched on Dahlgren's boyish face and employed it to bring the third man into the cordialities.

"Colonel Ulric Dahlgren, Third Division, Cavalry Corps, Army of the Potomac, Captain John McEntee, second in command, Bureau of Military Intelligence," Kilpatrick said, noting with approval Dahlgren's arched eyebrows indicating his familiarity with the BMI's impressive reputation. "I have secured the participation of Captain McEntee and a cadre of choice men handpicked by himself to accompany on us on our mission. Indeed," Kilpatrick continued, "not a man shall ride down upon Richmond that is not individually selected by his regimental commander. We shall have the best four thousand horse soldiers in the United States Army."

Dahlgren assayed McEntee's manner as pleasant but betraying not a trace of insight into the man's thoughts, mood, or attitude.

Then into the room stepped Brigadier General George Armstrong Custer. Tall and strapping, from vigorous Teutonic stock, Dahlgren observed him to be not at all the pale dandy some of Custer's detractors portrayed him to be, with a dazzling blue, red, and gold uniform and luxuriant strawberry blond curls spilling down onto his broad shoulders.

Rare was the day Dahlgren felt himself to be intimidated by any man, including a president. But an electric charge entered the room with Custer as sure as Dahlgren stood atop one of the finest handcrafted wooden legs in America.

Ulric Dahlgren, at twenty-one, might be the youngest colonel in the Federal army; George Custer, twenty-four and every bit as fearless and reckless and, despite finishing last in his West Point class, infinitely more knowledgeable as a military man and almost without peer as a horseman, was the youngest general.

Though none of the four men held strong religious convictions, none smoke or drank. So Kilpatrick, motioning a guard he had stationed outside the room to close the door, moved quickly to a crude map of Virginia he had spread across the table.

Dahlgren marveled as the refinements of Kilpatrick's plan poured out.

"The courageous—and, I might add, persecuted—Miss Van Lew has again sent word from Richmond, through certain of Captain McEntee's operatives," Kilpatrick said, canting slightly his sandy-whiskered head toward the government agent, "that a mere one or two thousand of our horse approaching from the north could land on the Pamunkey River at dark, ride in unmolested—and take Davis."

For a few seconds, despite themselves, a hush overcame all four men, even Kilpatrick. Perhaps the enormity of the endeavor found at last a berth in the minds of the bold group. As quickly, however, Kilpatrick plowed ahead.

Custer would lead his famed Michigan Wolverine cavalry brigade southwest toward Charlottesville to destroy a railroad bridge and supply depot; this provided part of an elaborate infantry-cavalry diversion to the west of Lee's Army of Northern Virginia, which was spread along the south side of the Rapidan, northwest of Richmond. The Federal sleight of hand was designed to open the way for Kilpatrick's force, including Dahlgren, to scoot east around the Rebel right and head south toward the Confederate capital.

At Spotsylvania, Dahlgren would peel off to the west with five hundred troops and hit the James River twenty-five miles to the northwest of Richmond. Kilpatrick, meanwhile, would pound straight south toward the capital.

"John Babcock, one of Captain McEntee's most accomplished officers, has secured a black freedman well acquainted with the James from Richmond up to guide you to the best crossing," Kilpatrick said, turning to Dahlgren and in a heartbeat judging him one final time as equal to the job, despite his youth and lack of military training. "You shall cross the river where most appropriate and enter Richmond from the south, where you will face scant resistance."

The more scant even than usual, because Kilpatrick would by then have engaged, along Richmond's northern perimeter of defense with his larger force and six cannon, what hardscrabble home guard and militia the Rebels could scratch together.

Dahlgren and his men, meanwhile, would storm the Rebel prisons of Libby and Belle Isle, free the thousands of sick and emaciated Federal prisoners, and shepherd them east, down the Peninsula toward Federal lines in that sector.

Kilpatrick and his larger force would merge with them and provide covering fire wherever circumstances dictated.

"And . . ." Dahlgren said, stuttering just a bit, ". . . the—other directives— upon release of the prisoners—"

"The prisoners themselves are to carry out, in as timely a fashion as possible," Kilpatrick said, gravity now weighing his voice more heavily. Custer and McEntee exchanged a silent glance, Custer chewing at his lip, disagreement filling his eyes and wanting to graduate to his lips, but not quite able to find the proper form for the advance.

"Sir," Dahlgren said, the word managing to escape a catch that had formed suddenly in his throat.

When Dahlgren emerged from the secret lair, the aroma of freshly cut pine filled his grateful nostrils, even over the assorted smokes, perfumes, hair tonics, and beverages. *Now to find the pious Captain—soon to be Major—Marley,* he thought, *of whom General Hooker spoke so glowingly.* An instant passed before anyone took note of him. In that moment he heard a nearby officer instruct a dutifully impressed Baltimore belle, "We've had precious little use for this 'Opera House,' as they call it, till now, though we filled the building to capacity a few nights back for a remarkable performance by a man from that famous acting family, the Booths—Wilkes Booth, I believe it was, yes, that was it, John Wilkes Booth."

●◇ ●◇ ●◇

Stringfellow was drawing as much attention from the Yankees in his taffeta as he had in his panoply of other disguises throughout the war, such as dentist, student, and Federal horse soldier. And as usual, the name Frank Stringfellow, as in "Stringfellow the spy and murderer" was the farthest name in the world from anyone's lips.

At first the "other" ladies evidenced a bit of reticence toward him. After all, his diminutive figure and strikingly attractive face—added to the mysterious aura he exuded—might prove troublesome for some of them who did not have beaus, and some who did. Once word circulated that he was a tragedy-struck belle of some sort, who had been summoned by a specific Federal officer for attention and consolation, envy and jealousy melted into curiosity, sympathy, and even concern.

"I'm so sorry for your recent misfortune," one fetching young Philadelphian said, taffeta whooshing as she laid a small gloved hand on Stringfellow's forearm. "Was it a beau?"

Stringfellow fluttered his eyelashes as Sally and her mother had cued him, blushed, and looked down.

"Oh, do please forgive me," the Philadelphian said, patting Stringfellow's arm gently. "How often I feared for my Hector's safety and paced, sleepless, in the night watches when he was out west and far from me." Then the pleasant amber showers of candles and Chinese lanterns washed over her fetching face, along with rapture at the happy conclusion to the story, at the news that Hector's corps had been transferred back to northern Virginia, and that he was expected through the door any minute!

Stringfellow conveyed a dutiful expression of shared relief for his new friend, while calculating in his mind which additional corps Lee's already massively outnumbered command now had stacked against him. The scout might not be able, at this ball, to reckon which corps, but the men to whom he would report the information certainly would. For as late as this morning, no Confederate intelligence report betrayed even a hint of such a movement.

The Virginian managed to fend off the numerous attempts of Federal officers to escort him to the dance floor, with the excuse that he must wait on his brave and considerate escort. Finally the most oafish of the suitors—bald, overweight, nearly fifty, and intoxicated with brandy—refused to take no for an answer. When heads began turning in Stringfellow's direction as the volume of the slurring major's determined petitions mounted, the scout realized an unappetizing sojourn to the dance floor was the better part of valor—and the best chance to prevent his entire mission from vaporizing along with, perhaps, his life.

A worse dancer Stringfellow had never had the misfortune to witness. The major stomped on his feet, kneed his thighs, bumped repeatedly into him with his full weight of probably two hundred fifty pounds, and showered his smooth face with a stream of spit, saliva, and sweat that gave Stringfellow concern that the Marstens' carefully applied facial powder might be rinsed away.

At one point the Virginian caught the bemused expression of a cigar-puffing officer observing the ridiculous scene. *Indeed, to what lengths do I travel for the cause of my dear Confederacy!* Stringfellow thought with a wry inward smile. The smile was scotched in its incipiency when something of the cigar-puffer's mien caught his attention. *It is that Pinkerton man I nearly had to kill when escaping Alexandria last year!* The remembrance came crashing home to him. For a moment the scout's heart seemed anxious to come pounding up out of his throat as he struggled to maintain his calm. When he thought it safe, he shot a glance toward the Pinkerton man. Thankfully the agent forfeited no inkling of recognition. *And, indeed, how on earth could he!* Stringfellow thought, the wry smile again threatening to hatch itself across his face.

Fortunately, too, the human brandy snifter stumbling all over him did not allow the scout a word in edgewise, so he did not have to risk orally betraying himself. When the major began to berate Army of the Potomac commander Meade for his supposed shortcomings, Stringfellow even decided to encourage him along a bit.

"When indeed is General Meade going to move forward and end this infernal war!" Stringfellow blurted out, surprising even himself with the passion resident in his voice. "It is all anyone is asking." He looked up into his partner's dilated eyes. "So many of us have lost so much."

The major nearly fell over himself at this opportunity. He looked first one way then the other, his head bobbing like an apple at the county fair, before leaning forward and saying, in the most surreptitious tone he could muster, "Allow me to share a confidence with you, my darling. Once this God-forsaken winter is finally behind us and we launch our spring campaign against Bobby Lee—" Stringfellow was not at this point certain whether this revelation or his own consciousness would outlast the other, as the major's overwhelming garlic-tinged breath swept through the scout's tortured nostrils and sinus cavity—"we'll have a real fighter leading us."

As Stringfellow reeled at the noxious fumes, now emanating only inches from his face, the major said, "I'll be bound that the war is over by summer."

Stringfellow rallied himself, ignoring the nausea welling up into his throat and deciding to bestow upon his dance partner a battlefield promotion. "Why, Colonel, how splendid!" Then, coyly, laboring to keep his voice high: "I realize it is probably out of the question, but, well, how unladylike of me would it be to inquire of a military secret from so gallant an escort as you?"

A light beamed in the Yankee's face. "Why, you must hail from Baltimore, dear. Your accent—it is quite like some of these Secesh women around here." Then, as quickly, the light flicked off. "You just keep your ear to the ground, madam," he said. "One of my old messmates is high up in Stanton's War Department, and he says the deal is all but certain. When it all breaks, you'll have to *grant* that I was right!"

The "colonel" roared at his own verbal nimbleness, showering Stringfellow anew with what for all the world looked, at least coming out of the man's mouth, like tiny pellets of cottage cheese.

For a moment, sweat streaming down his smooth round pate, an air of solemnness seemed to envelope the Yankee. "Of course, this great raid that's been garnering all the gossip at Willard's and all the speechifying here—Meade will probably receive more credit than he is due for that, though I know for a fact he had nothing to do with it and— Oh, heavens, ma'am, I'll have to excuse myself. I've got to be going . . . er . . . that is, thank you for the dance, ma'am."

Before Stringfellow could protest, he was back at his seat and the wordy major was trundling toward the door, to relieve himself outside in some manner the scout was certain, but in which, he could not be sure.

Already midnight had passed. Despite another in a long parade of frigid evenings this winter had foisted upon Virginia, the Opera House felt like a smokehouse, and rivulets of sweat cascaded down Stringfellow's back. He fanned himself and mulled over the torrent of information he had consumed the past couple of hours. At least one Federal corps—*the Fourth!* he realized, fretting himself for not remembering earlier, *It must be the Fourth*—returned east against Lee . . . U. S. Grant, the fierce victor of Fort Donelson, Fort Henry, Shiloh, and Vicksburg, assuming command of the Army of the Potomac . . . and the big raid, likely on Richmond, of which Stringfellow and others had heard whispers and fragments for months, he had heard more than one reference to that this evening. What arrested him was that it now appeared to be imminent.

"Madam, I'll be asking you to come with me."

Stringfellow, continuing his fanning, looked up. It was the lieutenant who had approved his entry to the party. But this time, the man was in no mood for dancing.

"Why, Lieutenant, my escort would never forgive me," the scout trilled.

The lieutenant's jaw tightened. "You know quite well the captain will not be your escort tonight." He lowered his voice a shade. "Will you come with me quietly, or shall I notify the provost guards?"

Stringfellow knew trouble had arrived with the lieutenant, but his still-powdered face registered only polite compliance.

As he neared the door, the lieutenant behind him, Stringfellow caught sight of a small gold cross pinned to the tunic of a much-decorated Yankee captain. Unlike the rest of the colorful ornamentation on the man's uniform, the tiny item reflected brightly the light from a nearby lantern.

Wayne Marley would step no further into this den of iniquity than he must, and then only until his hopefully brief conference with Ulric Dahlgren was completed. He wore the little cross "Old Prayer Book" Howard had sent to him while he recuperated in the hospital from his Chancellorsville wounds, but he would like to have had his Bible with him as well.

Stringfellow believed with his whole heart that never could he have come through so many toe-to-toe tussles with the Grim Reaper unless a merciful Providence had been guiding and delivering him, for such purposes as he knew not. That brightly shining little cross—on a Yank uniform—brought a smile to the scout's face with his acknowledgment that, as so often He had, God was reminding him of His constant and superintending presence. As Stringfellow moved through the now-mild, torch- and lantern-lit night, revelers all around, he rehearsed in his mind the psalm he so often had in the crucible of danger, the words of another young warrior-poet from a different time and place:

> *Whither shall I go from thy spirit?*
> *or whither shall I flee from thy presence?*
> *If I ascend up into heaven, thou art there:*
> *if I make my bed in hell, behold, thou art there.*

Comfort swept over his small frame, so much so that he had to stifle a chuckle at contemplation of how God might view the prayers of a man deceiving and lying to others while dressed up as a woman, so that he and his fellows might be better able to do them harm!

No such mirth informed the Yankee lieutenant's countenance. "Alright, madam," he said, his voice tense and his words chopped. They had passed behind a stand of elms on the far perimeter of camp. The lieutenant glanced back toward the Opera House, which still poured forth light, music, and merry voices. Then he walked to within a couple of feet of Stringfellow. "I cannot say what your gambit is, but I have learned that some of our pickets fired at some Rebel guerillas as they spirited a kidnapped Federal captain across the river two nights ago."

The lieutenant searched Stringfellow's face, turned in the direction of the camp lights that now illumined it, for reaction. Seeing none, he proceeded, his words coming low and awkward. "After some investigative work this evening, I learned what you of course already knew. That captured captain is your supposed escort, also missing since night before last."

Stringfellow looked the lieutenant in the eye. "I do not know what to say, Lieutenant. It is true that the captain has not shown himself tonight."

"Well, I'm going to tell you what I think happened," the lieutenant said, without mirth. "The captain intended to deliver that pass to you, but he got himself captured. This country is riddled with Mosby's scum. They managed to get you the pass anyhow, and you're here doing their bidding."

Stringfellow remained silent for a moment, attempting to gauge the man before him. When he spoke, his words came steady and deliberate. "In that case, Lieutenant, why didn't you arrest me back at the Opera House?"

The Federal had not prepared himself for that question.

"I believe it's because you're a true gentleman," Stringfellow continued before the Yankee, now blushing and shifting his feet, could summon a response. "And you don't truly think I'm a spy, do you, Lieutenant? You think I'm a lady. And just to show you how much I appreciate your trust, I want you to face that way—that's it, back toward that ole Opera House, and close your eyes for just a teensy minute."

The lieutenant, now thoroughly bewitched, loosed a goofy smile and did as he was told. Stringfellow took up his skirts and plucked out his derringers. "All right, you can look now, Lieutenant."

It was not what the Yankee had hoped to see. "But—"

"Out here, in the wide open?" Stringfellow said. "Why, you ought to be ashamed of yourself, being a gentleman and all." Now he cocked the derringers. "I am Frank Stringfellow, scout for General Jeb Stuart. And you are now my prisoner, Lieutenant. Do not try anything at all, for I shall shoot you dead sure as the turning of the earth."

The lieutenant was speechless.

"We're going to walk nice and proper to my buggy, Lieutenant," Stringfellow said. "And we're going to get in, and we're going to head south."

Such were the shock and jumble of fragmentary thoughts imbuing the lieutenant that he walked as though in a trance back through the festive camp and to the buggy, where Stringfellow motioned him into the seat. Not until they came to the picket down near the Rapidan did his mind begin to engage itself. When the lieutenant hesitated to speak as the sentry shone a lantern into the buggy, Stringfellow poked him in the ribs with one of the derringers.

"I . . . I'm escorting this young lady on her way," the lieutenant stammered. "I'll return presently."

The sentry smiled and saluted. As they rode on, Stringfellow heard the guard cackle behind them, "Have yourself a fine evening, sir, hee-hee—but watch out for Rebs."

Stringfellow had developed through his many close encounters with Yankee bullets and hangmen's ropes the eye of an eagle and the nose of a bloodhound in apprising men. He had discerned an ever-so-slight shift in the lieutenant's demeanor at the picket post. Still that prepared him in no way, as they came to the river, for the numbing shot the Yankee landed from out of nowhere with the heel of his fist across the scout's jaw. The blow knocked Stringfellow nearly out of the buggy. Struggling to shake the fog from his ringing head, he pulled himself up, only to get caught across the side of the head with another blow as the lieutenant flailed away with his fists. Reeling back, sprawled halfway out of the buggy, Stringfellow sensed somewhere in the back of his mind that the horse had bolted—and was heading back in the direction of the Yankee picket station!

Even as the lieutenant continued to swing wildly, Stringfellow, stunned and hurting, summoned every ounce of will in his less-than-one-hundred-pound body and began to slash at the Yankee's face with the derringer. For several sickening seconds, the two pounded away, grunting, and gasping, some blows landing, some cracking against one another, others missing, as the out-of-control buggy bounced and careened down the road, headed straight for the Federal pickets.

Finally, Stringfellow, taking another hard blow across his forehead, felt his strength—and consciousness—slipping away. Blurting "God help me!" he reared back and launched one last mighty blow at the lieutenant, which connected with crushing finality across the bridge of the man's nose. Stringfellow had not the strength for even one more blow, and he fell against the back of the seat, summoning all he had just to raise the derringer and point it at the Yankee. All he could do now to save his own life—for he would surely be hanged as a spy by the Federals, probably from the ceiling rafters during the last dance of the night at the Opera House—was squeeze the trigger. Then he heard the lieutenant moan and, after a moment, when Stringfellow's vision cleared, he discerned the man to be sprawled on the floor of the buggy, clutching his face, blood trickling through his fingers.

Stringfellow emitted a sigh of relief, then realized the Yankee picket post was right around the next bend in the road, no more than one hundred yards ahead and closing fast. He started to leap from the buggy when he saw the reins, slipping over the front dashboard! Somehow, despite all the tumult, they had remained in the vehicle, but now they were— Stringfellow lunged for them, but they slid over the dash. He lurched down, the charging horse peppering his face with dirt and rocks, thick dust choking his throat and searing his eyes. With one outstretched, lace-gloved hand, he snagged the tip end of one of the reins as it fell away and jerked with all the strength he had. At first the horse fought him, ran on, but as Stringfellow pulled back with his shoulders, his entire upper body, the hocks of the angry, frightened animal skidded to an ugly halt, slinging more dirt and rocks all round.

Seeing the lieutenant had lost consciousness, Stringfellow sprang from the buggy, grabbed the other rein, and sweet-talking the huffing, snorting horse as well as even Sally Marsten could walked him gingerly around to where he again faced south. Then the scout jumped back into the buggy, and with no more than a light flick of the reins and two snaps of his tongue against the roof of his mouth, he had horse, buggy, and Yankee moving, even as the Federal picket less than seventy-five yards away cocked back the hammer on his .57 caliber Enfield and tried to discern what was afoot around the curve just to the south.

For General Lee himself would need to know what sweet "Sally Marsten" had learned this memorable night.

•◆ •◆ •◆

"But why me, when you have every man in the Army of the Potomac with a horse at your disposal?" Marley asked Dahlgren as they stood in the same little room where the younger man had an hour earlier met with Kilpatrick, Custer, and McEntee.

"Why, Captain, you have a long and distinguished record, dating back to your duty with Stonewall Jackson in the Mexican War," Dahlgren said, his face animated. "Every superior under which you have served, including General Hooker, writes and speaks glowingly of you. I'm frankly at a loss as to why . . . well, why you've not advanced through the ranks more rapidly. We shall, however, now start the ball rolling on that score."

Dahlgren pulled a file from his leather valise, retrieved a single sheet of paper from it, and handed it to Marley.

"That is your commission as major—Major," Dahlgren said, a smile stretching across his thin handsome face as he extended his hand to shake Marley's. "May I add that that order comes with sanction from the *highest* levels of our government."

Marley, shaking the proffered hand, perceived the glint in Dahlgren's eyes. Something big was indeed afoot.

"And there is something else, Major Marley," Dahlgren said after a moment, all pretense and airs vanishing. "It is said you are a man of . . . an unusually devout faith. Well, I, during my convalescence that is, had much time for contemplation of and meditation on the *weightier* matters of this life—and the next life. That is to say, Major, I spent many hours reading in the Scriptures, more perhaps than heretofore I have ever in my life."

Marley listened as Dahlgren, rarely at a loss for the most articulate expression, grappled to complete his thoughts.

"I guess I should say I felt that coupled with your record and your reconnaissance and scouting capabilities," Dahlgren said, "I cannot but think it is to our—to my—advantage to have a man like you with me along the way." Now the airs returned. "Anyhow, we shall see, shan't we?"

"I'm indebted to you for your trust," Marley said. "I'll do my best to uphold the confidence you've placed in me."

Outside, mounting his horse, Marley thought to himself, *"It is said you are a man of . . . unusually devout faith."* Tears filled his eyes that he, such a rebellious, oft-backslidden doubting Thomas should have been so well spoken of by others. That he should have been given such encouragement by God that He, the giver of all gifts, was not yet through with Wayne Marley.

A few days later, Dahlgren sat alone in his tent. The temperature was unseasonably mild for late February in northern Virginia, which pleased him, because his "partial" leg did not ache. He pulled out his timepiece and clicked open the gold cover. Twenty minutes till four. He must be up and at it. The column was to leave at 5 P.M.

He dipped his pen in the inkwell, then signed the letter lying on the crude camp table before him. Somewhere outside a bugle sounded as he scanned the missive, completed only moments before.

> Dearest Father,
>
> I hope this correspondence finds you well. I again thank you for the love and consideration you showered over me during the long days of my recent convalescence. Now I take pen in hand to share extraordinary news with you. I have not returned to the fleet, because there is a grand raid to be made, and I am to have a very important command. If successful, it will be the grandest thing on record; and if it fails, many of us will "go up." I may be captured, or I may be "tumbled over"; but it is an undertaking that if I were not in, I should be ashamed to show my face again. With such an important command, I am afraid to mention it, for fear that this letter might fall into the wrong hands before reaching you. I find that I can stand the service perfectly well without my leg. I think we will be successful, although a desperate undertaking. If we do not return, there is no better place to "give up the ghost."
>
> Your affectionate son,
> Ulric Dahlgren

Word reached Lee, in Richmond for consultations with Davis, that three large contingents of Federal horse were headed southwest from the Northern lines near the Rapidan. When Lee also learned that the great scout Stringfellow himself had secreted information back from behind enemy lines that a large cavalry raid was headed into the heart of Virginia, designed to "turn the Confederates' table upside down and spill all their dishes onto the floor," his first primal thoughts flashed where always they did, not to himself, not to his army, not to Virginia, but to the safety and happiness of the wife and daughters he must again leave alone in the face of war so that he might return north to command his country's army

CHAPTER 17

WHEN MARLEY CLIMBED INTO THE SADDLE AS DUSK DESCENDED over northern Virginia on February 28, 1864, nearly five hundred of the best horse soldiers in the Federal army climbed into their saddles with him as part of Dahlgren's command. Later that evening thirty-five hundred more would mount up with Kilpatrick. From across the Army of the Potomac—and the North—they came, handpicked from Pennsylvania, Maine, Michigan, New York, Ohio, and Indiana. Every man and every commander—all four thousand of them—had excelled at making war and came on direct recommendation of one or more of his superiors.

Kilpatrick had assembled a hard, tough, veteran column of physically imposing warriors who could match the best Billy Sherman and Little Phil Sheridan's western armies had, or even what Jeb Stuart with his dwindling forces and gaunt horses could now throw at them. And they planned to see no one remotely so martial as Jeb and his boys.

When they rode out, the temperature was so mild that not a man wore his overcoat. As a light southerly breeze kissed his bearded face, a resurgence of pride and resolution in the purposes for which he had again donned the blue coat swelled Marley's chest. *It is like the old days,* he thought, brimming with a joy he had nearly forgotten. *It is good to believe again in what we are doing. And such an undertaking—surely the Lord himself must be pleased that we are not only following his admonitions to visit the prisoners; we are bound to free them! Indeed it is a good day to live. And even a good day to die.*

For Marley now felt, with his renewed spiritual vigor, his work these past months teaching the Bible to the men, and his selection to this breathtaking quest into the teeth of the Confederacy, that were his life to end this very night, he would consider himself to have fought a good fight, finished his course, and finally kept the faith. *Hopefully Old Jack is smiling away up there somewhere, even though*

I'm raiding Richmond to free many of the prisoners he himself fought to capture, he thought.

A sudden revelation came to him. *More than any other man I have ever known, I wish to be like Tom Jackson.* Indeed, Marley realized with a twinge of regret, the color of a man's uniform matters little when compared with the condition of his heart. Then a bit of his joy slipped away, but only a bit.

"Fine day for a ride, wouldn't you say, Major?"

Marley turned to see Dahlgren pull up to him.

"Yes, sir," Marley said with a smile.

"I've questions for you when this is over and we are back in Washington with our freed thousands and our glory," Dahlgren announced with all the bright promise of a spring dawn. "Questions of a . . . religious nature . . . about the Bible."

Marley smiled. "It would be my highest honor at any time and anywhere to discuss the Scriptures with you, Colonel."

Dahlgren studied him for a moment as they rode, the younger man easy in the saddle despite his wooden leg, which was strapped to the horse. "You knew Stonewall Jackson well, they say."

Marley canted his head and glanced down for an instant, then met Dahlgren's gaze. "Yes."

Dahlgren seemed to find his words with difficulty. "How . . . that is to say . . . what sort of a man was he?"

Marley thought for a few seconds. "A man who loved God," he said simply.

Dahlgren stared at him. "Yes," he said.

"Yes," Marley said.

Dahlgren nodded and gently spurred his horse, the magnificent coal-black stallion. "We shall talk again," he said.

"Sir," Marley said, nodding once and saluting. "Oh, sir."

"Yes?" Dahlgren replied, slowing his horse.

"Why so large a quantity of oakum, turpentine, and explosives, sir?"

Dahlgren's lips widened almost imperceptibly. "Well, one of our assignments—straight from the very top of our government—is to burn Rebel supplies, rolling stock, rail depots, and the like."

"Yes, sir," Marley said quietly, saluting again.

Still, he wondered that several wagonloads of such materials were necessary, especially on what, from the light provisions assigned them, looked to be a lightning raid and over very soon.

●◆ ●◆ ●◆

"Sir, we have confirmed three separate Federal commands proceeding past the Rapidan toward Madison Courthouse," one of Davis's advisors said.

Lee looked up from the desk in the court building across the street from the capitol square in Richmond, where he sat addressing correspondence to various government departments. "Three?"

"Yes, sir. Sedgwick, Birney, and that flashy Michigan horse soldier, Custer."

Lee turned to the wall map of Virginia. *So many objectives they could have,* he thought. *They could be intending mischief farther west, in the Shenandoah. They might be creating a diversion for action elsewhere.* He rubbed his snowy-whiskered chin with his hand. *Or they could be rounding our left flank in order to move—here.*

"Sir," Davis's advisor said, "The president will see you now."

A wave of relief passed over Lee. *That means he is working today in his regular office, in this building, not in the president's home.* This meant the respiratory afflictions that often required Davis to attempt to work and hold meetings in the makeshift second-floor office off his bedroom had relented, at least temporarily. Often Lee feared that Davis's woeful physical ailments would force him from office—or kill him. *He has many flaws, as do we all,* Lee thought, *and he is criticized from all corners, but who else could keep this besieged country from flying into a hundred pieces? Lord God, I pray Thy sovereign hand to hold him up and guide him along the way in wisdom, understanding, and knowledge.*

Then Lee realized that with such a combination of known threats on the move against him—and whatever else might yet be afoot—he must return on the morrow, Leap Day, February 29, to his field headquarters near Orange Courthouse to the northwest. And he must endeavor as soon as he could to determine where lay the true threat. *I shall send Jeb Stuart toward Charlottesville and I must keep the rest of the army in position on the Rapidan,* he thought, divining the map before him. He was wrought with uneasiness.

But I believe those people are coming straight for Richmond, and they are coming now, and it is not Custer or Sedgwick or Birney.

His face reddened as he realized, *I must return to my own camp while this benighted city lies naked before the enemy, and my own wife and daughters squarely in the center of it.*

◆◇ ◆◇ ◆◇

Custer drew Jeb Stuart's horsemen and the attention of the Confederacy as he kicked up dust out toward Charlottesville. As Kilpatrick left Stevensburg with his force, Dahlgren and his five hundred hit the Rapidan, the river shimmering like polished onyx under the evening moon. They surprised and overwhelmed the small Confederate picket, sent word back to Kilpatrick, then galloped south toward Spotsylvania Courthouse.

Two Confederate scouts, comrades of Frank Stringfellow's, had an even more momentous night. No one caught so much as a whiff of them as they observed the entire Rapidan proceedings. Then the two stole a pair of Federal horses during the brief tussle, rode at the rear of Dahlgren's column for a while, then spurred off to report to Wade Hampton that, Custer notwithstanding, a Yankee force was indeed heading in the direction of Richmond.

Dahlgren and his men raced through the dark. They hit the sleepy junction of Spotsylvania just as dawn peeled back the pitch veil of the night watches to reveal the Yankee raiders.

Both the old broken nose and the shot shoulder reported faithfully and achingly for duty to Marley as they always did when cold or wet were in the wind. He pulled alongside Dahlgren as he spotted a second-floor window shutter jerk shut. "Sir, is there weather coming?"

Dahlgren possessed his own barometer. Rubbing his wooden leg, he nodded. "Another reason we must hasten toward Richmond. And even if we have been as yet undetected, I would wager the fair folks of Spotsylvania will prove faithful harbingers to the Rebel government of our arrival."

That afternoon, farther south, Dahlgren called a brief halt, one of the few since the journey began. Marley, checking the two Colts and the carbine he carried, eyed the young colonel as Dahlgren walked the black steed along the column. *He does not lack resolve, I'll grant him that,* Marley apprised. *He carries himself with spirit and has an air about him that even these veteran, elite troopers seem to recognize and be steadied by.*

"Major," Dahlgren said a few minutes later, approaching Marley, who fed oats to his grateful horse from a bag, "I want you to pick a man and ride a half mile ahead of us. We're into serious country now, and I need your eyes. I don't want any surprises. Three shots if you find trouble and can't get back to us."

When he resumed the brisk ride, Marley eyed the gathering banks of low, charcoal-colored clouds scudding toward them from back over his right shoulder. And he saw more of what he had seen all day—once-verdant fields and hills now blasted into colorless, winter-war ugliness, and a sparse, underfed populace of women, children, and old men, their faces wan and lined beyond their years.

This country and its people are being dragged down the ladder to destruction and devastation one rung at a time, he thought. *How detestable the face of war, and how shamed we as a people, North and South, for failing to solve our differences without it.*

As Lee's train rumbled north then northwest out of Richmond and into the country on the rickety Virginia Central rail line, sentiments flooded over him of Rooney. How he wanted to see the big strapping boy again. *Such a man, such a responsible leader Fitzhugh has become after all,* Lee thought. He remembered his son's years of irresponsibility, of debt, of leaving Harvard College without a degree. Now pride merged with the pain of separation and uncertainty that had swelled up within him. *How is he bearing up, wounded, in prison, never again to see on earth his loving wife or babies?* Then he offered silent prayer for the young man, and for all of his children, near and far. Especially did he pray for Agnes. *Sweet, quiet Wiggie. She still grieves for Orton,* he thought, frustrated at how little he seemed able to ease the pathways of life for his children, especially when war raged all around them.

Yet in spite of having me as their father, they all seem to have turned out exceedingly well, he thought with a mixture of guilt, relief, and thanksgiving toward God for His merciful intercession on behalf of every member of the family. *And Precious Life, still just seventeen years of age, and yet how she increasingly fills the yawning void left by the loss of our gentle Annie.* Then in spite of himself, he laughed right out loud at the recollection of Custis Morgan, the feisty little squirrel whom Mildred had determined would fill another void, the one created when the Lees had to leave all their family pets at Arlington.

Such an incorrigible little critter is this Custis Morgan! Lee thought, his mind lost to the martial conversations of other officers holding forth near him. Lee found less applicability in Mildred's drawing the first name of the animal—the rodent, Lee corrected her—after her eldest brother than in namesaking him for the famous Confederate cavalryman General John Hunt Morgan, who some months before had famously escaped from a Federal prison camp. *Indeed,* Lee thought, *this rodent is continuously escaping from his own cage and running roughshod through the house.*

He retrieved pen, inkwell, and paper from an aide, and as war raged around him and rent his family with death, prison, separation, and homelessness, began to write a heartfelt letter to Mildred.

> Precious Life,
>
> How much I enjoyed the most recent visit, and availing myself of the opportunity to become better acquainted with the newest member of our family, the redoubtable Custis Morgan. Upon some reflection, I proffer this suggestion for yours and Aggie's culinary satisfaction. To wit, a robust and nutritious soup, squirrel soup thickened with peanuts. Custis Morgan in such an exit from the stage would cover himself with glory.

Lee felt as proud of himself for this missive as he had any for some time.

"General Lee, sir, coming up on Frederick's Hall Station," he heard a voice say.

Just a little while to Orange now, Lee thought. *I've got time to count Mary's socks.* He pulled a large cardboard box up from the floor and began to count the fruits of Mary's Franklin Street factory. She had "yarn scouts" seeking and sending her worsted wool from every state in the Confederacy. The shipments came regularly, though Lee was able to bring this one with him. His orders to Taylor were to distribute the socks to the neediest soldiers in each regiment. This time of year, the closing weeks of winter, was the most grievous for the men; thousands had little or no covering for their feet. The Federals had learned they needed no great strategies for following the Army of Northern Virginia's trail. They need only follow its bloody footprints.

"Ah!" Lee exclaimed, drawing the curious glance of a nearby officer as he stared at the enormous collection of socks. *Once again she has done it; she has miscounted. I have twice counted one hundred and two pairs and she has indicated a total of one hundred and four. Where can those extra two pairs be?* He leaned over, looked around the floor and on the empty seats adjacent to him, his countenance growing darker. *No! I know perfectly well—they are not here. She has miscounted again!*

Never would Robert E. Lee's wrath over the most insubordinate officer, the most foolish military blunder, or even the most tragic—and preventable—battle folly exceed that which boiled up within him when Mary Lee's sock count was off. But he would convey his displeasure to no man.

Cooling down, he shook his head. *I must not allow my anger to rise over the matter of miscounted socks,* he thought, ashamed of himself. Then he caught a glimpse of a little Baptist church tucked clean and white in a stand of pines. Fronting the church was a pond that sparkled and drew the attention of two little girls in white calico dresses. *What a glorious world God Almighty has given us,* Lee thought. *How thankless and ungrateful we are, and how we labor to mar His gifts.*

Marley heard the train before he saw it, as he trotted his horse along a narrow road abutted on both sides by tall, thick woods. By the time he reached the clearing along which the tracks were laid, the train was chugging past. He and Quayle, the shrewd Indiana corporal he brought with him, ducked their horses into the wildwood at the edge of the road. Marley hopped off and ran to a position of cover where he could observe the train. His lone eye, grown razor-sharp through years of solo duty, caught an arresting sight— gray uniforms, truly gray, and clean, with lots of yellow piping, of the sort only high-ranking Rebel officers could now sport. He was back in the saddle in seconds, whipping the withers of his horse with the reins and spurring him like he rarely had before. The Hoosier, clueless as to what Marley had seen, could barely stay with him.

"Sir!" Marley shouted toward Dahlgren, riding at the head of the column, while still fifty yards away. Marley charged his horse so close to Dahlgren that when he jerked the reins back, the animal skittered to a halt on his shanks. "Sir, a train just passed, heading from Richmond toward the main Confederate camp. From what I could tell, it's a very important train."

Dahlgren stared at him for an instant, then spurred the black and shouted, "Let's go!"

The whole column, the sound of the train whistle in their ears, thundered down the road toward the rail crossing. When they hit it, Dahlgren, in the lead, turned his mount toward the train, its smoke still visible in the distance. He charged down the tracks. After a moment, he reined up.

"Who? Who could it be?" he asked Marley, at his side.

"Don't know, sir, but I saw lots of gray—not butternut—some braid. We know the Rebs are running only the trains that have to run, and we know that General Lee has been in Richmond the last few days but is expected back to his headquarters at Orange Courthouse any time, sir."

A glint escaped from Dahlgren's eyes. "We—you—have a knack for knowing a lot, don't you, Major?"

Marley did not know what to say.

"Well, that's one reason you're a major and on this expedition," Dahlgren said. "But I fear that without more substantiated information, chasing out cross-country after a train, in the opposite direction of our assigned mission and in enemy territory, when we actually do not know who is on it, could prove counterproductive to that mission—even if we catch the train, which we would."

Marley could understand the decision, but the feeling gnawed at him as they began instead to tear up track and cut telegraph wires, that something big was on that train.

◦◦ ◦◦ ◦◦

"Mama, here are the items from which we may make, uh . . ." Agnes was not sure exactly what indeed they *would* make from the items.

"Coffee?" Mary asked.

"Well, these all will color water."

Mary motioned her to continue. Her arthritic bones told her a fresh wave of cold air had blown in outside—and so did the descending temperature in the family's first-floor sitting room. Not enough materials, wood or otherwise, were available to keep more than one or two fireplaces burning, even on the coldest days, and burning low at that.

"Acorns, carrots, corn, cottonseed, dandelion roots, okra seeds, peas, peanuts, rice, and roasted rye," Agnes said, rattling off the list. She folded the paper in her hands, then looked again at Mary. "The last appears the most popular," she added quietly, "but actually, I alphabetized them."

Mary peered at Agnes for a moment, an odd pain causing her to flinch. Then, including Mildred in her statement, she said, "Dears, it only makes sense to use those sweet potatoes someone left at our front door last night, since we have learned that the sediment left at the bottom of the cup after sweet potato coffee makes such strong soap for cleaning the curtains and carpets." She motioned toward the kitchen. "And Mildred, please—"

"Yes, Mother," Mildred said, rising from her wing chair. "Give most of the sweet potatoes away." Her Roman nose crinkled a bit. "For people who now have less, we must surely give away more than anybody in the Confederacy."

Mary stared at her. "God has given us more than almost anyone in the country." When Mildred attempted to reply, she said, "Never be so foolish as to think that God's primary blessings are material in nature, dears."

At that point, Custis Morgan terminated the conversation by leaping from a position of complete concealment behind the sofa where Mary sat. He ran onto the sofa, raced up her arm, snatching the winter cap she wore off her head, then pivoted and retreated from the room with no less rapidity than any Yankee army Mary Lee's husband ever chased from Virginia.

Agnes's eyes appeared ready to pop from her head; Mildred could barely suppress a giggle while sputtering, "Mama!"

Mary Lee's eyes burned like Stonewall Jackson's before a battle. "That's nothing, Mildred Lee. Why, night before last, your Custis Morgan sprang from the fireplace and pulled my shawl right off me while I was taking my rheumatism medication!"

On the evening of February 29, the low dark scudding cloud banks, that a few hours earlier claimed Marley's attention, gave birth to a steady downpour of cold rain, whipped around by winds that felt as though someone were slashing his face with sharp icicles. Still riding south ahead of Dahlgren's column, he pulled his soaked hat low and his caped Federal greatcoat up and around his cheeks, warding off the miserable elements as best he could. Then snow began to fall, snow which, as Marley feared upon its arrival, soon became sleet. All this, plus everything around him was black as pitch. At one point he discerned the ghostly outline of a small country church steeple. *How I wish I were in there,* he thought, his eyes shut to mere slits, and real icicles forming and multiplying over his beard, coat, and hat. *In there, with a fire, light, and God's people, building one another up instead of here to tear everything down.* He was the one supposed to watch and scout, and he could see nothing. He did not know if he were among woods, hills, or towns, though even solitary homes seemed few and far between. No lights shown, only darkness.

At nearly two o'clock in the morning, near Goochland Courthouse and still a few miles north of the James, he found his way along the road back to Dahlgren. "Sir, up ahead is a crossroads with a small store. If you've a mind to rest a spell anytime before Richmond, this might be the place."

At the crossroads they couldn't even get a match lit in the unrelenting storm, so all Marley could detect of Dahlgren was his voice. "Very well, we'll make a short camp here."

Marley knew that the dark, wind, cold, rain, and sleet that kept peppering all their stinging faces, would pose difficulty for Dahlgren even to dismount from his horse. So the Pennsylvanian swung out of his own saddle and found his commander—more precisely, his wooden leg. Helping the towering young colonel down, he asked, his voice barely discernible above the roar of the evening, "Are you not too tired, sir?"

Dahlgren made it to the ground; Marley could feel the man turn toward him and could almost see the winsome boyish smile through the dark. "We'll have some supper and two hours' sleep," Dahlgren said, "then you'll see how bright I am."

He is young, Marley thought, lowering his head as he searched for a bit of shelter, *but he is a good man, and we need many more like him if we are ever to win this war.*

Hours before, Stringfellow's comrades had raced their foaming exhausted mounts up to Wade Hampton's headquarters house and reported their observations. Exercising that peculiarly American practice of taking the initiative when events dictated and orders were not available, the hulking South Carolinian ordered every horse soldier he could find—three hundred of them— into the saddle. Exercising that peculiarly Southern practice of hurling oneself into a numerically superior foe, he did just that—his men lighting out after troops more than ten times their number.

●✧ ●✧ ●✧

As the night watches grew deeper, accompanied by the bitter storm, Lee found sleep elusive. He sat up in his cot. The elements pounded against the tent he insisted on over the comforts of a warm bed in Orange Courthouse. Like Washington he desired to remain among the men who froze, bled, and died for him and their desperate fight for liberty. Feeling smothered at having been in his tent for many hours, he poked his head out of the flap. Instantly the swirling storm snapped it back inside. Stung, he dried his forehead, cheeks, and ears with a towel.

He now knew that Custer was churning toward Charlottesville on his left flank and that another Federal force had driven through Frederick's Hall on his right flank. Marshall had delivered a further report just before Lee turned in that yet another force was rumored farther east, around Beaver Dam Station. The Federals all seemed headed in one direction—south.

If in fact such a force exists around Beaver Dam, they may be even now coming against Richmond, he thought, a fresh chill gripping him. *And what of the Frederick's Hall contingent—are they moving against Richmond? Or us? Are they a decoy? And what is Custer about? Will Jeb find him? Even if he does, being so outnumbered and with such haggard horses, will he be able to do anything with him?* Then the pounding on the tent grew so ferocious that Lee could not maintain his train of thought. The roar . . . the wet . . . the chill . . . and his mind was returning to the Pedregal. Nearly twenty years it had been, and yet he knew that still the legend of Bobby Lee and the Pedregal grew with each passing year in the hushed whispers that carried across the decades through the ranks of the Federal army, and now, perhaps, that of the Confederacy.

Where others had failed as Winfield Scott and the United States Army pursued Santa Anna toward his capital of Mexico City in the Mexican-American War, Lee had single-handedly crossed on foot a hellish, five-mile-long stretch of volcanic lava called the Pedregal. He had crossed and recrossed it in the dark, with all its jagged igneous rock and sudden steep holes, in a raging storm whose lightning provided his only light. And the next step at any time the entire night could have been the one that brought a Mexican bullet or sword. All while going thirty-six hours without sleep.

Lee also managed during those efforts to guide American troops into position to win two of the war's most pivotal battles, Contreras and Churubusco, which set the stage for the final victorious assault on Mexico City.

He could barely remember the commander in chief's assessment of his exploits: "The greatest feat of physical and moral courage performed by any individual in my knowledge."

Now he wondered if that dauntless soldier still existed.

Blessedly the storm had relented when Marley awoke a few short hours later, the morning of March 1. The trees around him dripped, and the air retained its chill bite, but the wind, sleet, and rain were no more. As he struggled to his feet, the stiffness of a man soldiering in the field in his mid-thirties warring against him, the Pennsylvanian heard muffled grumbles from some of the troopers. "Insane . . . beyond the pale . . . crazy, we'll never smell Richmond . . ."

As the aching weariness spread like a cancer through him, Marley was inclined to succumb to similar cynicism. Then, in the predawn shadows, he caught sight of Dahlgren, already being helped up onto his saddled horse. A bolt of shame coursed through him. *Who could complain of weariness,* he thought, *when looking at that brave young man, still weak from his wound, minus a leg, and riding along quietly and uncomplainingly, vigilantly watching every incident of this march?*

Then Marley realized that of all the men with whom he had ever campaigned, only Stonewall Jackson could match Ulric Dahlgren for hard courage.

"Major," Dahlgren summoned Marley. "You will continue to be my forward eyes. I have already sent Captain Mitchell and a hundred men down the Kanawha Canal this side of the James to wreak havoc on canal locks, mills, and whatever else they find. We shall proceed east along James River Road to Jude's Ferry, whereupon our Negro guide, so helpfully recommended us by Captains McEntee and Babcock, will guide us across the river. From there, as you know, we shall enter Richmond from its soft southern underbelly and effect release of the prisoners, even as General Kilpatrick attacks from the north."

Despite the cold, the fatigue, the uncertainty, and above all, the unremitting danger, a sparkle lit Dahlgren's eyes, even in the dim early morning. "Proceed as far as Sabot Hill," he ordered Marley. "You'll find it on your map. I intend to pay a social call on its owner." Starting to pull away but detecting the quizzical expression on Marley's face, Dahlgren added, "Why, the master of Sabot Hill is the Honorable James A. Seddon, Secretary of War for the Confederate States of America. And I have it on good authority he sleeps in his bed even as we ride toward him."

Dahlgren's splendid black, sensing momentous tidings, reared up. "Ride, Major Marley," Dahlgren called, contagious excitement swelling his voice and coursing through the men around him, "Ride!"

CHAPTER 18

THE FIRST TOOTHACHE OF JAMES SEDDON'S ADULT LIFE DROVE him early from his wife's bed, left him bereft of sleep, and brought him to the brink of cursing his Maker.

It also accelerated his departure for a meeting with Jefferson Davis in Richmond, to allow time for a stop by the dentist's chair. He thus descended Sabot Hill at midmorning and turned east on the river road no more than five minutes before Marley and Quayle arrived at the same spot.

"Just servants and Mrs. Seddon, sir," Marley said a few moments later as Dahlgren stumped toward the main door of Sabot Hill. Dahlgren, disappointment creasing his smooth lean face, surveyed the fat white columns running down both sides of the front portico. Then he turned and took in the view, facing south. Even in the morning murk it was breathtaking. The big house stood atop a steep, tall hill, at the foot of which was the river road—not visible from the front door—on which the Federals had ridden in from the west. Beyond that were railroad tracks, trees, and the James, which was swift-running and, it appeared, significantly above its banks. This caught Dahlgren's eye.

"Have Captain McEntee make ready his Negro," he said. "We'll need to find his crossing and find it quickly. But first," he winked, "I must leave my card with the lady of the house."

Suave, brave, and handsome Ulric Dahlgren was twenty years the junior of Sallie Bruce Seddon and brimming with confidence and panache. Yet when she herself answered the great oaken front door of Sabot Hill—the servants were too frightened at the sight of four hundred Yankee horse soldiers to do so—her beauty left him for a moment without breath.

"Madame," Dahlgren said, removing his navy blue hat and bowing low, "Colonel Ulric Dahlgren, at your service."

Sallie extended her hand and curtsied as prettily as though she were being introduced before all Virginia.

"Surely you are not little Ully, son of Admiral John Dahlgren?" she said, her green eyes dancing with light.

"At your service, ma'am," Dahlgren replied, bowing the more sweepingly.

"Why, your famous father was a dear beau of mine in my girlhood days," Sallie said, with such charm that her glow threatened to melt "little Ully" into a puddle where he stood. "Do come in, and let's reminisce of better times," she said with the whitest smile Dahlgren had ever seen.

Unbeknownst to him, as Sallie was dispatching one servant for a choice bottle of twenty-year-old blackberry wine and crystal goblets, she was sending another on Sabot Hill's fleetest horse for Richmond.

Marley, without asking permission, stationed himself in the marble-floored foyer, in sight of Sallie and Dahlgren as they chattered in a nearby drawing room. He posted other guards, armed to the teeth, on the front porch and all around the house.

Marley had lived in Virginia for a decade before the war and he knew Southerners, male and female. His blood pressure climbed with each passing minute. *Why is he doing this?* he thought, with great apprehension. *We are no cavaliers on this mission, and I am wagering Mrs. Seddon is no damsel in distress.* Now Marley narrowed his gaze toward the open-doored drawing room. *The young man believes he is winning her, but it is her charm that is intoxicating him, more so than any few drinks of blackberry wine. He'll forget himself and that every minute Richmond grows farther away and Confederate defenders closer.*

Perhaps Dahlgren was not all as lost as that, but Marley had deciphered by the time he decided to enter the drawing room that Sallie Seddon, far from feeling any urge to rush the invaders off, seemed intent on playing the gracious hostess to them for just as long as they might allow her.

"Do remember me to your gallant father," Sallie said as she finally saw Dahlgren to the door.

"And my compliments to your husband. He is indeed a fortunate man," Dahlgren replied. "You have my assurance that no harm will come to your properties."

Her smile was as murderous as it was dazzling.

"Sir," McEntee said as Dahlgren was helped up into his saddle, "this is our guide. He is Martin Robinson, and he is a black freedman, formerly of these parts, who purports to know the location of the Jude's Ferry crossing of the James, not far from here."

"Yes, Major, your capable colleague John Babcock—of Pinkerton fame, I believe—wrote me," said Dahlgren, "promising that Mr. Robinson is the very man we want. So we shall see."

Dahlgren eyed the youngish black man, a composed and neatly dressed fellow who sat a saddle well. "Help us to do good today, Mr. Robinson, and you'll be richly rewarded for your efforts. Lead on."

Then they were pounding back down the hill and turning east onto River Road.

Marley and Quayle cantered ahead with Robinson, who said nothing, his eyes fixed on the adjacent river. The Pennsylvanian wondered how the main raiding force under Kilpatrick was faring. Along about now, he believed, Kilpatrick should be firing signal flares heavenward to indicate his position before the lines at Richmond. *But these skies,* Marley thought with trepidation, glancing up, *even with no precipitation, are hanging over us like leaden blankets. We could not discern a flare shot even a mile away. As hard as we've ridden, we still have to be at least twenty miles out, and a bit more from the northern defensive fortifications that Kilpatrick is probably facing.*

A few minutes later Robinson slowed his horse. Marley gauged that the freedman's intent expression had grown bewildered. When they reached the water, all they saw was rushing, swirling brown current—and lots of it—far above its normal banks. No ford.

None of the men said anything. Robinson walked his mount along the shore. Marley's eye swept the river. Across the way he saw an unmanned ferry tied to a tree. After a couple of hundred yards, Robinson, his countenance now stricken, turned and rode back. Now the earth rumbled with the approaching hoofbeats of Dahlgren and the column.

"Could you be mistaken?" Marley asked with mounting anxiety. "Could we be in the wrong place?" he pressed Robinson. "Water's awful high here."

Dahlgren rode up. At this point Robinson was staring out at the river, his mouth wide open. *The poor man appears as though he is in a state of shock,* Marley thought, his horse shifting and snorting beneath him.

"Are you quite certain this is the spot of the crossing?" Dahlgren asked after apprising the situation.

Robinson could only nod.

Dahlgren stared at him, the Federal's own black stallion now uneasy as well. "Perhaps there is another spot nearby where we could cross."

Robinson shook his head again as it dropped down to his chest.

Dahlgren turned to McEntee. "Captain? What do you make of this?" he said quietly.

McEntee chewed a drawn lip barely visible under his black moustache. "I don't know, sir. We checked him out, and he proved absolutely reliable. John Babcock, as sure a man as we have, as nimble inside Richmond as he is in Washington, vouched personally for him. He lived for years just a few miles back, near where he rested this morning. He crossed the Rapidan just night before last, with all manner of information on enemy troop placements. He even lived in Richmond more recently and escorted north some of the few men who did escape from Libby Prison."

They're not discussing the crossing; they're discussing Martin Robinson, Marley thought with a start. Now the darkening sky began to toss out cold sprinkles. A dark expression spreading across Dahlgren's genial features, an expression Marley had not before witnessed, chilled the horseman further.

"You realize you have not kept your portion of our agreement," Dahlgren said. Robinson, stricken, nodded slowly. "I must now execute my part of the agreement. I must hang you."

Marley blinked. *Surely he did not say—*

"You have jeopardized the success of this entire mission," Dahlgren continued, fury creeping into his voice. "A mission approved—even called for—by no less than President Lincoln. And not only this mission, but perhaps the course of the war to preserve the Union itself." Now Dahlgren shook with anger. "Hang him with his own reins," he said.

For a moment no one moved, the entire group stunned. Marley shook his head and opened his mouth to object. "I said hang him with his own reins!" Dahlgren screamed.

A lieutenant flew from his horse and called the names of three men to assist him. They ordered Robinson from his horse and marched him to an ancient oak with enormous boughs stretching out like the wings of Pegasus.

"Sir," Marley said, fumbling for words in his stupefaction. "Sir, this man has made a mistake, true, but by all appearances an honest one—"

"Major," Dahlgren said, Marley unable to divine whether the young man's eyes or words were more freighted with poison, "proceed down the river road. We've an appointment to keep in Richmond with General Kilpatrick and we cannot now cross the James."

Marley did not move.

"That is a direct order, Major Marley," Dahlgren said.

"Let's go, sir," Quayle said quietly.

Marley, his square jaw locked like flint, was on the point of challenging Dahlgren further when he glanced over and saw that Martin Robinson already dangled by his neck from the oak. Sorrow sweeping over him, Marley realized he could do nothing for the poor man; he could still do something for thousands of other poor souls in those stinking Richmond prisons. He consoled himself that he would bring the incident to the attention of the authorities upon his return to camp. *I shall present these events to the president himself,* he thought, wrath filling him. *Maybe our generals, maybe our congressmen, maybe the Stantons and the Sewards of the world will tolerate this, but I know one man who will not.* Afraid of what might pour out if even he opened his mouth, he jerked his horse around and rode away without a word.

Dahlgren left Robinson swinging in the growing breeze that blew in from the river that rushed over Jude's Ferry, a key crossing point over the James for better than a century, but now, for one of the few instances of that entire period, so thoroughly submerged by high waters as to be invisible. Forty-eight hours earlier or forty-eight hours later, it would have accommodated Ulric Dahlgren—and Martin Robinson—just fine.

When Mitchell's destruction party hit Sabot Hill an hour later, they were not privy to social banter with Sallie Seddon, so they were not aware of Dahlgren's promise of no harm being done to her properties, and they burned the barn, stables, corncrib, cellar, and every other outbuilding on the property to the ground. They raced from there to the next plantation, just to the north, Dover Mill, owned by the widower of Sallie's deceased sister. Again they burned down barn, stables, and every other outbuilding. This time they torched the main house as well, but house slaves extinguished the blaze. Again they fired it, as nannies, children—black and white—and elderly slaves—male and female—cowered or cried in the road out front. The flames leapt higher this time even as rain began to pour, and again the house slaves, joined this time by field slaves, all acting of their own volition, pitched in to stop the blaze.

"Why in the h— are you fool darkies putting out the fire?" called Lieutenant Samuel Harris, formerly a steam engineer.

One elderly lady, bent by rheumatism, stood to her full four-foot, eleven-inch height and shook her walking stick at Harris. "We 'uns may be slaves, but this be our home, too, and what you Yankees going to do, feed every slave in Virginia after you burn them out? Give 'em beds and work and takes care of 'em, sick or not, young or old?"

Crimson streaked Harris's face as other soldiers nearby, some of them tucking geese under their arms, hooted and hollered at him.

"Some liberator you are all right, Sammy!" one sergeant yelled as he reared back with his saber, then slashed it through the thin neck of a fleeing gander, sending forth a geyser of blood and propelling the head over fifty feet through the air.

The children clung to the older blacks, and one white aunt, frightened and whimpering, but generally well-collected for what they were witnessing, as the Federals began a contest to see who could decapitate the most geese. Meanwhile other soldiers tried a third time to fire the house. Again the servants put it out.

"Well, looks like to burn down that blasted house, we're gonna have to kill half the slaves with it," Mitchell growled at Harris and another lieutenant. "Let's just move on." Harris, incensed, engaged a group under his direct command to smash out all the windows in the house and clean out the plantation's considerable wine cellar. Mitchell had already ridden on, so several of the troopers stuffed their saddlebags with the expensive—in some cases, vintage—bottles and rode out gulping wine as they went.

Something stirred up the children as the final squad of Mitchell's men completed their massacre of the geese. One last goose, large, fast, and beautiful, seemed to be a favorite of all the children. For the first time the little people were screaming that the soldiers would not hurt the bird. But two troopers, hearing none of the pleas because they were locked in a ferocious competition to see who could first wield his blade so as to take off the goose's head, unintentionally rode the creature down and crushed it under the hooves of both their horses before either man could unleash a good blow at his prey. Staring for a moment at their bloody crushed victim, the anger of both was kindled against the other, and they began slugging each other with their fists. Only the provision of several bottles of rare, imported wine for both men from their considerate sergeant calmed them.

However, there was no consoling the sobbing children over their dead pet goose, Elmer, who had been destroyed ten feet from where they stood.

"Man, the Yanks are h— on poultry," Harris said as he wheeled his mount and galloped away.

"Lookee here, sir," one of his sergeants called to Harris, flagging him down a ways from the main house. "This here is the Dover grain mill, sir. Reckon how many Rebs this critter feeds?"

Harris's eyes widened as he rode to the impressive structure, more than two hundred feet long, and all brick. "They say it's one of the biggest gristmills in the county," the sergeant said, "with a sawmill attached that's powered by a one-hundred-horse-power steam engine. I guess you know all about that, huh, lieutenant?"

At least the day won't be a total waste, Harris thought. "I'm gonna light the first torch," he said with glee, hopping down from his horse. Indeed they fired the mill, which would never again be of service to provide food or anything else for anybody.

Mitchell dispatched other detachments of horse to fan out in all directions, shooting every cow, horse, chicken, goat, sheep, or anything else that walked on four legs, could be ridden or eaten, and could not be slung over the pommels of their saddles. The column's progress was best evidenced, however, by the roiling smoke and the stench of fire that followed after them as they scorched a blazing trail through a district possessed of some of the grandest homes in the Old Dominion.

Agnes would bring out the dress at different times. Sometimes late at night when the house was asleep. Sometimes during the day, upstairs, when everyone else but her wheelchair-bound mother, downstairs, had left. She would comb her thick dark hair, pin it up, pinch her cheeks to give her flawless features the color for which she had no "makeup" products to attain, and then she would waltz from room to room, in his arms, as they had done one sweet night at Arlington when the perfume of the lilacs wafted in from the gardens and woods and neither of them had suspected it would be their only waltz ever.

The gown was a rich blue-and-silver brocade, and he had brought it to her on his last visit, though it had been secreted with one of the servants so the family would not know. And none of them knew even to this day.

So she would turn and step as the minutes passed, her arms held just so, feeling his arms around her.

No living soul had ever seen her in Orton's gown.

She had removed it, handling it no less gingerly than she would have her own babies had she any, and packed it away in its secret place when she heard Mildred burst in the door, returning early from church. As Agnes ran downstairs, her sister gave her the report that Papa had been captured by Yankee raiders. Mildred burst into the tears she had pent up the whole walk home. Mary's already sickly face grew pale. Even Agnes fancied that part of a tear formed in one of her own eyes.

After they consoled Mildred for a moment, Mary said, steel in her voice. "Your father is a gentleman, a general, and a Christian, but I do not believe he would consent to capture by the enemy."

Then she pulled away and wheeled out of the room.

What frights, what specters, what terrors will each new day bring? Agnes wondered, her stomach hollow as she held Mildred's tear-stained head to her breast.

At that moment Lee, in his tent, dipped his pen in a vat of pokeberry juice. *Ah, those people have not yet ruined the pokeberry bushes around Richmond, and they have not yet snatched me away.* He, too, had heard the rumors of his capture.

Agnes had been on his mind, even more since the loss of Annie and now Charlotte, and since his observation of her undisguised sorrow during his Advent season visit. He wished he could hold her to himself as he had when she was a little girl and her sensitive spirit had been wounded by one thing or another.

> My precious little Agnes,
> I miss you already, especially when I realize I do not know when
> I shall again be allowed by Providence to see you. I wish you were
> with me, for, always solitary, I am sometimes weary, and long for

the reunion of my family once again. But I will not speak of myself, but of you. . . . I have seen the ladies in this vicinity only flying from the enemy, and it caused me acute grief to witness their exposure and suffering. But a more noble spirit was never displayed anywhere. The faces of old and young were wreathed with smiles, and glowed with happiness at their sacrifices for the good of their country. Many have lost *everything*. What the fire and shells of the enemy spared, their pillagers destroyed. But God will shelter them, I know. So much heroism will not be unregarded. It cannot be allowed to be unregarded. We must think upon it and write about it and speak of it, that when we are called home by our heavenly Father, those who follow might understand the precious treasure that their mothers and fathers, their grandmothers and grandfathers, paid in defense of their beleaguered homeland.

Your devoted father,
R. E. Lee

Dahlgren assigned Quayle leadership of a five-man contingent to deliver a dispatch to Kilpatrick. The written order apprised him that the James could not be crossed and suggested that the two Federal columns synchronize attacks on Richmond at sunset.

Marley, now with a Michigan corporal, veered away from the river and rode parallel to it a ways to check the higher ground over which ambush might come. He sent two more men ahead of the advancing column on the river road. A mile or two from the river, he came across a tidy little white-framed church tucked amid a forest of oaks and pines. A solitary fir stood sentinel out front of the church, whose sign Marley now noticed said "Hebron Presbyterian Church, 1843."

His eye brightened for the first time all day, and he rode to a window. Looking in, he saw a sturdy pulpit of white wood, elevated in the Puritan—*the biblical*, he thought—way; sturdy brown wooden pews and a high white balcony; sturdy white square posts anchoring the corners of the chancel. It all looked so sturdy. *I should be in there instead of out here*, he thought sadly, *out here where*— He now observed, at the far end of the building, a opossum sniffing around a bottle of Madeira that had been smashed against the outside wall of the sanctuary. Then he noticed several other wine bottles, some empty, some smashed, littering the churchyard. Gunfire swung him around and he saw, in the field behind the church to the west, some of Mitchell's men shooting down a small herd of grazing cattle.

That is to starve the Army of Northern Virginia whose host comes out against us, Marley knew. *But how can such action starve an army and fail to starve women, children, and the aged?*

With a small prayer for Hebron Presbyterian Church and its pastor and congregation, he spurred his horse back toward the river road. When he came to it, the column was approaching. McEntee rode up to him.

"Mind if I ride out front with you for a spell, Marley?" the government man asked.

"Suit yourself," Marley said, galloping ahead.

At half past three, a steady rain now falling, the wind picking back up, and the temperature going back down, Marley spotted the main van of Mitchell's column. The two groups merged near the little community of Short Pump, eight miles west of Richmond. Campfires were made where the pines and oaks offered shelter and hiding, and Dahlgren huddled with Mitchell to revise their Richmond strategy.

After reporting to Dahlgren, Marley, wet, cold, and still seething over the hanging of Martin Robinson and striving to keep from confronting Dahlgren about it, filled his tin cup with coffee and went for a change of horses. Physical, mental, and emotional exhaustion weighed him down. Thankful for the steaming coffee and going for another, he again met McEntee. The man had not said two words to him since they met, and now he seemed to be hovering around Marley.

"I was headed for a quick stretch of the legs. Care to join me?" McEntee asked. Implicit in the man's tone and eyes were a stronger admonition.

Marley nodded and, after ordering his new horse fed with a bag of stolen Rebel corn, followed McEntee a surprisingly long distance to a clearing that overlooked the swelling river.

"Time is short, so I'll make this quick," McEntee said. "How is it that with all we have planned for the Rebs you're so prickly about the hanging of one n——, and one who may yet prove to be the undoing of this entire mission?"

Marley stared at him, for a minute thinking to reprove the man for butting into someone else's business and convictions. Something, maybe just his fatigue, prompted him to respond.

"Nothing we have 'planned' for the Rebs has anything to do with the hanging of that black man—that free black man—who risked his life for us just to be on this mission," he said, color rising on his bearded, weather-beaten face. He pointed back toward the main camp. "What was done to that brave volunteer brings shame to this fine unit, to the Army of the Potomac, and to the United States of America. I did not think such treatment of Negroes was what we were about in this infernal war." Noting how taken aback McEntee was by the force of his response, he lowered his voice a bit. "Anyhow, I was under the perhaps mistaken impression that our plans have more to do with our own people than the Rebs."

Now it was McEntee, his eyes wary, who regarded for a moment his own response. He never drank coffee, Marley had noticed, or smoked, or drank alcoholic spirits, or cursed. He seemed a supremely capable soldier and intelligence officer, though Marley was doubtful of his having had any spiritual conversion.

"I find it curious that you would not consider the momentous deeds we hope to undertake in—against—Richmond and against the secessionist leaders," McEntee said, glancing about to make sure no one else was within earshot, "as possessed of an import tantamount to that of the release of the prisoners."

Marley blinked. He shook his head as though to clear the fog from it.

"Major?" McEntee blurted before Marley could speak, the BMI man's voice solemn as a death knell. He actually took a step toward Marley. "Major, you are aware of our plans against the city itself and the leaders of the Confederate government?"

Marley's mouth dropped open. McEntee scowled and uttered the first oath Marley had ever heard from him. Now Marley saw that McEntee himself, rough and ready and sure and hard as he was, for the first time evidenced the strain of their quest.

"Major Marley," McEntee said in a plaintive tone, stretching his arms outward, palms open, "you do not mean that neither Kilpatrick nor Dahlgren informed you Richmond is to be put to the torch and Jeff Davis and his entire cabinet hanged where we find them?"

Marley thought he might faint. "Richmond . . ." He did not even hear the latter portion of the sentence. "What part of Richmond?"

McEntee's eyes were glassy. "What part? Why, all of it."

Marley dropped his coffee cup and took a couple of steps away, grabbing his temple with a dirty yellow-gauntleted hand. Sheets of rain blew over them, and the wind rushed against them from the river. He had no idea of anything to say.

"I . . . I assumed because of your rank you knew," McEntee said, stepping again toward Marley. "I . . . it has been on my own conscience and I thought that you, being a Christian man, might be . . . able . . . to help me . . . sort out . . . what appears . . . er . . . a most difficult course to justify."

Now McEntee saw that tears ran wet down Marley's face.

"Major Marley—"

"There can be no justification for such barbarism," Marley shot, spinning to face him, then striding past him toward the main camp. Before he had even left the clearing, waves of Federal horse, Dahlgren at their head, began to rumble past. *No bugles because of where we are,* he remembered.

"Where you been?" a New Yorker Marley knew hollered at him. "Dahlgren's been looking all over for you. Kilpatrick's engaged to the north. We're going to free the prisoners. You better get to the front quick."

After the man raced away, Marley stood for a moment as the rain thudded down on his thick, soaked wool hat and the shoulders of his blue greatcoat. In the distance to the northeast echoed the sullen rumble of guns. He wanted no part of this glorious "raid." Then another group raced past, one man carrying Old Glory. *Yes, that is who we are,* Marley thought, *and what sort of patriot am I to cut and run when all looks dark? Is that not when men of conscience are most needed? Perhaps I may be able to help thwart these dark deeds. I shall in no way stand idly by for more Martin Robinsons. Oh, Lord Jesus,* he thought, trembling, *for a whole city.*

Then he found his horse and was up in the saddle. As he pulled the reins to go, McEntee rode up.

"Such orders cannot have originated with Kilcavalry," Marley snarled, anger filling him. "He may like them, but he has not the wits to create them."

McEntee's jaw twitched.

"Was it Pleasanton?" Marley pressed, his horse rearing. "Meade?"

"They are not even aware of the . . . these plans."

Marley stared at him as more riders, hundreds of them, thundered past. "Well then, who is above Meade?" His eye narrowed. "How high?"

"High," was all McEntee could manage.

Then they were off for Richmond, mud spattering their horses' bellies and their own faces and coats as the rain poured, the wind howled, the sleet began, and the thunder and lightning blazing from the blackened sky provided the perfect *coup de grâce* for a day which bore increasing resemblance to a masterpiece from the canvas of the devil himself.

CHAPTER 19

THE CLANGING OF THE TOCSIN EMERGENCY BELL SENT A shiver to the marrow of Agnes's being. She had never heard it before. And now, twice within a few hours. Late this morning, Richmond's entire military defense force of six hundred men had moved into place against Kilpatrick's three thousand choice horse soldiers. A couple of hours ago, the sullen growl of guns began. She could hear them now. Every few minutes the windows would rattle at the concussion of a particular blast.

What if the Yankees broke through? Dread spread through her. *Oh, how can they not this time? We have only a few hundred, and they have thousands.* Reports and rumors, swirling wildly through the dark, stormy, unreal melee in the capital of the Confederacy, posited the size of the Federal force at anywhere from five to fifty thousand. Such a sledgehammer, with no significant Southern forces close enough to help, at least today, could not be kept out of Richmond this time. *For two years they have strived to overcome this brave city,* Agnes thought, *and today they shall do it. But what will they do once they are here? What if they free their benighted thousands from Libby and Belle Isle? Thank God they are still Americans, and many of them Christians. Surely despite their many previous depredations against our land and people, we can trust them to act as gentlemen among the helpless civilian thousands of our capital.*

The bell was so close! She could glimpse it, despite the burgeoning storm, through the leafless linden tree branches from her second-floor bedroom window. It was no more than a couple of hundred feet down the gentle slope of Franklin Street and across Ninth Street at the southwest corner of the Capitol grounds.

Then Mildred was flying up the stairs, more like Rooney or Rob, two at a time. "They're coming!" she shouted. "The Yankees are coming!"

She burst into Agnes's room and ran to embrace her. "Oh, Wiggie, they're coming!"

Agnes grabbed her arms and forced her back. "Have they broken through our northern defenses?"

Mildred gawked at her. Her words came quietly this time. "No, Wiggie, there are more of them, and these are coming from the west. Already they have captured Secretary Seddon's family and burned his plantation and most of those along the river. They are destroying everything in their path, and we have no one but the home defense brigade to stand before them."

Agnes stared at her, the room seeming to spin around her. She knew how paltry was the home defense brigade to stand before a regular army force, especially one so powerful and capable as to have made its way all the way to the very gates of Richmond. Her grip on Mildred's arms grew so firm that the younger girl cried out. "Oh, they're coming, Wiggie," Mildred said. "Mama wants us downstairs now."

Agnes dawned her shawl, then her coat, and followed Mildred down the stairs. *Never ever have I been so cold in my life,* she thought. *Oh, when will it be warm again? And what will happen today?*

Within minutes the strangest collection of manhood Agnes believed she had ever seen began to file up Franklin toward the west, past the Lees' rented home, from their mustering point near the tocsin bell at Capitol Square. They were old men of seventy, boys of thirteen and fourteen, and ex-soldiers with one empty sleeve or a crutch where a leg should have been. They were sickly office clerks and factory workers and business owners and schoolchildren, many of them over sixty years or under sixteen. The civilians wore ragged coats; the ill, wounded, and few furloughed regular soldiers wore burlap sacks or strips of rawhide or carpet over their shivering, often barefoot, bodies.

Many had already walked miles in the frigid air to their place of service. Now they would walk more miles, knowing that nothing and no one had been able to stop the foe against which they came out. Even counted with their brothers now heading west from the armory, arsenal, navy, and Tredegar Iron Works "battalions," their numbers paled against the nearly five hundred elite Federal cavalry, handpicked from regiments across the Army of the Potomac.

They alone now stood in the gap for everything and everyone they held dear.

As Agnes, standing at the front window with Mary and Mildred, watched them march past, beset by hunger, cold, fear, and this most hellish of winter days, her heart began to swell within her. A sharp pain it was. She did not at first joy in the realization that it was a pain, and that pain meant life, and that meant her heart might yet have a chance. Tears streamed down her cheeks. *How brave they are,* she thought, *how gallant. Oh, they are everything Papa ever taught us our Christian men are to be.* And then her mother and her sister were calling out to her from somewhere, and sleet and rain were stinging her face, and she was slipping over the icy ground, stepping through the short iron gate, and standing in the street as their defenders marched past. She did not know what to do, but she wanted in some way to help them. Finally, when one smelly man with a hat pulled low on his grimy bearded face looked at her with hollow lost eyes, she threw her arms around him as she never had any man since Orton. She hugged him so hard that he dropped his rifle and stood limply in her embrace.

After some moments she remembered herself and pulled back, and all the men who passed stared in stupefaction, realizing that it really was Agnes Lee, *his* daughter, and one of the most beautiful women in the entire Confederacy, who had hugged that man.

And that man, his own heart not yet redeemed, but now full of hate and venom for the foe he blamed for the loss of all the kin that had remained to him on earth, that man felt a human touch and love for the first time in years. So unknown was it to him, whose own mother had detested his birth and whose father had beaten him from infancy, that he could not then comprehend its meaning. But as he picked up his rifle and turned to resume his march up Franklin Street, the tears Cole Culpeper wept like a child in front of all the other men were matched by the first flicker of hope that perhaps he actually meant something to somebody, even if he did not yet know whom.

Marley could not catch Dahlgren. The column was hurtling headlong toward Richmond in the gathering dark. A parade of thoughts raced through his head. He could not focus on any of them. Plus, he felt sure his body was on its final stretch of coherent action unless it entered into an extended period of sleep. He did not believe he had slept for more than three hours in the past forty-eight, every minute of it hard, cold, and rife with tension. Suddenly shots sounded from up ahead. They were scattered, but as he rode on, he heard groans and nearly flew from his saddle as his horse cut around downed men. More shots sounded from the trees on either side of the road on which they raced, the famed Revolutionary War thoroughfare Three Chopt Road, and now Marley was amid the bushwhackers. *Sharpshooters,* he thought. *We are in for it now if they have sharpshooters already placed.*

On they galloped, minié balls sizzing through the column. Marley drew a Colt, kept his head low, and rode hard. He did not know it, but up ahead, Dahlgren himself had churned into the advance rank, the Fifth Michigan, which had been bloodied, then faltered and regrouped, then charged ahead.

A moment later Dahlgren halted the rain-drenched column. Shouting to be heard over the storm and the crackling of hidden rifles, he ordered them to form ranks for a charge. "The Rebels have established a line across our front. We shall ride over it, and we shall ride into Richmond!"

Then he was leading them across a shadowy field. Marley, shouting and firing his Colt, charged forward with the other hundreds. Suddenly a line of yellow flashes appeared directly in front of them, at a distance of no more than fifty feet, knocking down men and horses and scattering the Federals right and left. Some of the defenders fell back, but most stood their ground. Dahlgren, regrouping, ordered another charge. More yellow flashes, more men and horses down, more sleet, wind, thunder, and lightning. Then finally, Dahlgren himself, shooting down two men as he cleared a stone wall, led the Federals through the now-retreating Confederate line.

The scratch group of Southern civilians, mainly comprised of the Richmond Armory Battalion, on foot against the best horse soldiers in the Federal army—outgunned, outtrained, outequipped, and outnumbered better than two-to-one—fell back yard by yard, body by bloody body. *Better that I should come out here against them than my wife and daughters in our dear home back on Grace Street,* one middle-aged shopkeeper thought to himself, leveling his ancient flintlock to fire an instant before two Yankee riders shot him down.

As Marley, not far from Dahlgren, got over the wall, he heard a shot from behind him and felt his hat fly off him. A one-armed Virginian, bleeding on the ground from four separate wounds, had launched one last shot that missed Marley's scalp by the thickness of a dime.

"You all right, Cole?"

Culpeper, keeping his eyes narrowed against the stinging sleet, saw Ethan McDowell on his gray charger. "Yeah, but I'll be even better soon's I jerk you off that mount and take her for myself," he barked in rustic good humor.

Ethan laughed. "Something tells me won't be long 'fore you've scared yourself up another mount, Cole Culpeper."

Indeed he would already have done so had the blasted tocsin bell not gone off even as he was relieving a man of his money and coat on that Shockoe Bottom wharf down by the river. So drunk had Culpeper been that his foggy brain did not immediately establish a connection between the bell ringing and the sudden tumult of men running, horses racing, and wagons clattering in every direction. All he knew was that he was having a devil of a time removing his victim's heavy wool greatcoat from the man's body. Cursing, he finally got it off, clutching the unconscious man's fat wallet in one hand. As he started to put an arm into the coat, he felt a crushing pain in the back of his head. Next thing he knew, Ethan was helping him up from where he had fallen. His own victim's money and coat were gone, and the man himself beginning to stir.

"I don't know what you've gotten yourself into this time, Cole Culpeper, but I do believe fighting the Yankees is less risky for you than living in Richmond," Ethan said, laughing.

"Oww!" Culpeper cried. His head felt as though it had been split open with an axe.

"Yeah, I'm sure that lump you got yourself was well-earned," Ethan said with feigned gruffness. "Let's get you out of here before Winder's home guards decide Richmond's safer with you in a jail cell than marching out against the Yanks."

Then he had ridden double with Ethan till they reached Capitol Square. There he mustered in with the departmental batallion, and he began to march. For miles he marched. He did believe he would begin no longer to fear hell because he had now marched right through hell and seemed to be surviving it. His aching head, vomiting stomach, and shaking legs could attest to that.

But something . . . something good had happened . . . yes, that girl, that Lee girl. Some of the men said it was Annie Lee, and some said it was Agnes. Others said both of them had died, leaving General Lee brokenhearted, and that it was a young cousin of his named Margaret or Martha. Culpeper did not know anything except that he had been on the point of quitting, his legs actually buckling so he could fall to the ground and sleep where he was, when the closest thing to an angel he had ever seen had wrapped her arms around him and hugged him. Never could he remember his mama or anyone else, other than Cousin Emma, holding him like that.

It was something different and apart. It was not desire, for he knew she was beyond anything he had ever seen, something so good, so fine, so beautiful you could never have it no matter how bad you wanted it. But what he did have was the feeling of her long gentle arms around his filthy, lice-ridden neck. Here was a woman, a fairy princess, who deserved to be spoiled and pampered and adored. And he had the soft safe folds of her blouse—*Why wore she no coat or bonnet?* he wondered—against his scarred, bearded face. And he had smelled just the lightest trace of lilac about her, which he remembered Cousin Emma wore. Yes, he confessed to himself for the first time ever, he *had* loved Emma. He had loved her dearly, like no other in his life. Then he began to weep again, for the second time on this march, and the second time he could remember doing so since he was a child.

There was no time for tears now, for a terrific fusillade raged somewhere up ahead, and that ramrod-straight Englishman, Major Ford, who sat the saddle of his majestic white stallion—*Why would an Englishman wish to lead us into battle?* Culpeper wondered—had his sword in the air as he rode up and down the line, barking orders in the stormy din.

A frown creased Culpeper's unkempt, tear-streaked face. He turned to the man next to him. "Why, it's comin' on full dark. They ain't expectin' us to fight now, are they?"

The "man" next to him was fifteen-year-old Miles Cary. The boy's big, shouldered Springfield gleamed in the gathering dusk. Every man in his family and every branch of his family as far out as he knew was either fighting in the war or had already been killed. Now he, the eldest who had not yet fought, had pulled away from his sobbing mother, raced out of his house, and marched west on Cary Street for miles until he was out of Richmond. There was no one left in his family to stand against an invader who had shown no leniency toward life or property in other Virginia expeditions and could be expected to show none against his home community, which happened to be the capital of the Confederacy.

"Believe our ranks have filled out since we started," Cary answered, his voice steady as the James running out into the Chesapeake. Indeed the ranks of the unusual assembly had been swelling by ones and twos ever since the column left Capitol Square. "We've got majors and colonels in the line serving as privates." A singularly nasty burst of fire rippled from the direction of the battle. Everyone looked that way for a moment. "The fight sounds like it's over around Ben Green's farm," Cary continued. "We'd best be ready, sir. They say we are the final line between the Yankees and Richmond."

As he watched wagonloads of furniture and frightened women and children hurrying past, along with men riding emaciated horses and driving scrawny cattle, everyone and everything trying to keep from the rampaging Yankees, even Culpeper could not but be shamed by the boy's response.

Dahlgren, reloading his pair of Colts as he rode, stayed at the head of the column and turned it south along Westham Plank Road. Marley, so weary he felt like crying, his inner thighs raw, bleeding, and screaming in pain from days of ceaseless hard riding, watched the dim giant figure with a mixture of revulsion and grudging admiration. *How can he still be upright?* he marveled. *He has only one leg. He must still be weak from such a horrible wound. He has never held command of so large a group, and the energy-sapping pressure weighing upon him is incalculable. Only his youth, natural vigor, and relentless will can have kept him in the saddle conducting the operations of an entire column of men in the most dangerous territory in the Confederacy, longer than any but the most capable of men could have done.*

But more riding, more fighting, more endurance remained. A fleeting thought reminded Dahlgren that the son of Admiral John Dahlgren could do no less. *Surely Father shall hear of our doings on these far fields,* he thought, *and perhaps, withal, he shall be proud.*

The Confederate authorities in Richmond had already heard of Dahlgren's doings, and those of Kilpatrick with his larger force of three thousand on the city's north side. Provost Marshal Winder, divining that the Federals intended to liberate their thousands of comrades from Libby and perhaps Belle Isle as well, ordered an enormous cache of gunpowder planted in the basement of Libby, the larger of the two prisons.

Major Thomas Turner, the Libby commandant, buckling on his sword, called the ranking Federal prisoner, General Neal Dow, to him and pronounced the grim news: "I do not expect to live if your cavalry get into the city. I shall stick to my post of duty until Kilpatrick reaches here, then every d—— Yankee in this place will be blown to h—"

Dahlgren and his men engaged in a vicious, running battle with the fleeing defenders. Marley saw a yellow flash from the forested shadows to his right and felt another minié sizz by, inches from his face. He fired and fired at the spot and heard an invisible man scream in pain.

A fourteen-year-old Richmond boy fell, ridden down by a Federal. "Mama . . . Mama . . ." he gurgled as his young life ebbed out amid a faceful of mud and blood. Twenty feet away, a sixty-four-year-old friend of the boy's grandfather grimaced as blood replaced the air in his punctured lungs. *Oh,* he thought, trying to rise despite the excruciating pain, *what will become of my daughters and granddaughters if they unleash the prisoners on Richmond?* His last coherent earthly thought was a prayer that God would keep his beloveds safely in His arms.

A shotgun blast from behind some trees tore the rider next to Marley screaming out of his saddle. Then Dahlgren had them forming ranks again. Marley could see a number of the retreating shadows melting into a fenceline fifty yards ahead. Now the Federals were charging again. *This is crazy. We cannot even see them,* Marley thought. *But we have come this far, and it has all cost us too much to turn away now. We must fight our way through! We must!* "Yahhhh!"

As Culpeper, Cary, and McDowell, now dismounted in the departmental battalion skirmish line, leveled their rifles from behind the fence, Culpeper silently cursed his participation in the entire ridiculous scenario. Then he remembered the unearthly presence of the Lee girl, and he remembered why his precious Emma and the children had had to take to the open road in the teeth of winter. And he knew what to do.

"You b——s!" he screamed as Alabama Captain John McAnerny, a wounded regular army man, gave the order for the skirmish line to fire. Twenty Virginia rifles barked as one. Scared, cold, wet, and exhausted from little food and walking miles in a howling winter storm, they were now organized, along with the remnants of the armory battalion. Their shots were not in vain, as several Federals flew from their saddles. The rest thundered on, straight for the fence. *Got me one,* Culpeper knew in the back of his mind as he hurried to reload. But there was no time. The Yankees were all over them and he was swinging his musket like a club, knocking one rider out of the saddle, then smashing the horse of another full in the face. The animal screamed and collapsed in a heap, throwing the rider straight into Ethan as Culpeper's rifle splintered into pieces.

The Federal came up on top of Ethan and stuck a Navy Colt in the Virginian's face. Before he could pull the trigger, Culpeper piled into him. As the two rolled through the muck, bullets whizzing past, horses rumbling by, and men screaming, groaning, and shouting orders, Culpeper was galvanized by a fury far eclipsing even that which possessed him at Gettysburg. He jerked his Bowie knife from its scabbard inside his right boot and slit the Yankee's throat from ear to ear. Then he ripped the dead man's Colt from his hand and raised it to fire at a Federal looming over him, pistol in hand, on an enormous stallion gleaming black even in the smoky dark. It was Ulric Dahlgren.

Culpeper got his gun up quicker and pulled the trigger. It clicked on an empty chamber, then another. "No!" Culpeper cried as he raised the pistol to hurl it at Dahlgren. Ethan tried to pull Culpeper away by his shirt as the skirmish line was retreating for its life, but Dahlgren fired, knocking Culpeper flat. The Federal's black reared in the midst of the cacophony as Ethan, crying out, bent to assist his friend. When Dahlgren got the horse back under control, he was facing the opposite direction he had been. He turned in the saddle and fired again, dropping Ethan like a dead oak. Another Reb, bayonet brandished, leapt over his bleeding mates and charged for Dahlgren, who shot him, too, between the eyes. Then Dahlgren wheeled, gun raised, and raced on.

Cary saw all this, his eyes filling with horror. He stared at the bloody pile Dahlgren had left. For the first time in his life, the boy hated. Screaming and crying, knowing fear no longer, he took after Dahlgren on foot. "Please, God, please God in heaven, let me catch that man," the boy sobbed as he charged, choking on gunsmoke, stumbling over fallen men and horses, bullets flying all about him. Just then a blinding flash erupted across his entire field of vision, an enormous concussion shook him, and the air around him was rent with the slashing of more Confederate miniés. So loud was the explosion that deafness consumed his ears as one eardrum burst into a green ooze. Thus he could not hear the screams of more Yankee riders and the screeches of their horses.

McAnerny had deployed fifty men in a firing line, and they had fired as one at his command. As the stunned Yankees stood, their horses rearing, the ragtag fifty Confederates, of whom no more than half a dozen had ever fired so much as one shot at a living person, hustled back and knelt, reloading behind a second group of fifty, who stood their ground, rifles aimed and hammers cocked.

"Fire!" McAnerny shouted again. Another volley tore through the halting Federal ranks, emptying more saddles and tumbling more raiders off collapsing horses to the mushy earth. Now Dahlgren ordered the Federals, seasoned and battle-hardened, to dismount and advance on foot. They returned fire as the second Confederate line fell back. Several defenders fell, but as they did, McAnerny, reopening a chest wound that had nearly killed him at Mine Run, called out again and the first firing line unleashed another hail of bullets right into the faces of the Yankees. More men fell as thunder crashed and lightning fulgurated from the pouring heavens.

Dahlgren drew his saber and prepared to renew the attack.

"Sir!" Marley shouted. He was on foot, holding his horse by the reins he had brought over the beast's head, as was every remaining Federal, save Dahlgren. "The fire is too heavy, we must retreat. This is regular infantry, sir."

"No, sir!" Dahlgren hollered down at him, his face set like granite. "The United States cavalry shall finish what we have begun! Advance, men!"

Just then, Miles Cary, in a headlong rush and shrieking the Rebel yell, slammed his bayonet into the pommel of Dahlgren's saddle. Neither horse nor rider was hurt, but the black reared again, nearly throwing Dahlgren off. When he came back to earth, his saber flashed down at the boy, who ducked, then dove at the towering Federal again. This time his blade ripped through Dahlgren's trousers, skimmed along his wooden leg, plowed through his saddle and saddle blanket, and pierced the black's side. The animal cried out and reared yet again. It took all Dahlgren's remaining strength to stay in the saddle.

But rage filled young Cary, and he plunged his bayonet at Dahlgren again and again, the Yankee commander desperately fending off the blows with his saber. Marley, his keen eye just making all this out, rushed toward the two just as the Confederate riflemen fired again. This blast took out a whole new group of Federals and slowed Marley just long enough for Cole Culpeper, bleeding from his side, to throw himself into the Pennsylvanian. Marley hit the ground with a thud, the air pushed from his lungs. He saw Culpeper's Bowie and feverishly scrambled out from under him and fired, hitting the Confederate and knocking him down again.

Five-foot, five-inch young Miles Cary—deaf, tear-streaked, sweat- and rain-drenched, and straining to the point that his groin ruptured into a hernia—reared back, then plunged his bayonet into the boot of Dahlgren's wooden leg. The Federal, dislodging the blade with a slash of his saber, and hearing other screaming Rebels approaching on foot, decided he had had enough. He wheeled the bleeding black around and galloped away, Cary still running after him, shouting the nearest thing to curses he thought his mother would permit if she were there.

Now Marley was back in the saddle and racing away, Northern horse soldiers all about him doing the same, as more Rebels from the skirmish line and the retreating armory ranks charged into them on foot from behind, the hideous refrain of the Rebel yell their serenade.

Culpeper, grimacing in pain, cursing in anger, and now bleeding from his hip, too, rose from the ground and saw two riderless Yankee horses running toward him. He stopped one and swung, grunting, up into the saddle. He smiled as he felt the wooden stock of a Spencer repeater protruding from the saddle holster.

"Cole!" It was Ethan McDowell, his right shoulder sagging where Dahlgren's bullet had clipped the flesh high and narrowly missed breaking his collarbone. "What the heck you doin' bleedin' all over that poor Yank horse?"

"It's 'bout time I got me a mount to fight this war on, Ethan boy," Culpeper said. "Now I aim to do me some real killin'—yiiahhh!"

Carried by the Rebel yell, a Yankee steed, and a burgeoning hate he found comfortably filled the gaping chasm in his soul, and with four holes in him from flesh wounds where bullets had entered and left him, Culpeper gave chase to the now-fleeing remnants of the most elite cavalry force in the United States Army.

Quayle and his contingent had been bushwhacked and killed by Wade Hampton's scouts. That mattered little, however. For Kilpatrick, the capture of Richmond within his grasp, had lost his nerve and retreated, only to be ambushed and chased headlong across Virginia by Hampton himself and his brazen band of warriors, who numbered less than one-tenth the Yankee force they chased.

Mixed praises, singing, sighing, laughing, and weeping wafted to the high ceiling of Saint Paul's Church in Richmond later that evening, where Agnes and Mildred sat amid an enormous prayer service gathering. The Rev. Charles Minnigerode had just announced that, at dear cost, the sons, grandsons, fathers, and grandfathers of the city had laid down their lives before the powerful Yankee invaders. At least for this day, they had saved the city and perhaps the Confederate States of America.

No one among the assembly yet knew the half of it.

CHAPTER 20

LEE KNEW THE FEDERALS HAD LAUNCHED A CONCERTED ATTACK on Richmond. He knew their cavalry numbered in the thousands and that they must be aiming to release the enormous collection of suffering soldiers in the Libby and Belle Isle prisons.

And what if that objective is attained? he thought, pacing his tent at midnight. *The Belle Isle company would likely pass near—perhaps right over,* he thought with a shudder—*the street where lies our house.* His whole body tensed, he stared into the amber hue of one of his tent lanterns. *Shall I go to them? I cannot leave my family—*

He was on the verge of leaving when Taylor entered the tent. The younger man knew Lee well enough to know when trouble marked his soul.

"Sir," Taylor said. "The latest reports we have indicate at least two separate groups of raiders have attacked Richmond but that all elements of the enemy have been driven off by home defense units—with heavy losses on both sides."

Taylor saw the question in the gentle brown eyes.

"Other than on the northern and western outskirts of the city, no civilian enclaves have been breached," he said.

Lee nodded slightly and turned away. Taylor recognized his dismissal.

Sitting down at his writing table, Lee admonished himself. *How often we fret at our own lack of power to effect what is right when instead we should be praying to God, who is supremely able both in that task and in comforting our poor frail hearts,* he thought, shaking his head. He laid aside a recent copy of *The Southern Churchman,* the Episcopalian magazine; he had been reading in this issue about "The Second Coming of Christ." He opened the leather-bound prayer book–hymnal with large gold crosses embossed on the well-worn front and rear covers. The daughters of his former chief of staff, R. H. Chilton, had given Lee the book as a Christmas gift in 1862. He treasured its many helpful sections. A lectionary aided in his systematic reading of the Scriptures. Epistle and Gospel selections appeared for Holy Communion every day of the week, year-round, in the Christian calendar. All one hundred fifty psalms were laid out in a manner to be read through every thirty days. The Articles of Religion, the Catechism, and the Apostle's and Nicene Creeds provided the theological and doctrinal instruction he saw so many professing Christians downplay and which were so valuable and satisfying to him. Hymns and prayers were listed for every conceivable occasion of life, including morning and evening prayer services, bad weather, famine, illness, holidays, infant baptisms, burial of the dead, and that to which he now turned, "In Time of War and Tumults." His thoughts now ran not to himself but to his wife, daughters, and sons as he opened the trusty book. *Ah, here it is,* he thought, finding the well-worn page and smiling inwardly as a man would when coming across an old friend he has not seen in some time.

"O Almighty God, the supreme Governor of all things, whose power no creature is able to resist, to whom it belongeth justly to punish sinners, and to be merciful to those who truly repent; Save and deliver us, we humbly beseech thee, from the hands of our enemies; that we, being armed with thy defence, may be preserved evermore from all perils, to glorify thee, who art the only giver of all victory; through the merits of thy Son, Jesus Christ our Lord. Amen."

Marley had never been colder. The cold ran right down into his bones. He could barely ride because he now had no feeling in his hands or feet and little in his arms or legs. In a way this was good, because what portions of his body were still sensate hurt with a pain he had never before experienced.

It was bad in a way, too, because he had to ride; he had to ride for his life. They all did. He knew the Federals no longer had the initiative. There would be no crashing the gates of Richmond, no freeing of the prisoners, no whatever else Dahlgren and those above him had envisioned for this raid. Just what had they planned? The urgencies of the current predicament shoved such speculation out of his mind for the time being. If he did not get out of this, it would matter not at all, to him at least, what anyone had planned for Richmond.

Marley's face was also numbed, whipped, and slashed to stupor by the relentless sleet and rain, not to mention boughs and branches hanging out into the black road like long invisible swords of ice. His battered face no longer felt pain from these branches, but several times they almost knocked him out of the saddle. If that happened to a man, which it did to quite a few, as Marley purloined from their thuds and desperate cries, and if his horse bolted, that man would not even make it to a Rebel prison camp. He would die shivering in the road if he was not first shot or trampled.

No one could see anything in the dark, but Marley needed to because he was back at the front of the column. Dahlgren had them moving north, away from Richmond and toward Hungary Station. But it seemed as though every passing minute brought its own special twist of horror. For one, Marley could not go a quarter of a mile without his horse stumbling into trees or other fallen debris. Whether felled by the chaotic weather of the evening, by the Rebels, or by what, Marley did not know or care. But it slowed the Federals' progress to a virtual crawl.

At Hungary Station Marley heard Dahlgren's voice behind him.

"We'll rest here for a spell. I want to meet with Mitchell when he gets up here," Dahlgren said.

Marley had to hand it to the young colonel. From the sound of his voice, he still exuded strength and confidence. How, Marley did not know, for he himself wondered how much longer he could remain upright in the saddle. Just then he heard the body of some unseen trooper thud against the sticky, soggy road. Whether the fall awoke the man or not, Marley could not say.

But Mitchell did not arrive. Dahlgren, conversing with voices Marley recognized as McEntee's and Major Edwin Cooke's, now second in command, grew anxious. He finally ordered Marley and another scout back to find Mitchell, who was supposedly a mere half mile or so back with all but the hundred men riding with Dahlgren.

Marley rode and rode. He never found Mitchell. After an hour or so, fearful of himself getting lost, he returned to Dahlgren with the sad news. Dahlgren at first said nothing. After a moment, he said, quite slowly, "We'll rest for an hour and then move on."

As the night watches passed, then the morning, word spread like a wildfire that at least a portion of the Yankee raiding force was north of Richmond, skedaddling east, pursued and tormented by Confederates like a vicious but wounded animal on the run from hunters. Again, as the call rang out, volunteers of all stripes, their anger rising despite this *coup de grâce* to the worst Central Virginia winter in half a century, streamed across the countryside to confront the invader. Home guards, militia, furloughed regular soldiers, schoolboys, farmers grabbing their rifles and heading straight off their land on horse or on foot, even a number of black men, free and slave—all for a crack at a raiding party they had by now heard had left a trail of flaming devastation in its wake.

Ethan McDowell had lost enough blood by the time he got his flesh wound tended in Richmond that morning that he could barely walk. But he could stay in the saddle—even with one arm in a sling—and that was where he spent the day, galloping after the Yankees with, at first, two friends. By the time they reached the Pamunkey River, a little over fifteen miles northeast of Richmond, their band had grown to a dozen. As they dismounted to feed their horses, Ethan, his own wound oozing from the ride, saw a man with bloody clothes sitting on the ground, his back against the wooden front wall of a small store. A smile spread across his now-stubbled face. He walked toward the wounded man. "You take a mess of killin', Cole Culpeper," he said.

Culpeper looked up through squinting eyes. Recognition sparked in his pale face. He had to clear his throat to speak, and when he did, his voice was raspy. "You should talk. Look at you, bloody, bent over, one arm no use to you. How in the h— do you expect to stay in a saddle?"

"Looks like I'm doin' a better job of it than you are, bub," Ethan shot back. "From what I know of *these* bluebellies, ain't no one sittin' on his brains like you are is gonna catch 'em."

Culpeper's head dropped in frustration. "Ah, I can't catch 'em. Been after 'em since the battle last night. Got me some doctorin' this morning, but— Ah, I don't even know why I'm chasin' these fools. I been tryin' for months to get outa this war, not back in." He shook his head and sighed as Ethan hooted at him.

"Well, they put two holes in you. That's not reason enough?"

"I got four holes in me," Culpeper said. For a long moment, he stared at the ground, his eyes glassy and his body slack. Then he stirred, grimacing. "Darn you, Ethan, get me up, boy. Help me onto my horse."

"*Your* horse, you big lummox?"

❦ ❦ ❦

After resting, Dahlgren had ridden his diminishing column all night, skirting Richmond to the north. No more than a hundred men still rode with him, along with a few slaves, some on horseback, most afoot. He wanted to get clear of any significant Confederate forces and outrun the pursuit back to General Benjamin Butler's Federal lines to the east. Toward midafternoon, the precipitation thankfully ended. Marley and the two scouts riding out front with him reached the Mattaponi River twenty-five miles northeast of Richmond. The three wore Confederate uniforms, assigned them by Dahlgren, in hopes the gray might provide them an extra instant of surprise that might balance the scales in their favor in case they ran face-to-face into a Rebel force.

Marley stared down into the rushing, brown Mattaponi. Steep banks abutted it, thick woods providing a snug canopy all round it. He recognized the same predicament as with the Pamunkey earlier in the day and the James before that: a river difficult to cross even with a boat, which was not in evidence. Dahlgren sent search parties along the Mattaponi in both directions. One located an old flatboat that Dahlgren ordered used to ferry his men across the torrent.

After Marley and an advance party crossed, McEntee urged Dahlgren, while helping him from his horse, "Sir, we need to get you across first."

"No," Dahlgren said, "I go last." Before McEntee could respond, the younger man planted his lanky frame against his crutch.

When half the men had crossed, musket fire crackled from the woods across the river. Dahlgren's miserable, exhausted troopers, on both banks, broke for cover, a couple of them shot before they made it. Dahlgren's color rose as he stood against his crutch. "Get me on my horse," he said, to no one in particular. "Get me on my horse!" he shouted, spotting one of his men ducking behind a clump of trees a short distance away. Stooping, the man hustled to Dahlgren as minié balls whistled past.

Marley, fatigued to the point of collapse and hugging the ground across the Mattaponi, saw Dahlgren step his horse out toward the water, defiant of the fire directed toward him. "We are the United States Cavalry," he shouted. Then, turning round toward his own men as he drew a revolver from its holster and cocked the hammer, "Step out as men, I say!"

As bullets cut through the misty frigid air, missing his head and chest by inches, Dahlgren began firing toward the thicket from where the Confederate gunsmoke roiled. Marveling at such defiant gallantry, Marley pulled out both his own Colts and, along with Federals around him and those on Dahlgren's side of the river, began to blast away at the enemy. Within minutes they had driven them off.

God help me to see my family again, Marley prayed as he swung his stiff body and legs again into the saddle to resume the ride. No more than half a mile later, three riders appeared fifty yards down the road from Marley and his two fellow scouts. At about thirty yards, one of the riders hollered, "Are you friends or enemies?"

Marley hesitated, then responded, "Friends."

At that point the rest of the Federal column emerged around a bend in the road behind him, and the riders turned their horses to make their escape. Marley swung his Spencer repeater out of the saddle holster and began firing. The other two scouts did the same. Two of the three fleeing riders fell from their saddles. The third escaped.

Marley stifled a curse. *Who knows to whom that third rider will report?* he thought. Shoving his rifle back into its holster and drawing one of his pistols again, he rode forward. His heart sank when he reached the downed riders. Neither appeared more than fifteen years of age, possibly as young as thirteen. How sick he was of this war. But he had no time to contemplate, as more gunshots sounded somewhere back down the road, perhaps near the rear of the column.

The escaped rider and lots of other Confederates had seen the Dahlgren column since daybreak. Indeed that rider would have ridden through the lower echelons of hell to reach Lieutenant James Pollard, commander of the Confederate cavalry's acclaimed "Lee's Rangers," a company of Virginia sharpshooters. The sobbing fifteen-year-old boy's younger brother was one of the other two riders, cut down by gray-coated Yankees. A close friend of the brothers, thirteen-year-old William Littlepage, had just joined Pollard's band on foot, along with Edward Halbach, his schoolmaster and commander of the school's military company. Littlepage consoled his distraught mate.

Pollard had chased Dahlgren all day, drawing recruits as he went like bees to honey. When word went down the line that two young boys had been killed by enemy riders posing as Southerners, the fury mounted on all fronts.

"That's just like them people," Culpeper growled to Ethan as they followed Pollard on a short cut geared to get ahead of Dahlgren and lay an ambush for him just south of Stevensville in remote, forested King and Queen County, well to the northeast of Richmond. From having detested his own army and its generals and given not a whit about who they were fighting, Culpeper was now gathering offenses toward the Yankees like a downhill-rolling stone picking up moss.

"Man, I'd give anythin' for another cup o' that burnt-bread coffee I had me this mornin' when that doc was sewin' me up," Culpeper said as Pollard positioned them and dozens of others in trees, on the ground, and behind bushes along either side of the thickly wooded road just north of King and Queen Courthouse.

"My big brother, Horace, was always a big coffee drinker," Ethan said. "Guess he doesn't get much coffee in Fort Douglas."

"I didn't know your brother was in a Yankee prison," Culpeper said.

"Got word from home just last week," Ethan said, running a cloth down the barrel of his rifle. "My baby brother, Felton, hasn't been heard from since Mine Run. Got word of that too." He held the rifle up to the light of the orange sunset behind him and peered down the barrel. They had not seen the sun for days. "I don't know how my little sister Rachel Anne's ever gonna weather all of it."

About a mile north Dahlgren ordered the seventy men remaining under his command to stop and rest in a wood. His eyes streaked with red, he called Marley to him. While Dahlgren's black servant laid out a bed of fence rails and blankets for him, he handed Marley a cup of steaming black coffee.

"I want you to ride ahead," Dahlgren said. "These fields and woods are crawling with Rebs, but if we continue south down the peninsula on this road, sooner or later we're bound to run into Butler's lines."

Dahlgren paused and looked Marley in the eye. "Wayne, I want to thank you for your superb work during this mission. It has been difficult, but once we are safely home, I intend to recommend you for a promotion."

Marley did not know what to say. He wanted to ask about what else had been planned for Richmond, but the time did not seem appropriate. He looked down at his boots. "Sir, I . . . thank you, sir."

Dahlgren smiled. "Now, my friend," he said, laying a hand on Marley's shoulder, "I regret that while you ride further yet, I shall be catching myself a quick rest, that I might be in some shape to lead this column home." He stepped away, then turned back. "I still wish to discuss the Scriptures with you once we have shaken the mud of this treacherous swampland from our boots, Wayne."

"It will be a pleasure, sir."

Marley gulped down a second cup of coffee to help him get his tired bones back into the saddle. Before he could, he heard his horse snort. "Oh, boy," he said gently, stroking the animal's neck. "I know, you're tired too. And I know you're tired of all corn and no oats too. Perhaps before too many more miles, we'll both have earned ourselves a long rest."

Groggy despite the coffee, Marley and his two scouts rode into the dark. A mile down the road, they heard a host of rifle hammers cock, from both sides of the road, and a steady voice that meant business hail them, "Halt there, Yanks. You can't see us, but we can see you, and if you don't get your hands up, we'll kill you, sure."

Three hours later, Dahlgren broke camp. "Where can Marley be?" he asked McEntee and Cooke.

"It must be trouble, for none of the three to have returned," McEntee said.

They moved out, full of foreboding as cold rain began to fall anew. A few minutes later they approached the same spot where Marley had been captured. Cooke, in the front rank of fours, sensed something amiss. He halted the column. For one long moment nothing sounded but the rain. Every man tensed and drew in his breath.

"Who are you?" someone shouted from the front rank.

Dahlgren, divining the import of the occasion, and suspecting the presence of more Rebel youngsters and perhaps farmers and others too old for regular army service, a mix he believed could be coerced, spurred to the front, whipping out his Navy Colt. "Surrender or I will shoot," he shouted. He leveled the pistol and squeezed the trigger. The gun misfired. He had not time to try again, for a deafening volley of fire crashed out from the right side of the road. Men and horses fell up and down the Federal line, the terrorized survivors charging through the rainy, smoke-choked, bullet-filled dark in search of an escape.

Pollard, Halbach, and his friend whose brother had been killed by gray-coated Yankees, the wounded Culpeper and Ethan, twenty-five of Lee's Rangers, and various others, some of whose property had previously been prey to Yankee depredations, blasted away as fast as they could reload and shoot again.

Among the dead left behind was Ulric Dahlgren, his torso riddled with buckshot and dead before he hit the muddy road, facedown. The last thing he saw, illumined by the flashing sheet of gunfire as he fell, were the connecting elm boughs arched across the road overhead from both right and left like a giant locked gate between him and heaven.

Some days later when Admiral John Dahlgren received the news, he remembered the Scripture he had learned in his own boyhood that chronicled King David's grief at the loss of his most beloved son.

"O my son Absalom, my son, my son Absalom! would God I had died for thee, O Absalom, my son, my son!"

CHAPTER 21

TAYLOR HAD BEEN AROUND LEE LONG ENOUGH TO SENSE, sometimes even to anticipate, when the dark moods were coming. Major Venable, with more years of living under his belt, and before that Major Chilton, Lee's previous chief of staff, had warned the younger man. Still, as is the way with young men, he had had to learn the hard way that, indeed, the majestic monument of benevolent kindness the Southern people had grown to revere was, after all, a man like all others. *Well, certainly not like all others,* Taylor admitted to himself. *At least he desires not to be like all others, which in itself sets him apart from very nearly all others.*

Ah, but the dark moods did come, did they not? *And how could they not?* Taylor reasoned. *For man is man, made by God in His own image, but with feet of clay and full of sin. To be other than that would be to be other than a man.* And no matter how tenaciously the general endeavored to be other than that, to control his feelings, to restrain his anger toward irresponsible subordinates, corrupt government officials, or the maddening frustrations and obstacles in the Southern fight for independence, he had inevitably to return to that station he seemed so determined to escape. *And when he does return, when this world of woe forces him back, he is angrier about it than a wet hen. And he can behave just about like a wet hen at those times,* Taylor thought, his own anger rising at the now nearly white-headed man sitting on the other side of the tent flap. *I have to give that old man a report I know he does not wish to receive, a report that will kindle his anger more than it already is. And when he lashes out, I shall be made to feel I am to blame for the entire blasted situation! Am I to be held accountable because the Confederate Commissary Department seems more adept at delivering the delicacies of life to Richmond's wealthy class than in preventing the starvation of the army whose blood and toil keeps those elites in their luxury?*

"Do come in, please, Major Taylor," came the voice inside the tent.

Taylor blushed, angry and embarrassed to have been divined as he was about to turn and leave until later.

"Yes, Major, please forgive my earlier unkindness to you," Lee, seated on his camp chair at his writing table, said as the younger man entered the tent. "You are not to blame for the unwelcome tidings you must often deliver. Such a cross display shames me, not you."

Now Taylor did not know what to say.

"Did you have something to report, son?" Lee asked. For the first time Taylor noticed the general's eyes were moist. He peered closer. The faint tracks of wiped-away tears remained on the old man's cheeks.

"Uh, no, sir," Taylor stammered, "just checking to see if you needed anything, sir."

"Thank you, no, Walter," Lee replied. Taylor could not remember the last time the general had referred to him by his Christian name.

Perhaps my delicate sensitivities warrant my dawning skirts and petticoats rather than boots and trousers, Taylor thought, shamed by himself, not Lee, as he walked slowly away, still holding the report. *The wonder of it all is how that one old man in there, and not because of anyone in Richmond or out here or anywhere else, has kept an army in the field, an army that consistently batters so titanic a foe. And he has so operated that army that neither it nor the people for whom it fights have yet starved, when we have so little food production remaining, virtually no industry in operation, and the Yankees have slowly strangled from us any succor from abroad.*

Lee returned to his gloom. He reached both hands around to his lower back and pressed the pain with his knuckles. *Hello, old friend.* He had decided that perhaps the lumbago would prove more tolerable if received as an intimate and welcome friend rather than a detested adversary. *Yes, you are quite lonely without me on nights as cold as this,* he thought.

Before him were the latest pile of letters, several of them from his own soldiers.

"Our horses receive five pounds of corn daily, not ten, and instead of ten in hay and fodder, nothing at all . . ."

"Only fifty men in our entire regiment have decent shoes, and the weather has been frigid without one minute's respite for many weeks. . . . I know not how flesh-and-blood men can continue to suffer for so long without relief."

"Once our pride and glory, once sleek and fast and unmatchable by the best the Yankees could bring against us, our poor gaunt rides now eat the bark off trees, devour empty bags, scraps of papers, and all the small debris of the camp."

"Though born a gentleman, hunger has forced me to steal, and my guilt to conceal my name . . . enclosed you will find, for you, my meat ration, as partial penitence for my sorry deed."

"Fully half the animals in General Stuart's entire horse artillery have died this winter. We are unable to replace them, and those which remain are in various stages of disease and/or dying."

"I complain not for myself but only for my men. Their daily ration is barely four ounces of fatty bacon or salt pork and one pint of cornmeal (often bug-infested) per day. Earlier this week, they suffered two full days without any food at all."

One final letter gripped Lee more than any other: "I beg the general's forgiveness for my presumption in penning so forward a communication. I write only to ask the general if he is aware of the want to which the soldiers have been reduced. However, if the general is aware of our situation, then we shall be content that some reason exists for the shortage."

That is still the way of our people, he thought with a mixture of affection, pathos, and wryness. *Those who work the land look to the landowner when in need.* He placed the wrinkled letter, written on yellow wrapping paper, back on the pile. His head drooped to his chest. *From where do we get such men?*

"Sir?" It was Taylor again. "A courier just delivered this for you, sir, from Secretary of War Seddon."

Lee put his reading glasses back on and opened the packet.

Custis Lee had himself ridden out to face Dahlgren's raiders when they crashed into the western outskirts of Richmond. He arrived just after the fighting finished, the dejection he had long felt through not serving the Confederacy with a combat command growing keener. He knew the high estimate his father held of his abilities as an advisor to President Davis. And he knew the valuable service he provided his father by offering him eyewitness apprisals—and appraisals—of the goings-on in the highest levels of the government.

He also knew, regarding a post in the Army of Northern Virginia, his father's opposition to "officers surrounding themselves with their sons and relatives," and the general's belief that the practice endangered the public good. He followed the same practice with Rob, who rode in cousin Fitz Lee's cavalry, despite Mary Lee's urging her husband to find a post for the young man on his undermanned staff.

Still the suspicion that his father did not hold a high regard for his aptitude as a field commander gnawed at Custis. Yet how could he initiate such a conversation? So he did not share the relief and joy of his family upon his return home, cold and soaked to the bone, the morning after Dahlgren had been driven off.

"Who was that officer I saw leaving as I rode up?" he asked Mildred, happy to give her something to do besides continuing in her embrace of him.

"Oh, a Captain so-and-so from North Carolina," she said. "He seemed a nice enough boy. And handsome and from a good family as well."

Custis eyed her, waiting for the rest.

"Oh, it just doesn't seem fair," she pouted, glancing to make sure her mother and sister were no longer within earshot. "Marching off to who-knows-what, possibly—very possibly—never to return, and *she*—" This, while canting her head toward upstairs. "—she can't even be cordial. Doesn't smile, barely converses. All the boys say the same thing. Wiggie's a-*loof*, she's re-*served*, she's *haugh*-ty, she's con-*cei*-ted." All this spoken with exaggerated flourish.

Custis's eyes twinkled just a bit. "While our Precious Life is here and none of those things."

She looked at him, and he was not sure if she would burst into the girlish laughter he so loved or continue to pout. She decided to pout a bit longer. "Well, I don't feel like I know her anymore. She always helps Mama, she always helps me, she always helps everybody—then she just goes back up to that horrid room and sits staring out the window."

Brother and sister stood for a moment in silence.

"George Washington Custis Lee, bring me those wet garments before you catch pneumonia," Mary's voice boomed from another room.

They shared the same thought. How could such a tiny, shriveled woman racked with pain and wheelchair-bound, possess a voice that could still exude such power when she wished for it to do so? "Come, Life," Custis said, a rare smile forcing itself on him. "Let's us go and see if we can scare up some of Mama's sweet potato coffee."

●◇ ●◇ ●◇

Never had Lee read anything remotely commensurate to what he had just completed. He called for an aide to prepare Traveller. This would take thought and prayer, and often he did both best when riding his favorite horse through the solitude of God's creation. A few minutes later, as he rode a short distance out from camp to collect his thoughts, the old specter returned to him of what he should like, someday, to be. *I wish I had a little farm of my own, where we could live in peace to the end of our days,* he thought. *Some quiet spot where I could work the land and earn my daily bread.*

Yet how could such a destiny be possible for him in a world that had come to what he read in those papers? Cresting a hill, the sweet aroma of cedars filling his nostrils and his soul, he shook his head and looked out at the beauty of his native land. *The world is changing, Virginia old girl, and I fear neither of us is prepared to change with it.*

How could they? he marveled. How could they, Americans like himself, some of them with strong connections, even family lines, in the South, conceive of such a scheme as Colonel Dahlgren's captured documents indicated? But he had read the deathly lines himself in today's March 5 newspaper account sent by Seddon, his heart growing tight in his chest for the first time in months.

None other than thirteen-year-old William Littlepage had found on the lifeless body of Ulric Dahlgren a planning notebook outlining for himself the actions to be taken once the Federal expedition had control of Richmond. Littlepage also gleaned a variety of documents and papers that, like the notebook, contained writing in Dahlgren's hand. The youngster read none of them, but passed them on to his commander and schoolmaster Halbach, who did. Shocked, he gave them to Pollard, who couriered them directly to Lee's nephew, cavalry Commander Fitz Lee, who took them in person to President Davis.

"We hope to release the prisoners from Belle Island first," the text identified by Dahlgren's writing as his speech to his men read, "and having seen them fairly started, we will cross the James River into Richmond, destroying the bridges after us and exhorting the released prisoners to destroy and burn the hateful city; and do not allow the rebel leader Davis and his traitorous crew to escape . . . Ask the blessing of the Almighty and do not fear the enemy."

In another document, addressed to Mitchell as he led his column of destruction along the north bank of the James: "Horses and cattle which we do not need immediately must be shot rather than left . . . The bridges once secured, and the (Belle Isle) prisoners loose and over the river, the bridges will be secured and the city destroyed. The men must keep together and well in hand, and once in the city it must be destroyed and Jeff. Davis and cabinet killed."

How foolish to have kept such a chronicle on his person in the execution of a desperate mission in enemy country, Lee thought, amazed and horrified. *Indeed their intent seems to have been to "unleash" a vengeful prison populace on the defenseless city to accomplish the dirty work—a populace their own ranking officer, Federal General Dow, has referred to as "the scrapings and rakings of Europe."*

He sat quietly for some minutes, watching an eagle circle overhead and feeling a light, stimulating breeze against his face as the sun dipped below the Blue Ridge to the west. *In nearly forty years of military service to my country—to my two countries—I have failed to learn what it means to "destroy a city,"* he thought. *And what of the people? What of the families and the children when their city is destroyed? What becomes of them?*

He feared that to dwell further on the matter would assure the onset of tears, so he patted Traveller's neck and turned him back toward camp.

Others possessed no reticence on the matter.

"My own conviction is for an execution of the prisoners," said Braxton Bragg, Davis's close friend and new chief military advisor.

"My own inclinations are toward the execution of at least a portion of those captured at the time Colonel Dahlgren was killed and publication of these papers as its justification," said Seddon. At the request of Davis, who stood against his own cabinet in opposing the execution of the prisoners, Seddon asked Lee for the benefit of "your wisdom and experience."

Indeed up and down the line of Confederate command, they wanted those one hundred troopers who had ridden with Dahlgren until the end—nearly all of them captured the morning after his death—killed.

And Davis, Lee thought, *will endorse whatever action I advocate.*

Of course the Richmond newspapers weighed in on the matter. One ridiculed the South's "milk and water" prosecution of the war, its determination to carry the fight only to the Federal armies, exclusive of the Northern people and their property. Another admonished the Confederate army, in the event of a future march into enemy territory, to throw off "their restraints of a chivalry proper with a civilized enemy," but which only brought about the contempt of such a savage foe. Dispense with "all rosewater chivalry and sentimentality," the paper exhorted, "and make war afar and upon the rules selected by the enemy."

Such words are directed toward . . . me, Lee realized. For he knew it was he who was the bulwark against such practices by the Army of Northern Virginia. He felt pressed in upon from all sides by friend and foe. For a long while he had recognized the disapproval of some of his military subordinates, Confederate politicians, and Southern press alike over his adamant refusal to war with innocents, since the North had increasingly engaged in that practice over the past two years. *What to do?* he wondered, tense and fretful.

He stopped Traveller in his tracks. *And just what* would *they have done to us, to our people—to my people—had they succeeded in their objectives?* Lee thought, his chest aching. *Of what would a country capable of such villainy have been capable?*

"Can this be the America for which I bled?" he spoke aloud.

A separate report from Hampton, who had savaged Kilpatrick's fleeing force, sent a new chill down Lee's spine.

"My observations convinced me that the enemy could have taken Richmond, and in all probability would have done so but for the fact (of an) intercepted dispatch from Dahlgren to Kilpatrick, asking what hour the latter had fixed for an attack on the city, so that both attacks might be simultaneous," Hampton wrote. "I regard the force to defend Richmond inadequate as at present located, and if a determined and concentrated attack is made, grave apprehensions of the result are to be entertained."

Marley fared better than most of his mates. He wound up being taken to the home of Captain Richard Bagby. That man had participated in the ambush of Dahlgren but only in time off from his normal work—pastoring a nearby Baptist church.

"I'm sure you boys were merely transporting those Confederate uniforms in your saddlebags as souvenirs," Bagby said, a merry glint animating his gray eyes. "I know you wouldn't have been wearing them earlier as you rode ahead of Dahlgren's column, in order to confuse those who would do you ill."

Marley and his scouting mates glanced at one another, then at Major Cooke—whom Bagby captured after the Federal asked for food at Bagby's overseer's house—as they sat around Bagby's dining table with their "host" and other armed Confederates.

"Well, let's be about more edifying business, shall we, gentlemen?" Bagby said, looking around the table as he cocked the hammer on one of the largest pistols Marley had ever seen and rested it on the linen cloth next to his plate. Then Bagby prayed over the food as few besides a Baptist preacher can do. Moments later, Marley, Cooke, and the other Federals were urged to feast on the Lord's bounty, as half a dozen Confederate triggers remained cocked around the room.

Later the group sipped acorn-roasted coffee as some of Bagby's neighbors stopped in to meet the surprise guests. Marley said little, exhaustion having so overtaken him that it seemed almost a relief to have been captured. *In any event,* he thought, chuckling to himself and sipping the dull, but hot, beverage, *if one has to be captured, the Rev. Captain Bagby seems about the most acceptable sort I could imagine to accomplish the task.* That, and a hot, nutritious meal, genial conversation, and, as it turned out, clean sheets and a warm bed.

The next morning, after a steaming breakfast of eggs, bacon, and biscuits, sans salt and butter, of which none were to be found anywhere in the region, Bagby sent the Federals on their way with an escort armed to the teeth. Just before they went, he called Marley aside.

"Major, I believe it was your saddlebags that contained these," he said, producing the worn old Bible and his dog-eared copy of the Westminster Confession of Faith, replete with both the Larger and Shorter Catechisms, the Ten Commandments, and the Apostles' Creed.

Marley blushed, then nodded his head. Bagby smiled and put the books back in a small bag. "I'd tuck this in the pocket of your overcoat," he said. "With God's help, I don't think most Southern boys will see any reason to separate you from them." He gave Marley a sly, knowing grin. "They'll probably think these books will help make you a better Yankee."

Marley smiled back.

"I thought right off you were a Christian man," Bagby said. "Then we found the Bible and saw who inscribed it to you. How on earth did you come to know Stonewall Jackson so well that he would pen such an inscription to you?"

A half smile crinkled Marley's tanned, bearded face. "That's a long story, pastor."

Bagby pondered that for a moment, then said, "Believe it was Old Jack himself that said, 'War is the sum of all evils.'"

"Believe it was, sir," Marley said with a nod.

"Well, one of its greatest evils is throwing brothers against one another like this," Bagby said with feeling. "You should be staying on here and coming to Sunday meeting with us, Major, having fried chicken with us at Sunday dinner— though there aren't many chickens around here you boys haven't already enjoyed—" This was said with a sparkle in his eyes. "—and joining us for Sunday night prayer meetin'. Oh, we use the London Confession of 1689, but it only differs with you Presbyterians' Westminster on baptism and church polity. You and I believe in the same sovereign God, the same sufficient Christ, and the same persevering Holy Ghost, do we not, Major?"

"That we do, sir," Marley said, heartened.

Bagby's countenance sobered.

"Major, I'm not sure to which of those hellish prisons you're being taken, but believe it or not, though my name may not carry enormous weight in government circles, I should tell you I have some old seminary brothers that do. I intend to alert them before this day is out to a certain Federal cavalry officer for whom immediate exchange would appear a necessity."

At this Bagby canted his head toward Marley's eye patch.

"No, no, sir," Marley said, "That would not—"

Bagby raised his hand. "Major, I must insist you be silent. You are my prisoner, after all. I know God can use a man like you anywhere a'tall, but I suspect sending you back north will present a better opportunity for your continued employment in His service than freezing and starving to death in Libby or Belle Isle."

Now the parson presented his hand to shake. Marley took it, warding off a sudden onslaught of tears and saying, "Thank you, sir."

"Good Providence to you, brother Marley," Bagby said, looking him in the eye.

"You too, pastor," Marley said.

Bagby smiled and turned away. After a few steps he turned back. "I don't know what all you boys had planned for Richmond," he said, "but you should know that the prisons there are indeed horrifying. I know, I been there many times ministering to the prisoners. But you should also know that no one—best as I can find out—is purposely tormenting or depriving them. The people of Richmond are starving, too, Major, slowly but surely. And there's refugees from all over Virginia in the streets every night—lots of 'em—just as cold as your comrades in those prisons that have half the windows broken out. I . . . I just thought you should know that if you didn't already." He stood for a long quiet moment, his brow furrowed, deep in thought, before he spoke again, staring at the ground. "I 'spect when the day is done, we're all to blame for this awful war."

Then he walked away and was gone. The sentiments were poignant, and some of the words thought-provoking. But arching over everything was a warm, sure feeling that spread through Marley. He glanced upward. *Yes, you are still with me, are you not, Sir?*

To ensure no repetition of the Kilpatrick-Dahlgren raid, the Confederate authorities moved the entire Federal prison population resident in Richmond out of the capital within thirty days of the attack. They were moved by train to a new prison camp redolent with the aroma of freshly cut pine, verdant woods, sparkling streams, and a subtropical climate, all the elements necessary for a much healthier existence for the prisoners. It was named Camp Sumter. It lay in a lovely part of south Georgia, not far from the town of Andersonville.

Among the readers of the Richmond newspapers, which spewed venom against Kilpatrick, Seward, Stanton, Lincoln, the entire United States, and especially Dahlgren, whom they christened "Ulric the Hun," was a tempestuous actor who had, since the commencement of the war, performed before both Federal and Confederate audiences. A member of the most famous stage family in America, East Coast theater impresarios roundly hailed his thespian range and power and predicted he would soon be considered the greatest actor of his generation.

A twenty-five-year old Marylander with Confederate sympathies, though he never belonged to the Southern army or any Confederate organization, his fury

grew the more he read of Dahlgren's audacious mission. By the time he finished reading, John Wilkes Booth was for the first time galvanized to lash out at
a Federal government he now believed had careened into tyranny.

CHAPTER 22

BECAUSE OF THE INTELLIGENCE FRANK STRINGFELLOW GLEANED at Washington's Birthday Ball, Lee expected the arrival from the west of Sam Grant. That unassuming West Point graduate had been decorated for valor in the Mexican War. Since then, however, he had failed in a series of business ventures and even in his military career, the latter due, so the story went, largely to the depredating effects of a struggle with the bottle in which he too often finished on the short end.

Now, however, Ulysses Simpson Grant appeared to be the Ajax that Lincoln and the United States government had for years sought. Grant had notched some of the Federals' first significant victories of the war at Forts Henry and Donelson. He had won the west's most important battles at Shiloh and Vicksburg. And he did it all, and much more, by exhibiting a tenacity that rendered the term *pit bulldog* too frivolous a euphemism.

Lee had made a career of divining the strengths and weaknesses of adversaries. So when he saw the North's most audacious—and successful—commander coming east as the newly appointed commander of all Federal armies, and the first lieutenant general in the United States Army since the First War of Independence; when a telegraph from Longstreet confirmed Stringfellow's intelligence that an entire corps was transferring to Virginia from Tennessee; when other sources informed him that trainload after trainload of new recruits were pouring into the Federal camps along the Rapidan, he prepared for three attacks.

He expected a diversion of some sort out west in the Shenandoah Valley; a move against the flank or rear of his army, probably just to the east of Richmond on the James; and a trip-hammer smash against the main line of the Army of Northern Virginia on the Rapidan.

Indeed Lincoln had told Grant he wanted the war won and he wanted it won quickly. His reelection battle loomed in November, a contest that if held today he knew he would probably lose because of the bloody failure of the war thus far. And he would lose it to the probable Democratic candidate General George McClellan!

Grant received from Lincoln a promise of breathtaking implication: whatever he needed to attain victory, and the freedom to employ it however he saw fit.

Coming east with Grant was the new cavalry chief of the Army of the Potomac, Phil Sheridan, a volcanic-tempered little Irishman as fearless as he was ruthless.

Withal Lee found his spirits roused by the arrival of such worthy opponents.

Taylor noticed it. "The Tycoon, as we on the staff have grown accustomed to calling him, has been complaining somewhat," he wrote his fiancée, "but he seems to have brightened in anticipation of a clash with the present idol of the North."

The task now before Lee, however, brightened him not in the least. The fate of nearly one hundred Federal prisoners, and perhaps scores of Confederates languishing in hellish freezing Northern prisons, rested on the words he wrote on the paper before him in the next few minutes.

One of those Confederate prisoners was his own son Rooney.

Yet Lee knew his duty was to do that which would best serve God and his country. *Fitzhugh's life is in God's hands, not those people's,* Lee thought, *as ever it has been.* Possible reciprocations against his son could not be a factor in his decision. Nor could the specter of "setting an example" be considered when future similar acts might be contemplated by the Federals. Nor the fact that much of the Confederate government, press, and citizenry cried out for the execution of Dahlgren's captured raiders.

No, the counsel for which he was sought must be based on the merits of this case alone. One part of him cried out for swift and permanent justice against those who would have left his defenseless daughters—and his sick, crippled wife—and tens of thousands of other noncombatants without provision or shelter in the midst of a howling winter storm.

But even as that voice strained for hegemony, another silenced it and won the day in the battleground of Lee's soul: "Blessed are the merciful: for they shall obtain mercy."

And how I need mercy, O God, he thought, sadness filling him. *How I continue to squander that which Thou hast bestowed upon me; how, as the prayer says, I continue to follow the devices and desires of my own heart, and leave undone those things which I ought to have done, and do those things which I ought not to have done. But Thou, O Lord, have mercy upon me, miserable offender. Spare Thou those, O God, who confess their faults. Restore Thou those who are penitent; according to Thy promises declared unto mankind in Christ Jesus our Lord.*

Hope breaking across his somber heart now like the morning sun cresting the Washington City horizon and flashing white through the front windows of Arlington, he dipped his pen in the inkwell and commenced his response to Seddon, the Confederacy, the world, and history.

> I concur with you in thinking that a formal publication of these papers should be made under official authority, that our people and the world might know the unchristian and atrocious acts they plot and perpetrate. But I cannot recommend the execution of the prisoners that have fallen into our hands. Assuming that the address and special orders of Colonel Dahlgren correctly state his designs and intentions, they were not executed, and I believe, even in a legal point of view, acts in addition to intentions are necessary to constitute crime.
>
> These papers can only be considered as evidence of his intentions. It does not appear how far his men were cognizant of them, or that his course was sanctioned by his Government. It is only known that his plans were frustrated by a merciful Providence, his forces scattered, and he killed. I do not think it right, therefore, to visit upon the captives the guilt of his intentions.
>
> I presume that the blood boils with indignation in the veins of every officer and man as they read the account of the barbarous and inhuman plot, and under the impulse of the moment many would counsel extreme measures. But I do not think that reason and reflection would justify such a course. I think it better to do right, even if we suffer in so doing, than to incur the reproach of our consciences and posterity.

> R. E. Lee
> General

Thus Marley lived to see the squalor of Libby Prison, which had too many prisoners, too many rats, too much disease, too little food, and too few windows remaining that had not been broken to keep out the bone-chilling winter winds. Night after night he shivered in the throes of restless sleep; even his overcoat had been confiscated by an illiterate prison guard who himself had no coat, suffered a frostbitten toe, and who immediately donned the coat to wear himself.

Marley lay among the very men he had attempted to liberate. He had cleared none of them out of Libby, but he noticed that the exposure and disease running rampant among them was clearing out plenty of them. Opening his Bible one night with blue fingers—the guard had taken his gloves as well—he silently thanked God that he had fallen into the hands of the Rev. Captain Richard Bagby. Marley and the cluster of Christian men who huddled close around him, drawing warmth from one another's stinking bodies, still suffered, but they were reminded by His Word that God was yet their defender, their shield and buckler and high tower, and even if they could not discern His hand in all this, that strong hand was assuredly working for their good amid the suffering.

The suffering of Lee's own men woke him at night, preyed on his mind during the day, and prompted him to tell Davis in a March meeting at the president's office, "My anxiety on the subject of provisions for the army is so great that I cannot refrain from expressing it to Your Excellency. I cannot see how we can operate with our present supplies. There is nothing to be had in this section for men or animals. My commissary officer begs to report the army has no meat and only one day's ration of bread. Unless there is a change, I fear the army cannot be kept effective and probably cannot be kept together."

He arrived at 707 Franklin still weighed down by the supply issues, particularly as he continued to hear reports of the North's mounting production of supplies, food, and every manner of material.

Then he saw Rooney. *Can it be him?* Lee wondered, nearly mouthing the words aloud. *He must have lost a hundred pounds.* And a wife. After a brief attempt at a manly son-to-father greeting, the sullen, emaciated young man, finally released from Federal prison by exchange, burst into uncontrollable sobs in his father's arms.

He had shed not a tear in the presence of any other soul prior to this.

"There, there, that's a good boy," Lee said, patting the stringy hair that when he last saw it had been so bushy and soft. "She was a wonderful, godly young woman, wasn't she? She was the best. We could not have loved even Annie more, could we?"

Now Rooney's sobs nearly became screams of anguish. "No," he choked, "we couldn't have." Lee felt hot tears running down his own cheeks. *Oh, to preserve one's children from the trials and tribulations of this sad, fallen world,* he thought. *But someday, someday, after we have raised them up in Thine admonition, heavenly Father, Thou shalt bring them to Thine own breast, and indeed, there shall be no more tears, shall there, Sir?*

Father and son spent many hours together, walking the nearby capitol grounds in the cool twilight, talking in Lee's study, remembering precious Charlotte and the babies as they stared at the fireplace for which they had no kindling to burn. Rooney cried much, Lee spoke little, and when the evening was done, the son was exhausted enough to sleep through the night. But the father went to the breast of his own beloved wife, though they slept now in separate rooms, and wept upon that breast no less than his son had wept the entire day because a son never grows old enough that his heartaches do not become the heartbreaks of a loving father.

The next morning, Lee, with Agnes, Mildred, the just-returned Mary Custis, Rooney, and Custis, attended Lenten services held by Dr. Minnigerode at seven o'clock in the lecture room of the church. Lee had prayed his duties would land him in Richmond during at least a portion of the Lenten season so that he might attend the sunrise services, which always strengthened his heart for the day to come and helped him follow his own admonition that "No day should be lived unless it is begun with a prayer of thankfulness and an intercession for guidance."

The Lord had answered with Davis's directive calling him to the capital to discuss supply issues, the coming spring campaign, and General Grant. This while no less than five of his children resided at "the Mess," as the Lees' rented dwelling had come to be known.

The lecture room filled to capacity each day, with the throng spilling out into the adjacent hallways. When the Lees returned home, Mary and a simple but warm breakfast awaited them. They talked of everything—whom they saw at that morning's service, when the weather might warm, the new Federal commander, Grant. Mary pressed for details on every point of Minnigerode's address, glad at heart to see the chairs around her filled again with her beloveds, especially her husband at the head of the table as he led the family prayers, invoking God's protection of Rob and offering thanks that the war had taken no more of the family.

Lee observed that Rooney and Wiggie remained quiet. *Their hearts are with others not present at table with us today,* he thought sadly, wishing he could take their pain onto his own shoulders.

One morning as the family members left the room, Mary signaled Lee to remain. She produced a three-day-old *New York Times* given her by Mary Chesnut. The paper lay open to the editorial page, where sprawled in bold letters the words "The Rebel Calumny on Colonel Dahlgren." Lee's eyes opened wide as he read on. When finished he looked Mary in the eye.

"So those people are saying the offending passages of the Dahlgren papers are forged, that our government has deliberately misled the entire world and attempted to cast onto that young officer unjust and lasting infamy," he said.

Husband and wife sat in silence for some moments before Lee looked at Mary and again spoke. "Did you know that, after all that happened, after this brave city rose on its last tottering legs to stand off those people's handpicked thousands, that they accused our soldiers of murdering Colonel Dahlgren, and they sent a further expedition that burned the entire town of King and Queen Courthouse to the ground, and took some dozens of prisoners, at least half of them civilians?"

Mary said nothing, noting the rising color on Lee's broad forehead and the small, rapid nods beginning. She knew his confusion and disgust with the North's discarding the old chivalric notions of warring only against those able to defend themselves, but . . .

"I do not consider Richmond a suitable place for you," he blurted, leaning toward her, the gentle restraint that usually marked him suddenly gone, "and never has that case been made more exceptionally than with this recent affair. Nor ought anyone to be here unless business or occupation for the country compels them." Now his head went from the staccato vertical nods to broader, horizontal shakes. "In addition to other considerations, you run the hazard of assault and siege, which you are not in a condition to undergo."

How passionate he still is for my safety, Mary thought, the sentiment endearing her husband to her anew. Though he appeared intent on a response from her, she knew him well enough to know that he had needed to say what he did, but he knew no suitable answer, at least one that had not already been offered many times previously. There was simply no acceptable alternative, short of leaving Virginia—and being separated further from him. This she would not do. So she smiled and, with difficulty, cupped a gnarled hand around his bearded cheek. He blushed, but his eyes softened, and she thought she detected a trace of whimsy at one corner of his mouth, struggling to be seen through the fluffy snowy growth.

After a moment she laid the same hand on the New York paper. "It says their own correspondent saw the documents in question the day the raid began and that they said nothing of murder, arson, or other such calamity," she said.

"It appears that though we might be done with the Dahlgren Raid," Lee said with a sigh, "it might not be done with us."

●◇ ●◇ ●◇

On March 30, Davis ordered Lee to inquire of Meade as to what knowledge the Federal high command had of Dahlgren's intentions.

"I have the honor to enclose photographic copies," Lee wrote of the explosive documents, "one of which is an address to his officers and men, bearing the official signature of Colonel Dahlgren, and the other, not signed, contains more detailed explanations of the purpose of the expedition."

Lee asked "whether the designs and instructions of Colonel Dahlgren, as set forth in these papers . . . were authorized by the United States Government or by his superior officers, and also whether they have the sanction and approval of those authorities?"

●◇ ●◇ ●◇

That Sunday Confederate generals abounded in the Sunday morning service at Saint Paul's Church. But not everyone considered the worship of God a desirable attribute in their leaders.

"Somebody counted fourteen generals in church today," Mary Chesnut told one of a dozen of her friends who sat in her dining room at Sunday dinner.

"She suggested that less piety and more drilling of commands would suit the times better. There were Lee, Longstreet, Morgan, Hoke, Clingman, Whiting, Pegram, Elzey, Gordon, Bragg, and—oh, I forget the others."

Fortunately the battle-weary, pressure-rent soldiers' receipt of Word and Sacrament did not prevent Mrs. Chesnut from arriving home in time to preside successfully over the serving of gumbo, ducks and olives, supreme de volaille, chickens in jelly, oysters, lettuce salad, chocolate cream, jelly cake, claret cup, and champagne.

Indeed some there were for whom the war had not proven nearly so severe as for the field soldiers who ate green corn, or the homeless women, children, and slaves who wandered down sleet-whipped country roads.

Mrs. Chesnut would perhaps have been the more put out had she known all the piety afoot in the contents of another Lee letter. This, a general order to the entire army by request of President Davis, the House, and Senate, ordered their observance of April 8 as a day of "fasting, humiliation, and prayer." Lee ordered all military duties, except those absolutely necessary, suspended for the day. He told the chaplains to hold services in their regiments and brigades. He "requested" the officers and men to attend.

"Soldiers!" he wrote, "Let us humble ourselves before the Lord our God, asking through Christ the forgiveness of our sins, beseeching the aid of the God of our forefathers in the defence of our homes and our liberties, thanking Him for His past blessings, and imploring their continuance upon our cause and our people."

The same day Wayne Marley, having lost twenty pounds in less than a month and having gained an unyielding case of diarrhea, walked out of Libby Prison with five other Federal officers and boarded a packet boat headed down the James to Fortress Monroe.

Clutching his Westminster Confession of Faith—he had with regret but not doubt left the Bible given him by Stonewall with his fellow prisoners—he voiced silent thanksgiving to God for His plenteous mercies, that he would not have to witness the further horror of how soldiers died in a filthy, rotten prison, and that he was leaving before his deteriorating body was added to their number.

●◇ ●◇ ●◇

Culpeper was a hard Valley man, with a hard Valley body that at age twenty-six still took little time to heal. He had four holes in him, had lost a bucket of blood, and had pushed that lean body to the brink of expiration by the time he helped in the Dahlgren ambush. The next morning, while the other Confederates rounded up Dahlgren's exhausted men, Ethan had helped Culpeper to a nearby farmhouse, where he finally collapsed and slept for thirty-six hours. The family's comely teenaged daughter mostly tended to him, but Culpeper was dreaming about Emma when he awoke, and it was she to whom his fevered thoughts ran, the more with each passing day. He thought of Emma and his Upper Shenandoah fields, and Emma and the summer sun and how he had seen it shining off her golden strawberry hair one day near the spring behind the house when she took off her bonnet because a bee had gotten in it.

Long would he ruminate on Emma, but always, whether awake or asleep, coherent or fevered, his remembrances and his fancies would end with the specter of her and the children staggering down frozen country roads—wind, sleet, and rain slashing them to early, agonizing deaths.

Then his hate would grow more than it had ever been, which was saying something. Cole Culpeper had always been a good hater, had always found it easy to hate and had with this war found more and more things to hate. As the comely teenaged girl he barely noticed nursed back his strength, something he considered one of the few bright spots through these days of healing and hating, occurred the day before he rode off with Ethan to join Jeb Stuart's cavalry under Hampton.

A certain renown had gathered around Culpeper's name due to his exploits during the Dahlgren affair. Word spread ranging from his being a one-man wrecking crew in the Richmond battle, to riding through a storm with four holes in him to help kill Ulric the Hun. Even Hampton knew about him—and wanted him. Ethan, with his family connections and his own reputation as a hardy horse soldier, met with Hampton, his brigadier and friend. He offered a sympathetic version of Culpeper's leaving his former infantry regiment "to go save the death-ravaged family farm" and secured his friend a slot in the regular cavalry, especially since he brought his own Yankee horse, saddle, and tack.

Culpeper's "bright" spot, however, was something else. Ethan had heard while at Hampton's headquarters that one of "Kilcavalry's" troopers had been told by a black Federal guard upon returning to Alexandria that the trooper was not authorized to ride through the town's streets. The white man drew his saber and killed the black man on the spot. As a result, furlough for Kilpatrick's entire exhausted force was canceled.

I hates most folk, and I hates Yankees more, but I sure hates darkies too, Culpeper thought, buoyed by the report.

"Let's get outta here and back to the war, Ethan!" he chortled.

"You said it yourself," Ethan said, scratching his head. "For a man who fought so hard to get out of this war, you're sure an eager beaver to get back into it."

Culpeper only smiled at him. But he was thinking, *Me, with a horse under me again and ridin' with Wade Hampton, oh, I'll be able to do me a heap o' killin' now.* For the first time in many months, he felt true, unvarnished joy.

"Ma'am?" he asked his lovely neglected nurse. "Y'all wouldn't happen to have a quid or twist 'roun'chere, would ye? I don't need nothin' to spit in."

The Federals, from Kilpatrick to the highest reaches of the United States government, disavowed knowledge of any supposed scheme to burn Richmond and slaughter the Confederate leadership. The New York City newspapers and others continued at the forefront of Northern denunciation of what increasing numbers of people in the North believed were Rebel lies, forgeries, and treachery.

Those publications avoided their earlier proclamations, made prior to the conclusion of the raid, that Kilpatrick and his men would "sack," "loot," and "plunder" Richmond.

In mid-April, Lee received Meade's response to his inquiry about the Dahlgren affair: "Neither the United States Government, myself, nor General Kilpatrick authorized, sanctioned, or approved the burning of Richmond and the killing of Mr. Davis and cabinet, nor any other act not required by military necessity and in accordance with the usages of war."

Lee, surprised to find that his predominant emotion was a sort of offended disappointment rather than relief at Meade's statement, forwarded the correspondence to the Confederate leadership in Richmond.

❖❖ ❖❖ ❖❖

Meade did not include all of his thoughts in the missive to Lee. A growing uneasiness covered the victor of Gettysburg and the commander of the Army of the Potomac. Finally he felt compelled to share it with his wife.

"This is a pretty ugly piece of business. In my reply to General Lee, I necessarily threw odium on Dahlgren," Meade said. "This, because *Kilpatrick's*"—Mrs. Meade could not fail to cipher the disdain with which her husband uttered the name—"statement challenged the veracity of the Dahlgren papers, as published by the Confederate authorities. But I regret to say that Kilpatrick's reputation and collateral evidence in my possession rather go against this theory."

Meade sighed with the weariness of a war that had lasted way too long. "However, I was determined that my skirts should be clear."

❖❖ ❖❖ ❖❖

Meanwhile trouble festered like an unwanted sore in the heart of Captain John McEntee, who through endurance, horsemanship, and craft became one of the handful of men, who had ridden to the end with Dahlgren, to escape back to Federal lines. He knew that what his government and the Northern newspapers were saying was not what Dahlgren—one of the bravest men McEntee had ever known—had told him. One sunny morning in early April, having told no man what Dahlgren told him and with his insides churning over the matter, the normally ice-veined government man showed up unannounced at the quarters of Army of the Potomac Provost Marshal Marsena Patrick.

The tale McEntee unfolded to his old friend, secure from the ears of anyone else, helped McEntee sleep better that night, but it kept Patrick awake until nearly dawn. During those troubled night watches, Patrick rose from his bed, crossed to his writing table, and lit his oil lamp. Then he wrote in his private diary of the interview that no newspaper, North or South, would ever obtain.

"McEntee has the same opinion of Kilpatrick that I have and says he managed just as all cowards do," Patrick wrote. "He further says that he thinks the papers are correct that were found upon Dahlgren, as they correspond with what Dahlgren told him."

CHAPTER 23

THE MORNING OF MAY 2, LEE RODE TO THE CONFEDERATE observation post atop Clark's Mountain, at the front of his army. He looked across the Rapidan to the north through his field glasses to the ocean of Federal tents spread like an endless blanket of late spring snow over the fields of Culpeper County.

One-hundred-and-nineteen thousand Federals faced him. Butler's army of thirty-five thousand more readied to move up the peninsula toward Richmond. To counter these forces, Lee, his mind alone producing the tactics and strategy that would endeavor to save a nation, had received Davis's permission to bring Beauregard north to defend Richmond and Longstreet east to shore up his own army.

Lee's throat tightened as he recalled the return of his Old War Horse's veterans from Tennessee. He meant to look quietly on, not interfering with their drill, allowing his presence to convey his appreciation to them of their return.

They would have none of it. It began with a scattering of "It's General Lee!" followed by a few throaty yells, then the swinging back and forth of tattered regimental and battle flags. He removed his hat and raised it to them. As the cheers became a roar, he blushed, wishing to hide himself, not wanting the day of their return to shine light on him.

Then, by dozens that became hundreds, then thousands, the First Corps of the South's first army—not one of them a Virginian—unleashed a collective Rebel yell that carried for long minutes, clearing the area for miles around of fowl and animal alike, a screeching wail the sheer volume of which he had never before witnessed. When these who had charged the Peach Orchard and Devil's Den and uncounted other ramparts for him began to pour tears onto their ragged, colorless uniforms, the ground on which Traveller stood started to rumble, and the hills that rose around him to shake.

Hot wet tears streamed down his own face. *My tears have come to evince themselves with unwelcome frequency,* he thought, *and I wish they would all go away.* He heard a First Corps chaplain some feet away say to an officer, "Does it not make the general proud to see how these men love him?" Lee winced and dropped his head. *Proud,* he scoffed to himself, stifling a sob that had clawed halfway up his throat. *Proud? When they could be so much more had they a true captain like Washington?* Proud. The very notion provoked in him the urge to retch. He forced his head back up to honor them with his attention. *How unseemly would it be for one so unworthy to effect the conceit of pride,* he thought, having no conception of why men so brave and suffering would in any way esteem such a flawed commander as himself.

Even with the return of Longstreet, Lee's command would total no more than sixty-four thousand soldiers, barely half the number of his foe. Elsewhere he knew the entire Mississippi River now lay in Federal hands, rendering the sprawling Trans-Mississippi South lost to the Confederacy as a source of supplies. The Federals held Chattanooga, Tennessee, gateway to the southeast Confederacy. They had also triumphed in the New Mexico Territory, Missouri, Kentucky, and that part of Virginia west of the Allegheny Mountains—now christened the new Union state of West Virginia—and their naval blockade choked more life out of the Confederacy with each passing month. And intelligence reports told him William Tecumseh Sherman had an entirely separate one-hundred-thousand-man army ready to march on Georgia from Chattanooga.

Indeed, a few weeks before, Lincoln had ordered the Northern states to provide him with *seven hundred thousand* additional troops to throw against the already vastly outnumbered Confederates. *Such numbers,* Lee thought, shaking his head, barely able to comprehend their enormity, *while we have so few . . .*

All these matters weighed upon his mind, though President Davis had, despite much public clamor, refused him any authority except that over the Army of Northern Virginia. Still, despite the man's limitations, he refused to go hard on Davis. For one, the president had lost his second small son, his treasured four-year-old Joseph, who fell to his death from the balcony while momentarily unattended. *That poor man,* Lee thought, filled with empathy. *How grievous the loss of one so small.*

He began to catalogue in his mind more substantive defenses for Davis. *Our men—and women—have fought long and well to preserve the right of our eleven countries to govern themselves in the sovereign manner they intended when each joined the United States, without undue intrusion from a distant central government. Yet how difficult for such a confederation to coordinate itself to fight as one! His Excellency faces continual threats from individual states to pull out of the Confederacy altogether if scattered outposts of troops so needed here and elsewhere are moved from those states, even temporarily. And the citizens of those states, having seen what the enemy has done to Virginia and other unhappy scenes of war, threaten their own leaders if their local detachments are moved where needed.*

With reluctance he had come to agree with the sentiments of a Virginia colleague in the War Department who said, "Certainly no deliberative body ever met in this state with less of statesmanship in it than the Confederate Congress." *Indeed,* Lee thought, resisting the tide of contempt rising in him, *it sometimes seems as though our congressmen are unable to do anything except eat peanuts and chew tobacco.*

Which way will they strike? he wondered, returning his mind to matters over which he might exert at least some small influence. *Across Ely's and Germanna Fords, like Fightin' Joe Hooker did last year? Or southeast, around my right, toward Fredericksburg, like Ambrose Burnside the year before? Or west, to threaten Richmond through the back door? Sam Grant has won a lot of battles in this war, and he has never gone for a leg when he thought a throat was to be had. He will come for me, not Jeff Davis, because it is the Army of Northern Virginia those people must destroy to win this war.*

"They shall come across either the Germanna or Ely's Fords and into the wilderness again," he told Taylor. Then he recalled the great and terrible Chancellorsville campaign over the same ground exactly one year before. It had nearly won the war for the Confederacy but resulted in the accidental death by his own soldiers of the man considered across the world the greatest general in the war.

His brown eyes twinkling in the sunlight, Lee turned to the younger man and said, "Perhaps Old Jack's ghost still stands as defiantly over the same ground."

Despite all that has happened, Taylor thought, *the death, the suffering, the deprivation, the separation, never have I seen him, and the army that is him, more calmly and firmly determined to be victorious, with God's help.*

Late that night in his tent, finished with the day's labors, Lee read from Everett's *Life of Washington,* given him years before by Mary.

How his spirit would be grieved could he see the wreck of his mighty labors! Lee thought as he rose from his knees after prayers and slipped into his cot. *How the fruit of his noble deeds has been destroyed, and how his precious advice and virtuous example have been so soon forgotten by his countrymen.*

He paused in reflection. *How would he have acquitted himself differently than have I wore he my boots? Surely he would have done much differently. Surely he would have been much the better general and inspiring leader than have I been. Oh, Father, that I might approach being for my people what he was for his.*

His last thoughts before sleep overtook him were, *I must read again from the edition Mary edited of Mr. Custis's* Recollections of General Washington. *How I do wish I could have known him, been around him, seen what he was really like . . . I would be so much better a general and a man, if . . . I could have known him . . . known him and . . . known my father . . .*

●> ●> ●>

The next day Lee and all the South continued to wait for the massive assault they knew was coming. As he rode Traveller through the camp that afternoon, returning the unceasing hailings of his men when they saw his approach, he silently thanked God for having poured such heavy rains from the heavens through middle and late April. The refreshing of the earth, completed by days of warming sunshine, had both delayed Grant's attack and allowed grass to grow for the Confederate horses, who had begun to resemble a sickly mob of four-legged apparitions.

He saw a cluster of men emerging from one of the thirty-seven log chapels that now checkered the camps of the Army of Northern Virginia.

Ah, I believe that is young Jones, the Baptist minister, Lee thought, cheered.

"Good afternoon, General, sir," the pastor said, reaching up to shake Lee's hand as the two dozen or so lean men who had been with him in the chapel, several of whose "uniforms" hung from them like mere rags, went their various ways.

"These worship houses seem to be occupied every hour of the day and night," Lee marveled. "Three o'clock in the afternoon on a Thursday and you have such a throng about you in there."

Only then did Lee notice that Jones's smooth cheeks ran wet with tears.

"Dear pastor, what troubles you?"

Jones looked up at him, his eyes watering over. He canted his head and pointed a finger back toward the disappearing soldiers. His words came raspy and low. "Those . . . men . . . sir, those skinny, diarrhea-infested, lice-ridden men, and boys—"

"Who are they?"

"They are Harris's Mississippi Brigade, sir." Emotion so choked Jones that he had difficulty continuing. "Their self-sacrifice and the name of Mississippi deserve to be written in letters of gold on one of the brightest pages of the history of this war."

Steadying himself, Jones rose to his modest height, inches shorter than Lee, and continued, "They have resolved to deny themselves one day's ration every ten days and give it to the poor of the city of Richmond. I have seen nothing in the history of this war more sublime than these noble men, cut off from supplies from home, thus offering a portion of their scant allowance to the poor of the city they have so long defended. Why, General, sir, you cannot but see yourself those brave soldiers are already half-starved."

Lee stared after them. One skinny little fellow broke into a trot and headed toward one of the camp's many open latrines. How often had he seen that trot—had even done it himself more than a few times—as a man rushed in desperation to relieve himself before he messed his trousers. Sometimes a man made it, and sometimes he did not. When he did not, and the army was on the march, it might be hours before his pants could be soaked in even dirty water. On a hot summer day, with the sun blazing and the horseflies buzzing and a man's constitution already melted down from the inability to hold fluids or solids, well— *What sort of man do we have that does not stop even when he is blind with fever, often not until he falls flat on his face into the dusty road?* Lee thought. *Why do they keep marching? They do not have splendid Traveller here, or the best doctors close by, or a comfortable cot in a nice tent as have I. Perhaps I should begin sleeping out among them. It does not seem right that I should have such comforts while they, who carry the destiny of our people on their bowed shoulders—*

Lee noticed that Jones had turned, head down, to leave.

"So our revival indeed continues, pastor?"

Jones turned back, his face brightening. "Oh, yes, sir, does it continue. Why, General, sir, I've reports from other ministers that brigades all over the South—in Tennessee, Texas, South Carolina, and all over Virginia—are seeing men, many men, some of the worst men, sir, embracing Christ and His cross and turning their backs on their wicked ways."

Seeing Lee's own countenance brighten, Jones plunged on. "Why, sir, I have received mention from more than one brigade that their gambling and profanity are now almost entirely confined to the new recruits fresh from home. You are the soldier, sir, but my understanding is that camp life may normally be expected to breed demoralization of all stripes; yet such activity is very greatly counteracted in our noble army."

Lee thought about that for a moment. Jones saw the shadow of a smile flicker across his bearded face. "So our brother Stonewall Jackson's greatest triumphs may yet prove not to have been those he accomplished on the battlefield."

"Yes, General," Jones said, "you may rest assured that the revival so fueled by the example and efforts of the great Jackson continues. Composite estimates from the various pastors and chaplains indicate that fifteen thousand men in the Army of Northern Virginia alone, this past winter alone, first trusted in Christ for salvation and deliverance from the terrors of the minié ball."

So might my "greatest triumphs," too, prove, Lee thought, as he rode off, doubting that any of his on the battlefield or off would long endure in the memories of men.

That night, though nearly prostrate with exhaustion, through sheer force of will, Lee kept his eyes open long enough to write letters to family. Their writing was the joy of his day, and he had looked forward to it since he arose hours before dawn.

He thanked Mary for her continued toil at producing socks for his needy soldiers. He knew the strain on her during the many hours each week her house was filled with other women knitting socks. More so, he knew she insisted on knitting herself, which brought pain to her ruined hands, arms, and shoulders every moment she did it. Still, with the eye to detail that had helped garner the Army of Northern Virginia world renown, he wrote, "How can it be that the number of socks you enclosed scarcely ever agrees with your statement? The latest shipment contained sixty-seven pairs rather than the sixty-four you indicated."

To "My precious Agnes," he wrote, "I think of you all, separately and collectively, in the busy hours of the day and the silent hours of the night, and the recollection of each and every one whiles away the long night, in which my anxious thoughts drive away sleep. I wish indeed I could see you, be with you, and never again part from you. God only can give me that happiness. I pray for it night and day. But my prayers I know are not worthy to be heard."

Then, to Custis: "Our country demands all our strength, all our energies. To resist the powerful combination now forming against us will require every man at his place. If victorious, we have everything to hope for in the future. If defeated, nothing will be left for us to live for. My whole trust is in God, and I am ready for whatever He may ordain."

In the portion of his nightly prayers devoted to the salvation and welfare of his enemies, he devoted especial attention to Grant, Sherman, and Lincoln. "I know not whether any of them have found the grace and mercy resident only in embracing the cross of the Savior," he prayed aloud, "but I would pray, Sir, that if not, even now Thou would draw them to Thyself, to make them Thy trusted servants; and if so, that Thou would illumine them to Thy will, convict them of sin, and grow and mold them daily through the Sanctifier's fire, as Thou would with me, Thy woeful and unworthy servant."

The next morning, as dogwood blossoms perfumed the Virginia spring, Federal armies poured across Ely's and Germanna Fords, up the Shenandoah Valley, into Virginia from the southwest, and up the James against Richmond.

CHAPTER 24

THE FORCES OF U. S. GRANT AND ROBERT E. LEE CRASHED together for the first time on May 5, 1864. Seeking to utilize the tangled maze of scrub oak, pine, cedar, and secondary brush and undergrowth known as the Wilderness as a balance to the Federals' great numerical superiority in men and artillery, as he and Stonewall had done one year before over the same ground, Lee allowed Grant to cross the Rapidan uncontested, then lurked in the Wilderness, waiting for him.

Conversely Grant no more wished a fight in the Wilderness than he wished all his teeth pulled without gas. But Jeb reported back to Lee his scouts' precise positioning of the enormous invader, and Lee heaved his two available corps, of A. P. Hill (Stonewall's old nemesis) and "Old Baldy" Ewell (Stonewall's old subordinate) into the forest against the Federals. Initially surprised, the Federals later gained the initiative and mounted a series of bloody charges all afternoon and evening. Thousands on both sides fell, and the Southern lines bent, then bent some more, looking as though to break. Every time, though, they held.

They held as the sun rose on May 6. Lee had waited all the previous day for the arrival of Longstreet's corps from Gordonsville, a few miles to the west, to help the battered corps of Hill and Ewell. At 5 A.M., with Longstreet and his men nowhere in sight, the Federals opened a blistering fire all along the Confederate line, from only yards away. Suddenly the stunned, sleepy graybacks, their front jagged and unable to organize a firm, straight line in the tangled forests all about them, lurched into retreat. Amid the early-morning shadows, roiling gun smoke, and whistling bullets, Lee rode Traveller out into the middle of the road along which the oft-valiant South Carolinians of Samuel McGowan retreated.

"General McGowan," Lee cried out, shocked, "is this splendid brigade of yours running like a flock of geese?"

"General, these men are not whipped. They only want a place to form, and they will fight as well as they ever did."

Where is Longstreet? Lee wondered, recognizing trouble the likes of which he had not seen since the Federals pursued him south after Gettysburg.

"Longstreet must be here," he said to another general, the nearest thing to panic he had felt the entire war afflicting him. "Go bring him up!"

But he was not there. Lee's face grew red as speckled beams of golden sunlight pushed to be seen through the hot churning tableau.

"Oh, where can he be?" Lee muttered, breath coming hard and his chest tightening as Hill's bloody, exhausted troops retreated past, the fire from the approaching Federal attack grew louder, and bullets now began to take down men around him. His officers screamed orders, waving their sabers at shell-shocked troops who had reached the limit of their physical and mental endurance. Bugles blew, horses reared, and his artillery raked the woods in front of them, now filling with what appeared to be a swarm of blue locusts. His ears ringing from the din around him and his eyes pouring tears from the smoke that had descended like a dusk at dawn, Lee turned toward the rear, toward where he had hoped to see Old Pete approaching in all his dour, gloomy competence. *They are less than two hundred yards away,* Lee saw. *If he does not show soon, today may be the day that—*

"Git! Git you ladies!"

Who— Lee wondered.

"Clear out ladies, we're goin' thisaway, where the fight is," lanky forty-five-year-old Robbie Witherspoon, whose homestead near the tiny community of Bristol, Texas, saw more bluebonnets than people in a given year, growled, shouldering one of the fleeing Confederates out of his way.

Lee's eyes sprung wide with hope at the sight of a small cadre of lean men in hole-filled hats and colorless rags for uniforms.

"Who are you, my boys?" he cried, his heart pounding, as the group, growing now, approached him, legs churning.

"Texas boys!" Witherspoon and a score of others hollered.

As if in salute a whole battery of Confederate cannon only yards from Lee unleashed a volley that shredded a company of Federals who had emerged not more than a hundred yards down the road. So loud was the salvo that two of

Lee's officers were flung off their horses, and several others had to cling for dear life to keep from being thrown.

Hood's Texans, Lee thought with glee. *How often they have done just such a thing. Longstreet has made it.*

"Hurrah for Texas!" Lee shouted, his face lit up brighter than the July sun on that Lone Star prairie where he commanded the Second United States Cavalry those years before the war. His voice boomed so loud that it carried over the simultaneous blasts of another Confederate battery and an explosion of rifle fire from both the Northern and Southern sides. He pulled the gray hat off his tousled hair and swung it round and round like a Texas lariat. "Hurrah for Texas!"

This transfixed Taylor. *Never in the entire war have I seen him exhibit behavior remotely similar to that,* the younger man thought. So extraordinary was Lee's behavior that several other officers, knee-deep in one of the greatest firefights they had ever witnessed, and horses still bucking, stared in stunned stupor at their commander.

Lee stood up in his stirrups and hollered, "Texans always move them!"

Hearing this, Witherspoon turned to the grime-faced men of his squad and announced, "I would charge hell itself for that old man." Every man jack who heard him nodded his assent.

Then Lee shouted for them to form ranks for the countercharge. Within seconds they had and were rushing into the blinding cauldron before them that brewed and dispensed death—slow death, quick death, bloody death, and always death that ended a man's earthly life but also widowed a wife, orphaned a child, broke the heart of a family, a community, a town, maybe even a country.

They had rushed into that cauldron many times before. Never before had Lee rushed into it with them.

Oh, no, Witherspoon thought, panicked at the sight of Marse Robert, just a few men down from him at the left end of the line, high astride the great Traveller, his face glowing like a sheet of bronze, riding straight into battle with the Army of Northern Virginia!

> *The king is the land*
> *and the land is the king.*

Witherspoon could not remember being more afraid for anyone other than his wife and five younger children back home, and his four soldier sons who fought in every corner of the South, one of them already dead and another missing. "No, General Lee, no, sir!" the leather-faced frontiersman screamed, his heart in his throat.

But Lee's only fleeting thoughts on the matter, before his attention became fixed on the enemy line, were, *General Washington would have done no less . . . nor would have . . . my father . . .*

"Go back, sir!" several voices cried.

Then the voices were a chorus resounding over the tumult of battle. For they were a proud, ancient people, most of them of or molded by Anglo-Celtic stock. Those of them who did fear joined with those who did not to mock fear and pain and reveal those impostors for the laughingstocks they were. And they would fight with no less their whole heart to protect their king from peril than they would to throw themselves full into the same.

Their cheers and their charge slowed, and they shouted by hundreds, "Lee to the rear! Lee to the rear!"

One general tried to intercept Traveller, but Lee rode right through him. A major tried the same and was knocked from his horse by a ball to the skull. Witherspoon realized Lee was getting to the front of everyone. The Texan threw down his long gun and rushed after his general. They were nearly halfway to the Yankee line and lead filled the air. One bullet took off Witherspoon's hat, and another tore the bullet pouch from his hard, slender waist. With a last lunging gasp he dove for Traveller and caught the reins in one hand. The great warhorse thundered on, barely slowed and dragging Witherspoon, who held on with all his strength, trying to keep his legs clear of Traveller's. Neither master nor beast were aware of anything in creation but getting to the blue line.

Finally Venable caught Lee's reins from the other side. "General," the old veteran spoke, his voice as easy as molasses and as soothing, "you've been looking for General Longstreet. There he is, over yonder."

Stopped now, Lee turned and saw the hulking Georgian. *Ah,* he thought, returning from where he had been. He looked at Venable, then down at the sweating Witherspoon, as bullets continued to pepper the air, the roiling gun smoke their only veil. He nodded at both, drew rein, then rode away, accompanied by the volcanic roar of the men who loved him and would charge anywhere *for* him, but nowhere *with* him.

Witherspoon, charging forward through the inferno, his Rebel yell shrieking forth from that mysterious dark abyss deep in the throat that was never home to any other sound, shot one final glance back over his shoulder at Lee. The thought at that moment seizing the simple Texan sprung from the trackless, faraway American frontier was common to many another man on the long gray line that memorable day. Most could not have put it into words, though one did. But their full hearts sang it out, as to make certain future generations would never forget. As bullets and canister ripped the air and men on every side of him, knowing that every step he took might be the last he ever did, Witherspoon thought, marveling, *Never have I beheld a grander specimen of manhood. He looks as if he ought to be, and is, the monarch of the world.*

Inspired by Lee, wanting so badly not to disappoint him, not to let the old man down, the Texans did indeed move them. And the Army of Northern Virginia dealt the Federals one of their worst drubbings of the entire war, even as the Southerners stopped all the other Northern incursions into Virginia. Indeed the Confederates, just as they had been nearly the same time the year before, were on the verge of inflicting a catastrophic defeat on their foe. And just as the commander of the fateful attack had been shot down by his own men then, so did it happen again.

And all within a few miles of the precise spot.

Last year Stonewall Jackson had fallen. This time James Longstreet was shot through the neck, again by battle-seasoned Confederates. And again Lee's army won a decisive, blood-drenched victory, but not a war-altering one. And this, as Providence would have it, would be Marse Robert's last such opportunity.

Grant was stopped cold in the second day of fighting, which continued unabated from sunup to sundown and into the evening. He suffered eighteen thousand casualties in his two-day eastern debut. Lee had seventy-eight hundred.

For days the stout, cigar-chewing Federal commander had admonished his new subordinates to quit worrying about what Bobby Lee was going to do next and to start worrying about what they were going to do. Late in the evening after the second day of fighting, when his two flanks, both of whom Lee had turned, were secured, Grant went alone to his tent. There, alone, he wailed and sobbed and wept, his body shaking till Chief of Staff John Rawlins, standing not far away outside Grant's tent, began to fear for his commander's well-being.

Purged, Grant composed himself and an hour later was whittling a chunk of wood around the campfire with his staff.

The Army of Northern Virginia held its collective breath. Would Grant retreat to lick his wounds as had so many other Federal commanders? Would he attack? Would he maneuver? If so, east to Fredericksburg? Or south, toward Richmond, to Spotsylvania?

Lee eyed the brilliant thirty-one-year-old brigadier from Georgia who rode with him over the ravaged Wilderness killing grounds the next afternoon. *Young John Gordon, trim and standing tall, is proving to be one of our best generals,* he thought to himself. *And he will get even better. And with Longstreet out of action indefinitely, and both A. P. Hill and Richard Ewell ill, he had better do so.*

It seemed as though his eyes had been blind with tears for days. And he did not foresee any change in that condition until the army moved away from the Wilderness. For the smoke of musketry and cannon had given way to that of burning trees, flaming brush, and—

Yes, Gordon sees them too, Lee realized. A cluster of men, perhaps the size of an entire squad, now petrified, sat, lay, and crawled as a fresh breeze that brought with it the fragrance not of dogwood blossoms as it should have but of roasting human flesh blew through them. Last night such a breeze had blown fire over those men, and hundreds, maybe thousands, of others blue and gray, wounded, frightened, or perhaps just cornered in the wrong spot at the wrong time, all over the Wilderness. Today's breeze was disintegrating the victims' ashes and scattering them over the remnants of other dead men and horses.

"Grant is not going to retreat," Lee said, breaking a quiet that had grown morose. "He will move his army to Spotsylvania."

Gordon's eyebrows arched in surprise. He had heard no such talk from anyone at any level of the army. He himself had hoped to see Grant skedaddle like all the previous Federal commanders.

"But," he said, attempting not to stammer, "has any evidence come to us of such a move?"

"None at all," Lee replied, his voice mild. "But that is the next point at which the armies will meet. Spotsylvania is now General Grant's best strategic point." Lee knew it would situate Grant between Richmond and the Rebel troops.

Gordon could no better understand Lee's ability to divine the intentions of his adversaries than could they themselves. *And it is not as though men with no intelligence or aptitude lead the Northern armies,* he thought. Yet time and again, when events were analyzed, Confederate successes could at least in part be traced to Lee's skills of intuition.

A few hours later Jeb confirmed for Lee that indeed Grant had packed up and moved away, around the Confederate right flank, toward Spotsylvania. Jeb as much as said that he realized the news constituted no surprise for Lee, as such a movement, if successful, would place Grant between Lee's army and the Confederate capital. *A fine, smart boy he is,* Lee thought, smiling at the remembrance of the merry, cinnamon-bearded cavalier who under his command in 1859 had stormed the murderous John Brown's redoubt, captured him, and thwarted his efforts to incite a slaughter of servile insurrection across the South.

Confirmation from such a trustworthy source as Jeb Stuart did brighten Lee. But he had long since ordered Pendleton and his artillery to clear a shortcut for the Confederates through the Wilderness, so that he could be waiting for Grant when the Federals hit Spotsylvania.

"We must beat them there tired as our boys are," Lee told Taylor as they moved out, realizing how difficult it would be to do so, as the Yankees were already well down the road. "If those people gain Spotsylvania ahead of us . . ."

Taylor waited for the rest of the sentence. It never came. *The main Yankee army closing on Richmond without our aid . . .* Lee thought to himself instead.

He knew what had been attempted with Kilpatrick's little band of less than five thousand. What might happen at the hands of the entire Army of the Potomac?

◆◇ ◆◇ ◆◇

It took brilliant screening of the Federal forces by cavalry commanded by Lee's nephew Fitz, but he did beat Grant to Spotsylvania, barely. There, on May 8, Lee hastened to employ the engineering skills chiseled through years of such projects as his rerouting the Mississippi River a quarter of a century before and thus saving the frontier community of St. Louis, Missouri, from floodwater destruction. Indeed, Lee's pioneering use of trench and fortification systems was gaining worldwide notoriety in military circles.

They would, a half century later, prove the primary inspiration for the gigantic trench warfare of the First World War.

As constant a companion of Lee's as the air he breathed was the awareness that one break in his lines anywhere at any time could trigger a sequence of events ending the Confederacy as a nation within one day. He felt God had dispensed sufficient grace to him for the task, but contemplation of the fearful weight resting upon his shoulders cowed the men around him, who did not even possess the responsibility, and it kept him mindful of his utter dependence upon God, as periodically accentuated by aching arms, a pounding heart, and a constricted chest.

As Lee rode with Taylor along the fortifications that ringed Spotsylvania and its key crossroad leading to Richmond—fortifications that would stretch seven miles around—he caught sight of a short, husky black man, handsome and dressed in a gray Confederate officers' uniform as crisp and tailored as any of his own staff, replete with gleaming sidearm hanging at his waist. Lee observed the man supervising a large detail of men, both black and white, as they constructed some of the most impressive breastworks he had ever seen.

"Good day, my man," Lee said. "Fine works you have going here."

When the black man looked up and saw Lee astride Traveller—the two by now were approximately equal in fame before the people of the South, black or white—a winning smile spread across his face.

"General Lee, sir," he said, walking toward the commander. "Sergeant Jason Boone, Company K, 41st Virginia infantry, at your service. It is indeed an honor, sir," he continued, his speech nearly as articulate as Lee's, standing to attention and presenting Lee with a crisp salute.

"It appears General Grant will have a job of work ahead of him to crest these emplacements," Lee said.

The smile returned. "Ah, with the general's indulgence—the man has not ridden for Robert E. Lee that can build a better abatis than Jason Boone."

"From where do you hail, Sergeant?" Lee asked.

"Suffolk County, sir, freeborn, with forty acres and twelve young'uns—so far, sir," Boone said.

"I regret we keep you so long from your family, Boone," Lee said. "God be with you, sir."

"And you, sir," Boone replied, returning the salute, then turning back to his men. "You heard him, men. Let's get General Grant's welcome ready for him!"

"Have you heard back from the president on your latest request to free all the slaves that wish to take up arms with us?" Taylor asked as they rode along.

Lee's face screwed up just a smidgen as he nodded his head.

"I just don't understand it," Taylor said. "The Yankees have an inexhaustible supply of men, sir—white, black, European—and they never take the field unless they have us outnumbered at least two-to-one. We need men so badly, and he won't even let us arm the freedmen on an unofficial basis. And we've got fifty-seven thousand of them from Virginia alone."

"As you know, black volunteers serve in a multitude of capacities throughout the Army of Northern Virginia, some of them in the regular infantry," Lee said. "General Jackson in particular utilized them to fight—but never under compulsion, only if they volunteered. I have from reliable sources he had at least two thousand of them spread through his corps at Sharpsburg. They have proven themselves as dependable as the white soldiers. They have much for which to fight as well; we offer them freedom for their services, and as defenders of our homeland, they, too, shall hold a station of honor in the South once our independence is secured."

Lee removed his hat in response to a seemingly endless line of soldiers—blacks, parsons, and chaplains sprinkled among them, Taylor noticed—who saluted, waved, and shouted greeting to him as he passed. "The president has many responsibilities and constituencies in his capacity," Lee said. "We must remember that and exhibit a spirit of forbearance." He looked Taylor in the eye. "And I shall continue to pursue the matter with him."

They rode along for a few moments, glad for sweet spring air to breathe after the inferno of the Wilderness.

"Soon the Negroes would all have been free anyway," Lee said, sadness filling his voice. "Slavery was growing impossible to support here, financially or morally, as it did in England and other lands. But some of those people were set for a fight one way or another, slaves or no. Still we should not have allowed them to goad us into one."

What could happen when two great American armies, led by two great American war chiefs, locked in mortal combat? For it was Grant, of Fort Henry and Fort Donelson and Shiloh and Vicksburg and Chattanooga; and Lee, of the Seven Days and Second Manassas and Fredericksburg and Chancellorsville and the Wilderness. There was no room for give, and thousands of the bravest men in American history, North and South, paid the price in blood and death for the stubborn resolution that would one day make America master of the world.

Grant's thousands attacked on May ninth and again on the tenth. Still, with a vast numerical advantage in everything from guns and men to boots and hats, he who had never met his match in the west could not move Lee. The Federal guns were quiet on the eleventh, leading Lee to believe his foe was again sidling around him to the east, intending to get between him and Richmond.

But confidence filled Grant, as he chewed on his cigar, that he was one knockout blow away from disposing even more thoroughly of the Army of Northern Virginia than he had his earlier foes, and ending the Southern Rebellion. "The enemy are very shaky," he wrote Washington.

With the first rays of dawn on the twelfth arrived one of the most horrifying days in American history. Grant launched a massive assault on a vulnerable protrusion in the Confederate line called the Mule Shoe. For sixteen straight hours the two sides fought with cannon, rifle, musket, pistol, knife, and bare hands. So total was the effort of both sides that for five hundred yards in the middle of the line, only a mound of earth separated them. Men climbed atop the parapet and threw down rifles with bayonets attached like spears at one another. Soldiers reached over and dragged their enemy by the collar, by the shirt, by the hair, by the neck, across the parapet as prisoners. And they stabbed one another blindly with bayonets, swords, and knives that they rammed through small openings in the thin barrier between them.

Two ancient oaks unfortunate enough to stand in the way of America's war with itself were shot completely off the bases of their trunks a few inches above the ground, solely by bullets and minié balls. Both tree trunks were nearly two feet in diameter.

God, thought Lee, up since his normal campaign rising hour of 3 A.M., as he watched the hellish day wear on, *this horror is like watching George Pickett's assault up Cemetery Ridge last all day.* Men slipped in blood and gore that sloshed as high as their ankles, and stacked their dead comrades in piles behind them to get them out of the way so they could shoot more of the enemy. Not missing a touch on this day, the devil stirred a pouring rain into his witches' brew to complement the choking smoke and deafening din.

Seeing that the Federals had taken the Mule Shoe, now baptized by blood, water, and fire into the American chronicle and legend as the Bloody Angle, and that they were about to roll up the center of his line, Lee's face grew scarlet, and his head began to nod in its way. He removed his gray hat and turned his warhorse into the face of the surging Federal attack.

Gordon, now promoted to major general, commanded the center of the line. He saw Lee just before a bullet seared through the Georgian's coat, a half inch from his spine. Distracted a moment by that, Gordon looked back up to see his commander, Lee's chin now quaking and tears rolling down into his beard, spurring Traveller to lead the counterattack. The sight emblazoned a singular memory into Gordon that would remain with him until the day he died: *Him with uncovered head and mounted on old Traveller, he looks a very god of war.*

"General Lee!" Gordon shouted. "This is no place for you. Go back, General; we will drive them back."

A battle raged in Lee's heart between going forward and heeding his trusted lieutenant's eminently sensible advice. So great was the emotional tug-of-war and the drama of the scene that Lee burst into sobs in front of everyone. Gordon rode closer to him as a .57 caliber Enfield slug tore through the heart of a Confederate officer mounted less than ten feet away, then exploded the skull of another man on horseback just behind him, next to Lee.

"These men are Virginians and Georgians, sir," Gordon, spattered with blood, pled, a kindly current tinging his voice. "They have never failed. They never will." He turned toward the sweat-, blood-, and rain-drenched line. "Will you, boys?"

"No! No! No!" Their roar rolled through the woods and clashed with the onrushing Northern horde. Gordon stared at Lee, praying to God his commander would relent. "General Lee to the rear! General Lee to the rear!"

Lee paused. *But my boys,* he thought, his face tight with ambivalence, *they need me . . . General Wash-*

"Go back, General Lee, we can't charge until you go back!"

"We will drive them back, General!"

He still was not really convinced, but as the enemy fire mounted, knocking down more men and horses that hesitated, waiting on Lee to retire, Gordon muscled his horse between Lee and the Federals. Finally a tree bark-gnawing sergeant grabbed Traveller's reins and swung him around to the rear.

Gordon's men raced into the fusillade. Somehow they, too, knew the consequences of giving way to the Federals, and they fought with the abandon of the Scots under Bruce at Bannockburn, among which in fact were many of their own forefathers. The Federal advance was stopped.

Still, nearing 7 P.M. that night, the battle raged on. And Lee orchestrated the reinforcing of a part of the line that faced great jeopardy. But he could not stop at orchestrating. Once they were in place and hustling forward, he could not leave them. *They are too brave, fighting on with no food, hardly any water, no rest, constant terror. How could I stand safely back and send them into it yet again?* he thought. *I cannot leave them even if it costs me my very life. God's will be done.*

And so the white-haired-man-grown-old took Traveller and his lumbago and his rheumatism and his worn-out heart with him into battle, the men running with him, some hollering for him to retire, but unable this time to catch him because he rode out front of them.

Now the Federal artillery drew down on the approaching column, paying extra heed to the mounted officers in their lead. The exploding shot and blasting shell rose to such an ear-shattering hail of destruction that Traveller himself reared up once, twice, then again and again and again. Lee not only stayed firm in the saddle as a tornado of white-hot metal swirled around him, but his thoughts ran to the four-legged companion he had dragged into this inferno, and he sought to calm the terrified beast.

But Traveller, walleyed with terror, reared yet again. This time, as the animal's forelegs kicked high into the air, a solid round cannonball shrieked under his girth, between his legs, missing Lee's stirruped boot by inches, and exploding some feet away, riddling a cluster of charging, Rebel-yelling infantry.

Now another Confederate attack slowed as Lee's battle-hardened vets cried out to him, "Go back! Go back, General! For G—'s sake, go back, sir!"

His color high and his head slightly nodding, he looked down at his soldiers. "If you will promise me to drive those people from our works, I will go back."

Amazement for most of them, for this old man and his old horse and who he was and what he at that moment was again prepared to do, would not come until later, after the battle, and it would gather onto them as the years and the decades rolled along, like the gimps and stiffnesses of their old age. For now, all they would do was scream and charge and fight, heedless of whether they would live another second or another half century, if only they could hold the line for General Lee.

And hold it they did. At the cost of seven thousand casualties apiece for one day's fighting.

"I propose to fight it out on this line if it takes all summer," Grant said when he reached Spotsylvania. By the time he changed his mind, the Federal casualty total for the week had reached thirty-two thousand—the worst seven days of the war for either side. He broke off the engagement, pulled back, and again wheeled south.

But during the slaughter of Spotsylvania and the Bloody Angle, Phil Sheridan demanded to have the cavalry juggernaut he now commanded turned loose to deal its own destruction. Grant gave his approval. And so the hair-triggered Irishman, whose record of success in the west as a commander of horse had matched Grant's, announced that he was about to go "Thrash h— out of Jeb Stuart."

In the old spirit of knighthood and chivalry, Sheridan determined he would ride straight toward Jeb and draw him out in a cavalry "duel."

Not as much in that spirit was the fact that Sheridan thundered south not just to duel but for the expressed purpose of wiping Jeb Stuart and his boys from the face of the earth. And he took with him the largest cavalry force that ever rode a trail on the North American continent.

Sheridan would field nearly thirteen thousand sabers. Jeb could muster just over four thousand. And as Sheridan had slipped behind Lee's infantry, Jeb's hungry men and their crow-bait horses were all that stood between the thirteen-mile-long Federal column and Richmond, which now lay as ripe for the taking by such an overwhelming mounted force as a Georgia peach on the branch in June.

CHAPTER 25

WHEN DURING THE EVENING OF MAY 10 AGNES AGAIN HEARD THE tocsin bell ring from its loft less than two hundred yards away, she felt as though the Death Angel himself had come to pay a special call on a city that already had seen so much of him that its collective senses were growing numb. Shrunken hungry bellies had little food. The remnants of families decimated by war, famine, and pestilence had no wood for even the tiniest warming fires.

Two sorts of establishments flourished as they never before had in the history of the city: hospitals and cemeteries. Every foot of floor space not covered by furniture—and there was less and less of that that had not been consigned to the fireplaces—or people seemed now covered by wounded, maimed, or dead soldiers. And there did not seem enough earth in Hollywood, Oakwood, or any of the other cemeteries to plant the dead, so numerous were they.

For days all Richmond had quaked and prayed as the guns of war resounded a few scant miles southeast of the city. Federal General "Beast" Butler, as New Orleans Confederates referred to him for his earlier depredations of that city and its inhabitants, had steamed up the James River with a ten-mile-long force of amphibious vessels. General Pierre Beauregard, who had gained worldwide fame for his leadership at both Fort Sumter and First Manassas, stood against Butler. Beauregard was outnumbered ten to one.

And was it possible the despised Federal cavalry, which only two months before had come so close to obliterating the city and its government, could now be sweeping down from the north?

"Can General Stuart stop this Sheridan?" Mary, never looking up from her sewing, asked Custis as he prepared to return to his office in the capital after a scanty supper with his family.

So slow was Custis to answer that Mary at length joined Agnes, Mildred, and Mary Custis in fixing her eyes on him for his answer.

"Yes," Custis said. "General Stuart will stop him."

Mary knew her eldest son, and she knew when his words were more prayer than declaration.

●◇ ●◇ ●◇

Ethan and Culpeper wheeled into a too-familiar setting. A farm with blasted fields, slaughtered animals and fowl littering barns and dooryard, no men, and half-starved women and children and, in some cases, slaves. This particular home housed a thirty-four-year-old mother who looked twenty years older and three scrawny children under the age of twelve. Two others had died since April 1861.

Ethan, back in action as a field-ranked lieutenant, had been dispatched by Hampton to scout the movements of Sheridan's column. As he dismounted in front of the dilapidated farmhouse, he winced at the jarring pain in his still-tender shoulder and mumbled, to no one in particular, "Leastways Little Phil makes it easy to follow him."

Culpeper, tabbed by Ethan to accompany him and sporting a new buckskin shirt with a broad leather belt, both gifted him through the unrequited regard of his devoted nurse, knew what he meant. All day and all the day before they had followed the billowing smoke of structures great and small, and the endless trail of ruined stock left in its wake.

"Ma'am," Ethan said to the mother, removing his hat. "Have you a ladle of water for our canteens and a gobful of green corn for our poor mounts? We've assuredly been tracking Little Phil Sheridan for two days and nights now for General Stuart—" He saw only hollow sets of eyes staring back at him. "—and I'm guessing you've seen them since we have."

Culpeper did not look any of them in the eyes. If he had thought on the matter, which he did not, he would have realized that he looked fewer and fewer people in the eye the longer this war continued. Instead he gnawed his leafy cud, swallowed, and gazed around the dooryard. He counted a half dozen slashed and dead chickens, scrawny though they were. Not far beyond a rickety old field fence lay three emaciated and very dead cattle—*That white one was their milk cow,* he guessed—each of them hacked to death. The cows, and the legions of flies buzzing about them, were visible from where Culpeper stood because nothing grew in the fields but weeds and pine saplings.

"Them Yankees said they poisoned our water well because we didn't tell them where General Stuart was," the mother rasped. When she spoke, the jaundiced toddler in her arms, who had heretofore been asleep, roused and began to wail for food. "Think they was jestin', but it's sure enough hard to tell with folks that would . . ." Her gaze drifted around the dooryard and out into the fields.

Ethan felt ashamed even to be asking for water from this family. He pursed his lips and glanced toward Culpeper. The latter's face—leathery-brown and bearded, the limpid green eyes dead—betrayed no more than did the dust a moderate breeze kicked up from the field.

Ethan paused, then pulled his canteen, still one-third full, down from his horse and walked to the well. He drew up some water, sniffed it, tasted it, then filled his empty canteen with it. Then he drank deeply from the wooden gourd. Culpeper's eyes came alive. *What the—,* he thought.

Ethan walked back to his horse. He pulled something out of his haversack and handed it to the lady. Her fingers riffled open the small newspaper-wrapped packet to find four hard biscuits. Their genesis as flour and water mixed to dough and fried in bacon fat rendered them no less precious to her than had they been lush cuts of prime rib of beef. Her eyes opened as wide as Culpeper's—who knew Ethan had just forfeited the entirety of his rations for the next two days—and darted to Ethan's.

"Sir—" she began.

He was already back in the saddle, ignoring the hole Culpeper's angry eyes bore through him. "We've no sleep in the last forty-eight hours," he said, turning his gaunt mount's head away with the reins. "We'll rest in the trees behind your place so as not to draw trouble for you from the Yanks. Corporal Culpeper here will let you know if I take sick in the three hours before we move on. If not, the well is probably safe."

The woman had not thought she still had tears to shed, not since the second child died the day after she received word her husband had been killed at Bristoe Station. To her surprise, she learned she did in fact have at least the few she felt running down her cheeks as her infant wailed in her arms.

◦◇ ◦◇ ◦◇

A lot more Confederate soldiers would miss some "meals" after Sheridan torched Beaver Dam Station, thirty miles northwest of Richmond, along with fully one quarter of the entire rail stock owned by the Virginia Central Railroad—and half a million bread rations and nearly one million meat rations.

How will I feed them now, Lee moaned within himself, *with our corrupt*—he caught himself—*our inefficient commissary?*

Jeb knew that worse than this was the reality looming should he not be able to catch Sheridan before the Federals stormed into Richmond. He pushed his men and their horses to the limits of their endurance to catch up, all the while knowing in the back of his battle-seasoned mind the Yankee was likely moving on Richmond only to force the Confederate horse to confront him for one last-man-standing showdown. Still he had no choice, because he knew Sheridan was capable of galloping with his thousands all the way into the capital if the man chose to do so, and Jeb had no idea what he would do after he got there.

While his men ate nearly the last of their rations on the morning of May 10, Jeb rode past the still-roaring fires of Beaver Dam Station. The blaze offered searing testimony of what Sheridan had done behind Jeb's own lines. Anger, fear, and hurt pride combined against the Virginian. And he remembered that one year ago this very day God had summoned home his brother Stonewall. Nonetheless, Sheridan or no Sheridan, Richmond or no Richmond, he would see his wife and remaining children, staying at the house of a friend just four or five miles away.

Jeb's thoughts as he rode toward Flora were of how blessed he had been by God to have her. She had loved him and supported him through everything. Through the long, lonely years he served out west as an officer in the U.S. Cavalry. Through the rupture between him and her own father, who had forsaken Virginia to command Federal cavalry, and whom Jeb had sworn to kill on sight. Through the loss of little Flora, whom he named for the woman he loved so much he wanted another one of her.

Little Flora, his *la petite* . . . he still could not think of her without his throat tightening. His wife had sent word to Jeb while he was in the field the previous autumn that the little girl, who was the greatest treasure of his whole life, was mortally ill. "Please come to her," his wife begged. But Jeb had not. How could he have, when to leave would have heightened the prospects of defeat and a life he would be ashamed to leave for his children?

And so little, sweet Flora, who at age five already knew half her entire catechism, who personally cared for every sick, small animal within five miles of her home, and whose "Da-da" was her singular hero, had died without Jeb. He gulped at the remembrance, and a sob tried to escape his throat. He punched his horse with his shiny golden spurs, which he rarely did. *I must get quickly to my wife,* he thought, a mist filming his eyes.

By the time he reached the farm, he had been riding at a full gallop for five miles, and his lean charger was panting and lathered. All the while, as if it were a curse hung round about his neck like an albatross, was the pounding realization that every moment he detoured, Sheridan got closer and closer to Richmond, whose commander, Bragg, had begged Jeb to hold the Yankees off at least long enough so Beauregard could send reinforcements.

Indeed the entire war for independence could go up in the smoke of a flaming Richmond if Sheridan got to the capital and then marooned a starving Lee out in the field with no government or hope of resupply. But something compelled him to drive on. *I must see her,* he thought. *I must not miss another.* . . . He would not think of that.

There she is, he thought, a smile crossing his face when he spotted the familiar auburn tresses dancing about her shoulders as she hastened down the front steps, positioning her skirts.

How lovely she is, he thought, galloping right to her and marveling that she could be more radiant even than on that long-ago Kansas prairie where he met her, courted her with her father's permission, and wedded her—all within two weeks. *How I wish I had time to write her a poem,* he thought with regret, *but I have no time even to climb down from my saddle.*

And then he was leaning way down to her, limber and agile despite the broad, muscled expanse of his upper body, and he was wrapping one arm around her while the other kept the reins, not thinking that that was how it had always been—one arm embracing Flora, the other the cavalry. They kissed long and with much love, not saying even one word, for so much had always been said between them from so far away without words, save the oceans of rhyme and verse he poured forth on paper for her eyes and heart alone. Yet no fair maiden ever graced the environs of the Southland who felt more secure, complete, and requited love—and this from a man over whom all Southern womanhood seemed to fawn and swoon, and a man who reveled in their attention, their waltzes and reels, and most of all in his happy innocent banter with them.

Then the baby, Virginia Pelham, was in his arms and he was kissing her, and he was reaching down to shake five-year-old son Jemmie's hand, and then he was again kissing his Flora and smelling the feminine scents that had first pulled him down off his horse in 1855 and that made him want to even now.

Never had her unpainted lips felt softer or tasted sweeter—sweeter they were than the taste of life itself, of which he had always feasted with so full a heart.

"I love you," were all the words he could get out without bursting into tears or climbing down, in which case he feared he might be hours getting back into the saddle.

She knew how much more those three little words meant because she knew that the merry cavalier the South loved and the fearsome warrior the North dreaded was, after all, Scots-Irish, and thus imbued with the singular touch of gloom possessing that spirited Celtic race.

As he rode away, she remembered the words he had once written her and by which he lived—and might perhaps die: "I, for one, though I stood alone in the Confederacy without countenance or aid, would uphold the banner of Southern Independence as long as I had a hand left to grasp the staff, and then die, before submitting."

Flora reached up and grabbed the pommel of Jeb's chief of staff McClellan. "Please, Henry," she implored, her green eyes blurred with tears, "do take care of him."

McClellan looked at her for a minute, a jumble of thoughts vying to win their way to his lips. "These last two days he has talked much of you and of what you mean to him," he said, his words chopped and full of emotion. He saluted her, then rode off.

Indeed, though McClellan knew how much Jeb loved his wife and family, this sojourn somewhat baffled him, especially now that it appeared virtually impossible that they could catch Sheridan before he reached Richmond.

"Mama," Mildred said the next morning, May 11, 1864, as she rushed into the drawing room–turned–sewing factory where Mary sat surrounded by women with nimble fingers and worried hearts. "Custis says General Stuart cut Sheridan off just six miles north of the city, and he says that his men are tired, hungry, and jaded, but they are all right."

A chorus of relieved sighs filled the room, and someone whispered, "Praise God." But just then the sunlight beaming in through the window gave way to an enormous bank of dark clouds rolling in from the north. Mary stared at her daughter, judging the glow of the girl's smile to be a trace bright. Sure enough, after a moment, the smile began to crack around the edges, and Life's voice with it. Then she was sobbing and hurrying out of the room past Agnes, who had now entered.

Agnes crossed to her mother, her steps soft as a cat's, and handed her a flyer a boy had passed to her on the street.

> The enemy are undoubtedly approaching the city, and may be expected at any hour, with a view to its capture, its pillage, and its destruction. The strongest consideration of self and duty to the country calls every man to arms! All persons able to wield a musket will immediately assemble upon the public square.

The notice was signed by Virginia Governor William "Extra Billy" Smith.

"Custis told me the Yankees have cut the railroads south and that all the congressmen are scrambling to find horses on which to escape," Agnes said, her voice devoid of expression.

For a long moment silence filled the room. It was broken only when the sullen growl of cannon began to echo from a new direction—north. A couple of women in the room gasped. Agnes and her mother looked at each other. For once Mary, now looking up to where she heard Mildred's steps against the floor above, seemed uncertain what next to do. Agnes leaned over, held her mother in her arms, and kissed her on the forehead.

"I'll take Mildred back to church with me to pray again," she whispered as the roar of Sheridan and Stuart grew more ferocious. When she stood up, she saw tears in her mother's eyes, which she had never witnessed since the war began. But Agnes knew her mother, and she knew the tears were for Mildred, that Mary could not do more to comfort her youngest child, yet seventeen years old.

Jeb had reached the ancient abandoned stagecoach inn called Yellow Tavern around 8 A.M. that morning. And despite his visit to Flora and the children, he had employed hard riding and hard praying to reach it before anyone else in either the Confederate or Federal cavalry. All he had to throw against the Federals was Fitz Lee's two brigades; despite Sheridan's force looming three times the size of his own, he had ordered half his own cavalry to continue supporting and working for Lee's infantry up north.

He soon had his men dismounted and dispersed in a concave, or semi-V, formation, along a ridge on one wing, connected with the Telegraph Road on the other. That way he prevented Sheridan from either overwhelming him with numbers through a straight-on charge or from rushing past him.

Jeb had eaten nothing for two days. The act of feeding himself had grown increasingly difficult as the legions of half-starved men, horses, and civilians surrounding him grew with each passing day. After forming his men, he dismounted for a few seconds to relieve himself. Something caught his eye. He blinked to make certain he was seeing right. *Yes, there it is, right there, on the ground,* he thought in amazement. One of the largest, shiniest, juiciest-looking burgundy apples he had ever seen. *But how could you have escaped detection from these thousands of hungry fellows?* he asked the fruit as he lifted it from the ground. Already his mouth watered. No one could see him or the apple. No one except for his horse, who alerted him to that fact with a heartfelt nicker.

Shame flooded over him. *Yes, it is no mistake this lush fruit has fallen before me, for Thou hast blessed me with grace to receive the blessing of giving it to another,* he thought, his hunger replaced in an instant with contentment and joy. He walked to the animal, to whom he owed so much, to this animal and many more before him, some of them shot, some sabered, some shelled, *others just run into the ground and an early death while fame and fortune festooned me all about,* he thought, not now feeling like a very big man at all. *How many of you have we and this war hurt?*

So starved and deprived was the horse that Jeb did not even play around with it and the apple like he would have in happier times. He smiled and sweet-talked the animal and stroked its neck as it drooled its joy and chomped the apple down.

"Now you must put your delicious breakfast to good use and help me against General Sheridan," he said, squeezing and scrunching the horse's soft nose the way it loved to be tickled, then kissing the side of its face.

A few minutes later the Federals, firing spanking new seven-shot Spencer repeaters against the Confederates' single-shot mélange of muskets, rifles, and old smooth bores, slammed into them. For hours the battle joined off and on, here and there, as Sheridan probed for the weakest spot in Jeb's outmanned line, which was also outgunned three to one.

McClellan pestered Jeb all day long to stay out of the line of fire. Jeb would smile, then instead send his young subordinate out of harm's way with another in a series of messages to someone farther back in the lines. So unnecessary did some of them seem to McClellan that he grew convinced Jeb was actually trying to keep *him* beyond the range of the Yankee guns.

When the young man returned anew around midafternoon, so somber was his countenance that Jeb inquired what was the matter. McClellan did not wish to speak of it.

"Now, Henry, my good man," Jeb said, his eyes all dancing. "We may hold up both these armies and this entire war if we must, but I shall know the genesis of the tragedy that has befallen your face."

This did not provoke laughter in McClellan as normally it would have, but it did elicit a response from him.

"Are we to stand here, sir?"

"We shall stand as long as we are able, my friend," Jeb replied.

McClellan shifted in his saddle. "But sir, they are far too many for us, they are carrying Spencers, their horses are fit and fed. Why do you smile, General Jeb?"

"Why, Henry McClellan," Jeb said, his face dropping in mock disappointment, "and you, coming from such a splendid family, with such a fine education and all."

Now a look of perplexity gathered over McClellan's features.

"Raised with the Holy Bible and the catechism and the Prayer Book, even," Jeb continued, mischief alive somewhere in his face—perhaps nestled in or behind the cinnamon beard now grown thick as a briar patch. "And yet you have forgotten that if only you will fear God, you shall have nothing else to fear!"

McClellan did not know whether to laugh, cry, or cheer, so he just smiled and said, with meaning, "Thank you, sir."

Around four o'clock Sheridan believed he had found his weak point, and he flung Custer's Michigan Wolverines at the Confederate left. This did it, overwhelming that section of defenders and sending them into retreat. Even then, Jeb, the commanding general, had anticipated the trouble and had outraced his entire staff to the spot.

"Sir, you must not expose yourself so," McClellan, just returned, cried out as Jeb rode forward, nine-shot LeMatt revolver in hand, black plume fluttering, and scarlet silk-lined cape flowing in the breeze.

"I don't reckon there is any danger," Jeb said, his eyes twinkling like the old days. But he was thinking about Bragg's plaintive missive that noted without a forestalling of Sheridan's rampaging legions, the Confederates would not have enough time to get their reinforcements across the James from Petersburg to protect Richmond. *God, Sir, please help us to hold them off a bit longer,* he prayed.

Suddenly from up the road, where Custer and his men had advanced, a fearsome firefight exploded. *That's close up,* Jeb thought, turning in that direction as thunderstorm clouds rolled in overhead atop the choking mountains of gun smoke, *pistol to pistol, saber to saber—hand to hand.* He held his breath, knowing if Custer was not stopped, the whole Southern line would probably be rolled up and chopped to pieces. He did not want to think what might evolve after that.

After a few minutes he saw—emerging out of the smoke from the direction of the fight—riders in headlong retreat. *But what color are they?* he wondered, straining his eyes, desperate to know.

"They're Yanks, sir," McClellan called.

"Yiiiii-ahhhyyy!" Jeb shouted the Rebel yell like he had never before shouted it, joy and relief and pride in the First Virginia cavalry regiment filling him with energy and purpose. He rode to the fence that separated him from the road along which Custer had attacked.

"Here they come!" someone shouted. Now the bluecoats were riding in the opposition direction of Richmond, as fast as their terrified mounts could carry them. Into a gauntlet of fire they galloped as a row of Confederates rushed to the fence, packing pistols, muskets, and shotguns, which they poured into the enemy passing right to left before them.

"Steady, men, steady!" Jeb shouted as he leveled his revolver, his tall charger steady under him, and began to fire into the fleeing throng, which now included men on foot who had been shot off their horses or had them shot out from under them. "Give it to 'em, boys!" One after another he knocked them down, finally loosing the LeMatt's trump card, a single roaring .20 gauge blast, the shooting eye that had never failed him since he was a boy proving true as ever. *I think perhaps we have given Bragg the time he needed,* Jeb thought, lowering his empty revolver to reload as the Yankees flooded by in disarray, falling like tenpins.

Then he felt a searing pain in his midsection. Jeb knew at once he was shot, for he had been shot before, in the chest by a Cheyenne out West before the war. Still it stunned him, and as he grabbed his right side, his head fell forward, the big cavalry hat pitching to the ground, plume and all.

"General, are you hit?" McClellan cried out.

"I'm afraid I am," Jeb replied, his tone calm and steady. He tried to shake off the wound and rise back to his normal riding posture, but the pain and shock threatened to topple him from the saddle, especially when his horse, smoke burning its nostrils, and knowing something was terribly wrong, began to buck and plunge.

One of his officers grabbed the animal's bit and reins, and another helped Jeb down and got him seated on the ground with his back up against a big oak. McClellan pulled away the yellow sash, then gasped along with the other gathered officers. The spreading crimson stain told the tale: Jeb was shot in the liver.

"Don't worry, boys," he said, grimacing in pain as he perceived the panic on his men's faces. "Fitz will do as well for you as I have done."

Within minutes, that man, Lee's nephew, pounded up, leapt from his horse, and found Jeb's side.

Jeb, still wearing his snow-white doeskin gloves, laid a gentle hand on Fitz's shoulder, fearing the man would burst into tears. "Now you go take charge of the field," Jeb said with a smile. When Fitz started to protest, he said, "We need you. I need you to do that as I know you are able." Then, seeing the tears welling up and spilling out of Fitz's eyes, he patted his shoulder. "Go ahead, old fellow, I know you'll do what is right."

Fitz sprung to his feet, raced to his horse, swung into the saddle, and looked back once at Jeb. He started to speak, but his quaking chin persuaded him against it, and he spurred his mount hard and raced away.

At almost the same instant, from a different direction, an ambulance pulled up, peppered every step of the way by Federal bullets. As his men lifted Jeb into the wagon, the pain so seared his insides that he thought he would pass out. He clenched his teeth together to keep from screaming.

"Will you be all right, sir?" one young aide asked, his ashen face rent with emotion.

"Well, I don't know how this will turn out," Jeb said, "but if it's God's will that I shall die, I'm ready."

As the vehicle began to bounce away, every jolt a saber slashing through him, Jeb heard one of his officers exclaim to another, "We've got to get this ambulance out of here. Custer is reforming, and he'll be on us any minute."

Jeb looked up and saw a group of exhausted Confederates fleeing the field. Ignoring the hideous pain inflaming him, he sat straight up as bullets flew all around him, summoned all the strength of voice he had, and screamed, "Go back, men! Go back and do your duty as I have done, and our country will be safe." Somehow, over the din of battle, through the roiling smoke, and in spite of their rattled mental state, a number of the refugees heard his voice, slowed, and turned toward him as he continued. "Go back! Go back! I had rather die than be whipped!"

Unable to stay up any longer, Jeb collapsed. He thought if he prayed he might curtain out some of the pain and at the same time keep his wits about him. First on his mind to pray for were those men. *My poor, poor boys,* he thought, poignant sentiments filling him for them. Despite his wound, he had seen their faces—hungry, tired to the brink of collapse, frightened, and out-numbered. *Always outnumbered,* he thought. They had stood all they could. *Gracious heavenly Father,* he implored, *strengthen them to stand just a bit longer, or whatever is needed to give our people time to defend Richmond.* He wished he had his Prayer Book or Bible, just to hold against him through this journey of torture, but praying did seem to help.

Suddenly the volume of gunfire increased. Custer was mounting another charge, and Jeb's ambulance was right in its path. The escalating din hurting his ears despite his wooziness signaled the arrival of more trouble, but Jeb knew he could do nothing but pray the harder . . . *"The Lord is my shepherd, I shall not want. He maketh me to lie down in green pastures . . ."*

Fitz Lee had spoken few words to his men, but so heartfelt had they been that as the news of Jeb's wounding rushed through the two beset brigades, the Virginians regained their hearts and determined to go down as their captain had, to the last man, if that be what it took to stand against Sheridan.

A squad of them, seeing a whole segment of Custer's line heading straight for Jeb's ambulance, swooped between it and them, firing at the Yankees as they rode. On came the whooping bluecoats, confident as they had not been earlier in the war. One, then another of the Confederates fell, then another, and another, and another. One tumbled to the ground when his horse was killed. He came up shooting, even though he was now out of the line of fire as the ambulance and its pursuers receded into the distance. He emptied two Yankee saddles with his Colt before one of Custer's Wolverines, unseen, sabered him.

Finally only one Confederate rode between the ambulance and the Federals. He was eighteen years old. He wore rags for clothing and had emptied his bowels four times since dawn—if his daily average held out, he would have four more trips before sleeping. His left shoulder and right thigh had already been pierced by Yankee slugs. Weighing all of one hundred and twenty-five pounds, he felt faint and started to swoon as another bullet tore into his exhausted horse's left hindquarter. He knew the trail was nearly at its end for both him and his mount, so he determined to sell his life as dearly as he could, in hopes that Jeb Stuart, who alone had given hope to his otherwise dark and lonely life, whom he loved like the father he had never known, might somehow still be gotten to safety.

He tossed his empty revolver aside, swung the horse around, drew his sword from its scabbard, and rode straight at the dozen Federals that still pursued, the Rebel yell shrieking from his throat.

Shocked, the Yankees broke in all directions, two of their horses colliding and tumbling with their riders to the earth. The young Confederate swung the saber like a scythe on harvest day, taking down one Federal, then another, and chasing after a third before two others got their pistols trained and emptied their chambers into him.

He was dead before he hit the ground, but the remaining pursuers realized that the bullet-riddled ambulance had nearly reached the outermost line of Richmond defenses. Uttering oaths, they turned and headed back toward Yellow Tavern.

So savagely did the remnants of Jeb's men fight that after another hour of fighting and trying to divine a new point in the Rebel line to exploit, Sheridan gazed up toward the blackening sky out of which thunder rumbled and lighting flashed. No darker was the sight overhead than the mood his aides saw coming over him as he contemplated his next move. Just then a courier came pounding up. Sheridan ripped open the missive and read it. A Rebel dispatch had been captured, which indicated that significant reinforcements had been sent for from Richmond. He growled and, only after another peal of thunder, ordered his men to break loose of "this obstinate contest."

He did not know Jeb was down, but he knew he was getting nowhere on this field, and that more problems were quite possibly headed straight toward him. The destruction of Jeb Stuart's cavalry would have to wait until another day after all.

Sheridan was not happy about that, but his disappointment was mitigated by his next decision. That was the order for his entire force to head straight south down the Brook Turnpike as the heavens began to unleash a torrent of rain and the wind grew to such ferocity that it blew over whole trees.

Phil Sheridan was headed to Richmond.

CHAPTER 26

IT SEEMED AS THOUGH THE VERY JUDGMENT OF GOD HAD COME crashing down on them. Agnes feared that at any moment the huge stained-glass windows behind and above the chancel area would burst from the wind and fly into a million pieces about the sanctuary of Saint Paul's. More light danced into the enormous room from the fulguration through the stained glass than was provided by the few candles spaced along the walls. The Yankee blockade had left Richmond no more tallow for candles than it had any other supplies. And it had been years since the church had had fuel for its gas lamps.

When the storm grew so loud Agnes could no longer concentrate to pray and when the freakish swings of air pressure began to blow out the candles, her eyes looked upward. *Dear God in heaven,* she thought, clasping her hands, *perhaps after all Thou art allowing the prince of darkness to come against us.* After all, it seemed as though all the elements of nature had conspired to war against this monument to God's presence on earth. And could more be at work in the extinguishing of the candles than wind and air currents? *Father, I must know that Thou art still there,* she pleaded. A series of brilliant flashes through the stained glass illumined the wall above them, just below the ceiling that arched majestically over her. Only a second or two and the verses painted into the wall were burned into her mind. "Peace I leave with you, my peace I give unto you."

A wave of gratitude swept over her. Whatever was in the process of happening, in here, outside, or out in the city in whatever directions the Yankees were now threatening, God would remind her that He had not forsaken her. She would perhaps not yet be ready to believe that as she once had, but she would believe it for tonight, for this hour, for now.

Something, evidently very large, smashed outside, and she and Mildred and many others in the sizable throng drew in their breaths as one. A moment later Dr. Minnigerode announced during a lull in the storm's fury of perhaps

254

thirty seconds that the entire magnificent steeple at Saint John's Church some blocks to the east had been blown off the building!

Agnes and Mildred looked at one another.

"Mama!" they exclaimed in unison.

Sliding out from their usual seats in pew 111, on the tenth row of the left center downstairs section, next to the left aisle, they rushed out of the building, down the wide steps, right onto Ninth Street, and downhill the one block to Franklin. *Heavens,* Agnes thought, looking up through the lightning-illumined sheets of rain at the tocsin bell tower to her left, *it is ringing again. What—who—comes against this benighted city now?* They continued back uphill the block and a half to home.

They found Mary in her wheelchair in the downstairs sitting room, a letter in her hand and tears in her eyes.

"Oh, what will my poor husband do?" she mumbled, not seeming to notice how her dripping daughters were soaking the hardwood floor. "It seems God has turned His face from us."

Agnes took the letter and read, girding herself for more sad news from the front.

My Precious Annie,

I take advantage of your gracious permission to write to you, and there is no telling how far my feelings might carry me were I not limited by the conveyance furnished by the Mim's letter, which lies before me, and which must, the Mim says so, go in this morning's mail. But my limited time does not diminish my affection for you, Annie, nor prevent my thinking of you and wishing for you. I long to see you through the dilatory nights. At dawn when I rise, and all day, my thoughts revert to you in expressions that you cannot hear or I repeat. I hope you will always appear to me as you are now painted on my heart, and that you will endeavour to improve and so conduct yourself as to make you happy and me joyful all our lives. Diligent and earnest attention by you and Agnes to all your duties can only accomplish this. I am told you are growing very tall, and I hope very straight. Write sometimes, and think always of your

Affectionate father,
R. E. Lee

"Oh, Mama," Agnes said, moved.

"It's just that our children are all so very important," Mary said, "every one of them, even—" Now she choked up. "—even they who are gone." Her head bowed, and Agnes saw her body begin to tremble from the silent sobs now overtaking her. "So very, very important," she said softly.

Agnes saw a pile of freshly knitted socks stacked into a box on the floor next to Mary. A wave of affection for "The Mim," as coined by Lee, swept over her. *With all that she has suffered, she can be very difficult at times,* Agnes thought, *but so shamed I am with myself when I behold how much she cares for others; how much she does for others.* She put her arm around her mother. Mary felt as if she was on fire.

"Why, Mama," Agnes exclaimed, "how warm you are." Agnes placed a hand against Mary's forehead. "I believe you have a fever, Mama. We must get you to bed right now."

Terror so gripped Agnes's heart as she swung the wheelchair around and shoved it toward Mary's room that she felt she might be nauseous. *No, God, please,* she thought, *no, I can't bear it if Thou were to let anything happen to her now. Yet how can we do anything for her no matter what ails her? The Yankee blockade has left us bereft not only of medicine but of all the foods she is already in such need of—milk, fresh fruits, and vegetables—how can I even hope to help her? Oh, let my heart remain dead, Father, for I fear if Thou were to breathe life back into it, it would be filled to overflowing with the poison of hate.*

Not rain or wind or lightning or even Jeb Stuart could stop Sheridan and his mounted hosts. They thundered through the thin light and the downpour and over the outer Richmond defensive lines. They galloped on to the intermediate fortifications. There the fire increased, and the tocsin bell rang on like a mournful siren tolling the entrance into hell—just as it had only two months before when Kilpatrick rode to the same point and felt the same hesitation as he, too, stood on the brink of a breathtaking opportunity.

Silently Sheridan cursed himself for allowing Jeb—and his own pride—to tangle him up in an all-day fight that had apparently accomplished nothing except to give the Rebels time to rally their defense forces and daylight to disappear.

256

When he reined in his horse, he stood three miles from the capitol building of the Confederate States of America. *Ah, to have back that time!* he thought to himself. *Still, even now I can be the hero of the hour. I can go in and burn and kill right and left. Yes! But at what cost? Stuart no doubt sent additional couriers with news of our advance. Who and what awaits us? And who might close on us from behind if we tarry in the city?* He gauged that the storm seemed to be relenting but the light with it. *And withal, for what permanent advantage will be our sacrifice?*

Thus did the blood poured out by Jeb Stuart and his men—and perhaps the prayers of frightened women, children, old folks, and maimed in churches all over Richmond, many of which lost windows or suffered other damage, and one its steeple—provide the final balance that weighted the scales toward the reprieve of the city from possibly being transformed into one enormous bloody slaughterhouse, the horror of which could scarcely be conceived of by the American mind.

Sheridan had disrupted the plans of many Virginians over the past few days. One of them was John Wilkes Booth. His theatrical performance in Richmond this night had been canceled due to the alarm caused by the Yankee cavalry. Instead he sat in the dining room of the Spottswood Hotel and, amid the repeated intrusions of fawning admirers, read a set of *New York Times* and *New York Tribune* editions he had brought back with him from a recent performance tour up north.

Booth enjoyed the climate of intrigue at the Spottswood, an establishment now "as thoroughly identified with Rebellion as the inn at Bethlehem with the gospel." It amused rather than irritated him that here, "everything likely and unlikely is told you—and then everything is as flatly contradicted."

Tonight, however, he was not amused at all. As the storm raged, the tocsin bell clanged, and all Richmond held its breath, expecting that each moment might be the one that saw the Yankee marauders stampede into the city, he read, as had Mary Lee previously, the published editorial position of one of the United States' greatest newspapers: "The Rebel Calumny on Colonel Dahlgren."

After the horror the Yankees attempted to inflict on the defenseless population of Richmond, and after the swath of plunder and destruction they succeeded in leaving in their wake, their military, their press—and likely now their entire population, Booth groused to himself—*disavow any plans to burn the Confederate capital or harm the leaders of our government.*

Not only that, but the *Times* was publicly accusing the Confederates of forging the portions of the Dahlgren papers relating to such crimes, then attempting to pin their actions on the Federals!

Only with the approval of that backwoods baboon who dragged us into this unending nightmare could such infamy have been—and continue to be—allowed, Booth thought, venom filling him like never before. *To countenance such crimes, themselves only a continuation of their perpetrators' previous prosecution of the war, is in itself an evil scarcely fathomable by civilized people. But to then attempt to blame the intended victims of prevaricating the whole enterprise!*

Yes, he thought, the inhumanity of war further hardening his heart as it was millions of others, *it is Abraham Lincoln, he who considers me his favorite actor, upon whose head the guilt rests. Someone should return upon him and his mercenary horde of Black Republican pirates the evil they have visited on so many others.*

Because Sheridan had the Brook Turnpike, Jeb's ambulance had to travel by bumpy, sometimes slippery, back roads. He endured six hours of agony before the exhausted mules pulled the vehicle up in front of the home of Dr. Charles Brewer, whose wife was Flora's sister. Brewer lived a few blocks west of the capitol on Grace Street, between Jefferson and Madison Streets.

A tortured ride it had been for Jeb, and a tortured night lay ahead for him. He prayed to God for the strength to endure the pain that seared his insides, the fire that would not relent. As they carried him inside, the fragrance of a run of yellow roses wafted into his nostrils. So sweet was the aroma, so refreshing the respite from his suffering, that he nearly began to cry out of gratitude to God for the unexpected blessing, and in renewed appreciation of how marvelous a Creator was the Almighty.

Because Sheridan had torn down the telegraph lines north, Flora did not receive word of Jeb's wounding till after he arrived in Richmond. She had been the wife of a soldier for nearly ten years. She had known that nearly every day of that ten years could be his last on earth. Still, when news of his Yellow Tavern wound came, she had to sit and compose herself so that she would not lose control and descend into a fit of screaming. She did not know if she could bear losing Jeb after already having lost little Flora, but she prayed for God to carry her through whatever lay ahead.

●◇ ●◇ ●◇

Like his comrade Stonewall Jackson, piercing and prolonged pain beset Jeb. And as with Stonewall, Jeb's patient and manly endurance of it did not go unnoticed by those gathered around him.

Just after sunup the growl of guns to the north seemed to spark Jeb out of the mental funk which had beset him throughout the long pain-racked night. Members of the capital garrison and Fitz Lee's horse had ambushed Sheridan, attempting to keep him from getting away to the Yankee lines to the east.

"God grant that they may be successful," Jeb said, looking heavenward. With a resignation previously unseen in him by any in the room, he added, "But I must be prepared for another world."

Then into the room walked the President of the Confederate States of America, Jefferson Davis. His face grave and careworn from his many concerns and the recent loss of his own treasured son, he gently clasped Jeb's hand.

"General, how do you feel?" Davis asked.

Jeb, his ashen face brightening, managed a bit of a smile. He replied, "Easy, sir, but willing to die if God and my country think I have fulfilled my destiny and done my duty."

Jeb could not miss the feeling and affection for him resident in Davis. The president stayed for about fifteen minutes; the words he spoke were few but heartfelt and choice as "apples of gold and settings of silver." As he rose to leave, the tall Mississippian's eyes filled with tears, and he could only smile at Jeb, for the sobs fighting for release from his throat prevented him from speaking. After all, how could a president weep in the presence of those who looked to him for strength and leadership in such dark days?

●◇ ●◇ ●◇

Davis would weep for a very long time in the privacy of his room when he reached it, both for his dead son and for the brave boy, Jeb Stuart. *Too many such brave boys have we lost,* he thought, remembrance of how long had grown that roll of honor somehow having become a weight singularly shouldered by him. The spidery lines multiplying across his rugged face offered mute testament to his burden.

Because Sheridan controlled portions of the railroad, Flora was prevented from what could have been a train journey of less than an hour. All night and into the morning, the couriers sent to help her attempted to guide her the twenty-five miles to her sister's Grace Street home. With Jemmie and the baby in tow, she traveled the rail a ways by handcar. When friendly tracks ended, a wagon was found for the wife and children of Jeb Stuart. But because Sheridan had the major roads, they had to detour for miles out of their way. At times all that preserved Flora's coherent process of thought was the presence of her confused children, whom she clutched to herself as though never to let them go.

Henry McClellan arrived in time to receive Jeb's instructions for the dispersal of his property, most all of it to his wife, with his two horses to McClellan and another staff officer.

"You will find in my hat a small Confederate flag," Jeb said, "which a lady of Columbia, South Carolina, sent me, with the request that I would wear it upon my horse in a battle and then return it to her. Send it to her."

How Flora will giggle when she hears of it, he thought, trying to ignore a new paroxysm of pain and noting the twinkle in McClellan's eyes, even as a weak smile creased his own tawny beard. Such antics had always amused her, despite the geographical distance that separated her and Jeb their entire marriage. For though the eligible—and not so eligible—women in the Confederacy might throw themselves at the dashing cavalier with the dancing eye—and one side of his hat brim pinned up to the crown, the other festooned with a merry plume— he had only ever thrown himself at one, and he had loved her in every way a husband can love a wife. She would live her whole life resting in the peaceful preserve of that assurance.

"My spurs which I have always worn in battle," he added, "I promised to give to Mrs. Lilly Lee, of Shepherdstown, Virginia. My sword I leave to my son."

Throughout the day Jeb asked if anyone present had heard tell of Flora's progress in reaching him. Always the same answer came: sad shaking heads and whispered words of "No," "Not yet," "Surely she will arrive at any time now." He labored to calculate what route and manner of transportation would avail themselves to her and how long the journey would take.

Late in the afternoon he concluded that because of the disruptions and chaos rent by Sheridan, Flora might be until tomorrow arriving. He called Dr. Brewer to his side. "Can I last the night?"

Flanked by two other of Richmond's most respected physicians, Brewer shook his head and delivered the most reluctant prognosis of his entire career. "I . . . I'm afraid the end is near," he said.

Jeb nodded. "I am resigned, if it be God's will, but I would like to see my wife." He turned his head away and contemplated for the first time the possibility that death might arrive before Flora. *Thou knowest all things,* he concluded to himself, *and doest all things well.* He looked back to those gathered around him. "But God's will be done."

He peered over to one side of the bed at the Rev. Dr. Joshua Peterkin of Saint James Church, under whose preaching he had often sat. Peterkin had arrived soon after Jeb had the night before, Bible and Episcopal Book of Common Prayer in hand, and had not left.

"Might you lead us in singing 'Rock of Ages,' sir?" Jeb asked.

Jeb's former aide, the Prussian giant Major Heros Von Borcke, had heard of his commander's wounding while he himself still convalesced in Richmond from a bullet he took in the throat during the Gettysburg campaign. The wound would have killed most men. Von Borcke sat at Jeb's bedside all afternoon feeding him crushed ice and placing it on the burning wound in his abdomen. While Jeb struggled to join in the song, tears filled Von Borcke's eyes as the memories tided over him of all the days on the fields around all the campfires he had heard that once-lusty voice cheer his men, celebrate with them in victory, and encourage them in defeat, the last which had not been often. He thought of "Jine the Cavalry" the first time he ever laid eyes on Jeb; "Goober Peas" when they stunned the world with the "Ride Around" (George) McClellan; "The Girl I Left Behind Me" when they headed north to Maryland; "Old Joe Hooker, Won't You Come Out the Wilderness?" when Jeb took the fallen baton from Stonewall at Chancellorsville; and "Lorena" in the rain as they bled their way home from Gettysburg.

And now it was the immortal words of the great hymnwriter Augustus M. Toplady, and Thomas Hastings's melody, itself every bit as mighty as the words and message it championed:

Rock of Ages, cleft for me,
Let me hide myself in Thee;
Let the water and the blood,
From thy wounded side which flowed,
Be of sin the double cure;
Save from wrath and make me pure.

When the song was finished, Jeb took the Prussian's great bearlike hands. Now the Virginian's eyes welled up. "How gallant a comrade you have been, old friend, to me and to our lovely Southland. Now I must impose on your manly Germanic generosity once more." For a moment Jeb feared the exceptional emotions of the moment might get the better of him. Then he looked Von Borcke in the eye and said, "Kindly look after my family after I am gone and be the same true friend to my wife and children that you have been to me."

Von Borcke knew if even he opened his mouth to speak, he would wail, so he merely nodded, the tears flooding out of both eyes and down his bearded face.

Then the spark left Jeb's dancing eyes, and the earthly life he had lived so well began to make way for the life eternal toward which he had looked since that long-ago summer night when the heart of fatherless, twelve-year-old James Ewell Brown Stuart was consecrated to Christ. It had happened after he first saw what was true Christian manhood when that faithful Methodist preacher climbed into his walnut pulpit and preached Jesus and Him crucified.

"Why, Flora, my precious little daughter . . ." Jeb murmured, his voice filled with wonder, the crushed ice no longer needed, as the eyes of all present widened. "There is no one I would rather . . ."

The brave men in that room, who by now had seen much war and too much death, fought to a man to stay the sobs that boiled up from within.

For a moment Jeb seemed to return to them. "I am going fast now, I am resigned," he said, as content as ever he had been in his life. "God's will be done."

And so with her violets blooming and her linden trees flowering, Virginia grew sadder even than she had been as the famed warrior poet whose feats of daring had brought her renown that could not fade, passed into the upper sanctuary.

"Oh, how will we ever smile again?" someone in the throng covering the front of the Brewer home and the street beyond asked.

Please, Father, I must get to him in time to comfort him, to help him, Flora prayed, raw panic trying its best to overcome her. A couple of the expressions she had seen on soldier's faces between Richmond and Beaver Dam Station had with no words revealed through her feminine intuition how dire were Jeb's straits.

The crowd outside the Brewers' home had grown all day and into the evening. It filled the doctor's front yard and covered nearly the entire block between Jefferson and Madison. As her escorts called for the crowd to part and the wagon pulled up in front of the Brewers', Flora's blood ran cold. She did not even need to spy the sorrowful countenances of those who stood all around her in the dim light of the moon and a few torches. She could hear the whimpering, the crying, the wailing. In a way, perhaps, it helped her. It cushioned the shock of finding that her beloved had been dead these three hours.

Because Sheridan had destroyed so many bridges and the storms had continued, she and her children did not arrive until nearly eleven o'clock.

"All he wished at the end was to see you," Von Borcke choked out to her before he finally burst forth into such waves of agonized weeping that Flora actually hugged and consoled *him,* silently thanking God as her own grief came crashing down that He had in His love and mercy drawn Jeb through breakneck riding to her for their final brief visit. For she had not seen her husband in months.

The elegiac refrain of one of the grand old Scottish ballads Jeb loved so well had been in her head when she awoke this morning. It had remained there all day, despite the momentous events swirling about her. It remained there now as she stared down at the brave and loving man who had written her very poor poems brimming over with love from the plains of Kansas and whom she had been blessed to call husband for nine years.

> O ye'll tak' the high road and I'll tak' the low road,
> An' I'll be in Scotland afore ye;
> But me and my true love will never meet again
> On the bonnie, bonnie banks O' Loch Lomond.

Taylor marveled that Lee's battered constitution not only remained upright but continued to hold together a nation whose very existence teetered on the brink of destruction and to wage war against an opponent so mighty he had always doubted they could be beaten in the extended sort of contest that had now uncoiled.

But that constitution had and would increasingly give way here and there, at the suspect points in its armor, in the shadowy joints of its harness. So now it did again, as illness began to befall him in his tent at Spotsylvania. Trying to shake the fuzziness out of his head, he stared at the order he had penned announcing Jeb's death.

I can scarcely think of him without crying, he thought, feeling the emotions well up within him again. As his eyes filled with tears, he shook his head again. *I have an army to lead, I must retain my wits,* he thought, scolding himself to little avail. For within a few seconds, his thoughts had run again to Jeb.

When Taylor peeked cautiously in to check on him, Lee looked up and said, "He never brought me a piece of false information."

Taylor had heard him say the same words at least a half dozen times in the four days since Jeb died.

Lee wiped the fog that had veiled his reading spectacles, then read the words he had written.

"Among the gallant soldiers who have fallen in war, General Stuart was second to none in valor, in zeal, and in unflinching devotion to his country. To military capacity of a high order, he added the brighter grades of a pure life guided and sustained by the Christian's faith and hope. The mysterious hand of an all-wise God has removed him from the scene of his usefulness and fame. His grateful countrymen will mourn his loss and cherish his memory. To his comrades in arms he has left the proud recollection of his deeds and the inspiring influence of his example."

The famed "Poetess of the Confederacy," Margaret Junkin Preston, the sister of Stonewall's first wife, and his close friend herself, dipped a rusty nail into a dish of persimmon juice to gift the generations to come one of the great memorials to the man Federal General John Sedgwick called, "The greatest cavalry officer ever foaled in America."

> Think of the thousand mellow rhymes,
>> The pure idyllic passion-flowers,
> Wherewith, in far-gone, happier times,
>> He garlanded this South of ours.
> Provencal-like, he wandered long,
>> And sang at many a stranger's board,
> Yet 'twas Virginia's name that poured
> The tenderest pathos through his song.
> We owe the poet praise and tears,
>> Whose ringing ballad sends the brave,
> Bold Stuart riding down the years—
> What have we given him? Just a grave!

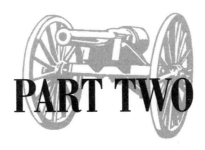

PART TWO

*The South is a land that has known sorrows; it is a land
that has broken the ashen crust and moistened it with tears; a
land scarred and riven by the plowshare of war and billowed
with the graves of her dead; but a land of legend, a land of song,
a land of hallowed and heroic memories.*
—Edward Ward Carmack

CHAPTER 27

GRANT DID NOT RELENT. LINCOLN HAD TOLD HIM HE WOULD provide whatever Grant needed if the North would win the war, but he wanted it won in time for his November reelection bid. Lincoln, who faced a challenger in his own party's presidential primary, grew increasingly pessimistic about his chances for reelection. As Northern casualties multiplied and the fourth year of the war dragged on with no end in sight, the pressure mounted on Grant from the White House.

So the Federal commander continued a series of flanking movements around Lee's right, intended to draw the Confederates into an open field fight where the vast Northern numerical superiority could be pressed to greater advantage. Lee would not bite, and each time the Federals moved to get around him, he adroitly used his shorter interior lines—and his renowned ability to divine the objectives of his opponent—to rush his troops to the key point just before they arrived.

But his own physical condition worsened. In the remorseless conflict of the last many days, the pain and stiffness in his chest and arms had increased. And the detested diarrhea had returned with a vengeance. *I hardly eat anything beyond boiled cabbage,* he thought shortly after rising at 3 A.M. on the morning of May 23, disgust filling him as he again emptied what little he had consumed into the chamber pot. Then he remembered all the men fighting for him and their country who were beset with the same or worse maladies. How often had he seen them, lined up, in clusters, in the woods, on the way to the woods, in the fields, sometimes wherever they stood. They had neither tent nor chamber pot. He reproached himself for lacking gratitude toward God and compassion and appreciation for his men.

When he sat back down at his writing table, the thought occurred to him of just how vast such problems would become if the Federals were allowed to maneuver him into a siege of Richmond. The prevention of just such a nightmare had presented a subscript to every decision Lee had made for months. Those who had diarrhea in the closing weeks of the Vicksburg siege, he thought with a shiver, were merely passing through the rats they had been reduced to consuming.

His fears—and frustration—were compounded by President Davis's categorical refusal even to consider the strategic abandonment of Richmond by Lee if it afforded the Army of Northern Virginia advantage in its prosecution of the war.

Enough of such morbid thinking, he said to himself. *It's time to be out and doing what can be done.* As his and Grant's armies massed on the North Anna River not far from his tent for another encounter, Lee paused to glance at the letter he had written late the night before to Mildred. It was a further plea to do the honorable thing and dispose quickly of the formidable Custis Morgan, who had recently wreaked a new round of havoc on the Lee home.

"It would be most grateful to his feelings to be converted into nutritious aliment for our wounded soldiers," Lee wrote, "and thus devote his life to the good of the country."

Ah yes, I believe I have conveyed just the message I desired, he thought, quite pleased with himself.

Later that day Lee watched through his field glasses as the Federals moved against the North Anna bridgeheads to which he had beaten them back.

"General Lee, sir?"

Lee turned to see a handsome man in his early fifties.

"W. E. Fox, and it's an honor, sir, to have you fighting on my land," the man said, reaching a sturdy hand up to shake with Lee. "We would be pleased to have you join us in the house for a brief refreshment, General."

"Thank you, kind sir, but I fear I will be here only a few minutes before events press me on," Lee said.

A glint entered Fox's eyes. "At the risk of being accused of bribery," he said, "may I add that my wife is roundly acknowledged for pouring the best liquid refreshment in the county?"

Lee, feeling weary, shook his head and said, with as much chivalry as he could muster, "Thank you, Mr. Fox, but I'm afraid I wouldn't enjoy myself for fear of bringing calamity down upon your lovely home."

When he saw the crestfallen expression on Fox's face—and the gray-headed face of a frightened woman, presumably Mrs. Fox—peering out a window, Lee continued, "Unless of course you have any buttermilk."

A smile as bright as the sun glinting off the massed Yankee bayonets across the North Anna beamed from Fox as he turned and gave the woman in the window a quick nod.

"I'll have to stay out here," Lee said as he climbed off Traveller.

"Please, take my rocking chair here on the porch," Fox said. It seemed to Lee as though the man had disappeared into the house, then reappeared with a pitcher of buttermilk and a plate of dark bread before Lee had even sat in the chair.

Lee could not disguise his glee. "Oh, my."

"I'm sorry we have no ice for it, and only stale bread to go with it," Fox said.

Lee poured himself a glass and took a long drink, then nodded, the residue of the liquid coating the snowy whiskers around his mouth. "Yes, I tell my daughters that buttermilk with ice is one of the most nutritious things available to them."

He noticed the woman from the window had not joined them.

Fox perceived his thoughts and said, "Since we lost both our boys at Gettysburg, she, well, she—"

Before he could finish, an ear-rattling explosion rocked the porch. Fox dove off the side of the porch for cover. After a moment, his wife's head appeared through a nearby window.

"Dear, are you hurt?" she asked, quite composed. Fox blushed, realizing he had landed headfirst in the dirt, with his posterior straight up in the air above him.

"Er, no, I believe I'm well, dear," he replied. *General Lee,* he thought, panicked. He got to his feet and swung his gaze back to the porch. There was Lee, rocking in the chair and finishing his glass of buttermilk, a thin veil of smoke wafting around him. Not half a dozen feet away, a yawning hole had appeared in the frame of the front door. A hole the size and shape of an unexploded round shot.

"General Lee?" Fox warbled.

Lee put down the empty glass, rose to his feet, and stepped off the porch toward his horse. He noticed some splinters and dirt on his uniform front and brushed them off.

Can he not have heard the cannonball that just passed within six feet of his head? Fox wondered, attempting without success to reconcile the stunning shot and Lee's nonchalant demeanor as the general climbed back into the saddle of an equally unperturbed Traveller.

"Please present my compliments to your wife, Mr. Fox," Lee said, "and add my appraisal to the others that her reputation is well-deserved. But just as I feared, I have brought danger with me to your home. So, much as I would relish another glass of your wife's delectable buttermilk, I must not bring further peril to you." With that he tipped his hat, then tugged the reins around to lead Traveller away at a canter.

Mrs. Fox emerged from the house. She stared at the minicrater gouged out of the front of her home. "Is General Lee well, dear?"

Fox, his back remaining toward his wife, stared after Lee as he disappeared. "Yes, he is, dear."

"Did he think awfully of us for endangering him?" she asked.

He put his arm around her shoulder.

"No, he feared the reverse."

For a moment, as the clamor of guns over by the river grew, neither husband nor wife spoke. Then, quiet as a mouse, she began, "Dear?"

He hugged her a bit tighter and looked down at her. "Yes, dear, he was delighted with your buttermilk."

The Confederates drove the Federals away again, but Lee's physical condition deteriorated. The next day he could not even get into the saddle.

"Sir," a flustered Taylor said, "please, if you must move about, allow us to fix up a wagon for you."

Lee said nothing but gave Taylor the look that the younger man knew meant, "You'd best stay out of my road, son." Still, Lee relinquished the reins and stalked back toward his tent.

Marshall stood nearby. "I hate it when he gets like this," he said.

Taylor knew if he opened his mouth he would be hard-pressed to shut it, so he passed Traveller on to an orderly, then walked toward his own tent. His stomach growled from hunger, and he missed his fiancée terribly, so he was in no mood for any of the "Tycoon's" childish tantrums.

Nearing his tent, he heard a rumpus coming from Lee's. *Can that be Venable?* Never had he heard the steady old major's voice so shrill. *Yes, that is Venable,* Taylor thought. He frowned as he heard Lee's voice booming the way it did during his fits of anger. Taylor shook his head. *What would our country think if they knew they had such a contentious old woman?* he thought, breathing contempt.

"You are not fit to command this army, sir!"

Taylor's head shot up. *Can that truly be Venable? Is he addressing the old man?*

He picked up the pace, heading toward Lee's tent. Venable flipped open the tent flap, then turned and shouted back toward Lee. "You had better send for Beauregard!"

Then from inside the tent: "We must strike them a blow!" Then coughing. Then, "We must never let them pass us again—we must strike them a blow!" Then convulsions of coughing.

Venable, not looking back, stormed past Taylor, growling, "I have just told that old man he is not fit to command this army!"

"Major Tay—!"

Lee had emerged from his tent. His face looked chalky white, and he held his chamber pot. Taylor could smell it from where he stood; he tried to keep from wincing.

"Major Taylor," Lee barked, "find the orderly who is to dispose of this, and ready me a carriage. I'll not be lying around here while—" A surprised expression covered Lee's face. Then it turned to agitation and finally despair before he wheeled and rushed back into the tent.

Taylor stood for a moment, trying to process the preceding sequence. He determined it was not worth the effort and returned to his tent. Guns were booming up at the front. *How big a God we must have to preserve us, as silly as we are,* he thought, shaking his head.

⚬◇ ⚬◇ ⚬◇

Silly was not the adjective Grant would have used to describe the Army of Northern Virginia or its leadership, as an aging man with a bad heart and leaky bowels, commanding his army from a cot, frustrated the Federal army's every move. After more flanking attempts and more Confederate countermoves and more desultory fights, Grant determined that one more full-blown attack would lick the Rebels once and for all.

His soldiers did not believe that. Thousands of them pinned scraps of paper to their uniforms. A typical note read: "Joseph Smith. June 3, 1864. Cold Harbor. I was killed."

His officers did not believe that. The fact that Rebel prisoners were skinny, hungry, barefoot, and lice-ridden gave them no hope that the Southern army was on the brink of surrender or disintegration.

But until the past thirty days, Ulysses Grant had been winning battles throughout the war. Angry and impatient at the Rebels' stubborn tenacity, he thought it time to win his most important.

Out of the 4:30 A.M. darkness on June 3, Grant launched the massed muscle of the Army of the Potomac—three Federal corps, totaling over sixty thousand men—against the heavily outnumbered Confederates.

But Lee had constructed an elaborate system of fortifications whose concave alignment lured his enemy into a staggering cross fire.

The blood of over seven thousand more Federals was the final reason for Grant at last to discard his hopes of defeating the Army of Northern Virginia in open-field combat.

So furious was the Confederate fire that the majority of those casualties occurred in the first *eight minutes* of fighting. The bodies were piled so high in some places that the bluecoats coming after them could not climb over. They blanketed five full acres of ground.

In one month of fighting, Robert E. Lee and the Army of Northern Virginia, Grant had absorbed the worst three defeats of his career. And he had suffered sixty thousand casualties. That number equaled the size of Lee's entire army when the campaign began thirty days before. Moreover, Grant could not fathom what he had come to consider Lee's near-clairvoyant divining of his (flanking) intentions.

The Federal commander determined to remove his battered forces across the James River. He would now get behind Richmond and cut it off from its railroad supply lifelines to the other Southern states by capturing Petersburg, twenty miles south of the capital.

For some weeks Grant's lieutenants were wary of launching further attacks for fear their soldiers would mutiny. Horror and rage flamed across the United

States at the unprecedented slaughter. Lincoln began to prepare himself for defeat in November.

"I think Grant has had his eyes opened," Army of the Potomac commander and Gettysburg victor Meade wrote to his wife, "and is willing to admit now that Virginia and Lee's army is not Tennessee and Bragg's army."

All this happened with an army Lee commended to corps commander A. P. Hill after Hill bitterly complained to him about mistakes made by Ambrose Ransom Wright, one of Hill's brigadiers.

"These men are not an army," Lee said, "they are citizens defending their country. General Wright is not a soldier; he's a lawyer. The soldiers know their duties better than the general officers do, and they have fought magnificently. Sometimes I would like to mask troops and then deploy them, but if I were to give the proper order, the general officers would not understand it. So I have to make the best of what I have and lose much time in making dispositions.

"You understand all this," he concluded, "but if you humiliated General Wright, the people of Georgia would not understand. Besides, whom would you put in his place? You'll have to do what I do. When a man makes a mistake, I call him to my tent, talk to him, and use the authority of my position to make him do the right thing the next time."

Late that night, after all his staff had retired, Lee pondered such notions, as well as their larger implications. He put a few of his thoughts on paper.

"The forbearing use of power does not only form a touchstone but the manner in which an individual enjoys certain advantages over others is a test of a true gentleman," he wrote.

"The power which the strong have over the weak, the employer over the employed, the educated over the unlettered, the experienced over the confiding, even the clever over the silly—the forbearing or inoffensive use of all this power or authority, or a total abstinence from it when the case admits it, will show the gentleman in a plain light. The gentleman does not needlessly and unnecessarily remind an offender of a wrong he may have committed against him. He can not only forgive, he can forget; and he strives for that nobleness of self and mildness of character which impart sufficient strength to let the past be but the past. A true man of honor feels humbled himself when he cannot help humbling others."

When he finished the writing, he added it to scores of others in his scuffed old leather valise. No other living soul would lay an eye on any of them while Lee still lived.

CHAPTER 28

WAYNE MARLEY WAS SENT TO THE SHENANDOAH VALLEY IN MAY as chief of scouts for General David Hunter, commander of the Army of West Virginia. The assignment cheered him, for through the ten years he lived there before the war, the Valley had coiled its way, unnoticed, around his heart, as it had many others before him. Indeed, in the three years since he had departed north from his Lexington home after Fort Sumter, his thoughts had run increasingly to the lovely verdant expanse that poet Maggie Preston had called "Virginia's loveliest valley, hushed by her embracing hills."

Now spring had returned with the dogwoods, and he thanked God every day for again having good food and water to drink. The month in Libby Prison had shaken him. He did not plan ever again to be taken prisoner. Only by the grace of God—and likely, Rev. Richard Bagby—was he released so soon, else he would have been on a train headed south to that spanking new Rebel prison down in Georgia. He thanked God for that release as well. He several times wondered who or what delivered him from the hangman's noose that everyone from the Richmond newspapers to the prison guards to the leaders of the prisoners themselves had believed was certain.

God must have work remaining for me to accomplish, Marley thought, savoring the verdant sweetness of the air as General Hunter's column approached the Blue Ridge, headed east across the mountains for the key Confederate transportation and military center of Lynchburg. *Hunter,* he remembered, *yes, indeed abundant work remains to be done.* He looked back over his shoulder. The pastoral tableau was smeared with the smoky testament to Hunter's sacking and torching of much of Lexington. Some of Marley's fondest memories in life were of those days after the Mexican War when as a twenty-one-year-old cadet plebe he had joined Stonewall, who was a professor, at the Virginia Military Institute. *Yes, I surely know why old Tom—Stonewall—loved this valley so,* he thought.

A commotion back on the Federals' left flank caught Marley's attention. He pulled out his field glasses and peered at what looked to be at least one hundred black men being herded out of some woods toward the column. Suddenly one of the blacks broke in a dead run back toward the woods. To his horror Marley saw a puff of smoke, heard the report of a Sharps carbine, and saw the man fall. A moment later a cavalry sergeant he knew galloped toward the front of the column from the direction of the incident.

"Sergeant O'Riley," Marley called. "What's the ruckus back there?"

O'Riley skidded his horse to a stop, saluted, and said, "Impressing us some volunteers, sir."

"What?"

"The coloreds, sir," O'Riley explained. "General Hunter has ordered us to draft all able-bodied slaves we liberate between the ages of eighteen and fifty who won't enlist voluntarily, to serve as noncommissioned officers and soldiers. All our armies are doing it, sir."

"But what the devil is going on back there?"

"Well, sir, a lot of these coloreds seem a might cowardly," O'Riley said, pushing his kepi back off his forehead. "They don't cotton to fighting for their own freedom, even when white men are dying for it. That lot back there cowered in the woods rather than serve. So we went in and conscripted them."

"And the man we shot?"

O'Riley shrugged. "Begging the major's pardon, sir, but I reckon it's just one less n—— to bring in the spring corn for the Rebs—not that they'll have much to bring in this year."

Indeed Hunter had done his worst to the Shenandoah. *And he, a valley man himself. It does not figure,* Marley thought. The grim general looted, pillaged, and burned his way south clean through the Upper Valley. But not much figured about Hunter. Rarely had Marley met a more venomous and spiteful man. And his most brutal wrath seemed directed toward his own homeland.

Hunter had held aloft, as though it were a prize or trophy, a heartrending letter sent to him by one Henrietta Lee, whose home was one of the myriad he razed. "Your office is not to lead, like a brave man and soldier, your men to fight in the ranks of war," she wrote, "but your work has been to separate yourself from all danger, and with your incendiary band steal unawares upon helpless women and children, to insult and destroy."

Marley had already discerned that affection for Hunter was rare even from his own officers. The last two days had also planted the troubling specter in Marley's mind that Hunter might be as lacking in judgment as he was in temperament. *The trashing and firing of civilian properties has long been a stain on this army's honor, but I fear we tarried far too long in so remote a district of this struggle,* he thought nervously. He was thankful Stonewall did not haunt the valley like spring before last. *But those Rebels we still face can't have been unaware and uninterested in our activities.*

He heard a series of angry oaths erupt behind him in the column. Well, he suspected they were oaths. The outbursts, from two or three different soldiers, were in German. He looked back to see one mounted man dive at another, clearing him out of his saddle, the two of them flying to the ground. *How different this army is than three years ago, or even two,* he mused. *Then, most of us were so idealistic. It seemed more like a crusade than a vicious fight. Now most of the best men are dead. Too many of those who remain are either indifferent to the causes for which we fight, if not downright hostile, or just plain ignorant of them. Our ranks fill daily with an endless stream of Germans and Irish, fresh off the boat, the one not able to speak English, the other despising all things English. Now, too, the blacks pour in.*

He thought of Lee's dwindling forces set against this escalation, plus a Northern navy and blockade while the Confederates had no navy. When convalescing at home in Pennsylvania from his prison maladies, Marley had read the official white population figures for the warring sections when the war broke out. The North had twenty-two million whites, the South just over five million. All he could figure was that the Federals needed more godly men in positions of leadership. The most disturbing trend he had noticed was a general hardening of the humane aspects of the soldiery. Some of that, he knew, was inevitable, and perhaps necessary after years of war. But some of it was downright frightening to him, as he observed the mounting violence against defenseless noncombatants, what would previously have been considered by the American people barbarous and uncivilized behavior, even in war. And the mysterious designs of Dahlgren and Kilpatrick on their Richmond raid still troubled him, though he had grown uncertain on how or whether to report his concerns.

What does it portend for the future of this war, he wondered, *for the future of our country?*

"We must destroy this army of Grant's before he gets to the James River. If he gets there, it will become a siege, and then it will be a mere question of time." Taylor and others had heard those words from Lee many times. Now Lee exercised every means at his command both to determine what Grant was about and how he might render a blow to drive this Yankee army out of Virginia.

Alas, military responsibilities never could monopolize his attention. *Poor Mary,* he thought, willing his eyes to remain open long enough for him to write her, well after midnight. Typhoid diarrhea had now afflicted both her and eldest daughter Mary Custis. *Typhoid,* he thought, shuddering. *Gentle Annie . . .*

This, coupled with his wife's numerous other ailments, concerned him more than he had ever been about her health. Too many good friends who had never seen a battlefield had succumbed to illness and disease the past three years. Too many family members. Most of all these were much younger and healthier to begin with than his bent, crippled wife. And just as the past winter had been one of the coldest on record, the summer was one of the hottest and dryest ever in Richmond. "I do not see how you will be able to live in Richmond; you had better be looking out for some part of the country where there are some provisions," he wrote Mary. He thought of the meager rations he had insisted on Custis cataloguing for him. "How Custis, yourself, three girls, Billy, and Sally can long live on a fourth pound of bacon and a pint and a half of meal I cannot see."

Even many of Mary's friends in Richmond besought her to follow her husband's advice. She would have none of it. "What is to prevent our being cut off and forestalled from returning when we desire?" she asked Agnes and Mildred from her bed one afternoon when they yet again entreated her to leave. "Where—" she began when a wave of coughing wracked her shrunken body.

"Oh, Mama," Agnes said, helping her sit up.

"Wh . . . where but in Richmond is there any possibility—any," Mary said, her eyes blazing with defiance, "of my seeing Robert?"

Thus concluded the conversation.

◦◊ ◦◊ ◦◊

Now events pressed in on Lee from all sides. Unbeknownst to him, while he regained his strength and his own diarrhea went into remission, Grant snuck nearly his whole army away from its positions on the night of June 12–13 and had them across the James on pontoons by sunup of the 16th. Meanwhile Lee wanted some of Beauregard's troops from Petersburg to provide him the capacity to exercise offensive options, as would the Army of Northern Virginia of old. But Beauregard, as outnumbered proportionately as was Lee, envisioned the opposite scenario to help him hold his line. Davis was caught in the middle.

Further, though Lee expected a move by Grant south across the James, he feared that even if that move came, it might be a ploy to draw him south, thus allowing the Federals an open road into Richmond.

On top of everything else, Davis would not allow him to leave the capital, so he could not maneuver.

What Lee could do, he did. The destruction of the Upper Shenandoah Valley, which had now earned Hunter the Confederate sobriquet of "Black Dave," and the subsequent dallying by that officer, presented Lee both the information and the time to exercise anew his famed knowledge regarding the designs of even distant foes. Correctly anticipating Hunter falling next upon Lynchburg, Lee dispatched a scratch Confederate force under former U.S. Vice President John Breckenridge west to that location, followed by a larger force commanded by new corps commander (replacing the ailing "Old Baldy" Ewell) Jubal Early.

Ever scenting the trail of offensive opportunity, Lee planned for Ole Jube to then march down the Shenandoah as had Stonewall two years before. They would reclaim that verdant "Breadbasket of the Confederacy"—and the Virginia Central rail line—before crossing the Potomac and moving on Washington, while Lee launched a counterattack to drive Grant away from Richmond!

He also sent Wade Hampton and his cavalry northwest in pursuit of the rampaging Sheridan, whose mounted horde was moving to link up with Hunter. Such a prospect so alarmed Lee that he felt he had to stop it even at the expense of emptying his depleted lines of fully a quarter of their strength.

Once again Lee rightly reckoned the next step of his adversary. Thinking, praying, reading his maps, and putting himself inside the boots and mind of Phil Sheridan, nearly a quarter of a century his junior, he placed his index finger on the map at Trevilian Station.

Then came frantic reports from Beauregard that the Federals were pouring in around the Petersburg lines. Lee rushed south, his men flush from the costly but favorable series of Wilderness campaign battles, and marching in cadence to the song they knew he loved.

> How firm a foundation, ye saints of the Lord,
> Is laid for your faith in His excellent Word!
> What more can He say than to you He hath said,
> To you who for refuge to Jesus have fled?

For a couple of days, Beauregard, shining more brilliantly than at any other time of the war, held off Federal forces that ranged anywhere from twice to quadruple his size. In less than a week, Grant suffered ten thousand new casualties. But many more tens of thousands came on.

Siege, Lee thought as he rode Traveller across the Appomattox River into Petersburg; the specter he had for so long fought to prevent. A hollow feeling filled his stomach, and he felt it begin churning like a harbinger of new horrors with the chamber pot. *Unless we can find a way to strike a fearsome blow at those people, our end is now inevitable, and it shall come inside the thirty-mile-long ramparts we must now build around Richmond and Petersburg.*

❖ ❖ ❖

"Our poor Papa," Mary said to Agnes, sharp stabs of stomach pain tinging her words, as her daughter applied cool wet rags to her fevered forehead. The distant growl of guns floated in with the linden-spiced spring air through the open veranda doors that faced south from Mary's bedroom. "All he has wanted for as long as I can remember is to have his family around him on a small Virginia farm, and land to work with his hands. No end of cream and fresh butter and fried chicken—"

"—and not one fried chicken, or two—" Agnes chimed in.

"—but unlimited fried chicken!" they said in unison, bursting into giggles like schoolgirls in a way either rarely did anymore.

Other than it consigning his hip wound to a perpetual dull ache, Culpeper enjoyed riding with Ethan McDowell, because he had lots of action and a friend with whom to engage in it. The tales of partisan ranger derring-do had begun to attract him, chiefly because those roving bands of mounted irregulars had little accountability to anybody and thus a much longer tether on which to wage war. In fact when Culpeper raised the possibility to Ethan of "hitching on" with such a group, Ethan had told him Jeb Stuart said John Mosby's Rangers was the only such outfit he knew of that was efficient.

"And General Hampton said General Lee tried to get Secretary of War Seddon to abolish all partisan rangers," Ethan added. "He said General Lee calls the whole system 'unmixed evil.'"

"Well, I don't know nothin' about generals and secretaries and the like, but I know this," Culpeper said as he brushed down his thinning Yankee mount one day, then rested his arms on the horse's back, his glinting green eyes boring in on Ethan. "Them bluebellies is killers, murderers, and vermin. And this idea I hear General Jeb and General Lee trot out that we're some sort of Christian knights—" Ethan cringed as he saw Culpeper's face begin to seethe in rage. "—well, I ain't no Christian knight, and if them d—— Yankees want killin', I aim to give 'em just as d—— much of it as they can handle."

With that he swung up into the saddle.

"Which way do you think you're goin'?" Ethan asked.

"Yesterday, our boys sent Custer flyin'," Culpeper said. "They got his own wagon with all his fancy duds in it. I don't aim to miss out on such a hoe-down today."

"But we're scouts," Ethan said, "we best be—"

"You do as you please," Culpeper cut in, drawing a Colt .36, one of two he had pilfered from Federal officer corpses. "I ain't missin' this fight."

With that he rode toward the Confederate position that overlooked Trevilian Station and thwarted Sheridan from both the Virginia Central rail line he wanted to tear up and the turnpike he wanted to head west on to reach "Black Dave" Hunter.

"I've created a maniac," Ethan said with a sigh as he mounted and followed Culpeper.

Over and over Sheridan's dismounted troopers tried to breach the Confederate line. Hampton's men—and those of Lee's nephew Fitz—made a bloody mess of them. That night the incensed Sheridan broke off the battle and his entire mission of hooking up with Hunter. He retreated back east toward Richmond.

A pleased Lee named Hampton to succeed Jeb as chief of cavalry.

Culpeper fired his twin .36s and the Spencer repeater he had added to his collection from a captured Federal horse soldier until he had no ammunition remaining for any of them. Cursing, he searched for more until Ethan brought him the news that the two of them were ordered west by way of the Virginia Central to meet Early in Lynchburg.

"Why us?" Culpeper asked.

"Where we from?" Ethan said.

"The valley."

"Wonder where Jubilee's goin'."

"Think?"

"Let's go find out."

"Yi-aah!"

It was the loudest Rebel yell of the day for Culpeper.

"Black Dave" had proven immensely brave when confronting the fertile fields of the Upper Shenandoah or the women, children, and old folks of Staunton and Lexington and other Valley villages. But when, ready to pounce on the tiny force of former U.S. Vice President Breckenridge, he learned Old Jube and his two divisions had just hopped off the train in Lynchburg, Hunter decided to excuse himself from further activity in that theater.

This disappointed Early, who lit out after him and chased him through the Blue Ridge, then across the Shenandoah. Recurrently along this way, the Confederates came upon blacks, by themselves or in pairs or small groups. Some had fallen into the Federal column on their own; others had been forced by the bluecoats to come along and perform such duties as tearing up railroad track. Now most of them were dropping out and drifting back to their homes.

Hunter proved more adept at eluding the profane Early than engaging him; the Virginia Unionist did not stop until his Army of West Virginia, now twenty thousand strong, had arrived back in its namesake state.

Suddenly, with Grant at the gates of Richmond, as had been McClellan two years before, Early found himself with a Shenandoah Valley wide open to him all the way to Maryland. And that is precisely the direction he headed.

Indeed, as if in recognition that with them the towering shadow of Stonewall Jackson was again cast across the Valley, Ole Jube marched a whole segment of his column past Stonewall's grave at the Virginia Military Institute.

But this time VMI lay in ashes with Old Jack. Hunter had fired nearly the entire campus, along with the VMI faculty homes, the library of Washington College, and former Governor John Letcher's home. And he had cannonaded the town. The lean, bronzed faces of the mostly barefooted brigades grew grim as they began to see just what sort of war Sam Grant was hell-bent on waging.

Two faces grew grimmer than the others. Swinging through Valiant, one of the biggest plantations in Rockbridge County, as the rest of the army marched through Lexington, Ethan and Culpeper found the big house ransacked and plundered of every conceivable valuable. All the outbuildings had been torched, and every animal on the place, including dogs and cats, slaughtered.

Mrs. McDowell and Ethan's older brother Felton sat on boxes in the despoiled room that had once been one of the most beautiful parlors in the Upper Shenandoah. Broken glass littered the floor, and flies and bees buzzed through the house. Everywhere the stench of smoke still poisoned the air.

"Your father was killed at that battle they call the 'Bloody Angle,'" Mrs. McDowell said, grave but composed. "We received word two months ago that Horace died—froze—in that Yankee prison, Camp Douglas." Not seeming to take stock of how all this registered with Ethan, she turned to her other son and said, "but we can be thankful Felton has returned to us, when we thought he was lost as well."

Only then did Culpeper notice that Felton was one arm shy of a full set.

Ethan stood stunned in the middle of the room. Then Culpeper noticed a queer expression come over his face. "Where is Rachel Anne?" he asked his mother.

"Your sister is upstairs," she responded, not looking at him.

Ethan glanced that direction, then walked to his mother, bent over, wrapped his arms around her, and hugged her. After a few seconds she said, "My, you smell a fright, Ethan McDowell."

Surprised he pulled back. "I . . . I'm sorry, Mother. We've been out on the trail a long—"

"We've no clothing left to give you, but we can wash those you're wearing in the pond behind where the corn crib used to be. The *Yan-kees* cut the ropes to the well buckets, then poured bags of our own salt down them."

Culpeper noticed that the word *Yankee* was the only one she had spoken with any emotion since they entered the house.

Without a word Ethan walked to the stairs, then climbed up them. Culpeper saw that the carpet on each step had been slashed with sabers.

Ethan found his sister in her room. It was empty except for a chair, a few boxes, and several items the Federals had evidently smashed. She stared out one of the windows, all of which had been smashed out. She wore her mother's white wedding dress and nothing else—under the dress, on her hands, feet, or head. What she did wear was a triple coating of lipstick and facial makeup. Dull greasy strands of her once-downy and lustrous mane dangled in her eyes.

"Rachel Anne," he said.

She did not even look at him.

"Rachel Anne," he repeated, touching her shoulder. She neither spoke or moved or otherwise acknowledged his presence. He noticed that her hands and feet were filthy. He wrapped her in his arms as he had done his mother and hugged her. Like her mother, she in no way responded.

"Are . . . are you all right, Rachel Anne?" he asked, his voice threatening to crack.

Still she did not respond.

He hugged her once more and kissed her on the forehead. It tasted saltier than the rancid bit of meat he had gobbled down this morning. Then he left her.

"What about the servants?" Ethan asked his mother when he got back downstairs.

"The house servants stayed; the rest are gone," she said, death in her voice.

"All of them?" Ethan said.

She gave a weak nod.

This did not surprise Culpeper, for the McDowells had the worst reputation for treating their slaves of anyone he had ever known. In fact he could not think of anyone else he had ever known who didn't treat their blacks—house, field, or driver—with affection and respect. It just didn't make sense. They were too valuable, though it took the devil himself to get many of them to do much work. He always figured that was why most of the slaves would either stay at home, or, if they went with the Yankees, come back. Most just had it too good at home to want to go make it on their own somewhere else. He considered his an objective view on the issue, since his family had never owned a slave, nor had most of the folks that lived out near his farm.

A few minutes later Ethan and Culpeper were back in the saddle, headed north down the valley for Staunton. Ethan, usually so free with a joke or a story, said nothing at all. Culpeper realized he himself now smelled smoky like the McDowell place. He checked the chambers on his pistols and looked over the Spencer as they rode. He had found some ammunition, but he needed more. Lots more. Culpepers of other generations had scouted for Washington in the Army of the Revolution and Andy Jackson in the War of 1812. They had fought and killed Indians in this same Valley in the French and Indian War and before. He knew he could do anything they had done. The longer this war went on, and the fewer of his friends and family survived it, the more he felt a part of it, and the less he felt a farmer. *Farmer,* he scoffed to himself. Farm what? With whom? No people, no money, no land now probably, with the Yankees running roughshod all over the Valley and gone. He was going to collect himself all the ammunition and all the food he could safely load on his horse. He was going to kill Yankees to get every bit of it. And he was going to enjoy doing it.

All this he thought as they rode through the wreckage of the country between Lexington and Staunton. When they reached Staunton, they found that "Black Dave" had sacked that town as well. Culpeper realized he had not seen a smile on the face of any white civilian since they arrived in the Valley.

Still Ethan said not a word.

Within a few days Grant would notify Washington City that a Federal host should be assembled "to eat out Virginia clear and clean . . . so that crows flying over it for the balance of the season will have to carry their provender with them. . . . Hunter should make all of the Valley south of the Baltimore and Ohio road a desert as high as possible, . . . and the people should be notified to move out."

CHAPTER 29

KNOWING WHAT FEATS THE CONFEDERATE CAVALRY WAS CAPABLE of accomplishing in the Shenandoah Valley, even without Jeb Stuart, Marley turned and rode back east to the rear of Hunter's retreating twenty-thousand-man column. He wanted his best outriders assaying the pursuit, and he feared that with Valley-reared scouts riding point for Early, his own troops might fall into ill tidings.

He allowed himself a few pleasant glances around the emerald-carpeted vale, the Blue Ridge before him shining violet in the noonday sun. As an eagle soared across the azure expanse above, a verse from one of the psalms leapt into mind: "O LORD, how manifold are thy works! in wisdom hast thou made them all: the earth is full of thy riches."

His earlier fears, for a few moments forgotten, proved well-founded enough that he landed smack in the middle of a Confederate ambush that killed two of his men and dehorsed him.

"I can give you a new cowlick, Yank," an amiable Southern voice called out as Marley drew his revolver and scrambled out from under his dead horse. So well concealed was the man that Marley had no idea where he was.

They did not shoot him; in fact they treated him like a gentleman. One of the barefooted ones even agreed to swap him back the leather-bound Westminster Confession of Faith in his saddlebag for his boots.

From what Marley was beginning to hear about his next destination, he had a hunch the Confession might be even more valuable to him than his boots at that Reb prison down in Andersonville, Georgia.

◆ ◆ ◆

Culpeper could not remember having more fun. As he and Ethan scouted their way north down the Valley of Virginia, ahead of Old Jube's thirteen thousand—half of whom marched barefoot—they rode each day until exhaustion compelled them to drop and sleep where they stopped. From one end of the Shenandoah to the other, those folks who remained, and who had just reaped the greatest harvest in the history of the Valley, cheered the motley band with the rope-muscled legs, the tawny beards, and the glinting eyes.

"All we need for this to be a perfect ride, Ethan, is some Billy Yanks to pot," Culpeper said one clear morning as June became July and they boiled some Yankee coffee. He rubbed his side, always the sorer of his wounds in the morning. His hip would be the worst in the evening.

But Ethan's words were still few. Culpeper had noticed him poring over a battered old Bible at night. He hadn't seen the Bible before.

"Say, I never seen a McDowell with a Bible in his—or her—hands 'cept for Sunday show," Culpeper laughed as he drained one tin cup and poured another.

Ethan glanced up at him, the hazel eyes alight, but then did not respond.

"Well, leastways it's good ridin', good country, not many fools tellin' us what to be about—and I just know there's a big fight a'comin' sooner or later," Culpeper practically shouted. He looked out across the valley from their high, sheltered spot. "Yi-ahhhh!"

"Cole Culpeper, you'll get us both killed sure, someday," Ethan finally spoke.

"Well, anything to get a word outa you, Ethan. Gits mighty lonely ridin' all the way down the Shenandoah Valley with no better conversation than my own."

Ethan could not help cracking a grin at that. "Come on, you crazy oaf. Let's see if we can scare up some Yanks for Jubilee."

They had to ride out of Virginia, across the Potomac, and into Maryland before they did. But on July 9 on the banks of the Monacacy River, where the road forked off to both Baltimore and Washington, with the whole world holding its breath—when only days before they thought the war between the American states all but finished—Old Jube crashed into the only force the United States could stand between him and the gates of the capital itself. The Confederates rolled over a contingent half their size commanded by Major General Lew Wallace, who would one day be governor of New Mexico and write the greatest-selling novel of the nineteenth century, *Ben Hur.*

Culpeper killed more Yankees, collected more guns and ammunition, then raced with Ethan all the way to a ridge from which they could see through their field glasses, no more than a quarter of a mile away, Fort Stephens, standing on the outskirts of Washington.

"Well, if that don't put blood to pumpin' back through you, Ethan McDowell, I jest dunno what will," Culpeper said, awed by the spectacle. "Not even our lame-headed officers have been able to foul this one up."

"Would you look at that," Ethan said in hushed tones. "Just a few weeks ago, you and I were spilling our blood to keep them from overrunning our own capital, and even then they almost did it. I just can't believe it."

"Well, you better believe it, you old granny," Culpeper hollered, pulling off his hat and whopping Ethan over the head with it. "Don'tcha know Old Jack'd be proud to be with us at this moment?" Then a strange expression came over his face and he glanced around, his voice hushed. "Why, I think he might be, Ethan."

Ethan stared at him, at all the rifles and pistols and bullet pouches and cartridge boxes and canteens he wore, then furrowed his brows and shook his head, surrendering another reluctant smile because of Cole Culpeper. "Stick to scouting, Cole," he said with a laugh, reining his horse to turn around. "You're a bust as a philosopher."

"What the hay's a philophoser?" Culpeper called after him.

Mary at long last surrendered to her husband's relentless haranguing to remove herself from Richmond to a safer place less likely to lie in the path of fighting. Agnes and Mildred helped her onto a canal boat, and they rode it eighty miles west. They disembarked at Bremo, owned by friends of the Lees and perched above the James.

Better weather, more and better food, and environs that featured seagulls and deer rather than Yankee cannon combined to improve Mary's health, as Lee had predicted.

One day she sat rocking out on the porch overlooking the river when Agnes brought a smuggled *New York Times* to her. As usual Agnes said little, but her mother could sense something amiss in the paper. Agnes had it opened to a sprawling letter from Admiral Dahlgren, Ulric's father. He was telling the world he had seen photographs of the documents found on his son's body purporting to order the burning of Richmond and the killing of President Davis and the Confederate cabinet.

"He claims the papers are forged lies, that they bear the signature of someone with handwriting other than his son's," Mary read. She looked up at Agnes.

"I presume he is accusing our people of forging them?" She continued reading. "Barefaced, atrocious forgery, . . . the wickedness of the act is only equaled by the recklessness with which it has been perpetrated."

She folded the paper up and handed it back to Agnes. Her eyes blazed, and there was an edge to her voice Agnes had rarely heard, even during the war. "'A more fiendish lie never was invented,' he says. By whom? The thirteen-year-old boy who found the papers? His pastor-schoolteacher to whom he gave them? Brave Pollard who brought down Dahlgren? Your cousin Fitzhugh? Your father? The president? These are the people who had access to his fair son's papers."

Agnes sat in a rocking chair next to her but did not rock. *What has it all brought us?* she thought, watching the tranquil river glitter in the summer sun. *Our honor and duty and chivalry? Now the world will brand us with infamy for concocting the crimes our hateful enemies wished to perpetrate against us. All while we cower and starve and die more and more with each day that passes.*

But these thoughts she shared with no man, only God.

"Bremo is lovely, but she is no Arlington," Mary said to break the silence five minutes later.

"Indeed," said Agnes.

●◇ ●◇ ●◇

Marley smelled the camp before he heard it, even before he saw it. The aroma was not to be described with words. No one who was not there would ever understand how different it was from anything ever smelled before or after. No one who was not at Andersonville could ever know its horror.

After leaving the train, he and the carload of new prisoners entered a building detached from stockaded, thirty-acre Camp Sumter. There Marley first saw Captain Henry Wirz, the prison commander. He stood erect and above medium height, with a black beard and handsome bronzed face encompassing china blue eyes. Roughness coursed through both his European dialect and the words he spoke to his new prisoners.

The most comforting information Marley gleaned was Wirz's assurance that prisoner exchanges, which the Federals had halted a couple of months before, would soon resume. "Before this hot, humid south Georgia summer is finished, we shall all hopefully be rid of one another."

After passing through an assimilation station and having the contents of his saddlebag inspected—the Confederates who captured him had been so impressed with his boots and spurs that they had let him keep everything else, even most of his money—he was formed into a column with the one hundred other new prisoners and marched through the single gate into the camp.

Now the stench proved unbearable. *I will have to cover my face with my bandanna as soon as I get squared away,* he thought, tears forming in his eyes as a reaction to the acidic air.

"Hey, how'd your old lady let you get away wearing her slippers?"

Marley's head whipped around to find the source of the high, nasal, unmistakably New York City-brogued mocker. *He's a cocky little pigeon,* the Pennsylvanian thought with contempt, spotting the man standing amid a cluster of ne'er-do-wells, *and I've seen a thousand just like him, street and wharf trash, probably dragged into the Grand Army of the Republic by his heels.*

Marley counted himself fortunate to have saddlebagged the sheepskin house shoes he wore in the field at nights on his sore feet after peeling off his boots.

Suddenly a musket blast from the rampart above the gate sent a shiver through him and drove him to duck low. One of the guards, a skeletal youth no more than sixteen, had fired down into the milling mass now enveloping Marley. A murmur rippled through the prisoners, and he caught a glimpse of a filthy man, wearing what appeared to have once been a blue uniform, lying dead on the ground near the stockade fence perhaps forty feet away.

"Simms crossed the deadline."

"Simms crossed the deadline and they shot him."

Before Marley could process this, a commotion erupted nearby, but in the opposite direction, toward the center of the camp. He turned just as a prisoner, eyes rolled back in his head and blood spurting from a knife wound in his chest, fell into him. Marley, his saddlebags slung over one shoulder, instinctively stepped back as the man fell facedown to the muddy ground. Two other prisoners knelt over him, rifled his pockets and clothes clean of contents, and disappeared into the crowd before Marley even comprehended what was happening.

"Welcome to Andersonville, Wayne," a hearty voice sounded in his ear as a huge bearlike paw clasped his free shoulder.

"Al, Big Al Hill," Marley said, bewildered by the stunning sequence of events. "One hundredth Ohio, you played the harmonica for us at Libby."

"Yes, sir," the hulking Hill said, casting a smile down on Marley from his nearly six-and-a-half-foot-tall frame. "You and me been to Libby, man; now we in hell."

⚬⟡ ⚬⟡ ⚬⟡

"I'm tellin' you it's him, Ethan," Culpeper insisted as his comrade sighted the parapet above Fort Stevens, now barely more than two hundred yards straight ahead, with his spyglass.

Many figures milled about the point Culpeper had indicated, and thin plumes of gun smoke enveloped the whole scene, but for just an instant, Ethan caught sight of a black-suited man so tall he towered over all those around him, a man with a high stovepipe hat atop his head.

"Oh, that surely could be him," Ethan uttered, almost in a whisper, excitement flooding his chest. Suddenly a man stepped in front of Abraham Lincoln, then fell out of sight as the report of Culpeper's rifle crashed in his ears.

"I think I got him!" Culpeper chortled.

Ethan lowered his spyglass. "Did you just try to pot President Lincoln?"

Culpeper was on his feet, unable to stifle his glee. "I think I took down Abe hisself!"

Ethan grabbed him by the collar and shoved him back behind cover, just as a Yankee sharpshooter's bullet ricocheted off the tree trunk Ethan stood behind.

"If that was Lincoln," Ethan said, "and I'm not saying it was, you hit another man who stepped in front of him just as you fired." Culpeper was crestfallen. "And besides, I'm not believing it's right for us to be shooting at their president, of all people."

"What do you mean, Ethan?" Culpeper protested. "Lookee what that Ulric the Hun boy tried to pull on Jeff Davis."

"So, much as you hate Yankees, you want to start fighting like them now?" Ethan asked. Culpeper didn't know what to say to that. "Come on, we shouldn't be up on this skirmish line. You know the orders from General Early. The Yanks have finally been reinforced, and we're pulling out."

Culpeper could not have looked more stricken if told Jubilee had ordered him to serve out the remainder of the war as an unarmed chaplain.

"But we're—we're here, we're right here, Ethan," he protested. "We'll never in our lives get another chance like this to turn the Yankee capital upside down."

His eyes lit up anew, and he grabbed another loaded rifle, then proceeded to take aim at the parapet. The man in the stovepipe was turning to step down from the parapet, but he was still visible. "There he is again, Ethan!"

Culpeper pulled back the hammer with his thumb and had his index finger on the trigger when Ethan slammed the heel of his own hand down, knocking the rifle away and causing Culpeper to loose a wild shot.

The blaze in Culpeper's eyes was matched by Ethan's.

"We don't fight like that," Ethan growled, his stance signaling his willingness to physically prevent his friend from firing again at the fort.

Fury filled Culpeper, and he started to shake his head and speak when a bullet from the fort took his hat off him. He dove for cover.

"Let's ride, Cole," Ethan said. "You and me are supposed to be back out in front of this army as we head back toward the Potomac." Feeling Culpeper's anguish at all this, he added with a half smile. "Don't worry, bub, we're not going home. We're just heading back to the Upper Valley—temporarily—to keep the Yanks guessin'. We'll be back here sure."

Culpeper said nothing, because Ethan McDowell was still the only friend besides Emma he had ever had. And he owed much, even his very life, to him more than once over. But if any other man had done what Ethan just did, he would have killed him. Cutting loose from this gentleman officers' army and throwing in with a partisan ranger band was looking better all the time.

It must be the heat, Taylor thought to himself as he heard Lee quarreling in his tent with Marshall. *That, and he's outraged to be bottled up like this, with not enough troops. Grant won't leave, and Davis won't let us leave to maneuver. He wants to go back on the offensive and he can't. Good time to write to my fiancée.*

He strode into his own tent and proceeded with the letter to his fiancée, Betty Saunders, that he had begun the night before in Richmond. A smile formed at the corners of his mouth and grew wider, drawing his dark moustache and goatee closer together. Today he would not complain to her about the Tycoon; he wanted not to think about the Tycoon any more than he had to; he was sick to death of dealing with the Tycoon, placating his trifles, humoring his moods, "Doing the work of five men!" he finally shouted aloud. He scolded himself for continuing to cling to such thoughts and forced himself to begin writing on another subject.

"Those scamps in the trenches pass their time circulating these preposterous stories and find some credulous enough to lend a listening ear," he wrote. "I should not omit to mention that General Burnside has some thousands of Negroes underground—not dead and buried—mining our works. Some of our fellows actually overheard them digging about fifteen feet deep and as many yards in front of our lines of entrenchments."

From somewhere in the camp wafted the melody of open-air hymn singing. He looked back at the sheet of confiscated Yankee writing paper before him. "At least so they say. No doubt these important facts will be announced to the public ere long, as was the death of Grant."

"Lieutenant Colonel Taylor?"

He hurried to seal the missive, thinking, *at least I had a few moments free of the Tycoon.* He kissed the envelope, then passed it to an orderly as he hustled from the tent, shaking his head at how important satisfying the Tycoon remained to him, and at the ridiculous notion of the powerful Yankees resorting to underground excavation in order to move the Confederates out of their way.

At 4:44 A.M. on the morning of July 30, 1864, America's fratricidal slaughter descended another rung down the ladder from Christian enlightenment toward spiritual darkness.

Lee, poring over maps of the Petersburg and Richmond lines in his tent on the lawn of Violet Bank in Petersburg, heard a distant, but volcanic, explosion. Across the tent from him, a tea cup and saucer set given to him by a little girl in Mississippi rattled ever so slightly. *I believe that came from the southeast, beyond Petersburg,* he thought. He stared at the china, wondering how it had ever arrived intact all the way from Mississippi and shuddering at what he knew would be the devastation unleashed in that faraway blast.

Within seconds, staff and line officers were running and riding in every direction. Soon an officer with red hair flowing out from under his hat and down onto his shoulders roared up on a lathered mount.

"General Beauregard presents his compliments, sir," the huffing officer said, saluting. "He begs leave to report the enemy have blown up a sector of General Elliott's line and, covered by the explosion's fire, have advanced many regiments into a huge crater resulting from the explosion."

"Are they to our works yet, son?" Lee asked.

"Yes, sir, and attempting to advance on Cemetery Ridge, sir."

Cemetery Ridge, Lee thought, wincing. He dispatched Venable to facilitate getting two brigades to the site of the explosion and shot instructions to every other officer in sight. Then he climbed up onto Traveller and called out to everyone within hearing, "Our line must be restored at once or Petersburg will fall. And if Petersburg falls—" A chorus of distant cannon fire interrupted him and he galloped, alone, toward the scene. He found Beauregard, and the two of them made their way to the upper windows of a house perched on a high ridge only five hundred yards behind what had already been christened "The Crater."

Peering through his field glasses, he caught his breath. The whole sector was engulfed in blood, fire, flesh, steel, and gun smoke. Through the haze he counted the flags of fourteen different Federal regiments. And there in the middle of thousands of surging, shooting, slashing men, was a crater in the earth fully one hundred seventy feet long, seventy feet wide, and thirty feet deep. From out of it protruded portions of wagons, rifles, cannon, accoutrements, and the arms, legs, heads, and torsos of men—many men. Standing in it were thousands of blueclad soldiers, packed like sardines in a crate. He looked closer through his field glasses. *That appears to be an entire division of black soldiers, skirting around the crater and marching straight for our lines,* he thought.

Lee heard an eerie wail that began low, then spread, and finally caught hold of the breeze above and carried over the whole region. The Rebel yell, but with a savagery he wondered if he had ever before heard. His men, seeing that blacks—some of them former slaves—confronted them, tore into the Federals with something akin to madness. They destroyed fully one-third of the black division, and these bluecoats, along with white divisions elsewhere along the line, were driven back to the edge of the crater.

Still, they hold the crater and portions of our line on either side of it, Lee fretted. *We must drive them completely away, or with their superior artillery they will re-form and drive on Petersburg.* He sent his order to the Alabama general who would lead the next counterattack: "Tell him if he does not take the crater on this next charge, I shall re-form our men and lead them myself."

◆◆ ◆◆ ◆◆

"I got 'im," one Texas sharpshooter called to his fellow eagle eye, perched up in the next tree over behind the Confederate lines.

"Nah, let the feller go," said the second sharpshooter. "I think I'd ruther just sit up here and watch 'im hoof it. I never seen a man could run that fast before. 'Sides, one runaway black man don't exactly make an invasion o' Petersburg."

"He do run like a bat outa hades," the first man said from his tree. "All right, we'll leave 'im be. Guess if he gits too ornery, they'll take care of 'im there in town anyways."

By the time sense returned to the first-time-combat-frenzied head of black Federal infantryman and former slave Elijah Sledge, he had made it all the way into Petersburg, alone and carrying his Enfield, its bayonet dripping with Confederate blood from the initial Federal attack at the crater.

"Sakes alive, here he comes again," the first Texas sharpshooter drawled to his compadre.

"I'da never believed that feller could run any faster than he did on his way in there," his friend said, "but durned if he ain't got rockets under his feet on the way back out."

❖❖ ❖❖ ❖❖

If twenty-year-old Private Zach McClintock had any say in the matter, the crater would be taken. Caked with dirt, gunpowder, sweat, and blood, he tapped Alabama Captain James Featherstone on the shoulder.

"Captain, they blew up our South Carolina regiment," McClintock said, grimacing in pain. "I'll get on my hands and knees and beg if need be so's I can go in on this charge with you."

Featherstone looked him up and down, dumbstruck. "Y . . . you—" he began.

"I want to get even with them," McClintock persisted.

Featherstone thought about that for a moment. "How high did they blow you?" he inquired.

"I cannot say, but as I was going up, I met the company commissary officer coming down, and he said he'd try to have breakfast ready by the time I got down."

❖❖ ❖❖ ❖❖

Now the Confederates crashed forward, fearsome as Beelzebub's hordes from perdition. They drove the Federals down into the crater—or back to their own lines—and hundreds of Confederate riflemen, along with mortar guns and cannon, unleashed a ferocious fusillade down into the gigantic hole where whole regiments floundered, unable to advance, many of the packed men unable even to raise their weapons to shoot.

The Confederates shot and bayoneted and bludgeoned in all-out hand-to-hand combat until all their adversaries who remained had surrendered. Then, nearly insane with rage, they continued to kill the blacks who had surrendered, only stopping when threatened by the brandished swords and pistols of their own Southern officers.

Perhaps a Federal general best described the explosion, so impersonal, so modern, that gouged out the crater: "Without form or shape, full of red flames and carried on a bed of lightning flashes, it mounted toward heaven with a detonation of thunder and spread out like an immense mushroom whose stem seemed to be of fire and its head of smoke."

Born of eight thousand pounds of gunpowder, it killed over three hundred Confederates; Lee suffered fifteen hundred casualties in all.

But Grant lost over four thousand men, twenty regimental flags, and another battle. And the disgust and in some cases betrayal the Confederates felt after being victimized by what they considered a cowardly "trick" and facing a division of black soldiers, and the Southrons' reaction to it, drew down further the shutters that had heretofore, even on the battlefield, let in the light of Christian charity.

Back in the bloody Richmond hospital wards where she was commander, Phoebe Pember, a name now known North and South and even across the Atlantic, sat up late, reviewing the new patient lists by lantern light. She paused, remembering the jolting realization to which she and many of her nurses had today come. To this point in the war, the Southern men and boys they had tended, even those maimed and dying, had behaved with rare exception as perfect gentlemen. Her heart was touched in ways too ineffable to express when she saw men with savaged, often incomplete bodies, straining not to utter so much as the slightest oath in the presence of her and the other nurses.

Now, in a manner so sudden, so unexpected, they had come streaming in from the Battle of the Crater, cursing their enemy for "blowing us up while we were dead asleep." Their eyes glinted, and their teeth clenched, and smiles crossed their filthy faces as they displayed the stocks of their muskets, to which blood and hair still clung. They told Phoebe that after firing, without waiting to reload, they had gripped the barrels and fought hand to hand.

"We took the whites prisoner and we killed the n——s," one blood-drenched young man boasted, himself shot and stabbed.

"Our own Negroes, many of whom have laid down their lives serving in our own army, hate the traitors of their race who have turned coat and come against us," said another. "They cheered us for slaughtering them."

She blew out the lantern and began to weep softly in the dark. *They are not my darling boys any more,* she grieved. *What this hateful war has taken from them can never be recovered.*

CHAPTER 30

WHEN CULPEPER AND ETHAN PEERED THROUGH THEIR FIELD glasses and saw the President of the United States, they did not know that the whole world looked on with them, transfixed.

Many words were written, more spoken, and the great seats of European governments stirred all over again.

"The Confederacy is more formidable than ever," said the London *Times*.

"Whose escape downriver had been prepared from which capital, complete with steaming warship at the ready? Jefferson Davis's? From Richmond? No, Abraham Lincoln, from the Federal capital of Washington City," crowed another London publication.

How on earth could the Army of Northern Virginia, whose exploits the world had followed from chapter to chapter ever since Stonewall Jackson raised his arms in prayer on Henry House Hill, be at the very gates of Washington City!

"How can they be still in this war?" one king asked his most trusted courtesan.

"Why did God see fit to apportion Robert Lee so infinitely much more majesty than any of the rest of us?" an archduke wrote into his diary.

"I want all our generals studying the strategies, tactics, and operations of Robert E. Lee," a field marshal ordered.

"Lee . . . Lee . . . Lee . . ."

"He has so few and they so many," eighty-year-old British Prime Minister Lord Palmerston said to his guest, the strapping colonel with the most ascendant military star in the British Empire. Palmerston knew the younger man well, and knew he had camped with Lee and the Army of Northern Virginia prior to the Fredericksburg campaign. He had called the colonel to his office to solicit his insights as the British government sought how it might leverage the

299

current threat on the Federal capital to its best advantage in its dealings with the United States.

"He has so little and they so much," the genial old aristocrat continued. "With his own capital starving, without succor or aid from anywhere on earth, and surrounded by this enormous Yankee horde, the ghost of Stonewall Jackson suddenly storms down the Shenandoah Valley and across the Potomac into Maryland, wiping every semblance of enemy opposition aside, only to stand at the entrance to Washington."

Palmerston paused as though in weighty reflection, then said, thumping the walking cane he held in his hand on the polished oaken floor, "By jove, I'm bound there has been no such excitement around the colonial capital since we burned it down in 1814!"

Nothing sounded in the room for fully five minutes, save the noonday tolling of Big Ben across the Thames. Then Colonel Garnet Wolseley spoke.

"Neither did what Alfred accomplished against the Danes accord with human convention," he said. "Nor Henry V at Agincourt, nor Drake against the Armada, nor Lord Nelson at Trafalgar."

Perceiving a satisfied expression dawning across Palmerston's face, Wolseley added, "Nor the feats of the Maid of Lorraine against our own fathers."

Now Palmerston's patriotic countenance fell. "Such deeds are the craft of God, not man," said Wolseley. "As means to ends over which He alone holds proprietary rights, but by which many are blessed."

"But the Southern Confederacy cannot win," Palmerston said, shaking his head. "It remains a point of debate whether they shall starve first or be reduced to rubble by the North's guns."

"Win?" Wolseley asked. "With respect, excellency, by whose measure win? Did our brave brothers who delivered their wives and children to safety on lifeboats, then stood in formation and sang on deck as the Birkenhead went down into the shark-infested waters that consumed every last man *win?*"

Now the eyes of the man who would one day command all the famed legions who defended the British Empire kindled with fire.

"I have met with many of the great men of my time," Wolseley concluded, "but Lee alone impressed me with the feeling that I was in the presence of a man who was cast in a grander mold and made of different and finer metal than all other men. He is stamped upon my memory as being apart and superior to all others in every way, a man with whom none I ever knew and few of whom I have read are worthy to be classed."

I guess I showed him, Taylor thought with a smile to himself as he stormed out of Lee's tent on August 1. He was galvanized by having finally told the Tycoon what he thought of his ceaseless minute instructions, often ladled with the pettiness so common to sick old men, all while Taylor, even by Lee's gauge, did the work of three men.

So galvanized was he that Taylor tripped over a tent peg and landed flat on his face in the dusty hard dirt. John Gordon, the majestic young Georgian general, about to enter Lee's tent, looked down at him, a puzzled look crossing his handsome features.

"Hello, General," Taylor said, looking up, his lip bloody. "General Lee, I believe, is expecting you, sir."

Gordon walked past, thinking it better for Taylor to move beyond the embarrassing scene as quickly as possible. Taylor sprang to his feet before anyone else could arrive and rushed to his own tent, ignoring an offer of water from an orderly.

He already simmered over the revelation in Betty's last letter, which lay before him as he sat down on his camp stool, that someone had asked her if she had seen any difference in his attitude or behavior because of his "high position."

"In the first place," he now wrote, wielding his pen like a rapier, "a Lieutenant Colonelcy is not such an exalted position even though the individual is at the right hand of the 'greatest man of the day' and privileged to receive benediction from the ever-flowing font of his wisdom and character." *And able, at the individual's choosing, to touch the very hem of his garment,* he thought acidly to himself.

Oh, how angry it makes me when I allow myself to be placed in a position where I appear to such disadvantage with him! Taylor thought, daubing his split lip with a rag, then combing his mustache and goatee before his small travel mirror. *How unreasonable and provoking he is at times!*

"Ahh!" he shouted, reaching again for the pen. He had to pour it out to someone else, and only Betty could he trust with such volcanic revelations that he had come to believe would actually scandalize the South were they to find their way to those ink-splashed rags in Richmond.

"I might serve under him for ten years to come and couldn't love him at the end of that period," Taylor wrote. "I don't intend though to take up my paper and your time with any account of my grievances concerning the 'greatest and best (?) man living!!' . . ."

He completed the missive as quickly as he could, placed it in one of his used envelopes, and got it to the mailbag in time to be taken out that day. He whistled all the way back to his tent, where he found Lee standing at the entrance. Tears filled the Tycoon's eyes, but a smile spread across his beard when he saw Taylor.

"Ah, Walter," Lee said. "I've only one, but I should like you to have it."

So ravishing was the peach in Lee's hand that Taylor could for the first time understand why Eve was susceptible to what must have been just such a fruit in the Garden. Surely it was the largest, prettiest, juiciest-looking peach he had ever seen.

Ah! But he is a queer old genius, Taylor thought, taking the fruit, his heart pounding and his mouth watering at the prospect of savoring the best piece of food he had tasted in months.

The concern written on Big Al Hill's face spelled trouble to Marley. He had seen no more shootings or stabbings through his first day at Andersonville, upon which the descent of the sizzling summer sun would soon bring closure. He had, in fact, as Big Al guided him along the grid of dirt "streets" around which the camp was laid out, seen the flourishing of commerce. Miniature "markets" abounded in booths, tents, caves, huts, out in the open, and in holes dug in the ground. Marley witnessed the sale or barter of food, blankets, whiskey, tobacco, and water; the "tailoring" of tattered uniforms; and real estate transactions for forty or fifty square feet of land.

He had seen, too, white men, always with faces so darkened by pitch, pine smoke, and dirt as to be hardly distinguishable from blacks, walking ankle-deep in fetid sloughs even as they inhaled the rancid air; he had seen men choking on their own vomit, suffocating on their own blood, and having bowel movements through their pants where they stood, because one place seemed no worse than any other.

"Oh, but the day is the period for leisure at Andersonville," Big Al said with a knowing nod as he, Marley, and six other men sat in a circle outside their "she-bang," a makeshift shelter they had built with pine branches and limbs, and in which, because of Big Al, Marley now joined them as a resident.

Besides, two of their number had met their demise in the past week; one from scurvy, the other from the raiders.

"And the raiders will certainly be on the prowl tonight," Big Al said, "likely in force."

"On the prowl?" Marley asked, chewing on a piece of hard cornmeal.

"Careful of that," Little Al Tate, the bespectacled group accountant-businessman warned Marley. "Rebs love that cornmeal, but it goes through our boys like green apples through a gander."

"Well, guess I'm a might fortunate," Marley said. "I lived in Virginia for ten years before the war, and I must have eaten a ton of the stuff."

"Fortunate ain't the word, friend," Bill Hankins, a Kentucky cavalryman said. These were the first words Marley had heard him speak. "There's men all over this camp, and over in the hospital, spillin' their insides out 'cause they can't digest cornmeal. They're used to wheat. Over a hundred men a day are dyin' in this hellhole."

"Men, we've seen that when we're careful about our cleaning habits, what water we drink, and staying away from tobacco and spirits, we stay fair healthy," Big Al said. "Am I right, Bill?"

Hankins looked at him for a moment, then nodded.

"But tonight, we best be havin' our thoughts geared to Curtis and Collins and the raiders," Big Al said.

"I take these raiders to be a big gang that has banded together to have their way," Marley said.

"Big?" Little Al piped up. "Sometimes it seems like half the camp is raiders."

"Course it's not that many," Big Al said, "but they do have several hundred men attached to them in varying degrees. What makes them so fearsome is they that they're highly organized, and they act in concert against much smaller groups of men."

"They rob, they intimidate, they extort, they attack," Little Al said, his eyes narrowing, "and they kill with no more thought than they'd give to swatting one of these swamp flies we got around here." With that he smacked a huge mosquito against his cheek, smearing blood clear across that side of his face.

"They're worst of all at night," said rail-thin Sam Simmons, a Chicago dentist before the war. "The darkness does not like the light, and it—and they—flourish at night."

"Just like one big street or wharf gang from any of them big Eastern cities," Hankins growled. "What do you expect from 'em? They're just actin' like they do at home, when they can get away with it."

Big Al eyed him. "I'm from one of them big Eastern cities, Bill," he said.

Hankins blushed. "Said nothin' 'bout you, Hill. But every one o' the raiders I know of *is* an easterner—a New England easterner—New York, Massachusetts, Rhode Island, Pennsylvania."

"Well now, most of us from around Canonsburg, the part of Pennsylvania I come from, would take exception to being accused of coming from New England," Marley said.

Perceiving Hankins's frustration, Big Al said, "Look, it is true, there's enmity that's developed between a lot of the easterners and westerners here. But boys, tonight, all of us—East, West, South—" He looked toward Hankins. "—wherever, we got one concern, and that's being ready for anything those scum might try against us."

"Is there something special about tonight more than other nights?" Marley asked.

"The raiders know the decent men in the camp are forming a police force—with the aim of bringing them down," Little Al said.

This conversation was amazing Marley the longer it went. Simmons divined this from his expression. "Rebs got eight hundred men to spread over this whole place," he said. "The camp, the ramparts, the guard towers, the bakery, the offices, the hospital, the guardhouse, the roads in and out, foraging parties; it goes on and on."

"They can't ride herd on—" Big Al began.

"Thirty-something thousand men in a stockade built for ten thousand," Hankins said bitterly.

"Bill—" Big Al started again.

"No, you listen to me," Hankins blurted, "Johnny Dunne and Fred Stillwell were *my* friends that died out of our group these last days. It's that Wirz's fault, him with his fancy uniform and his fancy European airs," he said, his voice growing vengeful, as he pointed in the direction of Wirz's office. "And it's them murderin' Secesh butchers in Richmond's fault. They could stop all this if they'd a mind to; they could split us up into other camps. They got 'em. But—"

"Any day now the Rebs will come around on the exchange agreement, and we'll all start getting swapped out of here," Little Al cut in.

"That's right, fellows," Simmons said. "Rusty, that boy that guarded our section of the stockade parapet, the one that caught gangrene on his private parts, he told me before they took him to the hospital that they're close enough to resuming exchanges that the Reb higher-ups told Wirz not to build that new addition to the stockade."

"Rusty," Hankins said. "He that skinny little redheaded boy, maybe fifteen?"

"Fifteen, maybe sixteen," Simmons said.

"Maybe," Hankins said. "Yeah, well he died last night in that flea trap the Rebs call a hospital. He lived right down the road from my uncle's farm back home."

"Oh," Simmons said, saddened.

"That makes three Rebs that have met their demise while guarding our little section of the rampart," Little Al said.

"Four if you count Ole Dickey," Simmons said.

"No, Dickey didn't catch gangrene till after the Rebs moved him to supervisin' burial details," Hankins said. "Least in the face he didn't."

"What beef have the Rebs with the exchange policy?" Marley asked. "I saw a report said they've got more men dying in our Camp Chase than we have dying here."

"They don't want coloreds included in the exchanges," Big Al said. "Leastwise, they don't want them included one-to-one for white soldiers."

"Howdy, men," came a new voice.

"Limber Jim," several of the group said.

Big Al introduced Marley to "Limber Jim" Laughlin, the lanky Illinois horse soldier upon whose broad shoulders the organization and forming of the police force had fallen.

"Expecting trouble tonight?" Big Al asked.

"You can count on it," Limber Jim replied. "Our spies tell us the raiders plan a sweeping attack tonight to crush our effort before it can do the same to them. Well, they'd better do it tonight, because in the next two days, I plan to have enough men deputized to haul in Collins and Curtis and the other leaders and bring 'em before a real live Federal military court."

"Wirz going to let you send them out of here?" Simmons asked.

"No, we're gonna do it right here in the camp," Limber Jim said.

"Fat chance o' that," Hankins said. "You and our other so-called 'leaders' probably won't even live through the night."

Limber Jim eyed him, then turned to Big Al. "Coordinate your patrols with our other men in this sector, Al. And all you men—sleep light, with at least one hand on your weapons."

Then he was gone.

Patrols? Marley thought to himself. *Weapons? Against our own men?*

"Dan, you're patrolling first watch with Morgan and some other men from the Iowans' cave," Big Al said to Dan Swenson, a man sitting next to Marley; the silent Swede was as tall as Big Al and even bigger-boned.

Swenson nodded.

"You take my club to go with your knife," Big Al said. Then he turned to Marley. "So what do you think of your first day in Andersonville, Wayne?"

Marley did not say what he was thinking; his body was screaming in a way it had not in months for a slug of the alcohol that had nearly killed him before he quit it. He felt the eyes of the men on him as dusk settled in with a coral canopy.

"Guess I expected the Rebs to be my enemy here like they are everywhere else," he said.

"Oh, they are," Big Al said, as a chorus of shouts indicating a brawl sounded not far away, "but at Andersonville, you got a whole lot more stacked up against you than just the Rebs."

CHAPTER 31

SO OFTEN HAD AGNES HEARD YOUNG LADIES AND GIRLS AROUND the Mess's neighborhood singing "When This Cruel War Is Over" from their front porches, that she knew every word of every stanza. As July at Bremo became August, September neared, and the war grew ever-longer, Richmond grew ever poorer, hungrier, and more doubtful of the future.

Yesterday a letter had arrived at Bremo from Mary Custis, still on the mend in Richmond from her typhus. *Life-threatening disease is likely the only thing that would keep her at home; she seems to pay no more heed to crossing enemy lines than she does stepping from one cobblestone to another on Franklin Street,* Agnes thought with a wry smile as she sat on the front porch and reread the missive. *Is there no end to how high these prices can go? Five dollars for a spool of cotton, twenty dollars for a yard of linen, nearly three dollars for a quart of milk, hundreds of dollars for one barrel of flour. Medicine impossible to find for anyone anywhere.* While ruminating on this, she heard a scream from inside the house, followed by a loud thud, then guttural moans. *Mama . . .*

Agnes rushed inside and found her mother sprawled facedown on the polished floor of the foyer, where her crutches had slipped out from under her. Her nose was bloody and one leg akimbo. The piteous groans emanating from deep inside her were the only signs of consciousness.

"Mama!" Mildred screamed from halfway down the stairs. "Oh, Mama!"

"Mama," Agnes said softly, cradling Mary's head. "Can you hear me, Mama?"

For a moment Mary lay there, not because she was hurt, though she was, but because a decision faced her. *I believe the Lord will be pleased to take me right here and now,* she thought. *Ah, how to die would be gain! And so weary I am. This would be the blessed end of it. No more sorrow, no more tears, no more cares, only eternal bliss, and reunion with Annie and Mother and Father and Charlotte and so many others. I can come now, can't I, Lord? But you have more for me to do, don't you? Yes, but the pain and sorrow and loss have overwhelmed me; they are all too much.*

So Mary decided to let go and be finished with it. As she relaxed and felt the warm darkness begin to tide over her, a passage of Scripture her husband had cited in his last letter as encasing the heart and attitude he desired, echoed through her listlessness.

"But now ye also put off all these; anger, wrath, malice, blasphemy, filthy communication out of your mouth. . . . Put on therefore, as the elect of God, holy and beloved, bowels of mercies, kindness, humbleness of mind, meekness, longsuffering; forbearing one another, and forgiving one another, if any man have a quarrel against any: even as Christ forgave you, so also do ye. And above all these things put on charity, which is the bond of perfectness."

Agnes's heart stopped as she felt no breath coming from Mary.

"Ma—"

"Lift me up, Aggie," Mary said, nose bleeding and eyes still closed. "I'll be returning to my room."

Mildred called a house servant, who brought Mary's rolling chair and helped the girls lift her into it.

"Call for a doctor, Will," Agnes said to the servant as she turned the chair and guided Mary to her room.

They cleaned her nose, which was not broken. The doctor determined she had a bruised rib. They brought her a weak broth, and Agnes spooned it to her for a quarter of an hour.

"Quit fretting, and hand me the letter on my night table," Mary said to Mildred, who stood wringing her hands. "Thank you, dear. And thank you for the broth, Aggie. Now I would be obliged if you'd leave me alone to read my letters."

The girls looked at one another, then Agnes said, "Mama, one of us will stay with you—in the room, at least."

"I'll not be fussed over," Mary said, her eyes sparking. "I'll ring my little bell here if I'm in need."

Trading defeated glances again, the girls kissed her forehead, then retreated from the room. Outside Agnes closed the door partway, then whispered, "We'll take turns sitting out here—"

"I won't be fussed over in here or out there in the hallway," Mary called out. "Now you girls run along and be about your business."

Exasperated, they fell back farther down the hall, where they stationed a chair as a forward listening post.

"Whatever you do, for goodness sakes be quiet," Agnes admonished Mildred as the younger girl began the first watch.

Mary unwrapped the packet of letters, all postmarked R. E. Lee, Headquarters, Army of Northern Virginia. She paused for a moment. *Oh, how dashing he looked when he last strode away,* she thought proudly. *Somewhat older and now white-haired, but, if anything, more physically vigorous in appearance. The same standard gray uniform, bearing only the stars on the collar worn by any Confederate officer; the cavalry boots reaching to his knees, and his handsome broad-brimmed gray felt hat.*

Ah, here is a fine letter, she thought to herself, smiling. *Those dark days in the rain following Gettysburg when we thought that at any moment those people might fall upon us before we crossed back over the Potomac, when Robert was thinking of me.*

> I trust that a merciful God, our only hope and refuge, will not desert us in this hour of need, and will deliver us by His almighty hand, that the whole world may recognize His power and all hearts be lifted up in adoration and praise of His unbounded loving-kindness. We must, however, submit to His almighty will, whatever that may be.

And desert us he did not, she thought, heartened. Now was a good time to read that particular letter, while she lay in pain, just as he must have been in pain in so many ways following that great disappointment in Pennsylvania, upon which so many hopes had ridden. She knew how often she had disappointed him when she failed to follow his wishes for her. When she returned to Arlington while he served at Fort Monroe, at Saint Louis, when he commanded the Second United States Cavalry in Texas; as she had remained in Richmond month after month during this war.

She had done what she had to do, for herself and for the children. Still, she should not deceive herself into thinking that she had not in some small way, at times, done it, unbeknownst to him—*maybe even unbeknownst to myself; though I doubt it,* she thought—to punish him for doing his duty and staying with the army when it kept him from Arlington. Why would he not just return and be master of Arlington? *Because he wants to work and serve as he has prepared himself,* she knew, *because he wants to be his own man and provide for his own family.*

It was part of what made her love him so, even when she did not return in kind. And it was part of what made her need him so, to know that what they had always believed still was true, when all the world seemed to be crashing down around them.

Yes, I need to know that, to know that he still knows that, she thought, opening another old letter. *And the girls need to know it.*

Agnes so needs to know it.

●◇ ●◇ ●◇

Matters pressed in on Lee from all sides. The war in the west, increasingly becoming the war in the south, went badly for the Confederacy. Federal Admiral David Farragut, a Southerner, captured Mobile Bay, Alabama, one of the few key Confederate ports still open.

Like Grant in the east, William Tecumseh Sherman had a larger, better-equipped army than anything his Confederate opponents could throw against him. He churned across Mississippi and part of Georgia and now threatened Atlanta, the most important city in the Deep South. Lee's old West Point friend Joe Johnston masterfully parried and delayed him. In the one full-scale battle they fought, Johnston's men slaughtered Sherman's charging westerners on Kennesaw Mountain. But now Johnston, whose bitter feud with President Davis had lasted for years, refused to divulge any plan to the president for saving Atlanta, and in fact was rumored preparing to abandon the city.

Davis wanted Lee's opinion about replacing Johnston as commander of the Army of Tennessee with Texan John Bell Hood, who served Longstreet so well as a division commander. A serious question it was, and Lee gave much thought to it. At length he advised Davis, "It is a bad time to relieve the commander of an army situated as that of the Army of Tennessee. We may lose Atlanta and the army. Hood is a bold fighter. I am doubtful as to other qualities necessary."

Grant kept up the pressure, working always to extend his lines farther around Lee's at Petersburg so as to gain the opportunity of a decisive flanking maneuver.

Lee's concern for his own troops mounted. Food and supplies had long been scant. Now, one by one, the Federals cut off rail and road supply routes. Plus, consigned to trench warfare, Lee did not have the ability to range his men as far afield to forage for supplies. And hygiene conditions in the fetid, sun-scalded trenches grew hideous. Increasing numbers of troops fell victim to disease, many of them dying.

Lee pleaded with President Davis that his men might only have soap.

As fall came, many of those men were now going elsewhere to find soap and food and other things. The government kept quiet the fact that at least one hundred men per day were leaving without permission for home. Rather than be angry with those who departed when he so desperately needed them, Lee felt deep sympathy and sorrow for them. For he knew why they were leaving. The letter before him spoke for them all.

> General Lee, sir, it has been a long, long time since I have begged anyone for anything, leastwise since my husband Horace starved to death two winters ago in the Yankee prison Camp Chase up north. But I am begging you now, sir, that if you are the compassionate man we hear tell you are, you allow my youngest boy Sam a few weeks off from defending Richmond to come back down to South Carolina and work the fields for us. It is only myself and my three young daughters left now and we are starving. Surely you, sir, with your thousands, can better spare Sam than can I with four starving mouths to feed. In the name of all that is dear to you, General, sir, I beg that you spare him, at least for a spell. Martha Beasley.

And so were hundreds of such letters flowing in to the army and the government from families—or the remnants of them—all over the South. Many of them came from the Shenandoah, where the Federals had finally availed themselves of their immense advantage in men and resources. Sheridan, with forty thousand men under his command, clobbered Old Jube and his thirteen thousand (*How recently we stood at the very gates of Washington!* Lee remembered with a pang) in a series of engagements, including Cedar Creek, that left the Valley under Federal control.

The bigger story coming to Lee out of that sector was that Sheridan had evidently commenced a program of total devastation against the Shenandoah, beginning at its north end and working south. Lee felt his chest tighten anew upon contemplation of the scale of human horror in such an undertaking. He shook his head slowly and thought, *I have lived too long when the American army decrees that it shall war against women and children, the aged and the sick, as a matter of strategy.* He lowered his head, and silent tears began to plink onto his small desk. *And I cannot stop them. I cannot protect my own people.* A surge of anger filled him, and he clenched his fists, wanting to bang them on the desk. Then he remembered the scriptural admonition to "Love your enemies, . . . and pray for them which despitefully use you," and he remembered that he had not been as faithful to pray for the Federals of late as he had previously been. *Perhaps if I am more faithful to do so, God, you might not be as provoked to provide such stern reminders to your poor servant,* he thought, shaking his head all the more.

Then came word that his son Rob had been shot in a fracas with the Federals outside of Richmond. He thanked God with all his heart the wound was not serious. He remembered that Mary was still on the mend from both her illness and her recent fall and that neither Mary Custis nor Custis sported good health during these days.

How much I have to pray for in these days and how little time to do so, he thought, remembering Martin Luther's statement about being so busy he would have to pray for several hours each day. Lee grabbed one more letter to read. Few were the people who knew how he detested paperwork of any sort, and in particular writing letters. Fewer still were those who knew that no matter how many letters he received—from the army, the government, private citizens, or whatever—whether one or a hundred a day, he would respond to every one of them.

As he read the last letter, he felt hot tears burning his eyes. A Reverend Mr. Cole of Culpeper Courthouse was writing to tell him that hardly a church still stood in that whole section of Virginia within the lines formerly occupied by the Federals. "All are burned to the ground by the United States," the pastor wrote, "and the materials used often for the vilest purpose."

Two churches at Culpeper Courthouse itself narrowly escaped destruction, but all their pews were removed and used as seating for the "Opera House" that housed the George Washington Birthday Ball where hoop-skirted Frank Stringfellow performed his deeds of derring-do.

"This fact was reported to the commanding officer by his own men of the Federals' Christian Commission," Rev. Cole reported, "but he did naught to halt or reprove it."

Lee sat for several minutes, attempting to ferret out how God would have him respond. Finally the thought came to him, a thought that became words when he wrote them to his wife on the matter: "We must suffer patiently to the end, when all things will be made right."

Marley had just begun his patrol when the raiders struck. They came crashing down, over a hundred of them, on the entire "neighborhood" to which his humble abode belonged. He was amazed at the array of weapons they brandished—knives, swords, clubs, axes, sharpened sticks, whips, even a few pistols. Over tents, campfires, and shebangs the raiders swarmed, like a herd of buffalo rumbling across the earth.

He and Big Al and the other men on their patrol dropped back to a preordained police rallying point on the street that ran alongside their shebang. When the raiders arrived, the police—which included Limber Jim and three other leaders of the antiraider forces, formidable westerners named Larkin, Key, and Corrigan—were ready for them.

The pitched battle proved as vicious as any in which Marley had ever participated, and he was a decorated veteran of both the Mexican War and the War of Secession. Grunts, screams, moans, thuds, ripping, and the general sounds of a melee of singular desperation filled the fetid air. As Marley fought, he stepped into and at some points rolled through dung piles in various stages of devolution. He had walked with his packed saddlebags slung over his left shoulder as a sort of shield. At first he had no weapon, but when one feisty little redheaded raider tore into him with a baseball bat, he parried the blows with his saddlebags, then shoved them at the bat, tangling the raider up long enough for Marley to leap onto him and take him to the ground. He glimpsed Limber Jim, a few feet away, wrest a knife from a raider and backslash him across the throat with it. *This is for real,* Marley thought. Having just entered Andersonville and being much bigger, stronger, and heavier than his foe, Marley yanked the bat from him and used the heel of it to bash the flailing man's skull to jelly.

He looked up to see Big Al standing tall, swinging a huge club and taking on all comers. There were several, since he, along with Limber Jim, Larkin, and some of the others had been especially targeted by the raiders. The hulking farmer laid two or three raiders flat before two others got onto his back and pulled at his arms, and a third plunged a knife into his side. Marley charged the knife-wielder, raised the bat, and brained him before he ever saw what was coming. Then Big Al turned on his other tormentors, grabbed them by their hair, and smashed their heads together until they were limp bloody messes. Clutching his bleeding side, he nodded thanks to Marley, picked his dropped club off the ground, and went after a raider he saw plunge a railroad spike into a man from the shebang next door to Big Al's.

The fight continued for several minutes, hand to hand, with no more mercy shown than would be exchanged with the Sioux or Pawnee out on the Great Plains. Marley charged after Big Al into a swirling pocket of fists, clubs, and blades that was raging near their shebang within a few feet of the deadline. He hammered another raider over the head, then felt a piercing pain in his left rear side. He whirled to see a swarthy, stocky scowler brandishing a knife and readying to stick him again. Before he could, Larkin ran a bloody saber he had taken from a dead raider clean through the man, who fell into Marley.

Then, twenty feet ahead, Marley saw a bloodied raider on his knees. Wounds gushed from his head, neck, and abdomen. The man appeared ready to keel over, but he held a derringer in one hand. He looked up onto the stockade, where stood a Confederate guard of no more than sixteen years, musket in hand, but not pointed. The lad's eyes were directed elsewhere, and he did not even see the man with the gun. *Why, he's taking aim at that Reb boy,* Marley thought, disbelieving. Screaming, he charged the raider bat raised high. The man clicked back the hammer. Marley screamed the louder. Just before he reached the raider, the man turned and aimed the derringer at Marley's head. A shot rang out, and the top of the raider's head disintegrated.

Noticing the brawl had quieted—"They're pulling back!" one of the police shouted—Marley looked up at the stockade. Another guard, about the same age as the one who had been targeted, held his smoking musket against his shoulder in the firing position. That boy had observed the whole sequence. He stared at Marley, then dropped his musket and fell to his knees covering his face with his hands and dissolving into sobs.

Other guards, and some prisoners, also had seen what happened. Within minutes of Marley's unconscious collapse onto the ground from his wound, he had been deposited into the hospital outside the camp. Before his eyes opened, he heard a conversation indicating that the power of the raiders had finally been crippled and would be even more when the trial of two dozen of their leaders began the next day.

The first sight that greeted his eyes was that of the Swiss-born commandant of Andersonville Prison looking down at him from next to his cot, his own eyes an unearthly sky blue reminiscent to Marley of Stonewall Jackson.

CHAPTER 32

SHERIDAN RAN ROUGHSHOD IN THE SHENANDOAH VALLEY, AND now Sherman had captured Atlanta. The news trickling in to Lee of what was following that conquest so horrified him that he thought it a good time to depart Violet Bank for a ride around the lines. *No,* Lee decided, *I will go see some of my friends and forget this destruction for a while. They always provide an effective antidote.* He was mounting Traveller to ride when Taylor approached.

"Sir, your, er, daily delivery has arrived," the young man said, looking up at him.

Lee's brow crinkled. *The boy is finding it difficult to keep pace with his tasks,* he thought, disappointed. *Such difficulty he now so often has in articulating his message.*

"From Mrs. Crump, sir, your daily bread delivery," Taylor said. *Must I now draw pictures for the Tycoon even on the simplest of matters?* the aide thought in frustration.

"Ah," Lee said, nodding. "I have written the dear judge's wife, begging her to cease sending it." He chuckled. "I told her we have plenty to eat and our appetites are so good that they do not require tempting," he added.

As Lee rode away, Taylor thought, *Some of us perhaps might appreciate a good round of temptation of that sort.*

Riding along, Lee pushed Sherman out of his mind to think on a matter closer to home. *Each day they grow more and stronger, and we grow weaker in numbers and all other ways,* he thought. *If only our government would allow me to abandon what is surely becoming the graveyard not only of the Army of Northern Virginia but for the Confederacy itself.*

Just then, as a balmy breeze ruffled Traveller's mane and refreshed Lee's face, the specter of his own father wafted into his mind from the deep distant mists of the past. *It must have been after his difficulties and before his wounding,* he thought, *because his face is bronzed and radiant.*

Lee would think no further on his father; certainly not to the remembrance of those "difficulties" being the repeated post-War of Independence and post-Virginia governor financial and investment failures of "Light-Horse" Harry Lee, and ultimately his debtors' imprisonment.

The elder Lee's "wounding" had been a permanent facial disfigurement and near murder, wrought by a mob who did not appreciate his criticism of America's War of 1812. He had called it an unnecessary fight with imperialistic overtones—such as the States' attempt to steal Canada from Great Britain by force of arms.

He was speaking to my older brother Carter and me, Lee remembered, *by the fireplace. It was winter, I believe, and he was holding forth about how to defend our Virginia; in this case, how to defend her when she is attacked by an enemy who controls the sea and who can escape by that avenue if defeated.* "Draw them to the interior," he told us, "at least fifty miles beyond the Tidewater, beyond the navigable streams, and then those ships will be of no use to him, and he may be struck a deathblow!"

Lee nodded with satisfaction. *Yes, to have Papa, and perhaps General Washington, with us now. . . .* His countenance dropped a shade as an odd feeling of loneliness overtook him.

Within days after that fireside visit between a father and his sons, Washington's famed cavalry chief had left for the West Indies. Six-year-old Robert, whom the elder Lee referred to as "always good" and possessed of a "happy turn of mind," would never again see his father.

Lee guided his mind back. *Our men at home on various pretexts must be brought out; if we can secure our entire arms-bearing population in Virginia and North Carolina, and relieve all detailed men with Negroes we may be able, with the blessing of God, to keep the enemy in check—to the beginning of winter.* Still he wished the government would accede to his recommendation of large-scale combat mobilization for Southern slaves, with freedom awarded them at the end of their service. *If we fail to do these things, the result will be . . . calamitous.*

Indeed the specter of Sherman refused to be kept at bay. He had conquered Atlanta, but what burdened Lee was his reputation for allowing his rough-and-ready westerners even more destructive latitude than did the eastern Federal generals theirs. It was Northern newspapers, not Southern, that had already tagged him with such unsavory epithets as "insane." Lee prayed for the protection and deliverance of the innocents of the South—physically and spiritually—

and for the spiritual regeneration of Sherman and his "bummers," as his foot soldiers had come to be known North and South.

Oh, there they are, he noticed, his heart suddenly lifted. The presence of a war that often hit far too close to home was balanced for many of the children of Petersburg by the frequent sojourns through their neighborhoods of the kindly white-haired general with the tired face, the gentle eyes, and the constant willingness to try whatever new games they threw at him. *Several of my regular friends are here today,* he saw.

"Hello, General!"

"General Lee, we have a new game for you today!"

"General Lee—"

Eight-year-old Polly Sturges never completed her greeting, because a Federal shell crashed into a house no more than a hundred yards away. The ear-numbing explosion dusted a couple of the children with earth. They had all heard shelling, but their own street was not normally hit. Polly's little sister Claire began to cry.

"There, there, that's all right, sweet darling," Lee said, jumping from his horse despite his aching sciatica and hugging her to him, even as all the children scrambled for a spot on him upon which to cling. His face grew crimson, and his head began its rapid nodding as he attempted to grind down the rage kindled in him at the foe who continued to war without apparent regard for the Polly and Claire Sturgeses of the world. "Do you know what my children used to do when I got scared or sad?"

"When you got scared!"

"We didn't think you ever got scared, sir."

"Why, yes, I'm very often frightened," Lee answered, "but not as much when I pray and read my Bible as I should. But my children would tickle my feet till their little fingers almost fell off."

"And you didn't stop them?"

"Stop them? Why, Jimmy, if they wouldn't tickle my feet, I would make them do it under threat of throwing them into the family jail!"

"The family jail?"

"Yes, well," Lee sputtered, trying without success to stymie his own grin. "Those people, when they set a house on fire—as I see they have down the street with that last shell—they tend to like to train their guns on that same spot for awhile." With this he turned, and with a sweeping motion, introduced a wagon drawn by two mules and driven by an orderly that had pulled up behind him. "So aren't y'all glad I brought the wagon so we can go play at head-quarters!"

Next to the explosion of the Federal shell, the cheer that erupted from those dozen children was certainly the most exceptional noise heard all day in that Petersburg neighborhood.

After an hour or more of playing every game his friends knew, as well as a few new ones they made up in attempting to prolong their visit to the head-quarters of the Army of Northern Virginia, the wagon was reloaded and the departure made from Violet Bank. This time Lee rode on the wagon, next to the driver, a position which was filled one-by-one by no less than eight of the children by the time they reached home.

Near her neighborhood, where due to shelling two homes now boasted only chimneys amid smoking black rubble, Polly lashed the mules to encourage them on.

"Don't do that, my little friend," Lee said, recalling the words of Proverbs 12:10 that his mother had first taught him better than half a century before: "A righteous man regardeth the life of his beast."

"Oh, I'm sorry, sir," Polly, not realizing she had erred, said, chastened.

A couple of minutes later, as the scrawny beasts trudged on, she forgot her lesson and struck them again.

"Polly," Lee said, compassion for animal as well as child filling his voice, "you must not do that again. My conscience is not entirely at ease about using these animals for this extra service, for they are half-fed, as are we all."

Seeing tears well up in her eyes, he hugged her to himself and said, "Don't fret, dear; if we remember they are God's creatures as well, we will rarely go wrong."

"You were brave not once, but twice tonight," Henry Wirz said in a fair English tongue to Marley. "You showed equal concern for the good regarding your own men and your enemy."

Marley did not know what to say.

Wirz produced two luscious burgundy plums and presented them to Marley, whose eye widened to the limit of its capability. The Swiss native raised his one good arm as if to silence Marley. "Before you object, Major, please. The plums I received as a gift; if you do not eat them, I will, at least I will eat one of them. And you, Major, with your loss of blood and your wound, you are in more need of this fruit than even your comrades in the stockade."

"But—" Marley began.

"I insist," Wirz cut in. "If not for you, then for the sake of those who love you back home. For you are not 'out of the woods,' as Americans say. Please," he pleaded, offering one of the plums, "if not for them, then for me, that I might not have your death on my conscience as already so many are."

Something, either in the man's words, voice, or expression—Marley could not tell which—at this point struck the prisoner, and he took the plum and inhaled it. Once he had done it with one, his hand seemed to grab the other with a will of its own and pop it, too, into his mouth.

"Courage should be rewarded," Wirz said. "I feared when I suggested the organization of the prisoner police force, with the aim—"

"You?" Marley rasped, the dull horrid pain of his wound only now making its presence known to him.

Wirz blushed, embarrassed. He glanced down. "I would not have mentioned it had I been aware the fact was not commonly known among the prisoners."

Marley's head spun. "I . . . I'm a new prisoner."

"Yes, I know," Wirz said. "Nevertheless, I am going to insist, providing you recover in a timely fashion from your wound, that you accompany the commission of prisoners being sent to plead with President Lincoln to reinstate the prisoner exchange cartel."

Now Marley's head began to pound.

"I know," Wirz said, "it is much for you to absorb at one time."

"But it's not President Lincoln that is holding things up—" Marley began, suspicion growing.

"Oh," Wirz said with a knowing nod. "The colored prisoners. Major, do you know how many white prisoners are tonight under the auspices of Camp Sumter? In excess of thirty thousand. Your president—through his emissaries—must do nothing more than resume the cartel unilaterally terminated last year by your Secretary of War Stanton. Then we begin the process—the immediate process of shipping all thirty-odd thousand home."

Marley thought about that for a minute, then summoned his energy to speak. "Captain Wirz, I may be your prisoner, and I may have a hole in my side from one of my own mates—I've got more scars on me from your boys than that—and I may be a little fuzzy in the head right now. But I'll not brook such talk from you, plum or no plum. You got that? I'll not be used by you for whatever it is you Rebs are up to."

Wirz smiled and pulled a rumpled sheet of paper from an inside pocket of his uniform. He opened it up and handed it to Marley. "That is your copy to keep, Major, though I shouldn't advise it for the sake of your own men's morale in the camp. But read it, and if you go to Washington with the others, confirm its veracity through your own channels."

> It is hard on our men held in Southern prisons not to exchange them, but it is humanity to those left in the ranks to fight out battles. At this particular time to release all rebel prisoners North would insure Sherman's defeat and would compromise our safety here.
>
> Ulysses S. Grant
> Lieutenant General
> Commanding Armies of the United States
> August 18, 1864

"One of our spies serving in your government copied the memo as he read it with his own eyes, then sent it through our lines," Wirz said.

Marley read the note through again and then again. He handed it back to Wirz and turned away.

"Major," the commandant said softly, "are you aware of recent entreaties of the Confederate authorities in Richmond for the delivery of food from the Federal government to the prisoners here at Camp Sumter? Food to be reserved for the distribution by and the consumption of the prisoners alone?"

Marley looked at him. Tears formed in Wirz's eyes. He whispered his next words, so not to be heard by nearby patients, nurses, or doctors. "I give half of my paltry salary every time I receive it directly to the purchase of food for the prisoners. Half, major. I and my government have shouted, we have bullied, we have begged, and we have wept for those in Washington City to agree to the resumption of the cartel—even on terms more favorable to them!"

Tears ran down into his ebony beard as he said, "God help you, Major Marley, for unless your government intervenes, I cannot. What can I do? I cannot *make* provisions. My own men, my wife and my three daughters have not enough to eat. They receive the same rations and the same medicines, such as they are, as the prisoners."

"Major?" One of the Confederate surgeons had approached Wirz and spoke in low tones to him, gesturing to his lame arm. Marley peered at the doctor and saw that one side of his face was disfigured. *Gangrene,* Marley thought, stunned.

Wirz, turning back to him, detected his expression and the cause of it. "Oh, yes, Major Marley," he said. "Not only our guards, but in particular our medical staff, fall prey to the same diseases as the prisoners, diseases for which your government so angrily denounces us. The rate of disease for the Confederates at this camp—for scurvy, gangrene, smallpox, dysentery, diarrhea, and all the rest—is almost identical to that of the prisoners. For the medical staff it is actually higher than it is for the prisoners."

Wirz noticed Marley glance at the commandant's lame arm. Wirz hesitated, then said, "I myself have contracted gangrene in this old wound I suffered at the First Battle of Manassas." For a moment his throat seemed to catch. Then he said, "Nearly two hundred Confederate personnel have already died at this camp—none by violent means."

Another officer now needed Wirz's attention. Wirz saluted Marley with his good left arm. "Excuse the intrusion, Major. With your permission we shall talk more at another time perhaps?"

Marley considered that, then gave a brief nod.

"Good, Major," Wirz said, turning to leave, "that is very good indeed." Then he stopped and turned back. "Oh, Major," he said. "Perhaps that young guard who did not die because of your actions is no more than a dirty brown shirt and denim trousers to you. But you should know that he is the only surviving son to his widowed mother of six boys, three of whom were killed in battle and two of whom have died in Northern prisons."

CHAPTER 33

NEVER IN THEIR YEARS OF FIGHTING HAD ETHAN OR CULPEPER seen anything to compare with it.

If they keep on, nothing will remain in all of Virginia, Ethan thought to himself, for he had not the life in him even to speak.

Old Jube had the pair scouting the northward steamroll of Sheridan's Army of the Shenandoah as it carried out Grant's orders that the Valley be rendered and "remain a barren waste." Miles north of Middle Valley Rockingham County seat Harrisonburg, the two Virginians had first seen the smoke roiling black as death—death for the Valley, for the Army of Northern Virginia, for the Confederacy. Like a batallion of fat dark ropes dropped to earth from heaven, the towering columns of smoke were arrayed across the horizon, from the Blue Ridge clear over to North Mountain.

Closer to Harrisonburg, as the air grew thicker, hotter, and more drafty, Ethan and Culpeper learned from one stricken, fatherless family of the supposed "murder" of Federal cavalry officer and Sheridan favorite John Rodgers Meigs by bushwhacking civilians.

Meigs also happened to be the son of Lincoln confidante and Federal Quartermaster General Montgomery C. Meigs.

"Shot him as he tried to surrender," the widow recounted. "Leastwise, that's the story Custer and his Fifth New York Cavalry broadcast when they set to work. Don't pass through Harrisonburg south or west, unless you've more provisions than you appear to have. They're calling it the 'Burnt District.'"

The enraged elder Meigs would have his son's body buried at Arlington. There, in honor of the lad, he christened a new section of cemetery on the grounds of the erstwhile Lee home—a section coincidentally encompassing Mary's beloved rose garden. Meigs ordered the treasured vines churned up and his son placed front and center. Soon a wave of other caskets filled the remainder of the old garden, commanded by an imposing bronze statue of John Meigs.

On direct orders of Sheridan, meanwhile, Custer set about the total destruction of the area from Harrisonburg south to the North River; the Valley Pike west to Mole Hill. The New Yorkers burned down every home, every barn, every store, every church, every building of any sort. They ate, stole, or slaughtered every four-legged creature they came across.

The vortex of the destruction was the area around the Rockingham County town of Dayton, near where the younger Meigs died. There dozens of sobbing families—mostly the usual complement of mothers, grandmothers, grandfathers, children, and maimed men—pulled as many valuables out of their homes as they could before the torches flew. Beseeched by one of his subordinate officers, Lt. Col. Thomas F. Wildes, Sheridan relented and spared Dayton. But the civilians at all points of the map around it stood weeping, screaming, or in dazed stupor as Federals, armed to the teeth, carted off family treasures by the armload and wagonload for immediate consumption or dispatching to their own families up north as souvenirs.

Scarcely a structure stood for more than three miles in every direction of Dayton.

Ethan and Culpeper barely eluded trailing elements of the vast Federal columns even while nosing their way along the back roads. So searing was the open air heat, that they rolled up both the sleeves of their sticky shirts and the legs of their trousers. They rode only a little ways into the Burnt District before the dirty smoke reduced them to blindness and waves of gagging and coughing. They had plenty of company as they turned to head away. A stream of women, children, and old folks, black and white, and a sprinkling of middle-aged white men filed out of the area on foot. The Federals had left them no horses or mules to ride, no wagons to load, only the few items slung over their shoulders in bags.

"Where are you headed?" Ethan asked one old man who held the hand of a little boy with glazed eyes and a smoke-smeared face.

"Nowhere," the man said, eyeing Ethan's horse.

Ethan knew that look. The man did not see a ride with it, he saw food. Ethan had already given everything he had to eat to the refugees. Culpeper had one biscuit left, which he planned to eat tonight. Ethan would have given them his horse except then he would be disobeying orders and Old Jube would know even less what to do against Little Phil than he did now.

The last sight the two scouts caught as they retreated up into nearby hills was that of two chimneys rising out of a pile of black rubble and orange embers.

"I hear tell some of our boys out in Missouri are liftin' Yank scalps, Indian-style," Culpeper, savoring stolen Federal tobacco, said that night. He and Ethan sat at a small fire in the hollow of a high hill whose population of lowland critters had ballooned as Sheridan blazed his trail down the valley. The birds, though, had all rushed south. There were no birds left anywhere around. The scouts drank chicory coffee that boasted no more punch than the tattered remnants of Stonewall's old Valley army. Ethan's leather-bound Bible lay in his lap, opened to the Psalms. "What sort of yowl you think we could get out of old Granny Lee if we took to doin' that to Sheridan's bloody legs, Ethan?"

"The last yowl you'd ever hear."

They sat in silence for several minutes. Nothing entered their ears except the occasional crackle of an acorn popping off an oak tree.

"I swear, Ethan, ain't that Old Virginny herself stingin' our eyes and noses?" Culpeper said, tying his dirty red bandanna over his face, pulling low the black felt slouch hat he'd taken off a Yankee corpse, and squinting.

After several more minutes of silence, Culpeper eyed the man with whom he had ridden down so many hard trails these last months and said, "Thinkin' on your old home place again, Ethan?"

Ethan thought about that for a long while before answering. "Yes, quite a lot, I have." He sipped more chicory, then said, "You've made reference a time or two to my family and their queer ways, Cole."

"Aw, I didn't—"

"No, you were right. And I've been thinkin' on that these last days, even more than on what we saw back there at Valiant. I saw what Pa left us, but it's taken me a lot more seein' up and down this poor valley to understand it."

"More chicory, Ethan?"

"Thank you, Cole." As Culpeper poured him another cup, Ethan continued, "I left Valiant soon as I could to go to the university in Maryland where Pa went. Didn't finish, but I stayed in Maryland till Lincoln invaded us. Did you know they started throwin' everyone in Maryland in jail or prison that didn't speak out loud enough for the Union? Why, Maryland was comin' out, but Lincoln and Stanton sent soldiers. They actually threw the entire legislature in prison and took over the state. Suspended habeas corpus for everyone."

"What the hey is habus corpeus?"

"Those are the reasons Maryland didn't come out, and those are the reasons I came home," Ethan continued. "The only reasons."

"Your Pa, he—"

"My Pa was a bad man," Ethan blurted, looking Culpeper in the eye, tears forming in his own. He said nothing more for a moment, as if surprised at his own words. "There, I have said it. My Pa—was a bad man. He was bad to me, bad to my brothers, bad to Ma. Bad to the animals, bad to the slaves. Like no one else anywhere around our parts, I suspect. But he had money and land, and he could sure smooth-talk folks into thinkin' how respectable he was."

"I ne'er did like him," Culpeper said from behind his bandanna. "'Scuse me, Ethan. That didn't come out right—"

"My little sister Rachel Anne, though, she always worshiped the ground he walked on. Any good there was in Pa, he showed it to her. She never saw his bad side, or never chose to see it. For some reason she was the one soul in this whole wicked world he truly wanted to be good for. Well, I know now it's men like him got us in this mess. It's men like him that have brought Vir—" At this, his throat tightened. "—that have killed Virginia."

Culpeper pulled his bandanna right off at that one. "Ethan, your Pa may've been meaner'n a cornered cur dog, but 'tain't no more his fault what's happened to Virginny than the man in the moon. It's Lincoln and his n—— lovin' scum what done all this to us."

"I hate Lincoln as much as the next man," Ethan said. "He's a pettifogging tyrant with his tariffs and his martial law and his war, and he's killed our Constitution dead as a beaver hat and wrapped it all up with religious cant—and him, an infidel. He's just the sort of ambitious, double-talking fool General Washington warned us about. Next thing you know, America will be off fighting other nations in other parts of the world, where our dog ain't in the fight. She did it to Mexico, she's doing it to her own South. Look out Europe, look out Asia."

"Ah, that's the craziest thing I ever heard in my life," Culpeper said with disgust, tossing the rest of his chicory, tin cup and all, into the fire.

"Yep," Ethan, ignoring him, said with a sigh, "men like Sam McDowell gave those Christ-hating Yankee abolitionists like the Howes and Wades and Stevenses the pretext to fire up the rest of the North to come against us. The North wasn't fed up with our slaves, Cole. They were fed up with us! But they needed the tariff money for the European products made from the crops we shipped overseas. If you don't think I'm right, ask yourself if Lincoln would have let us go if we'd have freed the slaves, *then* seceded."

"H— no, he wouldn'ta!" Culpeper shouted.

"And it's the biggest regret of my whole life to finally figure it all out," Ethan said. "Pa knew full well slavery was dying in the South; since Congress finally got the sense to stop the slave trade, the cost of slaves has gone up faster than the amount of work they do has gone down. Ma told me he said himself they just weren't profitable anymore. That's one reason he got frustrated and bullied 'em so bad. But the fly in the buttermilk is, slavery was dying—and would've died right along, with or without Lincoln's war."

"But I'll be hanged if I ever bit off one ca'tridge to fire so's I could save some rich boy's slave," Culpeper said. "Nobody in my whole part of Rockbridge County ever owned even one slave. I wouldn't want no darkie workin' my spread if'n I could have 'em!"

"You know it, I know it, the whole South knows it, but that doesn't matter a shake now," Ethan insisted. "Men like my Pa gave all our enemies an excuse to stir up the pot against us. The Yank industrialists who wanted our tariff money, the Federalists who wanted our power, the Emersons and Thoreaus who wanted our way of life, their apostate preachers who wanted our souls. And all Pa and his kind had to say to that was 'Let's fight,' because they thought seceding from the Union was their best chance to keep their slaves. Don't you see, Cole, he *wanted* war." He shook his head and bit his lower lip. "How blind they were. They would have wound up losing their slaves even if the Confederacy prevailed because it just won't work anymore. So now thousands of blacks will be turned loose all of a sudden without a clue in the world how to live as free men."

Culpeper was out of responses.

A wave of calm seemed to break over Ethan. "One thing I've learned from this ole book, though," he said, brandishing his Bible, "is that God's justice sometimes takes a while in coming, but it does come. You watch and see if 'Honest Abe' doesn't get his in the end too."

He put the book down, took a dreg from his tin cup, and stared into the fire. "Like ole Dr. Dabney said, God has chastened his people, and he has used his enemies to do it, just like in the olden days."

"Who is Dr. Dabney?" Culpeper groused, a surly mood enveloping him. He wanted whiskey. "All that readin' and book learnin' you done just fouled you up good, bub."

"No, Cole," Ethan said, nodding his head. "I think I finally figured some things out."

"Is that Dr. Dabney related to Dabney what rode with Old Jack?" Culpeper asked.

"One and the same," Ethan said.

Culpeper's face grew somber. "Tell me somethin', Ethan," he said, his voice dropping, as though he were in danger of being heard and embarrassed by others. "Was that Dabney a preacher boy?"

"One of the greatest in the whole country, and in the United States too," Ethan said.

"You caught yourself religion from him, didn't you?"

This stopped Ethan short.

"'Cause you carryin' that Bible the way you do don't count a whit with me," Culpeper said, his words gaining velocity, "nor readin' it, even. But . . ." He didn't seem to know how to finish. His eyes grew shiny, and it seemed to Ethan that for the first time he was getting a peek into his friend's very soul. "I . . . it's just . . . you actually seem to believe what's in that book, and I ain't never seed a McDowell do more'n carry it to church with 'em."

Now Culpeper stopped, giving Ethan a chance to respond.

"Well you're right, Cole," he said. "It was a sermon Dr. Dabney preached in camp while still Old Jack's chief of staff. But—" Now Ethan's own eyes misted over, and he closed his mouth and lowered his head for fear of bawling.

"What, Ethan? What is it?"

Ethan looked back up. Tears streamed down his cheeks, but the hazel eyes glimmered, and a smile curled up the edges of his gold-mustachioed mouth. "It happened after Gettysburg. That sad, horrible march back, with our hopes dashed and a hollow feeling in our empty bellies for the first time that maybe our independence was not as sure as we had thought. And General Lee—who of all men had lost so much, and him, riding so proud and tall still in the saddle, but us knowing his two broken hands still hurt him, and that he hurt in lots of other ways, too. Some Yank prisoner lay on the ground, his leg shattered by a ball, next to the road past which General Lee rode.

"Anyhow," Ethan continued, "this Yank commenced to shaming the general to his face like he was no better than a mangy yard dog, Cole, shouting 'Hurrah for the Union!' and 'Down with the traitors!' and the like. Everyone, dozens of men around there within earshot, Billy Yanks and Johnny Rebs both, all of us, were quiet as a church mouse all of a sudden, breathless at what Marse Robert would do."

Ethan paused for a moment, reflecting.

"Well, what, Ethan boy? What did he do?" Culpeper pressed, looking as if he would come across the dying little fire and shake it out of Ethan if he did not tell him the rest.

"He halts his horse and climbs down," Ethan said. "And he starts to walk toward this foul-mouthed Yank, his features set stern as stone. One man near me whispers, 'He's gonna shoot him; he's had a bellyful of the Yanks.' Another says, 'No, he'll slap him, then have him hided.'

"But the general, the head of the whole Army of Northern Virginia—the leader of the entire South, I'll be bound—his hopes and dreams for us all just crushed, well he walks right up to the man—who wore spectacles, I remember, and had hate smeared across his dirty face—and that Yank gets real quiet, real quick. And the general, he reaches down his hand to this Yank stranger, this private, and grips his hand and shakes it, and says to him, 'My son, I hope you will soon be well.'"

The remembrance of the act now so overawed Ethan that he did not know if he could finish. This time, though, Culpeper did not push him.

"Then the general pats him on the shoulder, just like a good father to a son—" Now Ethan's voice cracked. "—this real sad look on his face, and he turns and walks back to Traveller, gets on him, and rides away. For a moment or two, no one said anything. Then that Yank whose hand the general shook, he began to bawl like a little baby and put his head to the turf, and I believe he cried himself to sleep, right there on that wet, bloody ground."

Both Ethan and Culpeper sat transfixed. "But by then, other men, blue and gray, had commenced to sobbing too."

Culpeper stared at the dying embers, unable to process it all.

"That's why I'm still fighting when I know we'll probably lose," Ethan said, his jaw set like flint. "I'll fight for General Lee till the Yankees grind me to dust."

When Culpeper spoke, his words were no more than a whisper. "Yeah, I saw General Lee after Gettysburg too."

CHAPTER 34

A SURGE OF ANGER RIPPLED THROUGH LEE AS HE READ MARY'S letter. Just as he finished it, Taylor stuck his head into the tent.

"Oh, what can it be now, Colonel Taylor?" Lee barked.

Previously tolerant and accommodating of the chameleon-like moods Lee had developed in the past year of war, Taylor now ignored them the best he could and also ignored how his own attitude might appear to Lee.

"The latest deserter counts," Taylor said, purposely squelching any conscious acknowledgement of, and especially any reaction to, the Tycoon's latest letter and mood. After placing the report on Lee's writing table, Taylor noticed the big man's familiar stretching of his torso and lower back. *His blamed sciatica is acting up again, though I, Marshall, and Venable will bear the most suffering for it. The old man could horsewhip Armistead Long, and that officer would not utter a negative discouraging word toward his master.* Taylor sighed, his dislike for himself beginning to eclipse that he now held for Lee. *I am becoming like him,* he thought, entering his own tent. Sitting down, he shook his head. No, he knew better than that. Taylor, perhaps better than anyone else, had perceived the lengthening roll call of physical afflictions besetting the Tycoon. Sciatica, diarrhea, pains in his arms, neck, chest, back, those small aristocratic hands he broke when he fell on the Sharpsburg campaign.

The young man removed his glasses and searched his own heart. *I'm going to go stark raving mad if I don't marry Betty soon,* he thought. *She, and the thought of losing her—the thought of marrying her and her losing me—are driving me round the bend. But it would be the supremely selfish act of my entire life to marry her at this point, with the uncertainty that lies before us. Any sunrise may bring with it maiming, capture, death.* He lay back on his cot, his head aching at the sight of all the papers on his desk that demanded his attention. *How God's wrath must be kindled against us all,* he thought, his eyelids forcing themselves closed hours before he had planned to turn in.

❧ ❧ ❧

I cannot believe she has done it, Lee groused after reading the letter again. *Returning to Richmond yet again, against my clearly pronounced wishes. Surely she must have left almost immediately upon receiving my correspondence advising her in no way to return in the present uncertainty of events! She and the girls were so finely set up at Bremo.* He sat letting the steam build. *Now she is right back in the middle of the war!*

He had wanted all of them out of Richmond until the war ended, but of course Mary Custis had found an excuse to defy convention—and the wishes of her parents—by staying at the Mess first to recuperate from her illness, then just to stay. *When we want her to come somewhere, she won't,* he thought. *Then when we want her to leave, she won't do that either.* Rubbing his aching arms, he tried to determine whether he was more of a failure as a husband or a father. *Certainly there is little heed given to any counsel of mine from any quarter of the family.* Even Custis had long chafed against his father's counsel to flourish where he was in service to Davis and the government; then when opportunity came recently for a command in the Shenandoah, he spurned it, citing his lack of experience for the role!

Lee's jaw hardened as he realized how far back his wife had gone her own way. How many years he had eaten prairie dust while she stayed—all the children with her—back at Arlington. Then he remembered with embarrassment the towering reason for her first removing herself and her children to Richmond, and now returning again: "How else do I even have a chance ever to see my husband?" Implicit in the "ever" of that plaintive sentence were the unwritten words, "When because of your daring, boldness, and tenacity, every day brings with it the possibility that it might be your last on earth."

And, after all, who had left Arlington and insisted on an itinerant career with much danger, little pay, and constant separation? She was the one who fought against it, so they could all be together, so he could have the respect the Lees had once had and which she wanted so badly for him. For him and not herself, he knew truly in his heart.

All she has ever wanted is to be with me, and all I have done is keep us apart. And here I am, still doing that, though I love her even more than I did then. Now the pain edged back around his shoulders toward his chest.

Yes, as usual, it is all my fault, and no one else's, he thought sadly. *God protect her and my children,* he prayed, pushing aside the stack of paperwork and letters that seemed only to grow larger, and opening his Bible. Even as he felt the soft worn leather and turned to the Psalms, which like so many venerable old friends welcomed him back down their familiar trails and footpaths, he felt his spirit lighten and his resentment and disappointment melt away.

The Federal prisoners of Andersonville, under the silent watch of Confederate muskets, tried their own men on the grounds of the prison camp itself. Defense counsel included a couple of New York City's most renowned barristers, who fought vigorously on the accuseds' behalf.

After two weeks of testimony, arguments, and deliberation by the jury of prisoners, six of the raider leaders were convicted of committing crimes worthy of death by hanging. Close to twenty others had to run a brutal gauntlet of their fellow prisoners for their penance. Still, a rumble of disgust spread through the camp that no more men were hanged from the gallows built with relish by prisoners whom Wirz awarded extra rations.

After a few more isolated brawls, won with crushing finality by the swelling ranks of the Wirz-backed, antiraider, Federal "police" force, order was restored among the prisoners and kept by the law-abiding men of the North. Wirz paroled home Limber Jim, Larkin, Key, Corrigan, and a couple of the other leaders for their own protection. The mantle of camp leadership fell to Big Al's broad shoulders.

A week after the hangings, Marley walked straight from his hospital bed to one of the more fashionable "Market Street" huts. There met the commission of Federal prisoners Wirz would send to Washington City to petition Lincoln for resumption of the cartel.

"The Rebels have agreed to full participation of the free black soldiers in the exchange," Big Al, who would not make the trip, told Marley.

"Have you the strength to make such a trip, to present our appeals to the executive himself?" Little Al, who would make it, asked Marley.

The diminutive accountant and the others knew Wirz wished Marley on the commission; they had also heard Big Al laud his cool-headed leadership among the prisoners at both Libby and Andersonville.

The Pennsylvanian, recognizing anew his weakened state even as the question was asked, pondered the situation, feeling the watchful eyes of the other five "commissioners," as well as several of the other prisoner leaders.

"With God's help," he said at last.

"Indeed," said Skinner, not a commissioner, but assigned by Big Al to take notes for their meetings, "with the blessing of the Almighty, a great good for our men, our people, and all of humanity shall soon be accomplished."

"Here, here," a chorus of voices assented.

"Major Marley, if you'll stay a few minutes, I'll rehearse the particulars of the trip," said Edward Boate, chairman of the commission. Then he faced the rest of the group and said, "Gentlemen, we report to Captain Wirz's office tomorrow morning at eight o'clock, thence to General Winder, for our departure. May God bless our mission."

Despite himself, Marley felt his heart pounding in his chest. *President Lincoln himself,* he thought, scarcely able to believe the turn of fortune that had befallen him, *and I, so often in the very clutches of the Death Angel, I am going to meet that great man himself. Perhaps the Almighty yet has work for me to accomplish in this life.*

The next morning Wirz betrayed the first smiles most of the commission had ever witnessed from him.

"It gives me great joy to inform you men that, even as we proceed with your important mission, Colonel Robert Ould, the Confederate Commissioner of Exchange, has forwarded to his Federal counterpart the Confederate Congress's offer to deliver to him all the sick and wounded prisoners we have." Marley could see Wirz's struggle to stymie a smile that threatened to burst forth from the surrounding bonds of his black beard.

Wirz added, "Further, in order to make your government safe in sending the transportation, our government will not insist upon the delivery of an equivalent number of our prisoners in return."

The stares that greeted this pronouncement evidenced no more understanding than Wirz himself had as to why a good God would allow Camp Sumter and the war that had spawned it.

"Gentlemen, what I mean to say is, your government has but to provide the transportation for the removal of every sick or wounded Federal soldier in any prison in the Confederacy."

Wirz, having developed a rapport with Marley during the latter's weeks in the hospital, spied the uncertainty written on his face.

"Way—uh, Major Marley," Wirz said. "Does not such momentous information elicit some manner of response from you?"

Marley thought about that for a moment. "Well, Captain," he said. "Are we free to speak our minds?"

"By all means," the arm-maimed Confederate fairly shouted to the eye-maimed Federal.

"Well then, I reckon I'm curious as to what sort of alchemy you fellows are about now," Marley said. Whether it was the stricken look covering Wirz's face, the prospect of meeting Abe Lincoln and gaining the release of tens of thousands of soldiers, or his own wonder at the news Wirz just imparted, he would never know, but whatever the reason or reasons, Marley let go a chortle of laughter before saying, "But if it's true, I say let the respective commissioners of exchange loose to treat them for ending the war!"

Minutes later, Westminster Confession tucked inside his coat pocket and wearing cavalry boots loaned to him by Bill Hankins in exchange for his house shoes, Marley, along with Little Al, Boate, and the others, was en route to see Winder, then to board a boat north to the White House.

Being a German, a Baptist Brethren, and a pacifist in what was considered the Scots-Irish, Presbyterian, Confederate Valley of Virginia had not always been easy for Jacob Schumacher III. Neither had pastoring a people who spoke a "foreign" language and who had developed chasms between themselves as wide as the valley they farmed so well.

Valley folk had christened the German Baptist brethren "dunkards," or "dunkers," in reference to their novel (at least in that land) practice of "believer's" baptism. The "dunkers" also tended to oppose slavery, and these factors, in league with their German language and convictions against fighting under any circumstance, combined to keep life very interesting for the dunkards and their pacifistic Mennonite cousins during the War for Southern Independence.

As if Schumacher had not enough drama in his life, he found himself in the middle of an emotional powder keg pitting older dunkards committed to the German language and retaining German anabaptist ecclesiastical traditions against many of their younger offspring, who preferred speaking the language and engaging in the customs, at church and elsewhere, of the America that was the only home they could remember.

Schumacher's own eldest son, Jacob IV, had come to be known by virtually everyone as Jake. This did not please his father, nor did the now-eighteen-year-old's poorly concealed passion to devote his talents as Rockingham County's finest marksman and one of its best horsemen to the Confederate cause. For Jake Schumacher's blood was half that of his mother's, whose Rhinehardt lineage ran back, so the family lore went, to that eighth- and ninth-century Christian warrior himself, Charles the Great—the peerless Charlemagne—king of the Franks, emperor of the Holy Roman Empire, uniter of Europe, and founder of the First Reich.

At times it seemed to preacher Schumacher as though all the world were conspiring to move him and his people from the pillar of their faith that stood against killing. Even his golden-locked wife, Katarina, whose hand he had won twenty years before when nearly every dunkard and Mennonite in the Valley of marrying age had sought it, even she had come to feel that Virginia was her land and its people hers.

She had never uttered a single word to him on the matter, but he knew his Katarina.

Thus she supped in silence opposite her husband at the great spruce table hewn from the cloaken fairyland of the Black Forest. Over Schumacher's shoulder outside, a hundred yards away, she saw the sturdy cedar-framed church from whose pulpit he, his father Jacob II before him, and his grandfather Jacob I before that, had preached. Down one side of her dining table sat four sons and down the other four daughters.

"Son, if you trade your plowshare for a sword, your end will be just as Holy Writ promises," Schumacher said as he dolloped potatoes onto his plate next to the lamb, sausage, and beans. "Just as that which found Stonewall Jackson and Jeb Stuart." He fixed his piercing blue eyes on Jake. "Men as devout and chaste as we, I remind you."

The very "Yes, Father," Jake spoke belied the rebellion boiling within. The words he was thinking were, *Robert E. Lee has traded his plowshare too, Papa.*

An odd aroma struck Schumacher, over the host of them already present at table.

"My little Gretchen," he said, gentleness invading his voice, which could be very hard these days, especially when he addressed Jake, "do I detect at table that most redolent of fragrances whose admiration we so share?"

A scarlet wave washed across the pristine visage of six-year-old Gretchen, whose yellow pigtails spiraled down right and left. Supper conversation did not often include the daughter Schumacher had come to realize was the most thoughtful of all his children. In these last years, however, the little one had coiled herself around his heart as snugly as had even Jake his firstborn. When she asked blushing permission to be excused from the table and he heard the pitter-patter of her quick little feet up the stairs, he knew where she went and that she knew he knew.

Thus did Gretchen see the dust rising from the approaching Federal column even before Jake's keen senses detected the rumbling of the earth. She was unafraid, even though she knew more Yankees were coming and even though she knew they had burned many homes and many barns, some of them belonging to friends, some even to kinfolk of hers. After all, when the first group arrived yesterday, though the men's voices sounded loud and her mother told her to cover her ears for some of the words they said, once Papa had explained he was a friend of the Union, they decided not to burn everything down. The Yankees did take most of the hogs and a lot of the sheep, but that was only because they were hungry, Papa said, and he was more than glad to contribute his part to the Federal cause.

Gretchen had wondered how those soldiers could be so hungry when they looked so much bigger and cleaner than the skinny, dirty-looking "Secessionists" as Papa called them. But she had been more concerned that no one hurt Frederick the Great, her pet duck. Fortunately her thirteen-year-old brother John—Johann, the older folks at church called him—hid the bird just in case.

Now she wondered whether she should return her prized little lavender soap cake, brought back to her by Uncle Gerhard from the Old Country, to its drawer in the cedar chest, or whether she should hide it somewhere else, or maybe even tuck it inside her dress for extra special safekeeping. And then there was the matter of "Baby." True, Baby was worn and frayed, more white than pink in her old age, but Gretchen calculated she could not leave to chance the fate of she who had been, next to Mama and Papa, her most faithful companion since before she could remember. At length, as she heard movement and raised voices downstairs, she determined to trust Papa and God both and return the soap cake to its drawer and let Baby stay on her bed with her other two larger but less-revered dolls.

Papa's teaching about laying up treasures in heaven rather than on earth had borne much fruit in her heart. *It is only Baby and my lavender soap cake from the Old Country that I have not yet given up to God,* she admitted to herself.

Gretchen had scampered only halfway back down the stairs when her sister Susanna shoed her back up to the girls' room, under Mama's orders to stay put till the soldiers left.

After a quick prayer with his sons, Schumacher walked out front to greet his new visitors. He noted with disdain the grim countenance painting second son Eli's sixteen-year-old features. *Jake has been talking to him again about bearing arms to defend Virginia,* Schumacher thought, anger kindling in him, not so much against his eldest as against the insane world over which he held increasingly little influence, even with his own family.

He glanced over toward the main barn. Twelve-year-old Paul already had the Stars and Stripes up the flagpole. *At least that is properly done,* Schumacher thought.

"Sir, you'll need to bring all your people out to a place of safety," the Yankee captain said right off, saluting, and dismissing the American flag fluttering in the breeze with a glance. Schumacher noted the smoky veneer coating the faces and uniforms of the company of soldiers flanking the captain. In fact the whole lot of them reeked of smoke.

"Greetings, Captain. I am Brother Jacob Schumacher III, teaching pastor for the local German Baptist Brethren. We offer our hospitality and refreshment to you, the brave defenders of the Union."

"I am sorry, Pastor," the captain said, "but I'm under orders to put the torch to all these buildings." His eyes gazed around with a bit more focus. "And I'm afraid, with the mill there, and situated as you are right near the river—your farm's just in a key spot, sir—we'll not be able to spare the main house either."

"Sir," Schumacher said evenly, panic trying to overcome him, "this family has suffered greatly from the Secessionists of the Valley since the beginning of this war for our pro-Union, antislavery beliefs. Twice we have risked our lives to hide my eldest two sons from Rebel conscription agents. In recent months written threats have reached our home from unknown persons with pro-Secessionist sympathies. I refuse to believe that now, when the forces of the Grand Army of the Republic have arrived to liberate us, we should be attacked by men carrying the very flag we have never ceased so proudly to fly."

The logic and power of this pronouncement rendered the captain mute. He sighed and pushed his navy blue officer's hat up off his forehead a bit. He glanced around at his men. "Sergeant," he said to a trooper just behind him. "It is late, and we do need a place to bed down."

"We would be honored to provide—and serve—your entire force with a hearty supper, Captain," Schumacher said.

The captain looked at him, glanced again at the flag, then said, "Very well, Pastor. It does take some amount of sand to be flying that flag in these parts. In fact, if not for these scurrilous Reb bushwhackers nipping at our heels every step of the way down this valley, I'd leave some guards posted here for you. But the Rebs'd just kill my men and you."

"We have survived thus far, Captain," Schumacher said. "Please, you and your officers are welcome to sup with us in the house."

"Much obliged, but that won't be necessary," the captain said, climbing down from his horse. "We'll dine and sleep in your main barn if you don't mind."

"Certainly, Captain," Schumacher said, with a slight bow. "Jacob, Paul, clear a space in the barn for the captain and his officers."

The expressions he saw on those two sons' faces sent a shiver down his spine. For he reckoned rightly they would rather be killing the Federals than providing hospitality to them.

Marley arrived in New York City with the other commissioners and with a letter from General George Stoneman, chief of cavalry for Schofield's Army of the Ohio. Stoneman had been captured when Confederate cavalry under Joe Wheeler smashed a major Federal horse thrust toward Andersonville.

Stoneman pled with Lincoln, not for the exchange of himself or other imprisoned Federal officers, but for the men in the ranks who had "fought so gallantly in the field and suffered so much in prison." He assured Lincoln he was not being coerced by the Confederates to make a statement; being in Georgia, and gauging the condition both of the Southern people and military and the

Federal prisoners in the area, he was convinced the Confederates were unable to provide any better treatment for their prisoners than they were already giving.

To Marley's surprise, on the ship voyage north, with so much at stake on the trip and such a historic opportunity looming before him, his own thoughts ran increasingly toward the loneliness racking his body and soul. He had not spent significant time with any woman of substance, any woman of interest to him, for years. After serving with Stonewall and losing his eye at Chapultepec in the Mexican War, he had returned to Pennsylvania, rather fallen out with his rigidly abolitionist family, and wound up in Lexington at the Virginia Military Institute under Stonewall's classroom tutelage. What had begun with so much promise, however, somehow deteriorated into a drunken, brawling descent nearly to his death. For years he had wallowed in sin and self-pity until, with Stonewall's example and God's empowerment, at last he crawled out of his destructive pit.

But a long, grueling ordeal it had been, especially eschewing the bottle, which had gripped him like nothing else in his life. When during the frigid, failed Fredericksburg campaign he had seemed bound to return to his old ways, he had fallen under the command and into the comradeship of "Old Prayer Book" Howard, the ardent abolitionist, Federal corps commander, and a man born on the same day as Marley in 1830 and only thirty miles away.

With Old Prayer Book's encouragement, Marley's faith had strengthened, and he had even led Bible studies among the troops when he wasn't isolated on scouting work.

He had now been dry for over four years, but he ached for a woman—a wife—more than he had his whole life. *Perhaps God has determined I am close to being worthy of a helpmeet and is birthing an irresistible desire to that effect in my heart, so that even in my slowness and dullness I might recognize His will when He brings such a union to fruition?* Marley wondered that night in the dingy hotel room he shared with the rest of the commissioners, all of whom besides him were long asleep.

He had evidently thought enough on the matter in God's opinion, for the next morning Boate and two other commissioners turned up violently ill.

"We cannot go to Washington City," Boate gasped to him between episodes of vomiting, "and this mission must not be delayed even one day further. Of the three remaining commissioners, Al Tate has not the force of personality, and the other man, Lemuel Pardee, cannot well control the force of his personality."

Boate wiped his mouth with a kerchief and looked Marley in the eye. "You shall lead the commissioners in representing the forgotten martyrs of Andersonville Prison before President Lincoln."

CHAPTER 35

WHEN MORE FEDERALS CAME TWO DAYS LATER, GRETCHEN, NOW considering herself a hardy veteran of the war, did not bother to disturb her soap cake or Baby from their comfortable sanctuaries.

Riding in from a field where the last of the season's wheat had just been shocked, Schumacher found a smaller group of horse soldiers than before. He estimated their number at forty.

He also found a very different man in command, a lieutenant short of stature but with an upper body that filled out its dirt-caked, once-blue hussar's jacket like an oaken tree trunk. A crooked angry scar mapped the left side of his face from ear to cheekbone to chin. Schumacher spotted at least three revolvers stashed into his holsters and gunbelt, and suspected more. Two Spencers protruded from saddle holsters. A stash of haversacks and saddlebags were slung over his horse's back behind the lieutenant. Before he spoke, half his force had already dismounted and begun collecting hay and other incendiaries, and distributing them around the perimeter of all the buildings, including the big house and the church. A dozen or so other men rode ahead toward the mill.

"Bring all your folk out into the dooryard," the lieutenant opened in a brogue so clearly German that Schumacher pondered whether the man hailed from Saxony or Silesia. In fact the pastor asked the cavalryman just that, in flawless German.

The lieutenant glared at him, his scar seeming to blaze a brighter red. "I'll not say it again. Now get out of my sight. Hoffman, bring down that flag."

"Sir!"

A beefy trooper on a magnificent, step-trotting white stallion, more than seventeen hands high—*That can only be Jared Kruger's horse,* Schumacher realized with a jolt—galloped over to the flagpole, slit the cord with his saber, and brought down the flag.

"We are loyal Unionists, Lieutenant," Schumacher said, his voice shaking. "We have flown that flag the whole war and have suffered accordingly—"

"Corporal Rudd, take your squad and clean out the big house—inhabitants first, whatever else after," the lieutenant barked, ignoring Schumacher.

"Yes, sir!" Rudd hollered with glee. Then he shouted an order in German to a half-dozen troopers, all of whom rode to the front of the main house, dismounted, and rushed through the front door.

Schumacher did not know which way to go. Several Federals who had not ridden in with the lieutenant were herding Jake, Paul, and John in from the wheat field, the boys on foot.

"Found these just finished stackin' the season's wheat sheaves, Lieutenant Gruber," a corporal called. "Prettiest piles you ever saw, some of them shocks must be ten, twelve feet high."

"Leave one man here to guard those—boys," Gruber said, sizing up Jake and Paul in particular. He looked up at the wind vane atop the big barn. The breeze was blowing straightaway from the house. "The rest of you head back out and burn every shock."

"But sir, can we—" the corporal began.

"You'll get your chance for food and souvenirs after you fire the wheat," Gruber said.

"Yes, sir!" the corporal shouted, saluting. He turned to his squad and spoke briefly to them in German, then the whole happy crew, except the trooper who would guard the Schumacher boys, galloped back out toward the wheat field.

"Lieutenant," Schumacher said, but Gruber was cantering toward the church and calling over his shoulder, "Corporal Hesse, bring out all the pews. We'll use them for our own fires tonight. We'll stable the horses in here, then we'll fire everything when we leave in the morning."

This had now gone beyond Schumacher's capacity to process.

Katarina knelt in the middle of her upstairs bedroom, her hands interlocked in a circle of prayer with her three daughters and nine-year-old son Simon. Gretchen lay scrunched under the covers of the bed across the room, now clutching Baby and her soap cake.

"Thou has prepared a table before me in the presence of mine enemies," Katarina prayed as the sounds of heavy boots, laughter, and German voices drifted up from downstairs. She knew she had to remain calm as her ten- and fourteen-year-old daughters trembled in fear. "Thou hast anointed my head with oil . . ."

She heard spurs jingling and scraping as soldiers climbed the stairs.

"My cup runneth over—"

Suddenly the thick oaken door to her room, which she had left partway open, crashed off its hinges and flew halfway across the room, smashing the bureau mirror that survived a century each on both sides of the Atlantic as well as the wave-tossed journey in between.

The screams of her daughters rang in her ears. She had not time even to rise from her knees before an enormous, brown-bearded Yankee trooper, Navy Colt in his gauntleted hand, wrenched her arms and jerked her to her feet. "Get up, old woman," he began, his accent thicker than Gruber's. When his black eyes perceived her beauty, lust filled them, and he said, "Ah, such a fräulein as we have not seen in this whole Rebel valley." Enjoying his power over her, he growled, "Praying will do you no good now, pretty fräulein."

Another soldier snapped the locket her great-grandmother had left her from around her neck. Another clawed out all her pockets, the big soldier pinioning her arms behind her. As two other troopers ransacked the room, she fought off the urge to scream, and instead said, "Calm now, children, stand together in the corner."

"No!" the big soldier shouted, pulling her close to him. She wanted to retch at the stench of his sweaty body and whiskey-rinsed breath. "Everyone out of the house now, woman." Then he shoved her hard toward the door.

"Come, children," she said, motioning toward the hallway, though little feeling remained in either arm.

"Corporal Rudd," one of the troopers called from over by the bed.

Rudd, still brandishing the big gun, stalked toward him, cocking back the hammer. The trooper indicated the turned-down covers on the bed. Rudd pulled off one gauntlet. His eyes widened when he felt the warmth of the bed. He whirled around to Katarina and shouted, "You dirty b——, hiding one of your filthy Rebel b——s!"

Katarina gasped for the children hearing such language. Before she could react further, Rudd bent down, pointed his Colt under the bed, then looked under it, where Gretchen curled in the far corner against the wall, shaking.

"Ah!" Rudd shouted, reaching for her. Katarina screamed and ran toward him, claws bared, but two of the troopers intercepted her. Rudd reached for

Gretchen with the now-bare hand that did not hold the pistol, but she reeled back and kicked him so hard with a rosy little bare foot that she fractured two bones in his hand. Rudd screamed loudly, unleashing a torrent of oaths at Gretchen, thankfully in German, which she did not understand. Tears in his eyes, he rose up, the entire back half of the giant bed atop his broad-beamed shoulders. As Katarina fought and her other daughters screamed, one of the troopers managed to get a hand around one of Gretchen's furiously kicking feet and drag her out from under the bed on her back.

When he had her in tow, still kicking and fighting, Rudd let the bed crash to the cedar floor. He snatched her up, wincing at the shooting pain in his left hand. Still the Teutonic curses poured out. By now, terror so filled Gretchen that she could utter no sound, but she pressed Baby and the soap cake against her pounding little heart. Rudd wanted to hurt the child and hurt her bad, but too many civilian eyes were upon him. Gruber said Sheridan would trouble no man for anything he took or burned, but the people were not to be hurt.

The big German let out a guttural growl, then spotted the doll and the soap. "Ah!" he shouted again, reaching for them. Gretchen fought him until he had to lift her up and slam her down on the bed to wrest Baby and the soap cake away from her. He let out a hearty laugh and walked past Katarina and the other children, stuffing his latest prizes in a coat pocket. Gretchen screamed so loudly one of the other troopers had to restrain her. Katarina broke loose, stormed to the bed, hit the trooper in the face with such force that it broke her own hand and stunned him, and grabbed sobbing little Gretchen into her arms.

One of the other soldiers, now beset by shame, said, in broken English, "Please, frau, all must leave the house."

As Gretchen wailed into her breast, Katarina rose to her full, nearly six-foot stature, looked the soldier in the eye, and said, "May God in His perfect justice bring His judgment on the German peoples for what we—they—have done here today and to this valley."

That night all the Schumachers slept on the floor of the smokehouse. The cheers, shouts, and laughter of Gruber and his men wafted out of the big house, mingled with the smashing of glass and other items. Other soldiers camped out in the dooryard, the barns, the kitchen house, the corncrib, and the near cornfield. The aroma of beef, mutton, and pork filled the air. The Yankees butchered every cow, every hog, every sheep, every animal still on the property, then carved out their favorite cuts to roast on spits over fires kindled with the church pews.

Schumacher read to his family from his Bible, then led them in singing psalms and hymns. Jake would not look him in the eye and would not sing. The boy's whole body tensed and remained tense, his jaw fixed in rage.

"We may have our house and possessions burned," Schumacher said gently. "But let us not forget that so many of those dear men and women—and yes, even children in some cases—we have come to love through reading and talking about them, have had their very bodies burned or in other ways destroyed in faithfulness to our Lord. We who have chosen not to fight for one army in this terrible conflict and not to fight against the other, are left to suffer as good soldiers of another army, that host that shall truly and certainly triumph when the scales of justice are balanced by Almighty God; we are left to suffer with joy, and so model that joy that even those in utter spiritual darkness who fall upon us shall perhaps be moved by the power of God's Spirit to consider their spiritual bankruptcy and eternal hopelessness.

"So," he said, cradling a daughter in each arm, "we have nothing to fear, do we? For God has so decreed the very events that now befall us for His glory and our good."

Midnight neared and the commotion from the big house died. Schumacher recited various psalms from heart. "He shall cover thee with his feathers, and under his wings shalt thou trust: his truth shall be thy shield and buckler. . . . Though they slay me, yet shall I—" He looked around the faces before him. Except for Jake—and Gretchen, who slept soundly in her mother's lap—they were calmed, heartened, even joyful in countenance. "—yea, yet shall I praise His glorious name."

Gretchen had been all right by the time she went to sleep, but when she awoke and remembered what had had happened to Baby, she burst into tears in her mother's arms. Katarina watched through the open smokehouse door as her husband approached Gruber outside the big house. With a pang, she saw the Yankees fortifying the piles of hay, brush, weatherboarding, and other sundry wood items they had positioned around all the buildings the day before.

Two soldiers stood emptying the chaff from inside the family bed ticks into the piles. *They truly are going to burn us out,* she thought in amazement.

Had she any doubts, they were erased by the sight of her husband walking back toward the smokehouse, head bowed. Tears filled his eyes when he stepped through the door. He sighed, then announced, "We have ten minutes to bring out what we wish from the house." He flinched at the chorus of reflexive moans and groans that greeted his words.

"But I just want my Baby," Gretchen wailed into her mother's breast. Not even the soap cake mattered now.

Katarina looked out and saw the Federals parking one of the Schumachers' wagons near the front door of her home. Within seconds they were carting armloads of her family's belongings out and loading them into the wagon. Over in the barnyard, two Yankees sharpened their sabers on the family grindstone. The autumn breeze carried their jokes, bandied about in German to her, along with the hint of rain and the soot of distant burnings.

For a moment she feared her husband, sleepless for more than twenty-four hours, might break into sobs for heartbreak over his childrens' sorrow. Then to her amazement, her eldest daughter, seventeen-year-old Louisa, who must know she would never again play as she had from age five her great-grandmother's pianoforte she so loved, put her arm around her father and said, "Please don't fret us, Papa. We give thanks for our Lord and our family and our lives. Homes and barns we can rebuild. Crops we can replant. We must pray for these poor lost souls."

"Yes, Papa, all will come well in the end," said ten-year-old Marta, normally the highest-strung of all the children.

"All will come well in the end" were the words Schumacher had employed countless times to assure his children when times seemed darkest.

When Jake stepped forward and placed his man's hand on his father's shoulder and said, "We're all with you, Papa," Schumacher gazed around at them and burst into tears.

"Papa!"

"Please don't cry, Papa!"

"All will come well in the end, dear Papa!"

"I know, I know," he said, waving them off just a bit. "I know it will," he sniffed, "it's just that a man doesn't deserve to have such fine children, so many fine children." Despite himself, he burst again into tears, and they covered him with their young arms and their love.

After a moment Gretchen turned her own tear-streaked face, which struck him now as never before as the ghostly rendering of his own beautiful mother, up toward him. "And I shall be just fine, Papa. I know that God will take care of Baby just like He takes care of me. And if it's time for Baby to go to heaven, then, well, it will be a better place for her anyhow." Then she broke into laughter of all things and reached up and hugged him with both arms.

And so did they all. Then, en masse, they marched out of the smokehouse toward what God had laid before them, singing "A Mighty Fortress Is Our God," the immortal hymn penned by the German giant who had lit his own fire, the Protestant Reformation.

I have my family, my Katarina, and my Lord, and I am singing old Luther, who despised Anabaptists but loved Christ, Schumacher thought. *How ungrateful of me to desire more.*

●◇ ●◇ ●◇

Ethan and Culpeper arrived at the ridge overlooking the Schumacher farm by following the black trail of the Shenandoah rising in clouds toward the waiting arms of heaven.

And angry arms too, Ethan suspected.

"I do not believe this is a people versed in Scott," he said as he observed Gruber's men through his spyglass, preparing to fire the whole spread, church and all, while carting off wagonloads of booty, all as a soon-to-be-homeless family with a crowd of children looked on.

"Scott who?" Culpeper slurred, his cheek bulging with tobacco.

Ethan stared at him for a moment, a wry grin growing across the golden beard that had never succeeded in masking his boyish features. "Cole Culpeper," he said, slyly beginning to check, one by one, the four revolvers he now carried, "there's one man that would say 'tis a good thing you have no schooling."

"What in blue blazes are you yackin' about?" Culpeper said, swallowing.

"Ole Doctor Dabney," Ethan said, checking to ensure the several reload cylinders crammed in the pockets of his short butternut cavalry jacket had all their chambers filled with bullets.

"Yeh, I mighta knowed he'd be in there somewheres," Culpeper snorted, waving his hand.

"I think he had you specifically in mind when he said that to educate the mind without purifying the heart is but to put a sharp sword in the hands of a madman," Ethan said, suppressing a chuckle as he pulled a cross necklace Culpeper had never seen out from under his shirt and over his head.

"Well, you and 'Ole Dabney' and all the book learnin' in the world can't plow a furrow one lick straighter'n the dumbest Culpeper what ever shouldered arms," Culpeper said. "So—what the heck are ya doin' now?"

"I'd be obliged if you'd be delivering that to Rachel Anne if anything untoward should happen to me down yonder," Ethan said, handing him the necklace.

"Huh?"

"And tell her," Ethan started. Then his eyes grew far away for a moment before he pulled out two of his revolvers. "Tell her I was thinkin' of her."

"But you're not—"

"And I'd be mighty grateful if you'd lay down a bit of covering fire for me," Ethan cut in, "but wait till I get down there amongst 'em. I'm always amazed at how the element of surprise can scatter a covey o' Yanks."

Then he stuck the reins in his teeth, spurred his horse, and charged down the hill.

"Look out for the family!" he shouted back over his shoulder, his teeth clenching the reins.

"Git back here, Ethan, there's half a troop down yonder!"

➹ ➹ ➹

Gruber had not allowed anyone but Katarina into the house, and he called her out after only a minute. She had gathered only a few sundries and items of hygiene such as the family's tooth powder and toothbrushes.

"Please, sir, at least allow me to bring out some clothing for the children," Katarina pled, "the nights are getting cold."

Gruber bit his lower lip and glanced over at a nearby wagon. "Rudd," he said, "leave 'em that pile of blankets and bed covers."

"But sir—"

"Shut up, we've got a schedule to keep." He reined his horse to turn away, but Katarina could contain herself no longer.

"What sort of men are you?" she said, brushing away her husband's attempt to restrain her. "How can soldiers who ride under that famed flag war without mercy on defenseless women and children?"

"Lady, some of your Rebel bushwhackers slit the throats of four of my men no more than a mile back up that there creek road just yesterday," Gruber snarled, his scar aglow like a hot iron. "This whole area is a nest of Secesh vipers, led by that scum of the earth Al Lincoln and his so-called 'partisan rangers.' Yeh, you know the name, sure you do, he's a distant cousin to President Lincoln, no less. Well, forget about those blankets and bed things, and if you don't get movin' down the road with your family right now, I'll consider you in active violent rebellion against the Constitution of the United States, and I'll start hanging folks, beginning with your preacher husband. That's right, frau—we hung two Rebs yesterday younger than your oldest boy there, the one that looks like he's ready for a fight. Well, by G—, I believe he is ready for a fight!" Gruber flew off his horse and started for Jake.

"No, please," Schumacher pled, stepping between them, as Gruber whipped out his revolver.

"You're dead, boy," Gruber said to Jake, slugging Schumacher to the ground, then aiming the pistol at the boy's heart and pulling the trigger.

"No!" Katarina screamed in a blood-curdling wail as the gun exploded and Jake fell to the ground. She raced to the boy as two Federals nearby approached Gruber, who was on his knees.

"Herr loit-nant?" one asked in German.

When Gruber raised his head to answer, his men saw a thin line of blood trickling out one corner of his mouth.

O God, be not far from me, Ethan prayed, charging down the hill, as he aimed again, *return not my sword empty.*

His second shot took off the top of Gruber's head.

Then the Yankees were scrambling in all directions.

"Run!" Ethan screamed at the Schumachers, spitting out the reins. "Run!"

One Federal came at Ethan to his left. He aimed both pistols and knocked him down. As he rode past the barn toward the house, another raised a carbine at him to his right. He turned both guns on that man and blew him down before he could get off a shot.

Then they were all around him, firing up at him on foot, from horseback, from behind wagons and walls.

Let them be confounded and consumed that are adversaries to my soul; let them be covered with reproach and dishonour that seek my hurt.

He aimed his guns and cut down the closest one, who pitched back into another who had taken aim at Ethan, decking the second man. He felt a jolt, and his horse reared up. Someone from behind had shot her in the hindquarters. He whirled, saw a blue hat poke up from behind a water trough, and blew it into a pink mist. A Yank came running toward him on foot with a raised saber. Ethan aimed both guns at him and pulled the triggers. Both clicked on empty chambers. He slung the pistols into the man's face, knocking him down.

More bullets struck Ethan's horse, and she reared more violently. Ethan clung on only by his thighs, leaning forward as far as he could. When her front legs crashed back down, he nearly pitched over her head. Somehow he stayed on and jerked out two more pistols just as a Yank rode down on him, saber flashing. Ethan pointed both guns at the man's face and blew it to ribbons.

Then he felt a horrible searing pain slice through his back. *I'm hit,* he thought, angered. He swung the horse around to take aim. It was the corporal who had torched the wheat field, firing his own revolver. Before Ethan could draw down on him, the corporal shot him again, the bullet breaking a rib and careening up through his insides. Gasping, he reined the horse around and circled the corner of the nearest building—the church. The Yank chased after him and, seeing another clear shot as Ethan started toward the rear of the church, raised the revolver to fire again.

Just as he did, Culpeper's stolen Yankee Spencer cracked from up on the ridge, and the corporal pitched forward, the big bullet punching cleanly through his lungs.

Now a whole line of Federals from the direction of the house, and out of Culpeper's line of sight, began blasting at Ethan as he galloped along the wall of the church.

They compassed me about also with words of hatred; and fought against me without a cause.

One bullet took his hat off, another nicked his neck, and others smashed out every glass window he rode past.

Then he vanished behind some outbuildings. The line of Federals who had been firing at him let loose a stream of German epithets as they slapped new bullet clips into their repeaters.

Culpeper saw two Federals, sabers raised, galloping toward the Schumachers, who had moved clear of the big house and surrounding buildings and toward the road that ran alongside Cook's Creek.

"You bloody b——s," he breathed, wishing he could arrange for their deaths to be exquisitely slow. "I'll send you to hell on a shutter." He fired two shots within two seconds, each exploding the skull of one of the riders.

The singular unearthly shriek of a Rebel yell snatched his attention back down toward the house, where the firing mounted again, though the church and the billowing gray haze of gun smoke blocked him from seeing what was happening.

Ethan came thundering down the line of men who had fired at him as he retreated past the church. Man, horse, and Rebel yell one bloody mess, he had reloaded and had both hands filled again. Firing the pistols in tandem, he put down one soldier, then another, before they even saw him. Then the others were firing at him, but helter-skelter, with no time to aim. He shot another through the throat, then turned the horse and headed toward the main door of the church, where a cluster of Federals had gathered.

Firing both guns together, he killed one of them and winged another, then three others, firing as they ran, fled into a nearby field. One other Federal jerked open the front door of the church, leapt inside, and slammed the door shut behind him and locked it just before Ethan reached him.

Now the remnants of the firing line charged around from the side of the church, shooting as they came, rushing right into Culpeper's field of view. He raised the reloaded carbine just as several of their bullets tore into Ethan's horse, tumbling animal and rider to the ground. One Federal ran right up to Ethan, who had one leg pinned beneath his dead horse.

"You bushwhacking skunk," the man said, surprisingly in perfect English. He holstered his pistol and unsheathed his sword. He raised it with both hands and brought it slashing down toward Ethan just as the report sounded from Culpeper's rifle. The Federal sprawled lifeless and bleeding across Ethan. Another Yank approached Ethan, and Culpeper dropped him too. The others, realizing they were caught in a crossfire and unsure of how many guns were against them or from what direction, wheeled, found what horses they could, and lit out. Culpeper managed to knock another one out of the saddle as they turned down the creek road.

"Get up, Ethan boy!" Culpeper screamed from the ridge.

Grunting and groaning, Ethan squeezed out from under the beast just as Jared Kruger's beautiful, riderless, milk white charger trotted up to him, snorting but tame.

"Well, hello, boy," Ethan, his legs shaking, said, stroking the animal's neck. Then he saw the horse had been hit in the back during the melee. "Oh, poor boy," Ethan said, glancing warily around for Federal guns. He saw none. "Do you have one more dance in you, sweet boy?" Ethan asked him, tickling his nose by squeezing it, which seemed to delight the animal.

Then he swung up into the saddle, steadied the white, pulled the pins out to release the empty cylinders in his remaining two revolvers, and pulled his last two full cylinders out of a jacket pocket and popped them in.

He looked up toward Culpeper. *I'm going fast; I can't even see the hill he's on,* he thought.

"Let's go clean up the Lord's house, boy," Ethan said, turning the white. Then he spurred him hard and drove him right through the church's locked front doors, which crashed open, knocking one stunned Federal to the ground, senseless. A dozen horses were tied to various fixtures in the back half of the sanctuary. They began to buck and rear, a couple of them getting loose.

Another soldier, a few feet straight ahead of the door, raised a pistol and fired at Ethan's midsection. The bullet blew a hole in his shirt just above his belly, punching the wind out of him and almost knocking him off the horse. The Yank tried to fire again, but he had no bullets left. He reached for his carbine. Ethan, forcing his heavy arms up, aimed both pistols and fired again in concert, killing the man. He sensed stirring on the ground nearby and saw the man whom the doors had knocked down trying to rise. Ethan put two bullets in him. Another soldier fired at him from behind a tied horse ahead and to his right. One bullet sailed past Ethan's head, another sheared a sliver of skin off his mount's girth. When the man's head popped up, Ethan fired at him, but his sight was fading, and he couldn't get a good shot. Then more guns—rifles—exploded from the front of the sanctuary, up near the pulpit, and a window above the front door showered down on him.

Ethan pointed both his pistols at the horse behind which the nearer Federal hid. He fired at the animal's head, obliterating it, and the two-thousand-pound body toppled over onto the screaming trooper and crushed him.

Then Ethan leaned in the saddle, almost falling off it. The numbness in his legs moving up his body, he wondered with an inner chuckle who would last longer, him or the beautiful, bloodied charger he rode. He patted the horse once on his withers, spoke to him softly as the rifles resounded, then spurred him again and raised the smoking pistols, screeching the Rebel yell as he roared down the middle aisle toward the altar, reins flying free.

Let them be confounded and put to shame that seek after my soul: let them be turned back and brought to confusion that devise my hurt.

A hail of lead came against him. One bullet shimmied along his left calf, another hit the horse in the shoulder. At least three rifleman stood around the chancel area—no, four. Ethan aimed his pistols and fired at one of them, his view growing more hazy. Both shots missed, but this was as hot as the trooper wanted it to get, and he turned and ran out the side door to Ethan's right. The Confederate aimed again and plastered one of the three remaining Federals. Then another one, his rifle empty, raced out the side door.

One man remained, defiant before the pulpit. It was Rudd. Sweating and cursing in German, he flung his empty Spencer aside and drew his revolver, bringing it up to aim. "Ahhhh!" he screamed.

"Yi-ahhh!" Ethan screamed.

They fired simultaneously, Rudd hitting Ethan high in his right breast, and Ethan's two bullets blowing Rudd into the pulpit, where he smashed down, with the splintering pulpit, onto some chairs, two of which also broke into pieces. The entire chancel section of the church was wrecked.

Rudd lay on his back, his life's blood pumping out of his chest. Ethan sat on his horse, his shoulders sagging. He climbed slowly down and patted the animal on the hindquarters, sending him stumbling and bleeding out the side door. Then Ethan grabbed the dead Federal nearest him by his ankles and dragged him out of the church through the same door.

Staggering, he walked toward Rudd to do the same, but wavered at the altar, then collapsed onto the floor in front of it, face up.

For a moment or two, the only sounds in the church were the snorts and neighs of the walleyed Federal horses, all of whom had broken loose from their tethers and were now finding their way out the wide-open front entryway.

Then Culpeper stepped through the same space. Behind him the breeze cleared away the gun smoke as the sun broke out in a determined show of light over the tortured Valley. So thick was the smoke inside the church that he had to squint to make out the train of destruction strewn from one corner of the building to the other. Dead soldiers, dead horses, smashed windows, splintered furniture, spent shells, blood spattered everywhere.

As he gimped down the center aisle, plugging more bullets into the Spencer, his eyes took in the chancel area. "L— Almighty," he uttered in hushed, awed tones. "You done a job o' work today, Ethan boy." The area outside the church from which he had just come looked like a slaughterhouse.

Then he saw his friend, spread-eagled on the floor before the altar, in a growing pool of scarlet.

The strangest sensation tided over Culpeper, one he had not known in a very long time. He did not know what it was now, but it numbed him, clutched his chest, and brought boiling tears to his eyes. He stared at Ethan. Had he the words to describe the sensation, he would have explained to Schumacher as he entered the side door that here lay the only friend besides Emma he had ever known, and the only one who had ever saved his life.

Culpeper heard stirring from a pile of wreckage over behind where the pulpit had stood. Carbine at the ready, he stepped over to see Rudd, blind and nearly dead, blood soaking his chest and running out of his mouth.

"I—" the man gurgled. "I wish only to know his name."

Culpeper's jaw clenched. "Ethan. Ethan McDowell."

Rudd nodded faintly, then expired.

Schumacher had seen this, and so had Jake, a bandage wrapped around the crease on his neck from Gruber's bullet that Ethan had caused to go wide.

Katarina, standing near the door, had also seen it, as had Gretchen, whose hand she held and who now bolted from her and ran to Ethan.

She knelt down beside him, ignoring the blood that spread beneath her and stained her favorite dress. She stared for several seconds at the tanned boyish face. Then she reached out and touched his yellow hair, yellow like hers, then brushed it up off his forehead.

Her father came to her side. He held Baby and the soap cake, which he had taken from a pocket in Rudd's jacket. Baby had no blood on her, the soap just a couple of drops. Gretchen's eyes glinted for a second, but then she turned back to Ethan. She did not see the blood-drenched, bullet-riddled corpse. She saw a person like none she had ever beheld, or would again for the ninety-two more years she would live.

"Papa," Jake said, approaching his father, "the vandals are all killed or fled. But more may come, and I cannot stand by any longer and let brave soldiers like these play the man for me."

Schumacher's head swung around. "Jake, Son, it is the Lord who is our protector, not men. To be in league with—" His eyes darted toward Culpeper, who listened, carbine cradled in his arms. "—God cannot have spoken more plainly when he said that vengeance is his alone, Son."

Katarina watched, surprised both that her eldest child had grown so suddenly into full manhood, and at the surprise itself.

"Papa, I love you, and I respect you more than any man I have ever known," Jake said with reverence. "But—a man lies here who has today delivered us from killers who would have destroyed all of us and all we possess on earth." He paused, summoning his courage. "I ask your blessing, sir, that I may take up the mantle that has today fallen from his grasp."

Jacob winced, then looked away. For the first time, he noticed the leaking, bullet-punctured baptistry up by the front wall.

"I have always tried to raise you in a manner that would render you able to make your own decisions when you became a man. You are now eighteen, Jake, and while I do not agree with your opinion on the matter—" With this, he turned to Jake. "—it is with joy that I see standing before me a man more godly than ever I could have prayed for him to be. And if your conscience tells you that you can honor God and not disgrace him by pursuing this course—then, my son, you do indeed have my wholehearted blessing."

Father and son stared for a moment into one another's eyes before they hugged each other with both arms.

"Papa?"

Schumacher turned to see Gretchen holding Ethan's Bible. She had spotted it peaking out of his shirt just above his belly. A bullet had torn through the center of the leather front cover. She opened the book and saw that the black-stained hole burned far into it. She kept turning the pages. Finally, at the last book of the whole Bible, the Book of the Revelation of Saint John the Divine, she found the spent bullet, embedded in those pages and stopped in its unholy transit by the back cover.

Gretchen stared back at Ethan. "Papa?" she said again, not turning toward him.

"Yes, little one." Schumacher replied.

"Is Ethan in heaven now?"

That caught Schumacher short. "Why, yes, little one, I expect very much that he is."

Now she stood, turned to her father, and looked up into his eyes, her own gleaming bright. "Then I'm so glad he came today, Papa. Because before he came, I had almost forgotten that God was good."

They buried Ethan McDowell in the old Schumacher cemetery, first inhabited by Jacob I in 1794. As Jacob Schumacher III spoke words over Ethan, he felt the autumn breeze in his nostrils. For a moment the pungent aroma betokening the smoking Shenandoah gave way to the most fragrant scent he could imagine, seeming to come from down in the open grave where lay Ethan in his coffin. It was the scent of—lavender soap.

He was not much surprised, however, for it seemed the most appropriate place for such an offering to rest. After all, when they placed Ethan in the casket earlier, he had noticed the soft stuffed hand and a portion of its arm jutting out from under the clean shirt, from atop Ethan's heart.

At first the worn, frayed little appendage had looked pink to Schumacher. Then he had nodded, knowingly, realizing that no, it was by now much more white than pink.

CHAPTER 36

NOT UNTIL THE BURNT DISTRICT WAS BORN DID THE TRUE STORY of John Meigs's death make its way out. He had died a soldier's death in the service of his country, in a straight-up, face-to-face contest with regular Confederate horse soldiers, one of whom he shot.

The orderly upon whose story Sheridan based his retaliation had fled from the scene without so much as pulling his revolver to aid brave Meigs.

But as the fourth calendar year of the war edged into its final weeks, outrage begat outrage. The martial nature of Americans engaged in conflict over issues wherein they passionately believe themselves to be in the right asserted itself in a parade of horrors that amazed all of Christendom.

Lee's heart sank when, crossing the Appomattox River south back toward Petersburg from monitoring the recent fighting around Richmond, he remembered how subordinates of Early, had without Old Jube's permission torched more than half the entire Pennsylvania town of Chambersburg when its business leaders would not ante up two hundred thousand Federal dollars as partial reimbursement for the Federals' annihilation of the Shenandoah Valley.

We have worked so long and hard that our army, our people, might retain their honorable name, even if our foes squander their own, he thought, praying God's restraining hand against the commission of further such cruelties by his own people. He had heard the stories of unchivalrous acts in the western theater by rough-hewn Confederate irregulars or semi-irregulars such as John Hunt Morgan, William Quantrill, and "Bloody" Bill Anderson. He determined that the Army of Northern Virginia, or any force under his command, would never have such infamy attached to it.

He prayed anew for the Federals—many by name, others by regiment, still more by division and corps—that those in union with Christ would walk obediently after Him and that those not in union with Him would soon embrace Him in faith.

Lee prayed also for the physical protection of the Federals, rehearsing the scriptural promise that unless it pleased God, not one hair on any of their heads would be harmed by the Confederates or by anyone or anything else.

His concern mounted at the parade of Northern newspaper reports screaming about the supposed unchristian treatment of Federal prisoners of war down in Andersonville, Georgia. *I cannot believe our people are engaged in the torture and murder of brave soldiers captured fighting for a cause they believe to be right,* he thought, shaking his head.

Then he recalled the stories cascading south from Confederates released or escaped from Federal prisons such as Johnson's Island and Camp Douglas. The Federals, flush with the food, medicine, and blankets the Confederate prison camps so lacked, were reportedly engaging, even now, in a policy of retaliation, in which they purposely withheld the necessities of life from their prisoners.

He had been informed by wire, by letter, by oral report, and by eyewitness account that Confederate prisoners by the score were being allowed—in fact, being consigned by order of higher authorities—to die needless deaths through freezing, starvation, and disease.

Meanwhile, Grant, relentless and evidently unperturbed at the ocean of Northern blood he had spilled in the past six months, sought inexorably to exploit the weaknesses he felt certain must be present somewhere along Lee's thin, outstretched lines around Petersburg and Richmond. Soon, Lee wrote to Davis, the Federal commander would have one hundred fifty thousand men. Just a few days ago, as October 1864 closed, the Yankees, with great numerical superiority, had assaulted both Confederate flanks.

"On last Thursday at Burgess Mill we had three brigades to oppose six divisions," he wrote. "On our left, north of the James, two divisions to oppose two corps. The inequality is too great."

Fortunately Longstreet had beaten off one attack and A. P. Hill's foot soldiers and Wade Hampton's horse soldiers the other. *But how much longer can we hold them off?* Lee fretted, knowing the Federals grew stronger every day, while his nearly encircled little army all the while bled, starved, sickened, and deserted itself smaller.

"Unless we can obtain a reasonable approximation to his force I fear a great calamity will befall us," he wrote.

How difficult it was for him not to feel the weight of all the wrongs and sins of the war piled onto his shoulders. *I have control over so little of it all,* he thought sadly. Just then, now west of Petersburg, he sighted his new head-quarters. *Ah, a fine home young Taylor has selected for us, though I should not have allowed him to dissuade me from returning to my tent,* he thought, his mood brightening with renewed appreciation for just how capable was that young for-mer banker.

As autumn stripped the trees of Violet Bank of their foliage, that head-quarters had grown visible to Federal batteries. Plus Lee desired a post closer to Grant's left, which edged ever-closer to the key Southside Railroad line con-necting Petersburg with the Valley. *Ever-tighter the coil wraps around us,* Lee thought, his mood dampened, due partly to a spasm of the sciatica that now ren-dered equal pain to him whether lying, sitting, standing, or walking.

After leaving Traveller with an orderly, he found Taylor in the parlor of the splendid two-story structure, compiling updated totals on troop strength for Lee from the various regiments.

"General Lee, sir," Taylor said, rising to his feet. "I've a finely fixed room prepared for you, with a crackling fireplace. I managed to secure some butter-milk for you as well, sir."

"Not too nice a room, I hope," Lee replied, gazing around the parlor and noticing that Taylor seemed to have more than his desk moved into the room.

The younger man's mien fell. *Not too nice, indeed,* he groused to himself. *Nor too lacking either. Not too pleasant most of all, for the Tycoon is never so uncomfortable as when he is comfortable.*

"Ah, you are finely fixed," Lee said, his gaze continuing around the parlor. *He has pulled a bed in here, washbasin, his clothes, his work, everything,* the gen-eral thought. "Couldn't you find any other room?"

Taylor blinked. He purposed not to reveal the latest anger provoked in him by this impossible idol of the Southern people for whom his last vestige of patience in serving had just elapsed.

"No, I couldn't," he replied, looking Lee in the eye, dauntless. "But this will do. I can make myself tolerably comfortable here."

He did not bother to inform Lee that the owner of the home had moved Taylor's belongings from one of the smallest bedrooms into the parlor while the adjutant was out, and put Armistead Long in the bedroom.

Taylor's impudence struck Lee dumb. The general had no idea how to respond to such a statement and so left the room, stiff with pain from a jarring new episode of lumbago.

Marley could not remember ever being more excited. *I am going to meet the president himself,* he thought. *I am going to be respectful, but I am going to provide him with the information he needs to straighten out this Andersonville debacle.*

Marley's suspicion had mounted that some of Lincoln's top commanders were intent on a calculated, systematic, and unprecedented war of terror on the Southern people. He believed the Federals' suspension of prisoner exchange and its effect on Andersonville were somehow connected with this program. He also believed that once Lincoln knew of it the world would be turned upside down. "God give us the strength to do the right as we see the right," the president had said.

As Marley read the new Bible he had bought in New York, he wondered if through all the pain, all the suffering, all the longing, God had been preparing him for just this errand. *How many lives might be affected, how many saved,* he thought, looking out the window as the B & O train chugged through the dingy Washington suburbs.

And how much more sacred our cause will be if we maintain a course of just Christian war as Augustine first advocated, he thought.

"Hey, Wayne, weren't you in on that Dahlgren Raid?"

Marley looked up to see Little Al Tate brandishing a *New York Herald.* He nodded, taking the paper and reading the story Little Al indicated.

It was another blistering letter from Dahlgren's admiral father. Marley's eyes widened the further he read. The elder Dahlgren claimed to have seen a sample of writing from the documents found on his son's dead body that ordered the destruction of Richmond and the killing of Jefferson Davis.

The writing was not his son's, Dahlgren said. Even the boy's signature had been misspelled!

Marley looked out the window, perplexed. *But how can that be?* he wondered. *Could McEntee have lied to me? But why on earth would he? He seemed so earnestly disturbed. Could he have been misinformed, could he have heard incorrectly or misinterpreted what he heard?*

The Dahlgren raid had been at the top of Marley's list for disclosure to the president. Now he did not know what to tell him about it, if anything. *Is the appearance of this newspaper piece unlikely coincidence or God providentially guiding my actions in the matter?* he wondered. He did not know. He would keep the paper and consider the matter further. The opportunity to speak with the president of the United States was a once-in-a-lifetime opportunity, and he did not intend to speak rashly on any matter.

How ironic to find myself at Willard's, the swankest hotel in Washington City. A few days ago I was graduating from a filth-infested shebang to a hospital bed where I was tended by a Rebel doctor with gangrene, Marley thought. Wirz had facilitated the delivery of a significant cache of gold from Richmond to finance the Federals' trip and secure them accommodations suitable for men seeking a personal audience with President Lincoln.

Sitting at a small table in his room as Little Al and Lemuel Pardee slept on the bed, he looked over the final draft of the letter he would in a few minutes send by courier to the White House.

The correspondence—written, corrected, rewritten, and written again over and over the past three weeks by a team of nearly twenty Federal prisoners—was only one page in length. It beseeched Lincoln for a meeting with the commissioners to discuss the unfathomable situation at Andersonville and the prisoner exchange issue. Accompanying the letter would be Stoneman's letter, as well as letters from Wirz and his commander, Winder.

After the courier departed, Marley went to his knees and offered more prayers to God that justice would be done in whatever way would please the Almighty. Heartened, though sober, he stretched out on the floor to await the president's response.

None came that day, nor the next, after Marley had sent a short follow-up letter. The third day, still receiving no response of any kind from anyone, Marley inquired after General Hooker, who he remembered had favored him. But Fightin' Joe's misfortune of leading the Army of the Potomac against the Army of Northern Virginia when Stonewall Jackson commanded one of its corps, still had him—and his career—out west fighting Indians.

"Know any other big wigs in Washington?" Pardee asked.

"There's no one remaining in Washington I wish to know," Marley snapped. "Except the president, of course."

The three remaining commissioners discussed what next to do. They decided to deliver a third letter in person to the White House.

"They say if you get there early in the morning, you can get right in and visit with the president himself, in person, without even an appointment," said Little Al.

On the way they passed an empty establishment all three knew not to have always been as dark and quiet as now. Until eighteen months ago, two years into the war, it was the largest slave-sale market on the North American continent.

Little Al detected Marley's consternation. "Guess those folks took awhile reading our great emancipator," he said.

Marley winced at the slight against Lincoln.

"So what, little man?" Pardee, a Marylander and a slaveholder, said. "The Emancipation Proclamation had nothin' to do with our slaves in the border states. It only freed Reb slaves. Last time I heard, General Grant still had his darkies, and so did Mrs. Lincoln."

"Still, it seems a sight more at home in Richmond than Washington City," Little Al said, looking to Marley, scion of abolitionists, for support.

Marley gazed at the large old building. *The president must have walked right past that building every time he left the White House to visit our boys in the hospital,* he thought. "Well," he finally said, "it is shut down, and last I heard, Richmond's still isn't. Besides, freeing the slaves was not part of Lincoln's original presidential campaign, or one of his reasons for going to war. The old logsplitter always favored shipping them all back to Africa for their own good."

"Like h——," Pardee blurted. "Folks in our part of Maryland might be persuaded to *sell* our slaves to the government, but we'll d—— sure not turn 'em loose for nothin.' Why, all the money we got in the world is tied up in our darkies. We'd be dead busted and rootin' around these muddy streets for food with the pigs if we gave up our slaves."

Marley said nothing, but he remembered that though many men wore the same uniform, they wore it for many different reasons.

And dressed such, head-to-foot in crisp new Federal blue uniforms, the commissioners made it into the White House building and to the first guard. Acknowledging Marley's rank of major—and the ribbons and medals garnishing his chest—he invited them to wait, under the watch of another guard, while he saw about their letter.

The first guard returned several minutes later, sans the letter. "If you're staying at Willard's, they know where to contact you if they wish to, sir."

"We have to leave Washington later today," Marley said evenly.

"Then you might wish to leave a forwarding address," the guard said, tiring of his unannounced guests. "Sir."

Marley, his blood rising, glanced at the other two commissioners, then spoke again to the guard.

"We've walked, we've ridden horseback, we've taken trains, and we've sailed the ocean blue to get here from Andersonville Prison, mister. Now we've been here three straight days, sending important material over here every day, and we've yet to receive a peep from anyone on a matter in which I should think the Federal government would be most concerned."

"You've come from Andersonville?" the guard asked, impressed by that infamous word.

"Yes, we have," Marley said, "and we've authorization at high levels—"

"What levels?" the guard asked.

"General Stoneman, among others," Marley said.

"Well, you'll be notified if they wish to respond to your inquiries, I'm sure, sir," the guard said, attempting to usher the commissioners out.

Marley jerked his arm out of the guard's grasp. "We'll have a seat and wait, if you don't mind."

"Not in this building, you won't," the guard shot back. The "sir" salutations had disappeared.

"Do you understand that while you're parading around the dangerous theater of Washington City in your dress blues, over thirty thousand Union soldiers are rotting in that Georgia hellhole!" Marley shouted, his patience at an end.

The guard, a black rage covering his face, pulled out a whistle and blew it. Within seconds a half-dozen more guards converged on the spot, revolvers drawn and cocked.

"Now you can go to Willard's, or you can go to Old Capital Prison," the guard said. "It's your decision, but make it now because I've had a bellyful of you three."

Marley wanted to tear out the insolent cur's throat and for a moment considered whether to do just that. Out of the corner of his eye, he saw Pardee's fists clench and that man begin to move toward the guard.

"Fellows," Little Al said gently, "for the boys' sakes, let's be on our way."

Marley knew he had either to attack someone or leave; so, bitter tears in his eyes, he wheeled about, and with a sense of foreboding that ran much deeper in his heart than just about Andersonville, left the home of his president.

He never received a response to the letters he had sent and delivered, but he did receive a telegram just before checking out of Willard's and leaving Washington. It came from Wirz, offering that man's solemn hope that the commissioners had fared better than had the Confederate government in its latest effort.

In a desperate attempt to preserve the lives of the thousands of sick and wounded Federal prisoners in Andersonville, President Davis had authorized the release of every one of them, along with as many healthy soldiers as it took to fill a Yankee transport ship with fifteen thousand men. To receive them, all the Federals had to do was provide the ship. The Confederates would ask none of their own men exchanged in return.

Lincoln and Stanton refused to respond to the offer.

CHAPTER 37

AGNES COULD NOT HELP GIGGLING WHEN SHE HEARD MILDRED'S exclamation from the kitchen. *Try as she might, she will always lack domestic skills,* Agnes thought as she strode in to observe Precious Life's latest culinary disaster.

It was the "sweet potato" coffee; more accurately, the "leavings from the sweet potato" coffee. The faces of the two young refugee maidens helping Mildred and Mary Custis with Christmas dinner were both drawn up like corkscrews, after having sampled the brew. Within seconds its pungent aroma assailed Agnes's nostrils. Mildred turned to Agnes, her face plaintive. "Oh, Wiggie, it is indeed *aw*-ful!" On the verge of tears, she turned first angry, then burst into laughter at the mirth painted on Agnes's face. "Such an awful domestic I am!"

"If Papa were here, he would insist we feed that creation of yours to Custis Morgan," Agnes said, giggling the more. When Mildred's joyful countenance faded, Agnes caught herself. "Dear me, I have forgotten of your pet squirrel's escape." She pondered that recent event for a moment. "No, I believe Papa would recommend we feed Custis Morgan to ourselves."

"Agnes Lee!" Mildred exclaimed.

"Dears, it is time to bring your Christmas cheer—and our dinner—to the table," Mary Lee announced from the dining room.

Determined that the ever-increasing wartime scarcity of almost everything would not dampen the household's joy and reverence during the Advent season, Mary had captained the ornamenting of the Mess with cedar, holly, and arborvitae, gifted to the Lees from the plantations of friends. Everyone wore triple layers of clothing because they had fuel only for the fireplace in Mary's sitting room. Everyone, that is, but a scarlet-trussed, twelve-year-old visitor named Emily.

When the Lees sat to table, more places than plates were in evidence. A grandmother, her three daughters, and two of their children, including Emily, had refugeed in from the Valley two days before, where nearly everything they owned had been burned or stolen by Custer's men.

After learning the Yankees had "confiscated" every piece of clothing her best friend's family possessed—except for what the family wore on their backs—before they torched her friend's home, Emily had determined to avoid such a calamity. Minutes before soldiers arrived at her own house, she put on nearly every garment she owned, rendering her a waddling laughingstock before the Federals.

And laugh they did, at the plump, four-and-a-half-foot-tall child.

"She's wider than she is tall," one hailed.

"We wouldn't want any of yore dresses anyhows, fatty," hooted another.

"Yeah, none of my girls are near as dumpy as you," shouted another.

Emily had not spoken a single word since that day, and she still wore every item of clothing she had put on.

"That fancy-pants boy general with the long golden hair left the dunking German Unionists next door to us completely alone," the grandmother said bitterly upon her arrival. The Lee girls had watched as Mary leaned up out of her wheelchair and hugged the old woman, who burst into sobs, despite trying not to.

Nearly every house on Franklin now hosted refugees.

For a moment, gazing through the dim candlelight at the table's lack of bounty, Mary saw other Christmas spreads in other years. Christmases bright with joy and life and bursting with promise and hope. At Arlington. Then she looked around the room at her three daughters and the family they had had the blessing to aid, and thought of her three sons and husband, all in the field but all well.

"Oh God bless us," she prayed, "and make us truly grateful for these and all Thy bounteous mercies, and be pleased to continue them to us, and to engender in us thanksgiving and gratitude for all Thy unmerited favor and goodness toward us. In the matchless name of our Lord and Savior Jesus Christ, amen."

As the others started the lean processional of food around the table, tears came to Mary's eyes, and she forced back sobs.

"Oh, what is it, Mama?" Mildred asked. "What is wrong?"

"Nothing is wrong," Mary said, a smile appearing amid the tears that now ran down her face. "I am overcome at how good God is to us." Then Mildred and Mary Custis began to cry as well, overcome at His goodness.

"What is it, Mama?" Agnes, stone-faced, asked, noticing a different look taking over Mary's face that usually indicated something afoot. Mary looked down at her plate, which contained two thin slices of bread sandwiched around a wafer-thin piece of ham, and one half of a sweet potato.

"Nothing," Mary said, mischief in her eyes. "Y'all just commence to eating."

Now Mildred and Mary Custis suspected something to be brewing in Mary's head, and Agnes felt certain of it. The hungry refugees wolfed down their food before any of the Lees had started theirs, just as Mary had intended. She shoved her unmussed plate toward Mildred.

"Wrap it up, Life," she said. "I expect the good ladies of Richmond will be on the move in their wagons toward the trenches anytime now."

"But Mama," Mildred said, "aren't they collecting for the soldiers from folks who have food they don't need?"

"Yes," Mary said.

"We already boxed up and sent nearly every morsel of food in the house, Mama," Mary Custis said.

"Tarnation, Mrs. Lee," the grandmother sputtered, coughing from a cold that would soon blossom into bronchial pneumonia, her head dropping, "and me a-chompin' my grinders like a man-hungry mountain lion." Mary saw silent tears dropping onto the weary old woman's lap.

"No," Mary said with such force that all at the table took notice. "You have done your part by coming here tonight."

Somehow, those words, coupled with the look in Mrs. Robert E. Lee's eyes, restored to the weary old woman her dignity.

"Grandmama."

All present turned in shock to Emily at the sound of her voice. "I saved me a half 'o my sweet 'tater," she said. "I reckoned some child might need it more than me."

At this, Agnes rose to her feet, her eyes glistening and her untouched plate in her hand. She put it on a silver platter, along with her mother's. She turned to Emily and said, "I would be proud if it would be you who would walk with me till we find a wagon taking the food to our soldiers."

Emily's eyes lit up like fireflies on a summer evening.

"But only if you first eat your sweet potato," Agnes added, "because you will need some extra energy to make such an important journey on such an important night."

Emily nodded with vigor, then consumed the food. She felt the concern of her mother boring in on her.

"Besides, Ma," the girl said, "I'm the best-dressed for it. Why, I'm practically sweatin' as I sit here."

Agnes shot her sisters a wee glance, but enough of one that they knew their Christmas dinners were forfeit.

"Lots of people seem to be coming to life tonight," Mary Custis said, shooting Agnes a look of her own, along with her plate.

"Aggie, four boxes of newly knitted socks are by the front door," Mary said. "Are you able to carry those as well?"

"Judith, Sue Anna, on with your coats, daughters, and away with them socks," the revitalized grandmother ordered.

Mildred and Mary Custis stared in amazement at their mother after the front door closed behind the traveling party. The only words they could muster between the two of them were Mildred's: "My, Mama, how you have changed since you fell on your face at Bremo."

＊◇ ＊◇ ＊◇

Lee stared out the frosted window into the black night. *I did not believe Virginia could have a colder winter than last year,* he thought, chilled despite a couple extra layers of clothing and the fire in his room, *but she may outdo herself this year.* He could only imagine how frigid his soldiers were in their filthy, disease- and vermin-ridden trenches, with fear and the call of Yankee sharpshooters and mortar shells never far away. *I should not have let Colonel Taylor talk me out of my tent and into these surroundings that are exceeded in their lavishness only by his own.*

He turned back to his desk. The task soon before him chilled him the more. His old friend—father of twenty-three-year-old Sandie Pendleton, the brilliant former chief of staff for Stonewall who was killed three months before while attempting to rally outnumbered Confederate troops at the battle of Fisher's Hill.

"Sir?" came the familiar voice, in the open doorway.

"General Pendleton," Lee said, happy to see his fellow gray-headed Christian warrior.

"General Lee, sir," Pendleton said, shaking the proffered hand.

"Please, General, sit."

"Thank you, sir."

"And a happy and holy Christmas to you, sir."

"Yes, and to you too, General Lee, sir. While here on a separate errand, sir, may I say that I have been so disturbed by an omission which occurred when I had the privilege of dining with you day before yesterday that I feel bound to apologize if it was a misunderstanding of my own."

"Why, whatever for, General?"

"It was the failure on my part to ask a blessing at the table, sir," Pendleton said, his lantern jaw taut. "I expected to do so, and awaited your request to that effect, but did not notice one by sign or word. I may, however, have overlooked such intimation from you, or you may have taken for granted I would say grace. Or you may have for the time forgotten my sacred office under the military relations in which we commonly meet. In such case, however, I suppose you would have officiated yourself. At any rate, I believe there was some misunderstanding; and although not one of the more important matters of life, I would not have it go unexplained."

Lee, listening intently to the earnest petition, nodded his great lion head. "Yes, General, I had expected you to ask a blessing on our table, and turned to you with that view. It was my fault, I think, in not making a more pointed request, which I should have done. Finding you apparently preparing to take your seat, I failed to request your office, and as is very frequently the case with me at our informal camp meals, offered a silent petition of thanks."

"Ah, yes," Pendleton said, nodding. "There it is."

Such a good man and a good friend, Lee thought as the clergyman-general sat. *How awkward was the necessity to replace him in his prominent role over the artillery with the brilliant young Alexander. Any man would deserve compassion and courtesy in such matters, one worthy of such respect as Pendleton all the more. How inadequate I am to discern the appropriate actions in announcing such cases or to adequately protect the feelings and sensibilities of the parties involved. And now I must also deny his request for a paltry two-day furlough home at Christmas to baptize the baby son of his own brave boy, killed even as the child grew in the womb.*

"I asked to see you in person, General," Lee said, "because the sad duty falls upon me to deny your request for furlough. Those people are so numerous and active everywhere that I would be unfaithful to the authority invested in me to approve your absence. I am indeed sorry to add to the enormous tribulations besetting you and your dear family. But I must request that you ride over to inspect the heavy batteries at Chaffin's Bluff tomorrow, though it be as cold as we have seldom seen Virginia be."

The only betrayal of emotion from the rugged face that had grown more noble but no less handsome with age was the welling up of tears in the alert gray eyes.

"Yes, sir," Pendleton said, nodding. "Of course, sir. Even my family themselves are best served by such a course."

How many brave souls God has given us, Lee thought, ignoring a spasm of lumbago, his throat growing tight. *And how easy to recognize young Sandie's valor when such a man as this sits before me.*

"As you know, old friend," Lee said, barely able to meet Pendleton's eyes. "I lost my own gentle Annie . . ."

He was unable to say more. Nor could Pendleton. Both sat for a moment as the small fire glowed. Then they rose and shared the manly hug of Christian brothers and the deep but unspoken import conveyed by it. Pendleton turned to leave, but stopped in the doorway.

"Uh, if I may, sir," he said. "Allow me to assure you of the fervent prayer with which I more than daily commend you to God's gracious guidance and blessing."

"I am deeply obliged to you for that, General," Lee said. "No one stands in greater need of them."

Then his gaze drifted from Pendleton's eyes—to exactly where, that general could not tell—and he concluded, "My feeble petitions I dare hardly hope will be answered."

So cold was the ride back to his own quarters that Pendleton feared he might suffer frostbite. To remove the suffering from his mind, he recalled his moments with Lee and the manner in which that soldier seemed always, even when delivering such lamentable news, to uplift the spirit of him, a minister. Heartened, he reminded himself, *Our fallen nature finds it hard to realize how blessed are those whom God prepares and takes to himself and how peacefully we may walk with Him even in sorrow while waiting all the days for our appointed time.*

The twinkling of the clear night's starry host caught his eye, and he smiled in the dark. *Such pleasing solaces we can find in natural scenes,* he thought. *The sweet blue heavens speak of where the beloved of my heart now rejoices; the lovely landscape tells of scenes far more exquisite in which his ransomed spirit now and forever delights and where we hope to join him in sacred joy.*

In gratitude his thoughts turned back to Lee. *How little sin do I see in that man,* he thought, tugging the frayed collars of his officer's greatcoat close to his face against the biting cold. He pulled the saddlebags he had already packed for the now-canceled trip off his horse and threw them over his shoulders. *Yet how ceaselessly he remains aware of it.*

Lee returned to his desk to examine the reports cascading in about William Tecumseh Sherman's unprecedented depredations across the state of Georgia. That general had captured Atlanta, the "warehouse and workhouse" of the Deep South, in a victory that probably saved Abraham Lincoln's November 1864 reelection effort. Then Sherman burned over two hundred acres of the choicest commercial and industrial sections of the tortured city. And then he turned the entire white population remaining in Atlanta—men, women, and children, old and young—out onto the open road.

Can this be so? Lee wondered, unable to comprehend such a specter. *Can he be orchestrating such a calamitous campaign on Americans, without sanction from the United States government in Washington?* But there the story was, in newspapers from all over what remained of the unoccupied South. In letters, reports, and eyewitness accounts from some of the most respected generals, statesmen, and clergy in the Confederacy.

Sherman had just taken the Atlantic seaport of Savannah and presented it as a "Christmas gift" to Grant. Behind him, according to the reports, the Yankees had left a sixty-mile-wide swath of desolation—all the way back to Atlanta. The destruction included theft on an unimaginable scale, slaughter of what livestock and animals were not confiscated, the torching of innumerable buildings and homes, rapes, beatings, and intimidation.

"If the people raise a howl against my barbarity or cruelty, I will answer that war is war and not popularity-seeking," Northern newspapers quoted "Uncle Billy," as his troops affectionately called him, as saying. "We must make old and young, rich and poor, feel the hard hand of war . . ." Regarding his trek across

Georgia, he crowed, "I could look forty miles in each direction and see smoke rolling up like one great bonfire . . ."

From a multitude of candidates Sherman had handpicked Judson Kilpatrick for his cavalry chief. Keenly aware of the infamy pervading the Kilpatrick-Dahlgren raid against Richmond, he said, "I know that Kilpatrick is a h— of a d——d fool, but I want just that sort of a man to command my cavalry on this expedition."

"Permit me to say that the unprecedented measure you propose transcends, in studied and ingenious cruelty, all acts ever brought to my attention in the dark history of war," Hood, since defeated as Lee suspected he would be, wrote Sherman on the eve of his forcing out the population of Atlanta. "In the name of God and humanity, I protest."

"I'm going to march to Richmond," Sherman said. "And when I go through South Carolina, it will be one of the most horrible things in the history of the world. The devil himself couldn't restrain my men in that state."

This is not a man-to-man fight, between two armed forces; this is a war against the people, Lee thought. *Sheridan in the valley, Sherman in Georgia.* A shiver ran through him. *What fate awaits us if Grant breaches our lines here, and they all converge upon Richmond? I fear we are learning of a sort of war new to modern Christendom, a kind of war in which I am not equipped to participate. Oh, that the president would allow me to move out into open land and fight those people in my own way on ground of my own choosing before they are able to further consolidate.*

Taylor entered his room, his face alight with excitement.

"Sir, you must come see this," the young man exclaimed. Lee, his face grave and appearing older than Taylor had ever before seen it, rose without a word and followed his aide out.

In the front yard of the house, several of Lee's staff officers—Marshall, Venable, and Long among them—had gathered around a wooden barrel.

"Sir, it is a barrel of turkeys sent to you and your staff for Christmas dinner," Marshall announced, his breath billowing into white clouds in the bone-chilling air.

Lee stood there, all eyes alight and on him. Only Long seemed to retain a sense of calm.

"What a blessing to a portion of our brave men lying in hospital my fowl will be," he said happily.

Expressions ranging from Marshall's gape-mouthed shock to Taylor's grim, clenched jaw greeted his statement. Long nodded slightly, a wry smile bereft of surprise pushing out across his bearded face.

Lee said nothing further but remained standing on the wide front steps of the house, his expectant gaze traveling around the crestfallen group.

"Guess that hospital mess is pretty scant, eh, General?" Venable said.

"Pitiably so, I fear," Lee replied.

"Expect you better chuck my bird in there too, sir," Venable said, sounding as though he were telling the dentist to go ahead and grip the decayed tooth with the pliers and yank it out.

"Yes, sir," Marshall followed, "me too, sir."

And so did they all follow suit, until only Taylor had not spoken. Lee turned to him. "Ah, our brother from the parlor," Lee said, a mischievous twinkle sparking his gray eyes.

Taylor flushed crimson, glanced at the others, then, putting the bravest face on it he could, said, "General, if I may be so bold as to speak for my bird, I suspect he would be honored to accompany your bird on the journey of their final service to mankind—sir."

When Lee nodded his satisfaction at the offer, Taylor scolded himself that so modest an expression of approval from the Tycoon could elicit such joy and gratitude in him that he had pleased the old man.

The Confederates in the trenches had heard that the ladies of Richmond planned delivering Christmas dinner to them. As they celebrated Christmas Eve night by shivering, scratching, aching, and returning again and again to the stinking open latrines, the men conjured up culinary creations of fantastic proportion in their tortured minds. Oh yes, when the ladies of Richmond put their minds to something, not bread riots, food rationing, eye-popping inflation, or worthless Confederate shinplasters could deter them.

Depending on the man, his background, individual tastes, and current mental state, he might be salivating over the nearly palpable taste of beefsteak or roast duck, turkey or rack of lamb. His sandpaper-dry tongue might be tickled by the onslaught of cranberry sauce, Yorkshire pudding, pumpkin or pecan pie, or chocolate cake with frosting. His aching empty ribs might be warmed with the thought of cornbread dressing or fried okra, dirty rice or steaming grits.

Many a soldier thought of home, and of up and leaving for it this very night, for the loving solace, Christmas cheer, and feasts it promised. Then most of them remembered that such promises, along with many others, had long ago been broken by a people never dreaming that the grasping Yankees would not be beaten after a few weeks, certainly months. Never would they have imagined "those people" would spill oceans of their own blood, and still fight on after nearly four years.

So most of them stayed right where they were, shivering without sleeping—for the sharpshooters, mortar attacks, and random shells bursting overhead had for the most part curtailed such luxuries as sleep—in their hollowed-out holes or straining against the dark as their teeth chattered and they stood guard.

Some of them, though, walked, crawled, or ran away, as some did every night now because no matter what had happened to home, it would be better than the trenches—seven months of trenches now. Most important of all, nearly every man that served under Lee had somebody somewhere who desperately needed him, whether to bring in a crop, kill some game for food or clothes, or help give a wife or child hope that lasting on another day was worth the pain and suffering it took to do so.

And supper time had long since passed, without the ladies of Richmond or their wagons or heaping hot piles of food, and presently the time approached ten o'clock in the evening. Then midnight came, ushering in the day celebrating the Savior's birth, and passed. One o'clock, then two, then three. Of all the tears, all the blood, all the heartbreak and blasted dreams through the months, and now years, the forlorn sense that now spread along the Confederate trench lines around Richmond and Petersburg like a prairie fire catching a hot August wind, seemed to many the most crushing of all.

Sometime after 3 A.M., when even the hardiest Southern soldier shook his head in frozen numbed confusion, a single voice, thin, uncertain, even plaintive, cried out, "Is it them?"

He was at first answered by silence. Then, "Believe it is."

And, "It's them—they've come!"

Such a Rebel yell as had never been voiced, and never would again, exploded forth from deep within the souls of brave men who had feared this night might have pushed them over that indefinable line that steals the life from even the bravest of the brave.

They had never heard the likes of such a throaty roar, had the old men, the maimed men, the widowed women, and the fatherless children who mounted mules, rode wagons, and walked by the hundreds, afoot through the black Christmas morning of 1864, to bring their protectors all they had to offer them.

Which included not nearly so much food as had been hoped for, but grand amounts of love, encouragement, and hope. More than enough of these, in fact, to remind many a man that the horror of the trenches was bearable, at least for a few more days.

Indeed, truth be known, more than one man that Christmas morning, after consuming his spartan sandwich or gob of vegetable, might even have considered it a distinct honor still to reside in those trenches.

CHAPTER 38

THE DAY MARLEY LEFT WASHINGTON, THE WOUND INFLICTED UPON him by the raiders began to throb with pain. The discomfort grew as he trekked home to Pennsylvania by train. *Home,* he thought, disconsolate. *I am thirty-four years old and the closest thing to "home" I have is the house I left as a seventeen-year-old boy to escape to the army from an unfaithful father, an insecure mother, and a spoiled, social-climbing sister. All of them good, loyal abolitionists, of course.*

He wanted out of his home again, but the persistent pain inside his wound concerned the doctors. Marley shared with no one his suspicion that the depressed mental condition wrought in him by the ordeals of the past months, capped by the heartbreak of the Washington trip, had perhaps contributed to his physical demise. He tried not to dwell on the confusing frustrations that befell him and the other commissioners. Evidently the Pennsylvania newspapers considered Andersonville much more important than did the Federal government, for they rendered it ceaseless attention and denunciation. If their reporting was remotely accurate, the death count at Andersonville continued to increase. *It has only grown since we went to see President Lincoln,* Marley saw. One snowy January day he put the papers aside and thought, *Why did he not send for us? Did he even know we were in Washington? Stanton or Seward or one of the other parasites who feed on him shaded us, I am certain of it.*

He shook his head. *If I persist in pondering the imponderable, I will need to be committed to an asylum before I die of any physical wounds. The resolution of such an important issue must wait, and I must trust that our government, imperfect as it is, is at work to bring about good in this desperate world.*

Perhaps it would not have to wait for long. A telegram arrived from the office of United States Secretary of War Edwin M. Stanton in Washington. He desired a personal interview with Marley in his office at the earliest possible date.

ROBERT E. LEE

●◇ ●◇ ●◇

A more saturnine man Marley had never met. Of course, after cooling his boots for two-and-a-half hours in Stanton's waiting room, the Pennsylvanian did not find himself inclined toward forbearance. The inclination did not increase when Marley was shown to a chair across the desk from the secretary, who continued for some minutes working at papers before him without so much as acknowledging his invited guest.

So Marley began to consider to what he could compare the appearance of the man before him. *A bat, perhaps,* he mused, *or perhaps a muskrat. No, I believe he bears strongest resemblance to one of Siegfried's Nibelungs.* His gaze bore in on Stanton. *And are you, too, a creature of the netherworld, Mr. Stanton, hoarding your riches?*

"Your concern for your fellow prisoners was admirable," Stanton said, still not looking up, the sudden sound jolting Marley, "if misguided."

"Sir?"

"In just how bad a way do you take the Rebels to be, Major?"

Marley chewed that one over for a moment. "Bad enough to be barely able to feed us—or themselves, sir. Same with medicine." A pause. "And the other things we're blockading from them."

This last, finally, earned Marley eye contact. Stanton considered the implications of his words.

"Perhaps it appears a hard thing that we refused exchange," he said.

"Refused?" Marley spoke up. "Or refuse?"

"We cannot afford to do so," Stanton proceeded. "We should be forced to trade strong, well-fed, available Confederate soldiers for our own men now broken-down from campaigning and disease, their terms of enlistment expired and them gone home, not to return to duty."

Marley gave the second-most powerful man in the United States as hard a stare as he had ever given anyone. "So it is indeed true. It is we and not the Rebs at whose feet rests the infamy of Andersonville."

Stanton was displeased with the direction this conversation was headed. Was this soldier as upstart and impudent as he appeared? Or was the secretary impaired in his judgment by his recent lack of sleep? It appeared just another in an endless line of reminders that soldiers must be kept in their place, far from the levers of power. *Take that maniac Sherman, for instance,* he thought, spite filling him. *I'll see that man in prison before I'll witness him any closer to the gates of power than that red clay he marched through in Georgia.*

"Major Marley," Stanton said, his face darkening as it took in Marley's ribbon-and-medal-littered tunic. "You are a decorated and, they tell me, valorous man. And, I might add, a tenacious soldier who takes more killing than anyone I ever knew. But you ill serve yourself, your career, and, yes, your country, by meditating upon affairs of state—though I suspect such a course may indeed be within your capabilities *after* this wicked rebellion is finally vanquished. For now there remains the most important contest in the history of America to be won. And it is a contest that only soldiers can win."

Ignoring the rare utterance by Stanton of a compliment, Marley vaulted to his feet, truly shocking the secretary. "A policy like this is the quintessence of inhumanity, Mr. Stanton, a disgrace to the administration which carried it out, and a blot upon the country," he said, his concern for protocol melting with his belief in chivalrous men and noble causes. "You rulers make the charge that the Rebels intentionally killed off our men. I can honestly swear by eyewitness observation that they were doing everything in their power to sustain us. Do not flatter yourselves. You have abandoned your brave men in the hour of their cruelest need. They fought for the Union, and you reached no hand out to save the old faithful, loyal, and devoted servants of the country. You may try to shift the blame from your own shoulders, but posterity will place the responsibility where it justly belongs."

It was perhaps the first and only time that Edwin Stanton ever received such a riposte from a major in the U.S. Army, then sat by as the man stormed out of his office without a by-your-leave or even so much as a salute.

But in his mind the entire farcical scene served to lift Stanton's spirits. *This will no longer be my cross to bear,* he thought, a rare smile spreading across his thin beard, *with Sam Grant inheriting responsibility for this exchange business. Thank goodness our backwoods oaf of a president at least had sense enough not to let that wild-eyed trooper disrupt our attrition strategy for the Confederates. And besides, if our mercenary scum don't have the salt to stay in uniform and finish this job, they might as well rot in those prisons as go home.*

No matter now, he thought, rising to head home and prepare for the evening's theater. The celebrated Booth family was back in town to perform more Shakespeare. *Grant is going to reinstate the exchange anyway. No doubt that is Lincoln's doing, concerned as ever about his place in history. If the death totals*

I'm receiving for our prisoners out of Andersonville are remotely accurate, some-
body's place in history is going to be in ashes. And with several thousand more
reportedly dead since the gallant Major Marley and his "commissioners" set out on
their quest, I will certainly see to it that I am not the sacrificial lamb.

He glanced down at the upturned letter on his desk, from Sherman. "There
is a class of people in the South—men, women, and children—who must be
killed or banished before you can hope for peace and order," the commander of
the Federal Army of the Tennessee wrote.

Stanton nodded his approval. "And children," he repeated, his voice a whisper, though he feared not the opinion of God or man on the matter. He smiled
despite himself at the contemptible soldier's determined and devilish ingenuity.
How convenient Uncle Billy's words—and actions—for our war effort, he thought,
and for keeping his dangerous presence out of my path as we set about recon-
structing the South.

Performing *The Merchant of Venice* tonight before an audience comprised
of the most powerful men in the United States was far from Wilkes Booth's
mind. After all, he thought with disdain in his backstage dressing room, the
warmongering tyrant, Lincoln, had so enjoyed a previous Washington performance of Booth's in Charles Selby's *The Miracle Heart* that the president
rose at the play's conclusion and initiated a standing ovation that swept
through the entire crowd. Then Lincoln sent for Booth to join him in the presidential box.

It was delightful to spurn his offer and simply walk out of the theater, in full
view of presidential cabinet members, Booth recalled with relish. *Soon he shall*
indeed have that audience he so desired, but on my terms, and not in the presi-
dential box. I hear he also enjoys private shows in the White House Red Room. Well,
I'll give him a private show such as he'll never forget.

Indeed Booth's tireless work seemed near bearing fruit. Spending thousands of Yankee dollars of his own money and working countless hours—in
mortal danger from the Pinkertons and other Feds every step of the way—he
had cobbled together a devoted band of conspirators. They included associates
around the Washington area, including Southern-leaning theatrical stagehands
as well as "partisan rangers" of the most irregular sort inhabiting the northern
Virginia countryside.

Booth would need them all if he was to expand his clandestine war effort beyond the smuggling of medical supplies into a Confederacy desperate for them because of the Federal naval blockade. Booth's men were needed if Lincoln was to be snatched, unharmed, as Booth planned, taken over the Potomac, across northern Virginia, through Grant's formidable lines, and to the Confederate government at Richmond.

Though Booth had been unable to elicit any sort of positive response from President Davis or even anyone below him, no direct admonishment had reached him *against* taking Lincoln. He knew that before Ulric the Hun launched his barbarous raid on Richmond not only would the Confederate government have warned against any move whatsoever against Lincoln, it was distinctly possible they would have taken such steps as they were able to preempt such an attempt.

Booth had contemplated kidnapping Lincoln this very night, familiar as the Marylander was with the layout of the theater. And with no more than the president's footman and a cabinet secretary or politician or two usually with him, how easy it would be. But Booth had not been able to coordinate the plan with enough of his comrades in time to pull it off, so the mission would have to wait—again.

Now his brow furrowed as a stagehand announced the five-minute juncture before the beginning of the show. His eyes darted around the room at his father, Junius, and his brothers Edwin and young Junius, who occupied various posts across the political spectrum. *How many times has Lincoln been within my grasp, only to slip away due to some complication or other?* Booth thought. He remembered today hearing that General Lee was advocating the large-scale recruitment of blacks—*free as well as slave!*—for combat service in the Confederate armies. *Oh my, the Confederacy must be teetering on its last legs to be contemplating such a thing,* Booth thought, his stomach beginning to churn.

It irked him that blacks were already scattered throughout the Southern armies, some of them shouldering muskets, just as it irked him that Lee was compounding his own culpability in the event the Confederacy fell. *If only that vaunted "gentleman" had prosecuted the war in the North, when he had the chance, in the manner our enemies have in the South!* Booth thought, his fury kindling. *No less, no worse, just returning evil for their evil. The Northern people would long since have complained over their suffering such as has never yet been seen in the Western world. Why, they've nearly made Lincoln quit a score of times already! We simply have too d—— many good Christians playing at war while our heathen enemies destroy our civilization.*

Now he grew cold sober. *What good will it be to capture Lincoln if no one remains in Richmond to deliver him to but Yankee occupation forces? And what good would the act then be anyhow? No longer would any reason exist for which to bargain him—no unexchanged prisoners, no favorable peace terms, nothing.*

If not kidnapping, then what? Booth wondered as he followed his father and brothers out of the dressing room and onto the stage. Hearing those first sweet strains of the audience's excitement, he chuckled, recalling how some of the more pious in the community had decried the transformation of the old building after it burned in 1863.

It had been a Baptist church. The complaining religious fanatics warned that the wrath of a holy God would likely fall upon the corruption of his house into a "royal road to perdition," peopled by unsavory actors who vied with the preachers for the public's affections, and now named Ford's Theater.

For months President Davis had been lobbying the Confederate Congress to act on Lee's long-held desire for the purchase of thousands of slaves from their owners, with the intent of employing them as desperately needed combat soldiers, then emancipating them at the end of the war.

The vehemence of the opposition to Davis from the Congress, some Southern newspapers, and certain segments of the public jolted him.

"I think we must decide whether slavery shall be extinguished by our enemies, and the slaves used against us, or if we will use them ourselves at the risk of the effects this may produce upon our own institutions," Lee encouraged Davis as the two sat in the small office the president kept in his home for use on days when he felt ill.

Today he could barely sit up due to the pain of a neuralgia attack.

"The Negroes, under proper circumstances, will make efficient soldiers," Lee said. He cited previous cases from his own observation and recollection, as well as that of other Southern commanders such as Stonewall, Forrest, Longstreet, and Pat Cleburne, where blacks had distinguished themselves for the Confederacy, both in combat and combat-support roles.

They had covered the ground before, and Davis agreed with him. But the president faced powerful foes on the matter. "My own opinion is that we should employ them without delay and that we should grant immediate freedom to all who enlist," the Virginian added.

"Immediate?" Davis, ashen-faced, said, looking up.

"Yes, excellency," Lee said.

Davis shook his head wearily. "The Congress will not have it," he said. "At least not immediate."

Davis's head drooped. Lee waited for his next words. After nearly a full minute had passed in silence, the president, with effort, lifted his handsome head. "Let us speak more on the matter," he rasped, his shoulders hunched.

Lee nodded, rose, and walked toward the door. Halfway there, he turned and said, "You are a man of great courage, sir, and it is an honor to serve you."

Davis stared at him. So deeply did such a remark from Robert E. Lee move him that tears welled up in his eyes. "Th . . . thank you, thank you, old friend."

No man on earth but General Lee could have accomplished what he has done these past years under Jeff Davis, while preserving a working relationship and a friendship with that proud, difficult man, Marshall, today accompanying Lee, thought to himself as he rose from his chair when Lee returned downstairs.

Perhaps God would be pleased to accomplish together two objectives beneficial to the South and perhaps pleasing to him, freeing large numbers of additional slaves, which would lead to the preservation of our independence, Lee thought to himself on the ride back to Edge Hill. Hearing a Yankee shell scream overhead not far away, then explode, he recognized with disappointment that the Federals had extended their lines even farther west.

Back in his quarters Taylor presented Lee with three new cases of captured Confederate deserters. Each left him little choice but to approve their execution as an example to the many others now tempted. Depressed by that, he brightened when Long announced that one of the black cooks had requested an audience with him.

Lee smiled. "It must be preferable to the regrettable duty before me, General Long," he said to that startled officer. "Please show the man in."

"Sir?" Taylor, stepping through the doorway, asked. "A Negro cook, sir?"

At times Lee enjoyed baffling his own staff nearly as much as he did "those people's" commanders. He got to his feet and said, "I can scarcely imagine a more important man by which to be held in high esteem than one who cooks for you. Show him in."

A moment later a black man several inches shorter than the nearly six-foot-tall Lee, but of equally handsome face and form, identical age, and similar downy white whiskers, stepped past the bewildered aides and shook Lee's hand.

"General Lee," the black man said, "I been wantin' to see you for a long time. I's a soldier."

"Ah," Lee said, nodding his head, "to what army do you belong—to the Union army or to the Southern army?"

"Oh, General, I belong to your army."

"Well, have you been shot?"

"No, sir, I ain't been shot yet."

"How is that? Nearly all of our men get shot," Lee answered, his brown eyes twinkling.

Now a broad, knowing grin took shape across the cook's dark face. "Why, General, I ain't been shot 'cause I stays back where the generals stay."

This exchange, one old salt to another, delighted Lee and calmed his throbbing sciatic nerve.

Long and Taylor furnished their best smiles, more amazed and less able than ever to comprehend the man just appointed by Davis as commander in chief of all Confederate armies.

That night Lee wrote to Mary, complaining that he had twice tallied her most recent shipment of socks sent for his soldiers, and that she had indeed overcounted the total by five pair. The air cleared about that, he offered a far briefer summary of recent military events, then concluded, "I pray daily and almost hourly to our heavenly Father to come to the relief of you and our afflicted country. I know he will order all things for our good, and we must be content."

The next Sunday, returning to his quarters from church in Petersburg, he passed a team of mules driven by a Confederate teamster and with great difficulty hauling a load of lumber. *Poor creatures,* he thought, stricken. The words he had heard one of Longstreet's wisecracking foot soldiers spout the other day at one of Hampton's passing horse soldiers came to mind: "You look like you're a'ridin' a fence rail with legs, boy!"

How I detest this war that constantly mocks the Lord's Sabbath, Lee thought, *which without observing our Christian people may no more expect God's blessings than could the faithful Old Covenant Jews.*

The next evening he wrote the general in charge of the stable:

> . . . The mules were dreadfully poor, weary, and worn. One in particular, the off leader, could scarcely be gotten along. . . . There are many things of necessity that we are obliged to do on Sunday, but I think this stable might have waited. Existing orders require all work on Sunday to cease, except those of necessity, in order that man and beast have one day to rest.

As February unfolded, Lee followed the progress of Sherman's juggernaut as it stormed northward through South Carolina. The shouted songs of the sinewy, blue-coated western veterans resounded across the piedmont:

> Hail Columbia, happy land!
> If I don't burn you, I'll be d——d!

On the seventeenth, "Uncle Billy" captured both Charleston and Columbia, the state capital.

Lee felt his chest tighten as he began to examine the reports cascading in about Columbia. Fires had started among huge bales of cotton the afternoon the town fell. Sherman deflected criticism for the blaze to Hampton, now promoted to lieutenant general and dispatched by Lee to command cavalry against the blue marauders. But waves of eyewitness accounts reaching Lee, including some from Northern officers, swore the cotton fires had been subdued late in the afternoon and that new fires had begun at dark.

Those fires, said the reports, swarms of drunken Federal soldiers had ignited with torches, pitch, turpentine-soaked rags, and a myriad of other incendiaries, following their capture of a whiskey distillery. Hampton's own mansion, reputedly the finest in South Carolina, went up. As citizens, and some Federal soldiers, fought the blazes, more drunken troops thwarted their efforts by bayoneting their fire hoses and chopping them up with axes.

Dozens of churches—some of them specifically targeted—had burned, along with an Ursuline convent.

"Oh, holy! Yes, holy!" laughing Federal soldiers jeered the nuns, blowing cigar smoke in their faces as they watched their building's large cross crash flaming to the earth. "We're just as holy as you are! Now, what do you think of God? Ain't Sherman greater?"

One Methodist minister fled from his flaming parsonage holding a sick child in his arms. He had wrapped a blanket around the child to protect him from the bitterly cold night and the choking, smoke-rent air. A Federal soldier grabbed the blanket.

"No!" the pastor cried. "He's sick."

The soldier wrenched the blanket from around the now-exposed child and slung it into the flames leaping from the parsonage. "D— you," he growled, brandishing his bayoneted rifle, "If you say one more word, I'll throw the child in after it."

Lee read prominent novelist William Gilmore Simms's firsthand account that while the Federals sexually assaulted no white women, they raped droves of blacks. "Many of them were left in a condition little short of death," he wrote.

"Regiments, in successive *relays,* subjected scores of these poor women to the torture of their embraces," Simms reported.

Nearly three-fourths of South Carolina's entire capital city was left in ashes. Flocks of stunned, weeping, helpless, homeless women and children sat crouched everywhere among the ruins.

"As far as the eye can reach, nothing is to be seen but heaps of rubbish, tall dreary chimneys, and shattered brick walls," wrote seventeen-year-old Emma LeConte. She described the United States flag hoisted atop the South Carolina capitol building as "That hateful symbol of despotism."

"How I *hate* the people who have done this!" she exclaimed.

Lee sighed upon learning that though the well-known Christian General Oliver Howard had, along with Sherman, initiated attempts to douse the fires, Howard was wing commander of the Federal assault on Columbia, officially in charge of the occupation, and his soldiers were among the worst of the arsonists and looters.

"Old Prayer Book" evidently lost little sleep over the devastation of the city and the suffering of its people. Lee saw where the Federal had remarked that he was reminded of the old politician who, when asked if he had attended burial services for one of his arch foes, replied, "No, I didn't patronize the funeral, but I approve of it."

Sherman later summed up the matter by blaming the fire on Hampton, crediting "God Almighty" with starting "wind sufficient to carry that cotton wherever He would," and saying, "I have never shed many tears over the event because I believe it hastened what we all fought for, the end of the war."

Columbia . . . Lee thought . . . Randolph, Tennessee . . . Meridian and Jackson, Mississippi . . . Atlanta . . . the Valley of Virginia . . . we are nearly surrounded by Grant, and Sherman is coming straight for us. I must find a way to maneuver, to regain the initiative, even as my own government straitjackets me.

After blowing out the two candles lighting his room, he folded his aching body into bed, weathered a piercing spasm of lumbago, and lay awake for a very long time. *Merciful God,* he prayed, *what will they do to Richmond if we fall?*

With Federals on land and sea cinching the girth ever tighter, on February 20 the Confederate House of Representatives finally approved the purchase and enlistment of slaves, and the large-scale enlistment of free blacks. But they refused to include emancipation for the slaves in the package. The Senate rejected even what the House had approved.

Finally, on March 8, the Senate approved a bill similar to the House's.

Lee knew the historic measure would not please everyone.

"If slaves will make good soldiers, our whole theory of slavery is wrong," prominent Georgia statesman and former Speaker of the United States House of Representatives, Howell Cobb, protested.

The head of the Confederacy's Bureau of War, directly responsible for filling the army's ranks, complained that President Davis indirectly—and Lee directly—had pressured both the Congress and the Virginia State legislature to enact laws arming the slaves.

Blared the *Richmond Examiner* newspaper: "It is to be questioned after the recent innovations concerning the widespread employment of Negroes in the Confederate armed services, how good a Southerner is General Robert E. Lee."

CHAPTER 39

THE WAR HAD, AFTER ALL, DONE MUCH FOR YOUNG JAKE Schumacher. The guerilla fight he and Culpeper and other "irregulars" and "partisan rangers" were waging against the Federal hosts in north and central Virginia had grown savage. They had ridden away from the Shenandoah because they could not live off it and because they did not want their actions to bring further reprisals against their kindred in the Valley.

They had heard much of the exploits of Mosby, Stringfellow, and others. They had also heard a man could not only kill Yankees with impudence but also eat well off the scraps of the Federals' supply-line table that ran from Washington south nearly to the Richmond-Petersburg area.

Culpeper thrived so well in such pursuits that the Confederate government officially disavowed him and his ilk, and the Federals stuck a thousand-dollar bounty on his head.

No one seemed to appreciate a man who answered fire with fire, especially when his fire included repeated ambushes, hangings, and throat slashings of Federal troops.

One night two of Mosby's deft rangers stole undetected into Culpeper's camp. Of the havoc-wreaking little band Culpeper had put together, only he, Jake, and a tall, fearsome Cherokee Indian they and others on both sides of the war had christened "Chief," had not yet been killed by the bluecoats all of them now despised.

Mosby's men, Sharps carbines locked and loaded, strolled right up to the tiny campfire. Never before had anyone accomplished such a feat on Culpeper or any of his comrades.

"General Mosby says for y'all to clear out o' this country or he's comin' for you hisself," one of the Sharps-toters announced to his startled little audience.

When no one responded, the ranger said, "Y'all hear?"

Culpeper nodded. The portion of his tanned face not covered over in a tawny beard sprouting gray flecks, was now lined like a map of the Valley drawn up by Old Jack's mapmaker Jed Hotchkiss.

The ranger gave a short nod of his own and said, "Well, then."

He and his partner turned to leave. Culpeper, who had had his .36 caliber, cap-firing Colt pointed at the uninvited guests the whole time from under his sleeping blanket, cocked back the hammer on that gun. Mosby's men froze in their tracks.

"We'll leave," he said, "but you boys ever see us again this side o' h—, you better step aside."

The rangers, stone stiff, their backs to Culpeper, nodded, then started again to leave.

"You can pass that right along to the great Mosby too," Culpeper said.

This last prompted surprised looks from both Chief and Jake.

"We'll go to Richmond," Culpeper told them later.

"Richmond?" Chief said.

"Oh, it is a town now full of brigands, gaming men, and 'ladies' of the sportin' sort," Culpeper said. He plugged in a chaw he had taken that day off a dead Yank horse soldier and rubbed his sore hip. The haul from which the tobacco came proved extensive, considering the Federal transported the entire spread on his horse after securing it from a Fauquier County farmhouse his squad had just torched. It included a variety of woman's clothes—petticoats, dresses, undergarments, bonnets—as well as bed linens, curtains, bolts of cloth, and a family Bible. Jewelry filled the bluecoat's pockets, along with a note from a Massachusetts girl named Louisa May.

"Forever in your debt shall I be, my brave conqueror," read the florid script, "if only you will send home special tokens of your oft-proclaimed sentiments toward me from the Rebel homes you pacify."

Jake had shot the trooper through the neck. When he discovered the considerable plunder and the note, he took his hunting knife and slit the dead man's throat from one jugular to the other for good measure and to remind the Yankees the reward they could expect for such rapine.

Chief beamed with pride, for the strapping boy completed the task just as the Cherokee had taught him.

"Long as we watch for Winder's home guards, reckon we'll make out just fine in Richmond," Culpeper said.

"Then we can come back and kill more bluebellies?" Jake asked.

Culpeper and Chief swapped amused glances.

"Chief said he'd show me how to do a scalpin'," Jake said, "like he did to those Yank cav out in the Nations and Missouri."

Culpeper broke into a hearty laugh as Chief pitched him a pint of Yankee bourbon. "Go stand watch, Injun boy. We ain't as salty as we thought we was when boys can stroll right in on us like them two did."

After Jake left and Culpeper sucked down a long couple of swigs, he flipped the bottle back to the Cherokee.

"You never told me how you got all the way here from wherever it was they had you and your people cooped up," Culpeper said.

Chief tossed his grand, buffalo-like head and hooted. A curtain of black hair, corralled at top by a purple bandanna, fanned down around his broad-beamed shoulders. "Sure, valley man. You tell me how you got here, then I'll tell you."

Culpeper thought on that for a minute, then laughed himself. Who, after all, could figure a college-educated Indian who carried a war club and Bowie knife? "Gimmee another pull o' that red-eye, big man," he said. "Ahhh, yeh—I'm gonna sure miss plyin' our wares on these town-bred and city-born Billies." He stared for a moment into the fire. "You know, I wouldn't give a bent nickel for young Jake there even so much as carryin' Ethan boy's spurs. But d——d if he ain't turned out to be a good hand after all."

Indeed war had done much for Jake Schumacher. It had turned the governments and militaries of two nations against him. It had put a five-hundred-dollar Federal bounty on his head. It had even loosed him from the confines of the faith that had encompassed him and four hundred years of Schumachers before him.

Why, the Bible Katarina gave him when he left to fight, the Gutenberg one in German that belonged to her great-grandmother in Saxony, had served him well. For between the rum he had gulped down and the fire made from that large old Bible, he and his mates had gone to sleep with a positively warm glow about them that night a few weeks ago.

They had those Yankee foragers to thank for that batch. The graybacks caught up to the Feds while they were ransacking that widow lady's farmhouse over in Prince William County. The Yanks had already driven iron tent pegs through the foreheads of her last two hogs. When they came outside, Culpeper and his boys jumped the whole pack of them and slit every one open from one ear to the other. Strapping young farm boy Jake started it by leaping nimbly from the roof—just like Chief taught him—and taking down the last man out the door.

Yep, Culpeper thought, feeling a measure of satisfaction for his role in the process, *young Jake has blossomed into a mighty fine man to have along in this fight.*

CHAPTER 40

I MUST GO AND TRY AGAIN TO PERSUADE THEM, TO PERSUADE him, *of the necessity of our abandoning the trenches and linking up with Joe Johnston,* Lee thought. He put on his uniform, gauging each movement so as to avert a lower back spasm here, a throbbing hip bone there, an aching chest, shoulder, or arm muscle there. When finished, perspiration dappling his bronzed forehead, he thought to sit for a moment but feared the effort and piercing jolts of pain from bending, sitting, then rising again. *But I feel as though I must first rest my old bones in some way,* he thought, perplexed, when Taylor appeared at the doorway of his little bedroom office.

"Sir, I know you must be off to see the president, but three visitors have arrived—" Taylor began before Lee halted him with a wave of his hand. That sudden movement sent a thunderbolt of pain down Lee's hip and leg.

"Sorry, sir," Taylor said, wincing at the hurt in Lee's face. "I'll tell the little girls you are not feeling well." With that, he disappeared back through the doorway.

"Little girls?" Lee queried, looking up, his face alight.

Taylor reappeared. "Why, yes, sir. They lost their home in Nottingham County and have made their way to Petersburg, the three of them, with their mother and two brothers."

Pain and fatigue shoved aside, even if not forgotten, Lee said, "Well, of course, show them in, Colonel Taylor, show them in straightaway."

Lee stood there like a parched man in a desert awaiting an oncoming water wagon. He heard their giggles—*their precious giggles*—even before he saw them.

Then they were stepping through the doorway and forming horizontal ranks. *Oh, how lovely their little dresses,* Lee thought. He sobered upon spotting the telltale signs he had so often seen in the wartime clothing of Virginia's finest families. *And so lovely they must have been as well, as flowing damask curtains in their fine Tidewater manor.*

"General Lee, sir, I am Elisabeth," announced the eldest of the three, no more than eight years of age, as she curtsied with immense drama. Scarlet trusses wandered down over her shoulders, and battalions of freckles dappled her pearl cheeks. Lee bowed as low as his lumbago would allow him in response.

"General Lee, sir, I am Sallie," said the second, perhaps seven years of age, her hair finer than Elisabeth's, but just as long and so blonde as to appear almost white. She had not the physical beauty of her sisters; in fact homely would have been a kind description of her appearance. For that Lee considered her all the dearer and offered her his noblest bow and courtesies. Sallie performed her curtsy with an even greater flourish than her sister.

"General Lee, sir, I am Fanny," said the smallest, all but invisible behind billows of the blackest hair, most prominent dimples, and most angelic face Lee had seen since—*Annie.* His throat tightened, and bowing a third time, he knew he had best move the conversation on before his emotions got the better of him in front of three little girls. But before he knew it, Elisabeth was stepping forward, presenting him a basketful of eggs.

"They were laid by our own hens," she said proudly.

Next, Sallie advanced. *Well, I'll swan,* Lee realized, upon closer examination, *little Sallie has the brightest smile, and the loveliest voice of the three.* And she also had pickles, an enormous Mason jar full of them, supplied by her mother.

Last but not least, Fanny presented Lee with a basket of popcorn, "Grown in our garden."

Not to be outdone, Elisabeth stepped out again. "I also have a small wheel with me on which I spin for Mother." After a pause, she added, "Mother weaves all the cloth for my two brothers."

"Ah, how appreciative your mother must be to you for all you do," Lee said.

"Yes, she most certainly is," Elisabeth answered.

Lee gazed at the cornucopia spread before him on his desk, then at the three pixies. He saw at once they could ill afford to give up even so modest a bounty as they had brought. *I must devise a strategy for redirecting their plans, without leaving them—or their mother—the wiser,* he thought, rubbing his bearded chin.

"Where did you all live?" Lee asked.

"Near Eastville," the blonde said.

Lee's eyebrows arched. "Eastville? Why, Eastville is very near our dear old Arlington."

"Yes," the redhead said, smiling, her eyelashes batting. "We loved nothing more than riding with the whole family in the carriage past old Arlington after church on the Sabbath."

For a moment Lee thought he might cry. Instead he said, "You know what was one of my very favorite places on all of old Arlington to sneak away to, whenever I could?"

The three sets of shimmering green eyes could have shined no less intently had the Lord himself just returned in glory.

"The apple orchard," he said, his eyes growing as wide as theirs. He paused, seizing the moment. "And you know what I have found out behind this house?"

So gripped were the girls, they could only shake their heads no.

"The loveliest apple orchard you've ever seen."

The gust of their collective sigh was nearly enough to propel the entire group out to the orchard, which is where they shortly found themselves, much to the consternation of Lee's mess steward, who grew grimmer as each little girl's basket, lightened surreptitiously by only a small portion of its original cargo, was loaded to overflowing with the delectable burgundy fruit.

Soon Elisabeth, Sallie, and Fanny, eyeing one another's baskets to see who had the greatest haul, were curtsying again, then proceeding back to their rented quarters in a home that had already had half its (empty) carriage house torn open by a Yankee shell.

All the scene lacked in Taylor's eyes to complete it were gold, frankincense, and myrrh. *Except that in this case,* he thought, *he who was called upon appeared to revere the callers, if possible, even more greatly than did they he.*

Never would Lee forget his ride through a portion of the Confederate lines the next day en route to meet with Davis in Richmond. Most of his soldiers still wore more lice than clothes, and still they rose in their exhaustion and illness to exhibit the most remarkable shows of affection and respect for their Marse Robert. They doffed hats full of holes. They saluted with arms that had no covering past the elbows. They stood from where they sat or lay on bare, scarred feet.

But now they also bleated, "General, I have no shoes."

"I am hungry, sir, I haven't enough to eat."

"My family needs me back home, General; they are starving."

Lee met first with members of the Virginia delegation to the Confederate Congress. He painted a picture for them of the current military situation—and the condition of his troops—that they found as unbelievable as it was depressing. In the end they applauded Lee for his great accomplishments, exhorted him to stand firm, and offered their boundless confidence in the people of Richmond to withstand whatever calamities might befall them.

No doubt the people of Richmond would be better suited for such calamities were they partaking of such provisions as are many of our esteemed "statesmen," Lee thought, beset by more than a trace of bitterness.

When he arrived at Davis' regular office in the Confederate White House that evening, he met with the president, Longstreet, and General Breckenridge, the new secretary of war.

"I wrote last night to General Grant about the possibility of arriving at a satisfactory adjustment of the present unhappy difficulties by means of a military convention," Lee said, "and offering to meet with him to explore the matter."

"How do you assess the chances of such a meeting?" Davis asked.

"I am not optimistic about them," Lee said. "But we must try, your excellency. We currently have at best thirty-five thousand men able to fight. Grant has perhaps one hundred fifty thousand." Giving this a moment to soak in, he added, "And he can draw reinforcements from both Sheridan and—" This pause was involuntary. "—Sherman."

The room lay hushed for a moment at the sound of that name. Every man at the table knew the trail of devastation Sherman had left behind him in two states, now entering a third, North Carolina. They knew he had upwards of a hundred thousand of his own men. And they knew that the Army of Northern Virginia hung on one day at a time, one hour at a time, just to ward off the Army of the Potomac, ever expecting a cataclysmic Federal assault at all points along the line.

"There appear three primary alternatives," Lee said. "We can start a fight, the sooner the better; we can pursue peace discussions; or we can abandon our lines around Richmond and Petersburg and move to join up with Johnston in North Carolina."

Again the room, imbued with such big men and large opinions, fell silent. Every man knew the survival of a nation might hang on a sentence, even a word.

"In any event, it appears, short of an outright surrender, that we are destined to abandon our lines here at some point," Lee said.

After a moment, Davis asked, "Then wouldn't it be better to pull out of the lines immediately?"

"The artillery and draft horses are too weak for the soft roads. We will have to wait until they become firmer," Lee said. "In the meanwhile I am arranging extra rations for the horses."

Afterward, Lee rode to the Mess to see his family and have dinner. Rarely had any of them ever seen him so depressed. He said no more than one or two sentences through the entire meal.

Custis retired to his favorite chair next to the fireplace, which had one log burning on it this evening. He lit up a cigar and opened one of the evening newspapers. Lee stalked back and forth across the room, his small hands clasped behind him. He was as troubled as the night he had paced the floor above Mary at Arlington striving to decide whether or not to leave the U.S. Army, but to this condition was tonight added a boiling rage.

Finally the explosion Custis knew was coming erupted.

"Well, Mr. Custis, I have been up to see the Congress, and they do not seem to be able to do anything except to eat peanuts and chew tobacco, while my army is starving. I told them the condition the men were in and that something must be done at once, but I can't get them to do anything."

Lee increased his march from quickstep to double quickstep, and Custis spied his father's face glowing crimson and his handsome head nodding quickly.

"Mr. Custis, when this war began, I was opposed to it, bitterly opposed to it," Lee railed. "And I told these people that unless every man should do his whole duty, they would repent it."

At this he stopped to face Custis. "And now they will repent."

Even as so many of the best and brightest of the Confederacy's leaders had fallen, other men arose to fill their places. Not enough other men, but some, and many of these the sort of true Christian men Lee knew the nation needed now and would need the more after the war. Especially if the cause of Southern independence was lost, which he now knew, short of miraculous intervention by Almighty God, it was.

Foremost in the new rank of such leaders was corps leader John Gordon. This young man, so possessed of clarity of mind and breadth of vision, Lee had called for a private audience prior to his Richmond meeting with President Davis and the others. Lee had consulted Gordon as he considered the nation's plight and the strategic options available to it. How encouraging it had been to find Gordon's thinking so nearly aligned with his own.

Now it was Gordon who had formulated a clever, multifaceted plan to effect Lee's idea of a surprise assault against the Federals from the northeastern end of the Confederate line around Petersburg. Spearheaded by troops posing in the darkness as deserters, Gordon would attack the Federals' Fort Stedman, capture it, and use it as a launch point to gobble up three other forts behind Stedman. From there, with the blessing of an all-wise God, the Confederates might roll up the entire blue line.

The odds were long, but Lee felt refreshed again to have a brilliant young subordinate—this one not even schooled in the military arts before the war—come to him with audacious and reasoned stratagems and tactics.

Too bad we perhaps no longer possess the wherewithal to execute such missions, he thought sadly as he sipped sweet potato "coffee" in his Edge Hill headquarters room. Still, his critics in the Southern press and the Confederate Congress notwithstanding, he had been chomping at the bit to resume his natural offensive inclinations to "get at those people," to strike forth with one concerted blow, while enough of his men still remained and still retained enough physical strength to afford some hope of success.

He arose before 3 A.M., the morning of March 25, dressed, and opened the worn old Bible to one of his dear old friends. Psalm 120 was one of his favorite morning prayers. Its closing lines reminded him how the Southern people had wanted only to be allowed to go their own way in peace. And how Lincoln and the other Republican leaders had persisted in war no matter if it meant mortgaging the nation's finances for a generation, trampling underfoot the precious freedoms promised by its Constitution and Bill of Rights, rendering the American democratic experiment a byword before all the watching nations of the world and, worst of all, destroying the flower of a generation both North and South.

My soul hath long dwelt with him that hateth peace.
I am for peace: but when I speak, they are for war.

At 4 A.M., canopied in darkness, a solitary shot cracked like a broken bone in the still, dark morning watches. Gordon himself led twelve thousand of his men out of the grayback works and into the teeth of the Federal lines.

Though Grant had long expected some sort of desperate, death-rattle thrust from Lee, the assault stunned the Federals. Gordon's men stormed the front Yankee lines, poured into Fort Stedman, and shooting, stabbing, axing, and clubbing, shoved the bluecoats out and took possession.

Lee had confidence Gordon could take Fort Stedman, but he feared the combination of Grant's mounting strength and the steady evaporation of his own would render unlikely results similar to those that had earned fame for Lee's army that stretched to the farthest reaches of the world.

His fears came to fruition when forward Confederate storming parties failed to locate the three forts behind Stedman in the darkness. This allowed the Federals a needed respite to recover from a blow that, in the end, proved no better than a pale reprise of the once fearsome striking power of the Army of Northern Virginia. The Federals, regiment after regiment rallying forward, began to unleash a withering fusillade into the fort.

We are caught in a crossfire, Gordon realized, *whose fury mounts with each passing minute.*

Lee simply had no one else to send forth in support of Gordon without leaving entire sections of his line wide open to attack and capture.

So the Confederate attack stalled, then splintered under the weight of Grant's numbers.

When Gordon and the survivors staggered back into their own works, exhausted and out of ammunition, they were four thousand fewer than they had been four hours earlier, though they took nearly three thousand Federal prisoners.

Tears filled Lee's eyes as, astride Traveller, he watched the battered bloody remnants of his assault force return.

They have suffered too long, he thought mournfully. *We—I—have asked too much of them.* He listened as the guns from the Federal lines boomed, their volume escalating with each passing moment. *We have given the best we have to give.*

That night he wrote Mary, "I received your note with a bag of socks. The count is all right this time." *Indeed, for Mary and I to square on our socks count seems a greater feat for the Giver of all victory than our reversing the fortunes of war against those people,* he thought with satisfaction. "You will have to send down your offerings as soon as you can and bring your work to a close, for I think General Grant will move against us soon—within a week, if nothing prevents—and no man can tell what may be the result; but trusting to a merciful God, who does not always give the battle to the strong, I pray we may not be overwhelmed. I shall, however, endeavour to do my duty and fight to the last."

He paused for a moment as thunder sounded in the distance. A familiar flowing script winked up at him from a folded scrap of paper next to his letter to Mary. He smiled at the digression. "I enclose a note from little Agnes. I shall be very glad to see her tomorrow but cannot recommend pleasure trips now."

Then he turned his mind back to that which most truly weighed upon it. "Should it be necessary to abandon our position to prevent being surrounded, what will you do?" he wrote. "You must consider the question and make up your mind. It is a fearful condition, and we must rely for guidance and protection upon a kind Providence."

Sadness enfolded him as he finished the letter. *Yet again,* he thought, *my dear, crippled Mim is left to fend for herself in the maelstrom of war and tragedy, while her husband attends elsewhere to duties concerning all but his own family.* A pang of guilt surged through him. *But for the forgiving mercies and sanctifying grace of a kind God, I would be utterly ruined.*

Indeed Agnes was determined to escape the Mess and make the trip to visit the Meades, Lee family friends in Petersburg. To her father's vehement protestations, she uncharacteristically countered, "Papa, the Yankees have been shelling us in one fashion or another for nearly a year now, so I don't suppose I'll get apoplexy over it."

Truth be known, she cared little whether evil tidings befell her. If they did, she considered the further humiliation of Yankee capture or the agony of injury and possible maiming far more distasteful than the quick end to her silent suffering that a direct hit would afford.

"Wiggie, I tell you, you have put off your visit too late," Lee insisted.

Agnes could not be accused of failing to choose her fights, and so she did indeed board a train—with her father's tacit approval—at the Richmond station the afternoon of March 29, 1865. It headed south for Petersburg, where the front line of the fighting in the War for Southern Independence now raged.

◦◇ ◦◇ ◦◇

A few miles away Ulysses S. Grant put the finishing touches on the long-awaited attack he would launch against every point of the Confederate lines at Petersburg. He would fight his enemy in the trenches, he would fight them in the streets of the town, he would fight them from house to house and room to room if necessary, and he fully expected to end the war within the space of a few hours.

CHAPTER 41

AFTER HE STALKED OUT ON STANTON, MARLEY WOULD NOT HAVE been surprised to receive a transfer west to Minnesota or the Dakotas, to serve under some general like Hooker or Pope who had been "put out to pasture." Demotion to private and posting on the front line at Petersburg would not have surprised him either.

Had he predicted his next assignment, however, it would have been to one of the Federal prisons in Washington City or elsewhere, the destination, he had learned, of nearly fifteen thousand Northerners judged not to be treasonous or even supportive of the South, just not quite supportive enough of the North.

Instead nothing happened. *Perhaps,* he thought as the family barouche took him to the train station for the journey to a Republican political rally and fund-raiser in Philadelphia, *they have decided I can do the least harm if left to ride out the war at home, far from any opportunity to embarrass anyone—including myself. Having a well-connected family likely bodes well in my behalf, though it has not stopped the government from locking up scores of newspaper publishers, politicians, and other well-known sorts.*

Marley now chafed at his inactivity. Though increasingly concerned by the multiplying evidence of a dark pattern of war policy on the part of the Federal government, his irritation with the Rebels' refusal to quit the carnage had also mounted. *Perhaps harsh measures are, after all, called for, to end this seemingly endless mountain of slaughter,* he thought.

He had no more interest in the rally and fund-raiser than in returning to a Rebel prison camp. He would attend as the family representative. What did spark his interest was the exclusive big-donor gathering afterward with Ohio Senator Ben Wade. For sheer, single-minded pugnacity against slavery, secession, and seemingly all things Southern, Massachusetts native Wade had few peers, if any. At times even abolitionist champions Thaddeus Stevens and Charles Sumner seemed to pale against him for brute, pitiless fervor.

Whatever the opinion of the firebrand, and many opinions there were, his fame had grown nationwide, even to Europe. Southerners hated him, Northern Democrats feared him, and as Federal casualties mounted to gargantuan totals, Republicans increasingly migrated away from Lincoln's total-war-but-soft-peace pole and toward Wade's philosophy of utter destruction—of Southern people, Southern land, and Southern culture and civilization itself.

Marley's Andersonville wound began to throb halfway through the rally, as it usually did when he sat for long. In this venue he considered the pain a welcome deliverer from a hateful convocation even more painful to him. He remained outside the convention hall until the rally closed. Abolitionist friends of his family, exhibiting Marley and his military decorations like the trophy of a righteous crusading champion, guided him to the ornate parlor that hosted what, to his amazement, proved to be a gathering of less than twenty people. *My family is not so significant as to warrant my attendance among these elites,* he thought, uncomfortable and uncertain as to the purpose of his presence.

A moment later Wade entered, surrounded by an entourage of a half-dozen of the most prominent abolitionists and industrialists in the entire state of Pennsylvania. High-cheekboned and steely-eyed, Wade emitted a tenacity so palpable that Marley felt a current of energy charge the room. *Such must happen when this famous man brawls face-to-face with the lions of the United States Senate, and even the president himself,* he thought, for once awed by another man.

Then the soldier and his chest bunting were ushered before Wade, and that man was commending him, "Looks like you've killed yourself a mess of those d——d heathen slavers, Major Marley."

The immediate vulgarity jolted Marley, which Wade must have seen, for, still galvanized by the hand-clapping, foot-stomping roar of his adoring huge rally audience, he plunged on. "What? Can such a decorated soldier, who has wounds both apparent—" Wade indicated Marley's eye patch. "—and hidden, blush at a manly oath? Why, I bet those scum-sucking Secesh uttered worse as you kicked h— out of them at Gettysburg, Major, eh?"

The giants of Pennsylvania abolition and industry hooted their approval at these notions, and suddenly, shockingly, Marley found all their eyes on him and their ears awaiting his response.

"Your differences with President Lincoln have electrified the nation," Marley opined weakly.

For an instant Wade's eyes betrayed his approval of the remark; Marley, alone, perceived the politician's startled reaction as, *Mark yon man well.*

But it was "Ah, the *president*" that he responded, at once heartened to have a chunk of bloody meat thrown his way—especially in the view of a throng of the high and mighty—and yet near nauseous at the thought of a man for whom he had neither affection nor respect. Yet it was Marley on whom the spotlight shone. "Yes, Major, I understand your recent traffickings with the self-taught, self-styled frontiersman fared no better than have mine of late."

Before Marley could digest this, the whole gathering erupted into a laughter as raucous and prolonged as a Stonewall Jackson led Rebel yell. As his gaze swept the others, Marley realized, *They know, they all know of our petitions to the president on behalf of the prisoners.*

"So, Major," Wade continued, his gaze boring in on Marley, "Had you your way, what action would the Federal government initiate at the conclusion of hostilities, which may at any day be upon us?"

Marley shifted his feet, his dress uniform now feeling ever-so-much more stifling than it had mere moments before. "Why, I expect as we all do, Senator," he said, never more uncertain of his own words, especially considering his recent rampage against Secretary of War Stanton, "to effect a just peace, with the cessation of the institution of slavery, and an orderly return to the Union of the departed states." Feeling the color rise again on his forehead, against his will, as he searched the faces of the others, he added, "The Southern states, of course, reentering upon their acceptance of the franchise for the Negroes and their commitment to abide by the laws of the Constitution."

A few folks nodded their assent, but Marley perceived the overall response as tepid. Wade said nothing.

"What about it, Senator?" one Pittsburgh steel baron chirped, reaching for another whiskey off the proffered drink tray. "Will you invite the departed cousins home, to resume their schemes where they left off—at Fort Sumter, I believe 'twas, or was it Abe the Encroacher's nomination—while keeping their land and their now-freed slaves, and those in a worse state than before and harmless as their heeled hounds?"

"Here, here," a Philadelphia real estate tycoon chimed. "And will you pay the poor Negroes' poll tax the Rebels will assess them when they arrive to vote?"

"Or will you take the writing proficiency test the Secesh will require of them?" added a Harrisburg merchant.

"Let us pray that the vapid actions of that Encroacher will at last incite the benighted coloreds to a servile insurrection that will at once sweep him from office and forever remove the shackles from them and affix them upon those bloodguilty man-stealers who so richly merit them!" Wade exploded.

"Ah," one of the most prominent Unitarian ministers in Philadelphia said as Marley reeled, "you would encourage the oppressed to take their rightful place at the table of the family of man?"

Wade stared at him, and for a moment the steel man would have sworn he saw in the senator's eyes sparks flying from the furnaces of his own mill.

"Indeed," Wade began in a low, guttural growl, "if they could contrive to slay one-half of their oppressors, the other half would hold them in the highest regard, and no doubt treat them with justice!"

"Here, here!" the steel baron said, satisfied at last, returning his empty glass to the omnipresent tray long enough to clap his hands, before snagging another whiskey.

Everyone was then shouting, cheering, and slapping Wade on the back.

On his triumphal march from the room, the senator stopped, wheeled, and said to Marley, "You have blood on your mouth already, Major. I suggest—and I believe our dear Thaddeus concurs—that if you expect a role in the new nation befitting your abilities, you decide soon whether you have the stomach for more."

Wade did not wait for a response. Out of the room he went, greeted by a burst of new applause on the other side of the door. *Thaddeus?* Marley wondered, standing now alone. *Thaddeus Stevens, Republican leader in the House of Representatives? Was his name invoked in reference to me? And "new nation"? I wonder to which new nation Mr. Wade refers. South? North?* He pondered that for a moment, his head spinning from the unthinkable specters suggested by the oratory he had just heard. *Or—both?*

•◇ •◇ •◇

Agnes found the citizenry of Petersburg as little concerned over the shot and shell rocketing about their town as she.

"Why, good morning, Mrs. Rives," Mrs. Meade said as she and Agnes entered a grocer's market.

"And good morning to you," Mrs. Rives replied with a smile.

"The Yankees have been shelling us for a long time now," Mrs. Meade told Agnes as they picked about the spartan shelves, "and we have grown quite accustomed to it." Then she turned to Agnes and said, "I declare, for such a race as would send fire and steel into neighborhoods where innocent children play, the people of Petersburg would not *dare* be cowed."

Shortly after supper that night, Agnes heard the melody of horns out front of the Meade home. When Mrs. Meade flung open the door, a regimental band stood in formation, trumpeting "Carry Me Back to Old Virginny."

"Why, those boys can only be serenading you, darling Agnes," Mrs. Meade proclaimed.

"Surely no," Agnes said, blushing in full view of the band.

"Surely so," Mrs. Meade said, fastening Agnes's arm in her own. "If only I could take credit for having invited them here."

"Excuse me for only a moment, please, Mrs. Meade," Agnes said, breaking away and rushing to the dining room table, from where she brought a cluster of roses she had picked earlier in the day. She began tossing them to the band. This gallantry, and her stunning beauty, beyond even what any of them had heard tell of, spurred the musicians to an even more energetic output of "Aura Lee."

Flattered as rarely she had ever been, Agnes smiled until she noticed amid the shadows of eventide the strong facial resemblance the band leader bore to Orton. Then her smile faded and she appeared, again, the cool, aloof Lee girl known to so many would-be Confederate beaux, remote and untouchable, matchless in her beauty and comeliness, and utterly immune to the advances of any man, no matter how handsome, highborn, or brave.

•◇ •◇ •◇

She awoke the next morning heartened, for she was going to pay a surprise social call on her father.

When she arrived in the Meades' now-rickety carriage at Edge Hill, her mood grew as dreary as the day that poured rain all around her.

"And when do you anticipate the general's return?" she asked Long.

"I'm afraid I cannot say, Mrs. Lee," he answered. "We've word the Federals are up to no good out near the western end of our line."

Streaking shells, haunting band leaders, torrential rain—she wanted to see Papa. *And this poor man,* she thought, noting a slight twist to part of Long's face, *he has neuralgia, and even worse than I.* Now she hated to ask for anything, but she must.

"Can—may I ride in that direction," she asked. "Please?"

If ever the polished and urbane Long could have melted right away into a rain puddle all his own, in the midst of his own pain, it would have been at the sight of this flawless face transforming before his eyes into that of a plaintive little girl desperately in need of her papa.

"Oh . . . er . . . I'm . . . uh, oh I'm so sorry, Miss Lee," he stammered. "If there were any way—would you care to come in and wait?"

But her head moved ever so slowly from side to side, her lovely long dark lashes veiling downturned eyes. She wanted now to be alone, with the thoughts and ghosts that had grown most familiar, most comfortable to her.

Richmond had proven no good time for Culpeper, Jake, and Chief. The whiskey was worse, and far harder to come by, since they quickly squandered the considerable Yankee dollars pocketed in their affairs farther north in what, to Culpeper's disgust, had come to be known by both Confederates and Federals as "Mosby's Confederacy."

"Yeh, and if he'd seen fit to take some notes from Cole Culpeper, there wouldn't be any d——d Yankees *in* Mosby's lousy Confederacy," Culpeper growled one night as he took three cards in another sad hand of poker in Legion's, one of the smoky Shockoe Slip taverns he and his friends had lately frequented.

Chief stood behind him, hand on the sawed-off twelve-gauge he had come to favor. Across the room Jake accepted the ministrations of a comely lady of the street who, unbeknown to him, had before the war been scion to one of the richest plantations in Northern Virginia. McClellan's men had killed her father, Pope's men had burned her plantation and destroyed all the crops, Hooker's men had killed her husband, and Grant's men had killed her brothers. Her mother and her two infant children—hard winter on the open road had taken them.

All she had left were her beauty and her newfound opium habit. The former was fading as quickly as the latter was growing.

Culpeper cursed as he lost another hand and realized he had neither Federal dollars nor Confederate shinplasters enough to score even one more drink. Then he felt Chief nudge him. Across the raucous room he saw two familiar faces.

"It's that gimp-legged, bald-headed cur of Winder's again and his little midget lackey," Culpeper snarled.

"You one to talk about gimp-legged," Chief intoned.

A female friend of Culpeper's of the "sportin' sort" had alerted him a few nights before that the same two men had been asking about him and his friends one night just after they left Legion's.

"Better git," Culpeper said. He managed to grab Jake and depart the smoky tumult just before the home guards spotted them.

The three hustled through rain-soaked back streets until they arrived at a quiet wharf right on the James.

"Richmond's lost all its favor in my eyes," Culpeper said. When no one responded, he said, "Jakie boy, 'bout caught you a good one in there tonight, did'ja, boy?" When Jake remained silent, Culpeper said, "Ah, what's got you down, Jakie boy? Ya ain't spit out four words in as many days."

After a minute, Jake said, "I'm ready to get back to the fighting."

Culpeper stood in the dark. "Chief?"

"Guess we better be going somewhere," the Cherokee said.

Culpeper thought on it for a minute. "Yeh, what I hear, if we don't, we're liable to miss out on what's left of it," he said. "I admit to growin' grumpy myself if I go too long without a set-to with the Yanks."

"That—lady—back there," Jake said. "She told me some fellow for the Union let on to her Grant's getting ready to unleash all the hounds of h— against General Lee."

This brought several seconds of silence.

"D——d Yankee curs," Culpeper swore. "Reckon maybe we oughta be gettin' down to the lines at Petersburg. Can't go back north, and they ain't nothin' left out in the Valley—of a fight, that is, Jakie boy. And it sure as fire wouldn't do to git popped by our own mangy home guards when we can hook it up with the bluebellies. But doggone it, I wish we didn't have to starve to do it. We git vittles much better when left to fend fer ourselves."

Resigned to having concluded his days of active service in the Grand Army of the Republic, and amid the growing torpor of inactivity and boredom, his wounds—old and recent—ever more bothersome, Marley descended into a morass of self-pity over his continued state of celibate singleness.

And then one morning Marley's hedge of faith crumbled, and an old "visitor" returned. He shook it off that day, and the next, but on the third, he found himself preparing to leave the house and ride however far he needed in order to procure, without recognition, the spirits his body and soul again craved.

Leaving the empty house, his family all out of town, he came face-to-face with his old Andersonville shebang-mate Simmons. How lost did that man appear too.

"If something does not change, and quickly, I shall be back at my old drug habit," Simmons announced, revealing a terror of which Marley had not heretofore been aware. "The Rebs turned me loose on that boat for which we released no one from our own prisons."

Marley had heard rumors but did not believe the story true.

"And what of the others—" Marley began.

Simmons knew what he meant. "Big Al still stood tall last I saw him. Dan Swenson caught dysentery, but I expect he'll weather the storm. Bill Hankins . . ."

"What about Hankins?"

Simmons's spectacles fogged over. "Well, when word came back that President Lincoln refused even to see the commissioners, old Hank, he just sort of went downhill from there." Simmons pondered that for a moment. "Funny, isn't it, sir, how the fellows you would least expect . . . oh, well . . ."

After this meeting Marley established a Bible study for Federal veterans, some of them wounded and even maimed, at the Presbyterian church six blocks from his home near Canonsburg. Through the weeks it blossomed into a sizable gathering, bearing much spiritual fruit.

He still pondered the implications of Simmons's release, and the refusal of his own government even then to let loose the starving and freezing Rebels in

Camp Douglas, Johnson Island, and elsewhere. Since February, thankfully, Grant had ordered the resumption of prisoner exchanges.

That cheered Marley, until he learned through a socially prominent friend of his mother's that since January, the Lane Resolution had been in force as United States law. The Lane Resolution championed to passage in the Senate by none other than Ben Wade, read:

> Rebel prisoners in our hands are to be subjected to a treatment finding its parallels only in the conduct of savage tribes, and resulting in the death of multitudes by the slow but designed process of starvation, and by mortal diseases occasioned by insufficient and unhealthy food and wanton exposure to their persons to the inclemency of the weather.

CHAPTER 42

AS LEE RODE WEST TOWARD THE FAR RIGHT OF HIS outstretched line, the rain pattering off his broad-brimmed gray felt hat and dark gray cape, he thought anew how critical was the holding of the Five Forks junction that lay up ahead, a few miles beyond the Confederate lines to the southwest of Petersburg. Five Forks barred the Federals from the Southside rail line. Other than the short stretch connecting it with Richmond, the only track still open out of Petersburg was the Southside, which ran southwest. Lee knew the Southside might eventually mean escape for his starving, nearly surrounded army. It might eventually mean food.

When he arrived near the end of the Confederate line, his heart leapt as he discovered that the Federal left was "up in the air." He himself directed an attack that caught the much-larger foe off guard and drove them back. Meanwhile, in blistering action a few miles to the west at the western terminus of the battle lines, George Pickett's—he of Gettysburg fame—Confederate infantry and cavalry banged Sheridan's Federals back from Five Forks and the railroad.

Lee arrived back at Edge Hill late that evening. The one blessing he recognized from his body aching inside and out in so many places was that none of the pains allowed any of the others to exert their full import on his senses. His alarm at learning Agnes had come was washed away with a keen disappointment at not having seen her. So exhausted that he dozed off twice during its writing, he nonetheless addressed a note to her in the early hours of April 1.

My precious little Agnes:

I was so sorry I was not here to see you yesterday. I might have persuaded you to have remained with me. If you had have stayed or come out at four o'clock this morning I could have seen you with my weary sleepy eyes. Now I do not know when I shall have the pleasure of seeing you.

Your loving father.

◆◆ ◆◆ ◆◆

When Marley's orders finally came, they bore the signature of Phil Sheridan. Custer remembered Marley's actions during the Kilpatrick-Dahlgren mission and wanted him as his chief of scouts when his horse soldiers came against the Petersburg lines. "Little Phil" himself had caught wind of Marley's growing reputation after his service to "Old Prayer Book" Howard, "Fightin' Joe" Hooker, "Black Dave" Hunter, and others. And Marley's bold journey to the bowels of the White House itself on behalf of the suffering Federal prisoners at Andersonville, word of which had spread far and wide through the Northern armies, was not without its admirers.

Now he reported in person to Sheridan in the climactic act of the war.

"Pickett has pulled back to Five Forks, sir," he said. "He is again holding his works along White Oak Road, which connects at Five Forks with Scott's Road, our approach to that junction."

Seething mad at some of his own eastern generals, the recent rains and current mud, and most of all, at the dogged foe before him only a fraction of his own size, the Irishman exploded into a rage. He flung orders in all directions.

So late was Sheridan's attack that Pickett thought the day would pass without a fight. He found himself, along with cavalry commanders Fitz Lee and Thomas Rosser, several miles away at an officers' shad bake when the Federals, triple his numbers, overwhelmed his force.

As dusk came on, Marley rode toward Sheridan to report the new Rebel positions. A brigadier was reporting the capture of several Confederate guns as hundreds of Federal troops shouted their glee and waved their caps.

"I don't care a d— for their guns—or you either, sir!" Sheridan shouted at the brigadier. "What I want is the Southside railway." Then he turned to the crowd of soldiers and screamed, "I want you men to understand we have a record to make before that sun goes down that will make hell tremble!"

Marley thought better of delivering his report just now as Sheridan rose in the stirrups of his high-stepping Kentucky pacer, jabbed a forefinger north in the direction of the Southside, and concluded, "I want you there!"

Lee heard of the stunning reverse before the sun had gone down. He did not yet know how grievous the damage was as he began shotgunning orders. He wanted reinforcements to help hold the now-vulnerable Southside. He wanted his Old War Horse Longstreet with him from Richmond, with some men. He wanted more of everything, and hardly anything remained.

How easily I could get rid of this and be at rest, he thought, exhausted and aching to the point of nausea, as he pulled off only his boots and coat, to lie down just after 9 P.M. Though deathly aware of the peril now astride him, his army, and his country, had he known fully how desperate his plight was, he would likely have evacuated Petersburg that very moment.

I have only to ride along the line and all would be over, he thought. *But it is our duty to live. What will become of the women and children of the South if we are not here to protect them?* Just then, the sullen rumble of artillery reached his ears. *Oh, my little Aggie is still in Petersburg!* he remembered.

"Captain Clark!" he called.

Agnes stared out the upstairs window of her bedroom in the Meade home. Never in her life had she watched so fantastic a display as now blazed before her. From one end of the horizon to the other, as far as she could see in either direction, the flashing of Federal artillery illumined the starlit heavens like vast fulgurations of lightning. She saw it, she heard it, but nothing registered in her mind except a prayer that God, a God she now no longer understood or comprehended, would, if he did indeed have the power, keep her father safe. *He is somewhere out there,* she thought, breathless.

Now shells began to streak through the sky toward the very spot where she sat. One fell a quarter of a mile away. Then another an eighth of a mile away.

"Agnes!" screamed Mrs. Meade, bursting through the bedroom door.

Another shell smashed into the home across the street.

"Agnes, dear, we must be leaving this instant," Mrs. Meade said, pulling her up from the inside ledge. Another shell landed with a deafening explosion in the yard of the home next door.

Agnes noticed by the flickering light the threadbare lace collar and jabot fronting Mrs. Meade's ancient taffeta gown. *Why, I believe this was once a part of her trousseau,* she thought.

"Agnes, this brave man is Captain Clark, sent by your father to escort you back to Richmond," Mrs. Meade was saying.

Then the explosions and the flames were all around her.

At 1:45 A.M., the rolling crackle of picket fire augmented the growl of the artillery. It was picket fire which would not now cease, but Lee did not hear it, for he had consigned his considerable concerns to the sovereign ruler of the universe and thus gained a few hours of sleep.

Lee awoke first when A. P. Hill, ashen-faced and out of his sickbed, then Longstreet, as yet without his troops, arrived at Edge Hill. *It seems as though all the afflictions that have beset me these many months have converged at this moment,* Lee thought, stunned at the unprecedented pain wracking his body, from neck to knee, at this, the worst possible of all times. Despite the sounds of a gargantuan Federal cannonade thundering in the distance, he could not even rise from his bed. Rather he asked Taylor to lay a blanket over him, and much to his dismay, from a prostrate position on his cot conversed with Hill—himself frail, fevered, and shrunken, aching, nauseous, blood-poisoned, and kidney-dead from uremia—and Longstreet, still healing from being throat-shot, his once-beefy right arm hanging limply at his side.

Salty old Venable burst into the room. Through all their bloody campaigns and near-run escapes Lee had never seen him on the verge of panic—until now.

"Sir, our lines are broken," he breathed. "An infantry officer, wounded and on crutches, fled before the enemy at Harris's division headquarters just to our west. Wagons, soldiers, and teamsters—all are rushing past your very gate, on the Cox Road toward Petersburg—er, rather wildly, sir."

A cold chill shook Lee. He could hear—feel—the rumble of galloping horses and heavy cargo outside. *Pickett's defeat at Five Forks was worse than I knew,* he realized. *He has been turned. Harris's quarters are a mile and a half behind our lines. Those people are in the rear of our entire right.*

Praying for strength even as he rose, a searing bolt of pain surging through his back, hips, and thighs, Lee wrapped a blanket around himself and hustled through the house to the front door. Taylor stood there, gazing through the dim presunrise mists at a mass of men advancing from the far end of the open fields that abutted Cox Road. They looked like a winding, scurrying horde of red ants. A stiff breeze bracing him, Lee realized with a jolt that the front elements of the force were within a half mile of the ground upon which he stood. And they were coming straight at him. *Surely they are ours, in retreat,* he thought, squinting into the shadows. *Oh, I cannot tell; it is yet too dark.*

"Colonel Venable," he called, "reconnoitre that position. General Hill—"

Already, however, that corps commander, his long reddish-brown locks flying, had leapt into the saddle and galloped away, accompanied by his flamboyant courier, Sergeant G. W. Tucker. *How desperate he is to do his duty and uphold his honor and that of Virginia,* Lee thought. *How he has ever been so.* Then Lee remembered hearing how Hill had said during his recent convalescence that "I have no wish to survive the fall of the capital."

Oh God, Lee thought.

"Colonel Venable," he called again as that officer jerked rein to leave. "First caution General Hill to take care he not expose himself."

Turning back to the approaching line, Lee peered again at the wide line of oncoming soldiers. *They are blue,* he now saw, his chest tightening.

Next he learned Longstreet's troops from Richmond were as yet nowhere to be seen. Lee, channeling the plethora of pains that gripped his body into the sharpening of his mind, hurried inside, donned his full gray uniform, and buckled on his sword. He ordered Taylor to supervise the headquarters telegraph operator in the cavalcade of messages now commencing.

His brow furrowed in concentration, he examined the maps spread around his little office. After uttering a silent prayer to God for wisdom, he ordered a stand made at Fort Gregg and Battery Whitworth, neighboring earthworks a mile south of Edge Hill, in order to staunch the Federal stampede toward the Southside and the Appomattox.

After that, seeing the approaching Federal line had paused as a Confederate battery Lee placed the night before in the Edge Hill garden opened fire on them, he mounted Traveller, rode out the front gate, and across Cox Road to a good observation point.

Within moments a cadre of staff officers rode up. With them was Tucker, riding Hill's dapple-gray horse.

Ambrose Powell Hill, hero of Williamsburg, of Cedar Mountain and Second Manassas, of Sharpsburg and Reams's Station, was dead, shot through the heart with a .58 calibre Yankee bullet. Stonewall's old West Point classmate and erstwhile nemesis never knew he had actually ridden to the rear of the *Federal* lines.

Tears boiled up in Lee's eyes. *Jackson . . . Stuart . . . Hill. Such are the evils of war that the bravest and the best fall,* he thought mournfully.

"He is at rest now," he said, "and we who are left are the ones to suffer."

All present awaited their commander's next command. It occurred to more than one of them how deeply Lee felt the loss and how unusual those feelings were in so great a captain of war.

On came the orders: "Sergeant Tucker, go with Colonel Palmer." He turned to the other man, Hill's chief aide. "Go at once, Colonel, and get Mrs. Hill and her children across the Appomattox." As Tucker and Palmer turned their horses to leave, Lee spoke again, his voice cracking. "Colonel, break the news to her as gently as possible."

Hill's beautiful "Dolly" was sister to the famed Confederate cavalryman John Hunt Morgan, also killed by the Federals. She was seven months pregnant, and had two little girls, ages one and three.

At 4:45 A.M., Sunday morning, April 2, 1865, sixty thousand Federal troops, three entire corps, thundered forth from their lines in the greatest assault ever witnessed in the Western Hemisphere. They charged from the Appomattox River east of Petersburg, all the way to Burgess Mill.

The blue phalanx stretched twelve miles wide. Against them stood less than one-fourth their number of Confederates, and many of those were exhausted, ill, and starving, and no longer had muskets, more still no ammunition.

CHAPTER 43

ESCHEWING HER BELONGINGS, AGNES THREW A WRAP AROUND herself, took Captain Clark's proffered hand, and rushed down the stairs and out of the Meade house, dodging the flames that licked at her. The emaciated mule drawing their buggy was well-suited to the task of running away from flying, flaming steel.

No longer were the remaining citizens of Petersburg taking things in stride. The streets teemed with people, afoot, on horseback, in wagons. They evidenced a generally westward flow. Clark took the buggy straight to the train station, fast as the mule could move. Agnes gradually detected the officer's tense mien.

"Are you quite all right, Captain?" she asked.

Clark glanced at her as a shell exploded somewhere behind them. He said nothing. A few seconds later he had to use all his strength to yank the mule around a mother who had appeared suddenly in the middle of the road, carrying a swaddling infant in one arm, her other hand holding that of a three- or four-year-old. This near miss seemed to loosen his tongue.

"I'm concerned there'll not be a train for us," he said.

"Oh, please don't fret that on my account," Agnes said.

"But I do fret it," Clark replied, "for the general himself tasked me with delivering you home." Slapping the overtaxed mule with the buggy whip, he thought on the matter for a moment. "If the trains are all gone," he said, "we'll drive this benighted beast as far as he will go. Then I'll commandeer a horse for you for whatever of the journey remains."

Truth be known, Agnes would have been content to remain in Petersburg, close to her father. At the same time she did not want to appear ungrateful for all the consideration and effort being exerted on her behalf. So she said noting.

The crowds grew larger and louder as they neared the train station. At the end Clark had the foaming mule knocking people out of the way.

"Come back here, you ingrate!" one man—in a voice Agnes discerned was not Southern—hollered after Clark had driven the mule right into him.

Then Clark helped Agnes down from the buggy as the crowd swarmed round them and the whistle of a train screeched.

"Oh, it's starting to pull out," Clark breathed, distress filling his eyes. He grabbed Agnes's hand and tugged her along through the crowd.

"Hey, look out, soldier," someone exclaimed.

"There you are, ingrate!" sounded the angry voice Agnes had heard moments before. *He is not far behind us,* she realized.

Now Clark brandished his officer's revolver in his other hand as he cleared a path for them toward the locomotive, which had begun to move.

"Come on, Miss Lee!" he shouted, pulling Agnes hard. She saw the rear of the single-car train just ahead but moving off; an older man and woman were stepping up onto it. In a flash Clark knocked the couple sprawling headfirst onto the wooden platform floor, then picked Agnes up by her waist and shoved her up onto the little landing, into the arms of the elderly conductor, just as the car churned away. She saw Clark fall forward onto his face as several other people, lunging for the train, toppled over him, grunting, groaning, and calling out, a couple of them tumbling down onto the rickety tracks several feet below.

"Thank you, sir," she said to the conductor, shaken. She turned to step into the interior of the car but saw that people jammed every seat and every square inch of aisle space.

"Best you stay out here, miss," the silver-whiskered conductor said. "Safer out here anyway." She saw that he had a hefty old horse pistol stuffed inside the waistband of his trousers.

Lee hurried Traveller back to Edge Hill upon learning of Hill's death. As the battery out front boomed forth against the halted Federals across the field, he rattled off a series of instructions for Taylor to give the telegrapher. Taylor wrote as fast as his pencil could move, somewhat distracted at how calm Lee appeared. *It is as though he is cataloguing his intentions for the disbursement of a supply of prayer books or Bibles,* Taylor thought to himself.

"I advise that all preparation be made for leaving Richmond tonight," Lee concluded his message to President Davis. "I will advise you later, according to circumstances."

A few minutes later Yankee shells began to land about the grounds of Edge Hill. After the second or third one, Lee asked himself, *Are they targeting the commanding general's headquarters?*

His staff began scurrying. Soon one of the Confederate cannon was hit, shrapnel tearing through its crew. Then Lee, standing just outside the front door of the main structure, realized musket fire was peppering the house. Suddenly a shell screamed over his head and smashed into the house itself, upstairs, with a deafening roar. The entire structure shook, debris showered him, and every window in sight shattered from the concussion. So did the ladies' petticoat mirror behind him in the foyer, spraying the Oriental rug in front of it with a thousand sparkling shards. *Well, I'll swan, those people* are *aiming for us,* he thought, astonished but not afraid as flames burst forth from the house. *For me.*

Taylor and the telegrapher appeared.

"Sir, my operator can no longer work his instrument," Taylor said, "so we are hastening to Petersburg." When Lee evidenced no immediate intention to pursue a like course, Taylor exclaimed, "General, sir, will you not come with us?"

No, he would not; what he would do, to Taylor's amazement and consternation, was take a closer look through his field glasses at those people across the field. Then, as crews hurried to remove the Confederate battery before the approaching Federal infantry killed the remaining artillerymen and destroyed the cannon, Lee turned to watch Taylor and the telegrapher as they road east on Cox Road toward Petersburg. He blinked as a shell exploded within a few feet of them, ripping the legs off the telegrapher's horse and sending him flying with his equipment. The blow knocked Taylor's horse sideways, but it kept its footing and galloped on.

"General Lee, sir, you must be leaving," Venable said, bringing Traveller to him. Lee watched as what remained of the Confederate battery limbered up and rolled past him toward Petersburg.

"This is a bad business, Colonel," he said with a sigh as he mounted Traveller, no more nonplussed than if he had just realized Mary had miscounted a shipment of socks. In fact rather less so.

Lee turned back to the house as another shell screamed into it and exploded, this time through one of the first-floor window openings. Flames now engulfed the structure. *I really do not wish to leave,* he thought, his color rising.

Another shell landed in the front garden, and bullets began to sing past on all sides of Lee, Venable, and the other three or four men finally quitting Edge Hill, as the Federal infantry marched at the double-quick to within a few hundred yards of them.

"Sir—please," Venable pled.

Disgusted, Lee jerked rein and trotted to the gate, then left, down Cox Road. His dander up, he slowed Traveller to a walk after only a couple of hundred yards. *It has happened just as I told them it would at Richmond,* he thought. *The line has been stretched until it has broken.* But now the Federals knew who he was, and they unleashed a barrage of fire in his direction. One shell crashed to earth mere feet behind him, spattering him and his entourage with chunks of a screaming animal's flesh.

Venable saw Lee's countenance glow crimson and his head begin its rapid little nodding. Brown eyes ablaze, he returned his gaze to the onrushing foe and started to turn Traveller back.

Savior in heaven, Venable thought in desperation, *he is going to charge them!*

"Sir!" Venable shouted.

Lee, eyes still sparking, fearless, gathered himself. When another shell screeched past, reluctantly he moved on—still refusing any pace greater than a trot.

Venable emitted an audible sigh of relief as he followed. *I do not know whom I fear more,* he thought.

Culpeper had found the telling of falsehoods an easy companion to the host of other commandments he regularly broke. No falsehoods proved necessary, however, when he, Jake, and Chief reached the Petersburg lines. Lee's dwindling army needed more of everything—guns, ammunition, food, horses, wagons, and most of all, men. Culpeper simply asked where "the biggest fight" was, then proceeded on to that location—Fort Gregg.

When he and his friends arrived at the "fort," they found it to be nothing more than a small, partially completed earthen embankment ringing the gorge out of which it was dug. A wooden palisade containing loopholes through which the Confederates could fire topped it in some places, but not all.

Brigadier General Nathaniel Harris, his own field headquarters west of Edge Hill and his home back in Vicksburg both captured by Federals, had just over two hundred of his men in the fort, mostly his Mississippians, along with a small contingent of North Carolinians. Lee had notified him in no uncertain terms that for the Army of Northern Virginia—and hence, the Confederate nation—to remain in existence even till the end of the day, the men standing in Fort Gregg must buy it some time—with their blood. That time must be bought by two hundred fourteen men standing against six thousand.

After one of Harris's Mississippi captains had assigned Culpeper, Jake, and Chief spots on the ramparts, Culpeper checked his Spencer and his arsenal of pistols for the umpteenth time that day, partly to take his mind from the pain in his hip and side, both of which, unusually, throbbed in pain.

"I came to the war from college," Chief, staring out at the activity-laden Federal lines, announced when Jake left for the latrine and no one but Culpeper stood close by. "In Connecticut."

Culpeper's eyes widened in surprise. "Yankee Connecticut?" was all he could manage.

"My uncle sent me to the same school the brother of the great Cherokee Chief and Confederate General Stand Watie attended," Chief continued, still not looking at Culpeper.

The Virginian had no idea what to say to this.

"Found me a chunk of hardtack for us in a dead Yank's knapsack," Jake said, returning. He dropped the hard flour cracker onto the ground, then smashed it with the butt of his musket. It took three blows to split the cracker into a couple of pieces. He offered one to Culpeper.

"Jakie boy, ain't no coffee—of any sort—'round here to soak that hardtack in, so you might just as well heave it at the Yanks," Culpeper said. "That'll prob'ly do more to help us than eatin' it would anyhows."

After a moment Chief continued, still gazing out over the Federal lines. "My uncle was a chief in the Indian Nations. A man known throughout the Cherokee people, and even the other tribes the blue coat calls 'civilized,' for his truthfulness, his dignity, his wisdom. His slaves loved him like their own father."

Jake's head whipped around at this. "Your uncle had slaves?"

"Yes."

"Of the Negro variety?" Culpeper asked, amazed.

"Seven of them," said Chief, "three of whom asked him to buy them from other Indians. Many Cherokee chiefs own them. I own three myself."

"Well, if that don't beat all," Culpeper said, shaking his head. "Hey, Jakie boy, wonder what them New England Yankees'd think about that? The three of us standin' here squarin' off agin' their army, and the two white boys ain't never owned or wanted a slave, and the Injun chief has a whole flock of 'em."

"When I was five years old, I watched the blue coat murder my father in Georgia because he refused to leave the land of his fathers," Chief said, his handsome high cheekbones set like granite boulders. "When I was six, I saw my mother and both my sisters die on the noble Andrew Jackson's Trail of Tears. Last year the blue coat killed my uncle and burned out his entire village in the Nations because he would not fly their flag. All of these, my kindred, had forsaken the pagan gods of our fathers to follow the Jesus of the blue coat."

Culpeper and Jake stood speechless at these revelations, none of which had ever before been hinted at by the Cherokee.

"These things I thought you should know in case I fall today," Chief concluded after a moment, "that you might find a way to get word to my people back in the Nations."

"Well," Jake said, checking the chambers of one of his revolvers, "leastways we've one thing in common." He spun the cylinder around, then stuffed the gun back in his waistband. "The bluecoats."

The Federal cannon began to boom shells into the fort. General Harris called the tattered little band of Confederates around him. The men could see his heart was full, and for a moment he could not speak. He did not believe he would undertake such a hopeless mission for anyone on earth besides Robert E. Lee. He knew he would not ask the men around him to do so.

"Men, the salvation of the army is in your keep. Don't surrender this fort. If you can hold out for two hours, Longstreet will be up," the handsome, thirty-year-old Natchez native shouted over the burgeoning cacophony of Federal guns now plastering the fort. The Yankees brought dozens of cannon to the battle, the Confederates only two.

"Tell General Lee we'll not give up!"

Culpeper and Chief, shocked, turned to Jake at the advent of his raised voice. His teeth already clenched the end of a paper cartridge plucked from the cartridge box on his hip; he was pouring the contents, gunpowder, and a

.57 calibre Enfield ball, from the cartridge he had bitten in two, down the muzzle of his musket. He rammed it home with such vigor that Culpeper chuckled.

"Holy moley, Jakie boy," he cracked, "for pity's sake don't git so fired up you do what ole Bucky Ashton did back at Sharpsburg." Jake paid him no heed as shells streaked forth from the Federal lines and began to thunder their ear-rattling explosions over, under, and all around the Confederates. The boy replaced his rammer, pulled an explosive charge-laden brass cap from its pouch on the front of his belt, and stuck it where the hammer would strike it when he pulled the trigger on his Enfield.

"Yeah," Culpeper continued with aplomb, cramming in a reinforcement wad for the tobacco already packing his mouth, "ole Buck, he was the d——t musket loader you ever saw. Why, if he'd a throwed at the Billies half o' what he rammed down his muzzle that day, we'da chased ole McClellan all the way to Washington City."

Now Federal bullets were flying in among the Confederates.

"When we found his gun, it had eleven powder charges and bullets stuck down it," Culpeper said, trying to suppress his laughter. "If he woulda remembered the part about the cap and pullin' the trigger, he'da been a fearsome force to be reckoned with at ole Bloody Lane."

Chief stared at him as a Federal bullet took out a Confederate soldier on the rampart a few paces away. "What happened to him?"

Culpeper, sighting his carbine through a loophole in the parapet, picked out a target among the now-onrushing bluecoated infantry and squeezed off a shot.

"Why, after he give up on his piece workin', he jist piled into the Yanks with his old huntin' knife," he answered, watching his target fall. "We found a whole covey of 'em atop his dead carcass after the fight, all 'em cut to ribbons."

Chief stared at him again. "How come I never see you spit out any tobacco juice?"

Culpeper pinched off another shot. He glanced over at Chief and spoke low, as though divulging a closely kept secret. "Best part," he said with a wink.

The captain hollered for them to get in concert with the volley fire he was ordering. The next salvo tore through the Federal ranks, which consisted of three separate columns, each comprised of an entire brigade, advancing in waves and converging near the fort. The surviving bluecoats wheeled and retreated. A few minutes later they surged forward again. The massed Confederate volley, now working to precision, claimed a frightful toll. The

Federals fell back again, over ground now strewn with the still forms of their dead and the writhing, moaning forms of their wounded.

Now another brigade joined the assault, making a full division and bringing the odds to forty to one. This time, the entire force of eight thousand men came in one roaring charge. The Confederates fired as fast as they could, the wounded passing loaded rifles and muskets garnered from their fallen comrades up to the sharpshooters on the ramparts.

Then an officer was shouting at Culpeper and the others from the ground below. So deafening was the din of battle, they could not hear him, but he pointed his saber toward the north end of the fort, where Culpeper saw through the soupy haze teeming masses of Federals swarming in from both flanks.

"They're behind us, boys!" he shouted, pulling Jake and Chief away from their posts. "I think we're trying to form a square around that cannon down there." He glanced over the parapet. What he saw stopped him in his tracks. *My G—*, he thought, *five—no, six—regimental flags.*

They hustled down the embankment and raced toward where the one Confederate cannon still firing sat near the middle of the fort. Federal shells had splintered the other cannon and its crew. When they neared the men forming a square around the surviving piece, Jake fell with a groan. Culpeper and Chief saw him on the ground, grabbing his bullet-punctured left thigh. They dragged him over near the cannon. The Confederates around them unleashed a coordinated volley that blew down the front rank of Yankees now rushing them from both the south, where Culpeper and his mates had stood, and the north, the fort's rear that the Federals had discerned was lightly defended.

Then the Northern horde was among them and the fighting was hand-to-hand.

Culpeper fired every shot left in his Spencer and his four pistols. From out of nowhere, a stocky little Federal, bayonet brandished, charged straight for him. The Virginian reached to the ground to retrieve his Spencer, but not in time. Just as the Federal reached him, Chief stepped over, and swinging his stone-headed war club like a baseball bat, landed a blow of such terrific force that Culpeper could hear the side of the trooper's skull crunch like a boot on gravel. Culpeper grabbed the Spencer by its barrel and began to swing it. The head of the second Federal it crashed against splintered its stock, and Culpeper slung it aside.

Then he realized every Confederate near him except Chief and Jake was down and out of action, either killed or seriously wounded, shot, stabbed or clubbed, or a combination of the three. The bodies, blue, gray, and butternut, lay in heaps. Blood stood in pools and ran in rivulets all around him. He bled in a couple of places himself from bayonet cuts. *This looks like it's going down to the last man,* he thought.

He saw that the Federals now coming forward were more wary, at the single step, not double, but their solid, shoulder-to-shoulder ranks reached so deep that with the roiling clouds of gun smoke he could not ascertain their rear, on any side. He saw one narrow lane, leading out of the fort to the east, that seemed open. *It is like it was on the Yankee side of the stone wall at Cemetery Ridge,* he realized with a jolt. *If we don't run now, they'll cut us down, sure.*

"Come on, boys, let's git!" he said, nodding toward the escape route. Chief was a half step behind him, and Jake, using his rifle as a crutch, hobbled a step farther back. Halfway to the spot that exited the fort through a gap in the unfinished earthen embankment, Jake stopped and turned his head back toward where the fight raged. The fort was filling with the endless ranks of Federals, whose mass was squeezing the square formed by the remaining Confederates near the center of the fort in from all sides.

Now the fighting was bayonet-to-bayonet, musket-to-musket, hand-to-hand, and hand-to-throat.

●◇ ●◇ ●◇

Lee sat Traveller atop a rise toward Petersburg, peering through his field glasses at the smoking conflagration. Nearby Longstreet observed the tears swelling in his commander's eyes, then coursing down his bronzed cheeks before disappearing into the snowy white forest of whiskers.

My sons, Lee thought to himself, *my gallant sons.* As he watched their terrible end come, he marveled at how his heart could be filled to bursting with love for them, even as they went down to their deaths in smoke and fire and steel by his order.

●◇ ●◇ ●◇

"Don't fire that gun!" Jake heard someone bellow over the roar of the battle. He saw a mob of Federals, hundreds strong, facing the Confederate cannon. Only one scarlet-trimmed uniform crew member still stood, the gunner, firing lanyard in hand. So often had his gun fired and so fearsome had been the battle, that though the man had not been hit by fire, Jake saw blood trickling from his eyes, ears, and nose, caused by sound and concussion. "Drop that lanyard, or we'll shoot!"

"Shoot and be d——d!" the gunner shouted at them, jerking the lanyard. The cannon thundered forth double-shotted canister, shredding an entire section of Federals as it recoiled from the force of the blast. The gunner fell dead across the spot from which the cannon had fired, his body torn by a hail of bullets. Jake saw it all, transfixed.

"Jakie boy! We gotta skedaddle, bub!" Culpeper shouted, alarm filling his voice. But Jake was filling the chambers of his one non-capfiring revolver, then hobbling back toward the fight.

"No!" Culpeper shouted, moving to restrain the boy.

There was no stopping him. His rifle still under his left arm, Jake shot the first Federal he neared in the back of the head, as well as one next to him who turned and tried to bayonet him. Then a Federal officer shot him in the side, knocking him to the ground. A cluster of Federals converged on him, jabbing their bayonets into him like they were pitchforking hay into the barn for a Shenandoah winter.

Suddenly one of the Federals let loose a quick, high squeal as his head cracked open. Then the soldier next to him went down in a like manner, then the one next to him. The rest of the dozen or so bluecoats who had mobbed Jake ducked and backed off a step.

Chief, his big lithe body whirling through the Yankees, swung his war club round and round like a harvest-time scythe. The Federal officer who had shot Jake managed to fire the remaining two shots from his revolver. One hit Chief in the buttocks; the other hit one of the Federals in the groin. The latter fell to the ground, screaming in agony. Chief, in one swift, smooth motion, pirouetted and smashed the officer's skull; the man never saw the weapon and was dead before he hit the ground.

One towering black Federal, his bayonet dripping Jake's blood, charged Chief to spear him. The Cherokee stepped aside, then spun and smashed the soldier's skull from behind. Now the remaining cluster of Federals stepped back a pace before the fearsome Indian and his war club that seemed to strike like a bolt of lightning, the direction of its attack impossible to divine. Chief raised the club again and moved toward one cringing trooper when a Federal sharpshooter, firing from about fifty feet away, hit the Cherokee in the left shoulder, knocking him down.

Again the Federals were like vultures on a bloody carcass, but this time, before they could do much damage, Culpeper was firing his revolvers, the two he had kept from Ethan, into their faces at point-blank range. He emptied both pistols into them, and when he finished, every Yank in the group was either dead or had retreated from the area.

The same Federal sharpshooter who had downed Chief now took aim on Culpeper, but at the instant of his squeezing the trigger, a stray bullet from one of his own men pierced his heart, and he fell dead without a sound.

"Come on, you big lummox," Culpeper said, grabbing the wounded Indian under his arms and pulling him to his feet. Seeing the hole in Chief's posterior, he said, "I don't wanna know where that bullet is."

Then the cries of hand-to-hand combat over toward the cannon rose to a crescendo so loud that Culpeper and Chief both stared for a second or two in that direction.

"A good boy," Chief said of Jake, who lay dead, slashed by a score or more bayonet thrusts, a mound of dead Federals on and around him.

Culpeper winced at the sight, true feeling for the boy filling him. But he had felt for Ethan, too, and it was a dangerous habit to get into, at any time, but especially in war, feeling for people, even your best and closest friends. Then he felt the strangest urge to bawl, so instead he grabbed Chief and turned toward the opening out of the fort.

They had no sooner done so than the cries of a couple of squads of Federals sounded.

"They see us," Culpeper said as the soldiers rushed toward them.

"Go," Chief said, shoving Culpeper toward the opening.

"What the—"

"Go!" Chief repeated, turning to face the charging Federals. Culpeper saw the Cherokee was standing at an odd angle.

He is hurt bad, Culpeper thought. Then he found himself running toward the opening, crawling through it, and shielded by banks of gun smoke, bushes, and Providence, reaching the inner Confederate lines toward Petersburg.

Chief raised his war club as the first Federals neared him, but several shots tore into him and he hit the ground hard. He knew one bullet had broken his left arm, so he dropped the club, slipped his Bowie knife out of the inside of his doeskin boot, and came up to a sitting position. He ducked the first bayonet and lunged at the man, driving the knife up into his femural leg artery, twisting it, then pulling it out as the soldier fell. He rolled and did the same to another Federal. A third soldier bayoneted him in his lame arm. Chief slashed the man's wrist, dismembering his hand from his arm. Then he was cutting and slashing up at them with a ferocity rare for a Cherokee since his grandfather had gone down fighting the white eyes that took his land a half century before.

He never knew when the end came. Even though Cole Culpeper would not take the story of his death back to his people, it would somehow find its own way home to the Nations, as the legend grew across the blue coat armies of the beastly Goliath and his war club and Bowie knife, half man and half animal, whose infidel kind had bedeviled the westward march of Manifest Destiny and white Christian civilization far too long.

"Yes, it was a good death," the elders of his people would tell one another one Sabbath Day after worship. "After all, it is no sin to die fighting the blue coat."

CHAPTER 44

THE MEN OF FORT GREGG BOUGHT LEE HIS TWO HOURS, AND another besides, and when Gordon held the line on the left and Longstreet's men moved up on the right, Grant cursed that the Army of Northern Virginia had somehow fought its way through one more day. He could not fathom how an attack of sixty thousand well-equipped, battle-hardened troops supported by massed artillery could not carry the lines against a starving force one quarter their size, many of whom had no weapons. But when the sun set, Lee stood defiant before the Federals, still south of the Appomattox.

Only thirty Confederates were not killed or wounded at Fort Gregg. And they—exhausted, surrounded, and out of ammunition—were captured by the Federals.

Yankee casualties were more than three times the number of the entire Confederate force that participated in the battle.

Grant's only consolation was that when the next day came, he would repeat the entire operation. This time he would attack and attack again, until the Army of Northern Virginia was utterly destroyed.

Agnes remembered some rector, long ago, saying how important it was that Christians continue to do what they knew they should do, even if they did not feel like it—*especially,* she believed the minister had said, if they did not feel like it—and also during those times Christians might even question the veracity of the act they knew they should perform.

In such a spirit, her body aching from fatigue, she accompanied Mary Custis, Mildred, and a couple of VMI cadets to church and took communion.

As the quintet strolled past linden trees budding along the sidewalk and daffodils that winked out at them from the hedge rimming the capitol grounds, the conversation centered on this sublime Sabbath spring day.

"Why, it is the sort of day when delicate silks, that look too fine at other times, seem just to suit," Agnes heard one well-heeled Richmond matron proclaim from under her parasol as they climbed the majestic steps of Saint Paul's Church.

She could sense the cadets' eyes on her, try as they might, as had so many other men and boys, to conceal their attraction to her beauty, her elegance, her mystery, her fame.

"How beautiful she is," Agnes had overheard Lancy Blackford, Rob's brave and decorated compadre from their days in the Rockbridge Artillery, whisper about her recently to another soldier guesting at the Mess while on a short furlough, "but her older sister Mary Custis is more agreeable."

The other soldier had nodded his assent.

She sensed a hint of mirth bubbling up within her soul as they found their seats. *Yes, they have—and will—whisper and speculate and conclude,* she thought. *Let them conclude as they please. In the end I have no room for any of them; my heart, dead or alive, has only ever had a place for one.*

A few minutes later the church sexton marched down the aisle, nudged President Davis on the shoulder, and handed him a note. Despite the opening of the eucharistic celebration, Agnes's eyes—indeed those of most of the congregation—were riveted to Davis. And like she, many of them observed a gray pallor cover the president's face an instant before he rose and strode back up the aisle and out of the building.

As other government leaders exited, Minnigerode, his voice steady and pastoral and still redolent of his Hessian youth, encouraged the congregation to remain calm and take the sacraments.

But Agnes knew something serious was afoot. She and her sisters remained for the duration of the service, then hurried home.

"They say Papa's lines have been broken and that Richmond must be abandoned," Mildred breathed.

"I suspect that is more rumor like everything we've heard these many months," Mary snorted from her rolling chair. "Broken lines, evacuations, surrenders—how many times have we heard of them all, dears?"

Agnes said nothing, but she feared her mother to be in error this time. *I have seen how stretched our lines are round Petersburg,* she thought, *and I have seen how my father must ride in person through rain and darkness to observe our vulnerable positions. I have dodged the shells and flames of Yankee guns, and I have had to make my escape on a train when no other train remained upon which to escape. We are finished.*

Family friends confirmed Agnes's private suspicions when they arrived a few minutes later and announced the government was packing to leave the capital.

The panic and looting began about midafternoon. The Lee girls barred and shuttered their windows and bolted their doors as riotous sounds began to fill the air outside on a Sabbath Day that had dawned so lovely.

That evening Mildred rushed in, her face ashen. She stood motionless in the middle of the front parlor, then sat on the couch. She had left a few minutes before to check on an invalid widow friend the next street over.

"What is it, Life?" Mary Custis asked, going to her.

Mildred looked up. "It is—terrible—out there." Her sisters listened. As she continued speaking, her breath and words came in gusts. "One of Gary's cavalry, on his way out of the city, told me all our soldiers, all our police, all the men—they are all gone, all of them. The Yankee prisoners are gone, too, but our own criminals are running loose through the streets. They, along with deserters from the army and other riffraff, are rampaging from street to street, smashing windows, ransacking empty homes, stealing food and whatever else they can grab from every store."

Agnes and Mary Custis stood mute as Mildred caught her breath. *She will be in for a good long cry when she finishes this account,* Agnes, who knew her younger sister, thought. But Mildred continued on.

"The army tried to destroy all the whiskey, so the Yankees wouldn't get into it and destroy the city like Sherman's drunken bummers did six weeks ago in Columbia, but the rabble found it," she said. "The soldier told me he saw men, and women, gulping whiskey with their hands, out of their hats, out of their boots, some slurping it straight from the gutter."

A bewildered expression took hold of Mildred's face, as if she were struggling to retain her composure.

"The soldier reported also that fires are beginning to break out," she said.

The girls heard several sets of feet rush past in the street outside, followed by the sound of shattering glass.

Mildred crumbled to the couch in tears. Agnes held her and consoled her.

"Come, girls, let us pray for Papa and for our brave soldiers fighting against such odds." The Lee girls turned to see their mother, seated in her rolling chair, in the doorway. Agnes saw that her eyes were dry, but she also saw the faint imprint of tracks down her cheeks, tracks of tears that had been wiped away.

"For my part it will always be a source of pride and consolation to me to know that all mine have risked their lives in so holy a cause," Mary began. She prayed long and with much energy for many people. Several minutes into her prayer, a deafening boom shook every window in the house. The girls rushed upstairs and peeked out the back shutters. Flames and smoke, roiling toward the heavens, lit the night sky.

"That smells like tobacco," Mary Custis said.

"It's coming from the warehouses down by the river," Agnes said.

An hour later, in the midst of singing Lee's favorite hymn, "How Firm a Foundation," which somehow made it seem almost as though he were sitting right there alongside them, another earthshaking explosion erupted. Reaching their earlier vantage point, the sisters, despite the gargantuan smoke banks now enveloping the city, saw new flames leaping skyward behind those of the tobacco warehouses. This time, a constellation of other, smaller incendiaries rocketed through the sky, begetting yet more sparks and bursts of fire.

"I believe that is what remains of our navy, moored on the James, and its ammunition stores," Agnes said.

The girls watched in amazement as one airborne projectile after another streaked across the heavens, exploding in flame and fury, then sending showers of lava-hot shrapnel down on the city.

"It looks like when we used to celebrate the Fourth of July, only . . . more," Mildred whispered.

Though they had blocked every opening in the house, even the chimneys, the smoke began to choke the girls, and their eyes burned and watered. They could hear the dull, horrific roar in the distance of fire that no one could stop.

"Which way is it moving?" Mildred asked, her voice brittle.

"The wind is blowing it east, I believe, through the warehouse and dock district, thank God," Mary Custis replied.

"What," Mildred started, "what if the wind shifts—or other fires begin—close to us?"

Her elder sisters looked at one another, then at her. Her rigid countenance, milky as a full moon shimmering over the Potomac, belied the sheer terror, barely constrained, of a child for whom everything on which she has counted and trusted appears on the verge of disintegration. Mary Custis put an arm around her and pulled her close. "We shall be just fine, my little Precious Life. God wouldn't dare let anything untoward happen to Mama, now would he?"

"I'm going down to check on her," Agnes said, covering her face with a kerchief.

As she did, she heard through the shuttered windows the muffled sounds of . . . the most profane, vulgar singing and shouting ever to insult her ears. *Are the Yankees in the city already?* she wondered, peeking out a shutter that now had no window beyond it. *No,* she thought, revulsed, *it is merely our own looters, the dregs of a now-crushed civilization.*

Sorrow greater than any she yet knew would have filled her had she known the process of crushing her people was just beginning, rather than coming to completion.

"Sir, may I have a moment?" Taylor asked Lee that night at the home that served as the commanding general's temporary headquarters a mile west of Petersburg.

Taylor, Lee, and the rest of the staff had just completed preparations for the removal of the entire Army of Northern Virginia from Richmond and Petersburg, as soon after dark as practicable.

Lee had much to ponder. No more than twelve thousand five hundred men would leave with him this night. Every one of the five Federal corps south of the James numbered more than that. Barely more than fifteen thousand additional troops through the rest of the Confederate lines would move west to converge with him. But thousands of these were wounded, convalescents, home guards or local militia, hardly possessing the combat capabilities of regular soldiers, North or South. In addition thousands of them had no weapons at all, his cavalry was exhausted, and his supply trains, meager as they were, would stretch for thirty miles on the open road, hardly conducive to a rapid march.

To reach his initial destination, Amelia Courthouse, Lee would have to travel thirty-six miles. Grant's pursuit would need cover only nineteen miles to the same point.

Lee felt confident that if he could shove out from Petersburg and Richmond tonight without being detected and maintain a good marching pace, he could outleg Grant to Amelia. There he planned for rations to be awaiting his men, trained in from Richmond on the Danville rail line. After that he calculated as little as sixty-seven more miles to the Roanoke River around Danville, North Carolina, to hook up with Joe Johnston. He would accomplish this by moving from Amelia to Burkeville, where the east-west Southside Railroad crossed the northeast-southwest Danville line. From there, he would march—or perhaps train—along the Danville line, southwest to the North Carolina town of the same name.

By then circumstances would play a larger role in his plans than his own stratagems. But if he had his way, he and Johnston would turn in combination on Sherman, give him the shellacking he so richly deserved, then gather themselves and face off with Grant in the climactic finale.

He knew such a sequence contained many assumptions and counted on a number of events occurring, but he also knew that Grant would no longer have the benefit of his fixed semisiege position, his railroads, or the James River and his open lanes to the sea. And Sherman, he knew, had fought only one pitched battle against Confederate regulars during his entire parade of wanton destruction across the South. Joe Johnston had thrashed him in that one, leaving one face of Kennesaw Mountain carpeted in blue.

Oh, if only I can catch those people out in the open just one time on ground of my own choosing! he thought.

But now Taylor was asking a question Lee must have misunderstood.

"You want to say good-bye to your mother and sisters in Richmond, and what else?" Lee asked, focusing his attention on the young, very nervous adjutant.

"Er, my sweetheart is also there, sir," Taylor stammered, "and we have arranged—if possible, sir—to be married—uh, tonight—sir."

Lee could not hide his surprise, and Taylor shamed himself for even raising the subject with a man burdened by such titanic concerns, especially this man, with whom securing a furlough even in the best of times took Herculean strength and no little luck. *A man,* Taylor remembered, *who won't even allow himself the luxury of spending Christmas with his own family when both armies are in winter quarters.*

"Elizabeth's home is behind enemy lines, and she is alone in Richmond and employed in one of the departments of our government," Taylor said, his voice rising to a higher pitch than ever Lee had heard it, outside of battle. "Virginia knows no more loyal daughter, sir, and she wishes to follow the fortunes of our Confederacy, should our lines be established farther south."

"Yes, Colonel Taylor, you may go, and please give all my fondest wishes and congratulations to this most fortunate of young women," Lee said, his eyes merry.

On the verge a moment before of canceling his own request, Taylor now felt guilty for seeking to impose on the loyalty and friendship of a man who carried on his broad shoulders responsibilities so incomprehensibly vast that the very lines creasing his sun-burnished face, not to mention his white-shocked hair and beard, bore mute testament to them.

"Sir, look," Taylor began. Then his smooth face crinkled up. "What did you say, sir?"

Lee's eyes twinkled in the candlelight. "I said go, Colonel Taylor, and prove to that girl how much she means to you. Show her tonight that you are indeed worthy of the breathtaking act of her placing the rest of her life in your hands, son."

"Well . . . I," Taylor stuttered, stepping back, "I never expected you . . . that is, sir. Yes, sir!"

Then the young man who for these years had accomplished work that no three adjutants on any other general staff on either side of the war could have, turned, tripped over a chair, and ran smack into a courier, all before he got out of the house.

As Lee sat alone for a moment, pondering how he would get his entire army out from under the vice grips of Grant's gargantuan force tonight, now without even Taylor, he heard from outside what ole Stonewall must have intended long ago as he told the boys in gray at First Manassas, ". . . and when you charge, yell like furies!"

Yes, I believe that is how Stonewall meant a Rebel yell to sound, Lee thought. Now he discerned how his merciful Father in heaven had allowed such an unlikely event to occur that might, after all, be as much a source of soul-lightening for Lee on this somber night as for his young subordinate.

Well, perhaps not quite as much, Lee thought, smiling to himself, and remembering to offer a prayer of protection for Mary and his daughters.

The man about whom I have complained and grumbled more than any other my whole life, Taylor marveled after completing perhaps history's lengthiest and most passionate Rebel yell as he galloped away, hoping an ambulance train might be had for at least part of the journey north to Richmond. *That man proves perhaps the one general in the world who would consent to my departure on this blackest of all nights.*

Just before dawn the most stupendous blast Agnes had ever heard jolted her straight up from the couch where she lay, as nearly every window in the house burst. So loud was the explosion that for a moment she thought she heard the community alarm bell clanging from down at the end of the block. Then she realized with a shudder, *No, the tocsin has never sounded since I returned from Petersburg—and it does not sound now.* The ringing came from inside her head, from the mind-numbing din of the explosion.

Shutters blocked most of the windowpane glass from spraying the house, but some of them burst open, too, and the glass blew in behind them, littering the wood floors and rugs with a thousand jagged slivers.

Blowing in as well were steamy, sooty puffs of incinerated Richmond.

Oh, how hot it is, Agnes thought to herself, noticing the dampness of her back and the perspiration dotting her brow and upper lip. Just then a soul-piercing shriek lacerated the air from upstairs. *Life,* she thought, rising, her ears still ringing, to go comfort her younger sister. As she stumbled up the stairs in the dark, she slipped and fell on broken glass, pain slicing through her exhausted body as the glass sliced through her knees. Near the top of the stairs, an explosion thundered forth so fearsome that it shook the whole house and nearly toppled her over the banister. Crying out, she staggered toward the sound of Mildred's voice, now wailing as a whole series of tumultuous crashes rocked the city. By the time she reached Mildred, she could no longer hear her little sister's screams, though she lay mere inches away from her.

◦◦ ◦◦ ◦◦

Finally the explosions ceased, and the morning passed. As Agnes's hearing returned, one sound remained constant—the menacing growl of fire. Fire uncontrolled, fire consuming building after building, block after block. But the wind kept it to the south and east of the Mess, and the air, while putrid, was not so thick as to be unbearable.

Midway through the morning Mildred called out from her room, where she attempted to rest, "Has the wind shifted?"

"No, my Precious Life," Mary Custis said, soothing as a nightingale in the evening watches, from her vantage point at the shuttered rear window facing south toward the inferno. "Though that is little consolation now to Richmond," she said in a lower voice to Agnes, who sat nearby.

But Agnes sensed something amiss. She excused herself and walked downstairs, stepping gingerly through the field of glass.

"How is Life?" her mother asked her, from the parlor.

Agnes stepped into the room, where she saw Mary Lee scrunched over in her rolling chair, knitting socks for her husband's army. Agnes's eyes widened as she marveled, *No one in Richmond is perhaps less able to perform any worthwhile task at all at this point in time, much less one so industrious and productive.*

"Why, Mama, are you well?" Agnes asked.

Mary screwed up her nose. "I asked you how was your sister," she snapped.

"She is," Agnes began, "she is the sweetest girl in the whole world, Mama, much sweeter than any of us who remain, and she is watching that world crumble down around her."

"You and Mary Custis continue tending to her," Mary said, "and tell her she may come down here with me if she pleases."

Agnes stepped out the front door and beheld flaming brands of all sorts—wisps of paper, tar paper from roofs, rafter particles—swirling and wafting through the air at every level, all floating from the direction of the fires toward—*me.*

She gasped aloud and her blood ran cold. *I knew it,* she thought, *I knew something was wrong. Oh God, God, where are You? Where have You been for so long? And what,* she thought, stark fear mingling with anguish and fury as she looked toward the smoke-smeared sky, *what do You have for us now? Just who are Your people, and who are the heathen? Is it all fairy tales? Nursery rhymes?*

"Oh!" she shouted, clenching her fists as she turned back toward the Mess. *Arlington was not enough, and Annie and Charlotte and—and all the rest—You must now take what little we have left in this cursed world.*

Her anger forestalled some of the fear that would otherwise have swept her. *But how to let Mildred know?* she wondered.

Mildred had so little energy remaining, physical or emotional, that she took the news with an equanimity that heartened her sisters and mother. But the wind had indeed shifted, and the fire was now coming toward the Lees.

Friends came to the door. "You must leave now," they urged Mary, "the fire is less than two blocks away, and the wind may land an incendiary on your very roof at any second."

Mary Lee looked them in the eye, all of them. "I let the Yankees roust me out of one home," she said. Her glare turned to steel. "I'll not let them roust me out of another."

All were silent for a moment. Then Mary added, "Daughters, I'll be pleased for you to go with these good folks to safety."

But they, all of them, even Mildred, refused to leave their mother, or even to dissuade her from her own course.

●◇ ●◇ ●◇

The fire found the north side of Franklin first. No one knew how it leapfrogged over the street without first striking the south side of the block, where lay the Mess. But the wind carried something over there and got it started, a couple of doors to the east of the Presbyterian church that lay directly across the street from the Lees.

Neighbors and friends from areas more remote from the fire had mobilized with Agnes, Mary Custis, and now, the rallying Mildred, to form a bucket brigade. They watched out the front door and windows in stunned stupor as the fire blazed up the north side of Franklin, toward the west, toward the Presbyterian church. Then a couple of old men, a couple of young boys, and one teenaged girl climbed up on the Lees' roof and soaked it down with buckets passed to them from Agnes, Mildred, and a dozen others.

"Look!" someone shouted from the roof. "It's on this side of the street!"

The south side of Franklin had indeed caught fire, down the hill, this side of Ninth Street, across from the silent tocsin bell.

"It's coming this way!" the same voice shouted.

Then a scream—and the steeple from the Presbyterian church crashed to the earth in flames. The whole Mess shook from the impact.

Mary Custis, Agnes thought, panicked. She rushed out the front door and found her sister, breathing through a kerchief she held over her mouth and nose, on the top stone step where her mother had posted her. A large pail of water sat beside her.

The sisters could only stare at one another, then at the inferno raging across the cobblestoned street. All of the north side of Franklin from the Presbyterian church east, past Eighth Street, to Ninth, was in flames. Agnes shielded her face and eyes from the smoke and craned her neck to see down the south side of the street.

"Oh, no," she uttered.

"What is it?" Mary Custis asked, standing.

The roaring blaze had churned up the south side of Franklin, straight for the Mess.

Flames now danced from the house next door to them.

The sisters stood slack-jawed, mouths agape.

"I—" Mary Custis began, coughing and sputtering. "What do we do now, Wiggie?"

Agnes lifted her gaze toward the roof. She saw a fiery brand sail through the air from the Presbyterian church and land on top of the Mess. She gasped as sparks flew upward, despite the roof being doused.

"Fire! On the roof!" she screamed.

The bucket brigade drenched that whole section of the roof before flames could take hold. Agnes rushed inside to her mother.

"Mama," she said, "the Presbyterian church is burning down across the street from us. It is sending sparks onto our roof. The house next door is going down even faster. We must get you away to safety now."

Mary had replaced her knitting with her big family Bible, open to Psalm 91.

"I'll not be moved further," she said simply, turning back to her Scripture.

"Oh!" Agnes exclaimed, storming back out the front door, frustrated with her mother as never before.

More sparks arced over from the church and landed on the front steps, mere feet from Agnes and Mary Custis. They stamped them out. Then others flew over and they stamped them out, sweating now, scared, coughing, choking, their hearts pounding in their chests, rushing to stamp more out, watching others whistle through the air. Agnes was fresh out of ideas, solutions, and plans.

Oh, dear God, please help us, she begged, blind with tears and looking toward the house next door, a few short yards to the east, now engulfed in flames. Suddenly her dark hair cascaded over her face. *What?* she thought. She turned around, toward the west. A stout breeze whipped the hair back off her face. Her mouth opened. "Mary—Mary Custis," she said, "It's turned again, the wind has turned back toward the east!"

And so it had. So the great Richmond fire of 1865 came no closer to Mary Lee than that Presbyterian church across the street, which it destroyed, or the house next door to the east, which it nearly did, or the roof of the Mess itself, which it would like to have.

It was a most unlikely day to have found oneself praising God and thanking Him for His mercies and deliverance. But that is exactly what the women of the Lee clan did.

It seems even the flames of Richmond obey my mother when she uses that tone of voice, Agnes mused, marveling anew at the gnarled, wispy-haired little woman bent in her rolling chair who refused to be cowed—by Yankees, drunken hoodlums, or the fire that had just burned the heart of the former capital of the Confederate States of America to the ground.

CHAPTER 45

MARLEY HAD SEEN NOTHING TO COMPARE WITH IT IN ALL HIS years of fighting wars, whether against the Mexicans or the Confederates.

Sheridan had sent him with three handpicked scouts early the morning of April 4 to personally reconnoiter the Richmond-Petersburg lines and prove that the scraggly little band that had snuck away by cover of night was indeed all that remained of Robert E. Lee's mighty Army of Northern Virginia. Indeed the only army Marley found was his own. He rode straight through the deserted Petersburg lines, his eyes stinging from the smoke that had carried, en masse, all the way from Richmond. He boarded his men and horses on a northbound Federal train for the same ride Agnes had taken only a couple of nights before on a Confederate car.

The entire ride seemed as though it took place at midnight rather than noonday, so dark was the smoke-filled air. If not for the gaslit lamps in the Federal train, Marley could not have seen the hour on the timepiece he pulled from the pocket of his coat and held before his face.

Finally, he thought, *a clearing and light.* But it was not what he thought. *Dear God in heaven, that suffering city is still on fire.*

A couple of the men with him uttered soft oaths.

"Is this what the hell you preach looks like, Major, sir?" one of them asked.

Behold, the awful price of treason, Marley thought to himself. Still miles south of the James, he caught snatches of the downtown moonscape.

Tears filled his eyes. *But this is all too much. It should not happen like this,* he thought. Then anger. *These—d——d—Rebel leaders—please forgive my profanity, Lord—why will they not relent? It is over; they have lost; their entire civilization is being reduced, literally, to ashes, and they yet have armies in the field, killing our men—insanity!* He saw a couple of scarecrows in tattered butternut rags and bare feet sitting by a roadside as the train passed. One had bloody bandages around his head; the other's left sleeve hung slack and empty at his side. *Too many of their soldiers still refuse to stack arms, when they must know they no longer have any hope of victory.*

The train rumbled past a shambling little house surrounded by fields overgrown with wild weeds and secondary brush growth. A tall, slender woman with what Marley calculated had once been a beautiful face, carrying an infant and with three small children hovering around her, stood near a water well not far from the tracks. She looked up and saw him and his uniform. When she did, her countenance turned to stone. If hate had a face, he had just seen it. *The very people themselves!* he anguished. *I am now convinced if they had any food or medicine upon which to subsist, they would fight us for a thousand years or until none of them remained left to fight.* How thankful he was for Lincoln's naval blockade.

Another oath, from another of his three men as the devastation of the Richmond commercial district along the north bank of the James shuttered into view. Then all of them were mute. They had no words with which to offer even a reaction to what lay before them.

In some places fires still blazed. What buildings he could see slouched like dismembered corpses whose insides have been cleaned out. He peered at the dark holes where windows had been. *Corpses without eyes,* he thought. And no roofs either. *Headless corpses.* And over all, like a dread black plague itself, smoke of every conceivable hue clung to everything in sight, so thickly that only glimpses could be gained beyond a few hundred feet.

One of General Weitzel's, the Federal in charge of the area, staff officers met them at the closest train station to the center of the city that had not been destroyed by the fire. He seemed quite sanguine.

"We didn't," Marley began, "do this—did we?"

"Oh, no," the handsome young staff officer said airily, with just a trace of his old Prussian accent. "The Rebs did it, and we put it out for 'em." When a nearby officer cleared his throat at that statement, the younger man revised his statement. "Well, at least they blew some powder magazines and burned some tobacco that may have started some of it; appears several fires began, separate of one another. Looters and vandals likely started some—maybe most—of them. We ran Old Glory up the capitol building flagpole first thing, smoke or no, though."

What stuck with Marley was the queer enunciation with which the officer rendered "Old Glory."

"Are the Rebs all gone?" Marley asked quietly.

"No, there are hundreds of them still here," the officer said. "But they're out of the war. Some wounded, some crippled, some drunk, some begging us for food." He paused for a moment. "Most of them just sit there looking straight ahead, never saying a word."

"Hallelujah, General," said a grimy-faced black man of around thirty.

"It's Major Steiner, boy," the staff man said.

"Where we goin', boss?"

"You can go wherever you want now, boy," said Steiner.

The black man stared at him.

"Get used to it, contraband," Steiner chortled. "You're free now. It's the year of jubilo—ain't that what you boys call it?"

The black man stared some more, flashed an ivory smile that did not reach to his eyes, then turned and walked off, toward nowhere in particular.

"Criminy," the staff officer said, "not ten or a hundred or a thousand of him is worth one of our men that died. My father fought for revolution in the Germanies almost twenty years ago, and I have now fought for it here in America for four years, but never can I recall the Negro as part of it."

"Revolution?" Marley asked.

"Well, surely, Major," Steiner said, as if surprised by his question. "Just what would you suppose this has all been about?"

Marley said nothing as he mounted his horse and rode away. He had heard most of it before. Few Federal soldiers he knew cottoned to Lincoln's late-blooming innovation that they were fighting to "free the slaves." More than one mutiny over the issue following the Emancipation Proclamation was narrowly averted. But revolution? It had always seemed to him the Confederates were the revolutionaries.

Between Eighth and Fifteenth, from Main Street all the way to the James, and between Fourth and Tenth, from Canal Street to the river, all that remained were smoking rubble and hollow, wasted skeletons of buildings. Marley could not even enter most of the streets, so piled were they with debris. Every bank was destroyed, the biggest hotels, the biggest newspapers, the state and county courthouses and all their records, the arsenal, the largest mills, the Danville and Petersburg railroad bridges and depots, a dozen drugstores, two dozen groceries, and most of the shops and stores in the whole city. All or part of fifty-four blocks and nearly one thousand homes and businesses were no more.

Women, children, and old folks, some terrified, some in glaze-eyed stupor, some glaring with hate-filled countenances at him and other Federals as they rode or walked by, huddled everywhere—on sidewalks, in the trashed-out streets. Marley saw them scrounging through garbage and rubble for food, and beseeching one another, anybody—in some cases Federal soldiers—for water.

Until the day he died, he would never forget the scene spread before his eyes when he reached the capitol square. Hundreds and hundreds of people sat, stood, and lay on the grounds, on the wide front steps, up to the doors themselves. Children constituted a majority of the assembly. Some wept; a few appeared normal. Most sat mute with the tearless eyes that to Marley testified to a soul so encompassed with horrors that tears have fled away from it as surely as the spring harvests had fled away from the Shenandoah in great black heaps of smoke.

"What are all these folks doing here, Sergeant?" Marley asked a husky white soldier supervising a squad of black Federal troopers patrolling one section of the square.

"Doing, sir? Nothing, sir. Nothing at all. Nowhere to go, sir. Burned out, homeless, refugees, every story you can imagine, sir. Most of 'em just need food and water now, enough to make it through the day. Guess they're loyal Unionists again, huh, sir?"

Marley said nothing, but he thought, *We'll see about that when their bellies are full and they are back on their feet.*

Almost back to the train station, three young boys with grimy faces, ragged clothes, and two small, flaky-crusted pies hailed him. "Major, sir," the eldest, perhaps twelve, called. "Where you from, sir?"

"Pennsylvania," Marley said, heartened that some spirit remained in the city.

"Ever had Virginia quail before, sir?"

Marley smiled. "Matter of fact, I have. Lived over in the Valley for some years before the war."

This caught the boy short. But he forged on. "Well, sir, then you mayn't realize that the quail native to these parts is sure enough more tender and a might more flavorful to boot than that peculiar to the Valley—er, beggin' your pardon, sir."

Marley smiled. "So what is Virginia quail—native to these parts—going for today?"

The youth glanced at his younger confederates, then turned back toward Marley. "For you, sir, twenty-five cents for one pie—Yankee coin—forty cents for the two."

Marley's eyebrows arched. "Sakes alive, fellows," he said. "I am impressed you can produce such fine-looking pies at such a bargain, with what I hear flour is costing these days around Richmond."

The boy blushed and shifted his feet. "Well, yes, uh, thank you, sir, we do try to run a, er, a low-cost operation, Major, sir."

Marley smiled and nodded, then reached for his change purse. "I'll be bound, that's the best deal I've been offered this whole campaign."

As the young salesman handed the pies up to him, Marley noticed tears streaking the sooty face of the smallest of the three boys, perhaps nine years old. He also noticed for the first time how emaciated the youngsters were. *They look like grubby toothpicks with filthy rags thrown over them,* he thought, feeling pity. He wondered how many more just like them now roamed the streets of Richmond, attempting to scrape together a few pennies for themselves and probably the women of their families. *If they even have families,* he thought.

"What's wrong, son?" Marley asked the nine-year-old. "Wish you'd priced your pies a might higher? Tell you what, here's fifty more cents. I'll hope to get a couple more of these from you next time we meet."

To Marley's shock, the little boy burst into tears.

"Son," Marley began, shaming himself that he had not thought before how hungry the boys themselves must be for the pies. "Why don't you take one of these pies back—but keep the money. You can just owe me an extra when next we cross paths."

The boy wailed louder. "No, sir," he said, his eyes wild with grief. "It's just that—it was my puppy we had to kill to make them pies."

Lee and his men covered more than twenty miles on April 3. As he neared Amelia Courthouse the morning of April 4, he had yet to see any sign of Federal pursuit, though he knew they were coming. Rations for the entire army would be awaiting him at Amelia. From there the closer he moved to Danville, his new army headquarters and supply base, the shorter would shrink his supply lines. *Yes,* he thought, *we have a chance; if I can get my boys enough food to keep them marching, we will meet up with Joe Johnston. Then we will turn and have it out*

with those people, far from their own bases of operation, on ground of my own choosing.

He breathed in the fragrance of Virginia as a new spring bloomed. *Yes, it is good to be back out among the land,* he thought. *If only Mary and the children were all here with me.* He raised silent petitions to God, that he would guard and guide them, especially since fires had swept Richmond, and the Federals had occupied it. He did not know how close the fires had come to the Mess, though he knew they had burned much of the center of the city. Still he felt certain he would have heard of anything untoward happening to Mary or the girls. A fresh breeze blew across his face. *Yes, we should always attempt to get back out to the land.*

Even if it was land stripped and despoiled by the ravages of four years of war.

Then he reached Amelia and found abundant ordnance—ninety-six full caissons, two hundred boxes of artillery ammunition, and one hundred sixty-four boxes of artillery harness.

What he did not find was any food for his whole army.

No, he thought, his knees weak for a moment and his chest tightening on him. *It cannot be! I telegraphed orders to Richmond to train rations immediately to Amelia for our army. The Danville line between here and Richmond was certainly clear on the second, the day I issued the order. Oh, those incompetents in our government!*

His rage lasted only a moment, and no man saw it. Sorrow and dejection followed on its heels, and his dejection mounted with each rail car he inspected with his own eyes. *I just cannot believe it!* he thought. *We may have lost the war today, for want of food rations ordered days ago. Now we will have to halt and give those people the opportunity to catch us while we send foraging parties out all over the country to find rations.*

But the surrounding country was already played out, and the wagons brought in barely any food at all. Nonetheless when Lee pulled his scarlet-lined cape round him and led his army out the next morning, April 5, they smiled and laughed and joked, and they cheered him and told him they had never been more ready for a fight with the Yanks. They did all this as an hours-long spring thundershower drenched them.

Never have I been more keenly aware of how unworthy I am of such men, he thought as the echoes of their cheers resounded across the fields and hills. He noticed not as many raised their hats to him as had during previous such ovations. Then he realized why. *Most of them no longer have hats. They are bareheaded as well as barefooted.*

Tears welled up in his eyes as he realized that even though he had failed to provide even the food for them that they needed, they still chose to honor him in the best way they knew. As if in benedictory response, their familiar throaty choruses began to resound off the surrounding hills.

> When through fiery trials thy pathway shall lie,
> My grace, all-sufficient, shall be thy supply;
> The flame shall not hurt thee; I only design
> Thy dross to consume, and thy gold to refine.

They had marched and sung his favorite hymn, "How Firm a Foundation," many a time, but never had it sounded as sweet and forgiving as did it now.

But because of the delay, his son Rooney rode up to his father a few miles south of Amelia. He and Lee's nephew Fitz each commanded a wing of the cavalry that remained with the Army of Northern Virginia (Lee had sent Hampton south). If news could possibly be more sad than the absence of food at Amelia, then Rooney's news was.

"Sheridan is in front of us at Jetersville," Rooney said. "We estimate two full Federal infantry corps digging in to stop us."

And if their infantry is here, so is their artillery and so certainly is their horse, Lee thought, dread enveloping him. *All because some government—person—in Richmond did not get our rations to us.* His back and shoulders and hips and legs all pounded with pain from the constant riding and lack of sleep. But now he must face the fact that, because of the delay to forage, the Federals had not only caught up with him, they had blocked his route of escape.

Soon news came that rations awaited him in Farmville, nineteen miles away. *I do not believe those people could yet be between us and Farmville,* he thought to himself. *If we night march, I believe we can beat them there and feed my men.*

But Farmville was west, not south, and the slender thread of hope by which the entire Confederacy still hung lay in a junction with Joe Johnston down in North Carolina, and that was south. *It would seem to be the only course left to us,* Lee realized, standing in the open air and poring over the maps spread across his camp table. *From Farmville, we'll push on to Lynchburg, resupply, then, with the help of the great God of heaven, turn the corner on those people and move south.*

What followed was a night of horror. Since the Confederates had not planned to travel that route, Lee's scouts and engineers had not thoroughly reconnoitered it. One key bridge gave way to the stress of the heavy column in the black midnight, jamming all the artillery and wagons. But it seemed as though the stumbling, exhausted throng clogged the road every step of the way. Teams of draft horses broke down. More soldiers stumbled away to find food or home. Many others just sat, fell, or fainted dead away by the roadside, unable to march any further.

Lee learned from captured Federal spies that Grant and virtually the entire Army of the Potomac, as well as the Army of the James and the Army of the Valley, rested within a few miles of him. So his men, stretched to the limits of their physical and mental endurance, grew more prone to confusion and panic. At one point in the deepest of night, a crazed black stallion bolted through the ranks, a fence rail dangling from his bridle. Thinking all manner of things, Lee's soldiers began shooting at one another in the dark.

The next afternoon, April 6, Lee personally scouted the area around him. What he saw filled him with foreboding. *There can be no spot in the whole of Virginia more vulnerable to attack by cavalry on a column of infantry,* he thought, surveying through his field glasses the hills and streams that crosshatched the country.

Then his eyes came to Sayler's Creek, very near the Appomattox River and still a few miles east of Farmville. A battle raged across the creek, toward the rear of his column. His surprise was matched only by his concern.

Peering through his field glasses into the distance, he saw what appeared to be the largest herd of sheep he had ever witnessed. The Englishman Wolseley, again accompanying the Army of Northern Virginia as an observer, rode up to Lee.

"Are those sheep or not?" Lee asked him.

"No, General," the younger man with the keen eyes answered, "they are Yankee wagons."

But how can it be? he thought, incredulous. *Those wagons travel in the* rear *of their columns. That means their army is— I must ride to a vantage point where I can see what transpires in this battle.*

He worked his way up to a high ridge overlooking Sayler's Creek, and the Appomattox River Valley beyond. Never would he forget what he saw. For never had he seen it before. Rushing headlong up out of the bottoms, directly toward him, were the shattered remnants of two of his three corps. Teamsters on foot without their wagons, their horses galloping without their traces, soldiers fleeing with no guns, hardly any of them now with shoes or hats. In the distance, also coming straight toward him, determined, unstoppable, were line upon line of blue-coated infantry and cavalry.

"My God! Has the army been dissolved?" Lee exclaimed.

"No, General, here are troops ready to do their duty," one officer choked out.

"Yes, there are some true men left," Lee said, nodding and maintaining his composure. "Will you please keep those people back?"

His own troops did not turn back toward the Federals. But neither did they continue their retreat. They began to cluster around Lee himself and Traveller, like so many little boys running to tell their big brother of a gang of bullies who have just thrashed them bloody.

Lee saw that a score or more of sweating black faces comprised one section of the throng. These Virginia men, with musket and bayonet, had repulsed three assaults of white Federal cavalry on a wagon train they guarded. At last, overwhelmed by sheer numbers, most of the black Virginians—some of them free, some slave volunteers—had been killed, wounded, or captured.

My boys, Lee thought as he surveyed the teeming mass enveloping him, deep currents of emotion, feelings that had no words, coursing through him. *My poor, poor boys. They have given everything they have. How can they continue to give? I must help them.*

And then did the commander of all the armies of the Confederate States of America reach down and pull from the ground a tattered red Confederate battle flag that had been planted there by a color bearer as he fell dead at its base of four gunshot wounds. That flag which would much later be so reviled by men ignorant of history or principles or causes. That flag, the only Christian flag ever flown as a symbol of an American nation, its blue and white cross purposely echoing the flag of Scotland, which purposely chose it to represent the courage, sacrifice, suffering, and Christian faith of its patron saint, the martyred Saint Andrew, brother of the apostle Peter himself.

Saint Andrew, crucified on just such an x-shaped cross as General Robert E. Lee now raised before his men.

"Who will go with me to stop those people?" Lee called to his men, gathered around him now by the hundreds. "Who will help me to drive them back before we are consumed?"

"I will!" rasped Cole Culpeper, hatless, shoeless, without food for three days, and holding his bloody side where a Yankee horse soldier had sabered him. "I will," he repeated, staggering forward.

"I will, Uncle Robert!" cried another.

"So shall I, General Lee!" shouted another, bleeding from the nose and ears. Then turning toward the crowd, "Where are the men who won't follow Uncle Robert?"

And then came the shouts from a place deep within their souls, as they must have been with their fathers who charged forward behind Robert the Bruce on the long-ago fields of Bannockburn. They began in a tentative sort of way, thin and wavering, but then they gained heart and they grew to the extent that by the time someone had pulled the battle flag from Lee's grasp and rushed with it back down into the Valley of Death, hardly a man among them cared anymore for his life.

We cannot let down Marse Robert, Culpeper thought, stumbling forward with no weapon but his trusted Bowie knife. *Please, God, whoever or whatever You are, don't let us let down Marse Robert.*

Then Culpeper collapsed to the ground, facedown in his own blood. But others did not, and they ran screaming the Rebel yell Old Jack had taught them. They ran into sheets of fire and steel, and more of them fell wounded, and more of them died, and more of them surrendered to the bayonets and the repeating rifles that surrounded them.

But they did not again retreat, and they stopped the Federals once more as the sun set on another bloody day of death and destruction.

The events of April 6 cost Lee nearly eight thousand men. The corps of "Old Baldy" Ewell, Stonewall's erstwhile lieutenant, and Richard Anderson were destroyed. Ewell himself was captured. Gordon's men fought long and well and helped save what was left of the army.

That night word reached Lee that Custis's division had been wiped out.

"He is not still with our army, General," the courier answered Lee's anxious inquiry as to his son's personal whereabouts. "And the Yankees have not reported capturing him."

Lee had that report to complement one received earlier in the day, the one reporting Rob missing in action since April 2.

CHAPTER 46

WE'RE NOT LICKED YET, LEE THOUGHT STILL LATER THAT NIGHT AS he formed one last-ditch plan to escape and rally his beleaguered troops and nation. *We'll use the Appomattox River as a shield between us and those people, and we'll burn the bridges across it so they can't get to us. If any cavalry manages to swim across the water, we'll deal with them.* He stared at the map, rubbing his white beard. *If we can just make it into Farmville and get our food rations . . . Lynchburg . . . south to the Old North State . . . No sir, this army is not finished yet.*

They marched out from there, many of them having barely escaped with their lives only hours before at Sayler's Creek. Men fainted or fell by the roadside, crow-bait horses staggered, and mules dropped dead, packs on their backs.

But by the early morning hours of April 7, Lee's men began arriving in Farmville.

Venable and Marshall watched as he rode off alone from his Farmville quarters shortly after dawn.

"Where can he be going in that direction?" Marshall, the younger man, asked. "We have no army over there."

Venable considered a witty reply such as, "After all this while, you consult me on the mind of Robert Lee?" but he was tired and hungry and chose to save all his words for another time.

Hurting physically in all the usual places and maybe even a couple of unusual ones; concerned about the disposition of every aspect of his army, especially their slow starvation; wondering where the Federals were and when they would next strike; indeed wondering whether the nation he now led would last out this day; and fearing the worst for still-missing Custis and Rob, Lee put it all aside for one anonymous errand.

The widow, thin as a reed, blue-black crescents ringed beneath her eyes, opened her own door and stood in gape-mouthed silence at the unannounced presence of Robert E. Lee at her very remote doorstep.

Bowing, hat in hand, and forcing back tears, he said, "I have not time to tarry, but I could not pass by without stopping for a moment to pay my respects to the widow of my honored soldier Colonel Thornton and to offer my deep sympathy in the sore bereavement which you sustained when the country was deprived of his invaluable services."

But why? she wondered after he had gone, when she had thrown herself down upon the lonely bed no longer warmed by the one man she had ever loved in her whole life and who had been her best friend since she was twelve years old. *Why would General Lee come way out here to speak to me, a nothing he never met, about a cavalry officer he never met that died two and a half years ago at Sharpsburg? How did he even know this was Johnny's house? Now perhaps I finally understand why Johnny loved him so. Oh, God forgive me for cursing this man these last years,* she prayed, watering the bed with many tears.

When her tears were staunched, at least for awhile, she looked out the window at the red ball rising in the eastern sky. In one regard she was greatly relieved. *Thank goodness we are winning the war after all,* she thought. *General Lee would never have taken time to come see me if the army were in such desperate straits as we had been told it was.*

Lee had wrested control of his emotions back from his sobbing by the time he spotted crusty old General Henry Wise, marching his brigade, undaunted from the Sayler's Creek drubbing. He even managed to have his eyes dried before anyone could detect a thing.

The first thing Lee noted of Wise was the dried mud smeared across his face. *That man, no less than the former governor of Virginia, washed up in a mud puddle this morning,* Lee thought, his sorrow turned to mirth.

Wise's mood was anything but mirth. Hatless, he launched into a profane tirade, current company notwithstanding, about how his own superior officer had fled the fight at Sayler's Creek and left his men to fend for themselves. Lee cautioned him, with disguised levity, that he might be court-martialed and executed for such insubordination.

"Shot!" Wise crowed. "You can't afford to shoot the men who fight for cussing those who run away. Shot! I wish you would shoot me. If you don't, some Yankee probably will in the next twenty-four hours."

Still building steam, Wise proceeded to instruct Lee of the necessity to put his "poor men on their poor mules" and send them home in time for spring plowing.

"These men have already endured more than I believed flesh and blood could. I say to you, sir, emphatically, that to prolong the struggle is murder, and the blood of every man who is killed from this time forth is on your head, General Lee."

"Oh, General, don't talk so wildly," Lee said. "My burdens are heavy enough. What would the country think of me, if I did what you suggest?"

"Country be d——d," Wise roared. "There is no country. There has been no country, General, for a year or more. *You* are the country to these men. They have fought for you—and there are still thousands left who will die for you."

Lee stood silent for a moment, then smiled at the mud veiling Wise's fierce countenance. "Well, I'm glad to see at least one of my generals has his war paint on today."

After a brief meeting with Longstreet, Lee, having hardly eaten a bite of food for two days, managed to find a chunk of chicken meat and two slices of bread. Just as he opened his mouth to chomp down, Taylor announced the general had a caller: his teenaged nephew, George Taylor Lee.

"My son, why did you come here?" Lee asked.

"I thought it was my duty to come and volunteer to fight, sir."

"Have you had any breakfast, George?"

"No, sir."

Lee handed him the chicken sandwich as a group of officers approached to meet with him.

"Go somewhere and eat it," he told the boy, turning toward the officers, and ignoring his growling stomach, which would now growl longer.

Soon news came sad as any yet received. A key bridge ordered burned by Lee had been captured by the Federals before its destruction was complete. The episode meant two entire corps of "those people" now breathed down Lee's neck from the same side of the Appomattox River as he, along with the two corps that paralleled his movements across the river to the south.

Lee exploded with pent-up rage. *Our last hopes—frittered away because of more poor communication between our commanders!* he thought. He prayed for the Lord to steady him, then set about dealing with the new situation.

Unfortunately his solution included pushing his army forward, before most of them received any rations. *Most of them have been marching for eighteen hours, many of them have had little pause for forty!* he realized, grieved.

Even before Lee had his men moving, Federal cavalry fell upon what was left of their rear. These bluecoats had spearheaded the rampage at Sayler's Creek the day before. They planned to duplicate their feat today. This time, nephew Fitz's and son Rooney's horse soldiers wooed them in, then struck in concert from front and flank, cut them to pieces, captured their commanding general, and sent the survivors flying in a rout.

"Keep your command together and in good spirits, General," Lee told his son after the battle. "Don't let them think of surrender. I will get you out of this."

Just as I thought, Virginia is not licked yet, Lee thought as he rode away, proud beyond words of Rooney, of all his children. Of Custis and Rob. *Oh, merciful Creator, Custis and Rob.*

It impressed Rooney that he had never before heard his father utter the word *surrender.*

Late that evening Lee received a note from Grant, asking for the surrender of the Army of Northern Virginia, that further bloodshed might be averted.

He handed it without comment to Longstreet.

"Not yet," said the Old War Horse.

Lee agreed, but he also wondered whether an honorable peace might now be negotiated between fellow combatants, an honorable peace that might not be possible should the powers in Washington take hold of the process . . . or should any more Sayler's Creeks befall the Confederate army.

Keeping his own counsel, he penned a brief response to Grant:

JOHN J. DWYER

7 April 1865

General:

I have received your note of this date. Though not entertaining the opinion you express of the hopelessness of further resistance on the part of the Army of Northern Virginia, I reciprocate your desire to avoid useless effusion of blood, and, therefore, before considering your proposition, ask the terms you will offer on condition of its surrender.

Very respy your obt. Servt
R. E. Lee
General

Lt. General U. S. Grant
Commanding Armies of the United States

He told no one, including Longstreet, of his actions.

●◇ ●◇ ●◇

Sunshine bathed the entire country around Lee the next day, Saturday, April 8. He realized the Appomattox River was narrowing toward its source point, no more than twenty miles west; before then the Federals would be able to cross the river in force from the south, either to flank, broadside, or block him from the front.

He also knew that beyond the Appomattox headwaters, and the rail station just west of it claiming the same name, was a twelve-mile-long ridge dividing the lands drained by the Appomattox to the east and those drained by the winding James to the west. Across that ridge, or watershed, ran the Southside Railroad, on which a different set of food rations—provisions his men needed more desperately than ever—awaited him on trains sent from Lynchburg. Lynchburg lay on the James River, at the western terminus of the watershed.

We must *gain the watershed before those people cut us off,* Lee thought, poring over Jed Hotchkiss's map, *or they will have us hedged in front, rear, and left, and the James to the north will block us from escape to the right.* He paused to contemplate that eventuality. *Then it would all be over.* A chill coursed through him that he was a moment in shaking off.

He focused on the watershed portion of the map. *It looks as if our route of march will first intersect the Southside at—Appomattox Courthouse.*

The morning passed with a remarkable degree of solitude as compared to recent days. Shortly before noon Lee spotted an inviting patch of shade under a stand of pines, climbed off Traveller, and stretched out for a nap.

After a while Pendleton approached. *I have known Lee for nearly forty years,* the preacher-artillery commander thought, not relishing his errand; *yet I cannot say what his response will be to the message I must deliver.*

That message was that Pendleton had been selected to deliver the unanimous recommendation of a host of general officers who met the evening before.

Pendleton did not include the portion, also unanimous, speaking to the group's desire to shift any potential onus of dishonor from Lee's shoulders to their own.

"Surrender!" Lee flared, flying to his feet with an energy that at first heartened Pendleton at the demonstrative possibility of retained physical prowess in men their age. "I trust it has not come to that. We certainly have too many brave men to think of laying down our arms. They still fight with great spirit, whereas the enemy does not. And besides, if I were to intimate to General Grant that I would listen to terms, he would at once regard it as such an evidence of weakness that he would demand unconditional surrender—and sooner than that I am resolved to die. Indeed we must all determine to die at our posts."

Pendleton, chastened, gathered his composure, bowed, and said, "Every man among us, sir, I am confident, will discharge his duty and be perfectly willing that you, sir, should decide the question."

Watching Pendleton ride away in his frayed gray uniform, on his skinny brown horse, Lee fretted. *My old friend, my loyal and trusted old friend, who left his rustic pulpit for the terrors of this and many other bloody battles. And at his age.* Lee forgot Pendleton was a year younger than himself. *I was too hard on him. Never has he forsaken his duty, never has he given an inch for the right. And still he rides with me, even after I advanced brilliant young Alexander around him, even after he in his own sharp intellect must no doubt have recognized more than one professional snub from the commander himself.*

Lee rubbed the snowy chin whiskers. Indeed is not a missive from my own pen perhaps being read at this moment by General Grant? One centered on and specific in its employment of the word *surrender?* He shook his head, ashamed of himself. *We are all worn to a frazzle.* Then, as he had often before, Traveller, tethered not far away, sensed something amiss with his master and whinnied at him. "I am all right, my friend," Lee said, going to the gray. "But how are you?" He stroked the animal's black mane and his neck, and tickled his nose. "We must find a way to improve your diet, lest you wind up facedown in the road, suffocating on mud like those poor beasts I saw today."

When Traveller nuzzled his coat pocket, Lee said, "Oh, dear friend, I have nothing for you even in there today." He kissed Traveller's face and told him, "I must find a way to encourage General Pendleton, and reassert my regard for and gratitude toward him. Yes, we all need encouragement in these days, don't we, old friend?"

Then Lee walked alone for a ways, his melancholy advanced with a jolting realization: *Now both parties wish me to cease hostilities. Grant wrote that he did not wish for himself "the responsibility of any further effusion of blood." Then upon whose shoulders does it rest, when my own lieutenants petition me for the same end?* he wondered. *When what remains of our army, indeed, our whole country, staggers under starvation, privation, illness, and sickness of heart? Such decisions are too vast for one man. They need prayer, as old Stonewall would have given them, and the counsel of others, which he would not have.*

The relative quiet persisted the rest of the day, though Lee perceived that the Federals were likely racing forward on all fronts.

Soon after dark another message arrived from Grant. Reading it by the light of a candle Venable held, Lee's spirits rose as he read that because peace was the Federal's great desire, he would insist only "that the men and officers surrendered shall be disqualified for taking up arms against the government of the United States until properly exchanged."

Grant may have gained immortality for himself, along with the *nom de guerre* "Unconditional Surrender," from his victories at Fort Donelson and elsewhere in the west, but he had fought Robert E. Lee and the Army of Northern Virginia long enough to know that they were capable of generating a vast "effusion of blood" in short order if their commander felt the proffered terms too severe.

"How would you answer that?" Lee asked Venable, in the habit he often exercised of seeking immediate counsel from another in his presence, with access to similar information.

"I would answer no such letter," Venable said after reading it.

How many such luxuries are lost to a commander, Lee thought. "Ah, but it must be answered," he said.

Despite the continued presence of the word *surrender* in Grant's communiqués, Lee still hoped such correspondence might effect a peace based on terms more honorable and favorable to the Confederate cause.

He chose his words carefully as he again put pen to paper.

> . . . I did not intend to propose the surrender of the Army of Northern Virginia, but to ask the terms of your proposition. To be frank, I do not think the emergency has arisen to call for the surrender of this army, but as the restoration of peace should be the sole object of all, I desired to know whether your proposals would lead to that end. I cannot, therefore, meet you with a view to surrender the Army of Northern Virginia, but as far as your proposal may affect the C. S. forces under my command, and tend to the restoration of peace, I should be pleased to meet you at 10 a.m. tomorrow; on the old stage road to Richmond, between the picket-lines of the two armies.

Around nine o'clock the sullen grumble of artillery echoed over the hills from the Confederate front, which lay three miles southwest of Lee, between Appomattox Courthouse and the Southside Railroad. The old pang returned to his chest.

They have blocked our advance, he knew, though he could not bear even to form the words in his mind of what that sound, from that direction, meant. He said nothing of this occurrence, or a few moments later of the spectral-like reflections of thousands of Federal campfires emerging off the darkening horizon—to his front, rear, and left—*and the James to the north will block us from escape to the right,* he remembered.

Just then Pendleton came pounding up on his gangly brown. His report confirmed Lee's fears. Federal cavalry had swamped the reserve Confederate artillery at the far front of Lee's column. In one of the most furious close-up encounters of the war, the air ablaze with bullets and cannon shot, Pendleton had helped extricate just over half of the Confederates' sixty guns. But then he had to jump his horse and his own fifty-five-year-old self over a fence, landing in a sassafras bush, to elude a swarm of Federal horse soldiers.

Now they have the trains containing all our food as well, Lee realized, his heart sinking.

He called for his remaining commanders, Longstreet, Gordon, and Fitz Lee.

As he waited, the sweet scent of honeysuckle wafted into his nostrils. *Ah, the divine mercy of a kind God, to demonstrate such blessed loving-kindnesses even now,* he thought, remembering that no matter what happened in the hours and days ahead, *there is one who sticks closer to me than a brother.*

Leaning back and relishing the fragrance, he stared into the fire before him and thought of those who would not be at this perhaps last council of war, the captains that had fought and led his men so long and so well. Hood, Pickett, Early, and Anderson—now relieved of duty after having had their commands overwhelmed in key encounters by vastly larger Federal forces. Ewell—captured. Jeb, A. P. Hill, Garnett, Pender, and Stonewall—killed in action. Even Longstreet and Joe Johnston had both been throat-shot and nearly killed.

How I miss them, each and every one of them, he thought, only to himself. Then, catching a whiff of the pines all round him, he pondered what General Washington would do in this situation. *He suffered defeats as well,* Lee remembered, *many times, through the years. He retained his composure, continued to lead his men, and leaned on God for direction. But what if the roles had been reversed at Yorktown? What if it had been him whom war surrounded and outgunned? What if he had faced surrender or certain death, leaving his people without the leadership of himself and his men?*

The cold hard truth struck him that not even General Washington had faced an enemy who warred on innocent women and children, who warred on an entire people. *Indeed has Christendom ever in history witnessed such feats by its own?* he wondered.

Faint chortles of laughter drifting to his ears from soldiers somewhere upbreeze reminded him, *And a scrap of raw bacon or a handful of uncooked corn intended for the horses has become a good day's portion of food for our boys.* He recalled overhearing two Texas soldiers arguing over who had secured the best rations for himself; one had a fistful of roots, the other a wad of swollen twigs.

Images of Mary and the girls brightened his thoughts. He now knew that they and the Mess had survived, by the barest of margins. He thanked God every time he thought of it. *So is it best for them that I go down, sword in hand, with these brave men around me, to demonstrate our last utter defiance of the tyranny that has come upon us, even when we have no chance of victory? Or can I do better for them to negotiate the most honorable terms possible, then return to them, and be there and serve them for my remaining days?*

When put in such terms, his course, as often it did when he considered the various sides of an issue, seemed apparent. *But, like Stonewall and Jeb, I do not wish to survive the fall of my country,* he thought, looking toward the starry sky, emotion now filling him. *That United States flag in no way represents what it formerly did. How can I ever stand to again pay homage to it? And how could I ever exhort, by word and deed, my countrymen to do so?*

Oh, how ready he was right then to unsheathe his sword and lead his men against those people! *Would Thou permit it, God? Would it glorify Thee, sir?* He bowed his head, perspiration on his brow and tears filling his eyes. He knew the answers even as he asked the questions. *It would be for my glory, my desire, and not Thine, to effect such a course of action. Such would indeed be no selfless sacrifice. How strange indeed that events should transpire so that placing one's life on the altar of his country would become a selfish act.*

I know that the true sacrifice lies in the suffering and devotion ahead, the long years of suffering that await us under the heel of godless men with hearts consumed by evil. How much we all will be needed to help one another and to encourage one another not to allow our light to be dimmed, in order that men may see our good works and glorify our Father which is in heaven.

So there it was. He would determine to preserve the lives of his remaining men—and offer his own sword to General Grant—immediately perhaps, or more likely after one final attempt at escape, if his lieutenants asked for that, which he knew they would.

But I must confess these other sentiments to no one, he thought. *I must be sturdy for them and offer an example that would help them see their way.* This, as he realized nearly his whole body ached with hurt—*Well, here comes nephew Fitz.*

Fitz and Gordon sat on a blanket before the fire. Longstreet sat puffing his pipe on a nearby log. Lee stood across the fire from them, despite the throbbing pain that remaining on his feet visited on his legs, buttocks, and hips. The council met for hours; eventually, unlike those generals who had convened among themselves the night before, every man present advocated one course of action: attack, and attack as soon as possible.

Which is perhaps why these few have risen to command, Lee thought wryly.

Fitz Lee's cavalry and Gordon's infantry would assault the Federals in their front, tonight, as soon as the Confederates could form ranks. They would attempt to open an avenue through the Federals to the food trains and an escape route beyond. Longstreet's foot soldiers would follow, protecting the rear.

"If Providence deems fit," said Lee, "a part of our army, at least, might reach the mountains of Virginia and Tennessee, and yet join Joe Johnston."

A bit later, after the commanders had gone to their business, Lee laid his head on his saddle and pulled a blanket over him to secure a bit of rest. He heard horses nearby munching the bark off trees. *We have one final chance; if we fail, it is over,* he thought. *Indeed it* must *be over.* Another thought struck him. *It is now Palm Sunday.*

One of Gordon's staff officers approached him.

"General Lee, sir, General Gordon presents his compliments and asks where he should halt his corps tomorrow night," the officer said.

Lee could not hide a smile at the assumption implicit in such a request that the Confederates would indeed break through the Federal hosts. "Yes, tell General Gordon I should be glad for him to halt just beyond the Tennessee line," he said.

CHAPTER 47

GORDON AND FITZ LEE TOOK THEIR MEN FORWARD AT 5 A.M.
Unleashing the screeching Rebel yell their adversaries knew so well and which
yet made their skin crawl, the sound one Federal said "apparently has no hint of
brain behind it," they rolled back the first Federal line and captured two guns
and a number of prisoners. The Confederates, screaming, pursued their enemy
for nearly a mile.

Eyeing the dead and wounded Federals littering the ground around him,
Gordon saw, his heart leaping for joy, *They all have spurs—their infantry are not
yet in front of us! Now our entire train—artillery, ammunition wagons, and
Longstreet guarding our rear, can pass through to the west. Then we shall race
them to a rendezvous with Joe Johnston.*

Just then a bank of early morning mist that had shrouded Gordon's view of
the field beyond, parted, and to his everlasting shock and sorrow, he observed
dark blue Federal coats forming deep ranks—on foot—as far into the distance
as his eyes could make out.

He would later learn these men constituted a portion of a thirty-thousand-
man force, just arriving after an all-night march sagaciously called by Sheridan.
They had indeed arrived just in time to put the cork into Robert E. Lee's last
bottle.

Gordon's armed infantry and Fitz Lee's cavalry between them totaled no
more than four thousand men.

◆◇ ◆◇ ◆◇

Lee sat Traveller atop a hill overlooking Appomattox Courthouse to the east.
The mist and fog obscured his view of the fight taking place on the other side of
the little village. Even as he prayed for the physical safety of his men and the souls
of all those on both sides of the battle, his heart raced with the excitement he

could not stymie that always came when his men charged forward on the attack, in hopes of helping bring about the lasting independence of his country.

He had dispatched Venable to ascertain the progress of the battle, and now, around seven o'clock, his salty old aide rode up, his face longer than the escape route from Grant was proving to be.

Venable saluted, then conveyed Gordon's report: "Tell General Lee I have fought my corps to a frazzle, and I fear I can do nothing unless I am heavily supported by Longstreet's corps."

Lee said nothing, nor did anyone else. The first bright beams of sunrise began to peek over the woods to the east, but no birds sounded in any direction.

Gordon is one of the most brilliant, audacious commanders in the history of the Army of Northern Virginia, Lee thought, a sensation of numbness tiding over him. *If anyone in the Confederacy could clear a path for us, it would be he. Pete Longstreet, with his few thousand and no horse, already stands against two entire corps in our rear.*

His eyes traveled around the group, but he saw none of them. *Even if we could have forced our way one day longer,* he admitted to himself, *it would have been with great sacrifice of life, and at its end I do not see how a surrender could have been avoided. We have no subsistence for man or horse, and it cannot be gathered in the country. The supplies ordered to us from Lynchburg cannot reach us, and our brave men, deprived of food and sleep for many days, are worn out and exhausted. It is over.*

"Then there is nothing left me but to go and see General Grant, and I would rather die a thousand deaths," he said, the fullness of his voice and the gravity of its words prompting the several officers around him to look away.

"Oh, General, what will history say of the surrender of the army in the field?" someone asked.

"Yes," Lee said, "I know they will say hard things of us. They will not understand how we were overwhelmed by numbers. But that is not the question, Colonel. The question is, is it right to surrender this army? If it is right, then I will take all the responsibility."

He sat for a moment, petting Traveller's thinning mane and thinking, *How much you need a good meal and some rest too, old fellow.* He looked across the valley and the little village before him as the sun's rays chased away the last of the morning fog.

"How easily I could be rid of this and be at rest!" he announced, the passion of his voice alarming his aides. A desperate battle seemed raging within him as he shifted in the saddle and deep color flooded his face. The men around him sat paralyzed. Finally he let out a deep long sigh and said, "But it is our duty to live. What will become of the women and children of the South if we are not here to protect them?"

●◇ ●◇ ●◇

"Sir," Marley told Sheridan upon returning from his reconnoitering of Gordon's position, "Gordon is exposed on both flanks; Longstreet, with the van of the Rebel army, is jammed up on the road behind Appomattox Courthouse and on the other side of the river."

The Irishman stood surrounded by staff and line officers. His dark eyes blazed with fire. He saw how exhausted Marley was from his work in Richmond and his haste in answering Sheridan's summons to reach the front of the Federal line as it pursued Lee. Still he trusted no man more than this quiet, one-eyed Mexican War hero in the reconnoitering of a position.

Now Marley had confirmed his suspicions; Gordon was vulnerable to encirclement—and utter destruction. Already thousands of Federal foot soldiers were advancing against the handsome Georgian's right flank; now Sheridan would lead his horse against the left flank.

"We shall soon have what remains of the Rebel army sliced in two," Sheridan said. "We shall dispose of General Gordon first, and then we shall take care of General Longstreet." *Such a day as this never has dawned on the United States army since the founding of the Republic,* he thought, breathless and barely able to comprehend the magnitude of the drama he himself would shortly bring to pass.

He swung up into the saddle and turned to his gathered subordinates, his color and his voice rising. "Now smash 'em, I tell you, smash 'em!"

●◇ ●◇ ●◇

Porter Alexander, the twenty-nine-year-old who had superceded all others, including the veteran Pendleton, to become chief of the Army of Northern Virginia artillery, arrived, unaware of Gordon's predicament or Lee's decision.

Observing that the Federals had beaten his army to its most critical of junctions, Lee asked Alexander, in his way, "What should we do today?"

Alexander, the fire in his belly stoked by his own undaunted men, harbored no ambivalence. He promised Lee the artillery would do its part in fashioning an escape route west. When Lee informed him that surrender appeared inescapable, the younger man suggested the army scatter and report to the governors of their home states. He pressed his case, gathering steam as he went, with a series of arguments: surrendering Lee's army would result in the quick capitulation of all other Confederate forces; though Lee cared nothing for his own name or glory, Alexander and many others did for him, as well as for that of the Army of Northern Virginia; finally, his men wished to prevent Lee the humiliation of being told by Grant that the terms for peace were "unconditional surrender."

"If I should take your advice, how many men do you suppose would get away?" Lee responded.

"Two thirds of us," Alexander said. "We would be like rabbits and partridges in the bushes, and they could not scatter to follow us."

"With the few thousand muskets left to me," Lee said, "two-thirds of them divided among the states, even if all could be collected, would be too small a force to accomplish anything. All could not be collected. Their homes have been overrun, and many would go to look after their families."

Lee turned to look Alexander in the eye, but gentleness permeated his words.

"Then, General, you and I as Christian men have no right to consider only how this would affect us. We must consider its effect on the country as a whole. Already it is demoralized by the four years of war. If I took your advice, the men would be without rations and under no control of officers. They would be compelled to rob and steal in order to live. They would become mere bands of marauders, and the enemy's cavalry would pursue them and overrun many sections they may never otherwise have occasion to visit. We would bring on a state of affairs it would take the country years from which to recover. And, as for myself, you young fellows might go to bushwhacking, but the only dignified course for me would be to go to General Grant and surrender myself and take the consequences of my acts."

Alexander walked away, not just persuaded, but marveling. *He has answered my suggestion from a plane so far above it,* the young artillery commander thought to himself, *that I am ashamed of having made it.*

⋯ ⋯ ⋯

Lee received Grant's latest letter as he rode with Taylor and Marshall toward the proposed 10 A.M. meeting.

The words he read were not those for which he had hoped.

"I have no authority to treat on the subject of peace; the meeting proposed for 10 A.M. today could lead to no good," Grant wrote, adding his sincere desire, however, that Lee's surrender would prevent the loss of any more life.

Lee's heart sank. *He is forcing me to ask permission to surrender my own army!* Bitterer medicine he had never had to choke down. But choke it down he would. He knew it was the only course remaining to prevent the slaughter of those few brave men still standing with him. *I have long maintained that one's great duty in life is the promotion of the happiness and welfare of others,* he thought. *With such an opportunity as this to demonstrate that principle, would I concern myself with my own name and reputation?*

Only eight thousand seven hundred soldiers in the Army of Northern Virginia still shouldered muskets; the blue hosts surrounding them numbered over eighty thousand.

He had Marshall respond with a request for an interview concerning Grant's proposal of surrender of the day before.

Now, however, events began to move beyond Lee's ability to control them. When Marshall delivered his commander's response, he learned that not only was Grant nowhere near that section of the line, but that a full-scale attack was about to be launched from the east, or rear, by Gettysburg victor Meade, and too soon for Grant to be reached to countermand the order!

Lee sent Marshall with another letter, requesting a suspension of hostilities until he could meet with Grant. But the Federals advanced for their attack, warning Lee to withdraw his forces. He stood near Traveller and his flag of truce as the blue waves came into view. *I must avoid another battle,* he thought, *else those few still remaining will be killed or,* he shuddered at the thought, *marched off to Federal prisons.* The horror of such institutions as Camp Douglas, Camp Chase, and Johnson's Island had gained lasting infamy across the South, even as Libby, Belle Isle, and Andersonville had in the North.

The front of the Northern column was now within three hundred yards . . . then two. Still Lee stood his ground, with only Taylor—who had voiced his loathing of the very mention of the word *surrender* and was ready to go down fighting—his military secretary Marshall, and A. P. Hill's tough, hard-riding old courier George Tucker, who carried the flag of truce. They stood in full view of thousands of oncoming bluecoats.

A final warning came from the Federals, now no more than one hundred yards away, that they could not stop the attack and that Lee had better pull back forthwith. He refused to move, fearful that another battle would render only harsher surrender terms for his men—and wanting desperately to go down as a soldier, much preferring death in battle to a long slow humiliating death in peace.

At last, void of any fear for his own physical safety, yet realizing that to stay would exhibit his selfish old self rearing its pesky head again, he climbed into the saddle, reined Traveller around, and headed to the rear.

Meanwhile, four miles west, facing the Confederate front, Marley feared Sheridan might burst a blood vessel in his neck or forehead.

"D— them!" the Federal cavalry commander screamed at word that a ceasefire had been called by the Confederates and that negotiations might be in the works between Grant and Lee. "I wish they had held out an hour longer, and I would have whipped the h— out of 'em. I've got 'em; I've got 'em like that!" he raged, shaking his fist.

He now had Gordon nearly surrounded, and Marley, whom he retained nearby in case he needed his special services, could see his cavalry chief's anxiety mount as the prospect of his final, conclusive attack came into question.

"By G—, we'll smash 'em up anyhow, white flag or no white flag," Sheridan thundered, his voice rising. "We're going to finish this war right here and now, boys!"

Marley could not help but marvel at "Little Phil's" ceaseless energy and drive. *He is a hard, hotheaded, unforgiving little pagan,* Marley conceded, *but he appears just the sort of man called for to finally end this rebellion once and for all.*

Just then, one of Sheridan's aides rode up bearing a direct order for him from his superior, General Ord: Do not attack yet.

"Custer!" Sheridan screeched. "Get over to Gordon and inform him that I demand the immediate and unconditional surrender of all the troops under his command—now go!"

Marley watched the twenty-five-year-old brigadier's mien light up. *And there is only one Custer,* he thought. He remembered their first meeting with

Kilpatrick and Dahlgren at the George Washington Birthday Ball as he observed the golden locks that hung down to the man's shoulders, which themselves sported the largest straps he had ever seen on a soldier, the short blue sack coat, and the bright red scarf tied in front by an enormous gold pin with the humble words, "George A. Custer, Major General." He also noted the shiny spurs of pure gold mounting the boy general wore and how he handled the middling horse he rode as well as ever Marley had seen any mount handled. *That, and his ability to lead men and act decisively under fire are the essence of George Custer, and why he is here today,* Marley thought.

"Go with him, Marley," Sheridan barked. Marley knew Sheridan would issue no such order to flesh out Custer's entourage; Marley was to keep his keen eye open and bring back his appraisal of whatever he saw. *I believe this man's concerted objective today is to bring Robert E. Lee in as his own personal prisoner, after slaughtering every man still under his command in the Army of Northern Virginia,* Marley thought as he rode on.

Soon they reached Gordon, who scoffed that he would indeed not surrender his command.

"General Sheridan directs me to say, General," Custer said, "if there is any hesitation about your surrender, that he has you surrounded and can annihilate your command in an hour."

Gordon sat his saddle erect as always. The rumble of guns and the rattle of musketry resounded from the front, where the remnants of his infantry, now perhaps sixteen hundred men, still blazed away, their own numbers gradually being annihilated. He appeared no more overawed by Custer than he would have been by a gnat lighting on his wrist as he rocked on his front porch after supper on a Georgia evening.

"I guess I'm as aware of my state as General Sheridan is," Gordon said. "General Lee has requested a truce, and I have nothing to add to that. You may tell General Sheridan that if he persists fighting in the presence of a flag of truce, further bloodshed will be on his hands and not mine."

Custer sat his mount, seeming to Marley to wonder if that was all. Then he asked Gordon if he might see Longstreet. Granted that permission, he rode forward with Marley.

Within minutes Sheridan himself appeared, spoiling for a fight and headed for Gordon's position.

"That's a splendid uniform that little man's wearing, sir," one of Gordon's aides opined.

"Fancy horse too, sir," said another. "Believe that animal's been eatin' a sight better than any of us."

"I say his uniform's prettier than his horse," said the first aide.

Gordon had allowed himself the rare luxury of a smile at this banter until he spied out of the corner of his eye a scope-equipped Austrian rifle trained on Sheridan by a veteran Confederate sharpshooter.

"Put down that long gun, mister!" Gordon shouted. "That man isn't worth the lives of every soldier in my command."

"Let him stay on his own side," the feebleminded marksman blurted, launching one of the largest wads of tobacco spittle Gordon had ever seen.

"General," Sheridan said as he rode up mere seconds later, even as Gordon heaved a sigh of relief at the narrow aversion of catastrophe, "unless you offer the immediate and unconditional surrender of all troops under your command, I will destroy that command, which I now surround."

Gordon, noting with little admiration that Sheridan's "mounted escort" approximated the size of one of Fitz Lee's entire regiments, repeated the information about the truce and the ongoing negotiations between Grant and Lee.

"I've no knowledge of any such truce or negotiations," Sheridan snapped, shifting in his seat, his eyes darting in all directions. "I am here for your surrender, sir."

Gordon finally settled him down when he produced a written order from Lee on the matter. After Gordon agreed to Sheridan's suggestion to a ceasefire on their section of the front until they received word on the proposed conference, the two generals sat down to talk.

"We have met before, I believe, at Winchester and at Cedar Creek in the Valley," Sheridan opened.

"I was there," Gordon said.

"I had the pleasure of receiving some artillery from your government, consigned to me through your commander, General Early."

Gordon considered these comments, and what he perceived as the hint of cockiness in Sheridan's black eyes.

"That is true," the Georgian said, "and I have this morning received from your government artillery consigned to me through General Sheridan."

⊷ ⊷ ⊷

Arriving at Longstreet's "headquarters," Custer dismounted, marched straightway to the hulking Dutchman, and announced, loud enough for the Confederate's staff to hear, "I have come to demand your instant surrender. We are in position to crush you, and unless you surrender at once, we will destroy you."

Amenities evidently disposed of, Longstreet shot back, "By what authority do you come into our lines? General Lee is in communication with General Grant. We certainly will not recognize any subordinate."

"Oh, Sheridan and I are independent of Grant today, and we will destroy you if you don't surrender at once," Custer said.

Now Longstreet's staff witnessed such an explosion from their chief as they never had before and never would again. His eyes narrowing, he looked down at the shorter, more slender Custer and shouted, "I suppose you know no better and have violated the decencies of military procedure because you know no better, but it will not save you if you do so again. Now go and act as you and Sheridan choose, and I will teach you a lesson you won't forget! Now go!"

Feeling the eyes of his entire audience trained on him—along with not a few smirks and smiles—Custer wheeled and returned to his horse.

So far this day was proving to be one of the more remarkable ones of Wayne Marley's thirty-five years. It grew more so when, out of the reach of Longstreet's wrath, Custer asked for a Confederate guard to escort him back to the Federal lines. Eyeing a stand of splendid, if somewhat svelte, thoroughbreds ridden by Southern officers, Custer pointed to one and announced, "I should like to have that mount."

The officer to whom it belonged retorted, "Well, it's not for sale—or plunder." The Confederate eyed Custer's spurs. "I've wondered for some time if an old friend of mine is still alive. He wore the prettiest pair of gold-mounted spurs you ever saw. His father received them in the Mexican War. They belonged to Santa Anna himself. My friend is Frank Huger, and you're wearing his spurs, General."

Custer blushed crimson, again feeling the heat of several pairs of eyes burning in on him. He stammered, "Why, as it happens, I am safeguarding them for Huger; we were friends at West Point."

Colonel Frank Huger would die many years later, never having succeeded in retrieving his spurs from Custer, who insisted on continuing to protect them from harm until his own death.

Lee rode to the rear of his army as the Federals closed in from all sides. All morning long he had averted one final, devastating attack, which he knew would slaughter the brave remnants of his men, while attempting to secure an appointment with Grant. But Grant had not replied, and now Meade had huge masses of Federals wheeling into place for an all-out assault on Longstreet and the rear of the Confederate column.

Along that front Cole Culpeper, woozy from loss of blood and lack of food, stepped off a rickety caisson, drawn by one skin-and-bones horse—its former partner in harness had dropped dead of a stroke the day before—which had served as his ambulance back to the fighting from the field "hospital" where a surgeon had stitched up his saber wound.

The rail-thin graybacks he stepped among stared at his blood-caked shirt.

Culpeper stared back at them. Four of them were black, one of these wearing gray, one butternut, one blue, and one a patchwork effort that Culpeper adjudged to be mostly—*Well, he's got more blood on him than any other particular color.*

"I been shot, stabbed, slashed, shot, and shot some more by them vermin," Culpeper announced. "I aim to murder every Yankee I ever meet if'n I can get away with it, if I live a hundred years and peace is made today. There won't be no peace never between me and any Yankee if I can kill him without too great a risk."

A couple of soldiers nodded their bearded faces in assent, then turned toward where the Northern hosts formed before them, bugles blaring, drums pounding, steel clanging and jangling, their ranks stretching as wide and deep as the Confederates' sight could make out.

They killed Emma, they killed Lukey Boy, they killed Ethan, they killed Jake and Chief, and now, they better come and kill me, for I'll never be finished with the b———, he thought, the chance to kill more Yankees animating his whole body with energy and purpose.

He had lost the Spencer at Sayler's Creek and now carried an Enfield to complement the two revolvers he still had. As he began to load it, he saw, out of the corner of his eye—*It can't be,* he thought, with a shudder.

"Ethan?" he asked in a quavering voice.

"It's Felton, Cole," came the reply of a man with an empty sleeve.

Culpeper uttered an oath, then said, "For a second there, I thought something was way out o' kilter, 'cause I sure don't expect to see your brother where I'm a'headin'."

This brought a round of chuckles from the men nearby, which somehow transitioned into a shrieking Rebel yell that rippled clear down the pathetically outnumbered Confederate line.

"Just what in blazes are you doin' back in the war, Felton McDowell, with one arm and no sense?" Culpeper asked when the noise subsided a full sixty seconds later.

"Well, light me up, Cole Culpeper. I expect, even with one arm absent without leave, I look a sight better than you," Felton retorted. "Ole A. P. Hill had his bloody shirt, and I reckon you got yours."

This brought more laughter, except from a terrified youngster on the other side of Culpeper. "How old're you, boy?" he asked the youth.

"S-sixteen, sir."

"Ah, don't you sir me, boy," Culpeper scoffed. "You know, one o' the bravest men I ever knew was Jake Schumacher, and he wasn't no older than you."

"He weren't?" the boy asked, shaking.

"H—, no," Culpeper said, "may even have been a shade younger. Sure didn't have as steady a hand as you have there."

The boy smiled, heartened, as tears brimmed over in his eyes. "I'm all that's left."

Every man within earshot knew what he meant.

CHAPTER 48

LEE STRAIGHTENED EVEN HIGHER THAN USUAL ON TRAVELLER AS he watched through his field glasses the ocean of Federals tide forward. *Here they come,* he thought. The Scripture of another warrior, another king, came to him; the Scripture so worn in his Bible that he had to tape a strip of paper over it, on which he had rewritten its words: "Blessed be the LORD my strength, which teacheth my hands to war, and my fingers to fight." And the verse following: "My goodness, and my fortress; my high tower, and my deliverer; my shield, and he in whom I trust."

"Sir," Taylor called.

A rider bearing a white flag emerged from the direction of the Federal lines. He carried a message that Meade had agreed to an hour-long truce, with the hope all could be sorted out between Lee and Grant.

Over the next hour the two commanders exchanged more notes. With each moment that passed, Lee wondered if the next might be the one that saw the Federals renounce their truce, that saw "unconditional surrender" Grant change his terms or revoke altogether his offer to meet.

Finally, around a quarter past noon, Lee received word that Grant wished to meet him at a location of the Virginian's choosing.

"You needn't go yourself, General," said Marshall.

But Lee remembered how dishonorable his father had considered Lord Cornwallis's failure to surrender his army in person to General Washington at Yorktown. He would go himself, with Marshall, Tucker as truce flag bearer, the Federal courier, and his adjutant general, Taylor.

"Begging the General's pardon," Taylor said, his face grimmer than Lee had ever seen it. "I—would prefer not to be a party to—that is, sir, I have ridden twice through the enemy's lines today and would prefer not to do so again."

Lee saw the tears and nodded his assent, remembering Alexander and thinking, *I fear in some ways, this will be more painful for the young men—the young people altogether.* He did not know nephew Fitz, unwilling to surrender, had already escaped the Federal net with the remaining Confederate cavalry.

And so he rode to Appomattox Courthouse to meet U. S. Grant and perhaps his greatest of all dates with history.

When Grant reached the outskirts of the little village, he found Sheridan awaiting him with his retinue, which included Marley.

After friendly salutations, Sheridan informed Grant, "This is a trick, sir. We can whip them and end this business in five minutes if you'll let us go in."

"Yes, General," chimed another officer.

"Yes, by going in and forcing an absolute surrender of the enemy by capture," said another.

Marley could not suppress a smile. *He never gives up,* the Pennsylvanian thought. *How I would dread going to war against him.*

But Grant would have none of it. In fact that Midwesterner, who still remembered with awe Captain Robert E. Lee's legendary exploits at the Pedregal and elsewhere in the Mexican War, found himself falling under the same spell that befell most men when he came face-to-face with Lee at Wilmer McLean's two-story, white-columned brick house. In spite of himself, Grant felt awkward and nervous, the more so appearing in mud-spattered boots and kit, shaking hands and looking up at the barrel-chested Virginian in his best dress uniform (Grant did not know all the others burned in a wagon torched at Sayler's Creek), knee-high Wellingtons, and stainless-steel sword.

But the fire-breathingest Southron who ever sang "Dixie" could not fault Ulysses Grant for his prosecution of the surrender of the Army of Northern Virginia. He indeed allowed Lee's entire army to go their way, requiring only that they surrender their weapons and pledge not to take up further arms until properly exchanged—which would be never. In addition he allowed Lee's officers to retain their side arms, private mounts, and baggage, and all cavalry and artillerymen to keep their privately owned horses. And he provided twenty-five thousand rations to the Army of Northern Virginia, from the supply, unbeknownst to Lee, that Sheridan had scuppered from the trains the night before.

Cordial to one another throughout the two-hour conference, Grant and Lee treated the event in a manner that, had it been emulated later by the civil leaders of the United States, might have carved the name Appomattox into the history of the world as the ending of one war, rather than the beginning of another.

What actions in the McLean house followed the departure of Lee and Grant impressed Marley as an ominous portent. Led by Sheridan, and like vultures picking a bloody carcass, the Federals proceeded to conduct their own auction—of every item of value in Wilmer McLean's home, down to candlesticks and photographs.

Sheridan carted away, for twenty dollars in gold, the table at which Grant had sat. But it was Lee's table that led the Federal sweepstakes, garnering forty dollars.

McLean refused all Federal "offers," along with the gold coin handed him, which he slung to the floor. Seeing this the Federals began flinging their coin to the floor themselves as they selected items for "purchase."

Watching all this with a couple of other nonplussed Federal officers, Marley wondered why his comrades even bothered paying the coin to a man from whom they were stealing.

"Well, what would history say of us if we just took what we wanted without paying for it?" Captain Michael Sheridan, "Little Phil's" brother, hooted upon divining the thoughts behind Marley's screwed-up expression.

For sheer breathtaking creative genius and the ability to rationalize it in its extremity, the Yankee mercantile spirit puts all the European pretenders to shame, Marley thought, amazed.

Lee rode Traveller away, through sprawling ranks of hushed, awed Federals. Now, having ridden down the ridge that overlooked Appomattox, then through the river valley to the east, he neared his own lines. *There they are,* he thought, seeing the tattered cadavers that nothing on earth could force to quit him. *But how can I face them?* Feeling sobs rise in his throat, he thought to sidle on through to the apple orchard, where he would wait for delivery of the twenty-five thousand rations, and say nothing to them.

But they would have none of it. They tided toward him, heaving a hearty cheer, those few still with hats raising them. Then they knew something was wrong. Lee stared straight ahead, as if stricken. The gentle acknowledgments and greetings—the brown eyes ever signaling acceptance and manly respect—that he offered them without fail, whether riding behind the lines, along the trenches, or even when at the battle front itself, attempting himself to lead them into the fight . . . they did not now see these things.

But how they remembered them! Whether the high-ranking Tidewater aristocrat to whom Lee evidenced no arrogance, insecurity, or professional or personal jealousy; or the lowliest backwoodsman, mountain man, or hard-scrabble slaveless sharecropper—they all shared one sentiment: *He is* for *me.*

Stonewall said, "General Lee is a phenomenon. He is the only man whom I would be willing to follow blindfolded."

Even those who despised God, loved Lee that he wanted God, and what he saw as all the blessings and benefits of God, for them.

"General, is it true, are we surrendered?"

He felt as though he had been stabbed. He choked out a brief explanation before impending sobs forced him to rasp only, "Good-bye," and ride on.

Then they swarmed around him, by the dozens, by the hundreds.

"General, we'll fight 'em yet."

"General, say the word, and we'll go in and fight 'em yet!"

They touched his uniform, his boots, his spurs, his stirrups, or if they couldn't reach those, Traveller's bridle and reins, his mane and neck and flanks. Some managed to hold one or the other of Lee's small, gauntleted hands and look up at him, tears streaming down their leathery bearded faces.

"Blow, Gabriel, blow!" one towering scarecrow cried, slamming his musket into the red clay ground as men around him, according to their perspective on the matter, variously wept, cursed, groused, or sat on the ground in stunned stu-por. "My G— let him blow. I am ready to die!"

Wayne Marley had wanted to meet Lee; indeed, Sheridan had posted him in the apple orchard to help supervise the delivery of the provisions. *But he is worn and heartworn too,* Marley realized. *And I am nothing to him—nothing good, anyway.*

Standing with a cluster of other Federal officers, all of the rest of whom pro-ceeded to introduce themselves to Lee during the course of the day, he observed the old Virginian from a short distance away. Marley's old cynicism at the ready, he watched for the hint of aristocratic snobbery on the one hand, or self-serving sanguinity on the other. What he saw was a tired, hurting old man whose whole world had just collapsed down around his ears, meeting each and every one of dozens of Federals, most of them strangers to him, with courtesy and dignity.

Such was not the case with every Confederate Marley witnessed. One Federal colonel made a speech about "brotherhood" to graybacks hungering for their rations, then expressed his desire to General and former Governor Wise for good relations between the two sides. Wise, his "war paint" only slightly faded, announced, "There is a rancor in our hearts which you little dream of. We hate you, sir."

Toward sundown, after Lee finished his myriad of duties with officers North and South, Marley saw him take his leave of the Confederates and Federals alike who buzzed around him as so many bees around the hive, and mount Traveller to return to his tent, a mile or so to the east of the apple orchard.

Word of his appearance swept through the ranks like Jeb Stuart and Turner Ashby and the Black Horse Cavalry of old sweeping down on a doomed foe. Marley watched as they poured out of the woods, in from the surrounding fields, off the rutted roads by the hundreds. Generals on their private thoroughbreds down to barefoot privates formed ranks half a dozen deep on both sides of the road Lee traversed, the entire way to his tent.

No victorious Roman general walked a more honored train of triumph than did the defeated commander of the Army of Northern Virginia.

Whatever section of the line he neared would raise an ear-rattling cheer. Then Marley noticed something amiss. As soon as a new group would cheer and raise their hats or hands in affection, they would halt, their voices would quaver, and the sound would turn to . . . *Are they attempting the Rebel yell?* he wondered, leaning forward on his own mount. *No, not that.* He squinted through the gathering shadows and discerned that Lee's high bronzed cheekbones ran wet with tears. *He is crying . . . and so are they.*

All of them. Those that were not when they came to the road were when they saw his tears. Marley saw them bawling as they stood before Lee, as they sat atop their horses, as they threw themselves on the ground.

Remembering his many years in Lexington, his first reaction was, *They have always been a more demonstrative people than we; that attribute, and not just chains, bonds them to the blacks. Most of them, after all, are Celts.*

"I love you just as well as ever, General Lee!" one screamed.

Then Marley thought on. *No, it is not just that.* Thunderstruck, he exclaimed, aloud, "*He* is their cause." Then, to himself, as if in revelation, *He is their father.*

Coleman Culpeper, whose father had not cared enough to bestow upon him a middle name, shouldered his way through the wailing, eddying throng, tearing open his saber wound, and managed to reach up and grab Lee's hand.

Hoarse with grief and blind with tears, he bellowed, "Farewell, General Lee, sir. I wish for your sake and mine that every d—— Yankee on earth was sunk ten miles in h—!"

Thus Culpeper gave verbal expression to the emotion of love.

Among those who poured forth wrenching tears was the Rev. Dr. Brigadier General William Nelson Pendleton, the only soldier below the rank of major general in either army appointed by his commander as one of the commissioners to carry out the details of surrender.

Still guilt-ridden at having proposed to Lee, in an hour of overwhelming pressure, that he surrender his army, still suspecting he had never quite attained the level of competency in artillery command that Lee had believed he would, Pendleton knew now how the apostle Peter had felt when, despite betraying Christ, he was, alone among the disciples, summoned by name by the resurrected Lord to meet him in Galilee to continue their grand work.

Like Peter, Pendleton wept many bitter tears. And he knew that he would henceforth be a better preacher and a better shepherd.

He could not express to his boys what filled his heart, so he commissioned Marshall to draft the last General Order of the war to aid him in that task. Lee liked the letter, except for one paragraph he felt harsh and hurtful rather than conciliatory, and too likely to inflame Confederate bitterness toward the North. He removed that paragraph.

> After four years of arduous service marked by unsurpassed
> courage and fortitude, the Army of Northern Virginia has been
> compelled to yield to overwhelming numbers and resources. . . .
> feeling that valor and devotion could accomplish nothing that
> could compensate for the loss that must have attended the con-
> tinuance of the contest, I determined to avoid the useless sacrifice

of those whose past services have endeared them to their countrymen.

. . . I earnestly pray that a merciful God will extend to you his blessing and protection.

With an unceasing admiration of your constancy and devotion to your country, and a grateful remembrance of your kind and generous consideration for myself, I bid you all an affectionate farewell.

R. E. Lee
General

Twenty-eight black veterans in the Army of Northern Virginia refused all offers from the startled Federals for freedom and insisted on surrendering with Lee and being paroled.

There is a true glory and a true honor; the glory of duty done—the honor of the integrity of principle, Lee thought as he rode Traveller away from the camp of the Army of Northern Virginia for the last time. Taylor, Marshall, and Venable accompanied him, though a proffered escort of twenty-five Federal cavalry was courteously refused.

In the North a seething, roiling giant kicked at the traces fixed on it by Lincoln and his desire to move forward in union and order. Thaddeus Stevens, Charles Sumner, Ben Butler, George Julian, Wendell Phillips, Zach Chandler, Ben Wade, and a host of other Republicans, in some cases little more "radical" than Lincoln himself but without the constraints of executive leadership of a vast and diverse nation, considered military victory but the preparing of the way for the salvation of the nation *yet* to come.

But with Lincoln and his hosts and the nation flush with smashing battlefield triumph, the "Radicals" needed a spark to fire the public torch that would illumine a great new revolutionary experiment, an experiment outlined by no less than Karl Marx and Friedrich Engels in their *Communist Manifesto.*

Indeed the events of what history would call the American *Iliad* were well observed by Marx. Though he would cheer the goals of Stevens and his cohorts, he would say concerning 1861–65, "The war between the North and the South is a tariff war. The war is further, not for any principle, does not touch the question of slavery, and in fact turns on the Northern lust for sovereignty."

Others would say the fire from such a torch would consume what was left of those majestic designs envisioned and proposed by George Washington and the founders for a morally upright, self-disciplined people.

Ben Wade cared not a whit what others, or anyone, thought. Already he suspected machinations were afoot between Lincoln and certain factions in the South, certain of the familiar old fire-eating factions, to return the seceded states to the dominion of those who had led them out of the Union—while maintaining the disfranchisement of blacks!

That continued status for blacks in the North seemed not to hold as keen a concern for Wade and his fellow Radicals.

"If the Negroes could contrive to slay one half of their oppressors in the South, the other half would hold them in the highest regard and no doubt treat them with justice," Wade stormed to a group of Republican colleagues, repeating the words Marley had witnessed a year before.

From violent insurrection he turned to news that Lincoln would allow the Virginia legislature to reconvene and begin the work of rebuilding that ruined state and that a Richmond newspaper had actually printed an address from certain of those men to the people of the Old Dominion.

"There has been much talk of the assassination of Lincoln," Wade roared, "that if he authorized the approval of the appearance of that address in that paper . . . by G—, the sooner he is assassinated the better!"

Those words found the unlikeliest of allies in John Wilkes Booth.

On the very day Lee returned to the Mess, Booth's mind was awash in thoughts and musings. Would Lincoln's security be as lax as usual? Booth had learned from John Ford, whose theater Lincoln would attend that night for a performance of *Our American Cousin,* that neither Grant nor Stanton—with their more imposing retinues of guards—would join Lincoln as earlier planned.

Their wives refused to socialize with Lincoln's astrology-studying, seance-frequenting wife, Mary, who had publicly humiliated both women with her insults of them.

Ah, that is good, that is very good, Booth thought. He felt confident he could carry out his portion of the plan. But what of his supporting collaborators, those assigned to kill Vice President Andrew Johnson, Secretary of War Stanton, Secretary of State Seward, and the others most responsible for perpetrating one of history's most obscene wars against the true heirs of the Founding Fathers' vision, the folk of the South?

I have done all I can do, he thought as he made his way toward the theater. *They are men, and they must play the man and carry forth their assignments.* After the plot to capture Lincoln without harming him proved impossible to effect before the war wound down, the Confederate government quit the process, and Booth was on his own, forced to cobble together such organization as he could for his own, more sanguinary mission.

Then another, more sobering thought returned to him. How often he had spurned the counsel of others to protect his magnificent voice by warming it up as he should, by taking lessons he could well afford so that he might better control and cultivate it, and by giving it periods of rest.

So now the doctors all said the same thing: that voice, the wonder of its generation, was ruined. Oh, the people did not yet know; they attributed his occasional raspy sound, and his recent habit of cutting short, then eliminating, long engagements, to a pesky cold or bronchial infection. But a few of the more discerning critics, especially the poisoned pens in New York, Boston, and Philadelphia, but even some in the South, had begun to suspect something more serious.

His mind drifted back to some of those Northern cities, and how brutish and cruel they had been toward him in his early appearances when he erred onstage. Those in the "City of Brotherly Love" had actually booed him offstage—more than once!

Most horrible of all, they once screeched with laughter at him.

He recalled how different were Southern audiences in Richmond and elsewhere. From the start his impassioned sense of melodrama seemed to resonate with them. *No jaded sophistication for them,* he thought.

More than anything else, even as he captured their hearts, they captured his by their compassionate sense of forbearance toward him when he stumbled. His blunders, rather than sparking contempt and ridicule, seemed actually to elicit in Southerners a shared sense of pain and embarrassment.

When one evening in Richmond his lack of preparation produced a humiliating onstage mistake, he held his breath a count, awaiting their derision. When instead they remained silent, then applauded him all the louder at his finishing flourish, he began to love them as much as the heart of a vain egocentric was capable.

Still, as the Ford Theater doorman smiled in recognition and admiration while letting Booth pass, hardly anyone besides the actor himself knew that his career, so recently on the ascent like a blazing comet shooting toward the heavens, had already peaked. Never would lasting immortality and legend, the prospect of which had first drawn him to the stage, be his.

Never, that is, unless he were the man to kill Abraham Lincoln. *What a glorious opportunity there is for a man to immortalize himself by killing Lincoln,* Booth had long thought.

But something else propelled him up the stairs toward the balcony as the audience roared its approval at the frequent impromptu references to the president by Laura Keene and the other actors.

Caesar crossed his Rubicon, and Lincoln his Potomac, and thus two tyrants killed forever two glorious republics, he thought, making his way to a seat of his own as patron after patron's face lit up in gleeful recognition of the handsome and famed Wilkes Booth. *So shall the laws of history and the rules of nature alike pronounce judgment on the both of them.*

Soon he stepped through a bright yellow door leading to the narrow corridor behind Lincoln's box. He steeled himself with remembrance of Yankee depredations against the South, especially the Dahlgren raid and papers—which had born in him the willingness to translate his beliefs into actions. *Such vandals!* he thought, *such barbarians to war on women and children, even an entire helpless city; and him—him!—the enabler of it all.*

Then, as Booth had suspected, he stood alone at the door to the presidential box. An empty chair sat nearby. *The absent bodyguard,* the actor knew, having just seen the man filling a balcony seat, the play holding him in rapt attention. Booth took a deep breath and reminded himself, *I strike for my country and that alone, a country that groans beneath this tyranny and prays for this end. Ah, such a deliverance, such a supreme triumph for the South shall be this act!*

He entered the box, stepped without interference to Lincoln, placed the pistol to the president's head and fired, hurtled down to the stage, with a now-broken ankle shouted, *"Sic Semper Tyranis!"*—Death to all tyrants—fled across it and out of the building, leapt onto a waiting horse, and galloped into the night—all in the space of thirty seconds.

Rather than achieving deliverance or triumph for anyone except the Radical Republicans, Booth's violence, as violence with its multiple breakings of biblical commandments is wont to do, set in motion a staggering and largely irremediable chain of events that would in the end accomplish nearly everything he had sought to prevent.

"By the gods, there will be no trouble *now* in running the government," Wade crowed as the Congressional Joint Committee on the Conduct of the War, which he chaired, met with new President Andrew Johnson.

That man had just announced, "Treason must be made infamous, and traitors must be impoverished."

Robert E. Lee, who during those days would have begged for death rather than be called forth to again lead a people, indeed would be so called.

Little did he suspect that the nature of that calling would prove more necessary to the very survival of his people than had his leadership of them in war.

Independence, he and those people would learn, was but a rosy romantic fancy when one squinted down the hard dark vista of extinction.

PART THREE

"Blessed are the peacemakers: for they shall be
called the children of God."
—Matthew 5:9

CHAPTER 49

HE PLANNED TO SLIP UNDETECTED INTO RICHMOND AND HOME to the Mess. *I hope they are all not too angry with me,* he thought as he, Taylor, Marshall, two rickety little wagons, and now Rooney rode toward his brother Carter's house, where they would spend their third night on the road—Lee in the yard—on the way to Richmond. *How I wish I could have done better for them, for all of them.*

Across the road Lee spotted a boy of no more than seventeen leaving a crimson trail in the wake of his gimping bare feet. The lad mustered a brave countenance to salute, but his eyes betrayed physical agony.

Lee stopped Traveller. "Son," he said, "how far have you traveled in this manner?"

Stunned that General Robert E. Lee had stopped to speak to him, the boy did not at first know what to say. Finally he stammered, "Had a Yank mule bolted on me, sir. Couple of miles back."

"Colonel Taylor," Lee said, turning to that man, "do you think we have room in my office for this brave defender of Virginia?"

Taylor smiled and glanced at Lee's "office"—a captured little Federal ambulance, splintered by shot, and crammed with the belongings of other officers more than with Lee's meager headquarters materials.

"Why, yes, sir," Taylor said, stepping down to clear a spot for the boy.

Lee turned to the bleeding youth, saluted, and said, "My boy, you are too badly off for the long journey ahead of you. My brother Carter lives just up the road, and I'd gauge he wears about the same size shoes you do. We will find you a pair, but then you must go home and help me rebuild our Virginia. Will you do that, son?"

For the rest of his long life, many years of which were spent wearing a judge's robes in a Virginia courtroom, the boy would thank the Lord he did not burst into tears before General Lee when the urge seemed so overwhelming.

ᴏ◈ ᴏ◈ ᴏ◈

"But why did you not accomplish your own escape prior to the surrender, when it was still possible for you to do so?" a neighbor of Carter's asked Lee over breakfast.

The question embarrassed the general, and he remained silent. The man pressed him, however, so finally he answered, "How could I leave those brave men who never failed me in all our years together to their own bloody fate, while I attempted to effect a better one for myself?"

They passed scores of his old soldiers along the way, tattered, emaciated, barefoot, often limping, often ill, often maimed. Without fail the men saluted him or raised their hat or hand in the old way, or even called to him. But it seemed to start with the little girls, the brown-headed one and the tawny-haired one. *Why, her hair is the same color as Jeb's beard,* he thought. They appeared in the road not far after Carter's place, lurking behind their frayed little calico aprons and their scarlet blushes, and almost forgetting the bouquets of daffodils and hyacinths they bore him.

He had been able to choke out no more than "Hello, men" or "God bless you, good men" at the sight of his soldiers. But at the sight of these girls, perhaps in their tenth year, he climbed off Traveller, stifling a grimace at the spasm in his lower back, removed his hat, and bowed.

"It is indeed an honor, fair maidens," he said, in the manner of a man from Westmoreland County, but not one consigned in youth to a station one rung above genteel poverty, West Point his only avenue to a college education.

But they could only giggle, turn away, and begin to run, almost forgetting to hand him their offerings.

From there, word just seemed to move along ahead of them on the road. By the time he reached the James south of Richmond, the women of that part of the country had presented more food before Lee than he had seen since the lines were drawn 'round Petersburg.

And soldiers, even a few blacks, were beginning to tag along.

He tried to greet all but to look no one in the eye too long for fear he would burst into tears for the feelings boiling up inside him. When he first saw the ruins of Richmond, it took a concerted effort for him not to break down.

How much we have before us, he thought. *The country is utterly destroyed. The trains and their tracks are all torn up; the stores are shuttered, and there is nothing to place on their shelves if they weren't. The banks are closed; there is no mail, no gas, no public transportation, no transportation hardly of any sort. The whites are broke, the men dead or maimed, the slaves turned loose onto the open road by the thousands with no fields to work and no one with any money to pay them if there were, for our scrip is now utterly worthless.*

And how long will I be here to help? My heart, my chest . . . this old body is going fast . . . and an indictment for treason may already be awaiting me at the Mess. The Mess, he thought, hurrying Traveller a bit . . . *Mary, Wiggie, Life, Daughter, all of them . . . I must live and live long for them.*

Our only human hope is that President Lincoln, to resume peace and order in the land, will restore our states and our people with a gentle hand. Maybe then we may rebuild without being torn down even more as the Radicals in the North would like.

He rode past block after block of charred rubble, hardly a wall of any structure even as high as his eye level. Still the train of support behind him grew, faster now actually, as he traversed the center of the city.

"You are now escorted by Confederate soldiers, Federal soldiers, children, dogs, the people themselves," Taylor said to him, "and this is where I should turn off."

Lee paused Traveller and stared at the young man who had served him so long and well, who had alone done the work for which less formidable generals employed whole staffs. "Thank you, Walter," he said at last, only the second time he had ever used his aide's Christian name.

Tears welled up in Taylor's eyes. He accepted Lee's extended hand, but could not speak. All the petty vanities and fatigue-laden spats, all the anger-reddened faces, quickly nodding heads, and savage moods were forgotten as though they never existed. He offered a faint smile, his chin quivering, and tugged the reins to turn his horse away.

"Walter," Lee said, over the din of a cheer for him that had rippled through the burgeoning crowd, including Federal soldiers, "tell our returned soldiers they must all set to work. And if they cannot do what they prefer, do what they can. Virginia wants all their aid, all their support, and the presence of all her sons to sustain and recuperate her. They must therefore put themselves in a position to take part in her government, and not to be deterred by obstacles in their way. There is much to be done which only they can do."

Taylor, shaking with emotion, could only nod, lift his hand in a farewell salute, and go.

A good boy, Lee thought for a moment watching after him. *How merciful of God to have permitted him to survive. For he has been a leader, and he must be a leader now.*

Then the white-headed general was turning onto Franklin Street, and hundreds covered the porches, the sidewalks, the street clear to the next block. *Surely they are not all waiting for me,* he thought. And between them and the scores now following him, such a roar, such a Rebel yell, such an utterance went up as Richmond had never seen or would again.

As he rode up to three-story, red-bricked 707 Franklin Street, he saw only blackened chimneys rising from the heaps on both sides of the street—right up to where the Mess stood, unvanquished. His gratitude to God for this, coupled with his feelings for those who swarmed around him, hailing him, thanking him, touching his legs, his boots, and Traveller, compelled in him such deep emotions that scarlet washed over his face. His head began its quick little noddings, usually restricted to his "savage moods," as his aides had come to term them.

But he did not feel savage now. A grizzled Confederate soldier grabbed Traveller's bridle and reins while Lee dismounted. He made his way through the crowd, which opened for him like the Red Sea parting for Moses.

Someone held open the waist-high iron gate for him. Then he was climbing the stone steps, reaching the little portico, and nodding respectfully to the awe-inspired young Federal trooper posted there for the family's protection. He turned back toward the assembly, removed his hat, and bowed once more.

Then he was in the house, and though he saw Agnes and Mildred first, it was Custis to whom his eyes and his first hug went. *Thank you, God,* he thought, gratitude sweeping over him. Then he leaned over and hugged Mary as long and as firmly as he dared, kissing her still-soft lips. She felt his hot tears against her cheeks and thanked God that the man who had been her hero since she was a little girl still loved her. In fact he held her so long she nearly lost her breath, but she giggled instead!

As he hugged them each in turn—Agnes, Mildred, Mary Custis—he thought, *I am indeed more fortunate, and more undeserving, than any man in all of God's great creation; how insignificant indeed is our most fervent thanksgiving that the most high, the Lord of hosts, the great ruler of the universe, is also so kind and merciful.*

He uttered silent thanks that he could even entrust Rob's life—and eternal destiny—to a wise, overruling, and divine Providence.

●◇ ●◇ ●◇

Lee needed sleep and rest as much as he needed his family. He would wish for more when the announcement arrived before he even had opportunity to lie down: Abraham Lincoln had died a few hours earlier, of a gunshot wound to the head inflicted the night before at Ford's Theater in Washington.

A hush fell over the gathered family. Agnes noted that her mother offered no words, no change of expression, no reaction at all. Custis's face turned grave, and her father's pale.

After the extraordinary moment passed, Lee shook his head, and sounding like a weary crusader having returned at last from a bloody, unsuccessful quest, he said, "It is a crime previously unknown to this country, and one that must be deprecated by every American."

Seconds more passed before Mary said, "Let us come to supper."

The family held to their previously agreed upon arrangement and withstood the temptation to pepper Lee with questions. The toll taken on him by the war was evidenced in his lined face, his reserved actions, and his paucity of words.

Lee himself noted with foreboding, now at this meal and in the days ahead, how the female countenances around him grew hard as stone at the sight of a Federal, or even the mention of them or their acts or anything about them.

The exception to this was the royal treatment Mary modeled to whomever stood guard on the portico of the Mess.

The day after Lee's return, the family learned that upon word of Lincoln's death, gangs of Federal troops all over the city tracked down every ex-Confederate soldier they could find, in order to beat them senseless.

That night at the supper table, the conversation turned back to the ancestral family home.

"Mama, if we are able to return to old Arlington, what will you do about all the Yankee graves now there?" Mildred asked.

Mary spread a coating of butter, gleaned from a firkin left anonymously one night at their front door, across a slice of stale bread.

"My dear," she said, raising the food to her mouth in a quivering, gnarled hand, "I would smooth them off and plant my flowers."

Legions of Richmond residents and others who had fled to the city went to churches all days and hours of the week for solace, prayer, and meditation. Or they stayed in their homes, or wandered the streets—though, especially at night, the latter no longer proved the safest of endeavors. Then many of them from all of these groups would go to the only other place they knew to go—the Mess.

One afternoon a cluster of Northern "dignitaries" and their "lady friends" ordered their barouche stopped in front of 707 Franklin. A throng of smelly, bearded Confederate veterans sat on the sidewalk just outside the iron fence.

"Tell us, sir," one frock-coated sharper in a stovepipe hat that seemed half as tall as the man himself, addressed a soldier, "did ever you meet him—in person?"

A nearby soldier who had ridden courier for Lee looked up and said, "I did."

The Northerner's eyes widened. "What—what manner of man was—is—he?"

"Our leader," the soldier said. "Our leader then and our leader still."

A few days later, with several other members of their extended family now staying at the Mess, including the family of Lee's brother Smith, Agnes and Mildred scouted for food and other supplies among the stores and markets now open for business.

As Agnes stepped around mounds of rubble, she felt the still-greasy Richmond air on her skin. *Oh, how long must I continue to wash away these daily reminders of our conquest,* she fretted. *Of our shame.*

The sisters noted with disdain that opportunists come down from the North operated more than a few of the establishments.

"They have destroyed our city, our country, all we have," Mildred whispered, vitriol dripping from her words, "and now they have the gall to move in where our people were and take what little money we have for their own pockets!"

Just then she caught sight of the United States flag fluttering in the May breeze against the blue sky. Her face grew hard and grim, and she spat, "Behold their filthy rag."

Agnes said nothing to this, or to the guttural grunt that followed it. She was trying to follow Papa's example and be more charitable, more loving—not to hate.

"Well, hel-lo, ladies."

The sisters looked up to see two Federal soldiers, about the same age as they, both aware they cut dashing figures with their scrubbed handsome faces, clean blue uniforms, and accouterments.

Agnes nodded politely, but Mildred glared at them.

Unfazed, one of the soldiers said, "Might we have the honor of escorting you beautiful ladies as you make your way about your tasks?"

Stunned, Agnes and Mildred's jaws dropped open.

They have stolen old Arlington, Agnes thought, *nearly killed Rooney, brought about poor Charlotte's demise, destroyed the White House, captured Custis, perhaps killed Rob, and hanged—*

For the first time in her life, if she had been able, she would have taken the life of another. Instead she grabbed Mildred by the arm as her younger sister was about to spout something and made her way home as quickly as she could.

I am not like Papa, she fretted as she heard the Federals clucking behind her. *I don't think I can ever be like Papa.*

Within a few weeks Lee saw enough to fear that much more trouble awaited Virginia. He determined that Richmond was not the place where he wanted his family to face it. For instance, U.S. General Henry Halleck announced the Federals would prevent, by force of arms if necessary, any wedding unless the bride, groom, and minister swore the oath of allegiance to the Yankee government.

"We want to prevent the propagation of legitimate Rebels," Halleck laughed.

Crowds continued to mill about outside the Mess; Lee felt a virtual prisoner in his rented home. Unlike most men in the South, he retained some financial resources from stock owned in Northern companies but not enough to support living in Richmond.

Mary's continued physical deterioration posed his greatest anxiety. The summer heat and humidity had already begun their viselike grip.

"I am looking for some little quiet house in the woods, where I can procure shelter and my daily bread if permitted by the victor," he wrote his former staff stalwart Armistead Long, whose neuralgia now virtually incapacitated him.

He would accept the Federal invitation to apply for a pardon, though each day that dawned brought with it silent expectation of Federal troops arriving at the front door with an indictment for treason.

With the identification of the pro-Southern Wilkes Booth as Lincoln's murderer, now caught and killed himself, several other Confederate sympathizers arrested as conspirators, and the Radicals in Congress casting suspicion toward Davis and his government, a seething rage toward the South clutched much of the United States.

And already our people are crushed, Lee thought, peeking through upstairs curtains at the crowds outside. *Worse, a general bitterness seems to have gripped them.* The realization chilled him that, *it exists even in my own house.* As fury built in the North, being fomented, and seeking expression, he realized he and other Southern leaders must steer the people away from self-destructive paths.

He took pen and paper and urged President Davis, on the run from pursuing Federals somewhere south, in a letter: "A partisan war may be continued, and hostilities protracted, causing individual suffering and the devastation of the country, but I see no prospect by that means of achieving a separate independence. To save useless effusion of blood, I would recommend measures be taken for the suspension of hostilities and the restoration of peace."

More than one of his prayers were answered when Rob showed up at the Mess one day in mid-May. Then a letter arrived from a family friend, inviting the Lees to use a two-story, four-bedroom cottage named Derwent.

"Quiet and in the country, just like you wanted, Papa," Mildred said as they walked down the front steps of the Mess one twilight. Derwent promised cool woods, abundant fresh vegetables, and only a fifty-mile canal ride for Mama up the James by packet boat. "I do so like our nightly walking ritual, Papa," Mildred chirped.

"Ah, but does it not cut into your novel-reading sessions?" Lee asked.

Even in the gathering shadows, she spotted the glint in his eyes.

"Papa! I know, I should be reading histories and the classics, not my foolish romances," she said, giggling, even as she thought, but as my own life possesses no such luxury, where else am I to find it? "Papa," she advanced, eager for a new topic, "who were those shy soldiers that called on you after supper?"

"Why, they were two of our brave mountain men," Lee said.

"What did they want, Papa?"

"Well," Lee said, himself now a tad sheepish, "they came for sixty others of their neighbors, who they said were around the corner and shy about entering a private home in their reduced state of hygiene and clothing. But, well . . ."

"What, Papa, what did they want?"

"They wished for me to come home to the mountains with them, where they own land, and live among them, that they might work for me and guard me from my foes."

Mildred pondered this.

"But Papa, why did they leave carrying almost all of your remaining clothes?"

At this Lee felt a knot take hold in his throat; he was glad to spot the house he sought of one of his former generals. A moment later he knocked on the front door of the darkened home. Soon the door opened, and a smooth-shaven young man stood there, holding a lighted candle.

"Why, Channing Smith," Lee exclaimed, a smile spreading across his face.

Blood kin of Virginia Governor "Extra Billy" Smith, partisan guerilla in the ranks of the now-legendary Mosby, and one of the most daring cavalry scouts in the entire Confederacy, he ushered Lee and Mildred inside, where they exchanged salutations.

"As you know, sir," Smith said, his voice low for fear of Yankee eaves-droppers, "Mosby's Rangers have not surrendered. And well, sir, I bear a message from General Mosby himself, a message that is a question: What should the Rangers do, sir? Should they surrender or fight on?"

Lee considered the question as candlelight danced off the young man's honest features. "Give my regards to General Mosby, and tell him that I am under parole and cannot, for that reason, give him any advice."

Smith's discomfort with this answer was palpable. *The boy is seeking to know something more,* Lee recognized. A few seconds passed before Smith spoke again.

"But, General—what must I do?"

"Channing, go home," Lee said, "all you boys who fought with me. Help to build up the shattered fortunes of our old state."

"Yes, sir," Smith said, his voice an elegiac blend of relief and sorrow.

"They all come to you, Papa," Mildred said a few moments later back on Franklin Street as they neared the Mess. "Generals, congressmen, pastors, privates, and corporals—they all come to you wanting to know what to do next." Seeing him start to protest, she continued, "No, Papa, I have watched it for weeks and weeks now. They seek direction from you. And when will you ever find time to respond to all those who have written? The mails are not even running, yet we have bagsful of letters dropped at our door by folks on foot, on horse—even those people from the North." He sensed something come over her. "Oh—those people!"

"Oh, my dear little Mildred," he said, putting his arm around her slender shoulders, stung by such venom in the tone of his youngest child. "We must not harbor such hurtful feelings toward others. We must pray for them and put our energies into helping those in need."

"I know, Papa," Mildred said, shrugging, "but—"

The commotion came from the street right out front of the Mess. In the bright moonlight Lee recognized three or four normally well-mannered boys from the neighborhood. They had someone on the ground, beating him. "You dirty, filthy Yankee!" one screamed.

"No!" Lee shouted, running for the first time Mildred could remember since long before the war. "Boys, no," he said, pulling one of them off the pile by his shirt. The others looked up, then scrambled away from their victim.

"Shame on you," he said, "attacking an innocent little boy that has never done harm to anyone. If you are Virginia gentlemen, you will be kind to all, especially strangers, and that includes Northerners."

"Come, little fellow," Lee said, helping the tiny boy up from the ground, dusting him off, and noting his bleeding nose. "Let us go inside and get you some buttermilk. You other boys, go home now, where you should already be."

●◇ ●◇ ●◇

The next day Lee received word the Federals had indeed indicted him for treason, an offense punishable by death.

CHAPTER 50

IN WASHINGTON GATHERED THE POLITIANS, AND WHEN COMPARED, Grant, Sherman, and Sheridan would appear allies of Lee. They had had many enemies with which to contend. But the Grand Army of the Republic subdued their Southern foes. The actions of Wilkes Booth dispatched the potency of their Northern conservative Democrat adversaries. And now their own energy, ambition, and ingenuity would prostrate opponents within the Republican Party to which they belonged.

They had those attributes and one greater. He was a sickly, never-married, club-footed seventy-three-year-old attorney and congressman from Lancaster, Pennsylvania. The proclaimed sentiments of one of the greatest barristers of the generation that "His mind was a howling wilderness, so far as his sense of his obligation to God was concerned" would have garnered wide assent even among his allies. So would his hometown newspaper's declaration that "He had been all his life a scoffer at religion and a reviler of sacred things."

Rather, he thrived on the prospects of a different sort of societal transformation. History would call it radical and him Radical, but as Thaddeus Stevens doffed his black wig and retired to his chambers for the evening with his live-in mulatto "housekeeper" Lydia Smith, his vision for the United States seemed to him quite natural. After all, was it not the white Southern traitors and butchers of the nation's bravest men who no longer deserved a voice in the American body politic, whether at the voting box or elsewhere? Was it not the black freedman of the South who now merited that privilege—even if the Northern public would not allow it in Steven's own section?

Ah, yes, the winds of change are aloft, he thought as he nestled in with his companion, *and aren't they blowing in this direction, as well as toward confiscating those d—— Southern landowners' properties and distributing them to our loyal freedmen? And certainly the winds are blowing in the direction of the perpetual, legally ordinanced dominance of the loyal party of the Union, the Republican.*

496

Abraham Lincoln had been the most powerful man in America, and now Thaddeus Stevens, who had hated him, was. Presidential cabinet members and leaders of Congress would be mere lackeys for this man who knew his time had at long last come.

Even now, Secretary of War Edwin Stanton, a Democrat serving in the administration of Stevens's archenemy, President Andrew Johnson, as he had Lincoln before him, and Buchanan before that, was arranging the process by which Lee's indictment would result in his hanging. At the same time, erstwhile Army of the James commander and soon-to-be Massachusetts congressman, then governor, Benjamin Butler was *warning* a deathly ill Johnson against anything short of a death sentence for Lee.

Stevens reminded himself to arrange a meeting in Washington with that young war hero and officer of Sheridan's, who so impressed Ben Wade a few months before in Philadelphia, the next time he came to town. *Yes, we will need every good man we can get as the real war begins,* Stevens thought. *That Morley or Miley, or whatever his name is, comes from good stock, good abolitionist stock. Led the charge up Chapultepec Hill with that slaver and religious fanatic "Stonewall" Jackson too, they say. And most importantly, he comes from a Pennsylvania congressional district whose representative will retire next year.*

Yes, with men like that, and our Wades and Phillipses, I will see that Davis and Lee receive their just bloody reward, and I will dispossess those other thousands, who participated in the rebellion, of every foot of ground they pretend to own, he thought, smiling as he partook of his lover.

It was June 26, Lee's last Sunday at Saint Paul's Episcopal Church. He would leave on Wednesday for Derwent. With Agnes's help he lifted Mary up out of her rolling chair and began to assist her up the stone steps of the majestic edifice. Out of the corner of his eye, he noticed one of Richmond's most respected young leaders step out of a mule-drawn carriage, scrape a used quid of tobacco from his mouth, and flick it into the street directly fronting the church, all the while imagining himself not to have been observed.

So disgusted was Lee that he thought to speak to the man, but Mary, in that way wives have, detected his mood and laid a gentle hand on his arm. He looked down at her. He said nothing, but she read his face like he would have read one of old Jed Hotchkiss's maps.

"Chewing is particularly obnoxious to you, I know," she said. She also knew he had never tolerated the gambling attendant to card playing and horse racing, and had long since stopped drinking any type of alcoholic spirits, or even serving them, so difficult did he believe their temperate use and so titanic the human carnage he had seen wrought by them, by all these practices.

The heat and humidity rendered the coat and shirt covering his back a soggy mass.

"Oh, how miserable, even for this time of year, even for Richmond," Mildred said as the whole family reached the open front doors.

Even as the service began, a surly disposition pervaded Lee in the stifling sanctuary. Twisting his troublesome lower back as he bent to place Mary back into her chair at the top of the steps had not helped. He attempted without success to attain some degree of relief by stretching his back even more erectly than normal as Minnigerode opened the morning prayer service. Each time he attained a modicum of comfort, the call went forth to kneel for a prayer or recitation. And each time he stooped over, his back spasmed in rebellion.

His sweating continued unabated, now from the pain and general irritation as much as from the heat. *Oh, sometimes it seems as if the legions of hell themselves are arrayed against me as I attempt merely to worship my Creator,* he thought.

Lee's melancholy persisted even until Minnigerode began the liturgy for the Eucharist. When he did, a tall, dashing young black man sporting a gleaming suit of black broadcloth strode down the aisle toward the chancel rail. He showed no less purpose than if he were storming the Confederate lines at Petersburg, which in fact he had, with now a saber scar across his chest to show for it.

The cavernous sanctuary grew silent as a tomb when the man knelt at the rail, very near the altar, and cupped his hands to receive the bread Minnigerode would within minutes distribute. The man's hazel eyes glinted as he stared straight at the rector.

He seems actually to be daring our dear minister to issue him the elements, Mary thought. Anger kindled in her that this newly coined "Reconstruction" would challenge even the most sacrosanct of all the people's practices, without the least warning or the opportunity even to discuss the idea.

The many hundreds gathered in what they assumed to be a rare remaining refuge of their old beloved world neither moved or uttered a sound. Their shock ripened into mute rage as the black man's glint matured into an insolent sneer.

Even the blacks massed in the balcony cringed, angry that this upstart would not wait his turn, after the white folks, to receive the elements. They knew that his arrogance and the anger it roused in the white folks would likely result in unpalatable consequences for at least some of them, whether they were all "free" now or not.

And then Robert E. Lee rose alone from his seat next to the left aisle in pew 111, on the tenth row of the left center downstairs section. The nerves and muscles in his lower back and hips spasmed their own protest as he walked down the aisle to the chancel rail. As Minnigerode looked speechlessly on, the old general knelt near the black man, gave that shocked communicant a respectful nod of the head, and cupped his own hands.

A tremor ran through the congregation, black and white, who then began, by ones and twos, then five and sixes, to stand and take their own place at the Lord's table.

For the first time in his life, Elijah Sledge, that tall, dashing young black man, Federal veteran of the Battle of the Crater, in no way a believer of Christ, oblivious to the sacraments of bread and wine now being provided him by Minnigerode, and with hidden scars from his days as Sam McDowell's slave far worse than his physical scar, began to wonder if perhaps Christianity was, after all, real.

CHAPTER 51

THE LEES ARRIVED AT DERWENT NEAR THE END OF JUNE. THE remote abode sat nestled in thick forest, with miles more forest and country around it. *If the unintentional leader of a war for independence who now had an indictment for treason against the United States government hanging over his head could feel removed from that predicament,* Lee thought, *it would be at Derwent.*

He remembered that the fabled "Angel of Mercy," Florence Nightingale, had grown up on an estate in the valley of the Derwent River in Derbyshire, in that grand old country from which Lee's own people had come. He thought of his recent invitation to settle on an enormous English estate with no obligation or expense but to live there. In fact offers were cascading in, most containing hefty remuneration. He tried to picture himself as president of a large insurance company or board member of a powerful bank. And some of the juiciest offers came from the North!

I will never understand those people, he thought wryly as he pondered the specter of excusing himself from a Wall Street board meeting so that he might go be hanged.

Most of the offers included one other component as well—the very public use of his name. "My name is not for sale, for any price," he had written one persistent Northern industrial giant.

Mostly he slept, visited with his family, walked the gardens, and rode Traveller along the quiet lanes, visiting farmers who could scarcely believe the real General Lee had just ambled down the road to them.

His solitude at Derwent ended when typhoid fever struck Agnes. He did not believe she had felt well since Orton's death—*No, since she spurned his offer of marriage, because she knew I would not give my permission,* he remembered. But this, *Oh, Father in heaven, can I bear it if you take her as you took our gentle Annie?* He winced as he remembered how Annie was Agnes's best friend—*she and Orton. Of course, we all loved Annie best.*

As the hours he sat at her bedside became days, and those, weeks, he read to Agnes, fed her with a spoon, placed cold compresses on her superheated forehead and rash-reddened cheeks, held her, and prayed for her.

He also sorted out his feelings related to the United States.

One night, as late evening transitioned into the early morning watches, he sat next to his unconscious Wiggie while her perspiration soaked the bed and the rasping sound of her breath filled the room. The rest of the family had long since turned in. He thought back through all the years and, with a start, realized for the first time that of all seven children Agnes possessed the gentlest spirit. Her shyness, particularly since the loss of Orton, and her position down the ranks of her siblings age-wise had suffused that fact. *But I truly do not believe this sweet child could do damage to so much as a fly,* he thought. *And of all the children, she has stuck closest to Mary and given her the most careful and constant support. Better by far for sweet Wiggie if she goes home, but how will I stand it?*

Then gloom of a different sort returned, as it had repeatedly these last weeks. *We failed . . . we failed . . . we failed,* he thought, over and over. He had prayed for consolation from God. *How can I ever offer it to others if I do not have it myself?* Now he prayed again. And he remembered one of the maxims he so often had remanded to himself and to others: "Obedience to lawful authority is the foundation of manly character."

The South sought to *restore* lawful authority, he recalled, as had their fathers against the British when Parliament acted in ways to which it was not legally entitled and George III refused to properly intervene.

But now God has decided our course on the battlefield, no matter how bitter the portion, and the United States is all we have, if we even have that now, he thought. Concern rose in him as he recalled ominous suggestions by Thaddeus Stevens and other Radical Republicans in some of Mary's Northern newspapers that the Southern states should in no way be allowed easy passage back into the Union.

How many talented and otherwise virtuous men he had seen fall short of their God-given potential because of their rebellion against lawful authority! And how often was the worst rebel the most winsome and to all outward appearances of the most stable temperament and humbly subjected to authority. Yet underneath roiled defiance—toward men, toward country, toward God.

Daubing Agnes's wet forehead, he thought, *Yes, we failed, but in the good providence of God, apparent failure often proves a blessing. Our defeat and the devastation of our country are all very sad and might be a cause of self-reproach, if we were not aware that we have humbly tried to do our duty. We may, therefore, with calm satisfaction, trust in God and leave results to Him.*

He sat for a moment as Agnes's breathing calmed, assaying whether he truly believed such words, now that the time had come to live them. Joy filled him as he realized, in a manner impossible during seasons of plenty, that he did. *I will ask for a pardon, I will practice a spirit of forbearance and forgiveness—alas, how unlike me—and I will pray for God's direction as to how I might best be used of Him to rebuild what has been ruined, most especially the people. Oh, the people . . . how downtrodden they are.*

He knew his path would not be without its detractors, from all sections. Many in the South would decry his appeal for a pardon from the United States. "For what have you done to be pardoned?" they would ask. President Davis would never ask pardon. *Yes, poor President Davis,* he thought, *now captured and by Stanton's orders wearing leg irons in a dungeon cell kept alight twenty-four hours a day, seven days a week, while three armed guards—none of them allowed to talk to him—keep him under constant observation.*

And Lee was beginning to get an idea just how poisonous the sentiment toward him was among the Radicals in the North. For those Northern newspapers Mary somehow managed to get her twisted aching fingers around told the story.

"It is bad enough to be the victims of tyranny," she said the next day over breakfast, venom dripping from each word, "but when it is wielded by such cowards and base men as Butler, Thaddeus, and Turner, it is indeed intolerable. The country that allows such scum to rule them must be fast going to destruction. We will care little if we are not involved in the crash."

Lee said nothing. His thoughts ran back to Agnes, still comatose. *My life counts nothing,* he thought, *but my Wiggie—so soon it would be for her to be called home.*

◆ ◆ ◆

Reverend General Pendleton was glad to be back in the pulpit, his own pulpit, at the Grace Episcopal Church in Lexington, and to be rector of the parish named for one of his heroes, the great English reformer Hugh Latimer. More than ever he now felt kinship with that martyr burned at the stake by another oppressive government, that of Queen "Bloody Mary."

"Be of good comfort, Master Ridley, and play the man," Latimer said to fellow bishop Nicholas Ridley as the two stood lashed back to back against the same stake as the fires were lit beneath them. "We shall this day by God's grace, light such a candle in England as I trust shall never be put out."

"And indeed it was not put out," Pendleton thundered from his pulpit as water from the night's rain leaked through the church's roof into buckets placed all around the modest sanctuary. "Even as Latimer and Ridley, and the great Protestant archbishop of Canterbury Thomas Cranmer, and Rogers and Hooper and Taylor and Bradford and hundreds of others felt the hot flames of martyrdom three centuries ago in England, even as their families and their congregations, yea, most of their country and the vast expanse of Christendom, leaned under the weight of wicked rulers loosed from the broad great scriptural creeds and traditions passed to them; even then, God and the advance of his gospel and kingdom would not—*could* not—be forestalled.

"So let us remember," he concluded, distracted by the flickering of the only lamp still resident in the dim sanctuary, "in these—" Finally the lamp gave up the ghost, as it had threatened to do the entire morning. "—dark—" When the congregation, spellbound by Pendleton's voice and message, detected the hint of a smile on his face, they took leave to let loose a round of laughter. "—days—" Now the people, joined by Pendleton, erupted in mirth.

But the next instant he was again their prophet, priest, and king in miniature, the learned voice of West Point, the accomplished mathematics professor, the eloquent champion of traditionalist low-church Episcopalian theology, boomed, "Indeed, that candle lit by Latimer and Ridley and the others has never been—will never be—vanquished. For out of their ashes was the gospel saved in England and did come the Thirty-Nine Articles, the Westminster divines and Confession of Faith, the faithful Cavaliers, Puritans, and Pilgrims, and then, when it pleased God, our beloved America."

Now Pendleton leaned forward toward his congregants and lowered his voice, even as his passion yet rose. "And in these dark, nigh hopeless days of persecution and oppression—" With this, he cast a sharp look straight at the cluster of uniformed Federal troops who had clattered in five minutes before and now stood across from him inside the door leading out of the sanctuary. "—who among *us* will stand amid the fires of devilry, debauchery, and villainy and light such a candle of faith in our land as shall never be put out?"

His eyes chanced to land on the McDowells—or what was left of them. *Perhaps those of that clan who remain will better reflect the tenets of their supposed Savior,* he earnestly hoped. *How grim they look.*

He knew his sermon had not pleased the Federals, who began their armed occupation of Lexington several weeks before. Neither had last week's. Though none of them had so much as entered his church until now, a friend warned him that last week's sermon had "given great offense to the powers that be," who found it "very inflammatory," and that he had best "mend his ways" if he wanted to escape arrest and having his pulpit given to a "loyal man."

He knew they would receive the benedictory prayer he was now reciting with even less enthusiasm. They had ordered him—warned him—to pray for the President of the United States by name, as outlined in the Protestant Episcopal Church of the U.S.A.'s *Book of Common Prayer,* as done by Episcopal churches in the South before the war, and as all Southern churches were now ordered to do.

Instead he would pray for rulers and all in authority—a petition also comprised solely of content from the prayer book—as he had done each week. He had prayed and meditated long over the issue, especially since learning of the sword of Damocles now hanging over his head. But he could not in good conscience pray for Andrew Johnson when he believed no lawful, God-ordained civil authority existed in Virginia or the South; when he rejected the notion that military power could legitimately control men's consciences or prayers; and when the Episcopal church in the Southern dioceses had formally, and lawfully, omitted that prayer book petition.

The occupying Federals exhibited no more interest in the logic of Pendleton's prayers and preaching than they did in whether or not Grace Church remained open.

He had no sooner reached the vestry room to disrobe than they burst in on him, pistols brandished.

"You are under arrest for defying the laws and Constitution of the United States of America," the officer in charge announced. "Take that d—— robe off, Parson; you can preach your treason from a cell in the guardhouse."

Pendleton drew himself up to his full, better-than-six-foot height, looked the officer in the eye, and asked, "May I ask specifically which law I am accused of breaking, Major?"

"D—— the proprieties!" the officer shouted. "You can consider this house of traitors closed till further notice."

"Sir—" Pendleton began, stung by the profanity.

"Enough, d—— you!" the officer shouted.

A throng of parishioners had formed outside the vestry room as Pendleton left it with his half-dozen soldier escort.

The minister heard the plaintive calls of his flock: "Why, why are you doing this?" "What has our pastor done?" "Do you not know that General Grant gave him amnesty?"

But it was her face, the beautiful, shattered, empty face of Rachel Anne McDowell, at the front of the group. *I believe she had wanted to see me after the service,* he thought, melancholy flooding him. *I wonder about what, poor child.*

The first person Pendleton saw as he left the building and descended the front steps of the church, flanked by his "honor guard," was Cole Culpeper. The pastor's eyebrows arched at the sight of a Lexington-area man he had never before witnessed anywhere near the grounds of Grace Episcopal Church.

Pendleton had also heard in the wind that the Yankees considered Culpeper and others who rode with him toward the end of the war outside the scope of the amnesty. The Federals had in fact placed bounties on their heads, so heinous were the acts against Northern soldiers of which they were accused.

The surprise of Pendleton, who nodded greeting toward Culpeper, was pale compared to that of the latter at the sight of half a squad of booted, spurred, and armed-to-the-teeth Federal soldiers thumping down the stone steps with the senior minister of the church in their custody.

Worse, one of the soldiers, well below medium height but wearing three sky-blue sergeant's stripes on his shoulder, shot a long suspicious stare at him. "What's your name, boy?" the sergeant asked at length, stopping the procession.

Before Culpeper could answer, the officer said, "Are you from around here?"

"Uh," Culpeper fumbled, "was a long time ago. Just on my way home now."

"Where?" the officer asked.

Culpeper had known much fear and much hate these last years. Hate would return if he wiggled out of this jam, but for now he felt fear as he had never felt it. Just before the officer spoke again, Culpeper said, "Tennessee."

"I asked you your name, boy," the sergeant growled, placing his hand on the heel of his holstered revolver.

"Schumacher, Jake Schumacher," Culpeper said.

The sergeant looked doubtful. He turned to Pendleton and asked, "You know this man, parson?"

"I've never seen him around here before," the pastor answered truthfully.

"Reb soldier?" the sergeant asked Culpeper.

"Yeah."

"It's yes, sir, to you, boy," the sergeant blared, getting in Culpeper's face. "You understand I can do any d—— thing I want to you, boy? I can throw you in the guardhouse with the parson here, I can take a whip to your hide, I can string you right up from one of these big oaks! You understand me, boy?"

The sergeant's spittle now covering Culpeper's face did not faze him, but he had never been talked to like this—and allowed the perpetrator to walk away standing up. *Boy, if I had me just Ethan or Chief here, we'd take out this whole sorry detail,* he thought wistfully.

"Course he's a grayback," the Federal officer cut in, striding to Culpeper.

As he did, Culpeper saw several people emerge from the church at the top of the steps. Among them were one-armed Felton and Rachel Anne McDowell and their mother. He caught his breath at the sight of Rachel Anne. Then the officer was tearing the buttons off the butternut cavalry jacket Culpeper had taken from a dead Confederate trooper he found on the road back from Appomattox.

"What—" Culpeper began, scared, shocked, angry, and now humiliated to have Rachel Anne see all this.

"You boys will learn it's also a hanging offense to be sporting the accouterments of a murderous armed rebellion against the Constitution of the United States," the officer said. "And you better d—— well—" Mrs. McDowell and the other ladies within earshot gasped at the profanity launched in mixed company, and on the steps of the church, no less. "—not even *think* of carrying so much as a pocket knife on you. We catch you, and we're liable to dispense justice to you with whatever weapon you're carrying."

The officer could scarcely ignore Culpeper's darkening countenance. "You have something you wish to say about that, Dutchy?" he sneered. Before Culpeper could think what to say or do next, the officer's face screwed up, and he feigned nausea. "Holy Moley, Reb—did you boys quit bathing when you seceded?"

The entire Federal contingent exploded into laughter at this. Culpeper's eyes ran to Rachel Anne, who, ashen as death, averted hers. Never in the span of his twenty-seven years of often mournful, frequently violent life had he felt less a man. As the Federals hooted and hollered, he bowed his head, turned, and slunk away.

And, more even than before, hate was kindled in the heart of mother and daughter alike, maimed and minister, boy and girl, all watching the systematic castration of the manhood that had bled and died to defend their homeland.

After delivering Pendleton to his filthy little cell, the Federal officer returned to Grace Church and padlocked every door.

Culpeper had come to church to give Rachel Anne the cross Ethan left her and to tell her that her brother's last sentiments regarded her. Now he would not—he could not—even face her. *What to do with this cross?* he fretted. He had gone by Valiant earlier, where some of the blacks told him the family had gone to church. Though he knew Sam McDowell was the hardest man in Rockbridge County on slaves, and many of them had run off, those he saw who remained seemed jovial.

"Mrs. McDowell, and especially Mr. Felton, they been much improved in their attitude since the fightin' ended," one house servant Culpeper knew before the war told him. Then he lowered his voice a notch. "Actually, it's been since Marse McDowell ain't been around, sir."

"What with white folks and black folks both broke and scrimpin' even food these days," one field hand said, "we's just plumb happy to have a place to live and food to eat."

A few slaves who had earlier escaped had actually returned to Valiant.

Culpeper had already seen a couple of posters bearing his sketched likeness and the bounty offered, dead or alive, for his capture for "high treason and violent crimes against the United States government."

The posters mentioned that he hailed from the Lexington area.

That sergeant, and probably his captain, were mighty suspicious, he thought. *They'll be figurin' me out soon, maybe already have. I can't stay around here. What's left for me here anyhow? Emma is gone, and the children; Ethan is killed; and I have been shamed before Rachel Anne and half the town. I'll go to Tennessee and find my cousins.*

Swearing an oath, he realized he could not walk all the way to Tennessee—though he knew some men who were walking there from Appomattox, and others even to Texas. But not Culpeper. *Not while there's prime Yankee horseflesh to be had,* he thought, his feelings brightening.

He walked to the farm of a cousin of Rachel Anne's that he knew, intending to leave Ethan's cross there. But the place looked to have been empty for months, so he tucked the cross into an inside pocket of the dungarees he had peeled off a dead Confederate teamster just before Appomattox. Then he proceeded to the nearby North River that skirted Lexington to the east. When he reached the river, he fashioned himself a fishing pole and made himself a good catch, wary all the while for Federals. Several times he wept, which he had gone the entire war without doing, at remembrance of the day's humiliation.

After dark he did what he always did when fighting Yankees and in need of a horse. He stole one of theirs.

The road would yet grow darker for Culpeper, and for the South. And those roads would intersect, and beget lasting infamy, in Tennessee.

Intrigue. This would call for more intrigue, Edwin Stanton thought, rubbing his white-shocked beard as he grasped for a bright ray in what had just happened. Because no one in the highest echelons of the executive branch had been around Washington as long as he had, no one, he believed, knew better than did he what the country needed from that branch and, truth be told, the other branches as well.

Few people remembered Stanton had actually come into administration service as attorney general for fellow Democrat and President James Buchanan, years before the war. He had schemed, along with Charles Sumner, William Seward, and other Republicans, against Buchanan that conservative Pennsylvanian's entire term.

When Lincoln chose him as his secretary of war, Stanton loathed that president and his Republican agenda, but he took the job—and schemed with Buchanan against Lincoln until that man's death.

His intimate intercourse with the Radicals so soon after Lincoln's death evidencing separate plots with them against Lincoln, Stanton remained as war secretary under Democratic President Johnson—and attained a new level of vigor in his intrigues against him, this time with Stevens and other Radicals.

Now, however, all his labor toward procuring a length of hemp for Jeff Davis and Robert Lee at last crowned with not just the cooperation, but the hearty support of congressional and military chiefs alike, the one man he had by design sought to circumvent had rendered the entire enterprise stillborn.

Ah, and he'll be after my own job before long, Stanton thought, rage again coiling 'round his heart, *or others will be after it for him; and then, the White House itself.*

The very specter of that seedy, cigar-reeking little lush Grant attaining to such lofty heights—*and over my loyal, trampled carcass, no less*—brought Stanton very near to retching. *His audacity to threaten resigning from the army when he knows how much we need him to implement our agenda,* he thought, *to threaten such if we arrest Bobby Lee of all people, and thus break his promise to that man of "immunity"—what humbug!*

Still, all was not lost. The House was licking its chops to get Lee in front of them. *Why, they'll have him convicting himself with the words of his own mouth,* Stanton thought, *and that traitor Davis too!*

Meanwhile, another matter pressed itself upon him, though only one voice seemed to clamor about this one.

Yes, the famed admiral has spent himself defending our honor—and protecting our place in the histories, Stanton thought, a wry grin asserting itself. *But somewhere in that warehouse full of Confederate government papers we have appropriated are the original "Dahlgren Papers," so-called. And I mean for no one—least of all that crusading old shellback—to lay eyes on them but me. We would not, after all, wish to discourage his patriotic fervor in defending the good name of our flag and country.*

CHAPTER 52

THE DAYS PASSED AND AGNES HOVERED NEAR DEATH. LEE tended her by day and Mildred by night. Mary Custis, in her thirtieth year and having lived apart from her parents most of the war, shook off Derwent like a set of loosed shackles and struck out for Staunton, north of Lexington, to visit relatives. Custis, himself thirty-three, traveled to Richmond, as well as the Virginia Military Institute in Lexington, in search of employment.

Then Lee noticed Mary's own condition growing worse. She could barely rise from her bed; when she did, a new degree of agony accompanied the least movement. Now he and Mildred worked themselves to exhaustion to care for both Agnes and Mary.

One night, as they prepared Mary for sleep, she looked up at Lee, the pain that had gnarled her unhappy body shouting at him through her eyes. And yet when she spoke, it was not of her own infirmity, as rarely it was. "The *New York Tribune* quoted Senator Zachariah Chandler as proclaiming before that august body that the only rights left to Southerners were the constitutional right to be hanged and the divine right to be d——"

How much happier we all would be if our earthly days were complete, Lee thought, his own physical pains working in consort with his fear and exhaustion over his wife and daughter's conditions and his uncertainty over the future to drive him to the brink of despair. *But let us not be weary in well-doing,* he reminded himself, *for in due season we shall reap, if we faint not. God, grant Thy frail servant the strength to tend my loved ones as they need.*

He staggered to his lonely bed and fell upon it, not even knowing when he did.

The next morning, a friend delivered letters from Rooney and Rob, with encouraging news about their first corn crop on the old family plantation over at Romancoke.

Minutes later came another friend and another letter with news from Washington. Grant had warned Stanton some weeks before that if Lee, or any Confederate officer paroled by the Federal commander, were arrested, Grant would resign his commission.

And then, even as he was thanking God for his tender mercies and loving-kindnesses, Lee heard the word perhaps more special to him than any other of his life. It was weak and quavering, but it was alive and it was for him: "Papa?"

When he walked into her little room, with its mingled scents of perspiration, medicines, fear, and love, he saw again a wan, frightened little girl sick and needing her papa. He had seen it before through the many years. *How often I have not been there to see it,* he thought, rue filling him even as tears of thanksgiving to God brimmed over in his eyes.

He held Agnes's frail body to him as tightly as he deemed safe and choked out, "How ever could I get along without my little Wiggie?"

When he heard the soft little sound that had always seemed more like the cooing of a pigeon than the giggling of his most tenderhearted child, he felt as though all were right on earth and in heaven and that if God loosed any more blessing on him, he would not be able to bear it.

Then, within a few days, a visitor arrived from Stonewall's old hometown, Lexington, across the Blue Ridge Mountains at the upper, or southernmost, end of the Shenandoah Valley.

It was Judge John Brockenbrough, who had indeed known Stonewall.

"I have been commissioned by my fellow board members at the Washington College to inform you of your unanimous election by the board on August 4 to the presidency of our school, General Lee," Brockenbrough said, for once in his life nervous to the point of stuttering. "The annual salary is fifteen hundred dollars, in addition to a house and garden, and one-fifth of student tuition fees, which are seventy-five dollars apiece."

It seemed to Marley another in a ceaseless parade of follies mothered by what Stonewall had called "the sum of all evils"—war. *But there it is,* he thought. His summons to Washington to appear as a defense witness on behalf of Camp Sumter commandant Henry Wirz, now in the Old Capitol Prison awaiting trial for war crimes against the United States.

Nearly thirteen thousand Federal soldiers had died at the South's Gehenna, Andersonville, and the Republican Congress determined that Wirz would atone for them with his own blood. Through a military tribunal handpicked by Radical leaders, rather than a civil court of the people, they also intended to establish that a conspiracy to murder Federal prisoners ran upward from Wirz through Confederate prison authorities, Secretary of War Seddon, all the way to President Jefferson Davis.

Marley was happy to speak on Wirz's behalf and even happier to get away from home for a spell. But he was not prepared for what he found in Washington. The entire city—the government, the press, the lobbyists, the galleries, the ladies of society, and those not at all of society—appeared h——bent on gaining the blood of Henry Wirz.

Not even the consul general of his native country, Switzerland, would lift a finger for him.

"But we have some formidable factors working for us," Wirz's attorney Louis Schade told Marley in the former's walnut-paneled Washington office the evening of the Pennsylvanian's arrival. "No one has established the slightest evidence of any sort of organized effort by anybody, and certainly not by Jefferson Davis or other high Confederate officials, to harm Federal prisoners. As to the charges against Captain Wirz of murder, 'in violation of the laws and customs of war,' of one hundred and fifty witnesses thus far for both sides, all but a dozen or so have sworn definitively that Wirz never murdered or killed any Union prisoners with his own hands or otherwise."

Rather than buoying Marley, this bothered him. "But . . ." he began, "what about those dozen?"

Schade waved his arm. "Good grief, man; they're worse for the government than the others." He held out one hand and proceeded to tick off one finger at a time as he recited his litany of evidence. "In nearly every case where a murder was claimed, not a semblance of a name could be offered for the victim. In the few cases where a name was given, no such person could be identified."

Schade's eyes narrowed. "I'm as loyal a Union man as they come, sir. I'm for everything Sheridan did, and Sherman too. But I'll not abide the employment of a pack of liars and opportunists to accomplish the Radicals' dirty work for them. And the way they've used the press to stir up the people!"

At this Schade pulled a bottle from a lower drawer in his desk and poured its amber contents into two crystal glasses that sat on a tray atop his credenza. Marley shook his head when Schade held one out to him.

"I'd heard as much," Schade said, nodding and pouring the contents of that glass into the other, then sipping, not gulping. He sighed and looked out his window as the sun set across the Potomac. "They're building a monument to General Washington yonder," he said. "You can see it rising from the ground." After a moment, he added, "Would that we had a Washington among us today."

"Or a Lincoln?" Marley asked, the question surprising himself as much as Schade.

"Or a Lincoln," Schade repeated, sipping again. "Now there's a question. Caesar crossed his Rubicon . . . and Abe Lincoln his Potomac."

That must be strong bourbon, Marley thought.

Indeed Schade was only beginning.

"What to think of the man," he said, "who illegally financed and continued a war without congressional approval; who usurped Congress's right to order a naval blockade; who threw fourteen thousand Northern, not Southern, citizens in jail, including the entire Maryland state legislature, when none broke an existing law; who shut down over three hundred Northern, not Southern, newspapers, thus demolishing the First Amendment rights of a free press; who ordered the arrest of the eighty-five-year-old chief justice of the Supreme Court when that man resisted the president's tyrannical revocation of the American citizens' privilege of habeus corpus; and who presided over the waging of the first total war against a civilian population in centuries by a Christian nation, altogether doing such violence to the Constitution as may never be repaired." This time Schade gulped his elixir. "And I agreed with him every step of the way."

"Is our government capable of initiating the sort of enterprise the Rebels accused us of in the Kilpatrick-Dahlgren raid?" Marley asked, preferring to address the institution rather than the man.

Schade stared at him, then rallied reinforcement to his empty glass. After gulping again, he eyed Marley. "They say you helped Stonewall Jackson fire the cannon that first made him famous in the glorious prosecution of our 'Manifest Destiny' against the Mexicans."

Marley gave a slight nod.

"And how would pious old Stonewall have assessed the United States government's potential for such acts?"

"But Admiral Dahlgren seems to have disproved the Rebel accusations," Marley said. "No less than Henry Ward Beecher has proclaimed Ulric Dahlgren a hero and a martyr from his Brooklyn pulpit."

Schade offered a wry grin before sipping some more. "They say you helped the dashing Ully too."

This time the trace of a blush tinged Marley's features as he gave another nod.

"And how would pious young Marley assess the United States government's potential for such acts?" Schade asked.

When no answer appeared forthcoming, Schade said, "Sure you don't want a slash? Came as a gift to me from one of our gallant 'political' generals, you know. He said it had been well stored these fifty years in the wine cellar of a Jackson, Mississippi merchant. Fortunately the flames of Uncle Billy's fires did not reach it, though they did destroy the building and the surrounding neighborhood above it."

Agnes's strength and vigor returned to her more grudgingly than spring returned to northern Virginia after a hard winter. But the danger had passed, and Lee could turn his thoughts to the parade of offers pouring in to Derwent.

Longstreet had gone over to the Republicans and was now in the position to offer Lee the presidency of a large corporation, and the twelve-thousand-dollar salary that accompanied it, exclusive of expansive perquisites.

A top New York publisher exhorted Lee to write his memoirs—with the promise of large earnings from a passionate audience North and South.

There were many other offers. And there was Washington College.

He did not want to go. "If those people (the Federals) will just leave me alone," he wrote Rooney, "I shall endeavor to procure some humble, but quiet, abode for your mother and sisters, where I hope they can be happy."

He would farm, he would rest his weary body and mind, and he would write the history not of the entire war but of the Army of Northern Virginia—*I want the world to know what my poor boys, with their small numbers and scant resources, succeeded in accomplishing,* he thought.

Other than writing his memoirs, he would eschew administrative paper-work like the disease that had almost killed Agnes. *How much of that would come with the presidency of Washington College!* he thought, remembrance of his similar service as superintendent at West Point from 1853 to 1856 filling him with foreboding.

Still he fretted, while churning out a torrent of missives to people great and small all over the South, who wrote him for counsel on what they should do next. He wrote as many responses as he could each day, and yet at the end of the day the stack of letters would be taller, and that with no official postal service yet in place.

He had only just written Beauregard, for instance, encouraging him to take the amnesty oath and not to emigrate from America. Washington—he whose canal stock had founded the school, Lee remembered—served as he often did as Lee's exemplar. "True patriotism sometimes requires of men to act exactly contrary, at one period," he wrote Beauregard, "to that which it does at another, and the motive which impels them—the desire to do right—is precisely the same. The circumstances which govern their actions change, and their conduct must conform to the new order of things."

Washington, he explained, had fought with the British against the French in the French and Indian War and against them with the French in the War of Independence. The sons of the South had fought for her with fire and steel; now they must fight for her with love, forgiveness, and devotion.

"I think the South requires the aid of her sons now more than at any period in her history." Lee wrote, "As you ask my purpose, I will state that I have no thought of abandoning her unless compelled to do so."

The unwelcome sense was growing over him, like green ivy up an old Arlington column, that he might be dispensing the same advice to everyone but himself.

For weeks he prayed and contemplated as he read his Scriptures and prayer book, as he walked through the hushed woods, as he and Traveller roamed the roads around Derwent.

I need the words of one who knows the God of the Word, he concluded, riding over to Albemarle County to see Rev. Joseph P. B. Wilmer, an old friend and Episcopal clergyman with a godly wisdom as profound as any man he had ever known.

As sometimes happens, the counsel rendered by another in an important discussion proved less valuable than the manner in which the exercise opened the mind of the seeker. Lee found Wilmer to be insulted, on behalf of Lee, that such an offer might be considered by the Washington College board as worthy of Lee. The clergyman recited a litany of more conspicuous schools that would welcome him with ardor as their presiding head.

"But it is this door, and not another, that Providence has opened to me," Lee said, as though now attempting to convince Wilmer of the propriety of accepting the position.

Lee wished Wilmer's thoughts not on whether the school was worthy of him, but whether, in the rector's opinion, he was qualified to lead it.

Startled at this realization, Wilmer smiled and listened to what he would tell others was one of the most eloquent treatises on the importance of Christian influence in education he had ever heard.

Arriving back at Derwent, one last nest of doubt beset Lee about his capacity to lead an institution that he was beginning to believe had far more potential than anyone, even its leaders, credited to it. *Is this how God would best have me apply the abilities and energies He has allotted to me for my little remaining time on earth?* he wondered.

Then came a letter from Pendleton. It did not mention that Grace Church remained shut down by the Federals and that the congregation was having to do its best to worship and receive the sacraments in his own simple home. It did speak to his opinions regarding Lee as the president of Washington College.

"One great reason why I hope you may judge favorably of this invitation," Pendleton wrote, "is that the destiny of our state and country depends so greatly upon the training of our young men. And now our educational institutions are so crippled that they need the very best agencies for their restoration and for the revival of high aims in the breasts of Virginian and Southern youths.

"I have thought, dear general, while thus doing an important service to the state and its people," he continued, "you might be presenting to the world in such position an example of quiet usefulness and gentle patriotism, no less impressive than the illustrious career in the field."

Lee was grateful at this point as often he had been that God, in mercy toward and understanding of his slowness, dullness, and faithlessness, had shone so bright a lamp unto his feet and light unto his path that even he could not but see where he should next walk.

CHAPTER 53

SHE HAD WRITTEN HIM TWICE ALREADY SINCE APPOMATTOX, THE first time only days after his return to Richmond. They had not conversed since the war began because she had stayed in the North with her family. But when that first letter arrived from a Federal soldier, emblazoned with "Miss Martha C. Williams," Lee's heart leapt with joy and anticipation.

The C. stood for Custis. Orphaned daughter of one of Mary's cousins, Lee could remember the day five years before he and Mary were betrothed that Martha Custis Williams—"Markie"—was born. And he could remember her ever since.

Nature had imbued her with porcelain skin and flashing dark eyes and rendered her handsome of face and form. Her father had died a hero in the Mexican War, Mary Custis had become her closest friend, and she had more or less moved herself into Arlington from 1852 until the war.

And she was Orton's sister.

"She is a lively, warm girl," Mary's mother, Mrs. Custis, proclaimed in the early 1850s, "a Christian in name and deed."

The memory would ever abide with Lee of that sunny day in 1848, the year of revolution, when he returned to Arlington from Mexico and observed her comely shape silhouetted in the front doorway abreast the wide Grecian columns. *All of the joy of this day,* he had thought, *and with it, womanhood has descended upon Markie!*

Ever after, they had written one another, wherever and however either might be. Mary had always known, and she had always known more besides.

Then came the war, and Lee had not thought it appropriate to converse across the lines. She had respected that and abided by his wishes. Only did she write with the dread news of Orton's death, and Lee did not respond.

But now the war was over.

As he opened the missive, he smiled at the remembrance of Markie, in her family's Georgetown home across the Potomac, and Mary Custis, at Arlington, hanging various colored undergarments out their windows to signal when one or the other could or could not come over to visit. *How special was the old place,* he thought.

She worried over his sorrow, suffering, and loss.

"I know you sorrow for us, but you must not be too much distressed," he wrote back. "We must be resigned to necessity and commit ourselves in adversity to the will of a merciful God as cheerfully as in prosperity. All is done for our good, and our faith must continue unshaken."

She worried over his indictment. And she wanted him to travel to Europe with her.

"It would indeed be a great gratification to me to visit Europe," he wrote, smiling wryly at his own mastery of understatement. "But there is much to detain me here, and at present at least it is my duty to remain. I will not avoid prosecution the government thinks proper to institute. I am aware of having done nothing wrong and cannot flee."

Now he chose his words carefully.

"There is nothing, my dear Markie, that I want, except to see you and nothing that you can do for me except to think of and love me. It would require you to become a fairy and turn what you touched to gold to take me to Europe, but I would not desire you to change your nature for my benefit. I prefer you remaining as you are . . ."

Then Mary was moaning from the next room, and he was rising to go to her.

Culpeper ate better on the way to Tennessee than he had since his days raiding Federal supply trains and depots back in Mosby's Confederacy. With an old smoothbore musket he had managed to secret away from Appomattox, he shot squirrels, rabbits, a turkey, even got himself a black bear when he came through the Smoky Mountains. He lingered up in the mountains for a couple weeks, eating the bear meat, hunting, and fishing.

And he slept. Several times each day and night, for hours at a time. He saw only a couple of people the whole time, and those at great distance through his stolen Yankee spyglass. The sun, water, fresh air, good food, and natural poultices healed his body, especially the saber slash from Sayler's Creek.

But as the days passed, reckonings dark as storm clouds coming across the mountains filled his mind. He had hated the Yankees for a considerable piece of time even before his humiliation at Lexington. Now he began to contemplate how he might exact vengeance on them, at least as many of them as he could. He knew he could not go back to Virginia, at least anytime soon. But he could get down and assay affairs in Tennessee. *Some day I'll go back to the Valley,* he thought, a grim anticipation seeping over him. *And I got their names, those scum what shamed me. I'll track them seven ways from h— if need be, but I'll make them sorry they ever come to our Valley.*

He traveled through the verdancy of eastern Tennessee by the back roads. He knew if he ran into Yankee soldiers he could lose his squirrel gun. If suspicion kindled in any of them, he could lose his life.

As he got farther west from the mountains, he noticed more and more homes and outbuildings where only piles of rubble and scalded chimneys remained. After a while he wondered to himself, *Where are all the people living?*

He knew where the blacks were, at least many of them. On three separate occasions, the melody of chanted songs carried to him, followed by the rumbling of many pairs of feet, then the appearance of a large throng of black men, marching somewhere, with evident purpose.

He veered clear of the first couple of groups. When he saw the third, he hid himself until the crowd had nearly passed, and asked a man in the rear where was he heading.

"Land o' milk an' honey, boss. Yankeeman say march on down this here road till we reaches land o' milk an' honey."

Then he was gone.

When Culpeper came to the little towns, he saw one thing common to every white face, no matter the age or sex. *No one smiles,* he realized. *Reckon nothin' left for 'em to smile about.*

Twice he saw white women with children—in one case, a black man, woman, and child with them—begging bread. One woman caught his eye. Tall, slender, and beautiful, she wore a teal-colored velvet dress the likes of which Culpeper had rarely seen. Except this dress was faded, stained, and as tattered as the last regimental Confederate battle flag he had seen.

She's bound to be a widder-woman. I don't think them kiddies used to be barefoot, and I don't expect her slaves was as poorly dressed as she is now, Culpeper thought, surprised at how the fall of so beautiful a Southern aristocrat to such a lowly estate disturbed rather than pleased him.

Neither he nor the woman looked the other in the eye as he rode past. *Jehoshaphat, she smells too,* he thought, ashamed for the both of them. *Ain't that the worst of it all, for a lady?*

One cool late afternoon as autumn bathed the trees in splendor, he tied his horse to a live oak enmeshed in some woods by a clear stream and settled in for the evening. Near midnight he awoke. Sleeping with his hands around the musket, he had the gun up to fire before he was fully conscious. He heard a voice drifting up to him from downstream. *No, voices,* he thought, concentrating. *No, one voice speaking and others cheering and amen-ing like a Sunday meetin'.*

He crept along the edge of the woods, his path winding with the half-moonlit stream as the voices grew louder. Soon the woods thinned to reveal a field where a sizable crowd, cheering and shouting, surrounded a man atop a small platform and flanked by a raging bonfire.

A chill breeze carried the man's words right to Culpeper.

"My friends, you'll have your rights, won't you?"

"Yes!" came the chorus.

"Shall I go back to Massachusetts and tell your brothers there that you are going to ride in the streetcars with white ladies if you please?"

"Yes!"

They's all darkies that Yankee's talkin' to, Culpeper realized with a start.

"That if you pay your money to go to the theater, you will sit where you please, in the best boxes if you like?"

"Yes! Yes!"

Now the crowd—Culpeper estimated it at a hundred or more—jumped, leaped, and danced with glee.

Culpeper winced at the nasal New England twang of the white speaker as the man reached the crescendo of his presentation. "I tell you, there is corn and wheat and flour and bacon and turkeys and chickens and wood and coal in the state—"

"Yes! Oh, yes!"

"—and the colored people will have them before they will starve!"

The ovation now grew so deafening that Culpeper, who had charged the cannon at Cemetery Ridge and faced the fury of Fort Gregg, placed his hands over his ears. Even that act could not protect his damaged eardrums, so loud was the next roar.

"What the—" Culpeper began.

"Behold, the terrible price of treason!" the white man shouted as a black man, hatless, his hands tied behind his back, was pulled out front of the crowd by two huge black men in Federal caps and tunics, the latter unbuttoned and open.

Why, Culpeper realized, *that poor boy's wearin' Confederate gray.*

"When the call to arms came," the speaker continued.

"Yes!"

"When the time came for all true patriots, black or white, to rise up—"

"Yes!"

"—and stand for justice, right—"

"Yes!"

"—and freedom—"

"Yes! Yes!"

Now the crowd shrieked its approval. For the first time Culpeper spied the glint of glass being passed among the crowd and drunk from.

"You men—you and you and you—answered that call and paid your own ransom from bondage with your own precious blood!"

So animated was the crowd now that Culpeper feared they might descend upon the man in gray or perhaps even the speaker himself.

"While some—" The speaker indicated the man in gray. "—played the traitor and shouldered arms for Massa, to keep the brave men, women, and children of Africa crushed down in the miry clay of bondage, chained to a future of rape and torture and death—"

Culpeper heard a bottle smash, then another, and another.

"Yes, but behold now—upon whom have the shackles descended?"

The Massachusetts man tried to continue, but the din grew so loud he merely made a motion toward the two soldiers. They spun the man in gray around to where his back faced the crowd, then ripped the blood-stained back of his shirt off him to reveal a crosshatched pattern of raw yawning gashes.

"Behold," the speaker screamed at the top of his lungs, "the awful wages of cowardice and *treason!*"

Now the smashing of bottles multiplied into a tinkling chorus, and the crowd surged forward. It took the two bluecoats, and a dozen more, some brandishing rifles, to spirit the whipped black Confederate away before the crowd tore him to pieces.

Another white man, tall and redheaded, wearing a frock coat buttoned to the neck that glimmered in the light of the fire, and a dark Federal officer's slouch hat, stepped up to the platform to replace the first.

"Brothers and sisters," the man called out, raising his hands for quiet. "I am the Reverend James Sinclair."

"Yes!"

"The Reverend Colonel James Sinclair."

"Lord, yes!"

"Up north, they call me the Fighting Parson!"

"Oh glory, yes!"

"The men of the Freedmen's Bureau, like my brother here from the mighty state of Massachusetts, are your best friends in the whole world," Sinclair bellowed. "And more of them, many more, shall soon arrive from the blessed North, many of them from the patriotic Union Leagues of the great cities of Philadelphia and New York, to aid you in your continuing struggle to escape the bonds of those man-stealers who thirst for your blood—yes, who thirst for your very souls."

As the crowd rose to another state of frenzy and more bottles smashed, Sinclair held forth: "Indeed the top rail shall now be the bottom, and the bottom the top. You must now visit upon your hateful masters and your wicked spoiled mistresses, the murderers of Lincoln and brave Union men black and white, the hate and vengeance they so richly deserve. For as the Bible says, an eye for an eye, and a tooth for a tooth!"

The crowd was nearly beside itself, but Sinclair raised his hands so that he might deliver the *pièce de resistance*. "For it is you, my black brothers and sisters, to whom the Freedmen's Bureau and the Union Leagues will give the brightest and shiniest new rifles—"

"Oh!"

"—some of you, only those most loyal and brave to the Union and the Republican Party, maybe even the magnificent Sharps repeaters—"

A spontaneous eruption of applause burst so violently forth at this famous name that the Fighting Parson, glancing back at the Massachusetts man, decided the hour was ripe for him to whip open his frock coat and pitch it aside, unveiling his own Federal officer's uniform, glittering with medals, stripes, and epaulets.

Now the crowd seemed to explode as a volcano. Some shouted, some sang spirituals, others began to fight, still others to march in a wave away from Culpeper, toward the nearest town.

For a moment something gave them pause. Culpeper saw a tall, self-possessed black man of perhaps twenty-five years of age and garbed in a lush dark coat of black broadcloth leap up onto the platform.

"That be Elijah Sledge," someone said.

"Yes—tell it, young Elijah!" rang someone else's voice.

"In ten years, my brothers and sisters," the black man, his voice a study in controlled articulate fury, shouted, "our biggest problem will be what to do with the white folks of the South!"

At this, the chaos resumed, now punctuated by rifle fire.

Some new-fangled church, Culpeper, who hated churches, thought, eyeing Sinclair, as he passed out cigars to the blacks. Yes, he had long hated the Federals too, but he never had anything against the darkies. He and Ethan hunted squirrels in the old days with Lylburn Downing and Big Sam Russell and some of the other slaves from around Lexington. And if it hadn't been for the McDowells' old Mammy Burgess, Emma woulda been lost after she miscarried her second child.

But now, his mind raced: *I expect the bluebellies are riling them up to take what little folks got left. Land, work, critters. And what about*—the streetcar illustration was indeed vivid—*our women?*

A shiver passed over Culpeper like none other in his life as he realized the Yankees were arming the blacks and disarming the whites, and he hurried back to the live oak. *I'm freezin' to death,* he thought, as more shivers took hold of him. He wanted to saddle and ride, but he had to get warm first. He pulled the dirty coat he'd scavenged off a dead Confederate outside of Richmond over him, along with a blanket he had scrounged and his saddle blanket.

It could not be more clear to him now if bolts of lightning had descended upon him from the heavens. *Land sakes, we got us another war a'comin'. The d—— Yankees hate us, and they're gonna kick us now we're down. And they gonna use the darkies for their dirty work, and then they're gonna give 'em what's ours, includin' our women.*

The terror that had swept over him eddied, then hardened into stone, like most of the rest of him now was. *Oh, I hate 'em,* he thought, recalling the tall lady in the tattered teal velvet dress. *I hate 'em all, and I'm gonna kill all of 'em I can before they get me.*

It is easy to see why our Stonewall so loved it, Lee thought one mid-September afternoon as he rode up the Shenandoah Valley and into Rockbridge County, home of Lexington. Off to his left rose the Blue Ridge, purple in the noonday sun. To his right the Alleghenies provided the valley's western rampart. *Such a treasury of God's riches,* he thought, inhaling the harmony of fragrances. Awe, gratitude, and thanksgiving filled his soul. *Oh God, may the words of my lips and the meditations of my heart be always acceptable in your sight.*

But the war was here too—everywhere. The scars of the Southern land studded every hill with destroyed fences, every vale with burned bridges and scorched mills. *A hundred years from now, I wonder if those who come after us will think our generation and those before us built only chimneys and no houses around them,* he lamented, wondering to how many broken dreams, terrified families, and orphaned children the silent blackened heaps bore mute testament.

He recalled Mary's parting smile for him when he told her he would ride Traveller rather than taking the train to Staunton and the stagecoach from there.

"Husband, you do not like to part even for a time from your beloved steed, your companion of so many a hard-fought battle," she told him, eschewing the slashing pain elicited by the mere cupping of his bearded chin in her crippled hand.

Others held no tenderness in their hearts for Lee.

"The bloodiest and guiltiest traitor in all the South, that man we make president of a college," said the *New York Independent.*

One letter to President Johnson cried that Satan himself would not allow Lee to open the door of the college for its new students.

A brown slouch hat covering his snowy crown, Lee wore his only suit as he rode into Lexington—his last gray Confederate uniform, all military accouterments removed.

Soon he was welcomed into the home where he would temporarily stay. Within minutes, unknowingly emulating a habit of the other great Confederate general who had educated young people in Lexington, the bloody, guilty traitor had retreated from adult company and immersed himself in play with the children of the house.

Then word spread, and, the brown slouch pirated by a precocious violet-eyed seven-year-old named Rebecca Coffey, he found himself besieged in war games and wrestling matches by giggling, squealing little people from the entire neighborhood.

Wirz's old wound, coupled with the stress and deprivations of months-long solitary confinement, made the Swiss so ill that he had to be carried into the courtroom every day of his three-month-long trial. There, as Marley now saw, he lay during the proceedings on a threadbare couch.

"Major Marley," Schade said as he moved toward the climax of his questioning before the court of the judge advocate, "as previously mentioned, you are a highly decorated, oft-wounded veteran of the United States Army in both the Mexican War and the recent War of the Rebellion. During your stay in Andersonville Prison and hospital, and in your many conversations since that time with former fellow prisoners, have you ever witnessed or heard reference to any untoward behavior by Captain Wirz toward Federal prisoners; in particular, his murder or participation in the murder of any Federal prisoner?"

Marley's face reddened as a hush fell over the court. He surveyed the gathered officers and army lawyers before he spoke.

"Rather than any such behavior, what I *have* heard tell of and have personally witnessed was a dedicated and maimed volunteer officer frustrated literally to tears and weeping over an inadequate contingent of guards and a lack of supplies, including food, for both prisoners and guards. An officer whose prisoners and guards alike were sick from the cold and rain and had no blankets or other coverings. An officer with no wagons available to him to provide fuel to the prisoners. An officer who displayed to me, once bursting into tears as he did so, duplicates of numerous requisitions and appeals for relief to our prisoners that he had issued to Confederate authorities."

"So you would not endorse the testimony offered by some in this court," Schade asked, "that while Confederate officers and guards rested comfortably and ate heartily, Captain Henry Wirz not only deprived his prisoners of all human comfort and succor but actually participated in the murder of more than one Confederate prisoner?"

"Most certainly not, sir!" Marley exclaimed, his eye blazing. "More than two hundred and fifty Rebel guards, doctors, and officers died at Camp Sumter. That is a number in nearly precise proportion to our own losses at that prison." As those declarations rent the silent room, Marley swiveled his body to face the judge advocate. "I saw murders and killings aplenty, sir; but they were all committed by our own men. Our own living skeletons cried and begged the Rebels for medicine and food—and in the same breath cursed our government for refusing to exchange them."

As he left the witness table, Marley saw no small number of fellow officers glaring at him, their faces lurid with fury. *I have called my own comrades liars, perjurers, and criminals,* he thought, finding a seat near the rear of the courtroom. *And I have defended the man the whole North considers the archcriminal of the entire rebellion, perhaps even above Davis and Lee. How can such insanity have overtaken us? For we are the ones who are in the right, who have fought for the good. How little I understand.*

Later Marley noticed a sly grin spreading across the judge advocate's face as his final witness stepped forward.

"And now, gentlemen, the government's final and most compelling witness," the judge advocate said. A smile threatened to rupture the blue-coated counselor's sweeping black mustaches. They were waxed to the extent of their considerable wingspan.

"When the oral and pictorial evidence presented by this noble Frenchman and kinsman of no less than the Marquis de Lafayette are completed," he continued, his chest swelling with confidence, "any lingering doubts as to the evil perpetrated by Captain Wirz, and perpetrated on so historic a scale, shall have dissolved into the mists of that shameful legacy which now claims the hateful and traitorous Confederate States of America."

CHAPTER 54

THE WASHINGTON COLLEGE BOARD OF TRUSTEES INTENDED FOR Lee's inauguration as president in early October to go down as one of the most memorable days in Rockbridge County history. But Lee insisted on a quiet classroom ceremony with an audience limited to students, faculty, and local ministers and community leaders. Already townspeople had taken to cheering him and Traveller upon spotting them riding. Once, when a sizable throng sent up a Rebel yell that Lee expected could be heard clear to the Blue Ridge, he noticed the grim expression painting the watching face of the Federal officer who had arrested Pendleton.

"I shall be far more useful in contributing to the rebuilding of our Virginia if I am not cooling my heels in a Federal guardhouse," Lee told Traveller later as they ambled along an autumn-leaved lane outside of town.

Following his swearing-in, Lee seated himself behind the desk in the next room, designated as his office. Sitting alone after all had left, he looked over the student roster. *How do we repair the remnants of this fine institution?* he wondered. *How do we nurture it to survival? We have fifty students; our library, science equipment, and classrooms were destroyed by those people; and the community and supporters of the school have so little money that Judge Brockenbrough, its board president, met me in a suit of clothes borrowed from several individuals.*

He stood and walked to the window, which looked out over the lush, spruce- and maple-splotched grounds that sloped down toward town. *The grounds have mostly recovered from the war,* he thought, *but amid everything else, we inherit a narrow and inflexible curriculum formed for the prewar instruction of the landed, without regard to the varied courses students propose to follow in their lives' vocations.*

The old tightness tugged at his chest, and he returned to his chair. Sighing as he donned his reading glasses, he wondered if perhaps contemplation of a college's entire curriculum by him, who had never before been a college president, might better wait another day. Before arriving at a conclusion, his door flew open without a knock or warning, and marching straight to his desk was a fierce, crimson-faced warrior in perhaps his tenth, maybe eleventh, year.

"How may I help you, son?" Lee asked, amazed.

"General Lee," the boy blurted, "my pa wore the gray and died at the Bloody Angle for our country. No man in the South served more bravely, General!" Lee nodded as the boy plowed on, his countenance continuing to darken. "But my mama, who gave away almost all our furniture for firewood for the soldiers, and all our clothes too, and nursed many a one of them that was wounded, in our very own home, well, she hails originally from New York, sir. And now my friends play me for a Yankee and call me that horrible word every day, sir."

For the first time Lee detected a darkening crescent forming under the boy's left eye.

"I've come to you, sir, to plead my case."

Lee stared at the boy. "How splendid a father you had, son."

The boy's face screwed up. "You knew my pa—sir?"

"I know him now, as I see the son he raised standing before me."

For the first time the boy's armor began to erode, a mist formed over his eyes, and his chin began to quiver.

Lee stood to his full stature. The boy looked up at him, his courage melted to fear. Indeed when he who thought his days as a general were past spoke, a fierce danger suffused his words.

"The next boy that calls you Yankee, send him to me."

None did.

◦◦ ◦◦ ◦◦

As the days passed, Lee studied the old Washington College curriculum; interviewed faculty and trustees; collected information on what schools north, south, east, and west were now teaching; and prayed for wisdom. He also determined to meet with every one of his students.

The school's enrollment was not fifty for long, but no matter how high it grew or how long any student lived, none would ever claim that after having met Lee in his office, he ever after forgot their name even once.

During the war he had formulated overall strategy, then entrusted Stonewall, Longstreet, Hill, and the others with the tactics to carry it out. Now he set about crafting the curriculum, while letting the teachers do the teaching, with only occasional discreet observation by him.

He had sent Jeb and the cavalry out to scout the enemy and terrain. Now he dispatched his trustees to comb the country for financial support.

He had also had Taylor, Marshall, Long, Venable, and the other staff officers. Now he had only himself—only himself to answer every correspondence the school received, whether from old soldiers, prospective students, parents, businessmen, philanthropic organizations, newspaper reporters, or officials from the United States government.

One day in his office, he glanced at the wicker basket filled to overflowing with mail. He would never empty it, but he would never cease trying to do so either. He would respond to every letter he could, nearly every day till the end of his life.

Near the close of October, Lee met with the full Washington board of trustees for the first time since his swearing-in. Out of that meeting was born one of the most innovative college curriculums in all of America. The school remained primarily a classical college with a Christian atmosphere; it retained the core of its rich prewar classical program. But it also called for five new professors to train the sons of the South in the work needed to rebuild the land. They included professors of mechanical and civil engineering; practical chemistry, under which metallurgy and the chemical aspects of mining fell; practical mechanics, encompassing architecture and thermodynamics with much in between; modern languages, including Spanish, which few schools offered; and English literature, composition, and modern history.

When Lee's plan unfolded, it issued forth one of America's first collegiate systems of elective courses.

As 1866 neared, with more students—many of them battle-hardened Confederate war veterans—arriving nearly every day, word began to travel across the length and breadth of the continent and beyond that Robert E. Lee appeared already to be making a new mark in the country.

Unaware of this, and missing his family, none of whom but Custis had arrived in Lexington, he wrote to Mary, "Life is indeed gliding away, and I have nothing of good to show for mine that is past. I pray I may be spared to accomplish something for the benefit of mankind and the honor of God."

●◇ ●◇ ●◇

While congressmen and senators all around him exploded in fury, along with newspapers across the United States, Thaddeus Stevens allowed himself a wry little chuckle. *They have acted, after all, exactly as I knew they would,* he thought.

The former states of the Confederacy had enacted the Black Codes, laws designed to deal with the blacks of the South, tens of thousands of whom now gamboled aimlessly, with no plan for the future. The Black Codes did grant some new rights to those of African descent. For instance they established fairer employee hiring practices and allowed blacks the right to sue in the courts on their own behalf.

However, the codes also forbade blacks to vote or marry whites or to testify in criminal cases against whites, and they instituted generally strict vagrancy laws.

The North, who had had nearly four hundred thousand of the cream of its civilization wiped out by the "Slave Power," seethed with rage.

"We tell the white men of Mississippi that men of the North will convert the state of Mississippi into a frog pond before they will allow such laws to disgrace one foot of soil in which the bones of our soldiers sleep," blazed a pencil-necked *Chicago Tribune* editorial writer who had never been within three hundred miles of a Civil War battle.

Stevens had always enjoyed the *New York Herald*'s call "for the punishment of all individuals in the South by hanging," and for Baltimore to be rendered "a heap of cinders and ashes, its inhabitants—including old men, pregnant mothers, sick children, and babies—either to be slaughtered or scattered to the winds."

Then, too, he rather liked the famous words of New York City's Reverend W. J. Sloane, who preached from the pulpit of his Third Reformed Presbyterian Church that "It was better that the six millions of white men, women, and children in the South should be slaughtered than that slavery should not be extinguished."

Yes, Stevens thought, *Sloane was that rare man who avoided neither controversy nor condemnation.* When blistered in the Northern press for promoting such an atrocity, Sloane fired back: "I affirm that it is better, far better, that every man, woman, and child in every rebel state should perish in one widespread, bloody, and indiscriminate slaughter; better that the land should be a Sahara, be as when God destroyed the Canaanites, or overthrew Sodom and Gomorrah, than that this rebellion should be successful."

Ah, but churchmen make the best haters, Stevens thought, his smile fighting its way back to the surface.

He himself had long advocated the making of the South into a desert, and all that implied. When a less-radical fellow Republican objected to the unspeakable horrors this would visit on a vast host of innocent women and children, the Pennsylvanian riposted, "That is the result of the necessary laws of war."

Moreover, Stevens's network of informants had alerted him that when the delegations from the former Confederate states arrived in Washington for the opening of the new Senate and House sessions, they would be led by a host of former Confederate leaders. *The same rapacious curs who brought the d—— war crashing down on our heads in the first place!* he thought.

But he knew that, obstinate as they were, the ex-Confederates were not his chief adversary; no more, even, than that coarse, slave-holding clod Andrew Johnson, or the weak, Wall Street lackey Lincoln before him. *It is that d—able "Constitution" we must bring down,* he thought, his blood rising.

And Stevens was not in the least angry, because he had plans already in motion that would go far beyond thwarting the slavers' pathetic designs. Indeed they would convert the Rebels' own actions into newfound opportunities for bringing the complete remaking of Southern civilization into the image of the North one step closer. Rather, the image of the North as it was to be.

Already brilliant men had drawn up a plan worth following. This plan was imbued with a philosophy quite foreign to most Americans and to the history of America. *Of course, neither the philosophy nor its authors are American,* he thought, *and so they are not infatuated by that wicked abomination, the "Constitution," that our slaver "Founding Fathers" penned in their mercenary aristocratic zeal.*

Amendments, he thought, suppressing the cough that had become an increasingly frequent, and unwelcome, visitor. *Yes, amendments, that's the thing. Building on the grand work, making the great greater, a sort of "living, breathing" document ever more perfect, ever more inspiring and helpful to mankind.* Now he had to suppress laughter. Not for the objectives embodied in such sentiments, but for the ignorance and weakness of arrogant cowardly men who must be snookered into an end he, virtually alone, had the courage and breadth of mind to envision and, more importantly, to desire.

Indeed, "Constitutional amendments" will likely be swallowed by Americans much easier than "Communist Manifesto," he realized. *Ah, but how brilliant this Marx and this Engels! The revolutions of 1848—eighteen of them on the European continent alone—have not in the end failed after all; they have only emigrated to our own shores with the many faithful bearers of their glad tidings!*

He pulled the document out of his desk. There they were, all ten planks. So audacious were they that they took the breath of no less than he, Thad Stevens, even now. Well as he knew them, it still warmed his cockles just to read over them and imagine how different and better a nation would be the United States when they were married to it.

The Manifesto called for the abolition of private property. *We will, by d—, levee such a property tax that the government will be able to withdraw property use rights from any landholder who fails to pay it,* Stevens vowed. *We will deal with this European and aristocratic notion of property ownership; we will annul—yes, even abolish—"private" property. Then let the plantation owner, the industrialist, the cattle baron say his land is his own. If he does not pay his property tax, we will quickly see who is the true landowner!*

Remembering how much of the difficult work had already been done for him, excitement began to fill Stevens.

One of the few things Lincoln managed to accomplish during his desultory reign was the establishment of this Internal Revenue Code service. We will reinforce that useful organization and impose a graduated income tax on the former citizens of the Confederacy once we have abolished forever the traitorous political entities of Virginia, South Carolina, and all the others, and replaced them with occupied military districts. He thought how splendid it would be if the new service should prove a fraction as effective at extracting revenue from American citizens as his gambling colleagues had been at emptying his own pockets around their smoke-enveloped card tables in Washington and Lancaster. *That has hurt me, as the revenue tax must hurt the American citizen.* As Stevens peeled off his jet-black wig, another thought stirred him: *Someday, by the gods, these standards will be imposed not just on the South but on the entire nation—yes, the entire world!*

Laying the damp hairpiece aside and rubbing his pate with a towel, he returned to the Manifesto.

It abolishes inheritance, he thought, directing all properties to the state, rather than the deceased's heirs; *we will impose inheritance taxes.*

It demands confiscation of the rights of rebels and immigrants; we will revoke citizenship and the very legal existence of the states.

It demands control of the banking system by the (central) state; we will have a Federal banking act.

It calls for the Federal state to control communication and transportation; we will establish a railroad commission to fulfill this aim.

The Manifesto calls for a state-controlled economy; we will put price controls into place.

It calls for a state-controlled labor; we will impose wage controls.

It demands corporatized agriculture; we will fulfill it with a Southern land redistribution act.

It demands state-controlled schooling; we will accomplish this with revenues from the already-passed Morrill Tariff Act and by establishing state colleges located on land granted to them by us.

Stevens felt the European revolutionary Mikhail Bakunin had perhaps best grasped the enormous significance of the Manifesto when he said, "In the struggle between the North and the South, all true revolutionaries are of course on the side of the North. This may well be the revolution necessary to utterly usher in the new world order."

Either we will have this new world order, Stevens vowed, *or we will have our Constitution. We will not have both.*

As he heard Lydia returning from her dead husband's grave, he recalled how the voters of Connecticut, Michigan, and Kansas had just repulsed efforts to give blacks the franchise in those states. *How far we yet have to go,* he thought, bewildered at the unwelcome remembrance that, *all in all, we have more effective Black Codes in the North than the South has attempted to give itself.*

No state in the Union could boast the galaxy of renowned warriors that Ohio could. Grant, Sherman, Sheridan, and Custer hailed from the Buckeye State.

Grant and Sherman *still* owned their own slaves, Stevens knew, and Ohio law authorized the barrel of a gun and the tip of a bayonet if necessary to keep any black out of the state who was not already there.

◦◇ ◦◇ ◦◇

Schade had already dismantled the government's attempts to establish a conspiracy against Federal prisoners headed by no less than Jefferson Davis. So Marley cringed as the towering case Wirz's defender had constructed with his myriad of witnesses, soldiers nearly to the man as possessed of intellect and articulation as they were valor, seemed now to be crashing down at the hands of the Frenchman Felix de la Baume.

He not only swore to having witnessed Wirz's direct and indirect involvement in the torture and murder of several Andersonville prisoners; he also displayed sketches apparently rendered by another prisoner. These depicted several of the scenes to which de la Baume gave testimony.

Marley could hardly miss the satisfaction painted on military and civil officials around the courtroom. Neither could the frustrated, then desperate Wirz, as he lay ashen-faced upon his seedy couch.

Then, when de la Baume's testimony seemed complete, the witness suddenly stood, thrust an accusing finger at Wirz, and raged, "By the honorable name of my great-uncle, Washington's captain, the good and great Lafayette, I accuse you, sir, of abandoning all precepts of military honor, even all concepts of human dignity and Christian compassion, to perpetrate for purposes known only to you and your superiors, one of the most heartless and brutal reigns of terror known to the annals of world history."

As Wirz's head dropped and he began to weep, de la Baume tied the knot: "May God have mercy on your wicked soul, sir, for this court must not!"

The blue-coated assemblage could scarcely conceal its glee. Someone actually uttered, "Here, here."

Marley wondered how Schade would rebound from a testimony so devastating if for no other reason than it provided everything needed for a decision against Wirz, no matter how sizable the legion who had defended him and how suspect the few who had not.

Marley need not have worried. Rather than bowed, Schade seemed kindled to righteous indignation, and his closing argument, however little heeded by the tribunal, could never have been forgotten by them.

"And so now I ask you to consider a question that will be answered—if not by this tribunal, then surely by the judgment bar of American history," the Prussian native said. He roamed the floor fronting the tribunal, every sentence launched into the musty air of the courtroom and left to hang there before his audience before settling down on them like an unwelcome pestilence. But more sentences came, and then more after that, all the while less welcome.

"Who indeed is responsible for the many lives that were lost at Andersonville—and in the other Southern prisons?" he queried. "That question has not fully been settled, but history will tell on whose heads the guilt for those sacrificed hecatombs of human beings is to be placed."

Now Schade whirled and unleashed his barrage into the face of the chief judge, mere feet away.

"It was certainly not the fault of Captain Wirz, when, in consequence of medicines having been declared contraband of war by the North, the Union prisoners died for want of the same!"

Anger rose in the breasts of many in the room, but none dared utter a peep, and Schade was far from finished.

"How often have we read during the war that ladies going South had been arrested and placed in the Old Capitol Prison by the Union authorities because some quinine or other medicine had been found concealed in their clothing?" he challenged.

Back and forth he paced, the volume of his voice and the intensity of his argument mounting with each pass past the chief judge.

"Our navy prevented the ingress of medical stores from the seaside, and our troops repeatedly destroyed drugstores and even the supplies of private physicians in the South. Indeed, the destruction of railroads and other means of transportation by which food could be supplied by the few remaining abundant districts to those without it increased the difficulties in giving sufficient food to the prisoners at Andersonville. The Confederate authorities, aware of their inability to maintain their prisoners, informed our Northern agents of the great mortality, and urgently requested that the prisoners should be exchanged, even without regard to the large surplus which the Confederates were owed on the exchange roll from former exchanges—that is, without seeking any longer for a man-for-man exchange."

He stopped pacing, but his voice escalated the more. "Our War Department, however, did not consent to an exchange. They did not want to 'exchange healthy skeletons for healthy men.'"

Finally the end came, and Schade stood looking directly into the eyes of the chief judge as he concluded.

"History is just, sirs, and as Mr. Lincoln used to say, 'We cannot escape history.' Dare not forget that puritanical hypocrisy, self-adulation, and self-glorification will not save the enemies of liberty from their just punishment."

The unanimous verdict was guilty, the sentence hanging by the neck until dead.

CHAPTER 55

MARLEY HAD ATTEMPTED WITHOUT SUCCESS TO VISIT WIRZ IN HIS solitary confinement. Then he developed a friendship with the Swiss's priest-confessor, Rev. Father Boyle. The day before Wirz's execution, Boyle told Marley to come along with him and Schade that evening to visit the doomed man.

When Marley met the clergyman and the counselor at Old Capitol Prison, he discerned a heaviness of mood in both men. He attributed it to the impending execution but soon learned more was involved.

Federal guards initially denied Marley entrance, but Boyle's protestations that Wirz had only hours to live and that Marley was a decorated veteran of the Federal army and former prisoner at Andersonville, caused them to relent.

Wirz, sitting with bowed head upon his couch, his old wound necessitating the placing of his arm in a sling, brightened upon seeing Marley.

"Kind Major Marley," he said, "I have seen your welcome and honorable face these last days at my . . . my . . . trial." The last word seemed as distasteful to spit out as a sour prune seed.

"Captain Wirz," Schade said a few moments later, "an emissary from a member of President Johnson's cabinet has come to us to offer you clemency— provided you implicate Jefferson Davis with the 'atrocities' committed at Andersonville."

Wirz's eyes, bleary and red, widened. "What is the nature of this— clemency?" he asked.

Schade glanced at Boyle and Marley before answering. "Your sentence is to be commuted. You will be released to permanent freedom."

Marley was more dumbfounded than Wirz, but he resisted the impulse to speak.

Wirz, seeming to take some vigor from the startling development, rose and crossed to peer out the tiny barred opening near the top of the solid, locked, and bolted door. The thought occurred to Marley that if the room had contained a window, Wirz might have sought to look out that.

The Swiss turned back toward the men.

"Good sirs," he said, surprising Marley with the gentleness of his tone at so overwhelming an occasion, "I have always told you that I do not know anything about Jefferson Davis. He had no connection with me as to what was done at Andersonville. And if I knew anything about him, I would not become a traitor against him, or anybody else, even to save my life."

No one said a word. It appeared to Marley that Schade and Boyle were not in the least surprised at Wirz's response.

Wirz sat, his gaze falling on the blank stone wall opposite him as he continued. "For six weary months I have been a prisoner. For six months my name has been in the mouth of everyone. By thousands I am considered a monster of cruelty, a wretch that ought not to pollute the earth any longer. Truly, when I pass in my mind over the testimony given, I sometimes almost doubt my own existence. I doubt that I am the Captain Wirz spoken of. I doubt that such a man ever lived, such as he is said to be, and I am inclined to call on the mountains to fall upon and bury me and my shame."

Now he looked up at the three Federals, and a fire lit his china blue eyes. "But oh, my friends, while I wring my hands in mute and hopeless despair, there speaks a small but unmistakable voice within me that says, 'Console yourself, you know your innocence. Fear not; if men hold you guilty, God does not, and a new life will pervade your being.' Such has been the state of my mind for weeks and months, and no punishment that human ingenuity can inflict could increase my distress."

When he divined tears in the eyes of all three men, he shook his head. "Fret not for me, good men, for life such as I am now living is no life. I breathe, sleep, eat, but it is only the mechanical functions I perform and nothing more."

No one spoke for a minute. Then Schade said, his voice cracking, "Father Boyle will remain with you this evening, Captain, but can Major Marley or I be of service to you in any way?"

Now a shiny mist glazed Wirz's eyes, and it was he who with difficulty spoke. "Pl...please help my poor family...my dear wife and children. Cruelest war has swept everything from me, and today my wife and children are beggars. My little girls—" His voice broke, and he bowed his head. Marley could not see Wirz's face, and no sound came from the man, but he could see the Swiss's body quaking with sobs.

After perhaps thirty seconds, Wirz raised his head and looked them in the eyes, his own dry as he spoke. "My life is demanded as an atonement. I am willing to give it and hope that after awhile I will be judged differently from what I am now. If anyone ought to come to the relief of my family, it is the people of the South, for whose sake I have sacrificed all."

Two hours later Captain Henry Wirz, maimed, Swiss-born soldier of the Confederate States of America, mounted the scaffold erected for his execution. When asked if he had any final words, he looked the questioner straight in the eye and said in a steady voice, "Yes, that I die innocent of the blood of all I am accused of harming."

And then he was hanged.

The Wirz trial had proven a much happier affair for Felix de la Baume than it had for the Swiss. Immediately following his pivotal testimony, and even before the verdict was rendered, de la Baume was appointed to a choice clerkship in the Department of the Interior.

For some days after, de la Baume was the toast of Washington. His accounts of Andersonville and the demon Wirz led the pages of the New York City, Philadelphia, Boston, and Chicago newspapers. He could be seen at the Willard and Wormley hotels, the restaurants of John Chamberlain, John Welcher, and Sam Ward, and all the other best establishments of Washington with all the most powerful men and all the most beautiful women.

One night, amid an entourage of government officials and delusive belle-pretenders, he swept into the majestic National Hotel, where Henry Clay had died, statesman of an earlier era, a different era, one of compromise and peaceful, if at times uncomfortable, coexistence and true Union. Seated in a corner across the hotel's cigar smoke-shrouded dining room were Marley and Kurt Schumacher, handsome, thrice-wounded, and recently promoted major of Steuben's Seventh New York Regiment of Germans. They knew one another, both from service in the Army of the Potomac and their concurrent hospitalizations after Chancellorsville. They had chanced into one another one afternoon in a corridor outside Wirz's courtroom.

"Being a Catholic, like most Germans in America, I did not agree at every turn with your Bible teaching in the hospital," Schumacher said with an articulation and absence of foreign inflection that impressed Marley. "But I must tell you that it helped preserve me from the cynicism endemic in our soldiery the last two years of the war. And it provoked me to a systematic reading of my own Bible unlike, I am ashamed to say, I had ever attempted before."

The thought cheered Marley, who of late had begun to wonder if his attempts to follow in the way of Christ had impacted anyone in the Federal army.

"And that Bible you had, from Stonewall Jackson," Schumacher said, marveling. "Such a keepsake."

Marley was about to explain that the volume had returned home to the South when Schumacher said, "Why, I know that man. The one with the blond beard. But . . . I cannot place him."

Marley's eyelids and blood pressure rose as one. "That is the Frenchman, Felix de la Baume, the government's star witness in the Wirz trial."

"Ah," Schumacher said. "But I saw none of that trial. I have seen him in some other setting."

"That is no less than his new employer, James Harlan, secretary of the Interior, seated with him," Marley said.

"You appear less than impressed with the arrangement," Schumacher said.

Marley sighed. "Let's just say the appointment occurred in surprising juxtaposition to his—key—testimony."

Schumacher nodded. "It appears more of the ways of Old Europe than the waging of war for economic and political ascendancy have crossed the Atlantic." Before Marley could unravel that, Schumacher moved on. "So where to now for Major Wayne Marley, Mexican War veteran, Virginia Military Institute graduate, and favorite scout of Little Phil Sheridan—a career in arms? The priesthood . . . er . . ."

"The pastorate?" Marley put in. "I don't know what is next. I do not feel my spiritual impact on the Union armies provides any ratification of a calling to divine service." Catching a whiff of a delectable liqueur, he added, "Nor, even, my own personal piety, or lack thereof."

Before Schumacher could further press the question, Marley turned the tables. "And what of you, war hero Major Kurt Schumacher? Have they petitioned you yet in New York to yield your life to public service?"

Schumacher blushed, something Marley had never before seen him do. "Well, actually, not in New York, but in Wisconsin."

"Oh?" Marley said.

"Germans have been pouring into Wisconsin for years," Schumacher said. "The climate and topography are more nearly that of the Germanies than any other state in the Union. I myself have four cousins now resident there. Well, three; one fell at Fort Gregg."

"I'm sorry, Kurt; I did not know."

"A brave and terrible affair, that," Schumacher said, lowering his eyes. "Our men virtually massacred the Confederate defenders, but at an unspeakably high price." He paused, then added as he looked back up. "I am told my cousin fell next to a young man—a Rebel—whose papers identified him as a Schumacher as well. I have been thinking that my grandmother's brother—an Anabaptist— went decades ago to the Shenandoah Valley of Virginia, and I have heard that he sired a godly line of ministers, doctors, teachers, and farmers, but I do not know how to go about finding out."

Both men sipped at their water as laughter erupted from the table where de la Baume sat.

"One of my other cousins is a close associate of the powerful Wisconsin Senator Carl Schurz."

"Yes, a famous man, Schurz."

"A brilliant man, and a leader in particular of the German-speaking Wisconsonites," Schumacher said. "My cousin says his entreaties to Schurz— unbeknown to me—to encourage my moving to Wisconsin and standing for public office, in order to protect and advance the interests of our fellow descendants of the German states, have been met with great enthusiasm."

"Perhaps you might have a more positive influence on our government than I did on our military," Marley said. "Our adherence to the Augustinian theory of just war did not exactly blossom after my revival to the Christian faith."

"Perhaps I might," Schumacher said cagily as the waiter placed a steaming tureen of turtle soup before each man. "And perhaps you might."

"Me?"

"Through his support of and friendship with Schurz, my cousin knows others in positions of influence and power," Schumacher said, spooning the soup into his mouth. "He has learned that no less than Thaddeus Stevens has his eye on you for a Pennsylvania congressional seat soon to be vacant."

Marley nearly dropped his spoon. "Thaddeus Stevens? But . . . I've never even seen the man. And from what I hear, he's a vulgar gaming sort who cohabits, unmarried, with a mulatto—and he's a revolutionary to boot!"

"Just the sort of man who might profit from a positive influence, yes, my friend?" Schumacher said, his blue eyes twinkling, as he spooned more soup.

"Thad Stevens is hardly—"

"And if not that," Schumacher cut in, "perhaps a positive influence could be brought to bear against him."

Marley shook his head. "I begin to suspect Prussian—"

"Saxon," Schumacher corrected.

"—Saxon intrigue is afoot," Marley said, a wry smile forcing itself out from under his gray-streaked beard.

Schumacher's eyes flickered, and his latest spoonful halted in midair, then returned to the tureen. He grabbed his linen napkin and patted the corners of his mouth, his countenance turned hard as stone.

"Well, I only jested, Kurt—"

"I do indeed know that man," Schumacher growled. "And he is no Frenchman."

"What?"

"To my everlasting shame, he, too, hails from Saxony, directly. That pretender, that impostor, is Felix Oeser, cowardly deserter from Steuben's regiment, whose brave men purchased with their blood the luxuries with which he now sates himself."

Schumacher shoved back his chair and jumped to his feet. Marley grabbed his arm.

"No, Kurt, that is not the way. There are congressmen, senators, governors, generals, and worst of all, newspaper editors seated in this room."

Schumacher glared down at him in Saxon fury.

"Go to Harlan, tomorrow," Marley said, sounding calmer than he felt. "I'll go with you if you like. Between us, I should say we've a bit of pull, eh? If need be, bring your cousin, or even Senator Schurz into the circle. Do it the right way,

Kurt. That liar will be disgraced—and your chances for the future will not be jeopardized."

The hot blue fire of Schumacher's eyes cooled a shade, and he turned toward the impostor. The oath he uttered was long, vicious, and in German, for which Marley was thankful. After several more seconds the waiter appeared with the next course.

"Is everything quite all right, sir?" he asked Schumacher.

The latter looked back at Marley, then sat. "No, but that is the way of the world. Excellent soup, sir."

Marley released an audible sigh, then fixed his own gaze on Felix Oeser. Tears filled his one eye as he remembered the letter he had written hours before to Wirz's widow and two daughters.

"Kurt," he said. "I think we had best leave. If we don't, I fear I shall murder that imposter with my own hands."

Secretary Harlan fired Oeser when several other veterans of Steuben's regiment vouchsafed Schumacher's claims the man was a deserter.

The testimony of other Andersonville prisoners disputing Oeser's oral and pictorial accounts—testimony suppressed during the trial by the Federal tribunal—began to plague the impostor. But Stanton warned against reprisals beyond dismissing Oeser from his job for fear it might confuse public opinion.

Henry Wirz had been dead eleven days by the time Felix Oeser was escorted out of his well-appointed office in the Department of the Interior.

"At last, the archfiend Swiss Wirz has stretched a Union rope, General," Stanton said to Grant as the two dined on a whole hog that had come into their possession, prepared by the still semiofficial, but burgeoning Daughters of the Grand Army of the Republic.

Grant nodded, not looking at Stanton. A squadron of chilled wine bottles graced the table, as well as a large tureen packed with sweet potato pudding and heaps of corn sticks on platters. And the women had roasted another loin, garnished with strips of side meat.

"Despite all, declaring the prisoner exchange cartel void was a rare moment of inspiration for Father Abraham," Stanton said. Noting the ambivalent expression with which Grant greeted the remark, he added, "Wise he was indeed to act as he did, as soon as I conveyed to him our intelligence that so many Union soldiers were purposing their own capture in order that they might expect either exchange home—never to reenlist—or the safety of prison as over against the risks of the battlefield."

When these insights failed to elicit any improvement in Grant's mien, Stanton called for patties and chops from the roasted loin.

"The hanging is small consolation to the widows and children of our brave thousands though," the secretary continued, shifting tack.

"Small indeed," Grant said. "Regrettable to have had to leave our brave men to face such a plight."

"But quite impossible to have exchanged healthy men for healthy skeletons, right, General?" Stanton said, reciting Grant's own words back to him as a servant laid the steaming plate of patties and chops before the secretary.

Grant eyed the lode as the charred and oily aroma of fried and roasted meat wafted through the room. Though too greasy, the ladies' supper was proving infinitely more palatable than his present company. His demeanor rose when he received his own private plate of sausages.

"Yes, quite impossible," the conquering general said, gobbling rapidly and reaching for another glass of Madeira.

CHAPTER 56

A COUPLE OF WEEKS BEFORE CHRISTMAS, LEE ROSE ONE morning at the usual time of six o'clock, shaved, washed, and brushed his teeth, read from his Bible and prayer book and prayed, then breakfasted. All these he did each morning. But this was no typical morning. Mary, Mildred, and Rob were arriving from Derwent.

Soon he and Custis were greeting their packet boat at Lexington's Kanawha Canal dock. Then he was taking them to the new family dwelling. It was a home which had seen love and loss, laughter and sorrow, hard partings and tender embraces. If the Lees had believed in ghosts, which they did not, they would have expected this white-columned, red-bricked, two-story Georgian structure with matching one-story wings to harbor a flock of them.

In a distant generation, words would be carved into an iron plate affixed to the wall next to the front door of the house:

> Here lived
> Robert Edward Lee
> Thomas Jonathan "Stonewall" Jackson
> Margaret Junkin Preston,
> "The Poetess of the Confederacy"

The legacy of the house was all but palpable as Lee showed his kin through it.

"Is it true Old Jack lived here, Papa?" Rob asked as he wheeled Mary around.

"Why, yes it is," Lee said. "His first wife, Ellie Junkin, died in childbirth before the war. Her father was Dr. George Junkin, a famous theologian of Pennsylvania and president of our college until the war broke out and he returned north." He led them to one of the single-story attachments and into a modest bedroom where lived Stonewall and Ellie.

"It is as pleasant as it is profitable to contemplate his character, to recall his patriotism, his piety, and his unselfish nature," Lee said, his voice trailing off to no more than a whisper.

All stood gazing into the room, somehow finding in it a touchstone to a past they could now barely touch. The moment passed, and Mary began to grasp how hard her husband had worked to prepare a happy and whole home for her.

"Oh, dear husband," she said as Rob wheeled her into her own room, "it is completely finished."

"One of our one-armed veterans crafted your furniture by hand," Lee said. "Another daughter of Dr. Junkin's who lived under this roof, and whom you will all likely meet, drew up the plans for each piece."

"Who is that, Papa?" Mildred asked.

"Why, that is Margaret Junkin Preston, Precious Life," Lee said, "Wife of Colonel Preston, cofounder of the VMI."

"The 'Poetess of the Confederacy'?" Rob asked, marveling.

"*Beechenbrook*?" Mildred asked.

"That is she," Lee said.

Mary cast a whimsical glance toward Mildred. "See, Life, pious, puritanical, Scots-Irish Lexington may not prove to be as dreary as you had feared. Oh, dear me, husband, can this carpet under us be that which covered our floor at old Arlington?"

"Yes, it is," Lee said, gladdened at how happy she was.

Then she turned toward the front windows and caught her breath. Leaving Rob behind, she rolled herself to one of them and reached out a shaking twisted hand, tenderly as she would toward a baby's crown. Her chin began to quiver. "Why . . . why can these be the very curtains that framed our pleasant and beloved views at the old home?"

Lee stepped to her, laid a gentle hand on her shoulder, and said, "Those sweet remembered scenes, Mary, these are the curtains through which we saw them."

Now it was all too much, and as the memories swept over her, she burst into tears.

"Oh, Mary, dear wife," Lee said, kneeling to her and wrapping her tiny shoulders in his beefy arms. "Oh, no, I wanted it to be a happy day for you, my darling."

Mary managed to get control of the sobs racking her and shook her head. "Oh, but it is," she choked, looking around at her family. She could not staunch the tears, so she talked through them as they raced down both cheeks.

"To be here, with my husband and all three sons spared to me by the war; my Precious Life; Agnes and Mary Custis surely soon to be here. A beautiful new piano given to us by those who love us, a pantry stocked full for us by new friends. And a home, husband! With such sanctified remembrances of the old place! Oh—" Now the sobs burst forth again. "But, oh, now I am filled with thanksgiving to God for the privilege and blessing of starting a new place with you all!"

Just reading the letter her father had written, granting her permission to travel to Richmond before coming to Lexington, made Agnes feel closer to him, and to the other Christmas Eves she had been remembering.

"My precious little Agnes," he had written in his flowing fatherly hand, "it is very hard for you to ask me to advise you to go away from me. But in order to help you make up your mind, if it will promote your pleasure and your soon-to-be-married friend Sally's happiness, I will say, go to Richmond as you request and be a bridesmaid."

So here I am, in Richmond, on Christmas Eve Day 1865, she thought. *But my mind is back at Arlington, when I was eleven, preparing presents and putting up stockings. Oh, the sounds and smells and colors are even more real now than they were then!* she thought, staring at the snowflakes that rushed against the windowpane, then slowly melted away, to be replaced by more.

She closed her eyes and remembered the delicious anticipation of donning the new green taffeta dress Grandpa Custis had already given her that year. He could never, it seemed, deny her, but he drew the line at not allowing her to put on the dress till Christmas morning.

She giggled out loud as she remembered: *How I couldn't keep still a minute!*

And then Markie—and he—had come to visit with yet more presents and cider. Him . . .

She realized the persistent thumping sound was not that of horses' hooves coming up old Arlington's drive but someone now at the bedroom door.

"Come in," she said, standing.

In walked Sally Warwick, elegant scion of one of Virginia's most powerful families and Agnes's good friend since childhood. Her nuptials were two weeks away.

"Agnes, dear, all our guests are *awaiting* you," Sally said. She took Agnes's hand in her own. "Is my dear friend well?"

Agnes nodded and took the lead in moving toward the door. "Yes, Sally. I'm so sorry, the snow was just so beautiful that I lost track of the time."

Sally halted her. "Now you simply *must* share with me your true impressions of Colonel Campbell. Is he not one of the handsomest and bravest men *ever*? And to have attained such rank at so young an age. And he's from one of Richmond's *finest* families. Being of Scots-Irish blood, of course, he would probably say *clan*!"

Agnes managed a weak smile.

"Oh, my *dear* Agnes," Sally said, clasping her hand the tighter. "You think I am *patronizing* you, darling. We . . . I . . . well, we *all* just think you are the sweetest, loveliest girl *any* of us know, and we can't *bear* the thought of Virginia's noble manhood being deprived of one of her most *supremely* eligible maidens!"

But Sally loved her friend and knew her life, and she lowered her voice when next she spoke. "Nonetheless, it shall be as my friend wishes; I will not speak another word of Colonel Campbell."

The girls hugged and headed toward the hallway when Sally stopped and turned back to Agnes. Sally's hazel eyes shone with luminous transparency as she spoke.

"To earn your favor, he must have been cast in a more heroic mold than I can even contemplate."

Agnes's eyes filled with sudden urgent tears. She clamped her lips together so as to keep down the sobs attempting to charge forth from the bondage in which her heart had chained them these long years. Instead she nodded her assent, and Sally wrapped her in a long loving hug.

Just then another of Agnes's friends and Sally's bridesmaids, Lucy Anderson, appeared in the doorway, her face pallid.

"Why, *whatever* on earth could produce such a *ghastly* countenance on my gayest friend?" Sally asked.

Lucy, too, appeared on the verge of tears. Her eyes darted to Agnes—now drying her own eyes—rested there a moment, then moved back to Sally. "It's the United States Congress," she said. "They have rejected every senator and representative from the entire South who wished to be seated. They have sent them home."

Sally, who had had three male kinsmen killed by the war, narrowed her eyes, and her face took on a hard set. "What do the Yankees intend now?"

"Thaddeus Stevens—" Both Agnes and Sally winced at mention of the name. "—appears to have a majority of the Radical Republicans convinced to consider the former states of the Confederacy as conquered provinces rather than states to be welcomed back into the Union, minus slavery, as Lincoln and Johnson both desired. He is heading a so-called 'Joint Committee on Reconstruction,' which usurps authority from the senate and the house in dealing with the South."

Reconstruction, Agnes repeated to herself. *They intend to reconstruct us in their own devilish image, against which Grandpa and General Washington, were they here today, would fight with the last ounce of their being.*

Sally pulled her hands away from Agnes and clenched both her fists. Agnes did not believe she had ever before heard her friend speak in quite the tone she now did.

"Oh, those godless infidels, those imperialist blackguards! Blaming us for a war in which they invaded and crushed us, all to save their larcenous tariff. Coming down here now and turning black against white. Destroying the rule of law and God in order to establish a new god in the Federal government, to which we must now pay homage. Oh, how I hate them!"

Lucy turned to Agnes. "And Aggie," she said, her voice trembling. "The governor sent us word they have ordered your father to Washington to testify before them."

Agnes felt her knees might collapse under her. "B-but he has put away his sword and seeks only to aid in the reconciliation of North and South, and encourage and train up the young men so that they might rebuild our country," she whimpered.

Lucy bit her lip. "There are many others in the South they seek to destroy as well," she said. "Having taken the slaves, they now wish our land, our remaining property, our political, even our social influence—all to redistribute it to others."

"Such a notion for a government 'of the people, by the people, and for the people!'" Sally erupted, quoting Lincoln's famed words. "To take the wealth and possessions from one group and give them to another. Oh, whatever would the founders say if they knew?"

Lucy's voice dropped further. "Agnes, they apparently believe they can use your father—"

"Many *others*?" Agnes said in belated comprehension. "You think they wish to destroy Papa too, when he is trying to effect such good?"

Lucy did not know what to say. She looked to Sally.

That unhappy bride-to-be spoke the very words now heavy on Agnes's own mind.

"Oh, whatever are we left to do now?"

CHAPTER 57

CULPEPER'S SHAMING ON THE STEPS OF THE CHURCH IN LEXINGTON seared him like nothing else in his whole life. But as he continued westward through Tennessee, the pain subsided into a dull, if unpleasant, remembrance. What proved more pleasant was the sense of fearless disregard of any danger whatsoever that replaced it.

Though he did not now find life particularly distasteful, he no longer cared whether or how long he lived. If he had thought through the issue, which he did not, he would have concluded that one day, six months, or fifty years more of life would have presented roughly equivalent amounts of appeal for him, provided they also included a modicum of pleasure.

And pleasure for Culpeper now meant nothing much more than giving the Yankees just as much trouble as he could before they got him, which he assumed would not be forever but would be awhile. Despite his numerous war wounds, he did not actually believe any Yankee rode a four-legged animal who could contend with him in a straight-up fight. But he also knew something important about Yankees, and that was there were lots of them, and it seemed that the more of them you killed, the more rapidly they proliferated. Culpeper had never sorted that one out.

He *had* sorted out a near-mystical way of divining when any tobacco lay in proximity to him. For instance, only yesterday afternoon, he had come across one of them Dapper Dan "carpetbaggers" as they were called. They seemed to be multiplying across the Southland about as fast as the bluecoats could. Culpeper wasn't yet sure what these carpetbaggers were up to, but he had figured out one thing—you could almost bet they had more to eat and drink than did a Southern boy. And more tobacco too, though the manner in which the leaf had been adopted varied depending on the individual carpetbagger.

So Culpeper got lucky and found one with about a half a pound of uncut chew on him. So keen had the Virginian's senses grown during his years of living off the land while men sought at all times to relieve him of his life and horse, that he actually smelled the tobacco on this carpetbagger without even seeing it.

He didn't actually know which he enjoyed more, relieving the man of his leaf, or pitching him, bound with his own ropes, into the shallows of a nearby stream. That water was cold, and the Yank would be awhile even in getting out, much less getting loose, but Culpeper saw to it he wasn't in so deep as to be in real danger. Of course, if it had been a bluecoat, no telling what he would have done, but the end result would have been much more definitive.

Finding that little popgun derringer on the peddler was a pleasant surprise too, Culpeper thought, as he turned the carpetbagger's fine roan up his own cousins' drive. Popgun, maybe, but it would do the job in tight quarters, and he had plenty of ammunition with it too.

He reached his cousins' farm in Giles County, Tennessee, on Christmas Eve. Little Advent cheer appeared in the air. Only a couple of the spread's out-buildings, all burned by the Yankees during the war, had been rebuilt. Not one head of livestock lived on land that before the war supported over a thousand animals. Weeds, secondary brush growth, and saplings blanketed most of the two thousand acres that once supplied a bounteous harvest for four different Wallace families.

"The last critters I saw on the land were a dozen of our hogs whose heads the Yanks jammed through with iron pegs, just to kill them so our folks, our women and children, would have nothing to eat," Culpeper's "Cousin Jed" Wallace told him.

"Yeh, I seen 'em do that lots before," Culpeper said with a nod.

A rainbow-hued sunset captured their frosty gusts of breath in bold relief as the two rode toward the nearest town, Pulaski, to meet some of Cousin Jed's friends and scare up some Christmas spirit, or spirits.

No one in Culpeper's life ever brought a smile to his face quicker than Cousin Jed. The years they grew up together before Jed's widowed mother joined her extended family in Tennessee, and the few times they had hooked up since then, his cousin's sunny manner had provided a soothing elixir to Culpeper's often somber plight. On the ride out from Virginia, Culpeper arrived at the belated conclusion that it was because his cousin seemed always to have a smile on his own face, and a way of seeing the good—or at least the humor-ous—in just about any situation.

What Culpeper had not realized was that his cousin's cheerful manner, more than anything else, was what had brought the bitter Virginian out to Tennessee.

They found the half-dozen men—all Confederate veterans, most of them officers, and among the most prominent young men in the county—in the law office where one of them worked. Culpeper at first felt greatly out of place. But as the men drank apple cider heated by the stove in the center of the main room, some but not all of them spicing it with brandy, their good-natured banter began to seem more and more like Ethan's. *I wish ole Ethan boy was here,* Culpeper thought, accepting a slash of the brandy. *He'd fit in right nice with these learned fellers.*

But Culpeper himself had plenty in common with the men. All had lost friends and family in the war. All had lost much—some nearly all—of their pre-war possessions. Their financial situations, as well as their prospects for the future, now ranged from little to nothing.

And all but two had been wounded, ranging from twice to six times. Three would gimp for the remainder of their days, one of those on a peg leg, and one had lost an arm.

Culpeper said nothing for a full half hour. Then, buoyed by the brandy, he piped up. "H—, my name ain't Jake Schumacher like I made my Cousin Jed here tell y'all. Jakie was a brave boy back in the Valley of Virginia what fought the Yanks off their feet 'fore a pack of 'em finally brought him down. Me, I rode with Mosby, leastways till we had a fallin' out o' sorts, and I got me a fat Yankee bounty on my head for my trouble."

Silence greeted this revelation, until Colonel John Lester, a handsome ruddy-faced redhead, smiled and said, raising his cup toward Culpeper, "Huzzah."

In short order the entire group repeated the gesture.

The spontaneous, unanimous demonstration of acceptance from such respected men, most of them former officers, bound Culpeper in sacred trust to them and whatever they should desire to do. Tears filled his eyes, and he blurted, "Comin' from you boys, that means a lot. I know I ain't a book-learned man like y'all, but—others could tell ya if they was here today—no man will fight harder and stand longer with you than me. So if ye ever need it, me and my guns and knives and whatever little else I got are yours."

Another pause, then Captain John B. Kennedy, whose winsome looks and manner now startled Culpeper with their kinship to Ethan, said, "That include that fine chaw I smell on you?"

Culpeper, surprised at Kennedy's astute sense of smell, flushed slightly, then smiled and pulled a huge square out of an outside coat pocket. All but two of the men wished a plug, which he felt proud to provide them.

"You know, boys," Kennedy said, relishing the first chew he had tasted in months, "for all we seen and been through, I expect Christmas Eve couldn't be much better than this, now could it?"

The group agreed, as more cider and brandy were poured, and another of the men, hefty Frank McCord, editor of the near-defunct Pulaski *Citizen* newspaper, opened the stove grate. Soon the chewers in the group were finding their range.

"It's not the great sweep of the Negroes, either ex-slaves or those who have long been freedmen, who pose the chief difficulty," Lester said. "Oh, I admit the irritation of their wandering the countryside at night en masse, but most of them are still harmless enough. They are just bored, and some of them are hungry. It is not even the carpetbaggers or these cooperationists of our own people—"

"Scalawags, they are being called," McCord said, not chewing but consuming the most brandy of any in the group.

"Yes, it's not even them," Lester said. "It's some of these blue-coated Negro Union veterans still toting muskets and throwing their weight around."

"I should say," Captain James Crowe opined, puffing on a cigar one of his former lieutenants, and now expatriates, had mailed him from Cuba. "The Feds have them occupying us."

"Well that's just it," Kennedy said. "Even good black folk that helped raise us from the crib, worked our land, and protected the women and children during the war, they're being hornswoggled by evil men into foul and nefarious acts."

For the first time, cherub-cheeked, one-armed little Calvin Jones spoke up, his eyes ablaze. "Just yesterday, two of those Negro bluebellies, brandishing rifles with the bayonet locked on, shouldered my wife and seven-year-old daughter off the sidewalk into a slush puddle. There was a sheen of ice under the puddle, and my little Darcy slipped and fell face first and chipped a brand-new big tooth right in front. Since they fired our sheriff, I went to the bluebelly commander, or tried to. I practically had to get in a gunfight with two more cocky n——s to see him. When he heard the uproar, he finally came out. Then he just Yankee-doubletalked me and told me it was too bad about Darcy, but our kind had been forcing colored folks into the street for a long time, and they didn't complain, and we shouldn't complain too loud either."

This hushed the group. The only motion in the room was Crowe blowing smoke rings through the lamp-lit air. After a full minute passed, Culpeper launched an amber jet into the stove from six feet away—out of anger, not need, since he usually swallowed—and stood.

"Reckon I'll pay me a visit to this Yank vermin and carve my complaint across his jugular," he announced, turning to leave.

"Cole," Cousin Jed said, grabbing his arm and giving him a good-natured, but respectful, wink. "That ain't the way, boy. Sit down. We've got to bide our time and use our heads."

"Me, I got lots o' dead friends used their heads," Culpeper said without emotion. "Dyin' or livin' a bit longer is all the same to me."

"But it's not just you that's involved here," Lester said.

"He's right, Cole," chimed Kennedy. "Even if you are able to take down that snake, there'll be lots more Darcy Joneses that pay for it before the Yanks are finished with us."

When Culpeper saw he would better please the group by sitting, he did just that and swallowed. The remaining man present, Richard Reed, who had said not a word, leaned over without being asked and stoked the Virginian's cup with brandy, giving him a nod as he did.

"Boys," Lester said, smiling as someone replenished his own cup, "we all have sad tales to relate."

"That's right," Crowe cut in. "My own mama had a grand total of four chickens left the Feds didn't find when they stormed through during the war. Well, just last week, two of those blue-coated n——s came right up to her back porch and stole 'em, laughin' at her all the while as she beat at 'em with the scabbard of Papa's sword from the Mexican War."

"It's these oily Union Leaguers," Kennedy said. "Frank here says they've been trying to stir up folks up North for years without much success, so now they're moving down here."

Lester, failing to get the conversation moving in the direction he wished, grimaced and shifted in his chair.

"Actually this is only the beginning," McCord said, his eyes beginning to glow red. "I have a couple of good friends who edit papers in the North, and they have warned me a full-scale invasion of Union Leaguers, Freedman Bureau agents, and Yankee preachers is on the way."

"We've already had one out our way," Reed said, the sound of his gentle voice surprising everyone. "Came right up to the old slave quarters with nary an invite or a by-your-leave and started pouring 'em cheap whiskey and getting 'em riled up—against us. Next thing you know, two of 'em are laying a chunk of birchwood across my brother's forehead, then lighting out with his horse and scattergun and all the food in the kitchen. Haven't seen 'em since."

"What's these Union Leaguers' play?" Cousin Jed asked.

"They want all the blacks organized into the Republican Party and voting how they say," McCord said, pulling a fresh pint of brandy from his hip pocket and twisting it open. "They'll vote, the scalawags will vote, the carpetbaggers will vote, and ex-Confederates will be disfranchised." Seeing Culpeper's confusion at the word, McCord explained, "They'll get laws from Thad Stevens and the Congress branding us traitors and keeping us from voting."

"But Grant promised us—" Cousin Jed began.

"Then, the Union Leaguers will have their Negro lackeys voted into power across the South, put there merely as pawns to do the political bidding of those Republican pirates in Washington and kept there by the guns of occupying Federal armies. Then the Leaguers will take care of a few additional details," McCord continued, waving off Cousin Jed's attempt to spice his brandy with cider, "such as confiscating our land and redistributing it to the blacks." Now he looked right at Lester. "Along with our law, our tax money—and our guns. That's what my Yankee friends in the North, who are terrified at such plans, tell me."

Not tobacco or cigars or brandy could flush out a response to that dread herald.

Minutes passed before Kennedy, at a loss now for winsomeness, murmured, "With no land, no money, no law, and no guns . . . our women and children . . ."

Lester drained his cup and finally announced, "Let's start something to break the monotony and cheer up our mothers and girls. Let's start a club of some kind."

"A club?" Kennedy said.

"Yes, a club," Lester said. "Something to bolster everyone's spirits while we contemplate how to face our problems."

When the others saw Kennedy nod, they joined in support and agreed to meet a few days hence at the home of Colonel Thomas Martin, the town's most respected man, to flesh out the idea.

The dozen men meeting at Martin's once-splendid but now looted and defaced Pulaski home agreed as one that prospects for the new year of 1866 looked even worse than they had at the onset of 1865. They held this view not because of the past but because they had no confidence in the way the future was shaping up.

Fraternal organizations featuring secret rituals, clandestine ceremonies, and imaginative initiation rites had become a popular activity nationwide. Several of the men gathered at Martin's had friends who belonged or had belonged to such groups. A number of them found great solace during these lean days in the worship and service of their churches; in a number of cases, the war and the deprivations following it had served to heighten their level of faith. Still, they knew their Bibles encouraged rather than forbid wholesome fellowship and recreation and admonished them that, "A merry heart doeth good. . . ."

And merry they were that cold, clear January night when the snow fell and the full moon rose, many of them for the first time in months. Good, clean fun did not at this point provide Culpeper's chief motivation in life, or any motivation at all. But these new friends, all of whom he considered his betters, had for some reason chosen to bring him into their confidence and association.

Then Cousin Jed told him one of them actually knew the fame of Cole Culpeper in Mosby's Confederacy.

"Word spread quickly through the ranks," Cousin Jed said, his voice solemn and freighted with gravity. "Now they would virtually have you at the head of their column if they were to charge into battle." The Tennessean stared with seeming awe into his Virginia cousin's eyes—then slugged him hard in the shoulder with a closed fist and burst into laughter. "Ajax—no, Hector—Culpeper! Ha-ha!"

Culpeper was stunned. No one since Emma had paid him such mind. He hadn't the faintest notion how to respond, other than to continue accepting their invitations to socialize. *I'll keep my mouth shut so as not to show them how ignorant I truly am,* he thought as he and the still-hooting Cousin Jed dismounted outside Martin's home. *And I'll listen right good; they talk just as good as Ethan boy, some of them maybe even a mite better, and maybe I can finally learn how to talk like a gentleman.*

Lester, Kennedy, and McCord had been cobbling together the outline for a club since the Christmas Eve gathering, so the group had their organization named, bylaws written, and purposes outlined after only two hours.

And they had an oath of allegiance agreed upon, the gravity of which both Lester and Martin warned the men to contemplate before they swore to it. McCord read it aloud in his rich baritone:

> This is an institution of Chivalry, Humanity, Mercy, and Patriotism; embodying in its genius and its principles all that is chivalric in conduct, noble in sentiment, generous in manhood, and patriotic in purpose; its peculiar objects being as follows.
>
> First: To protect the weak, the innocent, and the defenseless, from the indignities, wrongs, and outrages of the lawless, the violent, and the brutal; to relieve the injured and oppressed; to succor the suffering and unfortunate, and especially the widows and orphans of Confederate soldiers.
>
> Second: To protect and defend the Constitution of the United States, and all laws passed into conformity thereto, and to protect the States and the people thereof from all invasions from any source whatever.
>
> Third: To aid and assist in the execution of all constitutional laws, and to protect the people from unlawful seizure, and from trial except by their peers in conformity to the laws of the land.

For a moment the group sat transfixed, as if doubtful they themselves could have crafted what sounded so sublime a document.

"God help us, and all who follow us, to uphold such revered ideals," Kennedy said.

"I cannot truly remember the last time such an aura of anticipation and carefree joy took hold of me," Lester said, amazed at the sense of giddiness enveloping him. "And I have no brandy, no spirits whatsoever, in me tonight."

"I've had no alcoholic spirits in me since I was sixteen," Kennedy said, "and it's the most fun I can remember having."

"I haven't been *without* spirits in me much of the past few months," McCord said, "yet I'm enjoying it immensely as well."

At this the group broke into boyish guffaws.

"Let's heighten the drama, the mystery of it even further," Kennedy said, leaning forward in the old canvas-seat camp stool that now provided one of Martin's more handsome parlor pieces. "Let's disguise ourselves in colorful costumes, ride en masse to the homes of our parents and sweethearts, and call upon them in silent serenade." Then, to the shock of the entire group, Kennedy's brilliant smile cracked, with his voice, and he choked out, his eyes filling with tears, "Precious little they have had to cheer them, and so much sadness and heartbr—"

He could not continue and lowered his head toward the scuffed, rugless floor.

"Indeed," Lester proclaimed, standing. "And I know just where, in this fallow season, we might find suitable apparel to go a-calling."

It was the widow of Kennedy's older brother who first heard the dozen horsemen rumble up. When first she looked out the window, she thought the luminous coating over all of them and their horses a reflection of the snow in the high fat moon flanking them. Then one of them dismounted and, with a familiar crippled gait, approached her front door, carrying something in his arms. Puzzled, she donned her robe and slippers and went to answer his knock.

Candle in hand, she at first gasped, then giggled at his strange attire. But she found no humor at all in the basket he placed in her hands. It contained a variety of fresh vegetables and jarred preserves, including—now she gasped again—peach marmalade.

She looked up at him, tears streaking down her cheeks. "Is that you under that gitup, Johnny Kennedy?"

But he only bowed courteously, then turned and gimped back to his horse, where he and every other rider touched a gloved hand to their heads in salute, before pounding down the road.

They wore hoods and robes of shiny white, sateen-weave cotton, and they spoke no word.

Her five children, each under the age of ten, were all ill and needed their sleep. But they were all even hungrier than they were ill, and she woke every one of them up, pausing only for a brief prayer of gratitude to a God she could not believe would let her family starve, even though until this very moment, it had looked as though the smaller children might.

On through the milky blue night they rode, from one shambling house to another, delivering baskets and sacks of what was needed to one dilapidated farm after another. This first night, benevolence held higher place than chivalry in the determination of visits.

Culpeper enjoyed riding the trail again with his fellow Southrons, especially outside the purview of the cursed Yankees. And these were soldiers, even though they weren't Virginians, with whom he would have relished riding in the war. He wished, in fact, he was back in the war with these very men. *Oh, wouldn't we mess up a few Yankee uniforms,* he thought with a laugh.

He noticed one oddity as they rode, though he wondered, especially as the hour grew very late, if it were his imagination playing tricks on him. It seemed as though several of the significant number of blacks he saw roaming the roads, even through the late hours, were stricken in terror at the sight of him and the other club members.

Sure enough, when finally they returned to Martin's house at nearly three in the morning, he heard Kennedy say, "Was my pea brain playing tricks on me, or did y'all think some of those Negroes we saw appeared a might frightened at our gitups?"

"Why, they were scared plum to death, Johnny," Cousin Jed chortled with benign amusement.

"I heard a couple of 'em call us ghosts as we rode by," McCord said.

"So did I," chimed another man.

"Les, should we get some different outfits?" Kennedy asked Lester. "We surely don't need to stir up any ruckus with the Feds when we're out just trying to have some fun. And every man here has good black friends—like your boy Zechariah, Les—suffering just like we are, who we don't want to harm, even by scaring them."

"Yeah, two of my best friends, Big Joe and his little brother Elisha, used to be my slaves," Cousin Jed said. "Some of them Union League-type Negroes have been making their lives miserable 'cause they still want to work for me rather than run me off my own land."

Lester's countenance had a weightier sense about it than the other men's.

"Actually, I'm not sure I'm concerned at the specter of some of these blacks getting a little spooked," he said. "A couple I saw that skedaddled into the brush were wearing Yank uniforms and carrying Yank long guns. No, I think I like our getups, and I know I like what we accomplished tonight," he concluded. "For now, I'm of a mind to go ahead as we are and see what happens."

"So what do you think about all this, pardner?" Cousin Jed asked, accepting a quid of tobacco from Culpeper as the two rode home.

Culpeper nodded his head. "It'll do some." Then, his voice not changing inflection, "But I ain't through with them bloody-legged Yankees yet, and I ain't through with their n——s either, if they get in my way."

"The second word does seem a fitting accompaniment to the first, all of us having the same Scots-Irish heritage that formed the backbone of our forefathers' fight for independence and our own," Kennedy said, inspecting the words he had just written on a scrap sheet of paper. He, Lester, and Martin sat around the latter's parlor room fireplace, which was the only one he could afford to keep going, even in these deepest shades of winter. "And the alliteration adds to the appeal."

"It's the first word that confuses me a bit," Martin said. "Isn't the Greek for a circle with no beginning or end—symbolic of our binding commitment to these principles, one another, and our people—*kuklos*?"

"Our rendering is a variation on it," Lester said.

The three men stared at the words as the fireplace crackled.

"Yes, that's it," Kennedy concluded.

Then, not intending to do so, they spoke the words in unison.

"Kuklux Klan."

CHAPTER 58

AFTER COMPLETING HIS OWN MORNING PRAYERS AND DEVOTIONS, those he led for his family, and breakfast, Lee determined to complete his latest letter to Markie. He had been interrupted at that task at least a dozen times in the past month. He petitioned God for a few uninterrupted moments in which to finish it upon arriving at his office.

All was quiet as he sat down at his desk. He wrote Markie his appreciation for her recent sending to him of the volume of Thomas à Kempis's *Imitation of Christ.*

As he pondered what next to say, his eyes came to rest on his well-worn coat-pocket-sized Bible he had placed on the top of the desk. The thought struck him that he could not remember when he first started carrying the book. *I know I had it with me during the Mexican War. I may even have had it at West Point.*

He thought farther back, to his boyhood at Christ Church in Alexandria. There, he recalled, they read the Scriptures to the congregation from General Washington's own Bible. *Of course,* Lee thought, smiling to himself, *they still had the general's family pew reserved for him.*

He stared at the small vat in which he dipped his pen. *What is this?* he wondered, sniffing it. *Well, we certainly are not yet again blessed with ink for our writing.* But as long as the substance, whatever it was, would allow him to convey his thoughts from his head to the sheet of paper before him, it would do.

> I have read some of your favourite chapters of *Imitation of Christ,* and hope I may derive from the perusal of the book, the good you desire. I prefer the Bible to any other book. There is enough in that, to satisfy the most ardent thirst for knowledge; to open the way to true wisdom; and to teach the only road to salvation and eternal happiness. It is not above human comprehension, and is

sufficient to satisfy all its desires. The difficulty is to conform the heart, the mind, and the thoughts to its teaching, and to obtain strength to bring the body under the control of its spirit.

Then, offering silent thanksgiving to God for his forestalling of visitors and interruptions, Lee composed the more difficult concluding section of his missive. In her last letter Markie had unleashed a torrent of emotion and sorrow to him. The war had rent her own part of the family asunder, though most of it stayed with the North. At the news their brother Orton had been hanged within hours of a drumhead court-martial, her sister Kate grieved herself to death— *like our beloved Charlotte,* Lee winced. But Kate left four small children, her husband was a Federal admiral commanding ships on distant seas, and it had fallen to Markie to become surrogate mother for her shattered nieces and nephews. How challenging the task was proving for still-single, now-forty-year-old Martha Custis Williams.

She had missed Lee terribly during the long years of war, missed his fellowship and consolation, if only from afar. With family illness, death, and her own neuralgia all afflicting her, she seemed to have nowhere to turn but him. At least nowhere she wished to turn. The unspoken theme of the correspondence blared at him from every page, if not every line: *She is so terribly, terribly lonely,* he thought with lament. *And yet I dare not—I would not—even acknowledge the presence of this, the clarion message of her entire life as it now stands.*

He shook his head. *She fretted so for us—for me—these past years. If not for the war, she might by now have been happily—* No, he must check his emotions, especially those lacking edification, and conclude the letter.

> I hope, dear Markie, that the anxieties pressing upon you have passed away. That you have found satisfactory schools for your nephews; that your neuralgia has left you, and that you have enjoyed peace and tranquility of mind. I cannot tell you how deeply I have sympathized in your sorrows; how I have grieved over your great grief; and how sincerely I have prayed that the Almighty hand of our Merciful Father should be always extended to you. In looking back upon the calamities that have befallen us, I cannot trust my hand to write the feelings of my heart, but bow in humble submission to His will, who never afflicts us

unnecessarily, or punishes us without a merciful purpose. His will
be done! I have endeavoured to do what is right, and in his eyes,
it never can be made wrong . . .
With constant love and affection

I remain your Cousin
R. E. Lee

"Jacob Howard is armed for bear," Stevens told one of the brightest of his
cadre of young Radical congressional protégés. "I have provided much of his
ammunition. I want you in attendance every minute that Robert Lee is giving
testimony. Then I want you reporting the results of his examination to me within
five minutes of its conclusion."

*I do believe I shall forego even my poker game tonight until I know what hap-
pens with Lee,* Stevens thought, more excited than he had been in weeks during
this, a season of many excitements for him.

Lee thought more of Arlington than he did facing a Senate subcommittee
comprised of some of the most powerful men in the United States. He decided
against even viewing it from afar, not certain—such confession he would utter
to no one—that his heart could withstand the sight of its despoiling. Besides, he
needed all his faculties directed toward his examination by Senate
Subcommittee Chairman Jacob Howard, tasked with oversight of the
"Reconstruction" process in Virginia and the Carolinas.

I wonder if I might find Markie, he thought. After much contemplation he
realized, *No, it would be out of selfish motivation. The reaction from the people of
the North could not have a happy effect on her.*

The keenness of his disappointment startled him.

A familiar but unwelcome old distraction had also reared its ugly head
anew. It concerned recurrent accounts in Northern newspapers that Lee had
not only broken his promise to free his father-in-law's slaves after that man's
death, but that he had actually supervised and in some cases even participated
in acts of physical brutality against them.

His public reaction continued to be governed by the thoughts he had long before shared with Mary: "I have not thought it proper to publish a contradiction, being unwilling to be drawn into a newspaper discussion, believing that those who know me would not credit it and those who do not would care nothing about it. It would lead to endless controversy.

"I will continue to trust God as my rock, and my fortress, and my deliverer," he told her, "and leave the correction of such lies to the return of reason and good feeling."

When she protested in pained tears, he held her in his arms and said, "We have to be patient and suffer for a while at least. All controversy, I think, will only serve to prolong angry and bitter feelings and postpone the period when reason and charity may resume their sway. At present the public mind is not prepared to receive the truth."

Nor, apparently, was Jacob Howard, his ears still ringing from fellow Michigan Senator Zach Chandler's admonitions to press forward with Lee to the end, if possible; that the nation would cry for the rope as the only sensible end for so blood-drenched a traitor.

Seating the gray-coated witness in a high-backed chair facing the subcommittee in the enormous high-ceiling room, Howard made it clear no immunity would protect the Virginian's testimony, that in fact the government reserved the right to use such to reopen its treason case against him.

The packed room sat hushed and tense as Howard glanced at the mound of letters sent to him by bereaved mothers, fathers, brothers, sisters, sons, and daughters of Federal soldiers killed by Lee's erstwhile Army of Northern Virginia juggernaut. His cheeks coloring, Howard narrowed his eyes and began the grilling. The host of witnesses knew, and hoped, that history might be made before their eyes this day.

Back and forth the two went. Would the South ante up the taxes necessary to pay off the war that had devastated it? Yes, it would. Would Southerners mix socially with Northerners come south to work among them? Most would prefer not. Would the Southern people object to the franchise for blacks? Yes. The South does not believe it is being treated as generously as it ought by the North? The North can afford to be generous, and President Johnson's (non-Radical) policy is the one Southerners believe will most clearly, surely, and speedily restore their civil government.

Lee detected a slight flicker in Howard's eyes and suspected the next question to be a favorite of the Michigan senator's, one Lee had been informed the man relished asking all the Virginians and Carolinians who had paraded before him the past many weeks.

"Should a war break out between the United States and any foreign power, such as England or France," Howard asked, unveiling his favorite question, "if there should be held out to the secession portion of the people of Virginia, or the other recently Rebel states, a fair prospect of gaining their independence, and shaking off the government of the United States, is it, or is it not, your opinion that the secessionists would avail themselves of the opportunity?"

As he answered, Lee determined not to scowl at Howard's studied application of the word *secession* and its variations. "I cannot say I have heard it. On the contrary, I have heard people—I do not know whether you would call them secessionists or not, I mean those people in Virginia with whom I associate— express a hope that the country may *not* be led into a war."

"In such an event, do you not think that many of that class of person whom I call secessionists would join the common enemy?" Howard said.

"It is possible. It depends upon the feelings of the individual."

For the first time a murmur ran through the packed crowd.

Howard had set up Lee the way he wanted to; now he would deal his blow.

"What is your knowledge of the cruelties practiced towards the Union prisoners at Libby Prison and Belle Isle . . . Andersonville and Salisbury?" he asked.

"I suppose they suffered from the want of ability on the part of the Confederate states to supply their wants," Lee replied. "At the very beginning of the war, I knew there were sufferings of prisoners on both sides, but, as far as I could, I did everything in my power to relieve them and urged the establishment of the prisoner exchange cartel, which was established."

Howard had not anticipated the cartel being mentioned. He opened his mouth to move the subject along, but Lee, gentle and steady, denied him the chance.

"I made several efforts to exchange the prisoners after the cartel was suspended," the Virginian continued. "I do not know why it was suspended. I do not know to this day which side took the initiative."

The crestfallen countenances on the men before him offered eloquent testament to which side.

"I offered to General Grant, around Richmond, that we should exchange all the prisoners in our hands," Lee said. "There was a committee from the Christian Association, I think, which reached Petersburg and made application to me for a passport to visit all the prisons in the South. I suppose they have my letter to them. I told them that I had not the authority, that it could only be obtained from the War Department at Richmond but that neither they nor I could relieve the sufferings of the prisoners—" Howard attempted to stop him but realized he had too many witnesses to attempt very hard. "—that the only thing to be done for them was to exchange them."

As a scarlet wave tided over Howard's face, Lee rolled gently and steadily on.

"To show that I would do whatever was in my power, I offered then to send to City Point all the prisoners in Virginia and North Carolina, over which my command extended, provided they returned an equal number of mine, man for man. I reported this to the War Department and received an answer that they would place at my command all the prisoners in the entire South, if the proposition was accepted."

Noting that a new murmur now rippled through the subcommittee itself, Lee completed his answer: "I heard nothing more on the subject."

One of Howard's colleagues rushed the examination in a different direction, which proved as fruitless as those before it.

Finally Howard paused and glanced at his colleagues. Lee divined that something of great import loomed.

Even Thaddeus Stevens's poker game hung in the balance, dependent on whether Robert E. Lee could now be proven a traitor to the United States.

"Suppose a jury was impaneled in your neighborhood, taken by lot," Howard said. "Would it be possible to convict, for example, Jefferson Davis, for having levied war against the United States and thus having committed the crime of treason?"

"I think it is very probable that they would *not* consider that he had committed treason."

"They do not generally suppose that it was treason against the United States, do they?"

"I do not think that they so consider it."

Lee's keen eye detected the fraction of a beat of a pause in Howard's questioning.

Ah, this will be important, the Virginian knew.

"State, if you please," Howard said, his voice full of gravity but sounding to Lee a shade tinnier than usual, "and if you are disinclined to answer the question, you need not do so—what your own personal views on that question were."

Lee gave no pause, recalling for the assembly the view of secession he had been taught at West Point in the 1820s.

"That was my view," he concluded, "that the act of Virginia, in withdrawing from the United States, carried me along as a citizen of Virginia and that her laws and acts were binding on me."

Neither this, nor hardly anything else he had told them over the past two hours, proved to be what Jacob Howard and his cadre wished. Frustration and weariness sheathed their faces. The thought struck Lee that as politicians, these men had more interest in promoting a particular agenda—whatever theirs might be, he hadn't a clue—than in finding the truth and promoting justice. They had had all they wanted of him, but he wanted just a bit more of them.

"I may have said and I may have believed that the positions of the two sections which they held to each other was brought about by the politicians of the country," he announced, the sound of his voice surprising the committee, some of whom had already risen to leave, "that the great mass of the people, if they had understood the real question, would have avoided it."

He looked straight into Howard's uneasy eyes as he concluded. "I did believe at the time that it was an unnecessary condition of affairs and might have been avoided, if forbearance and wisdom had been practiced on both sides."

"He dispatched them and their questions with no more aplomb than the archangel Michael batting away so many demons with his sword," Stevens's young protégé reported.

The old warrior cursed as he listened, and he cursed all through his poker game that night, even though he won back a portion of the small fortune he had in recent weeks lost at the same table.

❖❖❖❖❖❖

News of Lee's appearance—and return to Virginia—made Edwin Stanton no happier than it did Stevens. It looked more and more to him like the greatest traitors in the Southern Confederacy were going to escape virtually scot-free and certainly without the ropes around their necks they so richly deserved.

Indeed many in high positions of power and influence have in these hours of treachery and villainy escaped accountability for their actions, he thought, holding a large sheaf of papers in the crook of his arm as he stood before the fireplace crackling in his office.

He shuffled once more through the collection, which was official, secret, complete, and original, and had at long last been delivered to him just hours before by his personal courier. Names like Kilpatrick and Dahlgren, Davis and Richmond—and Stanton—filled them. One place alone seemed appropriate for their safekeeping, he thought, eyeing the fire and believing, even as perspiration dappled his forehead, that he felt a winter chill in the sweltering room.

A more vigorous blaze was indeed called for.

CHAPTER 59

HE BLUSHED AT THE ACCOLADES HER PEN RAINED DOWN UPON HIM in her latest letter. In a way Lee sorrowed for her, that she had not her own husband toward whom to direct such sentiments and emotions. *At least I, her hoary-haired old man of a cousin, can be a safe haven to harbor her human feelings,* he thought, happy that such pleasurable conversation and encouragement served beneficial—and justifiable—purposes.

"It seemed like old times to hear you talking again," he wrote back to Markie at the end of April 1866. "In my visit to Washington, knowing how our merciful God mixes in the cup he gives us to drink in this world, the sweet with the bitter, I had hoped I might have found you there. But you were far beyond my reach."

He paused, thinking how to write what came next. Then, "The changed times and circumstances did recall sad thoughts; but I rejoiced to think that those who were so prominent in my thoughts at former periods when returning from long and distant excursions, and whose welcome was so grateful, were now far above all human influences, and enjoying eternal peace and rest. I saw, however, other friends, whose kind reception gave me much pleasure; yet I am considered now such a monster that I hesitate to darken with my shadow the doors of those I love lest I should bring upon them misfortune."

His throat grew tight.

"I did not approach Arlington nearer than the railway that leads to the city. I know very well how things are there. I am very sorry that you still suffer from neuralgia," he concluded, emotionally drained. "I am easily wearied now and look forward with joy to the time, which is fast approaching, that I will lie down and rest."

Stevens awaited the arrival of the war hero and prospective congressional candidate. *He has only one eye, Ben Wade tells me,* Stevens thought. *The people*

will naturally assume the rebellion to have claimed it, not the Mexicans. Confound it, what is that man's name, Miller or Marlar? He sucked on a glass of bourbon and thought back over the raucous first half of 1866. *So much I have failed to achieve,* he thought with rage, cognizant that the disease—which doctors had pronounced his "dropsy of the chest"—now beating the life out of his body harbored no more interest in him finishing the work before him than did Johnson, the Democrats, or the Rebels.

For instance he wanted the Southerners' plantations chopped up and dispersed as forty-acre tracts to free blacks, but his own party had thwarted that.

How much sooner would I feel sanctioned to take my leave of this vain world, he thought, *if not for men anxious to embrace the representatives of Rebels, employ the unscrupulous use of patronage, and practice the oily orations of false prophets.*

Still, he admitted to himself as the bourbon began to warm and soothe, it could not be denied that much had been accomplished.

The Joint Committee on Reconstruction—the Committee of Fifteen as it had become known—had established itself as a revolutionary body no less faithful in his estimation than the Directory of the French Revolution. And he alone, among its gallery of American political titans, steered its helm.

The Thirteenth Amendment had passed, officially freeing all slaves in the United States—without a speck of financial remuneration to the slavers relieved of their "property," as those who defended that abominable Constitution claimed proper. *Some day, or year, soon,* he thought wryly, *the courts will overcome the Delawares and Marylands of our Union and free their slaves as well.*

Maybe even our illustrious Napoleon himself, the drunk little general Grant whom we must shortly win to our ways—and our next presidential ticket—will yet free his own slaves, Stevens thought.

Authorization for the Freedman's Bureau had been extended indefinitely. Moreover, it approved division of the former Confederate states into new districts and subdistricts beyond that. Commissioners, agents, and clerks appointed to facilitate the bureau's work, a corps that would number in the thousands, must attest to the "ironclad oath" of past, present, and future allegiance to the United States, effectively assuring those agents all to be in political accord with the Radicals.

The bureau and its employees would fall under the authority and protection not of the three constitutionally appointed branches of the Federal government but of the United States military.

Stevens seethed as he recalled President Johnson's objections to the bill. With no peacetime juries in concerned cases, no indictments required, penalties determined by the will of the court-martial tribunal, no appeals, and no writ of error allowed anywhere, "I cannot reconcile a system of military jurisdiction of this kind with the Constitution," the president thundered. "Where in the Constitution is authority to expend public funds to aid indigent people? Where the right to take one man's land and give it to others without 'due process of law' . . . with eleven states excluded from Congress, this bill is 'taxation without representation.'

"From these arbitrary tribunals there lies no appeal," Johnson concluded, "no writ of error to any of the courts in which the Constitution of the United States vests exclusively the judicial power of the country."

When Johnson vetoed the bill—which action the Radicals overrode—Stevens swore to the gods he would destroy the Southern slaver and his administration if he had to purchase additional time on earth from the devil himself to do it.

Then came the Civil Rights Bill, which among other things intended the worthy objective of combating discrimination based on race, color, or previous condition of servitude. President Johnson came against it with all his might for *how* it went about achieving its goals:

"They interfere with the municipal regulations of the states, with the relations existing exclusively between a state and its citizens, or between inhabitants of the same state," he said, "an absorption and assumption of power by the general (Federal) government which, if acquiesced in, must sap and destroy our federative system of limited powers and break down the barriers which preserve the rights of the states. It is another step, or rather stride, to centralization and the concentration of all legislative power in the national government."

In other words, Federal—Northern—government agents, rather than officials of the states, now owned the power both to enforce activities covered under the bill and to arrest offenders.

Johnson railed on, accusing the bill of establishing a massive force of Federal police agents, unlike anything before seen in America or envisioned by the founders, and "irresponsible to the government and to the people . . . Federal police in whose hands such authority might be made a terrible engine of wrong, oppression, and fraud."

Among the president's many other concerns was a fear that the enormous new bureaucracy would have "a vested interest in fomenting discord between the two races, for as the breach widens the Freedman's Bureau agents' employment will continue."

This time the Radicals had to contrive the bitterly contested removal of a Democratic senator, replacing him with one of their own, in order to overcome Johnson's veto.

Whether Johnson's concerns proved valid would be seen by the world in the months ahead.

Stevens snickered as he recalled how the promise of the Civil Rights Bill to keep more blacks from migrating to the Northern states had secured its support from a number of congressmen and senators in that section of the country.

And then had come the brawl over Stevens's vision for a new, Fourteenth Amendment to the Constitution. Generating the most vitriolic debate was his plan to disqualify any former Confederate, whether a corps commander or a free black digging trenches, from holding national public office or even voting until July 4, 1870. They would, of course, not be disqualified from other privileges such as paying their taxes to support the government in which they would no longer have a voice.

"Taxation without representation" was among the kinder epithets hurled at the Radicals by men of all political and geographic persuasions around the country. The hotter the invective, the more Stevens reveled in it.

When Congress took up the disfranchisement plank, Stevens decided it was altogether "too lenient" and moved the exclusion back to 1876, broadening it to disqualify any former Confederate from "all state and municipal as well as national elections."

He smiled at remembrance of how even those in his own party had thrown every objection at him their delicate sensibilities could conjure up.

"What of Lincoln's promise—written into law—of pardon and amnesty?"

"Are you willing to make the South a vast camp for four years more to have your way?"

"Won't we Republicans be accused of attempting to influence and control the presidential election of 1868?"

"This section of the amendment seeks to prevent the South's adoption of the entire amendment, and hence to keep those states out of the Union—it would make the South another Ireland!"

"I do not hesitate to say at once that the disfranchising section is there to save or destroy the Union—Republican—party," he answered, bringing the argument to its most primal application for his fellow politicians. "I should prefer it to extend to the year 18,070 instead of 1870, for until then should every Rebel who shed the blood of loyal men be prevented from exercising any power in this government."

"Can you build a penitentiary big enough for eight million people?" one congressman cried out.

"Yes," Stevens boomed, gasping for more air as he thrust a long bony finger at the man like a lance, "a penitentiary that is built at the point of the bayonet down below—and if they undertake to come here we will shoot them down."

Nothing slowed him, despite his illness. He laughed, he scorned, he mocked, he rebuked, he shook the long bony finger at them, and most of all, he intimidated and converted better but weaker men, and men of lesser conviction than he, to his paths.

The ramifications of his will reached far and wide. Moderate Republicans and Democrats alike rued the wholesale shoveling out of vast tracts of the national domain—a process prevented before the war by Southern politicians.

"Nearly all the grants of lands to railroads and wagon roads find their way into the hands of rich capitalists," an Iowa Republican senator bellowed.

Indeed out west the railroads—owned by the mightiest industrial captains in the United States—flattened everything in their way. Even pro-Republican publications wailed over their influence as the most formidable in any community and that they were poisoning politics across the country and overwhelming what sovereignty still remained to the states.

Back east, spearheaded by Stevens in secret sessions, Congress extended the policy of exorbitant tariffs pioneered by Lincoln and against which the South had fought so long and hard, finally seceding over it.

As the nearly 50 percent entry taxes had funneled hundreds of millions of dollars from the pockets of Southern farmers into those of Northern merchants, so they now did the same to Western farmers. The discerning saw that as political power had shifted from the South to the North, so it now shifted from the agricultural to the industrial, from the land and the villages and the towns to the powerhouse metropolises of the northeast.

"The Rebels must come in as new states or come in as conquered provinces," Thad Stevens proclaimed over it all as he booted and spurred the

Committee of Fifteen into a colossal force of world history. ". . . provinces not prepared to participate in constitutional government for some years. Then, no arrangement could be so proper for them as territorial governments, where they can learn the principles of freedom and eat the fruit of foul rebellion."

These notions choked down hard, even among many rank-and-file Republicans. What ultimately swung the moderate Republicans who constituted the balance of power in Congress over to Stevens's program was his deft answer to the question of when the Southern states might be restored.

"Why, when the Constitution is amended so as to secure perpetual ascendancy to the party of the Union," he told them, smiling, and smiling the more as the realization dawned on men less concerned about the blacks and more concerned about the Constitution than he, that his program, however little they cared for it, was their best engine for continued, even growing, power.

A cold fear gripped Marley as he waited in the anteroom to Stevens's office that this very old man embodied a very new America, that the words of one non-Radical Republican describing Stevens were providentially inspired: "Genius and audacity without wisdom, imagination but not sagacity, cunning but not principle."

Marley knew efforts were already in motion to facilitate his own election to Congress. He knew also that though the right side had won the war, right in postwar times appeared a bit thornier to discern. He planned to help ensure that those with the power to prosecute the right, did.

Stevens, suspecting as much, called from his office, "Come in, Major Marley."

How thankful Lee was to God for His blessings on his first year at Washington College. Financial donations had arrived in large enough measure to pay bills and salaries, purchase new equipment, begin restoration of the school's physical plant—including the addition of a baseball field—and allow an expansion of curriculum, faculty, and student body for the 1866–67 term.

Devout, twenty-four-year-old former Confederate artillery commander Edward Gordon, now studying for the Presbyterian ministry, would come aboard as superintendent of buildings and grounds and secretary of faculty, among many other duties. The faculty post entailed clerical support for Lee, by request of the faculty.

And the trustees insisted on planning for a new, larger president's house for the Lees, which would include outside porches to accommodate Mary and her rolling chair, as soon as funds were available.

Lee's first year had seen the student body nearly triple, to a final enrollment of nearly one hundred and fifty students. A prospective freshman for the fall semester sat before him in his office. The lad's final question was, "I notice that no written set of rules exists for the college, General."

"We have but one rule here, and it is that every student must be a gentleman," Lee said.

Soon it was two o'clock, and he was taking leave of that office. *I must get home and tend the rosebushes I have planted,* he thought. He had intended them as a serendipity for Mary, but amid her physical pain and infirmity, and the bright early spring, they had rendered her more homesick than ever for her roses at old Arlington.

Lee decided to take a circuitous route and walk down the hill past the location of the project that excited him most, the new chapel. He had been employing his engineer's skills for weeks already, drawing up initial designs for the building. He would put his own office in the basement. He felt good knowing he would be but a few steps away at any time from the chapel. And—Grace Episcopal Church lay just next door!

As he walked across the campus, bathed in warm sunlight and brilliant in spring foliage fragrant to the nostrils and the soul, he saw a student escorting a young woman who reminded him very much of Annie. He smiled at the faint but welcome token of remembrance. *Ah, but she is gone—for now,* he thought. *And Mary Custis stays away, and Agnes—my poor Wiggie—only a part of her remains with us.*

He looked up as a fresh breeze puffed a troop of dogwood blossoms past him, pursued by a pair of cardinals, bright scarlet in the sunlight. The pastoral scene, for which he thanked God as if His Almighty hand had crafted it for Lee alone, brought his baby to his mind. *Ah, my little Miss Mildred; she is my light-bearer; the house is never dark if she is in it.*

He gazed just beyond the new chapel site to the stalwart stone walls of Grace Church. *Poor General Pendleton,* he thought, *how hard it was for him to consent to signing the loyalty oath in order to get the church reopened, especially after finding his brave Sandie's grave defamed with vulgar and profane language carved by those people with their knives. But God bless him for putting his service as a shepherd to his flock before his own desires, however honorable their motivation.*

"Sir! General Lee, sir!"

Lee turned to see two of his best students rushing up, out of breath.

"General, sir," one of them said, "they have caught and jailed that Jonathan Hughes, the—man—who has been stealing all the horses out around the countryside these past months." The young man paused. "And they are about to lynch him, sir."

Lee nodded, then without a word headed straight for the courthouse, just a few blocks south. He heard the commotion more than a block away. An angry crowd whose size unnerved Lee surged around the building. *A show of this size means they are riding in from the surrounding country,* he thought. Then he saw white-haired jailer Thomas Perry, standing at the top of the steps leading down into the jail. Perry held the jail keys high above his head. Lee saw that the front rank of the mob stood facing and flanking Perry, hesitant to assault the respected old townsman. *He stands silent, like I would expect ole Tom Perry to do,* Lee thought, *but he could not be more definite about his willingness to lay down his life for those keys if he gave a speech saying so.*

Lee knew the situation had come to this partly because the bankrupt town and area no longer had any legal officials besides Perry, the Federal major, and one town marshal. And the Federal garrison had transferred nearly thirty miles north to Staunton. There had simply been no one to chase and catch Hughes, so his thievery against the emaciated county had mounted to a devastating level.

In a few minutes, someone will grab those keys from Tom, Lee thought, *and they may have to shoot him to do so. Dear God, see how many of our old soldiers are in this crowd—are leading it.*

A shudder ran through him as he saw that some of the men in the very front were gentle, mild-mannered sorts, brave in battle, but whom he would not have imagined capable of perpetrating so horrible an act. *They must be desperate,* he thought.

He began to move, alone, quiet, from cluster to cluster. "Hello, men."

"General Lee, sir!"

"Why, hello, General."

"God bless you, General."

"Is there anything we can do for you, Marse Robert?"

"Why, yes, my good men, let us be true to our name and to Virginia, and not take vengeance into our own hands, but trust in the law to take its course," he said.

One group after another would blush, then lower their heads in shame, not because he intended to shame them, indeed all the more because they knew he did not.

"Oh, General, sir . . ."

"We're . . . I'm . . . sorry, sir."

"Yes, sir, you are right, sir. Don't know what is wrong with us, sir."

Finally he was at their front, only feet from Perry, whose thin, ancient, now-shaking arms somehow still held up the keys.

"Hello, men," he said to the leaders, two of whom he knew to be among the bravest and best that ever rode with Jeb Stuart. When they saw him, they bit their lips and looked down. His eyes welled up as he observed the rags clinging to these men of valor. One of them began to cry.

"I'm sorry, General," he sobbed, unable to look Lee in the eye. "The Yanks took all our horses and mules but one sickly one, and she was all I had to plow for spring seeding. Cora May is eight months along with our fifth, and every-body's hungry, and—"

With this, he who had ridden around McClellan, battled through three different wounds to help Jeb keep the field at Brandy Station, and fought Sheridan's hordes at Five Forks until his horse was killed and he was shot, bay-oneted, and captured, crept away with lowered head, dappling the dirt street with his tears.

The other lionheart looked Lee in the eye and said simply, "Folks just don't have any horses to spare these days, sir. But we were wrong." Then he turned to the men around him and said, "Let's go home, men."

"Th—thank you, General, sir," Perry stuttered, lowering his numb arm.

"No, sir, thank you," Lee said with meaning, "for preventing us from forfeiting our honor."

●◇ ●◇ ●◇

Rarely had he been so grateful to arrive home. He needed some cheering up. Nearing the front porch, he passed one of Mildred's friends and her freckle-faced seven-year-old daughter, who had lush tawny hair tumbling almost to her waist. But try as he might whenever he saw her, Lee could never prompt so much as a nod of the child's head in acknowledgment of his presence.

"And how is Lady Grace today?"

The little girl had rarely spoken since word arrived two years previous of her father's death in Camp Douglas. She had smiled no more than a handful of times. Neither did she now.

Her mother cringed with embarrassment, but Lee's smile diminished not at all.

"Where is my little Miss Mildred?" he called out a moment later as he walked in the front door. "Where is my light-bearer, the one with whom the house is never dark if she is in it?"

But the first thing he heard was the sound of Mary crying. *Oh no, what can it be now?* he fretted, rushing to her.

She sat in her rolling chair before a back window.

"What is it, Mary?" he asked, leaning over to embrace her.

"Just now—right out this very window, I saw the same African thief that stripped my garden all but bare only last week," Mary exclaimed, turning those treasured brown eyes up to him as Mildred appeared. "This time, he took what little was left. And what could I do but sit here and watch him do it?"

His heart burned as she began to weep. "Oh, even in this little place of Lexington, every house has been robbed and even the spring plants pulled up out of our garden," she said. "And I know that they do not keep most of what they steal for themselves. They take it to that new Yankee store in town run by that ex-bluecoat Erastus Johnston, who rewards them for their larceny, then sells their stolen goods at extortionist prices."

Mary grabbed a kerchief in her trembling, gnarled hand and wiped her eyes. "Oh, Robert, if our poor people, helpless and disarmed as they are, could have realized all they were to suffer at the hands of the ungenerous and unprincipled party who are unfortunately now in power, they would never have relaxed their efforts to obtain their independence. Oh God, how long?"

Lee hugged her and ran his fingers through her silver hair.

"To express my true feelings," Mary said, sitting up, "would be at the risk of Uncle Sam's penitentiary. But as I neither feel nor owe any allegiance to him, except what is exacted by force, my conscience does not trouble me. We are protected neither in person nor property by his laws; nor do I feel any respect for the military henchmen who rule us."

He waited a moment before speaking. When he did, it was not just to her, but to Mildred, Agnes—who quietly approached, her face pale—and himself.

"We must not be too hard on the black folk," Lee said. "True, I have owned no more than a handful of slaves in my life; and we released these and those of Mr. Custis years before, or at least by the early stages of the war, paying the way to Liberia for all those who wished us to do so. But as you know, I have long maintained that in this enlightened age there are few who will not acknowledge that slavery as an institution is a moral and political evil in any country. I think it a greater evil to the white than to the black race."

"But Papa," Mildred butted in, "no one in our family or anyone with whom we associate has ever raised a hand of harm against a slave. You yourself have said they nearly bankrupted us at Arlington with their indolence."

Lee found a straight-backed wooden chair, pulled it close to Mary, and sat as he continued to speak. "It is true that the blacks, even when in bondage, were immeasurably better off here than in Africa—morally, socially, and physically. The painful discipline they have and are undergoing is necessary for their instruction as a race, and I hope will prepare and lead them to better things."

"You yourself have told us of the many affectionate letters you have received from former servants, some through the lines during the war, from those who went to Liberia," Mildred said.

Lee smiled at her, silently thanking God that she loved him so, when he had been with her so little of her life.

"The length of their necessary subjugation has been known and ordered by a wise, merciful God," he continued. "I said before the war that we must leave the progress as well as the result in His hands who sees the end, who chooses to work by slow influences, and with whom two thousand years are but as a single day; and that their emancipation would sooner result from the mild and melting influence of Christianity, than the storms and tempests of fiery controversy."

As happy as Mildred's defense of her father had made him, so sad did the familiar drawn countenance of Agnes's face render him. She stood alone and silent and beautiful in the corner opposite him.

"I still say that this influence," he forged on, "while we give it the aid of our own prayers and all justifiable means in our power, though slow, is sure. The doctrines and miracles of our Savior have required nearly two thousand years to convert but a small part of the human race. And even among Christian nations, gross errors still exist."

"Mama said that when you were up north recently," Mildred persisted, "a number of former slaves who knew you when you were there before the war, approached you with affection, shaking your hand through the carriage window, and the like. They would hardly have received you in this way had they looked upon you as fresh from a war intended for their oppression and injury. Oh, those abolitionists—"

"So far from engaging in a war to perpetuate slavery, I am rejoiced that slavery is abolished," Lee interjected. "I believe it will be greatly for the interests of the South. So fully do I believe this, as regards Virginia especially, that I would—" Now he peered at Mary. "—have lost all I have lost by the war, and have suffered all I have suffered, to have this object attained."

Mary looked him in the eye and nodded her head in assent. This reaction amazed Mildred. When she heard footsteps behind her, she turned to see Agnes leaving the room.

"It is regrettable, however, that the abolitionist has never understood," Lee concluded, his sad brown eyes tracking Agnes's departure, "that he has neither the right, nor the power of virtuous operation except by moral means and persuasion, and that if he means well to the slave, he must not create angry feelings in the master; that although he may not approve the mode by which it pleases God to accomplish His purposes, the result would nevertheless have been the same; that the reasons he gives for interference in what he has no concern, holds good for every kind of interference with our neighbors when we disapprove of their conduct," Lee said. Then, sighing, he added, "Still, I fear he will persevere in his evil course."

"Look," Mildred exclaimed, "another Negro is sneaking into our garden!"

Mary scoffed, wheeling herself around toward the front of the house. "No matter—his comrades have already absconded with everything worth taking."

CHAPTER 60

THESE OLE BOYS ARE LEARNIN' ME HOW TO LAUGH AGAIN, CULPEPER thought. With chill attaching itself to the nights as 1866 proceeded into autumn, he felt thankful to have the thick white linen sheets covering his buckskin shirt and denim pants, as well as the sacklike one covering his head as a hood. All had stitched onto them the Maltese cross now emblematic of the Kuklux Klan, or Ku Klux Klan, as some had begun calling it.

The scene unfolding before him could scarcely be described for someone not witnessing it, which would not happen anyway and, by the rules of the organization, could not.

"Recite the oath," Kennedy announced, his voice filled with ominous portent.

"This is an institution of Chivalry, Humanity, Mercy, and Patriotism . . ." the blindfolded man began.

As they were all cloaked, Culpeper could not see Cousin Jed's face, but he had known him since they were toddlers, and the posture of his body and the tilt of his head, even through the white sheets, revealed clearly as could have words the merriment festooning his kinsman's soul.

Detecting this, Culpeper had to bite his lower lip so hard to keep from exploding into laughter that it nearly bled. For it would not do to erupt into a laughter that would certainly have ignited Cousin Jed and probably would have swept through the other dozen costumed men in the room. No, not at the solemn initiation of a new Klan member, especially Jed's little brother—and Culpeper's cousin—Daniel Wallace.

But when Cousin Jed removed the blindfold and young Cousin Daniel perceived his own image in the cracked mirror before him in the lamplit back room of the tornado-ravaged old house just outside of Pulaski, Culpeper feared he might cry for the effort he was expending not to laugh.

Especially when Cousin Daniel saw the gargantuan hat atop his head—and the donkey ears rising from it. Near fainting or crying with fear himself, the eighteen-year-old Wallace boy burst into laughter, which ignited that long-suppressed act in Culpeper, Cousin Jed, Kennedy, Lester, McCord, and every other man in the room.

For the Ku Klux Klan was a joyful frolic in the lives of those who had lost kin, homes, limbs, and hope. The evening's subsequent adventures only grew in mirth.

"Lookee here, Cole," Cousin Jed, grinning ear-to-ear, called in a loud whisper from the doorless front entryway of the house.

Culpeper hustled to the spot as thunder cracked from the heavy night sky. He saw a cloaked rider at the front of the dooryard. Three black men on foot, one in a Federal uniform and carrying a rifle, stood in the road before the rider.

"Man?" the rider said, an eerie tenor to his voice. "You call me a man? Why, no man am I."

"Doggies," Culpeper whispered to Cousin Jed. "That sounds like ole Reed, the quietest one in the bunch."

"It is," Cousin Jed said, needing great effort to throttle his laughter.

"I am the spirit of a brave Confederate soldier—whom each of you men knew well—slain at Chickamauga," Reed tolled.

None of the black men spoke or moved.

Finally the bluecoat raised the rifle to his shoulder and, his voice faltering, said, "I may kill you again, ghost man."

Reed thrust a robed arm at the man, his index finger pointing as though a harbinger of imminent cosmic wrath.

"No bullet or a company of bullets can now do me harm," he bellowed with mounting volume, as a streak of lightning lit up the wind-sheared tree stumps around the house and a volley of fresh thunder crashed.

Culpeper and Cousin Jed held their breath as the bluecoat pondered his next move.

"Yea, drop yon gun," Reed droned, "lest ye condemn thy wicked soul to utter and everlasting damnation, oh foolish man!"

The bluecoat did not drop his gun, but he and his two comrades turned and ran as fast as they could for as long as they could.

"Did you see that?" Cousin Jed gasped to Culpeper.

"I saw that and more besides," Crowe said. Along with most of the other Klansmen in the house, he had wedged into the doorway to witness the amazing sequence. "Since we've been riding the night roads, they're all back to work, or looking to work, most in their old masters' fields."

"Well, we still best be careful," said Cousin Jed, growing serious. "We all got lots of good black friends, and I heard just last week a couple of the boys scared the livin' daylights out of 'em up on Parmalee Hill."

Kennedy whistled softly. "That would have been Calvin Jones and company. Never thought I'd see the little Baptist choirboy take so vigorous a hand in such matters."

"That's proving to be one expensive chipped tooth for the blacks," McCord said.

"Little Calvin Jones and company," at the heretofore-bashful Jones's persistent suggestion, had taken to riding as a separate unit, ostensibly to allow the club to cover more ground. Lester reluctantly assented to the division as word spread of the decrease in theft, idling, and harassment of white women by the blacks, and the concomitant increase in law-abiding and hard work in the fields.

Little Calvin had further metamorphized from his choirboy cocoon by engineering a series of original exercises that amazed his comrades, not to mention the blacks whom they targeted.

Such as that he would now unveil as Culpeper and the larger group joined Jones and his little knot of men a hundred yards down the road from the cabin of one of the black soldiers they learned participated in the Darcy Jones incident.

"McCormack here says the cur is just t'other side of that bend, coming this way, dead drunker'n a fence rail," Jones said.

"Here he comes yonder," Culpeper, with the best eyes in the group, said, catching a glimpse of the stumbling soldier in a flash of lightning.

The black soldiers did not know whether the mysterious white-cloaked riders who roamed the countryside at night were indeed spirits returned from Confederate battlefields. And they could not yet say, if they were, what effect .57 calibre Enfield balls might have on them. But they darned sure were not going to find themselves up against one without at least having a weapon to fire.

Without a word Jones spurred his horse, white-cloaked like all the other Klansmen's mounts, toward the cabin. Even in the rain and wind, the biting aroma of moonshine whiskey reached Jones seconds before the soldier himself did.

But it wasn't the whiskey that produced the sight now before the soldier.

"Greetings, soldier," Jones said as the man cringed before him, the stock of the Enfield hitting the wet dirt. "With all this rain these last days, I seem to be a bit soggy up top. Would you mind awfully holding my head for me for a moment?" He reached up and pulled off his hood—and the head inside it!

"Aaiihh!" the soldier croaked as Jones offered the white-cloaked bundle to him.

Never before had Jones heard such vulgar language from any man, black or white, Federal or Confederate, as what streamed forth from the soldier as he fled into the woods, flinging his rifle to the ground as he retreated. Cradling the large headdress-wrapped gourd "head" that had rested above his real head in one arm as he reigned his horse around to return to the group, Jones wondered how such a fool could have been brave enough even to force a seven-year-old girl into the mud.

The laughter of Jones's fellows only subsided when Culpeper announced his own proposal to round out the evening, as the storm grew to torrential proportions, the thunder now so loud Cousin Jed and the others could hardly hear the Virginian's voice over it.

"My esteemed colleague of the Old Dominion, if you are able successfully to pull off this scheme, I will personally fill your rubber bag for you next time with whiskey," McCord chortled.

"All I ask is for Cousin Jed here to come with me," Culpeper said. "I want one feller to fetch an upclose eyeball o' what happens."

And so the two of them rode to the hut of Happy Samples, whom Cousin Jed's friend and former slave Big Joe identified as the man who provoked a fight and beat him with a club the day before because he and his brother Elisha would not join the Union League.

Staying with Samples, they knew, was the agitator Elijah Sledge, whom several Klansmen, including Culpeper, had witnessed in close association with Union Leaguers and Freedman Bureau agents, and frequenting their assemblies.

Samples was slow to answer the door.

"He must have seen us comin' down the road," Cousin Jed said.

"We're jest thirsty travelers pinin' for a scupper o' water," Culpeper called from astride his horse.

The door creaked open. Samples saw what he feared he would. In a noble attempt at masking the terror he felt, he said, "All a thirsty man's got to do in this downpour is point his face toward the heavens and open his mouth."

"Well, now, cousin," Culpeper said cheerfully, "as you can see, that'd be just a might tricky, what with this here hood on."

"Whyn't you take off that blasted hood then and quit a'scarin' innocent folks," Samples snapped.

"You'll be pleased in jest a minute that I don't do that, friend," Culpeper said. "Now since you kept me waitin' such a spell, believe I'm gonna need a whole bucketful of water."

Samples's eyebrows shot up.

"You and yo friend gonna drink a whole bucket?"

"Didn't say that," Culpeper responded.

"Oh," Samples said, relieved, "yo and yo horses too." He peered at the mounts. "How they gonna drink through them gitups?"

"They ain't," Culpeper said. "And neither is my pardner. Now d— you, get me a bucket o' water, or I swear, I'll lose my happy temper, Happy."

"Say, how you know my name, mister? I know you?"

When Culpeper said nothing, Samples scowled, uttered a profanity, and stomped back through his door. He had to go out back, the storm soaking him every step of the way, and pump water up from the well he shared with several other blacks nearby. Cursing one long flow of epithets, he filled an entire wooden bucket, then added a lusty chunk of spittle and a not ungenerous stream of urine for good measure.

By the time he returned to Culpeper, Samples's surreptitious handiwork had significantly improved his demeanor, and he visited upon his uninvited guests just the show of hospitality as whose proverbial absence had won him his nickname.

"There now, see how that wets your pipes, boss," he said, flashing a smile so bright Culpeper could see it even though the lightning had ceased.

"Why, thank ye, Happy," Culpeper said, lifting the whole bucket to the small mouth opening in his hood.

Samples's eyes grew till Cousin Jed feared they might pop out of the man's head as he watched Culpeper, without pause, drain the entire five-gallon bucket.

"Yep, that's mighty fine, Happy," Culpeper said with a smile as he licked his lips. "Couldn't spare another could ye?"

Gripped with horror, beginning to suspect more indeed might be at play here than the prank he suspected from one of his white neighbors, Samples took the bucket and walked back through the hut to the well. After all, he was sure he had never heard this man's voice before, and he figured he could tell just about any man's voice, black or white, from around Pulaski, whether or not his head was covered with a white hood.

After Culpeper drained the bucket a second time and asked for a third filling, Samples remembered the persistent story, circulated by a growing legion of sources that he had to this point discounted, of white-cloaked ghost riders spurring their white horses through the midnight skies over nearby towns.

The fleeting thought struck him as he returned to the well that a full bowel movement was now in order and would provide the perfect spice to the pail. *But what if that b—— is a ghost?* Samples panted. *Story say ain't no bad black man escape; not at all, the spirits always follows them and catches them and ain't no living man hears from them again. And they leader—he ten feet high, his horse fifteen, and he carries a lance and a shield like Goliath of the Philistines!*

"Ah, lah-dee-dah," Culpeper hollered with joy, licking his lips again as he turned the empty pail upside down a third time, and the rain stopped. "I come a thousand miles in twenty-four hours, and that's the best water I had me since I was killed at the battle o' Shiloh. A man gets plumb thirsty in hell, Happy."

As if on cue, now came the greatest explosion of thunder Culpeper, Cousin Jed, or Happy Samples had ever heard, the brightest sheet of lightning, and a rain so full and hard it seemed as though God had pulled back the canopy for a second flood.

When Culpeper saw his host's knees quaking, he determined to deliver his sermon before the man fainted dead away.

"Leave Big Joe and his brother be," he shouted over the din. "They's lots o' room left in hell, and ain't no one I know there singin' psalms about it."

Samples could not speak then, nor could he when Elijah Sledge returned an hour later from an important Union League errand.

A delighted McCord, vowing to somehow make good on his promise to Culpeper—and in smooth Tennessee sipping whiskey—assured the Klansmen back at their ramshackle meeting place that the Pulaski *Citizen* would provide the community with full coverage of the "radical Negro" Obadiah Samples in that week's edition.

Culpeper and Cousin Jed laughed all the way back to the farm.

"But how'd ya fit the rubber sack and the three bucketsful of water you poured into it, all under your robe, without Happy seeing it?" Cousin Jed asked.

"Well, now, I can't show such secrets to a man lessin' he plans to put 'em to use," Culpeper said.

"Oh, I already got me somebody in mind," Cousin Jed said with that easy laugh.

The laughter ceased when they got home and Cousin Daniel told them Federal soldiers and Union Leaguers, black and white, had left an hour before, with the entire haul from the Wallace's secret cotton gin, set back in the forest behind the farm.

"Little Elisha came cryin' to me after, sayin' Happy Samples threatened him and Big Joe with lynchin' if'n they didn't spill where was the gin," Cousin Daniel said, himself near tears. "He felt so bad about it, he told me 'twas that Elijah Sledge put Happy up to it. And 'tis Elijah Sledge what is workin' with some of them carpetbaggers on some big doin's come this Saturday night."

Culpeper saw Cousin Jed's face had turned white as the hood he wore that evening and now had packed in his saddlebags.

"All of it?" Cousin Jed asked his brother, his choked voice barely loud enough to be heard. "Half the men in our—half the men we rode with tonight brought their cotton to us for ginnin', Cole, 'cause the Yanks been takin' it all, new and old, claimin' it as goods for the Southern war effort. And it was our first crop since before the war."

Cousin Jed squinted, the only light that of the oil lamp showing out a glassless window from the partially completed little cabin several of the Wallaces now shared as they built it. "Your eye's black, and you're bleedin' from the mouth, nose, and ears, Dan."

"The Federal commander said to tell you they confiscated the cotton as Confederate contraband, but they're still gonna tax us for it—for everybody's—as a penalty for hidin' it from 'em," said Cousin Daniel, ignoring his brother's observation, and knowing, as did Jed, that with no cotton there would be no tax money, and with no tax money they would lose the family farm. "They took the gin, too, and said if we snuck another back in there, they'd hang every one of us as unsur-inun-insurr—"

"Insurrectionists," Culpeper said.

Despite his numbed stupor, Cousin Jed stared at Culpeper. "Cousin Cole, never before heard you speak a two-dollar word like that."

"Oh, I know what that word means," Culpeper said, seething with mute rage. "I *am* that word."

Frank McCord published more in that week's *Citizen* than the feature on Happy Samples. High up on the right-hand side of the front page, next to the Samples story, ran the bold headline, "Shrouded Brotherhood! Murdered Heroes!"

Beneath it, in slightly smaller but still prominent print, appeared the words: "Fling the bloody shirt that covers you to the four winds. . . . Strike with the red-hot spear. . . . The skies shall be blackened. A single Star shall look down upon horrible deeds. The night owl shall hoot a requiem over ghostly corpses."

CHAPTER 61

HE FIRST SAW HER THE NIGHT HE WAS ELECTED. SHE HAD BEEN watching him for months from varying distances and settings.

Marley's first vision of her cut through the giddiness, the presence of some of the greatest names in the Northeast—senators, congressman, industrial captains, publishing magnates—and his utter amazement that a one-eyed, battle-scarred Christian and friend of Stonewall Jackson's, who had bitterly contested the co-opting of President Lincoln's programs by the Radical Republicans, could be standing at the finest hotel in Canonsburg, Pennsylvania, on this cold November night in 1866, elected to the United States Congress.

It even intruded on the thoughts that raced through his mind about launching a Bible study for Federal veterans—*and congressmen?*—from his own office in the United States Capitol Building. He believed such an effort might be used by God to bring far greater good to the nation than the best legislative efforts.

Other men, other Republican men, stood triumphant in important cities, north, south, and west this very night, as the setting of the stage continued for a new and very different America.

"The United States may remain a republic in name, but some eight million of the people are subjects, not citizens," said one sympathetic Northerner.

Marley had not thought himself still capable of experiencing the heady sense that enveloped him at the sight of such a vision as the woman who now watched him.

How fair is her skin, how long and slender her neck, how softly rounded her shoulders, how black her hair, how blue her dress, how brilliant the pearls around her throat, and—how low on her bosom the cut of her dress.

He shamed himself for such unchaste thoughts, even as the feelings tided over him anew of how badly he desired a wife.

I am reminded by her of someone I have known, somewhere, at some time, he thought. Then, shaking his head, he chuckled to himself, *Perhaps she reminds me only of someone I should like to know.*

Then she was before him, one of the other Pennsylvanian congressmen, Fitch, introducing her to him as "Miss Anne Nelson, one of our loyal Western Virginia Unionists."

Fitch, smiling and smelling of alcohol, chuckled, and added, "So wise indeed to have remained loyal, when one's Southern countrymen are proclaiming the 'Northern elections' the doom of their destiny, and their portion one of utter ruin and abject degradation."

Marley, noting her graceful smile and that she was perhaps the only person present besides him in the entire room not imbibing champagne or something stronger, offered the deepest and most formal bow he could muster. He felt a surge of elation in spite of himself when he saw the bow so impressed her she blushed and touched a kid-gloved hand to billowing black hair.

At the recital of his name, she curtsied and cooed, "Who does not know of the famed Colonel Marley—" Stevens had seen to that. "—and his many and legendary deeds on the fields of battle in two great wars?"

So charismatic was this opening flourish that Marley did not yet discern her cultured Southern brogue.

"I shall forever lament that I have not a heroic uniform like yours, Colonel and Congressman Marley," Fitch said, his voice not void of true regret. "But then, such a foolish sentiment may be at least partly informed by Gettysburg being the place of my birth."

"Gettysburg?" Marley asked. "Did you know Mr. Stevens when he lived there?"

"I knew him then, and I know him now, as I live but blocks from him in Lancaster."

"But . . . how can you be congressman from Lancaster when already Thaddeus Stevens is?" Marley asked, baffled.

Fitch laughed. "Indeed, I have said I am a newly elected congressman *from* Lancaster. I did not say I *represent* that region. No, I am the people's representative from one of the most verdant sections of that nasty little womb of fire-breathers, South Carolina."

Marley saw the twinkle in Anne's eyes, but he was lost.

"Of course, I have not yet seen my district," Fitch said, slurping champagne. "And I do not think I am inclined to see it anytime soon. When I received the letter from Washington informing me of my 'election,' I had to confess to my wife that I was not aware I had even been nominated!"

Then he was sweeping a pair of champagne glasses off a servant's tray and wading into a cluster of bejeweled young maidens, as Marley stared after him in stupefaction.

"I fear I may pose a dreadfully boring companion for you this evening, Colonel," Anne said, the syrupy drawl impossible now for even the giddy Marley to evade, as the two of them watched the other man depart. "I imbibe nothing more daring than that delicious Roman punch in those beautifully cut ice goblets."

Marley smiled. "I believe the most daring item of this entire folderol is a charming and beautiful Southern woman who drinks only punch."

Her well-crafted composure came close to crumbling at this, but as her eyes glittered, she smiled her devastating smile and took his arm.

"You'll not take offense, will you, Colonel Marley, if I am so bold as to suggest that you face more ruthless enemies now than ever you did in war?" she asked as she escorted him toward a knot of the most ruthless.

"If only I had such faithful mates as I did then, to guard my way," he could not believe he heard himself say. He suspected it was her eyes, the way they lit up like fireflies every time he said something. Then he realized her perfume was the most intoxicating he had ever smelled and that her voice possessed such a charmed melodious quality that he actually feared if he did not get some of that punch he might be hypnotized by her right there in front of all Pennsylvania.

"From what region of western—or West—Virginia do you hail, Miss Nelson?" he asked.

A different sort of glint flickered in her eyes before she said, "Oh, a part that no longer exists. Fortunately."

He wondered later about this statement and about much else of what she had, and hadn't, said. How she knew so many of the "elite" from his own state, and what was so familiar about her. He had no idea why was she even there, in Pennsylvania, tonight. Then he shrugged, thinking, *I suppose I will have time to sort all that out, as she seems quite looking forward to my escorting her to Kate Chase Sprague's New Year's in Washington.*

Altogether, she generated ever so much more cause for deliberation than had Thaddeus Stevens in Marley's short and unsatisfactory meeting with that man.

●◇ ●◇ ●◇

When the clock struck ten o'clock, Lee rose from his chair in the dining room, opened the door to the front parlor, and crossed to draw the shutters. By now his ways were known well enough in Lexington that only the greenest young—or not-so-young—beaux required the additional prodding of "Good night, gentlemen."

And hardly ever anymore did he need to replace Agnes or Mildred in their seat and continue the conversation until the startled courter perceived he had way past worn out his welcome.

Yes, sometimes it took only the ten chimes of that old clock for the splendid men who had come calling to be falling over themselves to grab hats and mufflers and gloves and be out of the president's home within a minute or two, and within seconds if possible.

How brave is our noble herd, Lee thought as they began to file out. Poor young Harry Wickham and poor old VMI professor and captain John Brooke, making the pilgrimage week after week to woo Agnes, always with the result reflected on their faces—and hers—again tonight. *And VMI post physician and widower Dr. Howard Barton, among the legion, with his three children and his unrequited feelings for our Precious Life.*

The next evening was Sunday, and Lee noticed a half hour after he returned home from evensong that Mildred had not yet arrived. A few more minutes passed when he thought he heard laughter from the front porch. *This is becoming a very un-Sabbath-like visit,* he thought, his anger kindled. He swung open the front door and detected his daughter's form—more womanly than he had remembered it—springing up from where she had been seated in the shadows on the front steps. A second figure, with a familiar gait and a loose sleeve, hurried away behind the bushes. *Maggie Preston's stepson Frank, who left an arm at Winchester and teaches our Greek and Latin at the college,* he realized.

"Ah, Papa, is it you?" Mildred, flustered, blurted out. "Was—er, was there anyone here while I was gone?"

"No, Precious Life," Lee said, sounding for all the world to Mildred like Moses bringing new proclamations down from Mount Sinai, "gentlemen do not visit at my house on Sunday night."

●◇ ●◇ ●◇

Part of his irritation with Mildred was that he had planned to complete his written response to Sir (later Lord) John Dalberg Acton's letter, which he had been attempting to do for nearly a month. He was determined to finish it tonight. Among other notable declarations, it was Acton, Lee knew, who had proclaimed, "Liberty has not subsisted outside of Christianity."

How insightful that Englishman's comments, a man who has never been south of Maryland, Lee thought as he read the penetrating words again, words to which Lee knew the unfolding Northern historical orthodoxy did not subscribe.

"Without presuming to decide the purely legal question," Acton wrote regarding Southern secession, "on which it seems evident to me from Madison's and Hamilton's papers that the fathers of the Constitution were not agreed, I saw in State Rights the only availing check upon the absolutism of the sovereign will, and secession filled me with hope, not as the destruction but as the redemption of democracy. The institutions of your Republic have not exercised on the old world the salutary and liberating influence which ought to have belonged to them, by reason of those defects and abuses of principle which the Confederate constitution was expressly and wisely calculated to remedy. I believed that the example of that great reform would have blessed all the races of mankind by establishing true freedom purged of the native dangers and disorders of republics.

"Therefore I deemed that you were fighting the battles of our liberty, our progress, and our civilization," Acton concluded, "and I mourn for the stake which was lost at Richmond more deeply than I rejoice over that which was saved at Waterloo."

Lee sat a very long time pondering those thoughts and their implications. Then, filled with the creeping guilt of his recent past and the regret of his distant past, he penned his response:

"All that the South has ever desired was that the Union, as established by our forefathers, should be preserved and that the government, as originally organized, should be administered in purity and truth. I had no other guide, nor had I any other object than the defense of those principles of American liberty upon which the constitutions of the several states were originally founded."

A few nights later he composed a response to Markie's latest letter in which she, an accomplished artist, asked questions about Traveller, with a view toward painting him. He began with a recitation of Traveller's physical features.

"My dearest Markie, if I was an artist like you," Lee wrote, "I would draw a true picture of Traveller, representing his fine proportions, muscular figure, deep chest, short back, strong haunches, flat legs, small head, broad forehead, delicate ears, quick eye, small feet, and black mane and tail."

Warming to the task and recalling anew how profound a friend Traveller had been through the most tumultuous events of his life, Lee's heart swelled with feeling as he continued. "Such a picture would inspire a poet, whose genius could then depict his worth and describe his endurance of toil, hunger, thirst, heat, and cold; and the dangers and suffering through which he has passed. He could dilate upon his sagacity and affection and his invariable response to every wish of his rider. He might even imagine his thoughts through the long night marches and days of battle through which he has passed. But I am no artist, Markie, and can therefore only say he is a Confederate gray.

"From the commencement of the campaign in 1864 at Orange, till its close around Petersburg, the saddle was scarcely off his back," Lee concluded, "even to when in 1865 he bore me to the final day at Appomattox Courthouse. You know the comfort he is to me in my present retirement."

Again Markie had dwelt at length and with much emotion on the subject of Orton. *The confusion, the bewilderment, the scars of unanticipated partings void of closure or resolution, scars still raw that would never quite close—how we are all beset on all sides by such hauntings,* Lee thought, pondering the toll levied on Agnes by Orton's death.

"My own grief," he wrote, "is as poignant now as on the day of its occurrence, and my blood boils at the thought of the atrocious outrage against every manly and Christian sentiment which the great God alone is able to forgive. I cannot trust my pen or tongue to utter my feelings. He alone can give us resignation."

Hours later, unable to sleep, he walked the cold grounds around the president's house, the bare tree limbs around him eclipsed by a pale winter moon. He knew much time would pass before he would be able to reconcile all the sorrow and suffering. And ominous new portents continued to arrive as harbingers of doom. This past summer racial tension between blacks and whites exploded into bloodshed in both New Orleans and Memphis. Largely Irish-African affairs, in each instance, both sides had received provocation. But the results were alike: virtual massacres of a sizable group of blacks by the whites, followed by heightened suppression of the white populations by the occupying Federal armies.

A shiver ran through him as he recalled disturbing rumors of ex-Confederate soldiers tracking down blacks who had worn—and in many cases still wore—the blue coat and lynching them as turncoat traitors to the South. He knew the rights and safety of the downtrodden former-Confederate population needed better protection than the Federals had provided, but these terrifying reports were trickling in to him from all over the South. *Dear God, that is not the way,* he thought, his chest growing tight.

So much of it all he felt crushing down on his own massive shoulders . . . Malvern Hill . . . Cemetery Ridge . . . even Fredericksburg, and the unspeakable slaughter of *those* people, stacked several men deep in places on Marye's Heights.

Only when he retreated to the Psalms, and shared the woes, the fears, the guilt . . . the forgiveness . . . of that other flawed warrior, did his spirit calm and he could sleep. Even then, his last coherent thoughts were, *I did not lead my people to victory in battle as did David. Oh, that I could help them in peace more than I did in war.*

On March 13, 1867, the First Reconstruction Act of the United States Congress resounded across the South like a fire bell at noonday. The handiwork of Thad Stevens and his minions now passed the once-sovereign state of Virginia, which birthed four of the first six United States presidents, out of legal existence. In its place, nearly two years after Lee offered Grant his sword at Appomattox Courthouse, they created Military District Number 1.

Every former Confederate state but Tennessee, with its Radical-controlled puppet governor and legislature, formed military districts.

Federal Major General John M. Schofield now held absolute and dictatorial authority to appoint, and remove, every public servant in Military District Number 1, from governor to courtroom bailiffs. Also vested in him was the power both to conduct the new voter registration Stevens wished for each military district and determine who was now eligible to vote—and not to vote.

The South reeled from the shock of the epic blow. Then shock gave way to fear and, as such things will, to anger—anger of a sort its people never felt the whole war, even to the bloody end.

"We thought the worst was already past and that the Yankees wanted us back in as sister states—ain't that why they say they fought us?" wagged tongues across the old Confederacy.

As the concussion reverberated through everyone he knew, Lee answered, with the condition that he speak in confidence, the request of a cluster of Lexington men for counsel on how to respond to the First Reconstruction Act.

"I think all persons entitled to vote should attend the polls and endeavor to elect the best available men to represent them in the convention, to whose decision everyone should submit," he said. "The preservation of harmony and kind feelings is of the utmost importance, and all good citizens should seek to secure it and prevent the division of the people into parties. The interests of all are inseparably connected and can only be preserved by our united wisdom and strength. I think it useless to offer arguments to show the propriety of this course. Its advantages are too manifest.

"It is extremely unpleasant to me, for reasons which I think will occur to you, that my name should be unnecessarily brought before the public, and I do not see that any good can result from it. I hope therefore you will keep my comments private but that you will try and allay the strife that I fear may arise in the state."

To Lee's mighty displeasure, his comments were printed, verbatim, two days later in the *Lexington Gazette*.

He did not know that a sizable number of men, in various locales around the South, and many of them brave men and good, put aside their thoughts of violence upon reading the "private" thoughts of Robert E. Lee, which spread like a Norther-blown prairie fire across all sections of the land.

Others responded in a different manner.

Somber news came from all quarters to the Klan's dilapidated meeting-house outside Pulaski.

"Our noble governor Parson Brownlow," said Lester, "is promising to enforce his Disfranchisement Law, barring us all from voting. Now I'm reading his own words from that rag he publishes in Memphis: 'If to do so it becomes necessary that there shall be violence and bloodshed, so be it.'"

"That our blood he's talking about, boys?" Cousin Jed queried, failing both to force a smile onto his own face and to inject a bit of levity into the conversation.

"We may lose what land we have left even before that happens," Lester said. "Brownlow is pushing for the dismembering of ex-Confederates' property into forty-acre tracts for former slaves."

"That—" Cousin Jed murmured, stopping when he saw Culpeper's eyes on him, not wanting to set a poor example for his visiting relative.

Culpeper had noticed a hardening of his cousin's attitude since the loss of his cotton and gin and Daniel's beating. *Reckon when a man ain't got nothin' left to lose, he jest don't rightly care what happens,* he thought, understanding the sentiment.

"I've got more good news," said Kennedy, whose own sunny demeanor Culpeper had seen less and less. "It seems the ex-slaves the carpetbaggers have elected to our city councils and our state legislature are voting the way their sponsors tell them."

"Well—what way is that?" Cousin Jed asked.

"The way that votes millions of dollars of bonds with scant value received for it, and Federal courts then telling the mayors across our states to levy taxes however big to pay the bonds off—"

"Holy—" Calvin Jones began.

"—at a hundred cents on the dollar," Kennedy finished. "My friends in Nashville and Memphis tell me if this keeps up much longer, every city or town in Tennessee will have to sell every item of any value it still owns—town parks, courthouse buildings, fire engines—and fire what few law officials we still have to pay these 'legislated' obligations."

"'Scuse me," Culpeper piped up, the rare sound of his voice in an official Klan meeting turning heads all around the dimly illumined room toward him. "I'm nothin' fer money doin's, but just where the heck are them millions of dollars goin'?"

"Last nigra state legislator I saw rode in his own two-horse walnut barouche, driven by the fanciest-liveried coachman you ever did see," Jones said.

"And the white carpetbaggers and scalawags are makin' the blacks look small by comparison," Lester said.

"I don't hardly blame the blacks," Kennedy said. "They want a chance like everyone else, and most of 'em are just taking the only shot they're getting right now."

"I don't blame any of 'em but the blue-coated ones," Cousin Jed groused, lowering his head. "For them, there's . . ."

"Hell yet to pay," Jones finished for him.

Lester raised his hands to slow them. "Lest we get ourselves riled up again, y'all know we've got fine news from the first national meeting in Nashville. Frank?"

"Fine indeed," McCord said. "Not only do we have Klan dens sprouted clear through Tennessee, but from the looks of what we saw at the Maxwell House Hotel, the more the Yanks shove us into the corner, the more we're spreadin' across the South. Why, General John Gordon was there, headin' up the realm in Georgia."

"How did he find out about it?" Jones asked.

"From his brother, who's the Baptist preacher down in Athens, Alabama," McCord said.

"Athens," Kennedy said, "isn't that where that Russian Yankee ran amuck?"

"Colonel Turchin," McCord said, "looted the town in 1862, built a heaping pile with the townspeople's Bibles and other Christian literature, then torched it; and his men went on a wild raping spree against the black women of the community. Then ole Abe overrode Turchin's court-martial and promoted him to general."

When silence greeted this dread remembrance, McCord proceeded. "Guess most of you heard by now that none other than the great Wizard of the Saddle himself, Bedford Forrest, has agreed to lead us."

"They named the position the Grand Wizard in honor of him," Crowe chimed in.

"Well, I expect we would know, bein' as half of us rode with him during the war," Cousin Jed said, though he managed a wink with words voiced harsher than he intended.

"Is it true they asked General Lee first?" Jones said.

"Yes, and I'm told that though he replied that his health prevented him from accepting the position," McCord answered, "he admonished us to keep steadily in the view of the great principles for which we contend and that the safety of our homes and the lives of all the South holds dear depend upon our courage and exertions."

"'Let each man resolve to be victorious,' he said, 'and the right of self-government, liberty, and peace shall find him a defender,'" said Crowe. "He also wrote a statement of his support but said that support must be invisible."

"Hence our alternate name of the 'Invisible Empire,'" added McCord.

"You men should also remember General Lee's absolute insistence that the Klan serve only as a protective organization for the defenseless innocents of our land," Kennedy added. "I am quite certain any other manifestation of the organization would void his support of it."

"Sometimes . . ." Cousin Jed began.

"Sometimes what?" Jones said.

"Well, blast it all, sometimes I wonder if General Lee plays a little too loose with these wretches what are doin' their best to ruin us all," Cousin Jed finished.

"Don't forget, men," Kennedy said, "General Forrest himself has had three men—and those are just the ones we know of—tried by the Klan and shot for violating his orders not to disturb or molest people. He won't tolerate it, and neither should we."

"Me, I'm startin' to think Mexico or Brazil look pretty good," Cousin Jed said. "Leastwise they hate the Yankees there too."

Culpeper heard the ambivalence in his cousin's voice. *He is fretting himself for being so down in the mouth,* the Virginian thought, not fretting him for it at all.

"Well," Lester said, "I think it clear the Radicals have no desire at all to 'welcome back as brothers' those President Lincoln said 'have never been away.' They want us and our old-school influences out of here. Mexico or Brazil—or England or France—suits 'em right down to the ground. And the simplest way to accomplish that is to take our land away from us through back-tax confiscation. If that doesn't work, this new 'income tax' the Yankee Congress has voted in on us will."

"Yeh, and when we been paying our property taxes all along, but to the Confederacy since 1861," said Jones. "They'll have to kill me to get me to pay again—especially to that den of thieves—or to get off my land either."

"And if we somehow manage to hang onto our land through it all," Lester added, "then when we die, they'll use this new 'inheritance' taxation to steal it from our children. One way or another they mean to get us out of here, and they mean to sunder the whole South from its birth ties to the land so they can redirect our orientation from the land to their Yankee capital. It's not Reconstruction, men, it's revolution, just like in Europe twenty years ago. In fact it's a lot of the very same schemers who tried that that are muddying the water now here in America."

The only response the group could muster to this was the gulping sound of an unusually large swallow of tobacco juice down Culpeper's throat.

"Well, I don't expect the ole Wizard would cotton to the Feds stealin' our land from us, then givin' it to the darkies," said Jones.

"Just remember," Kennedy said. "Bedford himself said 'Better Confederates did not live' than those 'darkies' that rode and served with us—the cavalry troopers alone among them counted sixty-five—and you knew them just like I did."

"And we've new concerns on our plate that command our attention," said Lester, trying as always to keep to business. "There's word suspicions are afoot among the Union and Loyal Leagues in the county regarding our local meetings and even the general area where we gather. I would propose we broaden the use of the loose brick in the back wall of the *Citizen* to make it a sort of mailbox to pass along announcements and information and to reduce the frequency of these assemblies."

After all in the group assented, Jones's soft voice sounded again.

"What with that skunk Brownlow and these carpetbaggers and bluecoat n——s, and now the Yanks trying to take what little we still have away from us, it appears we got us another war on our hands."

The whole room waited for Lester's response. "General Forrest told us in Nashville he receives fifty to one hundred letters a day, every day, every week, every month, from every Southern state, from men complaining, worn down, without hope, whose friends are killed, or even now being killed, or their families getting insulted, and they write him to know what they ought to do."

"So what did he say?" Cousin Jed asked.

"He said we have already lost nearly all but honor by the last war," Lester continued, "and that in order to be men, we must protect our honor at all hazards and thus preserve our homes and families and whatever else may be left."

The ensuing silence indicated with what import each man held Forrest's opinions and that all had turned toward his own thoughts and consideration of the additional levy such a course must likely demand of them. Then the mournful voice of Reed rose in the still night out by the road.

"What soul approacheth on yon road?"

In an instant they were at his side, pistols drawn and cocked. It was Big Joe from the Wallace place, astride an ancient scrawny mule. Culpeper saw that the lanky man's feet nearly touched the ground and that his breath came in frightened gusts.

"Mr. Jed," Joe blurted, knowing the other man from all the rest, even under his garb, "that rascal Happy Samples and that Elijah Sledge are lightin' the stupid n——s up over to the Brick Church, and they got a couple o' Yankees puttin' 'em all up to it, and one of them white boys be passin' out free whiskey and the other be givin' 'em Bible tracts, and Mr. Jed?"

"Yeh, Big Joe, what else, fella?" Cousin Jed said.

"They done whipped some poor nigras from the Cunningham place, and they wore white sheets to get up close to 'em so's they could snatch 'em and have you men blamed—and Mr. Jed, worst of all—"

"What, Joe, what, man?"

"They fixin' to scald our whole place out and some o' these other men's too."

Cousin Jed and Culpeper were already on the way to their horses.

"Jed!" Lester, knowing more than a dozen women and children, black and white, lived on the Wallace land, called out. When neither man slowed, Lester, now moving himself, said to the others, "Get to your horses. We best be there with them."

This time no one frolicked on the ride, no one paid heed to whom they passed, blue coat or no, and none brooked any tactics or strategy at all except to get into the presence of their enemies as fast as they could.

Happy Samples had learned how the rubber-bag trick worked, and he was plenty steamed about it, and plenty likkered about it too. He planned to toss the first torch through the front window of the partially built Wallace cabin. *Course, poor white trash ain't got a glass window on their tacky spread now,* he thought, guzzling more mash and grinning at the bound ex-Cunningham slaves lying on the ground before him, their backs raw from lashes, some of which Happy himself had delivered. His own sheet lay on the ground a few feet away.

"Riders a'comin'!" someone screamed. Samples felt the ground tremble before he heard the hoofbeats.

The Klansmen thundered into the churchyard before anyone had a chance to do anything. As the throng of perhaps thirty blacks scattered in every direction into the surrounding forest, several riders cornered the two whites. The squat little whiskey-dispensing carpetbagger cowered before the fearsome mounted specters. But the tall, thin Congregationalist preacher, his face creased in wrath, waved a Bible at them.

"'I have pursued mine enemies,' sayeth the Lord," he shouted, "'neither did I turn again till they were consumed!'"

Calvin Jones kicked the man's hand so hard it cracked from the force of the booted blow, and the Bible sailed into a nearby bonfire. Little Jones leaned over and, just as he had seen Bedford Forrest do to a Yank foot soldier at Shiloh, he hauled the parson up off the ground by the nape of his neck and collar of his coat with one hand and slung him over the crupper of his horse. Then he headed out into the woods.

"We know who you are, Mr. Carpetbagger," Kennedy said to the other white man, the Tennessean's voice no less amiable than it was at Sunday dinners on the Presbyterian church grounds. "And you have until sunup to be out of Giles County. If we so much as see you again—Union Leaguers, bluecoats, Grant's whole d—— army, we don't care—we'll stretch your neck for you. Now get a move on, and a good evening to you, sir."

All present marveled that so rotund a man could run so quickly, and so immediately at that.

There was nothing amiable about Culpeper or his cousins Jed, Ben, Red, and Daniel, all of them riding alongside one another.

"Where's Happy Samples?" Cousin Jed called out to one of the blacks who appeared sober and somewhat more composed than most of the others. When the man hesitated to answer, Jed tensed, then pointed his huge old Colt's dragoon at him and cocked back the heavy hammer. "Come on, mister. It ain't worth dyin' over. We'll get him anyhows."

The man pointed toward a clearing in the dense tangle.

"You ain't foolin', are you, mister?" Cousin Jed asked.

Before the man could shake his head, Cousin Daniel shouldered his horse forward and barked, "'Cause if you are, we'll be back, and there'll be h— to pay."

Then the teenager spurred his horse hard and led his kin into the darkness.

They tracked Samples for miles before the four sets of hoofprints split into pairs. They had all discerned which tracks were Samples's, and without a word all followed his.

As they came to the foot of a hill, a splotch of clouds drifted in front of the three-quarter moon, just long enough to obscure two new Spencer repeaters that would otherwise have been silhouetted atop the eminence. Several shots cracked out from them, knocking Cousin Daniel from his saddle. Before the reports finished echoing off the surrounding hills, Culpeper spotted one shooter's form and dropped it with a shot from his Springfield musket. Then he and his cousins Jed and Red charged straight up the face of the promontory. Cousin Ben dragged Daniel, his lungs blown open, to cover.

When they reached the top, Cousin Jed in the lead, they saw a body crumpled over a stump and had their pistols trained on him in the beat of a heart. But he no longer posed any threat. Cousin Jed flew off his horse and ran to the man, Red and Culpeper remaining in the saddle, the latter spotting two sets of hoofprints leading down the back side of the hill.

Cousin Jed found Happy Samples bleeding from the throat. He put his gun to the wounded man's temple.

"Tell me who just rode down that hill, or I'll finish you," Cousin Jed said.

"I'm already finished," Samples gurgled.

"Then I'll make you hurt bad before you go," Cousin Jed snarled.

Never had Culpeper heard such a tone in his cousin's voice; but then, never had he seen one of his cousin's brothers shot out of the saddle.

Samples attempted a wry laugh. "Ah, go get 'im for all I care. That fancy-talkin' Elijah Sledge brought me nothin' but trouble since he come to Tennessee—" His throat convulsed into a spasm of coughing that sprayed a dark mist over Cousin Jed.

"Who else fired on us, Happy?" Culpeper asked from his horse. "Wasn't just you, was it? You stink too much o' whiskey to get off that lucky a shot."

Samples coughed and gagged some more, then shook his head. "Nah, wasn't—me—was that high and mighty—"

"That Elijah Sledge?" Cousin Jed pressed him.

"I seen him another time," Culpeper said.

Samples laughed. "H—, you won't catch them boys on them nags you're a'ridin'. They got 'em brand new mounts from them Linkum boys, fit and fed, for leadin' the Unions up to your cotton, Jed."

"They?" Cousin Jed asked. "That pair what split off gonna meet back up with Sledge down the trail?"

"You'll never catch 'em," Samples repeated, convulsing in laughter. "H—, they headed all the way to North Carolina, to ride with Colonel Kirk."

Culpeper saw Cousin Jed's body tense.

"George Kirk?" the Tennessean barked.

"Nothin' but trou-ble," Samples sputtered, bleeding and dying.

Cousin Jed jumped up and saw his brother Ben clearing the top of the hill. Daniel lay facedown across his own horse.

Cousin Red swore an oath, and Cousin Jed stumbled toward his dead brother, stunned. His legs shook, as though his knees were about to buckle. Culpeper wondered if his friend would faint or burst into tears first. Instead the white garments again stiffened, and Cousin Jed said, his words slow and his voice hardly more than a whisper, "You take Danny back and bury 'im, Ben. Red, Cousin Cole, an' me are pushin' on till we take those miserable curs down." He turned, walked to his horse, and climbed back into the saddle, pulling rein.

"Ole Happy was right, Jed," Culpeper said. "We ride on now, we'll be afoot within a few miles—lessin' they pick us first."

Cousin Jed thought about that. "We'll push on steadylike and find us some better horses."

"You figure to do better for your family this way than stayin'?" Culpeper asked.

He thought about that too, and how his brother was a widower with no children, then said, "Ben, you take my Daisy Mae and the girls up into the hills, and you stay with 'em till I get back. I don't care if the Yanks burn the whole spread and flush it straight down the shoot to h— You keep my family away from them murderin' b——s. I'll deal with them when I get back. And you send Danny's wife and baby down to Oxford to her mama. You hear?"

"I hear, Jed."

"North Carolina, cousin?" Culpeper asked, doubtfully.

Cousin Jed sighed, then said, "Cole, George Kirk and a gang of bluebelly killers shot, stole, and torched their way clean across East Tennessee during the war. He was always smart enough to stay out of Bedford Forrest's reach, which is why he still draws breath today. But he cuts a wide swath wherever he goes. So if that murderin' Elijah Sledge is hookin' up with him, we'll sooner or later catch 'em. But I ain't aimin' to let Sledge get all the way to North Carolina anyhows."

With that, Cousin Jed spurred his horse down the hill toward the east. Culpeper sighed, thinking but saying to no man, *Guess I sorta thought this place might be worth settlin' down in.* Then he said, "Ben, can you find Happy a happy—and private—restin' place?" and followed after.

Which was just as well, because Governor Brownlow had a thousand-dollar bounty on both their heads before the next day was out.

CHAPTER 62

WHEN MARY CUSTIS RETURNED TO THE PRESIDENT'S HOUSE AT Washington College in the fall of 1867, she found her family immersed in efforts to raise money for repairs on and expansion of the dilapidated Grace Episcopal Church, which they had all joined.

Lee himself had been elected a church vestryman and headed the finance committee overseeing the effort to raise monies.

Conjuring visions of her wartime knitting army, Mary, bent and pained and churning with the energy of a steam locomotive, formed the Grace Church sewing society, which produced a stream of items that were packaged in Christmas baskets and offered for sale, the proceeds going toward the building fund.

The absence of children's Sunday school classes at the church had long bothered Agnes; now she and one of the V.M.I. professors were building one. And she was teaching the smallest children. *Not since dear Annie and I used to teach the slave children reading and writing and the Scriptures when we were girls at old Arlington have I felt so useful,* she thought one Saturday evening as she prepared the next morning's lesson.

Meanwhile, Mildred was attempting to master, at long last, the arts and sciences of domestic engineering and was preparing a late supper for the family when Mary Custis returned through the front door from her latest months-long travels among friends and other family.

"Ah, the prodigal daughter returns," Lee announced, in only partial jest, as he and Custis entered from the dining room. Mary and a couple of other sewing-society members had been debating, in the front parlor, the merits of raffling off a beautiful pincushion donated to the building fund by the mother of a Washington College student. After greetings had been exchanged with Mary Custis, the dialogue continued, only to be concluded with Lee's return from the dining room.

"No, don't raffle things for the church," he admonished them, stricken by the church resorting to such questionable tactics. "What amount would you hope to raise by such a plan?"

When Mary apprised him of the amount, he asked who was the sewing society's treasurer.

"I am," one of the other women answered.

Lee stared at her a moment, contemplating a not-insignificant amount of money he had saved in order to purchase himself a decent desk and chair for his office, which he needed badly, and a suit of clothes, which he needed worse. *Almighty and all-wise God,* he thought to himself, his eyes twinkling, *why should I be surprised that the amount saved and the amount here needed are one and the same? How much better may furniture pieces and clothing garments be entrusted to Thee.*

To Mary's astonishment, he returned from the modest little room he slept in next door to her bedroom with the full amount hoped for from sale of the pincushion.

The other ladies departed a bit later. The aching in Lee's arms, shoulders, and chest that Mildred's suitor Dr. Barton, as well as other area physicians, had determined stemmed from his heart and vascular system, bothered him worse tonight than usual. This partially prompted his extended questioning of Mary Custis regarding her extended absences.

She, worn to a frazzle from the long trip home, the last ten hours of which had been the bone-jarring stagecoach trip from Goshen, had heard it before, usually in good humor. Tonight, though, her own fatigue and soreness, and the occurrence of that monthly cycle she loathed, rendered her neither patient nor good-humored. She wanted only to go to bed. When her father persisted in delaying that act, she finally erupted.

"You have long questioned me on such matters," she said. Lee nodded. "You have long wondered how, when such breadth and depth of cordiality and companionship exist within these—and other—walls where we have resided, that I could deign to flit cross-country, without husband or chaperone or even your blessing."

Now she nodded as Lee wedged in a "Yes, we have—"

"These and many, many other things have you—have you all," she thundered, with a wave of her arm indicating the statement to include her mother, Custis, and Agnes as well, "long marveled at, worried over, and with innuendo and inflection both subtle and not at all subtle, pressed forth against me the compelling and satisfying verdict of a guilty conscience."

"Daughter—" Mary began.

"Just as I have for oh-so-ever long wondered," Mary Custis now shouted, "your cavalier sojourn away from a little girl of—was it five years old?—Yes! I should say I know exactly what it was, and for how long, and how that little girl felt the entire twelve months and sixteen days she was left with others while her parents shipped across country to an uncertain destination out west, with an undetermined date of return, and, in those days, a distinct possibility of never returning at all. Yes, I should say I have long wondered about certain issues myself, and found travels and separations from such parents who would ignore a little girl's screams and beggings and pleadings that they not leave her alone—for over a year—to be natural, without pain, and most satisfying!"

The only sound now heard in the front parlor was the faint thump of Mary's thimble dropping from her arthritic fingers onto the carpet. Silence followed for some seconds until what sounded like the firing of a small-caliber pistol in the kitchen.

Mary gasped, and Lee hollered, "Life? Life, are you all right?"

Then they heard Mildred's screams, from the kitchen, the dining room, and finally the front parlor.

Agnes and Mary Custis shrieked in unison when they saw their baby sister's face covered in crimson and looking more like she had been on the receiving end of a shotgun blast than a little pistol.

Lee rushed to her, croaking, "My sweet Precious Life—"

She fell to the floor, burying her messy head in her arms and bursting into sobs.

"Oh, I am hopeless!" she cried. "I am finished!"

Lee fell and enfolded her with his arms and body. "Oh, my dear, dear little Miss Mildred, what happened?"

Her body convulsed in loud long wails, and the others could barely discern the words when she whimpered, "I might as well be dead, as I could never be a good wife. I cannot even open a bottle of catsup without exploding it on myself and the entire kitchen—oh!"

He is not likable, but who can refrain from respecting the old lion? Marley marveled as he watched Thad Stevens, leaning against his walking stick, voice rasping, body trembling, the familiar bony finger thrust forward as if in accusation of all who would dare come against his sweeping vision for a new America.

Stevens had wearied of the thorn-in-the-flesh to that vision that was President Johnson and had engineered the historic—and historically unconstitutional—"Tenure of Office" Act. It threw a protective shield, primarily against Johnson, around the Republican-imposed bureaucracy that would oversee the Reconstruction. It also protected Congress from legal retaliation by Johnson; the Third Reconstruction Act disallowed Johnson any power to return any Confederate the right to vote.

And it forbade Johnson firing any member of his own cabinet unless the Senate approved the action. Marley—who with some reservation had followed Stevens's lead and voted for the Tenure of Office Act—and everyone else on all sides of the question knew the immediate objective was to prevent Johnson from firing the duplicitous Stanton, who served as the Radicals' in-camp spy within the presidential cabinet.

Then Stevens turned his guns on the United States Supreme Court, which had infuriated him by denouncing Congress's replacement of the citizen's right to a constitutionally guaranteed due process of law and trial by jury with autonomous military courts.

Marley, fearing to do otherwise would threaten the entire Reconstruction effort by undermining the military authority which enforced it—and thus void four years of bloody sacrifice by Federal armies—voted with the Republican majorities in the House and Senate to remove the Supreme Court's right to hear appeals by Southerners protesting their treatment under the various Reconstruction acts.

With the executive and judiciary branches thus hamstrung, Stevens and his juggernaut had cleared the field for both implementation and sustainment of their program of Reconstruction. Marley truly marveled at the scope and scale of Stevens's vision and his tenacity at carrying it off, all as the emaciated, pale, wheezing, and tottering man amazed his doctors with every day he lived.

Marley had arrived at the considered conclusion that one force kept Stevens's heart beating when it should long since have stopped: hatred for Andrew Johnson. This hatred matured into full flower when Johnson continued to defy the Republican-dominated House even as it began debating whether to impeach him for supposedly breaking the Tenure of Office Act.

So incensed was Stevens after this decision that he loosed Missouri Radical B. F. Loan on the House floor to preview the next evidence against Johnson.

"Andrew Johnson stood next in line of succession to Lincoln," Loan announced to the bewildered assembly. "He is a lifelong pro-slavery Southern Democrat and influenced by all the grosser animal instincts, complemented by a towering ambition. How should we be surprised that the Jesuitical leaders of the rebellion should prefer just this sort of man to hold the reins of government?"

Marley saw the color rising on the handsome blond head of his freshman colleague from Wisconsin, Kurt Schumacher. That man, like his mentor Schurz, had been suspicious of the demagogic Radicals from the start.

"But one frail life stood between them and the chief magistracy!" Loan hollered. "Then the crime was committed, and an assassin's bullet directed by Rebel hand and paid for by Rebel gold made Andrew Johnson president."

When Marley saw Schumacher move to rise, he grabbed his coat sleeve.

"Karl," the Pennsylvanian uttered in a loud whisper. "You can't do that, you're out of order, and worse, you're still brand new here—"

Schumacher glared at Marley as if ashamed of him, then jerked his arm away as he stood.

"I demand those hateful and treasonous words be taken down," he boomed.

With Stevens seething at what he had hoped would be another disciple, the rest of the House looked to Speaker Schuyler Colfax for a ruling. That genial lieutenant of Stevens's smiled, termed the language unexceptionable, then smiled some more.

When Loan launched into a diatribe against the Supreme Court, Schumacher shot to his feet again.

"Sir, do you not feel that your own self-respect and that of the House itself calls for the least shred of evidence on which to base so grave a charge?" the decorated veteran shouted.

Loan, stunned at the ferocity of the strapping Midwestern neophyte, stood dumb. So much blood rushed to Stevens's brain that it actually prevented him from unleashing a riposte against Schumacher, the likes of which the old warrior himself had rarely uttered.

Speaker Colfax smiled, then said, "The gentleman from Missouri refuses to answer further," and smiled some more.

After a straight party vote supported Loan, Ben Butler of wartime New Orleans occupation infamy, rose. He announced that stunning revelations were soon to be unveiled about Johnson.

Schumacher, booted as always, stamped out of the meeting in view of everyone and in offense to most.

Marley saw Stevens, near-apoplectic, jabbing his walking stick in the direction of Schumacher's departure and hissing orders to the Radicals at his sides.

"It is the Constitution rather than Mr. Johnson that is in danger," the London *Times* reported of such sequences.

Marley caught up to Schumacher that night at Kate Chase Sprague's soiree for the Washington elite. He had not seen her secretary of the treasury–father's forty-servant Edgewood mansion high atop a summit not far from the capitol. Anne Nelson had, and wrapped in an eye-stopping stole from Worth's of Paris, she giggled at his awestruck expression as their barouche, provided by Republican congressional lobbyists, arrived fashionably late.

"I was afraid you wouldn't be here," Marley said as he cornered Schumacher at one of the several mahogany bars.

"Oh, I'm afraid I am," Schumacher said, tossing down straight whiskey.

Marley saw no reason not to cut right to the bone. "Kurt, demonstrations like that one today—how can you believe they accomplish anything profitable for your people or your country? They only lessen your influence in arenas where you might otherwise be used to effect much good."

Schumacher drained the glass and slapped it down for another. When the black bartender attempted to refill it, Schumacher jerked the whiskey bottle out of his hand and did the pouring himself.

"Yes, profitable," Schumacher grumbled, looking up and down Marley's expensive new broadcloth suit and chunking back more drink. "Tell me, Wayne. Have you any idea where our esteemed colleagues Butler and Ashley are at this moment?" To Marley's baffled expression, he said, "I'll tell you where, my idealistic naive comrade. They are rendezvousing with a cadre of distinguished perjurers, forgers, and thieves to secure a series of false testimonies leading to the conviction of Andrew Johnson as a conspirator in the murder of Abraham Lincoln."

All Marley could do was blink.

"Not our government, right?" Schumacher said, filling his glass again. "Our government would not suborn witnesses to swear that Johnson himself corresponded, met, and collaborated with Wilkes Booth. Our government would not suborn witnesses to swear Booth had told them he planned the murder in league with Johnson."

A gale of laughter swept over them from a throng standing in the center of the room, Ohio Senator Ben Wade at their center.

"Our government would never dare depose an Andrew Johnson and replace him with that towering pillar of virtue and integrity," Schumacher snorted, gesturing toward Wade with his half-empty glass, which quickly emptied once again. "How fortunate are you and I not to be part of a government who would commit such acts."

Marley turned and saw Wade looking directly at him and flashing a rare, and ugly, smile.

"Ben Wade?" Marley could barely utter the words and digest the implications without retching.

"Ah, the only woman I have yet met in Washington as beautiful as Kate Chase Sprague," Schumacher said, attempting a smile and slurring his words.

Marley was glad for Anne's return from the powder room and Schumacher's exit. Had that diatribe continued much longer, it would have fouled the whole evening. Plus, Marley thought his friend in his tightness had spoken with entirely too much volume.

Fortunately time remained for punch in the second-floor library with an ensemble including Grant, who knew of Marley from Sheridan; dinner in the garden behind the house at a table adorned by a floral ornament costing a thousand dollars; and a face-to-face visit with the woman whose first baby's birth was a national event and its first words on the lips of mothers and daughters across the North.

"And here is the brave soldier whose sage silence and keen judgment are helping us rebuild our nation into a more truly perfect Union," said Kate Chase Sprague, the stunning tiara of turquoises and diamonds atop her head more than matched by the pale blue Parisian silk and pale pink silk overdress and the comely form encased by them. At his guileless surprise, mirth filled her breathtaking face, and she indicated Anne. "Brave Colonel—and so young he is, Annie!—my dear friend Anne, from one of Virginia's best old families, has quite brought me up to speed on how crucial the congressional hierarchy consider your judgment and leadership."

The lone remaining particle of sense resident in Marley's overawed brain prompted him to bow and say nothing but, "Such words from you, madame, are humbling indeed."

As they walked away, Anne embracing his arm, Marley said, "You did not tell me you were a personal friend of the most famous woman in America, and the most popular since Dolley Madison, Miss Anne Nelson!"

"Don't her eyes look as if they had been crying hard, but without the redness?" Anne giggled. "They are the most fetching eyes on earth."

"Oh, I can think of a pair I'd put up against them," Marley said, looking deep into Anne's sea-colored orbs.

"There is something in how, when she talks to you, you feel you are the very person she wanted to meet," Anne continued, her voice sweet and enchanting to him as a lark, "and I believe that is the secret of her popularity. Oh, what say we escape to the barouche and ride up to the Soldiers' Home, away from this silliness?"

He smiled at her, realizing for the first time that he wanted to see her every day and that he could not imagine the day coming he would not see her. Concern crept into the inner recesses of his mind that his Bible study for Federal veterans and congressmen was drifting farther away, even as he heard himself say, "That is the wisest of all the suggestions I have received tonight!"

The ride up to the dark lonely grounds Lincoln so revered was cool, and it offered Marley the happiest moments of his life up to now. When they reached the heights, looking out over the city, she nestled up against him. Old desires, old needs began to beckon him. They were strong, and he knew they must be fought off for yet awhile longer.

"How is it that everyone I meet seems to know all about me, and from the least objective perspective imaginable," he said, turning his mind a different direction, "and the more famous they are, the more glowing their report?"

"My darling, you have heard it from their own lips," Anne said, clutching his arm a shade tighter. "You have no one to blame but yourself, and all your famous exploits."

"But that's just it," he said, perplexed, "too many of my better-known exploits are more likely regarded as infamous than famous in these high circles."

"Not of late have they been," she corrected him. As he pondered that statement, she saw his brow crinkle again. "Stop it right now, Wayne Marley. You quit worrying. You have more than earned every opportunity and blessing that is coming your way."

Even though he was now attending her Episcopal church in Washington (whose winsome rector, steeped in all the latest tenents of German higher-critical theological thought, had welcomed him with warmth and hospitality), rather than his own Presbyterian, he had noted her embracing of some of his biblically fragranced words such as "blessing."

He managed a faint smile. "Oh, it's just that I wonder if Kurt Schumacher would agree with you at this point."

"Oh, so much phooey on that ole Kurt Schumacher!" she blurted, with more fire than Marley had yet seen. "Dear, that's what is so inspiring about you, that you want to be a part of doing what Kate said, of building a better country, and that you are willing to do what other men are not, just as you so often proved in battle."

She patted him on the forearm. "You must always remember, my sweet, such courage will never gain favorable reception from all quarters."

He grasped her lavender-kid-glove-covered arm and fought against her intoxicating cologne gaining too deep a beachhead in his mind.

"I cannot say I have not found a warm reception in the halls of Congress and in Washington generally," he said. "I believe I am beginning to understand one reason why."

"Darling," she said, with meaning, looking him close in the eye like she had never before done. Suddenly she pulled back, embarrassed.

"What is it?" he asked, cupping her chin in his white-gloved hand.

"Nothing."

"Yes, Anne, it is something—what?"

She looked at him, her lips parting. "Oh, darling," she purred. "It is true, I do have friends, many friends in this smelly little town, and in high places—for the life of me, I cannot fathom why, me just a silly ole country girl from the vanguard of the rebellion—but I hear over and over, without my prompting such comments in any way, and often when the speaker has no idea of my—" She batted her eyes. "—my high regard for you."

"What is it you are saying, Anne?" he asked.

She paused a beat, then said, "Only that—I believe, if you persist in maturing as you are in the arts of governance and in the service of your people and the country at large—well, dear, I truly believe your dreams are within your grasp, Wayne. That you are going to rise to the highest levels of power the nation can offer you and, what is more, leave a mark that will last on America for generations—why, even forever, dear!"

He could not speak; then a fellow Pennsylvania congressman was passing in a buggy and shouting, "Wayne Marley, is that you? Did you hear? He did it— Johnson fired Stanton, tonight! That'll do for hothead Andy, the Rebels' last mollycoddler!"

"What?" Marley gasped.

In his own shock, he did not detect the rage boiling in Anne. But he heard her words.

"Surely that is the final blow that besotted ruffian slaver can be allowed to inflict on our national harmony, Wayne Marley. You—look at me, my darling, it is true—*you* are the man who must lead those less brave and less honorable into doing what they must do—removing that creature from office and putting him in prison where he may no longer jeopardize our national future."

CHAPTER 63

THANKSGIVING TO GOD FOR HIS MANY AND SIGNAL MERCIES NEARLY overcame Lee as 1868 began and he contemplated the blessings—and protection—God had and continued to provide him.

The brick-and-limestone chapel so dear to his heart would open soon, as would a Washington College dining hall. The library destroyed during the war had grown to over five thousand books. The astronomy students now had a planetarium, the campus grounds had been restored to their prewar beauty and beyond. And the student body size had tripled from Lee's first year, to four hundred and eleven.

An innovative flair for education had blossomed in Lee that no one, except Mary, had even suspected. Praise poured forth from all sections of the country and from other countries. Lee launched a series of firsts in concentrated curriculum offerings never before witnessed in American education, which the academic power structure could not, and did not, ignore: photography, journalism, and a business school, among others.

Support, including the financial sort, burgeoned from the North. The North's most famous preacher, Henry Ward Beecher, brother of Harriet Beecher Stowe and proclaimer of Ulric Dahlgren as a "hero and martyr," rose before a crowd of New York financial titans hundreds strong and proclaimed, "I stand before you tonight and plead for Washington College, because it is in Virginia and because Robert E. Lee is its president. No one frets the course pursued by General Lee in former days more than I. But let us all give earnest pause to consideration of this: If we had been born in Virginia, raised in her institutions, educated in her schools, might we have pursued just so flawed a course as did General Lee or General Johnston?"

As the old pulpit fire and intellectual power that had propelled Beecher to international renown ignited, the hearts of many in the crowd who had come out of duty or curiosity or even social appearance, were stirred.

"General Lee now pleads for mental bread for his students," Beecher said, "devotes himself to the sacred cause of education, and seeks to kindle in his students a love for their country. Whatever his past transgressions, men question he might pervert the minds of youth. A thousand times, no! He shall teach a love of this American nation to all his students!"

When Beecher sat, the crowd rose as one and shook the foundation of the building with its ovation. Tears filled the eyes of many, for many reasons, and they determined to help those they had knocked down and who were struggling to earn their place back into the very country they had nearly destroyed.

Still, job offers cascaded in to Lee, their number continuing to escalate with the fame of his accomplishments at Washington College.

To one, which offered him a staggering amount of money for the worthy cause of promoting Southern commerce in New York, he told Mary, "I am grateful for the offer, but I have a self-imposed task that I must accomplish. I have led the young men of the South in battle. I have seen many of them die on the field. I will devote my remaining energies to training young men to do their duty in life."

The Lees also had found a treasured home at his old friend Pendleton's church.

All the while Lee felt the decline of his earthly body and its capacities, even as its pains and infirmities mounted, though he breathed few words of it to anyone.

"With the return of a new year, my mind reverts to you with fresh pleasure," he wrote Markie. "Although so distant, you are often present to my thoughts and always come to brighten reminiscences of the past." His heart growing full with remembrances of his life and of how dear she was to him then and now, he continued, "I hope the New Year may bring you every happiness and that all heavenly blessings may be showered upon your head! My interest in time and its concerns is daily fading away, and I try to keep my eyes and thoughts fixed on those eternal shores to which I am fast hastening."

He wrote her of Rooney's recent second marriage in Petersburg and of Lee's own hard illness caught while vacationing with Mary at the White Sulphur Springs resort area in what was now the state of West Virginia.

"By the mercy of God I was restored and came home by easy stages on Traveller, who was considerate of my weakness and suited his gait to my debility," he wrote. "I have never seen anything of the poem in his honor, and I confess I have never had any hope of his being immortalized except by your brush. That is my sure trust, and I hope you will not forget to append his tail to his likeness. How are you progressing with Traveller's portrait, Markie? He is getting old like his master and looks to your pencil to hand him down to posterity."

That so much good, so many repaired ruins could soon go crashing into the hard icy surface of Lexington's North River would forever amaze many a thoughtful observer of that long-ago world.

"I swear to you, Wayne Marley, if Edwin Stanton is not barricaded inside his own office, sleeping on his sofa at night," Schumacher said as he and Marley stalked down the first-floor corridor of the War Department, "I'll, well I'll—"

"Knock off the sauce?" Marley interrupted, looking him in the eye and smelling the stench of alcohol that clung around his friend like a wreath.

Schumacher's countenance blackened. "Well, now—"

"That's far enough, gentlemen," announced a captain of Regular infantry. At least a dozen uniformed Federals shouldered sixteen-shot Henry repeaters between the captain and the door to Stanton's suite of offices fifty feet further on. "What's the nature of your business here?"

Marley's jaw dropped. He turned to Schumacher, who could barely restrain his laughter.

Turning back to the captain, Marley said, "I'd like a word with the secretary, if you don't mind."

"The secretary's not taking visitors," the captain answered evenly.

"I'd be obliged if you'd mention to him that Congressman Wayne Marley is here," Marley said.

The captain's altered expression evidenced he recognized both the title and the name.

"Yes, sir," he said, turning toward Stanton's office. He returned a moment later and said, "You may go to the door, but no one is allowed inside."

"Ah, a long way you have come from Andersonville, Colonel and Congressman Wayne Marley," Stanton said from the other side of the door after Marley approached and hailed him.

"Yes, sir, Mr. Secretary," Marley said. "So far, I guess, sir, that you have never called on me to testify in your own investigation of Camp Sumter—or of the Kilpatrick-Dahlgren raid on Richmond."

Schumacher's eyes widened as nothing greeted those comments from the other side of the door but silence; then the recently immigrated Wisconsonite covered his mouth with a hand to keep from bursting into laughter.

"Er," Stanton murmured, "I believe the government will indeed have much more to say about the criminal acts of the late Swiss and the other Rebels at Andersonville; the Dahlgren matter, I believe you may consider disposed of."

When Marley appeared set to pursue that topic, Schumacher said, "Mr. Secretary, sir, Representative Schumacher of Wisconsin."

"Ah, yes, Schumacher, and how is Senator Schurz?"

Schumacher frowned, taking the remark as it was meant, as a snide insinuation that he served as a lackey of Schurz's, who had proved an inconsistent ally of the Radicals.

"How may we expedite a resumption of normal affairs, Mr. Secretary?" Marley asked.

"You may impeach and remove that dastardly buffoon who threatens the very foundations of our Republic," Stanton called.

"And which of the buffoons would that be, sir?" Schumacher said, suppressing a belly laugh only with great effort. Marley delivered a hard shot with his fist to Schumacher's upper right arm.

Stanton paused, then shouted, "Why which buffoon do you think, you ignorant Hun b——? The so-called 'President' Johnson!"

When Marley saw the smile vanish from Schumacher's squared-jawed countenance, he feared his friend was about to knock down the door and unleash his long-held frustration on Stanton.

"We are about to do just that, sir," Marley said, moving between Schumacher and the door. "In the meantime, some of us thought you might consider—in the interest of the happy and peaceable operation of the government, and only until the president's soon-removal is effected—perhaps transferring to other quarters."

Stanton said nothing.

"We are seeking every means possible of preserving the general peace, sir," Marley stammered, uncharacteristically wondering whether a touch of Schumacher's schnapps might not pose some merit at this particular juncture. "Some of the rumors of civil insurrection over the present series of actions are proving to possess some truth."

The tumult of the crowd thronging the street outside the front of the build-ing increased at that moment as if on cue, to the extent that the sound reached Marley and Schumacher.

"Captain Marley," Stanton thundered, "you take your Hun friend and get the h— right out of here, sir. General Grant himself has promised me that if any-thing of the sort portends, he shall deal with it no less decisively—and perma-nently—than he did the last such disturbance. And I believe you, more than most, understand just how effective the general has proven himself at such a strategy."

Now Marley did not know whether he or the smoldering Schumacher would go through the door first. Schumacher stared at him, waiting for his response. When none came, Schumacher turned to the door and said, "Listen, you miserable little rodent. I shall see to it that President Johnson remains in office long after this insipid little barricade prank of yours is over and you are off the public dole and, if I have anything to say about it, cooling your own heels in the deepest darkest recesses of the Old Capitol Prison."

After a few seconds, the voice on the other side of the door snickered, "Well, go to it, my besotted Hun friend, go to it."

Three days later, with Marley offering one of the more eloquent, if rea-soned testaments, Andrew Johnson earned the lasting notoriety of being the first American president ever impeached by the House of Representatives. Stevens, his very life hanging by a thread and appearing to be in a last-ditch race to outlast Johnson's White House tenure, marshaled his lieutenants, House and Senate, to prepare the case that would, he now believed, result in the senior body's vote to remove Johnson from office. And from there, Stevens told him-self, smiling broadly, to a very honorable, very respectable prison cell all his own.

"But I am more than just worried about Kurt," Marley told Anne as they partook of a ravishing dinner in the celebrated Wormley Hotel's dining room. "He seems intent on destroying his own career, even his name and reputation, all the while not even recognizing the unprecedented opportunity available to him to craft the very destiny of our nation, and that to a higher and more noble purpose."

She clasped his hand and turned her glittering eyes on him. "Kurt is a brave and good man, sugarplum, but, perhaps because of his mentor Senator Schurz, he is also terribly misguided. And now, as he sinks further into the abyss of drink, his judgment descends proportionately. What is important to remember, my dear, is that you cannot—you must not—allow anyone, even Kurt Schumacher, to drag you down."

When his gaze drifted away, she said, "Honey, something else disturbs you."

Toying with a well-mounted column of crab cakes on his plate, Marley said, "What with all this Stanton and Johnson business, and the problems down South, no one seems to pay heed that the economy of our entire nation is sliding so low that I fear if nothing arrests the decline, we may face a disaster even greater than the war."

"But, dear, I thought our nation prospered famously," she said, truly surprised.

He looked at her. "No, dear, who has told you that?"

She appeared confused. "I cannot say, truly. I have just heard it about."

"Well, such is not the case, and if it does not turn around, and soon . . ." he said, shaking his head. "I'm just worried that in our determination to quickly right the wrongs of our nation, we are having to break too many immutable laws of business and finance—not to mention human nature. I wish that the people would behave better, because when the government has to intervene on their behalf, it inevitably winds up costing everyone money."

She detected a perplexed look run across his face. "What it is, Wayne?"

"It just occurred to me that not everyone suffers when the government becomes more powerful. Some of those big New York money men like Jay Gould and Jay Cooke and Jim Fisk seem only to get richer. And I continue to hear disturbing accounts of odd goings-on in the gold market."

He looked into the eyes that had captivated him since the night he met Anne. *Has it been only a year and three months since I first set sight on her?* he wondered to himself, still finding it impossible to believe. "Sometimes," he said, clasping her hand as well, "I do feel I've known you forever, Anne Nelson."

She started to speak, then demurred.

"What is it, dear?" he asked.

"Propriety prevents the voicing of my true sentiments," she said.

"No," he objected, now squeezing her hands, "you may say whatever you feel."

"Well," she said, the window of her soul opening wide to him like the petals of a blooming flower, "perhaps you feel you have known me forever because I have been searching for you forever."

"I do love you, Anne Nelson," he announced.

She blinked, thunderstruck. No words would come. For the first time since he met her, she seemed to lose herself.

"No," he said, smiling and touching a finger to her lips, "you needn't say anything, Anne. I just—I just needed to tell you that, even though I had no idea I would until the moment I did."

She stared at him, pale with astonishment.

"Why, there's Speaker Colfax," Marley said, rising to flag him down.

Surprisingly Anne gave no evidence of hearing the announcement and little more of recognizing the speaker when he came smiling to her table.

If not for Agnes, Mildred, and Mary Custis Lee "breaking the ice," Presbyterian Lexington might never have embraced ice skating as a respectable recreation. To their delight, however, they found a long stretch of the North River above the dam alongside Lexington quick to freeze in cold weather and thick and hard when it did.

But the day "ex-bluecoat," Lexington storekeeper and American Missionary Association teacher of black freedmen, Erastus Johnston skated down the North River for the last time, it seemed that all of Lexington except the Lee girls skimmed along the ice.

Johnston had sensed hostility from some in the town, especially college students, since he came to Lexington in the fall of 1865. Others, particularly merchants, resented how his store prospered, with evident Northern capital backing it and suspected stolen produce supplied by local blacks helping sustain it. An even larger group did not so much mind his teaching blacks reading and other subjects as they did what they considered his Enlightenment-flavored view of American history and the destiny of America.

"Far from espousing the transforming doctrines of Christ, he promotes communistic revolution and the concentration of power away from the states and people to Washington," thundered one community leader. "He is a Yankee missionary, not a Christian missionary."

So, unbeknown to his American Missionary Association sponsors, he carried a concealed pistol with him wherever he went.

Snubbed by townspeople as he skated this steel gray February day of winter, Johnston proceeded down the ice toward the dam, where a group of local young boys and college students skated. One of them, twelve-year-old Todd Chandler, had watched the messages come to his mother during the war that first his oldest brother, then the second oldest, and then finally his father, had died.

His father froze to death without a blanket or shoes in Camp Douglas prison.

Five-foot-tall Todd had seen none of these kinfolk—or two uncles—return to Lexington, but he had seen ex-Federal Johnston arrive, and that after his army had sacked the town and stolen or killed every head of livestock the Chandlers still owned.

As several other boys and college students lobbed insults of no great import toward Johnston, little Todd remembered today would have been his father's birthday. "Go teach your darkies, Yankee-man!" he screamed, his voice rising above those of the others. Hot tears formed in his eyes as he observed the gloved, stocking-capped, thickly-clad Johnston sailing back and forth across the river and remembered the grizzly report of his father's miserable shivering death, which was allowed in retribution for the reports filtering in to the Camp Douglas authorities of Andersonville atrocities.

Suddenly Todd raced up to Johnston and hurled a vicious vulgarity in his face.

The storekeeper-missionary glared down at the child, then exploded with rage, jerking the boy to him by the collar of his coat with one hand, and whipping out his Remington pistol and shoving it in his face with the other.

"You hateful little brat," Johnston growled as Todd's eyes grew large with terror and his whole head began to shake, "if ever—ever!—you call me such a name again, I shall shoot you dead. Do you understand me? Do you?" he hollered, shaking the boy.

Todd could not see or hear anything beyond the dark open barrel yawning two inches from his face. He was so petrified that he could not even open his mouth, much less voice any words. A hot stream of urine began to run down the inside of his leg.

"What the h— do you think you're doing, you Yankee b——!"

Johnston whirled to see Todd's sixteen-year-old brother, Mark, skating up at the head of a pack of youths, their faces dark with fury.

"If you've a mind to shoot anyone, Yankee-man, why don't you make it me, not some little boy," Mark stormed, jacking the heels of both his hands into Johnston's chest so hard he nearly knocked him down.

"Listen to me, you young fools," Johnston shouted, "when are you going to learn this world is full of people different from you, and that it's no excuse to mistreat them, whether it's Negroes or Northerners or foreigners or whatever. You're all living in the wrong century!"

"Why you Bible-thumpin' hypocrite. He's a little boy!" Mark screamed, scarlet with rage and coming on toward Johnston for more; when the Northerner saw this, and the snarling squad of reinforcements on Mark's heels, then heard someone yell, "Hang him!" he whirled and skated away.

"Come back here, Yankee missionary!" Mark screamed, skating after him. Then more boys and college students swarmed into the pack, and Johnston heard the first shrieking chorus of Rebel yells he had heard since Gordon's ill-fated assault on Fort Stedman. Realizing now his mistake at pulling the pistol, he rushed for the riverbank, his heart racing. Slipping and tripping up its frozen sheen, he stumbled as a volley of rocks and ice balls showered him, a couple hitting the back of his head so hard they stunned him.

"Get him, boys!"

"Drown the n——loving cur!"

By the time Johnston got up to solid ground, a couple of strapping Washington College students had skated forward.

"Listen, Yank," one called, "you've got ten days to clear out of Rockbridge County. Look at me, Yank!" When Johnston glanced back over his shoulder, he saw the speaker thrusting an index finger at him. "And we will come and get you and string you up from the nearest oak if you breathe a word of this to your Yankee occupation commanders."

That night, this young man, another student, and three hard-bitten Confederate veterans pounded on the door of Johnston's store and hurled more insults at him, not knowing he was at a friend's house nursing his bumps and bruises.

Lee first heard that Johnston, whom he had seen around town and certainly knew by reputation, had pulled a gun on little Todd Chandler, then been driven off the river by angry townspeople. He knew more was afoot a few days later when Major General O. B. Willcox, commissioner for the subdistrict of Lynchburg in United States Military District No. 1, called on him after hearing from Johnston and interviewing him, other witnesses, and the mayor of Lexington.

Willcox gave Lee the names of three Washington College students accused of spearheading the actions against Johnston. Lee's calm demeanor gave no indication of the trepidation already filling him for his people and land at news of President Johnson's impeachment. He followed the depressing national news as little as possible, but Custis had felt compelled to apprise him of the watershed events in Washington. Well Lee knew who waited in the wings in the event of the Tennessean's removal. *One of the few men in the government with views even more extreme than Thaddeus Stevens and the Radical congressional majority,* Lee thought.

"Please accept my profoundest apologies and regret," Lee said, shaking his head. "I will attend to the matter immediately."

Before Willcox even left town, Lee expelled two of the students. The third, present during the incident but playing no role in it, was granted permission by Lee to withdraw.

Many in Lexington, and even some in his own family, questioned the expulsions. What *should* the young men have done when a Yankee soldier stuck a pistol in the face of a little boy? they complained.

Lee beseeched God all the more in his morning devotions, and at various seasons during the day, for peace, charity, and solitude to reign in Lexington, though he saw passions and anger barely constrained either by those loyal to North or South.

Johnston, who had moved to Covington, flew into a rage when no further sanctions ensued.

"You are partly to blame yourself," Willcox wrote him, "as you threatened to shoot a small boy when they first bothered you."

"That will not do at all," Johnston seethed, and he and his friends in Virginia and the North unleashed a blizzard of letters to newspapers and political leaders all across the Northern states.

As the story of the ice-skating row on the North River in General Lee's college town mounted in ferocity, it became a *cause célèbre* in the North. Donations to Washington College from the Northern states plummeted.

And as Andrew Johnson's presidency—and his remaining influence on Southern Reconstruction—hung by a thread, the story of Federal war veteran Erastus Johnston and Confederate General Robert E. Lee's rogue college and town found its way onto the floor of the United States Senate.

Thad Stevens, near death, offered homage to whatever power in the universe orchestrated such events and employed the information in his climactic sally against Johnson.

Marley found himself named to the committee tasked with preparing the House articles of impeachment to present to the Senate for their vote. Their approval of any plank would remove Johnson from office. Marley suspected his appointment was Stevens's doing. That man seemed to harbor an unusual affinity for him. Marley sensed Stevens fancied him, fellow Pennsylvanian as he was, as a sort of disciple who might be groomed to carry on the fight for revolution—under different terminology, of course—after his departure, which from the looks of him, Marley feared could not be too distant.

So far, Marley's voting, if not his passions, had gone Stevens's way.

The committee met a final time in late February 1868 before presenting its work to the Senate. The committee crafted ten articles of impeachment, nine regarding his firing of Stanton and one the president's speeches. Marley had wearied of Johnson's often-abrasive style, and he considered the man an impediment to positive reform in the country—partly because his refusal to compromise seemed to drive more moderates into the Radical camp—but a queasy feeling beset him whether the founding fathers would consider Congress's actions within the purview of their meticulous system of checks and balances among the three branches of American government.

The capital was electric with excitement and anticipation. Committee cochairman J. A. Bingham announced the rumor sweeping the city that a large group of armed men marched that very moment toward Washington from Maryland to protect and, if necessary, defend Johnson—and his possession of the nation's highest office—by force of arms.

Marley shook his head, divining the baselessness of the tale. *Both Stevens and Bingham are profane,* he thought, but he had to admit to himself, *Stevens is especially so.*

Stevens harbored no such hesitation. He stood and introduced his own eleventh article, a sort of cornucopia offering something for everyone. He designed it to catch ambivalent senators who were uncomfortable voting for any of the specific preceding articles.

"If my article is inserted, what chance has Andrew Johnson to escape?" he hooted. "Unfortunate man, thus surrounded, hampered, tangled in the meshes of his own wickedness—unfortunate, unhappy man, behold your doom."

CHAPTER 64

MARLEY REVELED IN THE WILLARD'S SUPPER AND COMPANY OF Anne, though the conversation threatened to steal from him the pleasure of both.

"But darling," she said, the diamonds around her neck and the sparkle in her eyes vying for the honor of blinding his vision, or at least his reason, "everyone knows Lexington has long been one of the hottest beds for treason in Virginia, even in the entire South. Who should know better than you? That Stonewall Jackson, his legions of protégés from the Virginia Military Institute—whose cadets, while still enrolled in school, killed many a good Union that awful day at New Market. And that is not even to consider the students at that Washington College and their reign of terror against the local Union faithful."

Neither Anne nor Marley had acknowledged his recent proclamation of love for her.

She touched his arm and gazed into his face. "And who was at the head of Stonewall Jackson and is now at the head of Lexington and Washington College and who knows what all? You know who—General Robert Edward Lee."

Marley shook his head as he gobbled custard. "Still, I can scarcely recognize the quiet, peaceable folk of Lexington I knew all those years—say, Anne, you do not have relations among the folk in that part of the Valley, do you?"

"No, sugar, mine are all farther north or west," she said.

"You just seem so like someone I have known, or seen, and somehow I keep thinking it might be someone I knew during my time in Lexington. Anyhow, they just don't seem the sort of folk we keep reading about in all these scandal rags. And I cannot believe all the New York and New England papers say about Lee is true."

"War does change us all, especially this awful war. And whatever is true and whatever is not regarding General Lee," she said, her words gushing forth much faster than he could process them all, "it is irrefutable that a gang of his college toughs—battle-hardened Rebel veterans to the man—attacked that gentle missionary merely because, as the Scriptures say, the darkness detests the light, and he was practically martyred trying to shed a ray of light into that den of murder and rebellion. I thank the Lord someone loaned him a pistol or the horrible beating he received would have been fatal, as they intended."

Marley stared at the empty dish of custard and contemplated ordering another, his third. He remembered his trousers all had to be let out another size this week, and that, as of this morning, he weighed thirty-eight pounds more than he did when he returned to Pennsylvania after Lee's surrender. *I shouldn't. Oh, I'll start that new eating program tomorrow,* he thought, signaling the waiter for another dish.

"All I know is that as Lee's stock plummets, Johnson's plummets with it," Marley said. "One more nasty scene out of Lexington, Virginia, and I should hardly think Johnson will have a prayer of staying in office."

She clutched his arm the firmer. "History, if it is truthful, will pronounce your efforts to that end among the most gallant and efficacious of any man in the country," she said, so moved that Marley's own heart was stirred.

"It is good to hear," he said. "Sometimes of late despite our successes, what with Kurt's rantings, I have found myself paying perhaps too much heed to a small voice that would seek my confusion and loss of resolution."

"I am convinced," she said, in a manner Marley and everyone he knew in Washington who knew her had come to find altogether convincing, "that all great men hear such voices. It is part of what makes them great, perhaps part of what God employs to render them more circumspect and imbue them with more wisdom than the vast expanse of their fellows not so wise."

When she says it, he thought, his head spinning from her, her words, and the wine of which he had for the first time tonight partaken, *I can scarcely not believe it.*

•◊ •◊ •◊

"Mama, would the church or the college even still be open if not for General Lee and all he and his family have done for both?" fifteen-year-old Francis Brockenbrough, son of Washington College's board of trustees president and judge John Brockenbrough asked his mother as they strolled home from visiting family friends.

"Both would certainly face more daunting times than even they are now," she said. How thankful she was the war had ended before Francis could take up arms, which he had wished to do since ten years of age. She had to forcibly restrain him at age eleven as he attempted to prevent the Yankees from looting their house when they rampaged through Lexington back in 1864. Perhaps the chivalric lessons of Thomas Malory and Walter Scott had been lost on many young Southerners with the demise of their land and the Christian ethos of just war, but they had not been lost on young Francis, who remained fiercely protective of his mother and his sisters.

She thought upon these things as they neared their home and saw a group of black men, one or two in Federal uniforms, the rest in civilian garb, clustered on the sidewalk near their front gate.

"Excuse us," Francis said, expecting the men to stand to one side or the other so he and his mother could access the gate.

"Excuse yourself," Caesar Griffin, the biggest of the half dozen or so men, said, his voice pregnant with challenge.

The Brockenbroughs stood their ground for a moment, certain the men would make way, at least to allow his mother past. When they did not, Francis's chin jutted out and his eyes blazed.

"Come, son," Mrs. Brockenbrough said, pulling him with her off the sidewalk into the muddy gutter, where she slipped and almost fell.

"You—" Francis raged at Griffin.

The other men laughed or remained silent, but Griffin said, "You what, little rooster?"

When Francis tried to go after him, his mother jerked him forward and thrust him around the men and toward the front door.

"Ma!" he shouted.

This produced an eruption from the sidewalk-tenders.

"Better git along, game little rooster, Mama hen's liable to peck your little eyes out!" Griffin chortled, bringing louder guffaws than before from his fellows.

For the moment Francis relented, bringing his mother great relief. But to her horror, when they got inside the house, he wheeled back out, slamming the door behind him, scooping a wooden broom off the porch, and marching toward the gate.

"Well, lookee here, the rooster returns!" Griffin said.

Francis, his face black with rage, kicked open the gate, shouted, "You're no gentleman, forcing a lady into the street, boy!" and clubbed Griffin over the head with the broom so hard it splintered into pieces and knocked him to the ground, silly.

The rest of the group, including the ex-soldiers, stood dumb with shock at the audacious boy. Francis raised the half of the broom he still held and whacked Griffin with it again. This seemed to return the big man to his senses. He pulled a revolver from under his homespun coat and inside his waistband, swung it up toward Francis, and pulled the trigger as the lad was about to deliver a third blow.

The blast struck Francis square in the chest, knocking him through the gate and flat onto his back on the ground.

A couple of the men swore oaths in their horror.

When Mrs. Brockenbrough emerged from the house and saw Francis still as a rotten log and lying in a pool of his own blood in her front yard, she began shrieking, "No! No! Please, God, no!"

"Now you gone and done it this time for sure, Caesar Griffin," one man stammered as the whole group, including Griffin, took to their heels.

As Francis Brockenbrough's life bled out onto a doctor's table, his older brothers marshaled nearly the entire body of their fellow Washington College students and fanned out in pursuit of Griffin. Soon they had him, a rope around his neck, marching him to the courthouse square.

A Washington professor and ex-Confederate officer persuaded them to deliver Griffin to old Perry, the town jailer.

By Sunday Francis still lived, but his prognosis looked the bleakest yet.

Word spread that a troop of students had already volunteered and been organized to storm the jail, drag Griffin out, and lynch him if Francis died. In fact it spread to the Lynchburg-headquartered Federal military commissioner for Lexington.

He beseeched Lee to head off trouble, neither man any more anxious than the other for further bloodshed that would draw yet more attention to normally tranquil Lexington.

Much too often have the actions of bad men, coupled with the people's raw emotions, resulted in such tragic scenes to us who call ourselves a Christian people, Lee thought, remembering horse thieves and ice skaters with pistols and now a boy lying near death after, in his mind, defending his mother's honor. *We must*

632

work even harder to cultivate in ourselves and our country virtue, forbearance, and Christian patience.

Now Federal troops marched back into Lexington, determined to prevent bloodshed. This shook Lee, confident that his students or anyone else in the community would not instigate violence but worried that so martial a show might provoke it. He did not know which chilled him more—the vitriol of those who hurled insults at the bluecoats, or the placid countenances of those void of expression, behind which he knew frothed a hate that knew no moderation.

I fear I have seen such faces under my own roof, he thought.

Custis displayed neither tendency, but Lee shuddered when Mary again raised her private concern with him about their eldest son's recurrent bleary and bloodshot eyes, which could not be attributed to lack of sleep, eye strain, allergy, or eye disease. It steeled Lee's resolution not only to forswear serving any spirits, but to advocate total abstention from alcoholic consumption.

Wretched disease, he thought, *mocker of all that is good and decent, plunderer of the honest and virtuous, destroyer of the faithful. God, in your mercy, let it not befall Custis.*

Lee received the military commissioner's request on a Sunday.

"What if violence *is* afoot?" Mary asked him that afternoon in the parlor. "Virginians have shown they have violence enough in their blood to turn the world upside down with it."

He glanced across the room at Agnes and Mildred, their countenances placid and void of expression.

Just then Custis stepped in.

"How is he?" Lee asked before his son, bleary- and bloodshot-eyed, even shut the door.

Custis sighed. "For the townfolk, he's on the mend. For us—he may not last till night."

Lee rubbed his aching chest.

Mary read his thoughts. "The boys can all be reached at the YMCA meeting tonight," she said.

He smiled his thanks to her, then retired to his room to compose a message for his students.

"I earnestly invoke the students to abstain from any violation of the law and to unite in preserving quiet and order on this and every occasion," they heard his words that night.

Caesar Griffin slept much more peaceably that night because of them.

Francis Brockenbrough survived his wound but was not out of the woods for many days. During several of those nights, the Lees heard pistol shots fired into the air.

We are too angry, too hopeless, he thought, trying to sleep one such night.

More trouble roiled when Federal Judge John Underwood in Norfolk, long the nemesis of former Confederate Virginians, ruled Griffin's ensuing conviction and two-year sentence unlawful.

"There is no lawful authority in Military District No. 1 other than we Federal judges," Underwood bellowed. "These ex-Confederate judges are usurpers."

He ordered Griffin set free with no further punishment.

All of Virginia, and much of the South, seethed with fury. So combustible did the admixture grow that Marley and Anne were informed one night by Kate Chase Sprague—eluding her gaggle of courters even as her drunken husband the senator eluded her—that her own father, chief justice of the United States Supreme Court, had headed to Virginia and overturned Underwood's ruling, giving Griffin back the two years in prison.

"Even though the man he shot was one of those vicious, unreconstructed Rebel soldiers from Lee's college, and even though the poor colored boy was very nearly killed and was only defending himself," she said, "Father believed it a just sentence and in keeping with the North's program of leniency and reconciliation with the secessionists."

"Well," Anne smiled, moving her full and richly painted lips toward Marley's chin, then at the last instant, as he braced for the soft touch, seeming to gather herself and pull back. Kate Chase Sprague's eyes twinkled at the obvious, and barely controlled, affection her two friends evidenced for each other. "Such lawlessness and obvious need for Northern intervention should render President Johnson's fate, and that of his policy of Reconstruction, all the more inevitable," Anne said, "especially with men the caliber of Colonel Marley hurrying them to it."

Not even Kate Chase Sprague could conceal her recognition of how imposing a national figure had this one-eyed warrior, who oozed gentlemanliness and good breeding, become. *He seems almost more akin to those grand Southern titans of the old school of gallantry who would come to Washington before the late war,* she thought. *Did he not live down there for some years? I will ask lovely Annie when there is an opportunity.*

Marley rose early the morning of May 16, 1868, and read long from the book of 1 Samuel. It occurred to him that, with the breakneck pace of his congressional work, the battles with Johnson, the Washington social engagements, the maintenance of relationships with his supporters back in Pennsylvania, and his deepening relationship with Anne Nelson—and his now-regular attendance at her stately but less than spiritually nourishing church—his Bible reading had eroded to less frequency even than his now-rare concurrence with Kurt Schumacher on the important votes of the day. He must, at now of all times, devote himself more faithfully to the Scriptures. And he must remember to pray with greater fervency and regularity for Schumacher's troubled, bibulous soul.

Marley arrived early at the capitol building. One of the first people he saw was Schumacher. As usual of late, that man had the aroma of liquor about him.

"So, today is your big day, my friend," Schumacher said.

Marley shook his head. "It is a sad day for all."

Schumacher smirked. "But *o contrare,* my comrade, it is the day for which you have long worked, the day you will finally rid yourself, rid our suffering country, of the tyrant whose heel clamps so ruthlessly down on the neck of freedom."

Marley frowned. *Of all times, an hour before one of the greatest events in American history,* he thought, *and out here, where we may be seen—and heard.*

"Oh, no secrets will be left, my friend," Schumacher said, divining Marley's thoughts. "And why should it bother you, eh, Colonel Marley? Why, you are about to become the first freshman congressman this century to receive a committee chairmanship. What is it the Bible says about growing in favor with God and man? And how God makes even the just man's enemies to be at peace with him?"

Marley reddened and glanced around, fearful of being heard, though he stood in a remote corner of the building.

"Well, know that your enemies are not at peace with you, my friend!" Schumacher shouted suddenly in Marley's face. "And that should be all the more frightening to you, as you know not even who your enemies are, Congressman!"

Schumacher's breath stunk of something even less fragrant than schnapps. Worse, Marley had a creeping fear the strapping German-American might at any moment physically assault him.

"Allow me to instruct you, sir!" Schumacher ranted on. "They are the communists and revolutionaries whose whore you are in overthrowing the greatest government in the history of the world. They are the people of the South we have conquered in war and now propose to vanquish—to destroy to the utter limits of their culture and civilization—in peace. No, you shut your d—— mouth right now, Wayne Marley, or so help me, I'll shut it for you, and you know I can do it, mister!

"They are the Africans you now betray to a future darker than any they ever have known before—by flinging them to the winds of a white South who once loved them but in whose bosom resentment and hatred now boil hotter every day and a white North who has always detested them, most of whose states will shoot them rather than allow them even to cross their borders. And your enemies are those across the world who dared hope our unique American experiment in constitutional republican democracy might birth a better, fairer way of life, but who will now, their suspicions confirmed of the tyranny they feared it would bring, revert to the old, failed, bourgeois but safe European models."

Now Schumacher's face was only inches from Marley's.

"But most of all, Wayne Marley, it is your country and its children who are now your enemies, even if they do not yet know it, because of what you, in the rare position and with the rare ability to do better *for* them, are doing *to* them as you wink and nod and look away from wrongdoing and instead grow rich and powerful and important and impress your pretty Miss Anne—"

At this Marley exploded, grabbing Schumacher by his collars and slamming him into the wall behind him. "You better shut up right now, you son of a b——," Marley screamed. "If you so much as utter her name again in this conversation, I swear I'll break your neck right here, so help me—"

"God?" Schumacher spewed back. "So help you, *God,* Wayne Marley? You think God is on your side in all this? Hah! You know much more about God than I ever did or ever want to, but she has you so blinded to all this—"

"I said shut up, Schumacher!" Marley screamed, slamming the other man's head into the wall.

"Or what, Marley?" Schumacher gasped. "What will you do—kill me?" Suddenly his tone softened. "Frankly, Wayne, at this point, you would be doing me a favor."

Marley did not know what to say. He loosened his grip and Schumacher pulled away, producing a metal half-pint flask from his coat pocket and gulping.

Not far away Marley saw that the towering brilliant Georgian, Ben Hill— one of the few Democrats the Radicals truly feared, though he had kept his comments very close to the vest for a long time—had observed the entire scene as he passed.

Never would Marley forget the searing look Schumacher gave him after he put his flask away.

"What you do, go and do quickly, Judas," Schumacher growled, before he turned and walked out of the Capitol building.

"What were you discussing with that drunken, Rebel-loving Hun?" Loan, passing by, asked Marley. The latter just stared at him, recalling with repugnance the Missourian's role in the now-discredited attempt to tar President Johnson with the murder of Abraham Lincoln.

"H—, I wouldn't give a bent nickel for that stupid German's future, in the House or anywhere else," Loan said with a smirk. "Thad Stevens has got his wagon fixed but good."

"What are you talking about?" Marley asked.

The galleries were packed, as was every open foot of space in the entire building. Marley looked up and saw Anne, resplendent in green, waving at him from one of the choicest of all the front-row seats. The great and the powerful of Washington, or their wives, surrounded her, Kate Chase Sprague right next to her. *How does she manage it?* he marveled.

Turning back toward the front, he thought, *I do need a wife, and I believe it will be her. She has shown me such love and support, and yet she has forestalled infractions of physical intimacy the measure of which I decreasingly find myself. But the apostle Paul himself made clear that to marry is better than to "burn," and however great Anne's discipline, mine is vanishing quicker than Andy Johnson's political career. When the political climate is stabilized, the Southern states in order, and Ben Wade—God help us—in charge, I'll ask her hand. Until then, I pray she retains her moral discipline, and that mine develops more in line with hers.*

The debate raged for days, occasionally lofty, but much more often low and partisan and vicious. Republican senators wavering in their commitment to convict Johnson were first wooed; next investigated, watched, and followed wherever they went, in hopes that untoward material might emerge with which to leverage them; then outright threatened and intimidated.

Marley found his views drifting toward the Radical extreme not by inclination but because he could not work with Stevens and the other House managers, or Charles Sumner and the senatorial leaders, if he harbored any semblance of moderation. *Then I would be thrust into the outer darkness and unable to do any good for anyone,* he told himself. He thought of Anne's admonitions that only God could have created so breathtaking a role for him to play in the history of His nation, even His world, and that to squander it would be tantamount to hiding his talents in a hole and cursing the God who gave them as a hard master.

Whenever ambivalence threatened his equilibrium, Anne's zealous encouragement and excitement lifted him past it.

"God is using you during some of the greatest days in our country's history to accomplish His will for the people," she told him, as if repeating the sentiment often enough would finally convince Marley to enjoy his role as a key lieutenant of the ruling Radicals.

As a key lieutenant of Stevens.

Then came the climactic day of final arguments. A bailiff passed Marley a note moments after he had taken his seat near the House managers' tables. "Hang Johnson by the heels like a dead crow in a cornfield to frighten all his tribe. General Neal Dow, Maine."

The highest-ranking Federal in Libby Prison when we tried to . . . to free them, Marley remembered. *What* was *intended that day by Dahlgren and Kilpatrick?* he wondered for the thousandth time.

Then a commotion erupted toward the rear. He swung around, fretting himself for allowing his weight to mushroom so that such a move required such effort.

Here he comes, he thought, breathless with anticipation, as four black chairbearers carried Stevens into the chamber like a Roman tetrarch borne into a subjected provincial capital.

Today Thaddeus Stevens would speak.

Never had the old lion toiled so over a speech. Bracing himself, he stood straight-backed before the House and packed galleries and roared forth his denunciation of the hated foe. After but a few minutes, he sat to continue; a half hour later he passed the speech to Butler to complete.

"Impeach this offspring of assassination!" the manuscript concluded. "And senators be warned that for any man daring to vote for acquittal, dark shall be the track of infamy which must mark the name and that of his posterity!"

Floor and galleries alike rose and boomed their approval. Marley could not resist looking up. Anne and Kate both cheered and clapped and blew him kisses. *Blessed indeed is he whose delight is in the law of the Lord, and who in his law does mediate day and night,* he thought, not knowing if it were possible for him to be any happier than he was at that moment.

It was commencement day at Washington College. *Is it possible we have already completed three years?* Lee thought as he took Traveller on a ride round the quiescent early-morning streets of Lexington. As the sweet fragrance of dogwood and lilacs filled the air, he came upon Mrs. Eunice Cooper, an older widow who had lost a son at Sharpsburg.

"Good morning, Mrs. Cooper," Lee said with a smile, tipping his hat.

"Good morning to you, General Lee," she said, excited at his appearance. "Sir, you are just the man I should like to see. Do you see this tree, General? This splintered tree right here?"

"Yes, ma'am."

"It was the Yankees did that, sir, when they shelled Lexington," she said, her anger rising. "This here tree is over a hundred years old, sir, and look what they did to it. What should I do about this, sir?"

"Cut it down, Mrs. Cooper," he said, tipping his hat again and nudging Traveller. He saw the grim shock with which she greeted his counsel, but it could not be helped. "Cut it down, madam, and forget about it forever."

We must forget, he thought to himself as he rode on. *We must forget and we must forgive if we are to escape ruin. Those people cannot ruin us, but we can ruin ourselves with the hate that is filling us.*

"Oh, hello, Susan," he blurted, snapping out of his musing and noticing tawny-haired Grace and her mother walking on the sidewalk.

"Good morning, General Lee," the mother said. Grace looked up at him, seemed to glare, then looked away.

I am glad that commencement is being held here in the new chapel, he thought that afternoon as the ceremony began. *And a much larger graduating class than last year. A much larger everything.* He knew that a sizable press corps was also on hand, from as far away as New York, New England, old England, and France.

Filled to overflowing, the building shone bright with newness and hope. Lee had taken his customary seat up on the platform when he noticed the five-year-old son of the Rev. J. William Jones wandering the front of the huge crowd, his chin quivering and tears filling his eyes.

One of Lee's favorite chaplains during the war, the elder Jones now shepherded Lexington's Baptist congregation.

Oh, the little fellow has become separated from his father and he is lost, Lee thought, realizing the program had begun and could not now be interrupted.

When all else failed, the boy looked up at Lee—besides his own father, his greatest hero in all the world—and fought the sobs that began to shake him. Lee motioned him up to the platform. The boy's countenance lit up like the sun Lee had seen break over the Blue Ridge this morning, and he rushed to the old general, sitting on the floor at his feet in full view of the whole assemblage. Soon Lee realized the youngster had fallen fast asleep, propped against his legs. He remained so throughout the ceremony. When time came for Lee to rise, shake the hand of the graduates, and present them their diplomas, he glanced down at young Jones, saw his eyes were closed and his breathing heavy, and proceeded to perform his duties from where he sat, every graduate coming to him.

As if on cue, when Pendleton closed the event with a prayer, the boy awoke and his pastor father collected him, determining to commit what he had just witnessed to writing, along with the growing legion of other such stories that had begun to collect about the acts of Robert E. Lee.

●◇ ●◇ ●◇

Word reached Lexington following commencement that the United States Senate had acquitted Andrew Johnson by one vote.

Hurrying home to share the news with Mary, Lee found Mildred's most faithful suitor, Dr. Barton, coming out the door, his face ashen.

"Why, whatever could be the cause for such a grim face, Doctor?" Lee asked, his words not belying the sudden dread befalling him.

Barton started to speak but had difficulty.

"Dr. Barton, what is it, sir?" Lee pressed.

"It is Mildred, General. Her condition is much worse than anyone suspected. She—she has typhoid fever, sir—in the advanced condition."

Lee was not certain if he was standing or sitting. All he knew was that typhoid fever had killed Annie and nearly killed Agnes, who had never recovered fully from its ravages. *Oh no,* he pleaded, *please, God, not my Precious Life, not yet.*

CHAPTER 65

MARLEY COULD ONLY MARVEL AT THE FIERCE OLD WARRIOR. *Unable to stand, scarcely able to walk, struggling even to breathe, yet bitter almost beyond sanity at the acquittal of Johnson, his whole being powered by hatred of the man, and without evident faith in the Savior who is his one hope for eternity,* Marley thought, *Thaddeus Stevens spearheads a new impeachment resolution.*

"My sands are nearly run," Stevens told the House, melancholy filling the voice he could no longer raise much above a whisper even in session, "and I can only see with the eyes of faith. I am fast descending the downhill of life, at the foot of which stands the open grave. But you, Mr. Speaker, are promised full length of days, and a brilliant career. If you and your compeers can fling away ambition and realize that every human being, however lowly or degraded by fortune, is your equal . . . truth and righteousness will spread over the land, and you will look down from the top of the Rocky Mountains upon an empire of one hundred million happy people."

Tears filled Marley's eyes as he wondered if he would again look upon Thaddeus Stevens shaking the foundations of Congress and the nation. *For all the old battle-axe's too-human failings, despite the "howling wilderness" of his spiritual state, he possesses less guile, littler ambition, and more single-minded selfless desire for what he sees as the welfare of his fellowman—all his fellowmen—and his country, than any other man of his generation.*

Tapping the gold-tipped cane that supporters from his congressional district gave him, Marley peered from under his towering new felt top hat. Anne gave him this, from a Parisian house, saying, "Oh, for no reason in particular, darling, just because you're you." He looked out the open window of his private barouche, this a gift from an altogether different, and anonymous, group. It had simply appeared one morning outside his Fifteenth Street apartment, a House courier presenting him with the deed of sale.

The Fourteenth Amendment to the Constitution passed the day before.

The rev—Marley caught himself as he watched the approach of Lafayette Square, realizing how few friends he now had outside the Square. *No, that is not the word I would wish used for it.* He could only think that the ongoing work of Congress was so often referred to as the "revolution" in the inner sanctum of the Radical hierarchy that the word had nestled its way into his own mind. *Reconstruction*—that *effort progresses with power and import for all the land and even, we hope, the world,* he thought.

Indeed. That Fourteenth Amendment, after more than two years of savage machinations, treachery, and influence-peddling, had finally passed into law. It bestowed United States citizenship upon all American blacks. It stripped the states of much of their power, including what they might use to deprive blacks or anyone else of the equal protection of the law. It prohibited all ex-Confederates who previous to the war swore loyalty to the United States from holding any elected office anywhere in the country. And it declared the war debt of the Confederacy invalid and that of the United States valid.

"But why must we continue to employ dishonorable means to arrive at honorable ends?" Marley fretted to Anne over lunch after they had found a private table at Mrs. Creswell's house. "Even with the old Confederate states required to sanction the Fourteenth Amendment and for it to become part of the Constitution before they could be readmitted to the Union—and whenever in American history has such high legislative extortion been employed?—not even then could we get it ratified."

When he saw her glass—and his own—were empty, he signaled the servant for another bottle of wine. "Then, when we ourselves required the support of three-fourths of the states to ratify the amendment, we wound up miscounting and declaring it passed, *still* one state shy of our own declared minimum of states!"

"Dear," she soothed him, reaching across the table and popping a caviar-spread piece of toast into his mouth. "Has not Mrs. Creswell simply outdone herself today? Oysters on the shell, clear soup, sweetbreads and French peas, Roman punch, chicken cutlets, birds, chicken salad, ices, jelly, charlottes, candied preserves, cake, fruit, candy, oh, on and on it goes—topped with your four favorite kinds of wines." He had stayed clear of anything alcoholic but wine, but in the weeks since he had taken that up, with now near-daily frequency, his voice had shown a propensity to rise precipitously once he had more than a couple of glasses down him. He looked at her, realizing that pleasing her had become as important to him as satisfying his own honor. *Maybe more important?* he wondered.

He was relieved when the icy new bottle, and friends, joined them.

He had just regained his equilibrium when a message arrived for him that Thaddeus Stevens's days in the Congress and on earth were completed.

How does she do it? Agnes wondered as she surveyed the spray of newspapers her mother had left out on the dining room table. *How does Mama procure the most powerful papers from all over the North? And why? When Papa won't even look at them and they surely must only madden her more than she already is. Oh, how they madden me!*

She began to sift through them. *Ah,* she thought, *these all have articles about the college . . . and about Papa.*

The *Chicago Daily Tribune:* "Washington College is a school run principally for the propagation of hatred to the Union."

The *New York Independent:* "Donations to Washington College from the North will buy implements for another and bloodier conflict and sharpen the knives wherewith to cut the throats of the givers."

The *Boston Evening Traveller:* "The arch traitor Lee's mission is to teach his students more treason, and to employ Northern donations for paying traitors to teach their d—— treason to the flower of Southern youth."

Then her eyes landed again on the *New York Independent.* An article by no less than William Lloyd Garrison, one of the most famous names in America. Founder and publisher since 1831 of *The Liberator,* so successful in inflaming a corps of Northern abolitionists on the slavery issue. One of the "Secret Six" who financed John Brown's infamous 1859 assault on Harper's Ferry, which her father and Jeb had thwarted. *How did I miss this story the first time?* she wondered.

"The South remains a section of universal ignorance that still wishes to rule in hell rather than serve in heaven," raged Garrison, never a man for understatement. "And who is more obdurate than Robert E. Lee himself? He at the head of a patriotic institution, teaching loyalty to the Constitution and the duty of maintaining that Union he so lately attempted to destroy! Has Lucifer regained his position in Heaven? If the South could reasonably hope to succeed in another rebellious uprising, and should make the attempt, who can show us any ground for believing that General Lee would not again act as generalissimo of her forces?"

Agnes shuddered upon remembering that the sentiments of the leaders of the United States government waxed darker even than these.

Oh, how can the college even survive with such enemies, with such hate directed toward it from those who hold all power in the land? How can we survive? she wondered. She could read no more. Flinching as a jolt of neuralgia tore across her face, she walked out of the dining room and up the stairs to the doorway of Mildred's room, open a couple inches wide. *There he is,* she thought, *old Lucifer himself. After another wild night of tending the deathly ill baby daughter who refuses even to close her eyes unless he holds her hand and can be trusted to be found next to her if she awakens at night. The obdurate arch traitor who pats her hand and swabs the sweat from her face all night after working all day at his breeding ground of treason.*

A surge of emotion filled her as she stared at the oldest and youngest members of her family. The hair of one was white as a mantle of snow atop the Blue Ridge and that of the other had all fallen out from the typhoid. *Dear God, how old he now looks,* she thought. *He can no longer even take Traveller for the long rides, such as to the White Sulphur Hot Springs this summer—if even we are able to go.* She prayed they would be able, as her own neuralgia, her mother's rheumatism, and her father's heart and circulatory ailments all cried for it.

She walked back downstairs, past her mother's room, where Mary sat rocking and staring out the window at her ravaged garden, everything planted in it this spring and summer now looted, twice over. *It isn't real, is it, God?* Agnes asked. *All that I have believed . . . all that I have been taught. It cannot be, for it is us Thou hast judged, we who grow poorer and sadder and sicker and die, and our enemies who prosper and grow fat off both our land and their own. For what does it matter to believe if these are the respective ends of those who believe and those who blaspheme with the very beating of their rotten hearts?*

She walked outside to the pockmarked garden, then turned and looked up toward Mildred's window. *Oh, where has it gotten him?* she brooded, a sudden wave of fatigue reminding her she had not yet vanquished utterly her own typhoid. *Where has it gotten any of us?*

●◇ ●◇ ●◇

Good and great God of heaven, Lee petitioned, *what will I do if I do not have my Precious Life to ride with along the paths of this lovely valley?*

He rehearsed in his mind some of their many journeys together these past months.

Their stepping out of the rain into the shelter of a little cabin where the woman scolded Lee for muddying her white floor, then nearly fainted when Mildred explained who he was after Lee had left to retrieve the horses. "Why, there his picture is," the lady exclaimed, "right there on the wall, next to General Jackson and President Davis! My Joe was a soldier in the Army of Northern Virginia."

Life's appearance in a crinoline hoop skirt at supper with friends at the end of a horseback journey to Bedford and her explanation to a startled Lee that, "Papa, surely I am old enough to pack hoops into my saddlebags without breaking them!"

His racing Traveller at full charge, then waiting for her to catch up on his slow old mare Lucy Long. "Life, tell me something," he would say, his eyes jolly and Traveller snorting, "tell me about those schoolmates Rob says have experienced every calamity but matrimony."

And her patient silence as they sat atop Sharp Top, having ridden higher up its face than anyone else ever had, while he gazed over the vista for long moments, the names, faces, voices, ghosts of men he had led to their deaths in a losing cause covering over his countenance with sorrow.

Lee prayed for her in his solitary morning prayers, he prayed for her with the family at breakfast devotions, he prayed for her during the day at the college, and he prayed through the night with her when she was conscious and over her when she was not.

Gradually, as imperceptibly as God's bringing new leaf to the Valley each springtime, Mildred's condition stabilized, then improved.

But she could not speak.

Finally the doctors gave her clearance to travel the fifty miles west to White Sulphur Springs, "the White," as they thought its rarefied clime would benefit her. Still she spoke not a word.

The day before leaving, Lee conducted a regular meeting of the college faculty. Word was afoot that the Republicans, despising the Democrat Johnson, would nominate Ulysses Grant for their ticket in the November presidential election of 1868. One professor launched into a bitter harangue against Grant the soldier, Grant the politician, Grant the ploy of Radical interests. When he tore into Grant the man, Lee thought of Grant's magnanimity at a time of supreme importance, and which few in the South remembered—Appomattox Courthouse. His eyes grew hard as any man present ever remembered them being, before or after.

"Sir," he said, "if you ever again presume to speak disrespectfully of General Grant in my presence, either you or I will sever connection with this university."

Indeed, it was a presidential election year, and the White's shining, white-wood, enormous columns, high-arching ceilings, and long wide porches brimmed with the most powerful men of the old Confederacy—and a burgeoning legion of the North's Democratic elite. United in their opposition to the Republican juggernaut, the two groups were discovering much common ground.

Less apparent, at first, were the batallions of Southern young people and their Northern counterparts, whom they welcomed with approximately the same enthusiasm Richmond greeted its Federal conquerors in April 1865.

The atmosphere tingled with romantic anticipation and political intrigue as old acquaintances were renewed and new ones struck.

The first evening that Lee appeared in the dining room, he escorted Reverend Pendleton's daughter Mary, with Custis and Agnes—she still stick-thin from the typhoid that continued to crouch at her doorstep—just behind them. All five hundred guests, North, South, and foreign, rose as one in mute tribute until the party was seated.

Seventeen-year-old Maryland beauty Christiana Bond, her eyes wide with awe, whispered to one of her high-born friends, "There is the hero of my dreams."

Her friend's eyes flickered. "There is the hero of all our dreams."

As the days passed, Mildred continued to improve, and as Lee found more time to socialize with the guests—particularly the young ones—he took note of the ungallant treatment of the Northern young people by those of the South. *Some of the greatest, and some of the best, families in all of the South are here,* he thought. *I know many of them, many of their young people. How ashamed we should be at our unchristian attitudes, our unchristian example*—he thought back to what those of the North had done to provoke such hatred and how miserably unhappy must be the lot of such people.

His great unspoken fear returned. *All that can destroy us is our own hate.* And his other great fear: *It is our young people who are the true haters. Oh, God of mercy and truth, forestall evildoing by our ene—by those people,* he caught himself. *And forestall evil thoughts by our people—by me.*

That evening Lee saw again how completely the Northern girls were shut out of the evening dances by the Southerners, greatly in the majority. He noticed one girl in particular, as did virtually the entire assemblage. Besides sporting dresses and gowns beyond the reach of all but a few besides Kate Chase Sprague, she possessed a beauty and charm so singularly striking that Lee inquired about her when he saw not a beau disturbed her solitary book reading in a parlor distant from the ballroom.

Custis learned her name, and that her West Virginia father had stayed with the Union, stayed home during the war, and grown fabulously wealthy. His neighbors had gone off to fight for the South. Those who survived lost all they owned.

As he watched the young beauty feign her best that the dance swirling about her and all its dashing young men held no interest for her his heart panged. *She has not read a page in that book she holds since I have watched her,* he thought. *Poor thing. How many like her, here and across the land, are punished, deprived, hurt, for decisions they had no voice in making?*

"It appears our Southern men hold nothing against the girl," Custis said, "but they fear the wrath of our women if they attempt any rapprochement with her."

The next night, seeing her again "reading" in her lonely remote chair, Lee excused himself from his table, walked to her, smiled, bowed, and asked the privilege of accompanying her in the evening's opening promenade.

Following the promenade, Custis and Agnes watched him escort the girl to a choice seat, in which she was beset from all directions by men of every section seeking an introduction and offering cards. As the girls and women of the South seethed with rage, Agnes said softly, "Only Papa."

●◇ ●◇ ●◇

The Democrats did not want Andrew Johnson anymore either, and they nominated Horatio Seymour to face Grant. They knew they had no chance to beat the Radicals without massive support by whatever Southerners were allowed to vote. So former General William Rosecrans, who helped lead the Federal forces that drove Lee and the Confederates out of West Virginia in 1861, came to the White. And he came to see Lee.

Rosecrans was one of the managers of the national Democratic campaign.

"General Lee," he opened, "everyone in the North knows you to be a representative Southerner, and everybody is perfectly confident in your truthfulness. General, if I could be authorized by you to say, on behalf of the Southern people, that they are now glad to be back in the Union, and loyal to the old flag, that statement would do a great deal of good in Congress. And I could use it to assuage the bitterness of feeling among the Radicals and make the Federal government much more lenient towards the conquered states."

Lee felt his color rise. *After all they have done, during the war and especially since,* he thought. *And now, even the best of them, would expect us to . . . No, they are only doing the best they know; and if they win, it will remove the troops from our land and be in every way better for our people.*

"Such consideration is a high compliment, General, especially coming from you, sir," Lee replied. "Yet I do not think I have the right to speak for the Southern people. I have held no office by their gift, except the very humble one of a teacher of youth. I have not even the right of citizenship, sir. Hence, I do not think I have any right to speak for the Southern people."

"But General Lee, sir," Rosecrans pressed, "the whole world knows that you *are* the South, sir. And that what you say is what the South says, or will, when they know how you feel."

Lee did not like the direction this was heading, but he did not wish to quash the man's efforts or what could come from them.

"General, you may know that many distinguished leaders of the former Confederate States are now at the springs, from various parts of the South," he said. "I believe from these men you could learn their impressions of Southern feelings and purposes."

Rosecrans liked this idea, and the two agreed Lee would arrange an introduction for the Federal with the other Southerners. It took place the next morning in the parlor of Lee's cottage. The Northerner's heartbeat jumped when he saw the assemblage Lee had gathered. Hampton . . . Beauregard . . . Alexander Stephens. The least conspicuous man present was Fletcher Stockdale, an old friend of Lee's from the Virginian's prewar United States Cavalry days.

Stockdale was "only" the ex-governor of Texas.

Rosecrans asked each man, in turn, the same question he had asked Lee. The mildness and uniformity of their answers unsettled Lee. *These are not men lacking such boldness as to speak their piece, whatever the consequences,* he worried. *Why do they not now?*

One after another they parroted the same chorus of contrition and gratitude for the prospective favor of the Union.

Finally there remained only Stockdale, the smallest man physically in the room at but a few inches over five feet tall, and just now crammed in a corner and not appearing at all appreciative for having to voice his own opinion before such an august group. So uncomfortable was he in fact that for a moment Lee did not think the Texan was going to give any answer at all.

"Governor," Rosecrans repeated, "have your gallant Texans no feelings toward the old government and the old flag?"

Finally, as the other men began to shift in their seats, Stockdale rose from his own—the first to do so. "I am sure that you may say this," he spoke. "The people of Texas will remain quiet, and not again resort to forceful resistance against the Federal government, whatever may be the measures of that government."

Rosecrans' face lit up like a Yankee Fourth of July fireworks celebration. "Ah! That is good news from our gallant Texas—"

"But, General Rosecrans," Stockdale cut in, to the surprise of every man in the room, "candor requires me to explain the attitude of my people. The people of Texas have made up their minds to remain quiet under all aggressions and to have peace, but they have none of the spaniel in their composition. No, sir, they are not in the least like the dog that seeks to lick the hand of the man that kicked him; but it is because they are a very sensible, practical, common-sense people, and understand their position . . ."

Finally an honest man among the bunch, Lee thought, noting the flush on Rosecrans's startled face, *and the least likely of the entire group at that.* When Stockdale concluded, Lee rose to his feet, and all knew the meeting was closed. One by one, the men filed out, Lee shaking each one's hand and wishing him a good morning. At the end of the line was Stockdale. When only he remained, Lee shut the door before him and held the knob with his left hand.

"Governor Stockdale," he began, "before you leave, I wish to give you my thanks for brave, true words. You know, Governor, what my position is. Those people choose, for what reason I know not, to hold me as a representative Southerner; hence, I know they watch my words, and if I should speak unadvisedly, what I say would be caught up by their speakers and newspapers and magnified into a pretext for adding to the load of oppression they have placed upon our poor people. And God knows, Governor, that load is heavy enough now. But you can speak, for you are not under that restraint, and I want to thank you for your bold, candid words."

"Thank you, sir," Stockdale said, gratified. He again expected to exit, but still Lee held the door shut, and again he spoke. When he did, the brown eyes flamed.

"Governor, if I had foreseen the use those people designed to make of their victory, there would have been no surrender at Appomattox Courthouse; no, sir, not by me."

Then, his head beginning its fast little nods and the color spreading over it like the Army of Northern Virginia swarming over an ancient field of battle, he announced, "Had I foreseen these results of subjugation, I would have preferred to die at Appomattox with my brave men, my sword in this right hand."

Stockdale stood stunned, knowing he had just heard something the likes of which Lee had never even before peeped in public. Lee lowered his head and, his face rent with sorrow, said, "This, of course, is for your ear only. My friend, good morning."

Rosecrans got his statement, and Lee and the Southerners got their concerns and desires aired before the whole United States.

Lee was still distracted in the ballroom that evening by what he had heard and what he had said. He wished no more of politics, now or ever. Rosecrans would indeed press the issue further with him by mail after Lee returned to Lexington, but the Virginian would henceforth pass the correspondence to an associate to handle.

For now, he would utilize his growing retinue of Southern belles to shield him from men North and South whose importunate, and uninvited, solicitations of his political views had grown intolerable.

In the midst of pleasant, humor-laced conversation with Christiana Bond and her friends, Lee spotted the just-arrived party of renowned wartime governor Andrew Gregg Curtin of Pennsylvania, who had been one of Lincoln's most trusted lieutenants. No one, least of all Christiana and her friends, seemed the least bit interested in making their acquaintance.

"Have any of you fair maidens met that honorable man yonder and his party?" Lee asked.

The girls shook their heads. Their eyes said more. Their eyes said, "Nor will we—ever."

But they escaped Lee's searching gaze behind their fans.

The escape proved only temporary as he said, "We are on our own soil and owe a sacred duty of hospitality."

Christiana's friend Jane Francis had tired of Lee's admonitions, the subtle and the direct, to reconcile with "those people." For days only her reverence for the Virginian and all he meant to her people had constrained her from revealing her sentiments. Being compelled to initiate social converse with one of the true lions of the Federal war effort that had cost her sixteen-year-old brother both his legs ended her reticence.

"Well, General Lee, they say General Grant is coming here next week," she said, ignoring the glares of Christiana and several of her other friends, her tone as cool as her smile. "What will you do then?"

"If General Grant comes," Lee said, Christiana thinking his eyes at once earnest and faraway, "I will welcome him to my home, show him all the courtesy that is due from one gentleman to another, and try to do everything in my power to make his stay here agreeable."

The fans grew busier. Lee was growing weary with the petulance—of all varieties, whether of rudeness or deception—of his people. His head nodding and glowing scarlet, he rose from his seat.

"I have tried in vain to find any lady who has made acquaintance with the party and is able to present me," he said. "I will now introduce myself, and will be glad to present any of you who will accompany me."

As Lee stood waiting, his court's devotion was little in evidence. Finally Christiana stood and said, "I will go, General Lee, under your orders."

"Not under my orders," said he, "but it will gratify me deeply to have your assistance."

As they proceeded across the ballroom, Christiana Bond, her arm in Robert E. Lee's, felt as though she could be no one but the queen of the world. *Oh, I know the whole room is watching, but I will not let on I see any of them,* she thought with glee.

In the dead center of the enormous hall, Lee stopped. Directly above them glowed a chandelier lit by dozens of candles. He looked her in the eye, seeing over Christiana's shoulder pale Agnes and her own friends, all Southerners, seated in their ranks across the room.

"You cannot conceive of the grief that fills me," he said, "at the spirit of unreasoning resentment and bitterness in the young people of the South, of the sinfulness of hatred and social revenge, of the failure to fulfill the duty of kindness, helpfulness, and consideration for others."

Christiana swallowed and glanced about, unable to stay his gaze. She caught sight of some pro-Federal Marylanders she knew who had cheered Lincoln's jailing of the state's entire legislature, including her uncle—for the whole war—when it readied to vote secession. When she again looked into Lee's eyes, the queen's mask was finally off. Through clenched teeth, her eyes fired with murder, she said in a low and slow voice Lee rued as far too old for her, "But General Lee, did you never feel resentment towards the *North?*"

He winced at the venom dripping from the last word. And he saw more glowing in her eyes than he wished. Reflecting in their anger the ranks of candles above, they flickered like a miniature torchlight parade through hell itself.

I have seen that look too often, he lamented, sighing. *Such a work we have before us, to recover our hearts. And what might Fletcher Stockdale think now, should he hear these sorts of lectures emanating from my lips?*

"When you go home, Christiana," Lee said, gentle as though he were nursing her very soul back to health, "I want you to take a message to your young friends. Tell them from me that it is unworthy of them as women, and especially as Christian women, to cherish feelings of resentment against the North. Tell them that it grieves me inexpressibly to know that such a state of things exists, and that I implore them to do their part to heal our country's wounds."

Tears filled her eyes, multiplying the ranks of candles in them, for she could not remember when she did not hate, only that it must have been before her friends and family began to be killed and maimed and imprisoned and shorn of their earthly belongings. She could only nod her assent.

He escorted her to the Pennsylvanians, who arose in one joyful mass at such a welcome from such a man.

"What do you think of him now, Christiana?" Jane Francis purred after Lee had returned her from the Yankees.

Young and lovely, charming and scarred, she thought about that as she watched him walk slowly back toward his room, alone and looking suddenly very old, to tend Mildred as he had tended Agnes and Mary and his mother.

"I never knew if Arthur was truly a man who walked the earth, or only a legend," Christiana said. "But now I know he is a man, and Camelot needs him desperately."

CHAPTER 66

ANOTHER AUTUMN ARRIVED. GRANT MET WITH KEY CADRES OF Republican Congressmen between campaign swings. The day arrived for Marley to meet with the nominee.

Marley, more than almost any man in the House, missed Stevens. He had held less in common with the man than almost any. The bridge between them had been their conspicuous absence of guile. When Stevens rampaged, Marley remembered what he himself was about and why. He needed that. Now, without it, seasons of ambivalence and guilt imposed themselves upon him with increasing frequency. Anne proved the best antidote to such funks, but some of the seasons now concerned Anne.

She for a long while preempted his proposal of marriage with assertions of her unworthiness of him, the dark past she could not yet bring herself to reveal to him, her desire that the revol—the Reconstruction—be consummated before they allow their own selfish plans to distract him from his historic mission. But his physical passion for her grew so acute, and the infrequent kisses they shared so inadequate, that his advances one night in the barouche forced her to physically resist him and to warn through a blizzard of tears, "Wayne, darling, sugar, if truly you love me, how can you place me in the predicament of choosing between dishonor and summoning a constable against my own true love!"

He drank more wine of late—increasingly more—than he read his Bible, but this incident sliced through the mental fog he began to suspect had enveloped him and prompted a proposal of marriage the next time he saw her.

"To retain my honor—and to properly esteem yours," he said, "I can do no other. We must marry, or . . ."

"Or what, Wayne, my love?" she said, her eyes glinting her alarm.

He looked down, fumbled with his hands, and murmured, "We must marry."

She pled for thirty more days to give him her final answer. He argued but relented, as always he did, with the advent of her tears.

Now the thirty days had expired, and she was in Paris with Kate Sprague. Marley swore under his breath at this and at the vodka and tomato juice that now demanded a place at his every breakfast. In fact some mornings it occupied the only place at his breakfast. He did not wish to advance beyond two of them, especially since he now took them with no ice. However, Anne's surprise departure at what should have been the most important of times—news of which she conveyed to him by telegram from the estate of Kate's husband in Narragansett—added to the meeting with Grant, plus realization that Stevens's death had rendered his own ascension in the party vulnerable to other Republicans who for various reasons hated him and/or Stevens, made a third drink seem the only sensible course.

He applauded himself for the decision as a warm blanket of well-being tided over him despite the autumn chill during the barouche ride to the capitol building. *I know she loves me,* he thought with satisfaction, *I have not been so long with her not to know. We will sort through it when she returns. And if somehow she says no?* Well, there was always more vodka and tomato juice in the morning, more wine in the forenoon, and more of that delicious brandy those Union Pacific Railroad lobbyists had been providing him in the evening.

Railroads, he thought, trying to avoid the thoughts now forcing themselves on him. Thoughts of how he and the rest of his party could no longer pretend the national economy presented anything but a gloomy tableau. Both the coal miners and the iron workers back in his district had perched on the brink of strikes for months. That recollection rendered the specter of a fourth drink worth considering. *Thank goodness for the big corporations,* he thought, or at least for their endless river of money. Not only had they tanked his campaign war chest to overflowing; they had actually delivered a mountain of money to his only formidable prospective Democratic opponent—in return for his staying out of the race!

He continued to be amazed that all they asked in return was his support on a key vote, just every now and then. Most of the time they left him alone to vote however he pleased—since he usually voted the way they liked anyway. *Their occasional requests are a small forfeit indeed in return for their fueling the birth and growth of a better America,* he thought. For the first time he began to understand what Anne and others meant when they talked of the giant mark he would leave before his course was finished. *Why, I do begin to sense the chances are greater of graduating from my congressional seat to a higher office than they are of my being beaten from the seat,* he thought in amazement.

Marley had met Grant at various functions and found him awkward and out of place in political-social settings. Now, with victory in the wind, the great captain of war smacked of confidence. Grant well knew how desperate were the Republicans, Radical and moderate alike, for victory. Defeat would jeopardize careers, power, financial opportunities, and everything for which they had worked these bitter past years of Reconstruction cold war. It would jeopardize revolution.

He knows he holds the whip hand, Marley thought as he observed his fellow Congressmen performing for Grant like trained marionettes. *He knows most of us would rather burn the White House to the ground as the British did in 1814 than turn it back over to the Democrats and their reactionary clients.*

"A pleasure to see you, Colonel Marley," Grant said. "No doubt you gentlemen are aware that Wayne Marley, a highly decorated veteran of our war in Mexico, was one of the best cavalrymen in all of the Grand Army of the Republic during the War of the Rebellion. Didn't you finish as chief of scouts for Sheridan?"

Before Marley could respond, Grant hurried on, folding in the rest of the men with his gaze. "And did you men hear of the bold impression left by General Sheridan on those moss-backed Prussians whose lines he toured this summer in France?"

Marley stiffened. He had heard. Evidently no one else at the table had.

"'We are shocked,' said the Huns after 'Little Phil' illumined them on our winning strategies of warfare, 'that this Sheridan and these Americans fail to wage war within the prescribed standards of Christendom,'" Grant said, chuckling. "Better for them, I suspect, that they limit their aggression to their European neighbors."

"I believe the unrecalcitrant rabble of the military district I now represent have learned as much respect for General Sheridan as have those in the Shenandoah Valley," said one of the former state of Louisiana's freshmen Radical representatives, native of a Hapsburg province, revolutionary, and not yet a citizen of either the state he represented or the country in whose Congress he served.

Grant smiled at reminiscences of the tempestuous little Irishman, whose outrages against the people of Louisiana had prompted Andrew Johnson to remove him as commander of that military district. "Little Phil," he mumbled, "whose self-proclaimed philosophy of war is to leave the enemy with nothing but their eyes to cry with."

Marley wondered if such was the case with the members of the Methodist church in Opelousas, Louisiana, which General, and now congressional stalwart Ben Butler boasted some of his Massachusetts brethren had converted to a "den of infamy."

"Uh, have you seen yesterday's *New York Herald,* General Grant?" a Radical congressman from New England inquired as he produced the paper from a crisp leather satchel.

"No," Grant replied. "They haven't come out for us too?"

Several around the table guffawed at such a supposition regarding one of the greatest of the Democratic Party's Northern supporters.

"Well, er, not exactly, sir," the New Englander said.

"Well, read what they say, man," Grant said.

"Sir?" the New Englander croaked.

"You've pulled it out," Grant said, "you read it."

Feeling all eyes on him and his stiff collar growing tight, the man cleared his throat and proceeded to read the front-page editorial.

"If the Democratic Committee must nominate a soldier for president—if it must have a name identified with the glories of the war—we will recommend a candidate for its favors. Let it nominate General R. E. Lee."

A couple of congressmen gasped. Grant said nothing, but Marley saw the color rising upwards from his neck.

"Let it boldly take over the best of all its soldiers," the New Englander continued, "making no palaver or apology. Lee is a better soldier than any of those they have thought upon and a greater man. He is one in whom the military genius of this nation finds its fullest development."

"Those b——s," one esteemed Midwestern congressman breathed.

"For this soldier," the New Englander read on, "with a handful of men whom he had molded into an army, baffled our greater Northern armies for four years." Now he looked up at Grant. "Uh, General—"

"Finish it," Grant said, his voice soft but the tiniest shade tight.

The New Englander cleared his throat once more, drank some water from the glass provided him, looked again at Grant, then read, "And when opposed by Grant, was only worn down by that solid strategy of—" He cleared his throat yet again. "—*stupidity* that accomplishes its object by mere weight."

Another congressman hurled a profanity and Grant blushed crimson, his jaw growing hard.

I have indeed heard all now, Marley thought, beginning to wish for more alcohol as a ringing started in his head.

"With one quarter the men Grant had," the reader went on, "this soldier fought magnificently across the territory of his native state and fought his army to a stump. There never was such an army or such a campaign or such a general for illustrating the military genius and possibilities of our people, and this general is the best of all for a Democratic candidate."

The New Englander stopped and started to put away the newspaper.

"Is that all of it?" Grant asked.

"Well—" the New Englander started.

"Finish it!" Grant shouted, slamming a thick fist against the dark cherry table.

"Yes sir," said the rattled reader. "Er . . . it is certain that with half as many men as Grant, Robert E. Lee would have beaten him from the field in Virginia, and he affords the best promise of any soldier for beating him again."

One congressman jerked the paper from the New Englander's hands and tore it to shreds.

"General, sir," another said, "you should send troops and shut those b——s down, just as President Lincoln would have done during the war, sir."

"How can they say such things?"

"They cannot be allowed to get away with such treason."

"What more eloquent—and obscene—demonstration could we ask for of the perils of our monstrous Constitution? With you as president, General, we must press forward with more amendments, more centralization, until such treason is rooted out and eradicated forever from these shores—if necessary at the point of a bayonet."

With a couple more oaths, the group's outburst sputtered to a close. For a moment silence reigned. Grant's anger appeared to give way to dejection.

Ah, how much more difficult to retain the people's acclaim as a politician than as a conquering general, Marley mused.

"What say you, General?" the Midwesterner asked. "Is Robert Lee the demigod for whom our people cry to lead them to the next plateau of our national destiny?"

Grant shook his head slowly and stuck a used unlit cigar in his mouth without seeking permission. Chewing on it, he said, his teeth clenched so tightly Marley could barely understand his words, "Lee had everything in his favor. He was supported by the unanimous voice of the South. He was supported by a large party in the North. He had the support and sympathy of the outside world. All this is of an immense advantage to a general."

Now the eyes of the victor of Shiloh and Vicksburg and Petersburg and Appomattox surveyed every man before him.

"There is a cry in the air that the generalship and valor were with the South," he said. "I myself have always thought Lee possessed of a slow, conservative, cautious nature, without imagination or humor, always the same, with *grave* dignity."

None could miss the emphasis Grant placed on the word *grave*.

"He is a large, austere man, and I judge difficult of approach to his subordinates."

Grant pulled the cigar from his mouth and peered at it. "I never could see in his achievements what justifies his reputation. The illusion that nothing but heavy odds beat him will not stand the ultimate light of history. I know it is not true."

Marley did not know if Grant's words or the accolades the other men in the room rained down upon him for them surprised him more. *Can he believe such tripe?* the Pennsylvanian wondered. *Lee beat the h— out of every other general he ever faced, and he beat the h— out of Grant until he had no more men or guns with which to do it.* Swearing with the Lord's name, he thought, *I know, I was there getting the h— beat out of myself through most of it.*

"Gentlemen," the Midwesterner said, a smile beaming from one side of his rugged face to the other. "Can any of us who are sane doubt we have our man?"

"Yeah, and it's d—— well not some aristocratic traitor," another congressman hooted.

"Then, General, shall we dispense with the amenities and retire for liquid refreshment?" the Midwesterner said.

As a chorus of applause echoed off the room's walnut-paneled walls, Marley thought, *At least this meeting has produced one sound idea.*

●◇ ●◇ ●◇

Indeed they had found their man. Despite the worsening economy, the Republicans for the first time ever won the Senate, the House of Representatives, and the presidency.

"Now we can really begin to accomplish something, sugarplum," Anne, back from Europe with no decision yet on Marley's proposal, told him with a gleeful toast of champagne.

The United States had experienced an impeached president. Now it would experience one with a corrupt administration, the most corrupt in American history.

Christmas morning 1868 dawned cold and bright pink, Lee's favorite time for riding Traveller. Patting the horse's neck as he rode along, he said, "I trust you are not still angry with me for leaving you here when we went to the White this summer, old fellow. But you know I have not held my age as well as you have." Traveller pranced even sprightlier. Lee glanced up as the sun peaked over the Blue Ridge and flung its golden beams over the quiet land. "And now you will be more annoyed with me, as I fear we must return early to perform special duties."

Lee was determined to make this the most special Christmas of Mildred's life. He could not allow the semblance of a thought to creep into his mind to fear it might be the last Christmas of her mortal days.

Rooney had left for his own farm with his second wife, Mary Tabb, a few days before, after a several-weeks visit in Lexington. *How gracious of Thee, heavenly Father, to have blessed him with another fine wife,* Lee thought. He chuckled at "Miss Tabb's" reported comments to the family that, "If George Washington himself, the father of his country, had arrived late for morning family prayers, I do not believe even he would have the unqualified good opinion of General Lee."

As the family advanced toward the dining room table for breakfast, Lee shook off the chill and chest congestion that had imposed themselves on him with an unwelcome increase in frequency in recent months. He would not let anything dampen this special day. *Heavenly Creator, in your kindness and mercy Thou hast brought all of mine to me this one day, except for Rooney and Tabb, who have been recently with us, and gentle Annie and sweet Charlotte, who are in your safekeeping.* He drank in the fragrance thrown off by the pine, spruce, and ivy trimmings Agnes and Mary Custis had placed around the table and sideboards. His heart rose as he watched each person's countenance illumine at the sight of the colorful packages he had earlier placed on the table, one or two for each of them.

Except Mildred. Still weak, Custis and Rob helped her to her seat. *How did she manage to get on her nicest dress?* he wondered, tears filling his eyes at the sight of Mildred's silk cap, which covered her still-bald head. *To have all of these here today, when we celebrate the birth of Thy son, our Lord and Savior, God of our forefathers, fills me with an inexpressible joy for Thy goodness,* he thought.

His gaze took in their faces—Boo, Rob, Daughter, the Mim, Wiggie, and, to his right, in the place of honor, his Precious Life, overjoyed when she saw that of all the more than dozen items she had mentioned as desirable for her Christmas gift, he had purchased one of the most special to her.

He only smiled, filled with that singular joy a father can know only when the love he has given a child has rendered in that child the unshakeable belief that her Papa is everything in a man he wished he were.

As each in turn opened his gift or two, Lee slipped away from the table and found the cache he had hidden at the back of the storage closet beneath the stairs. A large cache it was, and expensive. *Oh well, my Father,* he thought with a sigh, *I yet trust that Thou hast ordained a better time for the purchase of that new suit of clothes than I can myself.*

He would remember a few things in the hours he lay dying, and one of them would be the expression on Mildred's face when she saw him step back into the room, the entire massive upper half of his body obscured by the heap of presents so large and so weighty that Rob vaulted from his chair to help him carry them in.

No one, not even Mary at the opposite head of the table from Lee, knew what he had done, though she assayed his actions before any save Mildred. Her hand went to her mouth, a mouth drawn grim from years of sorrow, that she might not do something she had rarely done, bawl in the presence of her family.

To the eyes of the others, Mildred was now twenty-two years of age, but to Lee she was still sixteen, twelve, eight, four, two. Far more of value than all the honors he had ever won on any field of glory or in the testaments pouring forth from the lips of the great and the small, was the one amazed—and amazing— word he now heard uttered by his Precious Life.

"Papa."

He wanted to wrap her up in his arms, but no, that would spoil the moment and detract from what he wanted to be her time.

"Papa," she repeated, no less incredulous, and scarcely less thankful, than if he had delivered old Arlington itself to her doorstep, "you have bought *all* of the presents for which I asked. Every one of them!"

And everyone at the table rejoiced with her.

A happier breakfast and time of morning prayers none in the family could remember. Even Mary exclaimed, "I had not thought to speak of it until certain the effort would succeed, but our old friend Congressman James May of Illinois has arranged to initiate the return to us of the remaining possessions of General and Mrs. Washington bequeathed to me by my father, which we left behind at Arlington."

These included china given to Mary's great-grandmother Martha Washington by Lafayette himself.

"But wherever are they, mother?" Mary Custis asked.

Mary fought to forestall severity from her face. "They are stashed in a dusty corner of the United States Patent Office, bodyguarded by the brave placard, 'Captured at Arlington.'" Her face softening, she looked down the table at her husband. "With Papa's approval, Jim May suggests my putting the request in writing to President Johnson, under cover to Jim."

"By all means, Mama," he said, his happy face glowing all the more.

After prayers, Lee nodded at Custis and Rob and the three of them rose. After Rob saddled Traveller, Lee presented the horse with his own Christmas gift of a couple of apples, then mounted up. The cold clean air clearing out his lungs, he grabbed the enormous sack Custis hefted up to him, and slung it across his pommel.

Spying Mary in the open front door with Mary Custis, Lee called out with a mischievous grin, "Do I need to make sure you counted right?"

"I always counted right, Robert Lee," she riposted in feigned sternness, "right down to the last barefoot Valley boy in the dirtiest company Stonewall Jackson ever marched over the Yankees with."

Smiling and waving at Agnes and Mildred as they looked out a front window, he reined Traveller around and headed down the hill toward town. It was a bit late for Santa Claus to make his rounds, but if that jolly old man had flown in behind a team of reindeer from the North Pole itself, he could have been no more welcome by those on whom he called.

"Here he comes!" one of them screamed as the bearded old general appeared at the bottom of Washington Street. The fame of General Lee's Christmas ride had grown much faster these past years than the gift sack had been able to, and it seemed as though they were all waiting for him this time. He had gently circulated the request that children remain in or near their own yards or sidewalks, to avoid crowds that would complicate the distribution of presents; and most, he was glad to see, had complied.

"General, sir, thank you, General, sir!"

"Mittens—gee, sir, just like Old Jack's boys wore!"

"Oh, General Lee, none of us have had a dolly since before the war. Thank you, sir!"

On they came, in every yard, at every door, their upturned faces, black and white, scrubbed extra clean in honor of General Lee. No parent in all the South could have borne the shame of knowing he had seen their child with a dirty face or unclean clothes, no matter how tattered they might be.

"You look just like in your picture Pa put up on the wall, General. He lost both his legs at Chancellorsville, but he still loves you, sir!"

Chancellorsville, Lee thought, just as something drew his gaze over to a quiet two-story brick home right on the street. *Stonewall's old place,* he thought, his throat growing tight. *There was a man who loved children. I wish—if only we had not lost him—*

"That's . . . that's Traveller, isn't it, sir? I know him from the picture books."

On cue, the gray high-stepped, as always he did when he knew he was the subject of conversation.

Then the bright sun glancing off a fluffy mane of tawny, freshly brushed hair caught Lee's eyes.

"Well, hello, Miss Grace!" Lee called as her mother tried to shoo her away from the door and out toward him. But the little girl dug in her heels and refused to budge. Lee's heart sank, but he smiled and waved at her and called, "You must come visit us, Miss Grace." At this the girl's face screwed up in horror, and she whirled past her mother to disappear inside the house.

The gift bag always ran empty somewhere along the way, and the last children contented themselves with receiving a look, a smile, a genial greeting from the man whose picture they all had in their homes. But today Lee looked down into the bag after more than an hour, expecting it to be almost empty. *But,* he thought, *how can so many gifts remain? It looks nearly as full as it did when I left the house.*

Then another screaming cluster of little ones, these black, hurtled toward him from their small mean cabin.

None of the four children who lived there, all girls, had ever before owned their own doll baby, but all did after today. Their mother, left by both her husbands, worried from one day to the next where the next food would come from. She was so frightened now that perhaps honorable means to that end had played out that she shivered. Something drew her out to Lee.

"General, sir," she said, petrified, "beggin' your pardon, sir, but we have another in the house, quite shy, who has never ever had a doll—" Now the voice of the thirty-year-old woman, whom Lee judged to be forty, but to have been once quite beautiful, cracked. "—baby, sir. Might you—"

Before she could finish the sentence, Lee had a fat pink one with a pretty blue dress in her hands. "Thank you, sir, you are a good Christian man, sir," she said, nodding and smiling, her eyes filling with tears.

That night, as she read the Bible she had been too long away from, hope returned to her that perhaps honorable means still remained to earn the family's daily bread. And she slept soundly for the first time in weeks, hugging the fat pink one with the little blue dress that looked ever so much prettier on the doll baby than it had hanging in Lee's now-curtainless little bedroom.

"I do believe he knows all the children in Lexington," Pastor J. William Jones told his wife as their little boy, now six, raced out with his siblings to see Lee. Despite the gift-bearer's admonitions to the contrary, a train of children followed in his wake, many of them with their parents, some not. He knew when the presents played out, he would have to reverse his route and guide them all home.

Noting the wretched rags many of the children still wore, Jones fought back tears. "How badly we need him," he said as his wife, sensing the melancholy again enveloping him, wrapped her arm around him. *How badly* I *need him*, he thought. *I will write to the world what I witnessed here today.*

Lee did not return home till after noon. Kissing Mary as he came in, he asked, "How did you and the girls find time to knit so many mittens? I gave out over twenty pair of mittens to the children. Thank goodness too, their parents were practically weeping with appreciation, what with how cold this winter has been, and nobody can find any mittens to buy anywhere."

Mary stared at him, her face flushing.

"What is it, wife?"

"Agnes and I were fretting even after you left," she said, "because all of us together had only managed to knit five pair of mittens."

CHAPTER 67

CULPEPER AND HIS COUSINS JED AND RED TRACKED ELIJAH SLEDGE for months. They lost his trail in the mountains of western North Carolina, then heard he was headed up to Virginia. Turning north, they were set upon by a squad of Brownlow's "militia." Professional bounty hunters tracking down one group of suspected Klansmen and other pro-Confederates after another, they shot Cousin Red in the leg, then chased Culpeper and his cousins up into the Appalachians. A vicious game of hunter and hunted ensued through the winter of 1867–68. When it ended, Red had been shot again in the same leg and lost it, and all but two of Brownlow's men were dead, those two headed back for Tennessee on foot.

But word drifted up to the cousins that a new bounty had been put on their heads in North Carolina and more "militia" dispatched for them. So they headed north through the mountains into Virginia, biding their time and hunting and fishing for food.

"In some ways I'm much obliged to the Yanks for drivin' us to this sorta life," Cousin Jed opined as the three dined on bear meat one evening amid the high pines. "I actually think I'm puttin' weight on the longer we're up here in the mountains."

"You don't miss your family?" Culpeper asked as hot juice from the meat he gobbled dripped onto his buckskin sleeve.

Cousin Jed's eyes grew murky, and he looked out into the distant mountains. "Daisy and me," he started. "Well, it weren't never quite the same when I come back. And now, what with all the killin' and what's happened to my brothers . . . I just don't feel any push to go back."

"Ever?" Culpeper asked, struck by the notion.

Now Cousin Jed looked at his chunk of bear meat. "She wanted things back the way they was before the war," he said. "And I thought for a while we might could do it. But when them carpetbaggers and whatnot kept leanin' on us, then stole all our cotton, with promises to come back for everything else . . . and then when Danny . . ."

Cousin Red grunted, which was a wordy sentiment for him since losing of leg.

"Me, with winter comin' on soon, I'm ready to head back down and settle matters with this Elijah Sledge," Culpeper said, carving off a cut of chew with his Bowie knife. "I reckon that's what we come out for. I sorta cottoned to Tennessee, but if we're not gonna do that . . ."

"Then why sit around?" Cousin Jed said.

"Yeh," Culpeper said after a moment, struck that neither now nor for months had he witnessed a laugh or even a smile from his cousin. The Virginian pulled out one of his revolvers to oil. They were flush with guns again. It seemed the only natural way. Like killing Yankees, it seemed the only way anymore.

Slugging down boilermakers in a backwater saloon two weeks later just on the Virginia side of the state line, they heard his name mentioned in a pro-Radical North Carolina newspaper article chronicling the formation of two regiments of mounted troops under Colonel George Kirk.

"But that don't make sense," Cousin Jed protested to the reader, a frock-coated dentist who had so thoroughly drunk away his family fortune that all he had left to show for it was the grimy suit and shattered spectacles he wore. "That scum Kirk is nothing more than a murderin' renegade. Some o' them Tennessee Unions whine about Quantrill and Bill Anderson and their Lawrence raid—well leastways they were squarin' accounts after what Bloody Jim Lane did murderin' so many o' their kin in Missouri."

"I heard it was for that buildin' burnin' down on Anderson's sister and them other ladies in Kansas City after the Yanks jailed 'em there," Culpeper said.

"When the Federals had been warned the building was condemned," the dentist put in helpfully, his eyes clearly crimson even through the fractured spectacles. "And there is more, much more of substantial interest contained in this written piece, gentlemen, if I might trouble you for one of those fine concoctions you are imbibing."

Culpeper and the Wallaces looked at each other.

"You sassin' us, mister?" Cousin Jed asked in no friendly way.

"Why, no, sir," the dentist sputtered, "I sought only to impose upon you for a complimentary refreshment, as I find myself in temporary want of proceeds."

Culpeper leaned across the table. "I don't know what sorta moonshine you're pumpin', dandy, but we been on the trail a long d—— time, and if you're tryin' to shade us, it'd be the biggest mistake *you* ever made."

The dentist stared at them, his mouth agape. Then he stretched out his arms. "Could you please buy me one of those boilermakers if I keep reading?"

"Why h— yeh, pardner," Culpeper said, leaning back in his chair as a grin broke out across his bearded face, his whole body relaxing. "Just don't try to play us for the fool. We won't be trifled with."

The dentist, a bead of perspiration dotting his eyebrow, nodded with a stupid half grin.

"Another round over here, and one for the doctor too," Culpeper called to the barkeeper.

"It says here Governor Holden is calling for the troops, United States regulars, to be employed in arresting disturbers of the people's government program—that means what the black Republican Yankees want—" the dentist told his audience confidentially. "They are authorized to arrest and try by military court, and some number of counties are to be placed under martial law."

Then he looked them in the eye. "It says here our President-elect Grant would have it all. 'Let those men move against you, Governor Holden,' Grant says, 'and I will move with all my power against them.'"

His unsavory new friends finally startled into quiet, the courtly dentist tossed back his whiskey and drained his mug of beer and, emboldened, announced, "God forbid we should ever again witness that power."

Elijah Sledge had never met anyone quite like thirty-three-year-old Colonel Kirk. Half the time he was scared to death of the man, and the other half he thanked his lucky stars for the chance to ride with him. He wondered for what purpose Kirk carried the leather English riding crop so omnipresent it seemed an extension of his right arm.

It all started as the legends grew around Sledge's exploits at the Battle of the Crater. Charging the Rebel lines, cutting, slashing, and clubbing his way clear into the town itself.

"If more men, black and white, had evidenced such valor that day," North Carolina Senator John Pool announced in Governor Holden's office, "the Battle of the Crater would have been one of the great military triumphs in the history of Western civilization. Such is the cut of man called for in the work that lies ahead of us." Present with Pool were the governor, Colonel Kirk, a couple of key Radical state legislators—one black, one white—and Sledge.

It had not hurt that the primary proponent of the Crater legends was Sledge himself. He found an attentive ear among the white Radicals cobbling together Southern state legislatures chock-full of blacks whose actions they could orchestrate. So, too, had the praise of his own lips helped balloon Sledge's march down the aisle to partake of the Eucharist next to General Lee into an act second in magnitude only to Luther's nailing of the Ninety-Five Theses to the Wittenberg Church door in all of Protestant church history.

The governor put an arm around Sledge's shoulder and crowed, "Ride alongside Colonel Kirk with the rank of captain—" Kirk's entire body flinched at that. "—and rid our fair state of the scourge of these secessionist scraps from the table of humanity. Then your spot in the legislature of our great state will be assured, higher office even than that certainly to follow."

The Radicals, through gerrymandering, franchising blacks, disfranchising former Confederates, and just good old-fashioned bribery, held a lopsided majority in both houses of the North Carolina state legislature. Sledge had seen enough of that august body to reckon he not only wanted to be part of it, but that he could rise through its ranks to a place of real power. A not-insignificant percentage of the legislature could neither read nor write. For those in their ranks needing a boost in confidence, Radical railroad tycoon and former Federal General M. S. Littlefield opened a free bar right up the stairs from the House chambers.

"Drink up, boys! Drink up!" Littlefield would cheer as he laid out thousands for drinks—and recouped it a hundred times over when his statesmen-clients voted him control of the state's railroads, and millions of dollars in bond money for them. Such largesse left plenty of cushion for awe-inspiring contributions by Littlefield to their reelection campaign money chests.

The poorest among the Radicals drinks champagne and the shabbiest wear the most elegant of beaver hats, Sledge had seen. He did not see that as Littlefield amassed a fortune building the state's railroads—like other Radicals did in other Southern states—he also bought ownership in the railroad car company, purchased cars for the state from himself, paid himself with state funds, and more often than not managed to overlook the tiresome detail of delivering the cars.

"Jumpin' Jehosophat," Sledge had whistled when he saw black men and white, far less accomplished than himself, drinking for free from Littlefield's bar during working sessions, all the while moving about in the most stylish suits from New York and Boston, and dining—with never any expense to themselves—at the finest restaurants in Raleigh.

Next thing you know, some of these boys be gettin' themselves white women for wives, he thought, though he himself would rather be stomped by mules than follow that path. He wanted to see the grudging respect for him in their defeated eyes, but he did not want one under his own roof.

"I'll leave the politickin' to you gentlemen," said Kirk, stocky but athletic, a tremendous horseman, scar-faced from a Rebel sword, and decked out in full but filthy blue Federal cavalry uniform. He popped the riding crop into the palm of his yellow-gauntleted hand—he had not removed either gauntlet through the whole of his visit to the governor's office—as Sledge returned from his brief spell of daydreaming. "I got my money, and I'm ready to get this 'private army' together as you call it and deal with these Ku-Kluxers."

The sheer volcanic force of Kirk's will and personality, not to mention his fearsome war reputation, rendered every man in the room, even a United States senator and a governor, temporarily mute.

Kirk was already almost out the door, sans handshakes or toasts, and calling back over his shoulder, "You'll hear from me."

At first the heavily black composition of the six-hundred-and-seventy-man column pleased Sledge. *After all,* he thought, *our destiny should be in our own hands; else what in tarnation have we fought for?*

But as the weeks passed, and he observed their imbecilic behavior, doubts began to plague him. *Their utter insolent ignorance and foolhardiness is exceeded only by the other half of our column, the white trash, most of those illiterate, few with shoes before Grant outfitted them, and not many of them over eighteen years of age.*

Fully a third of the force hailed from outside North Carolina, mostly pro-Union states.

Sledge's disdain grew as the marauders rollicked through one peaceful town and village after another.

In Salisbury he watched widows beg Kirk not to torch their houses after his men looted them nearly bare.

In Newton he saw little children shrieking in uncontrollable terror as Kirk's troopers shoved their revolvers in the faces of unrepentant Rebel fathers and dragged them off to jail, falsely proclaiming loud enough for all assembled to hear, "We're very sorry, folks, since these men will never see their homes again."

In Yanceyville he witnessed the widows and children themselves threatened by Kirk with shooting if the men he was arresting as they led a Democratic Party political rally offered any resistance.

And not far from that town, he saw two white troopers returning from the wooded rendezvous they forced on a comely black teenager who lived in a remote shack with only her ill grandmother and six-year-old sister.

Smoldering with rage, he drew the revolver specially presented to him by a friendly black state senator (after confiscation from an unreconstructed Rebel).

"Whatcha doin' with that revolver out, boy?" Kirk asked, crop in hand, as he rode by.

"Er . . . looked like might have been some trouble over behind that cabin, sir," Sledge stammered.

"T'ain't none o' your concern, boy," Kirk said with a yawn, waving him along with the crop.

Sledge moved on, sullen as the sound of distant artillery fire. But he began to question for the first time if anybody at all was looking out for the black man. *The Southerners, with their friendly condescension, never really believing the black man capable of making it on his own anywhere closer than Liberia; and the Northerners, whose guns and bayonets ended slavery, even though most of them hate us and don't want us anywhere near their own section. Some choices the black man has,* he thought, the realization more bitter than poison berries.

Kirk purposed to exercise force in areas where the Klan and other Southern resistance groups had threatened or roughed up carpetbaggers, blacks, or others, or where such folk had met mysterious and untimely demises by hanging, shooting, or just plan disappearing. So undisciplined was his information-gathering network, however, that the bulk of his intimidation wound up occurring in the most peaceable areas, and where he did commence an operation in or near a town where confirmed night-riding operations had occurred, he inevitably punished people innocent of wrongdoing, while the guilty parties remained anonymous and safe.

The brutal hand that had seemed so effective in war worked against him in peace because the people who might otherwise have aided him, particularly for a price, were dissuaded from doing so, either through outrage at his actions or fear of reprisal of even a permanent sort by their seething fellows if found out to be cooperating.

"We'll just have to wait the scoundrels out," became the unofficial creed of North Carolina; that, and "We'll win the next elections."

After a while Sledge had to concede that Kirk's simple, rough-hewn manner seemed tailor-made for such a collection of rogues. *He knows how to command stupid dangerous men,* Sledge admitted to himself, *which makes them even more dangerous.*

For instance, it took the rape of only one white woman, and Kirk's killing of the one white and one black offender with his own revolver, to impress upon his men that no women—at least no white women—were to be assaulted.

This pleased Kirk's Philadelphia-raised Congregational chaplain, tall and fresh-faced twenty-eight-year-old Mortimer Hedgecock. Nonetheless, Rev. Hedgecock, whose own wife and two children accompanied him on the journey, purposed to caution the manly colonel at an appropriate time regarding the propriety of sexual assault against black women. *But it must be done at the right time,* the parson told himself, *if I am to carry my point without danger of losing sway on more important matters such as the ascendancy of that race to the dominant position in the new Southern society.*

Lee's stomach churned with concern as Markie's latest letter revealed to him how far her health had slipped. Already weakened, her solitary efforts at raising four energetic young nieces and nephews began to seem as though they would require her very life as forfeit.

"I am so sorry to learn from your letter of the 17th instant, which I have just read," Lee wrote her, "that your health is still feeble, and that the cares and anxieties of your life consequently weigh heavily upon you. I can well understand of what deep interest to you is the future of your sweet nieces and nephews. The disposition of them must be a subject of most earnest consideration, and its decision depends entirely upon what may seem for their good.

"I beg that you will fully weigh the last consideration in your letter," he continued, "including the delicacy of your health, the heavy care, and whether it would not be to their advantage to relinquish them, especially the boys, to their father. It is a grievous question, and you must decide it with all the lights before you, if you do not live with their father."

So wonderful a mother she would be as well to children of her own, Lee thought, reminded anew of the searchless designs of the heavenly power. *And so fine a wife to a husband of her own.* He sighed, then remembered the day's date, February 22, and all that it meant.

"I wish I had something cheering to tell you," he wrote on. "This day formerly brought great rejoicing to the country, and Americans took delight in its celebration. It is still to me one of thankfulness and grateful recollections, and I hope that it will always be reverenced and respected by virtuous patriots. The memories and principles of the men of the earlier days of the Republic should be cherished and remembered, if we wish to transmit to our posterity the government in its purity they handed down to us.

"Who can ever rival Washington in our esteem and affections?" he concluded, moved and wishing he himself could have left for his own needy people the palest shadow of so honorable a legacy. "The students of the college will have tonight in the new chapel the celebration of the Washington Society, and I hope the speakers will recall for our edification his great example."

He is a noble man, and he served our country bravely in the war, Agnes thought a couple of weeks later as VMI professor Captain John Brooke departed down the front steps of the Washington College president's house. *And he is wise and mature and responsible and very, very lonely. At least today he did not linger. Today indeed,* she thought, perplexed. *Odd that he should come on an afternoon rather than evening and not even stay.* Shaking her head, she sat in the parlor and opened the crisp new Richmond newspaper Brooke had left her.

Now she understood why he both came and left early. President Johnson had welcomed the opportunity to return the china and other Washington family articles to Mary, he and his entire cabinet, shorn now of the enraged Stanton.

That is what looked to happen, the newspaper reported, until, just before Congress adjourned for the year and Grant took office, the Radicals caught wind of Johnson's very open intentions. A few hours before going home, the Radical-controlled Committee on Public Buildings, which Arlington now was, jammed through a recommendation against returning the heirlooms to Mary.

Only minutes before adjourning, the full House of Representatives voted likewise.

"By what right does the Secretary of the Interior surrender these articles so cherished as once the property of the father of his country, to the Rebel general in chief?" the Radicals asked. "To deliver the same to the Rebel General Robert E. Lee is an insult to the loyal people of the United States."

Agnes stared at the paper, wondering if God decreed any limit to the amount of suffering a person might endure in his earthly life.

"Something is wrong."

Agnes's head swung up to see her mother sitting in her rolling chair in the doorway.

"Don't you try to bamboozle me, little miss," Mary said without rancor. "That paper has news."

Agnes tried to speak, but her lower lip began to quiver.

Mary's eyebrows arched. "It's our things, isn't it, Wiggie? They aren't going to give them back to us."

Without a word Agnes stood and took the paper to her mother, then reached down and embraced her. "I'm so sorry, Mama. I just don't understand."

Slowly Mary turned the chair around and headed down the hallway, never once looking at the newspaper, mumbling, "What would Martha and the General think about it all . . . what would they think?"

Lee thought plenty, and rarely had he faced so stern a struggle to maintain a spirit of kindness as he wrote to a friend of Congress's actions.

"It may be a question to some whether the retention of these articles is more 'an insult,' in the language of the Committee of Public Buildings, 'to the loyal people of the United States' than their restoration," he wrote. He sat back, praying for the grace to offer redemptive sentiments over such a rotten situation. A squadron of dogwood blossoms, some white and some pink, floated past the window of his study. Reminded that all things belonged to God, to be distributed and used as he saw fit, even as His purposes so often remained unclear,

Lee wrote, "But as the country desires the relics, Mary must give them up. I hope their presence at the capital will keep in the remembrance of all Americans the principles and virtues of Washington."

Then another painful memory struck him. "From what I have learned," he wrote, "a great many things formerly belonging to General Washington in the shape of books, furniture, camp equipage, etc., were carried away from old Arlington by individuals and are now scattered over the land. I hope the possessors appreciate them and may imitate the example of their original owners, whose conduct must at times be brought to their recollection by these silent monitors. In this way, they will accomplish good to the country."

How true indeed, he thought, *Stonewall's favorite passage of how* "All things work together for good . . ."

Then a luxuriant mountain of tawny hair illumined by sunbeams slanting in from a window across the hall caught Lee's eye. Standing in the doorway was nine-year-old Grace.

Lee could not conceal his surprise. He heard her mother's voice and realized she had come to visit Mildred.

"Would you like to come in, Miss Grace?" he finally managed.

Quickly she shook her head in the negative. Lee was afraid she would leave, but she stayed in the doorway, her eyes gazing around his study. When he thought her departure imminent, something caught her eye, and her whole face lit up like he had never before seen.

Lee turned and perceived the object of her gaze to be the pasteboard figure of a man in a costume of a century back, stuffed and hanging on the wall. *My pen wipe,* he thought, barely containing his laughter at the remembrance of the lovely young Lexington maidens who bestowed it upon him as a show of "our absolute devotion, Gen-rul Lee."

Grace stared at the figure, then at Lee. Then she stepped into the study toward him and asked, "Is that your doll baby?"

These were the first words she had ever said to him.

"Why, yes," he stammered.

To his utter and complete amazement, she now walked right to him, climbed up in his lap, and laid her head against his chest.

Lee did not know the last doll she ever received was given her by her father the day he left Lexington for the final time.

●◇ ●◇ ●◇

By midsummer 1869, Culpeper and Cousins Jed and Red had yet to get close enough to Sledge or Kirk to so much as lay eyes on them. The Confederate veterans were months learning the whereabouts of the marauding column. Southern loyalists gave them no trouble, but word spread of Cousin Red's being one leg shy. Once a Radical sheriff quizzed them. Then a Federal patrol not related to Kirk chased them for nearly twenty miles before they found a good spot to dismount and drive the Yankees away, two of their saddles empty. That incident, and the ensuing futile manhunt for them through that part of the state, cost more weeks.

By the end of August, all three of them were ready for a suicide attack on the head of Kirk's column. Tales of summary arrests by the Federal force, long jailings without trial, and torture of prisoners had swept the state and traveled even back to Washington, where Grant grew nervous as moderate Republican legislators began to join the Democrats' chorus of protest.

"I got sores growin' on my saddle sores," Cousin Jed said. "It's time to finish it."

"But that column is seven hundred strong," Culpeper said. "We'll git ourselves killed and not even smell Sledge."

And they did not know that Washington—the executive branch in Washington—now had Senator Pool on a short leash as complaints cascaded in from every congressional district in North Carolina.

"For God's sake, don't send troops here; the town is quiet and all works well. Avoid strife."

"We're Republicans, and we want the troops out of this section. It will kill us in the next election. Besides, we have no outrages of consequence here, and I have not heard of any for two months."

"Such men as Colonel Kirk do not do a political party any good. He is universally detested by the people as a military man. They fear and hate him."

"Kirk is very odious to a great many citizens of this county. I hope you will at once revoke his commission."

"I ask you, if you send troops to our mountain county, do not have Kirk over them, because in the late war the county was overrun by the very worst of troops, or men pretending to be such, under his command."

"We Republicans look upon Colonel Kirk as a man of bad character, and his continued presence is driving political support away."

With Pool's rope shortened, so was Governor Holden's, and thence that of Kirk himself. He determined to stage so spectacular a feat of Rebel subjugation that even if Washington forced the termination of his campaign, it would be pronounced a success, and him a hero.

"Sir," one of his captains announced one day as Kirk's men looted another terrified backwoods Carolina village, "this here marshal has a writ of habeas corpus from the chief justice."

Sledge watched Kirk scoff at the peace officer, a Republican appointee. "What the Sam Hill are you doing following me out here, boy?" the colonel said, menace dripping from his raspy, whiskey-ravaged throat. "And since when has that black-robed buffoon in Raleigh acted other than to encourage the carrying out of the laws of the great state of North Carolina?"

"Uh, sir," the captain said. "It's from United States Supreme Court Chief Justice Chase."

The marshal, sick to death of haranguing from citizens about Kirk and his band, shoved the writ toward the soldier, a smug look on his face. The expression vanished when Kirk whipped out his saber and waved the paper aside.

"Such business from Rebel-loving politicians is all played out," he crowed. Sledge's eyes arched in surprise at defiance so audacious even for Kirk. Something else preempted his attention. *That redheaded hussy still passin' time with our good chaplain,* he thought, confused. *Where that nice wife and children of his? And what is that hussy doin' here anyhows? Ain't nothin' but loose women ride with this outfit. Like to know what brand of gospel he's preachin' to her.*

Kirk turned back to his column, whose behavior proved so raucous as to almost give the impression a battle was raging within their own ranks. He shouted with another wave of gleaming steel—a roar that shook the hills around them building from his men almost before he finished the sentence—"Let's get the h— to Redemption and reconstruct us some Rebs!"

⊷ ⊷ ⊷

By now whispers carried on the wind that Kirk might not have his army much longer.

"If they break up before we get to 'im, we might never find Sledge," Cousin Jed said, panic etched in his face as Culpeper had never seen it.

"We've heard three different places now they're headed for a little town called Redemption," Cousin Red said, uttering approximately the number of words Culpeper had heard from him the last week. "I didn't spend the last two years o' my life and give up that leg to go home without takin' that black b—— down."

Culpeper gazed around the verdant hills. Cousin Jed, a dedicated chewer himself, was surprised at how enormous had grown the chaws Culpeper stuffed into his cheek.

"This place ain't near tore up as Virginia," Culpeper said, swallowing. A few more seconds passed and he said, "Guess I had supposed we might happen into some boys of the Klan-sort who'd give us a hand with our business."

"Believe the night riders are layin' low till Kirk clears out," Cousin Jed said.

"I still got no beef with givin' up the ghost over this cigar-store gentleman," Culpeper said, stretching in the saddle to ease the stiffness from old wounds. "But I don't fancy cashin' out without even gittin' a good gander at the man."

"Only thing most o' the Yanks in this part o' the state know about us is Red's leg," Cousin Jed said. "The one he ain't got, that is. What say we git in to Redemption ahead o' Kirk, and Red wait outside o' town with our horses?"

"We jist gonna walk in and walk out?" Culpeper asked.

"We'll help us to some Yank mounts," Cousin Jed. "That all right by you?"

"Well," Culpeper mumbled, stuffing in more chew, "I never sported strong feelin's *against* liftin' Yank rides. Got to Tennessee and a lotta other places on 'em."

"Then we go home?" Cousin Red asked.

"Then we go home," said Cousin Jed as they spurred forward.

The acts of Colonel Kirk and his men the day they rode into Redemption would be passed down on Southern lips for generations. And so would those of the few men who came against them.

CHAPTER 68

HOW SHE OPENS HER HEART TO ME, LEE THOUGHT, READING Markie's plaintive words. *I trust not too much, and I hope I do not encourage her so too much.*

"My dearest Markie," he wrote, "there is something in your last letter that prompts me to answer it at once. You must not think me one of those who 'cannot comprehend disinterested love,' and I know that your devotion to your nephews and nieces is caused by that and your natural affection alone. What I said in reference to matrimony was intended to be general, without reference to particular individuals.

"You must not say you will never marry. It may be proper as well as becoming in you to marry some of these days, and if you determine now 'never to marry,' it may make it difficult for you to do so. I hope therefore that you will come to no determination on the subject but leave it an open question, to be settled by circumstances. I am sure that no one would make a better wife than you, Markie, and you ought therefore to be willing to give the world the benefit of your example and conduct."

He could not say even in his own mind if he wished for her to wed or not.

Marley took Anne up one cool evening to their favorite overlook at the old Soldiers' Home. He tried to put out of his mind the riot at the family factory in Pennsylvania that spilled over into town and almost burned down his mother's home. For every triumph in Washington, loss, disappointment, and tragedy bloomed in every direction—not just in the South but now in the North and West.

Honest old Julian of Indiana, once one of Marley's closest cohorts in the Thad Stevens steamroller, now drew the fury of the Republican leadership as he bellowed how "The saddest part is that the public officials, both state and

Federal, are in league with the capitalists in making the rich richer and the poor poorer."

Even Carl Schurz, an original "Forty-Eighter" revolutionary and Kurt Schumacher's mentor, railed against the excesses of the Republicans' unchallenged power, and the corruption and destruction wrought by the vultures spearheading "Reconstruction." Along with many other Northerners, his suspicion grew that scoundrels and rascals were behind the confiscation schemes of Southern land.

Kurt Schumacher . . . Marley could not but wince at remembrance of the name. Schumacher, too, had turned against the Radical agenda—*against me personally,* Marley remembered with pain. *But too much of that brave man's rage was drenched in what I have been increasingly drenched in,* Marley frowned, the sweet residue of sherry on his tongue even now. *And he said things he could not and would not call back to people far less forgiving than I.*

So, certain Radical stalwarts strew information, some true and some not, like raw meat to carrion birds, to Democratic and Republican newspapers alike about Schumacher's drinking. And they "arranged" for a most embarrassing public—and press-covered—exhibition of his drunkenness immediately following.

Finally, within weeks, they arranged Schumacher's removal from office through party agents in Wisconsin. They tried, but failed, to arrange his conviction on trumped-up morals charges in Washington.

Marley never saw him again.

Julian . . . Schurz . . . poor Kurt . . . even Charles Sumner over in the Senate, Marley thought. *Money has indeed become the goddess of the country, and otherwise good men are almost compelled to worship at her shrine. Legislators everywhere, local, state, national, are bribed with money or controlled by corrupt rings. . . . Boss Tweed and his machine in New York . . . that ruthless John D. Rockefeller out in Ohio . . . the coal industry is not only black-lunged, but the most black-hearted in the land . . . the railroads through which we are sealing our "manifest destiny" are a blot upon mankind, a scheme for rich men to get richer through contracts and vast tracts of land given to them without the consent of the American people who own it, in return for gifts of money and demands for yet more influence.*

What will history say of our conceits and hypocrisy? he wondered. *And beyond everything else, what of "Jubilee" Jim Fisk—the traitor who made one fortune blockade-running Southern cotton during the war and another padding his pockets selling military material to our government. Both fortunes are drenched in the blood of our own brave soldiers. And then there is the multimillionaire Jay Gould. Their breathtaking financial speculations have Wall Street tongues wagging like never before in its history.*

Then Anne's voice, coming from next to him in his leather-upholstered barouche, was cutting through the fog of his concerns and worries and the sherry he had drunk down before leaving his office.

"Are you even listening to me, Wayne Marley?" she asked.

"Yes, yes," he said, "and wondering why you've not mentioned Kate Sprague of late," he said.

Anne frowned at the change of subject and the subject itself. "Oh, I just dearly love Katie, but that husband of hers, the senator—" She put her lips almost to his ear in the manner she knew tickled him when she spoke, as if to impart a secret of vast importance and danger. "Well, darlin', there are a passel of important folk known and respected by you and me who fear he has gone quite crazy." At the sight of Marley's turned-up nose, she insisted, clasping his hand, "No Wayne, truly sugar—crazy. With all his foolish talk about money becoming too preeminent with the leaders of our government and menacing the economic liberties of the people."

He took her kid-gloved hand in his other, looked her deep in the eyes, smiled, and said, "Have I told you lately, dear Anne, that I am just a mite crazy over you?"

She blushed and giggled. Even in the dim lamplight of the coach interior, her luminous eyes—which Marley thought seemed to change colors from blue to gray to green to combinations of the three, depending on her mood—sparkled. "Wayne, honey lamb, please don't patronize me on so dire a topic."

"I don't patronize you," he said. "And I don't fret Will Sprague's sanity, though I certainly question his judgment, not to mention an increasing array of his views. But there is much which I question these days."

"Oh, lamb," she said, "I do fear you question *too* much these days."

"It just seems every time we pass a new bill or amendment into law that concentrates more power in Washington, the nation's economy hiccoughs in choking it down," he said.

She eyed him. "That is not all that bothers you, honey."

He shook his head, looking out over the twinkling lights of America's capital city. "No, that is not by a long shot all that bothers me. For months, even as the national economy has soured while certain men and companies prosper, the price of gold has risen precipitously—actually, way beyond precipitously."

"What does that mean?"

"It means information has come to my attention that Jay Gould and Jim Fisk have poured oceans of money into the gold market," Marley said.

"I have met them both," Anne said.

"You have?" Marley said, startled.

"Yes, both are quite handsome—and dashing too, in singular ways—but there end the similarities."

"Oh?"

"Jay Gould is small, smooth, suave, refined, and perfectly mannered. You could almost mistake him for a Southern man," she giggled, "until you hear his soft New York twang. And Jim Fisk is big, robust, and rollicking. A suit of his European clothes would likely constitute more worth than you or I will ever draw in a year."

"They have something more in common," Marley said. "Their scruples."

"Truly, dear?"

"Yes—neither of them have any."

She blanched at the hard words.

"I have arrived at the considered conclusion that they seek to corner the nation's entire supply of gold," he said. "Then to raise it to whatever price they choose as they sell to merchants needing gold for the customhouse. And just today I receive word that Gener—President—Grant's sister's husband is knee-deep in it with them. And others, too, whom you and I both know, like General Dan Butterfield. Tomorrow morning Horace Greeley will run a front-page editorial in his *Tribune* claiming conspiracy and demanding the secretary of the treasury forestall it by selling several million dollars of the government's gold. I tell you, Anne, no matter which way this goes, a lot more people are going to get hurt, and probably badly."

Sighing and shifting, she said, "Horace Greeley—a more contrary man I do not believe I have ever witnessed. He just can't seem to make up his mind whose side he's on. I wish *he'd* go west and leave the young men alone. Well, phooey on him. Wayne Marley, I have always adored your devotion to honor and integrity; but I declare, sometimes of late you almost seem as though if there is not a cloud in the whole wide blue sky, you'll not be satisfied unless you bring on a thunderstorm."

He turned to her. "Is that truly how I seem?" he asked, alarmed.

Pity shrouding her face, she nodded and said, "I fear so, dearest."

He shook his head and said, "I'm sorry. It seems that as of late, the blacks and whites of my work have developed an irritating propensity to take on shades of gray."

She was answering him then, but he was again not hearing her. He could no longer stave off asking the question that would break their months-long agreement, which held that she would give him an answer on the question of matrimony when she arrived at one; and he would inform her if he could no longer wait for her answer. Otherwise they would not brook the subject.

His question broke both promises.

Pulling out the stone he wanted to be large and knew needed to be large to stand out among her glittering constellation of jewelry, he looked her in the face and said, "Anne Nelson, I'm fraught with flaws and foibles, but I'd be forever grateful if you'd have me and help me work 'em out."

She smiled at the stone he held. Then the smile went away as she stared at the enormous token of his love. After a moment a light breeze pushed through the opening in the curtains of the door, ruffling her black hair and the red ribbons he so liked her to wear. She looked at him and smiled again. When she finally spoke, he was so light-headed that he barely could fathom the words her bewitching voice purred, its tones smooth as molasses and sweet as honey.

"Yes, Wayne, I will marry you."

●◇ ●◇ ●◇

How often the past nine months had Marley lamented his allowing Anne to precipitate intimate—and consummate—physical relations with him. His first regrets centered on guilt, wondering if she felt pressured to the act in order not to lose him. Many other kinds of guilt followed, more kinds than he knew existed, including guilt long-dormant over his morally wronging other women prior to his becoming a follower of Christ.

And now our wedding night will never be what it might have been, he would think later as he went to bed.

It was just another reason why he looked forward to the claret at dinner tonight.

Culpeper savored a half-stick of licorice as he leaned against a wooden post outside the Redemption barber shop. He had not tasted licorice, or anything else with so much as a touch of molasses, since the war. He had had to trade two twists of tobacco for it. *Fancy that,* he mused, his mouth watering as he sucked the candy, *folks in North Carolina havin' to trade for tobaccy. Wonder if they's been a crop o' tobaccy brought in yet in this whole county since the war.*

Thinking to lessen his chances of getting spotted by the Federals, he got a haircut and shaved the beard he had sported in various stages of ferocity for nearly eight years. Between that and the bath he took in the little creek where he and his cousins camped last night, he was feeling pretty chipper, especially in the balmy early-autumn sun. He started to hum the tune of a song he'd heard from some other exiled ex-Confederates up in the mountains. As he hummed, the lyrics started slipping back to him, in ones and twos, then threes and fours, but he could not string enough together to make much sense of them.

"I like that song," Cousin Jed said.

"Yeh," Culpeper said, "can't remember hardly any o' the words, though."

"That's a good thing," Cousin Jed riposted. "Folks 'round here have had hard enough luck without havin' to listen to you sing."

Culpeper thought to spit on his cousin's boot, but a commotion from the village green—brown and dry and flammable from lack of rain—across the narrow rutted street captured his attention.

Such a spectacle as that spread before him on the green Culpeper had never before witnessed. There, in full view of nearly the entire village—men, women, and children—as they made their way this Sunday morning to their four small churches, Colonel Kirk's army cursed, spat, drank, and played cards. When one cluster of towns women passed in their frayed Sunday best, Federals, black and white, semidrunk from the long night before, hurled a chorus of catcalls and obscenities at them. By the time these women and other folk returned from church, several bluecoats, roaring drunk again, dropped their trousers in plain view and squatted to relieve themselves. The large throngs of their fellows around them hooted their approval.

"These 'soldiers' fit the uniform they wear jist about perfect," Culpeper suggested.

"What I'd give to have me General Forrest and fifty men here," Cousin Jed said. "We'd clear out the whole sorry lot of 'em. No, we'd *wipe* out the curs."

Then another ruckus started, up the road. A few seconds later, several of Kirk's troopers cantered to a stop in the street right out front of the barber shop.

"Those vermin—" Cousin Jed began at the sight of four bloodied white men lying stretched out on the ground, their wrists bound together and connected by ropes to the saddlehorns of the horses that had dragged them into town.

"That be Kirk yonder," he added. "One o' John Bell Hood's boys give 'im that scar at Franklin."

So many bluecoats pressed around the dragged men that Kirk finally pulled his revolver, fired two shots in the air, then pointed it at them. "If you boys don't git back onto that grass, I'll be forced to begin the dispensation of justice with my own men."

Grumbling and cursing, the mob turned and moved en masse back to their encampment, where, to the tinkling sound of smashing empty whiskey bottles, numerous fistfights broke out among them, no few between "officers" and rankers refusing their orders. One of Kirk's white troopers called out to a bespectacled townsman standing nearby, "What the h— are you lookin' at boy?" When the fifty-year-old man could only blush in terror, the trooper slugged him in the face, smashing his glasses and knocking him down. Then a half-dozen bluecoats piled onto the man.

"We tracked these men from the scene of their beating of three Union League Negroes," the lieutenant in charge of the dragging detail announced to Kirk as Federals dragged the semiconscious men to their feet. "And their killing of one."

"They killed one of our boys?" Kirk asked, his scar seeming to flush an angrier shade of crimson.

"Yeh, and they was just tuckin' these into their saddlebags when we come upon 'em," the lieutenant growled as he flung a pile of thick white linen sheets, capes, and hoods to the ground in front of the captives.

Slowly Kirk slid his revolver back into its holster. He gave a quick nod to some black troopers standing nearby with water buckets. They drenched the captives with them.

"You boys awake now?" Kirk whooped. "I hope ye are, 'cause I want you to know why we're gonna hang you from these fine oak trees in the common over here tomorrow morning."

Just then Rev. Hedgecock, in uniform but toting the largest Bible Culpeper thought he had ever seen, stepped to Kirk's side and whispered in his ear.

Kirk nodded assent to Hedgecock and turned back to the captives. "You men are in good fortune today," he said. "Our own travelin' parson here, the Rev. Mortimer Hedgecock, now a resident of the fine capital city of Raleigh, has reminded me that an old custom exists in certain parts of this here country: that the worst sort of criminals, the lowest type of desperadoes, the most evil-wrought enemies of order and the rule of law, are strung up in the most public place, right between morning and evening worship. Sort of a reminder to the gentlefolk of the community that God indeed uses the sword of the state to dispense His perfect justice."

A low rumble tremored through the growing crowd of townspeople, but the granite cast of most of the faces remained, as Kirk knew it always did when he came before them, no matter what he said or did. The more dispassionate, inscrutable white Southern faces he saw, the more he hated these people. *They will hate me today,* he promised himself.

Kirk smiled at the bleeding captives, one of whose skull appeared to be cracked, and all of whom appeared to have at least broken ribs and noses and probably more. He added, "Besides which, you brave Rebels will have the distinct privilege to be dispatched on your way to the fires of perdition by the lovely words of our sainted parson here. So no complainin' that we ain't merciful conquerors."

"Conquerors my a—," a thirty-year-old rustic who looked forty said pleasantly.

"Who said that?" Kirk blurted.

No one stirred.

Kirk screamed the Lord's name in vain as he repeated the question and stalked toward the crowd.

Not a voice sounded, not an expression changed.

"That skinny man there in the homespun said it, cunnel," said one of Kirk's black "sergeants."

Kirk nodded his head and slapped the crop in his gauntleted palm. "Captain Sledge, take these men to the town jail for questioning."

Culpeper and Cousin Jed snapped to attention at mention of their prey's name. Culpeper amazed his cousin by actually lobbing an amber wad of spit out onto the street.

"And Captain," Kirk continued, placing emphasis on Sledge's rank and surveying the still-growing, still-impassive throng of white faces. "Choose a Negro detail to escort the prisoners—including our smart-mouthed friend in the homespun."

"Yes, sir," Sledge said. Turning to a throng of carbine-toting black troopers, he said, "Jones, Bartlett, Thomas, Crawford, Jefferson, Samuels—let's go."

A tall, distinguished-looking man of about sixty stepped forward. "Sir, these men need to see a doctor, not—"

He was interrupted in midsentence by Kirk's crop, slashing down across the face of the homespun man as he passed. A second blow knocked the bloodied man to the ground. Kirk nodded in satisfaction and said, "Now you look ready to join your fellow traitors." He turned to the older man. "You have doctors here in Redemption?"

"Yes, I am Dr. Sam Garrett," the older man, shaken, said, "and Fred Cody, who I believe is delivering a child out on the McCullough farm just now, is as well."

"Fine, fine," Kirk said, slapping the crop ominously into his gauntlet. "You'll go with Sergeant Houlihan and Private Hornacek here that helped bring in these traitorous prisoners, fetch Dr. Cody, and proceed with him to tend to the darkies these traitors did harm to. I hardly think those murderers need a doctor where they're headed."

A burly white sergeant notable even amid his fellows for his shambling appearance and alcoholic stench, handed Kirk a sheet of paper on which were written several names.

"You're sure these are the names and addresses of the men we just jailed?" Kirk asked.

"H—, yeh," the sergeant growled. Then his voice dropped to where only Kirk could hear him. "One of the local Union Leaguers supplied the information."

"You trustin' a n—— for this?" Kirk asked.

"Well, h—, yeh," the sergeant blurted as if the legitimacy of his (quite illegitimate) birth status had been questioned, his voice back to full pitch and then some. "He knows what'll befall him if'n he aims to shade us."

Kirk smiled and said, his own voice loud enough for everyone to hear, "Lieutenant Taylor, now that you've brought in these low-down killers, take a platoon and fire their homes, one at a time, in the order they appear on this list."

"But Colonel," Taylor protested with a vulgarity unknown to the ears of many of the younger town folk, "we just got back from—"

"I'll throw you right in there with them other sad sacks, Lieutenant," Kirk interrupted, "and you'll swing alongside 'em too."

Taylor frowned in anger, then reached down from his horse for the list. A thought struck him and he asked, "Usual protocol for confiscation?"

"Yes, Lieutenant," Kirk said, "whatever you and the men can fit—sensible-like—on your persons or the backs o' your horses, without slowin' ya down on the road."

"Yes, sir!" Taylor shouted, saluting and turning to collect his detail.

Perhaps Kirk could not divine the feelings animating the crowd, but Culpeper had spent his entire life around such folk, and he suspected a bushel more trouble lay in wait for everyone.

"Ah, first blood always gits my constitution a'runnin'," Kirk said happily.

A bonneted, fresh-faced young woman broke from the crowd and ran screaming toward the prisoners, who were being dragged in various fashions through the street toward the jail.

"No, please, that's my husband! You can't do this!" she screamed, rushing to one of the bleeding men. Sledge, petrified at laying hands on an attractive white woman in front of half the town, turned a plaintive face to Kirk for direction.

"Deal with that woman, Captain!" Kirk shouted, thrusting his crop at Sledge.

"Ma'am, please," Sledge said, laying a gentle hand on the woman's shoulder.

"Get your filthy hands off me, you black baboon!" the woman shrieked, pulling away.

As Sledge stepped toward her, Culpeper and Cousin Jed stepped off the sidewalk and toward him. They had held off making a play for Sledge for fear of inciting a bloodbath that might wipe out half the town. *But this . . .* Culpeper thought, reaching for one of the revolvers tucked under the buckskin shirt inside his trousers as he heard a score of Federal rifle hammers click back when the crowd moved a half-step toward the jail.

"Ma'am," a young white trooper said, stepping to the screaming woman as the prisoners disappeared into the jail. "Please, ma'am, I'll see to it you get to visit your husband soon." Sobbing, she looked up at him. "Please, ma'am," he repeated, lowering his voice, "there's a lot of folks here could get hurt."

She hesitated, searching his face, then pulled away, sobs racking her body as several family members folded her in their arms.

Culpeper breathed a sigh of relief, swallowing and glancing at Cousin Jed, who pulled his hat down lower on his face. When Culpeper heard laughter, he saw Kirk shaking his head at Sledge. "Send a boy to do a man's job, I guess," the Federal commander said.

Beyond Kirk and the townspeople, Culpeper saw a mass of additional troopers, guns everywhere in evidence, drifting like a blue tide toward the street and the disarmed crowd. He bit his lower lip, then signaled Cousin Jed with a look that it was time to leave. His cousin shook his head. When Culpeper motioned more furtively, Cousin Jed broke eye contact with him, put both his hands in coat pockets, where he had pistols of his own, and started for the jail.

Oh, no, Culpeper thought.

Sledge emerged from the jail and approached Kirk. "Sir," he said quietly, "you'll get more from those prisoners tonight. They mostly passed right out. Couple 'em gonna die too, 'lessin they get a doctor."

Kirk pondered that. "All right, folks," he called to the crowd. "Beggin' the good reverend's pardon, we're gonna delay the necktie party till in the mornin'. That'll give the prisoners time to get presentable fer their hangin's. Meantime, the more vittles you good people can provide my men tonight, why the better I expect they'll behave themselves while in your fair town."

Silence enveloped the assembly.

"Now break it up, folks," Kirk said. Not one soul moved. "I tell you what, people," he said, his eyes narrowing as he placed his hands on his hips, "if you don't git a move on, and right d—— now, I'm gonna turn these boys loose on ya, and I swear to Satan, we'll not spare man, woman, or child."

But Culpeper could not pay attention to the crowd as it turned and walked away, filled with a supreme silent rage that the passing of decades or even whole generations would not kill, because he was pursuing Cousin Jed. Much as the Virginian himself wanted to give Elijah Sledge his just comeuppance, he could not bring himself to do it—or let it happen—at the risk of the whole community. *But if I hook it up with Jed, what if the bluebellies collar us and figure out who we are?* he worried, frantic. *Then everything is for nothin'. No, he's almost to the door; there's his guns—*

"Why, Jed Wallace!"

Culpeper stopped in his tracks a few feet behind Cousin Jed as a slender, loose-limbed man in a homespun shirt and thin, faded Confederate cavalry trousers, grabbed the Tennessean and shook his hand.

"Well, howdy-do, Matthew Miller," Cousin Jed mumbled, glancing nervously about at the Federals and shoving his pistols back down. "What're ya doin' in North Carolina?"

"You 'member how General Forrest ordered us to git back to livin' and git the war behind us?"

"Yup."

"Well, I met me a perdy little gal visitin' her sister over in Knoxville," Miller said, his gaunt tanned face glowing and his green eyes gleaming, "and, well, heck Jed, turned out Susie hung the moon for me, and her daddy had a parcel o' land here he give us to work. So here I be, with two youngin's and a third bakin' in the oven!"

As Culpeper joined the conversation, he and Cousin Jed saw a score of Federals form around the front of the jail as many more went around back.

"This my cousin Cole Culpeper, from up Virginia way; he fought with General Lee and rode with Hampton and Mosby," Cousin Jed said, his voice solemn as the grave. "Matt Miller here, he an' I rode with Bedford Forrest's Seventh Tennessee Cavalry."

Culpeper's and Miller's eyes locked the instant they clasped hands. A smile took shape across Culpeper's clean-shaven face. "Why shoot, Jed," he said, "believe we got us more'n just a cousin here."

Cousin Jed's eyebrows arched. He shook Miller's hand, and a familiar shake it was.

"I 'spect you boys won't want to miss out on what we got cooked up fer that Yankee b—— tonight," Miller said.

CHAPTER 69

IN THIS, AS IN SO MUCH ELSE, I SHOULD HAVE LISTENED TO MY Mary, Lee lamented while standing in her doorway one midnight and watching her sleep as sleep for him again proved as elusive as had Southern independence. *For I find I much enjoy the charms of civil life and find too late that I have wasted the best years of my existence.* Staring at the mound of covers under which lay her bent little form, he recalled how lovely she had been before illness and death and war and separation and bitterness had intruded. How her pleasant mysteries and surprises had multiplied from the night of their wedding. *We did have seven children together,* he mused, *and might have had yet more . . . had I but remained at old Arlington . . . as she wished and prayed and pleaded . . . oh, how much of my children's lives—of Mary's life—I have missed because I left old Arlington!*

He walked past his own bare, whitewashed room, then crept up the stairs and peeked in on Agnes, Mary Custis, Mildred—only now regaining her strength, and some of her hair—and Custis.

He had been so angry when Custis for the first time defied him and determined to enlist as a private in the U.S. Army if he were unable to secure an appointment to West Point. In no event would he remain at Arlington. How disappointment had festered in father and resentment in son, and how both had lingered . . . for years.

Lee stared in at the strange dark form. *Do I know him even yet?* He thought back over the years, then sighed. *Yet did he not follow his father's course, his father's actions rather than his father's words? Did he not leave his women at Arlington to join an army and pursue a career, neither of which he ever loved? And then, did he not return to his family . . . once Arlington was no more?* Arlington . . . how they had both set their jaws like flint to leave it; how they had longed for that which they chose to leave! *And how the ways of men are past finding out, even unto themselves.*

He marveled at the beauty of the new Washington College president's home as he lit the lamp at his study desk. *How kind they all have been to us,* he thought, *building a house for us nearly twice as large as the original, which was quite adequate. And such modern features—running water and hot air furnaces. And our greenhouse, cow house for the milk cow, and connected stables in the same brick as the house for the horses. It is so satisfying to have Traveller under the same roof as I!*

He stared at the omnipresent pile of mail on his desk. A couple of responses had just arrived with research information for his book *The History of the Army of Northern Virginia.* The letters related to the 1864 Kilpatrick-Dahlgren raid on Richmond, its darker aspects still vehemently denied by the U.S. government. *Never have I possessed the slightest doubt of the authenticity of those papers,* he thought, even though his lone voice had spared over one hundred of the captured Federal raiders. *Perhaps in my book I can furnish the most indisputable proofs that they were genuine and not forgeries.*

Back from abroad, Lee thought as he saw Jubal Early's name on one of the letters, *poor, bitter, angry man.* He snapped to attention when he read Early's letter. It addressed Admiral John Dahlgren's long-held, and very public, claims that the handwriting on papers indicating Northern plans to burn Richmond and slaughter Jefferson Davis and his entire cabinet did not match his son Ulric's and that in fact his son's forged signature was misspelled.

By examining his own photographic copies of the key documents, Early explained, he realized that the paper on which Dahlgren had written the infamous orders was so thin, some of his handwriting bled through it. In "touching up" the messy portion, the lithographic technician inadvertently created a slight, and initially unnoticed, misspelling of the uncommon name "Ulric Dahlgren."

As to whether the handwriting form actually matched the younger Dahlgren's, Early, having himself risen to the field rank of lieutenant general, scoffed at the notion that a Federal officer of high rank necessarily, or even likely, copied in his own hand the written lines on the pages from which he would read his men their orders. Considering the volcanic nature of the orders themselves—and the nature of men such as Kilpatrick and Stanton upline from him—Early posited to Lee the likely possibility that Dahlgren neither conceived of nor wrote the orders.

Lee sighed, lamenting anew all that had been lost, North and South. Then he saw that kingly offers of employment continued to flock in. From Georgia,

John Gordon offered Lee the presidency and splendid salary of his thriving Southern Life Insurance Company, whose board of directors included Wade Hampton and Ben Hill. *Good to see some of our men climbing back up,* Lee thought. *They will lead others out in this sad peace, just as they led them in our sad war.* From Louisiana, Longstreet had gone over to the Republicans and asked Lee's blessing. Lee would not give it.

He picked up the letter from Dr. Barton. It mentioned words like *rheumatism, arthritis, pericarditis,* a heart and circulatory system desperately in need of rest. He thought about that, about his constant pain, his constant fatigue. *Oh, God, ruler of the universe, I can barely walk from this house to the college, which is no more than one hundred and fifty yards. I will resign my position.*

"Papa?"

Lee whirled to see Agnes standing in her robe, nightgown, and slippers in the doorway, a sprig of dark hair curled down over one eye.

"Well, hello, my little Miss Wiggie," he said with a smile.

"Hello," she said, leaning against the doorjamb.

"Can't sleep either?" he asked.

She smiled and shook her head.

"I believe my Wiggie has something on her mind," he said, glad it was so, for it had been long since she had to come to him with anything on her mind.

She watched him for a moment, as if speculating his response to a proposed question. "Papa," she said, "I want us to go to Savannah."

"Savannah?" he said, startled.

"Yes, Papa," she said, the window to her soul opening to him as it had not in years. "Savannah."

"But . . . why Savannah?"

She thought about that. "Because—it is special to you. And it was part of your life before—" She paused, looking down. "—the war." After a moment she looked back up at him, to his great surprise a gleam in her dark eyes. "And because of Eliza Mackay."

"Eliza Mackay!" he blurted, startled.

"Yes," she said, giggling and crossing the room to place her hands on his shoulders. "Eliza Mackay, whom you adored and who adored you."

"But I haven't thought about her for years," he protested.

She canted her head. "Papa—I *am* still your daughter, and it is OK."

Despite himself, he burst into laughter.

"So then—it's settled?" she said, smiling with pride. "We'll go?"

He knew when he was licked. "I cannot say when, but yes, we shall go—but only because the doctors have already told me it would be a good place for me to go when I re—that it would be a good place for me to go."

Almost to the door, she turned back to him, stared for a moment, then burst into more giggles.

Greed, Marley thought, scowling, *greed, vanity, and more greed. Our country is awash in it. The slavers and their plantation kingdoms; the westerners—and the easterners buying west—and their land and railroad schemes; and everybody else with their influence and their factories and their mines—and their gold.*

Oh, he sighed, pouring himself straight bourbon from the crystal decanter he brought with him in the barouche. *They have done it now with their accursed gold, their accursed greed.* He slugged down the whole glass and poured another.

"Hurry up, Silas!" he shouted to his driver in the box seat up front. He cursed to himself as he remembered the words of Charles Dickens, whose entire corpus of books and other writings Marley had devoured: "Union means so many millions a year lost to the South; secession means the loss of the same millions to the North. The love of money is the root of this as of many, many other evils. . . . The quarrel between the North and South is, as it stands, solely a fiscal quarrel."

The Northern lust for *economic sovereignty,* Marley, draining his glass again, remembered Karl Marx describing it, *and he is supposed to be on our side.* He shook his head bitterly, not realizing how such words constituted anything but a criticism from the lips of Karl Marx.

We have broken every rule to give our people the freedom and opportunity for which they screeched, Marley thought, *and with these won, the people themselves break every rule. And now, breaking the rules, they have broken the gold market, left half of Wall Street in ruins, and sunk the entire nation into a financial depression like none we have ever seen before.*

He just could not believe it. "So stupid!" he shouted, his voice echoing off buildings right and left as Silas turned onto Anne's street.

Gould and Fisk had bought and bought until, yesterday, the gold price skyrocketed out of control, raising Cain with commodity prices and finally, today, wreaking havoc with the entire stock exchange. When the Grant administration finally unleashed four million dollars' worth of the Federal gold reserve, the gold standard crashed flaming back to earth, the fortunes of hundreds of investors and speculators great and small crashing with it.

"Nobody is in their offices, and the agony depicted on the faces of men who crowded the streets made one feel as if Gettysburg had been lost and the Rebels were marching down Broadway," read one telegram sent to Marley from New York late in the day.

No matter how many men go down, Marley thought, pouring himself another glass, *I'll wager those bloodsucking hyenas Gould and Fisk came out just dandy.*

Indeed both men in the end banked handsome profits off the affair.

Nodding to Sam the doorman and toting the now-quarter-full bourbon decanter and his glass with him, Marley took the stairs up to Anne's third-floor apartment three at a time. *Man, the world has turned upside down when such tragedies occur that make it difficult for a fellow even to savor his coming matrimony to the most beautiful girl in Washington,* he lamented.

And what matrimony. All had been patched up between Anne and Kate Sprague, and the Marley wedding promised to be the social event of the 1869 Christmas season.

Now that's odd, he thought, breathing heavily from the stairs and his extra now-forty-one pounds, when he saw Anne's front door standing open. He had never since he knew her seen it unlocked, much less wide open, when he arrived.

"Annie?" he called, stepping into her parlor. "Did you hear? Grant—what the devil?"

She emerged from the corridor that led to her bedroom, a route he fretted himself he knew now so well. When she did, she wore her mother's wedding dress, which she had shown him a few nights previous, with petticoats, hoops, train, and the veil, which obscured her face.

Every ounce of it was dyed black as midnight.

So shocked was Marley that in his already unsettled and semi-inebriated state, he dropped both the decanter and his glass, which he had just refilled. They smashed onto the polished oaken floor.

She walked across the room toward him, halting about midway. She pulled back the veil with a black-gloved hand to reveal lips and eyelids painted black.

Her hair, normally the blackest feature of her person, flowed in long luxuriant curls down onto her shoulders. Long luxuriant flaxen curls.

Marley's very skin crawled at the sight of her. When he saw her shining crazed eyes, eyes the color of the sea, that were cast in his direction, but no more looking at him than at the man in the moon, it crawled the more.

Shaking, he stepped toward her. Only then did he see the gun in her other black-gloved hand.

"Yes, I heard, honey lamb," she said, her voice high and tinny and unearthly.

"Annie, dear," he uttered, stepping closer, "that gun—"

"I heard because the man I truly loved, have loved all these last years, the man who delivered me from being hungry and dirty and alone and white trash-poor, the man who purchased me into Washington City society, Wayne, the man who purchased lil' ole me, who told me to fetch you for the Radicals because you were the best there was, the one they needed most, who told me finally I could marry you 'cause he had a wife he hated and could not; this wonderful, loving, giving, great-hearted man whom Europe killed first after his revolution failed twenty years ago and whom America has killed now—I heard because he is gone today, Wayne, killed by his own hand, right outside the Gold Room in Exchange Place in New York City, with a bullet to his beautiful head because he played too long in league with your tariff-thieving Yankee jackals."

"Christ in heaven," Marley choked, on the verge of tears.

"But sugar," she purred, "didn't you know? There is no Christ in heaven or anywhere else. My daddy told me there was, but my daddy lied to me. He lied to me about everything."

As he stepped to her, she raised the gun, checking him.

"It's all right, my sweet Annie," he said, sobbing, "I won't hurt you—I won't let you hurt anymore."

An ethereal smile spreading across her face, she said, "Oh, I know you won't, Wayne, I'm all through hurting now, dearest."

"But," he sputtered as she raised the gun, "I'll help you get through this, Annie, together we can be happy, we can—"

"Oh no, darlin'," she said, her voice sickly sweet as the drug-induced glaze now covering her painted face, "we cannot. Didn't I tell you? This is not an American tale, sweetie, this is a Southern tale."

Then she said one more word—"Valiant!"—and put a bullet through her own brain.

CHAPTER 70

OF ALL THAT HAD HAPPENED THROUGH THIS LONG INFAMOUS DAY in Redemption, North Carolina, the one act that would endure in the memories of the desperate band of men gathered under the pine trees in the woods near Cooper Cemetery seven miles northeast of town was Cole Culpeper's filching of a quart bottle of applejack and two full cuts of chew from passed-out Kirk troopers at the edge of town.

"Well, that's Cousin Cole," Cousin Jed shrugged, as the bottle came to him.

"I heard o' you," said a pipe-smoking man of flaming red beard and such enormous girth that Culpeper assayed any other two men around the small campfire could have fit into the space he took. "You raised a ruckus in that Dahlgren romp."

"That's sure him," chortled Cousin Red, with them now, himself taking a touch.

"You was shot already, right?" red beard asked.

"Aw," Culpeper scoffed, slicing a plug of tobacco with his small knife, not his Bowie, for Cousin Jed.

"I heard he rode with Mosby," said a little man with a salt-and-pepper beard past his chest and an empty sleeve. "Got a fat Yankee bounty stuck on him. Prob'ly still do."

"That right?" red beard asked.

"H——, Mosby said he'd shoot me hisself if I come near him again," Culpeper said, gobbling a chaw. "Arrogant little cuss."

"Hmm," red beard said. Then, pipe in mouth, he reached forth a hand the size of a bear paw for Culpeper to shake. "I'm Nels Drumgoolen, and I reckon we'd be proud to have you along tonight."

Culpeper, shaking Drumgoolen's hand, nodded.

"Tuck Dooley," salt-and-pepper said, offering his own hand. "You ain't aginst night ridin', Culpeper?"

"No," Culpeper said, "or women or children neither."

This drew a moment's silent contemplation from the dozen men around and near the fire before Drumgoolen, puffing his pipe, said again, "Hmm."

"Lorena Anderson has her cake baked and a pie too for them bluebelly guards," Matt Miller said. "Jed, you, Cole, Red, and the McCormack brothers here'll go with her. Me, Drumgoolen, Dooley, and the rest'll pay our respects to 'Colonel' Kirk; we know him to be domicilin' tonight two miles or more t'other side o' town with one o' the less reputable ladies of our community."

"Where's that n——, Elijah Sledge, Kirk's 'captain'?" Cousin Jed asked, his voice cruel.

Miller glanced at Drumgoolen, then said, "Don't know."

Motioning to Culpeper for another pull at the bottle, Cousin Jed said, "Well now, we didn't spend the last two years and come all the way from Tennessee to stir up a ruckus and let that darkie skedaddle out from under us."

The fire crackled and Drumgoolen sucked on his pipe. Overhead, through the pine boughs, Culpeper saw a sliver of moon peak out from behind speeding banks of cumulus clouds. Not a star was in sight.

"You boys smell rain?" he asked.

After a pause, Miller sniffed the air and said, "Good, anything that stirs the mix more is good for us."

"Jist be careful ridin'," Culpeper said, swallowing tobacco juice and thinking it was the worst-tasting leaf he had had in some time, and he had had plenty of bad leaf since the war started.

"Boys," Cousin Jed said, his eyes leveled at Miller, "you should know Cole and Red and me, we won't be out of the saddle tonight till we've laid Sledge low."

"Mister, maybe you oughta—" Dooley started, his eyes hard.

"No," said Miller, shushing him. "Jed, we'll do our best to get Sledge too. But we got a whole town under the gun here, man. You heard that lunatic yourself this afternoon. He won't spare woman or child—"

Cousin Jed stood up. "I come here to kill the cowardly scum what murdered my brother. And not friend or foe'll git'n my way."

As he turned to leave, Culpeper said, "Settle down, Jed. I heard one o' them Yanks moanin' on our way out o' town that Sledge is Kirk's pet and he don't ever let him out of his sight. I reckon where you find Kirk, well, that's where you'll find him."

Cousin Jed stared at Miller, who nodded and said, "All right, Jed. I'll lead the group with Mrs. Anderson. You, your brother, and Culpeper go with Drumgoolen and the others. Tuck, you come with me too."

Dooley was staring a hole through Cousin Jed. The latter, noticing this, said, "You want somethin' with me, mister?"

"Maybe I do," Dooley snarled. "Maybe I'm a 'wonderin' why this whole town's havin' to turn things around jest to fit with you Johnny-come-latelies."

"You better watch your mouth mister, or I'll clean it out for ya," Culpeper said, as pleasantly as a "howdy-do" on the front porch at eventide.

"Maybe you boys best clear on out," Drumgoolen said mildly, his pipe still in his mouth.

"No!" Miller shouted. "We gotta work together on this, we can't have different groups gettin' in one another's way—"

The thump of hoofbeats sounded from beyond the cemetery.

"That's Cunningham," someone said. "From the sound of his gait, must be riders comin'."

The lone rider was the Rev. Jeremiah Shanklin, thirty-four-year-old pastor of the Redemption Presbyterian Church, where Miller and a couple of the other men worshiped.

"How in blue blazes did you find us, parson?" Miller asked.

"Lorena—Mrs. Anderson—told me," said Shanklin, a tall, square-jawed sort who walked with a gimp. He wasted no time. "Men, you cannot do this."

"Beggin' your pardon, pastor," Miller said, his voice a note higher than Culpeper had heard it, "but we're gonna do it."

"Who are these men?" Shanklin asked, noticing Culpeper and his cousins. "These men are not from around here."

"Look, pastor, you know why Mrs. Anderson's husband Deke and those others are in jail right now?" Miller asked.

"They got caught committing violent acts they had no right to do," Shanklin said.

"No sir," Miller fired back. "Them blacks they dry-gulched was the ones that scalded out the Carter brothers last week."

Shanklin shook his head. "No, that was the Klan." He thrust an accusing finger at Miller. "It may have been you, Matthew Miller!"

"That's a lie!" Dooley shouted, leaping to his feet.

"Hold it, Tuck," Miller said, trying to calm the situation. "Pastor, those colored boys *did* do it. The carpetbaggers surely put 'em up to it, but they hate the Carter brothers anyway, 'cause they're black and Democrats and fought for the South—and they won't apologize for it or ask pardon from any da—er, any Yankee, sir, black or white. I got a hunch it ain't the first time they put on the white sheet around here, 'cause some o' what's happened we sure as heck didn't do. 'Sides, we got word two different ways them Union Leaguers fired on Deke and the others before they'd even shown a gun o' their own."

Confusion curled up Shanklin's face.

"It's goin' on all over the South, pastor," Drumgoolen said. "Union Leaguers and other Yankee sorts puttin' on the white sheet, then workin' their evil, all the while pointin' their fingers at us. They're the worst enemy the South has."

"No," Shanklin bellowed, "you men are the worst enemy the South has. Maybe not you men individually, because I happen to know pretty much all you've done in your night ridin', and I know who are the disreputable sorts against whom you've moved. But in other places, other towns, other states—white men, Southern white men, ex-Confederate Southern white men are out of control, men. Innocent folk are being hurt, and the Yankees won't have it. Don't you men know by now that if they have to, they'll burn the whole South out till it's just one giant desert?"

Miller sighed as the other men shifted around where they stood or sat. "Pastor," he said, "there's eighty thousand black Union Leaguers in North Carolina alone as we speak. It's them got that idiot Holden elected once, and they'll do it again. They got clubs all over the state drillin' night and day as military companies, armed with pistols and Bowie knives. They're gettin' ready for war, pastor. Sir, it's us or them. I don't like it any more than the next man, any more than most o' the blacks themselves prob'ly, but it's the Feds that have forced this play on everyone, sir. They're usin' the blacks to put us down so's they can build a whole new South right over us."

"I refuse to believe it has to be us or them, one or the other," Shanklin said.

"Carpetbaggers and Negroes were runnin' wild around here till we started night ridin'," said Drumgoolen, his voice calm, as he savored the aroma of his own smoke. "You know it's true, Pastor Shanklin, they busted up your own church. Fact is, it weren't safe for the ladies to walk to church—"

"And with what you've done, it's safe now?" Shanklin said. "What did our women—and children—encounter on their way to church today, Matthew? What did Lorena Anderson encounter? Can you stand there, look me in the eye, and say you men have improved the lot of our community? With that swarm of vermin nesting on the town common at this moment, ready to do who-knows-what tonight? Get a grip, Matt—*you* men are the problem—and as your pastor, appointed by God Almighty himself to watch over your souls, I adjure you to go home right now, you and you too, Tom and Billy McCormack, and watch after your kinfolk."

Tears filled Miller's eyes. "What choice has been left us as men, pastor?"

Pain etched Shanklin's handsome face as he closed his eyes, shook his head, and squeezed his temples with his hand, the back of which Culpeper saw was horribly disfigured. "Matthew, a Federal marshal was supposed to have arrived this morning from Raleigh to arrest this Kirk," Shanklin said a moment later. "That's right—I've been exchanging telegraphs with his office for weeks, ever since Kirk and his band arrived in the county. Well, they've plenty on Mr. Kirk and were already in the process of obtaining arrest warrants for him and his key officers. Perhaps they'll arrive tonight, or at least in the morning—"

"Before Deke Anderson and those boys swing?" Dooley said.

"I attempted to talk to Mr. Kirk before I came out here—" Shanklin began.

"What did he say?" Miller asked.

Shanklin shook his head as thunder rumbled in the distance. "He had no interest in talking with me."

"See?" Dooley blurted, getting to his feet. "I say it's time we git a move on, boys. That murderin' Fed may take a fancy to stringin' Deke and the boys up tonight just to impress his trashy new 'lady friend.'"

"Please, men," Shanklin said, spreading his hands, palms up in appeal.

"I think you better leave now, parson," Cousin Jed said, murder filling his voice.

Shanklin, his face and voice absent of fear, gazed around the group. "Why must you men do this when help is on the way?"

"Because we're rough men with violent ways, pastor," said Culpeper. "We're followin' the one road's been left us."

"You don't have to do this, man," Shanklin urged him.

Culpeper looked away from the cleric's gaze.

"Maybe we do, pastor," Miller said, his voice quiet as the tomb. "Maybe we do, sir."

Shanklin's jaw tightened. "I can do nothing about the rest of you—that is, I *won't* do anything; I won't speak to your pastors, those of you who have them. But Matthew Miller, Tom and Billy McCormack, I'll see you tomorrow evening at the church at session meeting—that is, if you're not in jail or a pine box."

The group stood mute as Shanklin gimped to his horse, then rode away.

"That dandy better get a grip on who is his flock," Cousin Jed growled.

"That 'dandy' got shot, stabbed, shelled, and burned fightin' for our cause," Miller said.

"Well, he better figure out whether his sheep are black or white," Cousin Jed said.

"He might say they're both," Miller replied.

Cousin Jed's brows furrowed. "I had a bellyful o' these troublesome darkies. I fought 'em at Fort Pillow, I fought 'em at home in Tennessee, then I come all the way to North Carolina chasin' the one what murdered my own brother, and what do I find? More darkies makin' trouble." He pulled out one of his revolvers and spun the cylinder, checking the bullet chambers. "I'm done with 'em, no foolin'. Now on, they better gimme the road when they see me comin'."

"Them Carter brothers bled, then got burnt out for the same flag we love," Tom McCormack spoke up, surprising all at the sound of his voice.

"They can go to blazes," Cousin Jed said. "Darkies got us in this mess, now they makin' it worse for us."

"I'll take the Carter boys' side against you seven ways from sundown, Mr. Hothead," Drumgoolen observed sagely.

Cousin Jed's eyes narrowed. "You playin' me for the fool, big man?"

Puffing his pipe, Drumgoolen said, "Oh, you'll know if I do that, Tennessee. Like I said afore—maybe you boys best just clear on out."

"Holy Moses," Miller said. "How can we fight Yankees if we're fightin' ourselves already?" He uttered a deep sigh and put his hands on his hips. "I'll lead the Kirk group; Tuck, you come too. Drumgoolen, you go with Lorena. Culpeper? Will you go with Drumgoolen?"

"I stay with my—" Culpeper began.

"Please," Miller said. "Jed told me about your Bowie. I want Mrs. Anderson to use it. And I want your gun with them."

Culpeper looked at Cousin Jed, who shrugged, then turned back to Miller. "Where is she?" Culpeper asked.

Miller's face lit up. "One mile straight down the road toward town, at the McCormacks'."

As everyone mounted, Culpeper said to Miller, "You know your plan is likely to get every man jack of us killed."

Reins in hand as he prepared to mount, Miller turned to Culpeper and said, "I ain't heard any better notions from you or your delightful cousins."

Still not having any, Culpeper asked, "What'll happen to your town if we make good?"

Miller leaned against his horse, reins still in his hands, and shook his head. "I don't know," he said, weary. Then he looked Culpeper in the eye. "But I know this—they burned down at least two more homes tonight, after the four Kirk said they was gonna burn. They may be burnin' more now. They may be killin' now. If we had anywheres near men enough that we could stand-up fight their whole blamed army, I'd pile in on 'em quicker'n fleas lightin' on a hound."

He stared up at the blackened sky. Thunderheads blanketed the moon as his voice dropped. "If we leave things be, Redemption may not survive this night anyways, and several brave men will die sure. Maybe we can get 'em chasin' after us, away from the town . . . and with Kirk gone . . . who knows?"

He looked at Culpeper before pronouncing his valediction: "They ain't no good options when a man's already got a mountain lion on his back, with his teeth sunk in 'im."

"Your kinsman seems a might touchy," Drumgoolen said as they rode toward Redemption with Lorena Anderson and her cake and pie.

The lightning now flashing as the wind rose revealed that they wore not white, but Federal blue.

"H—, the scum murdered his brother, stole all his cotton, then took his land after we left Tennessee," Culpeper said. "I don't 'spect that makes for kissin' cousins, now do it?" When Drumgoolen said nothing, Culpeper calmed down and said, "Funny thing is, ole Jed was the lightest heart in the family ever since we's kids. Always seemed to find the best side of things—even if there weren't one—and make you feel all right too. Knew his Scriptures too, before—and after—the rest of us. He just ain't the same, though, since . . ."

At that, his voice trailed off.

Drumgoolen enjoyed one final drag on his pipe before tamping it out. He put it in his coat pocket as raindrops began to patter on his slouch hat and navy blue rubberized cape and coat, which he had taken off a dead Yankee at the Bloody Angle.

"Guess who else fits that mold?" he said.

"Who?" Culpeper said.

"Tuck Dooley."

"Huh?"

"Yep, he actually did 'im some backwoods preachin' before the war. Didn't go to school much, but loved his Bible," Drumgoolen said, covering the exposed stock of his saddle-holstered scattergun with his raincoat. "Well, while some was findin' their faith during the war, he was losin' his, and he checked it plum in since then."

"Worse now in some ways," Culpeper said.

"Easier in some ways to git shot at than just to sit there and take it all, then go home and sleep in your bed," Drumgoolen said.

"Easier than to sleep sometimes."

"Easier than."

They rode a ways in silence, the rain coming on a bit stronger.

"Seems sometimes that dyin' is all that's left," Culpeper said, giving voice to sentiments he had never before shared.

"Oh," Drumgoolen said through the darkness, "'tain't so. Don't let 'em beat you down to that. They may take your life from you with a bullet—but don't let 'em take it from you before that."

Culpeper pondered these words as the darkness deepened and the rain came stronger.

Two miles outside of town, he—with his face unfamiliar to Kirk and his men or the people of Redemption—and Lorena left Drumgoolen in a grove of elm trees and rode on. Near the edge of town, they heard laughter, then screaming. They topped a rise, the wind swirling in their faces, and looked down to see a farmhouse and a couple dozen of Kirk's men wreaking havoc.

"The Caldwell place," Lorena said. In the dim light shed on them from the farmhouse and a dozen or more Yankee torches in the dooryard, Culpeper saw her pull the tattered blanket draped around her over her soaked head.

"Here, ma'am, take this," he said, removing his stolen Federal hat and offering it to her.

"No," she said. "You must retain your complete uniform so as to escape detection."

Another scream from down below commanded their attention.

"What is it?" she asked.

Culpeper pulled out his stolen Federal spyglass and squinted through the rain and dark. After a moment he grunted.

"What?" she asked.

"There a family grave plot down yonder?" he asked.

"Why, yes," she said. "The Caldwells have been on this land a hundred years or more."

"Well, our Yankee visitors—I heard Lieutenant Taylor's name again— appear to be diggin' up the coffins of the dearly departed—"

A high wail pierced the night.

"—and spillin' out the contents, while the children and their mother watch."

"Oh, God," she groaned. "Two Caldwell boys fell during the war, and Mr. Caldwell died a month ago of scarlet fever—and a broken heart."

"That would prob'ly be him they just unveiled," Culpeper said as more children's screams filled the night. "They seem to be on a treasure hunt for good coffins, prob'ly for some o' their own people."

"Moist as the ground is around these parts, they'll get no more than three good coffins from that graveyard, if that," she said. "Dear God in heaven."

Shutting out the screams of "Dad-da!" and "Daddy!" that now rose to crazed shrieks, Culpeper put away his spyglass and said, "Let's go git your husband, ma'am."

CHAPTER 71

AS MILLER SUSPECTED, WHEN LORENA ANDERSON, "ESCORTED" BY Culpeper, arrived at the jail, almost all Kirk's men—despite his vehement orders to the contrary—had gone elsewhere or passed out drunk. A steady drizzle fell on the latter; the heavier rain through which Culpeper passed had not yet reached town.

Four troops remained, all brandishing new but filthy revolvers. They had the aptly named Slim Curtis, who had protested earlier in the street to Kirk at his use of the word *conqueror,* standing on a table in the middle of what had been the town marshal's office (before the Federals fired the town marshal). Wearing his homespun, Curtis was the least-damaged of the prisoners; his hands were cuffed behind his back.

"If you don't tell us who is your leader—" one white Federal shouted.

"Your mother!" hooted a black one.

"—I'll break your d— spindly neck—tonight," finished the first Federal.

Observing this through the window, Lorena Anderson uttered a silent prayer that she would be allowed to pass her cake to the prisoners in their cell.

"Lookee at this!" hollered a third Federal, white, swigging from a whiskey bottle.

"A cake—and a pie—and a bee-u-tee-ful woman too!" shouted the second.

Affixing her most bewitching smile and turning all the Southern charm she possessed on them, Lorena said, "Why, boys, did you know I'm favored far and wide in these parts for my apple pies?"

"Apple—"

"—pie!"

Placing it on the desk formerly belonging to the town marshal, she said, "Now you boys better dig in, before all your friends catch a whiff."

"What about that cake?" the thus-far silent, white fourth soldier said, indicating Culpeper, who had almost managed to get past them and back to Anderson and the other prisoners.

"Why, boys, can't you let a lady bring her condemned husband and his friends a little ole piece of cake?" Lorena cooed, wanting desperately to see her Deke, but deciding against doing so because of the attention she knew would follow her back to his cell. "Besides, I'm much better known for my pies than I am my cakes."

"How come you're so cheerful when your man's fixin' to swing?" asked the fourth soldier, sullen, suspicious, and not nearly so drunk as the other three.

"Why," she said, sweetness oozing from every pore, as Culpeper slipped on back to the prisoners' cell, "could it be I trust that Southern hospitality will without doubt be answered by Northern gallantry and mercy?"

As the other three soldiers wondered what on earth she meant, the sober man said, "Hmmph."

"Well, eat up, gentlemen!" she said, moving toward the door as Culpeper reappeared

"Hey, who're you?" the fourth soldier said to Culpeper.

"Jake Schumacher," Culpeper said.

"Who sent you over with this smiley woman?"

"Lieutenant Taylor."

"Yeh?" the fourth soldier said. Then his face darkened. "Say, where is that lyin' jackanapes? He said he'd have men over here to spell us an hour ago."

"Well, I'll take you right to him, if you like," Culpeper said.

The Federal eyed his pie-wolfing mates, then said, "All right, let's go."

About the time the grim trooper wondered why Culpeper had him halfway down a dark alley, the Virginian smashed him in the face with the butt of one of his pistols. Lorena gasped and turned away as she saw Culpeper go to work on the fallen man's head with his boot and spur.

"Sorry you had to see that, ma'am," Culpeper said, dragging his dead victim behind a stand of large hogsheads. "But I reckon it'll go easier for your husband and them others without him eagle-eyein' 'em. Let's get back there."

Hurrying around the corner that put them back in front of the jail, Culpeper gasped when he saw the three drunken guards—all wielding pistols, pie smeared on their faces and dirty, unbuttoned tunics—stepping over the passed-out bodies of other Kirk men, leading Slim Curtis out of the jail.

"Can't I fetch my shoes?" Curtis asked.

"No, you won't have use for them long," the black soldier said.

A few seconds later, the drunken men had a rope up over a signpost and around Curtis's neck as the rain began to pour.

"Now, will you confess, skinny man?" one of the white troopers asked, putting the gun to Curtis's breast.

When Curtis closed his eyes and gritted his teeth, the soldier signaled his two cohorts, and they hoisted their prisoner up into the air, where he dangled, gasping for breath, his legs kicking.

"D—," the black soldier swore. "We really gonna kill 'im?"

The white soldier conducting the proceeding swore more oaths, saw Curtis was unconscious and purple, and ordered him back down as crashing thunder accompanied rain gusting now in sheets.

Shoving and kicking him back conscious, they hauled him to his feet.

"All right, you scrawny secesh jaybird," the soldier in charge snarled, cocking the hammer of his pistol and putting the barrel in Curtis's left ear. "You got one chance left to confess and save yourself."

By now a few other drunken troopers began to stumble up, and even a few sober ones, though the storm, alcohol, and lateness of the hour rendered the majority of them unaware of a scene about which most would have been gleeful.

Still Curtis said nothing, his neck bruised and bloody, but his face blank as a freshly wiped slate board.

Noting the dozen or so soldiers gathered around, and realizing Slim Curtis had decided to die rather than say a thing, the tormentor bellowed a stream of obscenities, knocked Curtis to the ground with his pistol, and shouted, saliva spewing from his mouth, "Then we'll hang your hide from that oak tree across the road till eight o'clock tomorrow morning, when we'll cut you down and bury you under the tree on which we hung you."

Hearing Lorena gasp, Culpeper bit his lower lip and wondered what to do. Concluding nothing could be done but perhaps rescue the remaining prisoners, he heaved a sigh of relief when some of the more sober soldiers persuaded Curtis's tormentors to relent till morning.

"Drag him back to jail!" said the chief tormentor, whom Culpeper heard referred to as Olson. "No, we don't need no help, we got the jail took care of just fine, thank you very much. You boys just get the h— outa here, and we'll take care of the jail."

Just as he suspected, when Culpeper peeked through the window, he saw half the pie remaining to be eaten.

"Nice pie, ma'am," he said to Lorena as they stayed out of sight in the shadows.

After a few minutes, wind, rain, thunder, and lightning alike escalating, everyone dispersed.

The last words Culpeper heard from them were, "That darkie Jenkins got him a game o' five card stud goin' over in that Baptist church."

The cacophony of weather drowned out the response.

Now nearly four o'clock, few of Kirk's men remained awake. The sleepers lay sprawled everywhere as the downpour washed over them—on the wood-planked sidewalks, in the street, on the brown town green, up in its trees, in the now-filling horse-watering troughs.

Soon the three drunken jailers were shambling out, Deke Anderson and his hurt, bloody comrades limping behind them. Peering closely, Culpeper saw his own Bowie knife, which Lorena had nestled into her very large cake at the McCormacks, pressed against Olson's back by Anderson. The other prisoners had the Federals' pistols concealed, but Culpeper spotted them all.

No other conscious Federals remained anywhere in sight.

"Psst," he called, waving to Anderson from the shadows.

Not knowing how either raiding party would fare, Miller planned a rendezvous back in the woods near Cooper Cemetery. If either or both parties failed to manage that by sunup Monday without bringing pursuing Federals with them, the contingency plan was for the jail rescue party, sans Culpeper, to get back to their homes—or someone else's—before the Federals detected their absence. The Kirk party, Anderson, and the other prisoners would head west to a mountain cabin of Miller's near Asheville and assess their next move.

Little had gone according to plan for Culpeper ever in his life, but when he, Drumgoolen, the Andersons, and the rest of their party reigned up in the woods half an hour before dawn, their three Federal prisoners bound, gagged, and tied facedown on stolen Yankee mounts, he wondered if perhaps this chapter might.

"I don't know whether to count this rain good or bad," Drumgoolen said to him as they listened to the storm roil.

"Good, I'd say," Culpeper said. "Kirk'll have trackers that can follow our trail wet or dry, unless we're far enough ahead of him, then the rain might wash our tracks away. And they sure can't see or hear us as well with this comin' down."

"It oughta slow up that drunken trash pretty good just gettin' off the mark," Drumgoolen agreed.

"I'd say if our boys get Kirk, I wouldn't give a plugged nickel for any o' the rest o' them Fed vermin gettin' much done," Culpeper said. "'Cept maybe tearin' up each other—and your town."

"Wonder when the government and the people will be on the same side again," Drumgoolen said.

"'Bout when Jed and Kirk give each other a big old smooch on the cheek," Culpeper said.

Drumgoolen guffawed.

"You know Miller, Jed, and them's got the Goliath end of the job with goin' after Kirk," Culpeper said.

With the slim gray light of rain-soaked dawn came the Kirk raiding party.

"What happened, Matt?" Drumgoolen asked.

"Oh we got 'em, we got 'em good, Drum," Dooley breathed.

"You boys all right?" Miller asked, happy to see Anderson and the other prisoners, hurting as they were. When Drumgoolen nodded, Miller added, "Kirk had the shack to himself with that little tramp Rowena Gore. Most his men must've gone back to town. The few that were there were mostly passed out in the lean-to by her folks' old place, fifty yards from the shack. Me an' Tink filled that skunk more full o' lead than one o' the Fightin' Bishop's cannon at Chickamauga."

"What with the rain and all, we was in and out and down the road 'fore those buzzards knew anything hit 'em," Dooley said.

"Turned out foregoin' our white garb to keep the heat off the Klan was a winner," Miller said, "'cause they couldn't see us anyhow, especially with our bandannas over our faces."

For the first time, Cousin Jed spoke up: "I'm goin' back in."

"Uh—we didn't see your Sledge fellow, Culpeper," Miller said.

"I scouted every nook and cranny o' that place 'fore the others went in," Cousin Jed said with a hangdog face. "The wretch was nowhere on the property."

"I advised him to wait for another shot—" Miller began. Culpeper shushed him with a raised hand.

"There's riders comin'," said the Virginian.

"There's no way—" Dooley started.

Culpeper leaped off his horse and put his ear to the soggy ground for an instant, then flew back into the saddle.

"Bunch o' riders, boys," he said.

"You hear 'em?" Dooley couldn't believe it.

"Comin' this way?" Miller asked.

"Does it matter?" Culpeper said, reigning his horse around to head away from Redemption.

"Cole!" Cousin Jed hollered.

"You'll git Sledge soon enough, cousin," Culpeper said, "prob'ly right in your lap."

The primal drive for survival drove even Cousin Jed, cursing, out of the woods and down the road. They rode as hard as they could, but day was here and the rain was no longer their friend; their horses began to slip and slide on the mucky trail. Heading up a steep grade a mile away, two of the horses reared up, their legs slid out from under them, and they pitched over. One was Lorena Anderson's.

"Lori," Culpeper heard her husband call in the soupy gloom. "Oh, Lord, no." Anderson began to wail. "Oh, Lord, please, no!"

Culpeper, stepping his horse back down the hill toward them, saw that her horse had landed on her, rolled over her, and slid off into a gully, leaving her with a crushed chest, blood streaming from her gaping mouth.

What a fine lady, he thought, stricken. Then he heard Dooley, at the crest of the hill, cry out and fly backwards off his horse, an instant before the report of a rifle echoed off the hill. Culpeper could see no one through the rain.

"Where are they?" Miller called.

"Don't know, but they gotta have a scope, prob'ly one about the size o' your whole arm, to shoot like that in this mess, even catchin' him atop the hill like that," Culpeper said. "And the ground's movin' like a whole passel of 'em are comin', close. We better move." Then another shot tore off half the face of Cousin Red's horse, and the beast collapsed to the ground onto its rider's remaining leg.

"Ahh," Cousin Red cried out. "I can't get out from under the big lummox, Jed."

"How the hey did they find us?" Tom McCormack shouted.

"Prob'ly that two-faced, smooth-talkin' preacher boy o' yourn," Cousin Jed said with venom.

"That's a lie," Miller snapped.

Culpeper whipped out his spyglass. He saw motion at the foot of the hill, a quarter of a mile away. He couldn't spot the sharpshooter. He turned and saw Cousin Jed, unable to get his brother, his one leg broken, out from under his dead horse. Deke Anderson was not leaving his wife's side. Billy McCormack's horse had fallen and snapped a leg. Drumgoolen was pulling the eighteen-year-old up behind him on his own horse.

Culpeper looked at Miller, whose eyes had caught everything Culpeper's had. But Miller's eyes were for an instant uncertain. The words were loosed before Culpeper even knew he had made a decision, for all of them.

"Dismount and git the horses down," the Virginian said. He reached around to grab his mount's bridle, then tugged it and the horse's head toward him with all his might with one hand while shoving the animal's neck down with his other, all the while still sitting his saddle. The animal snorted, then sank to his foreknees as Culpeper slid nimbly to the ground behind him.

"We can't outrun 'em in this muck," he said. "Least we got high ground and they're stupid enough to come right at us. We'll cut some down, then make a run for it."

Miller, the ex-Forrest trooper, parroted Culpeper's descent from his horse. The others got down in one manner or another, Slim Curtis when another sniper shot cut a swath cleanly through his throat with a brass-cased .50 caliber slug.

"Wait till I give the call," Miller said.

A few seconds later the bluecoats were slipping and sliding into Culpeper's view as he gazed again through the spyglass. *What?* he thought, startled at what he saw.

"It's Kirk at their head," he said.

"That can't be," Miller said.

"Fire, d——!" Cousin Jed shouted, loosing a shot that knocked Kirk out of the saddle.

"That boy's been shot all to pieces today," Culpeper said, shooting Miller a wry look.

Then the deafening chaos of combat filled the air everywhere around them. The front dozen or so of Kirk's force either fell shot or were knocked down by horses and men who were. Kirk crawled bleeding into a brush-rimmed hollow. His screaming, cursing threats spread most of the rest of the reluctant Federals like a net across the fields on either side of the road, now irretrievably blocked by a mass of screaming, screeching, flailing, bleeding men and horses. Culpeper and those with him began to pot the Federals one after another, but as they did, Yankee bullets tore into the Southerners' horses lying before them like breastworks.

Culpeper saw some Federals galloping away; he was surprised the whole lot of them weren't. Then he realized not many of them were still firing. He squinted through the pouring rain and choking gun smoke at his own men. Billy McCormack was gut-shot and a couple others were dead. Two of their three bound Federal prisoners lay bloody and still. A couple of horses had bolted away; all but one that remained looked as dead as his chances to live through this day, even this morning. The one still alive, Drumgoolen's, thrashed neck- and groin-shot in the muddy slime. The big man ended the animal's misery with a .36 caliber slug through the brain.

Culpeper looked around at Deke Anderson. That man sat motionless against his wife's dead horse, holding Lorena in his arms, his own forehead, neck, chest, stomach, and groin torn open by bullet holes.

"We better move on foot, or they'll close us out quick," Culpeper said to the others.

"Red can't move," Cousin Jed said, reloading his pistols and rifle.

"I ain't leavin' Billy," Tom McCormack sobbed, cradling his younger brother's head in his lap.

Culpeper thought about that as torrents of rain whipped his face. He heard Kirk shouting more orders, still spiked with oaths, the sheer ingenuity of their pith and cadence commanding the Virginian's reluctant admiration. The image—the feeling, actually—struck him of laughing with Emma as a cool rain blew into their smooth, creaseless young faces and drove them inside the empty line shack on the far edge of the McDowells' lush emerald Valiant.

Then the ground told the veteran Valley scout that more Federals approached from town, a lot more.

He looked at Miller and said, "We'll give the rest o' you boys coverin' fire. I 'spect I'd shimmy into them woods off to the left there and make a run for it."

Elijah Sledge was fed up with the abuse of women and the terrorizing of children. And that included in his mind the Rev. Hedgecock's own wife and little girls, quarantined by Lieutenant Taylor through the chaplain's surreptitious request to a little cabin out on the south edge of town. Taylor had thrown out the elderly couple who built the cabin and resided in it these past thirty-four years. He posted three white soldiers, more to keep the Hedgecock family in than anyone else out.

The good reverend, meanwhile, grew bolder in his public escorting of his little redhead, and the outfits he "requisitioned" from town stores and that she wore grew more lavish, at least as lavish as the meager stock of garments from Redemption's two dry-goods stores could be.

Taylor posted two black soldiers at the little redhead's tiny ramshackle flat, with clear warning they would breathe knowledge of the overnight visits of the tall, Bible-toting cleric at the forfeit of their lives.

Cousin Jed did not find Sledge at the Gore place because he had ridden away from Colonel Kirk and from Redemption, headed east for he knew not where. But Sledge knew—he thought—he was finished with Kirk.

Then the storm drove him off the road and under a live oak for the night, and he fell asleep. He awoke only when the first dim light came. As Providence—or the gods or whomever—would have it, he got back on the road just as Kirk and the hundred men he had managed to collect thundered up.

"Sledge, you black b——," Kirk snarled. "Where the h— you been while them Rebs been tryin' to send me to an early demise?"

Sledge's blood ran cold. He thanked those same gods when the frantic colonel continued, "You on their trail too?"

"Uh, yessir, cunnel," Sledge said, nodding with vigor.

"We had to beat it out of her, but Anderson's sister finally told us his wife was headed with the renegades to a cemetery a couple miles up the road here."

"Same as I heard," Sledge lied.

"Lucky I found me that little mulatto wench you had your eye on yesterday—now don't gimme that look; I caught you lookin' at her too," Kirk chortled. "Anyways, if it ain't been for Miss Lizzie, woulda been me and not that fool cousin o' mine they shot up in that Gore tramp's bed. Let's ride!" Kirk shouted, slashing his horse with his crop.

Sledge cursed Kirk and the gods and God and everybody and everything else as he followed his colonel's order to lead a forty-man contingent around to the other side of the hill behind the Rebels. Leastwise, he led the black half of that contingent. Kirk had also ordered the twenty or so whites he considered the most worthless—and expendable—of those he had on hand to ride with Sledge. These defiant characters refused to heed orders from a black man and rode apart, en masse, from Sledge, hurling insults at him and the other blacks.

I was almost away from that detestable bigoted oaf, Sledge thought bitterly. *Now, gosh sakes almighty, here I am getting ready to lead a cavalry charge for him straight into a pack of desperate Rebel riflemen. Maybe this charge will get me free of these madmen and into the State House where I can finally do my people some good.*

Matt Miller stared with overwhelming lust at the woods that stretched south far as the eye could see, even when the sun shined. He had no more doubt that he could outleg Kirk's undisciplined, horsebacked men than Culpeper had that he himself could. And Miller knew what sweet Susie would say. That was the only real hard part.

He turned back to Culpeper. "I reckon General Forrest'd have any of our scalps that he heard lit out," he drawled.

"Suit yourself," Culpeper said, realizing with a start that every Yankee in sight was hiding behind cover.

When Cousin Jed saw Elijah Sledge riding at the head of the troop that now rumbled over the crest of the hill and down onto them, his heart nearly leapt out of his chest.

CHAPTER 72

HEARING LIEUTENANT TAYLOR AND HIS FIFTY-MAN CONTINGENT gallop onto the scene just as the shooting between Sledge and the Rebels exploded up the hill put the first smile of the day on Kirk's scarred, whisker-stubbled face.

"Push right on through, Taylor, push right on up the hill," Kirk waved with one hand as he lay against a fallen tree trunk, his other hand staunching the flesh wound in his shoulder Cousin Jed had dealt him.

"Come on, you cowards!" Taylor hollered to the filthy mob of bluecoats following behind him.

It would have been hard to tell whether Sledge and his men or Culpeper and the ex-Confederates were the more surprised. Before either group knew it, the crest of the hill blocking both their views, the bluecoats were riding over their outnumbered foe.

Culpeper and his surviving mates threw up such a furious quick volley of lead into the Federals' faces that the whole front rank of their saddles was emptied, with the exception of Sledge. Cousin Jed drew a perfect bead on him as he passed and squeezed the trigger. Nothing happened; the rain had so dampened the powder charges on his .36 caliber revolver that none of them would fire.

Cousin Jed screamed, inconsolable with wrath, as he pulled out his .45 to reload it. A riderless Federal horse, spooked and snorting, careened away from Cousin Red and crashed into Jed from behind, knocking him sprawling.

Culpeper fired every bullet he had from every gun he had at the Federals thrashing around him, knocking one dead from the saddle, hitting another, and driving the others away. *Most of these scum have never seen battle before,* he thought with contempt as he saw perhaps half of Sledge's force retreating. *They scattered the instant they saw it was a fight.* Then he felt the whizz of bullets flying past him. *From down the hill,* he realized, turning and seeing Taylor and half a troop slipping, sliding, and scratching their way up the inclined swamp that

717

now posed as a hill, as water rushed down it from the rain that continued to pour.

If this ain't hell, Culpeper thought, grabbing for his rifle, *I don't wanna see it.* "Look out, they're comin' up the hill too!" he shouted, knowing even as the words released that it was too late. Cousin Red had time to unleash one more blast of his scattergun, which tore up two Federals and their horses, before a hail of bullets finished him. Drumgoolen, already hit in the leg, stood and took a slug point-blank in the chest, then dragged the shooter off his horse, yanked the revolver out of his hand, and put a bullet between the Federal's eyes with it before two other bluecoats emptied their own pistols into him. It took every bullet they had to put him down, and even then he was stalking toward them till he fell, his red-bearded face a sheet of rage.

A couple of other ex-Confederates ran past Culpeper for the trees to their left. A half-dozen Federals rode them down before they made it. Tom McCormack lay dead atop a lifeless Federal, into whose chest he had plunged his own hunting knife, all the way to the hilt.

The rain came down harder still, and that, the choking clouds of gun smoke, and the teeming mass of Federal horses, many of them riderless, precluded Culpeper from finding a rifle. Suddenly a white Federal was looming over him, pistol aimed straight at his face. Before the Virginian had time even to be scared, the man pulled the trigger. The hammer clicked harmlessly. Culpeper reached for the gun just as a pair of shots rang out from a few feet away, knocking the bluecoat out of the saddle. Then Culpeper saw that the shooter was a confused black Federal who, thoroughly rattled, turned to ride away, only to bump into another of his own men, who promptly shot him out of the saddle.

Culpeper pondered what to do next. *Why not just let it finish here?* he thought, unable to conjure one reason why his life needed to last beyond the end of this battle. Just then, a gust of wind—from the opposite direction of what it had blown these eight hours—pushed the smoke aside enough for him to see Drumgoolen lying on his back on the ground, his face relaxed and at peace, water rushing downhill all around him. *"Don't let 'em beat you down to that,"* Culpeper remembered the man's advice. *"They may take your life from you with a bullet—but don't let 'em take it from you before that."*

He heard Cousin Jed's angry voice and decided to make his way toward it. Another riderless Federal horse, shot in his left flank, stumbled past him, headed down the hill. One of the men who had been jailed with Deke Anderson fell to Culpeper's right, dead. Stray shots, mostly wild and errant, some fired blindly into the melee from Kirk's men still downhill, sang their siren song of death all around him.

For a moment the smoke and rain cleared just enough for him to see his cousin mount a horse, loaded .45 again in hand. Lieutenant Taylor rode up to Cousin Jed from behind and leveled his gun at him as he bolted away, only to be shot dead out of the saddle by Miller, standing a few feet away. Then a horse carrying a Federal slid down the bloody mud pit into Miller, knocking him down, then rolling over him. When, bleeding from the ears, he tried to rise, a stray shot meant for someone else finished him.

Culpeper grabbed Taylor's horse and lit out after Cousin Jed. As he rode, north and east and away from Redemption, he saw a number of Kirk's men riding off as well, in various directions, as the rain at long last relented, and he broke into rolling meadows. Behind him he heard a few bursts of gunfire. *They are finishing off whichever of our boys are still breathing,* he thought, numb.

Cousin Jed was perhaps a quarter of a mile ahead. *And that must be Sledge out ahead of him,* Culpeper thought. The rain had soaked the ground, but the sky was clearing, and Culpeper found the footing much surer, even on an unfamiliar horse, through open pasture land than it had been on the road.

Ahead, he saw Cousin Jed closing on Sledge. *No way he'll outhoof Jed, lessin Jed picked him the biggest nag o' the lot,* Culpeper thought. Then he saw Sledge, almost to the top of a low rise, tumble to the ground with his horse.

Look out, Sledge, Culpeper thought, watching Cousin Jed leap from his horse and land running on his feet before the animal had hardly slowed.

I couldn't win the last war, and I can't win this one, Culpeper thought ruefully, *but maybe I can hit a lick or two before my number is called.*

"Yiii-aaahhh!" he shrieked in the best Rebel yell he could muster after all the fighting and tension and rain and no sleep.

He saw Sledge, shaking himself off on the ground, reach for the pistol in his hip holster and stand. Just as he pulled it, Cousin Jed kicked it out of his hand, then backhanded him to the ground.

"Yiii-aaahhh!" Culpeper hollered again, riding up as Cousin Jed stood over Sledge, .45 in hand.

"Howdy, cuz," Cousin Jed said with a grim smile as Culpeper's horse skidded to a halt and almost fell on the wet grass.

"Howdy," Culpeper said.

Cousin Jed hauled Sledge up by his collar.

"Should we shoot the murderin' rodent first," he asked Culpeper, "or hang 'im, then shoot 'im?"

Culpeper noticed a Sharps carbine poking out of the saddle holster of his new mount. He pulled it out, jacked the lever, and felt a bullet slide into the breach.

Cousin Jed stuck his .45 back into his waistband, pulled his Bowie knife out of his boot, and held one of the two monstrous blades to Sledge's throat. "Or should we slice him up a bit first?"

"What say we let him go?" Culpeper said.

Cousin Jed whirled around. "Huh?"

Culpeper, holding the reins with one hand and pointing the Sharps vaguely in the direction of Sledge and Cousin Jed with the other, just nodded.

Cousin Jed smiled, his eyes lighting up. "Oh, you mean give 'im a head start, make it sportin'-like."

"Naw, I mean let the b—— scat, and let's go back to livin'."

His cousin's face twisted into a distorted mask of bewilderment. "Why, I declare such words surely surprise me comin' from you, Cousin Cole. What the Sam Hill you think them Yankees gonna do, just let us waltz back to Tennessee and start ginnin' cotton again, lettin' bygones be bygones?"

"I was thinkin' maybe—Texas," Culpeper said.

"H— fire, Little Phil Sheridan's rulin' them Texicans like Julius Caesar hisself; t'ain't no chance for us in Texas."

"Texas is a big place, Jed."

Cousin Jed had no such travel plans in mind, and the look on his face evidenced it. He turned back to Sledge, gripping the Bowie.

"Don't do it, Jed," Culpeper said. Now the Sharps was trained on the knife-wielder's chest.

Cousin Jed's mouth and eyes worked as he glanced at the terrified Sledge, whose own eyes were about to bulge out of his head—even as his first prayer since childhood silently begged God, if He existed, to show him mercy and give him another chance—then back at Culpeper. The Tennessean gnawed his lips as scarlet anger tided over his face and blue veins tried to burst the bonds that held them in his neck and throat.

"Why not?" he screamed at Culpeper. "Why the h— not!"

Culpeper's face grew grim. He thought about that. He thought about the long, long journey of blood and tears and heartbreak, of good men turned bad and bad men turned worse, that had cost him and his so very much. He thought of the lost love, the lost hope, the lost dreams he had tried so very hard to pretend he never had. *But I did have them,* he thought, his throat dry as a coffin, *I did have dreams of my own. I had lots of them.*

At last, he now realized, the long dark passage had very nearly cost him what once, he felt sure, sometime in the distant past, had been most important of all to him—his honor.

"Why!" Cousin Jed screamed the louder.

"Because we don't fight that way," Culpeper said, the echoes of that honor, nearly killed, demanding their hearing from a cold dark grave in the Shenandoah Valley where lay the scent of lavender and a soft little pink doll that from the wormy darkness had strength greater than cannon or bayonets or carpetbags or Constitutions that were torn into tatters, or even hate and despair and envy and fear, and that still meant friendship and kindness and love.

Something in what he said, maybe even how he said it, took the juice out of Cousin Jed. His face and heart sank, and the Bowie too. He flung it to the ground, where that wide double-blade of legend speared the sodden turf just as it would have speared it had no rain fallen in months. He walked, head down, to his horse, climbed into the saddle, gave Culpeper a brief nod, then drew the .45 and galloped straight back toward Kirk and his men. Culpeper, feeling suddenly quite alone, watched him for long seconds.

"Th . . . thank you, mister."

Culpeper looked down and saw Sledge, shoulders hunched, soaked to his weary bones, staring at him.

An overpowering sense of fatigue and gloom overtook Culpeper, and he sat for a moment without saying anything. Then the guns sounded back toward Redemption. Shot after shot, growing in ferocity, till he had heard more than twenty. A wry smile succeeded in getting a foothold on his face, but it could advance no further than that. Finally the firing tapered off into silence, just as the most beautiful rainbow Culpeper had ever seen arched across the sky above him.

He looked down at Sledge, who appeared himself as though he would collapse any second. *The wrong man o' those two died,* Culpeper thought as he spurred his latest well-fed Yankee horse into a slow trot and headed north without a word, toward Virginia.

On the way, he realized a Federal bullet had torn open his trouser pocket that contained Ethan's cross. *I'm sorry, Ethan boy,* he fretted, near grief over the loss.

And he remembered a few more words to that ditty he heard the boys hiding up in the mountains sing.

> I can't take up my musket and fight 'em now no mo',
>> But I ain't a'goin' to love 'em, now that is sartin sho';
> And I don't want no pardon for what I was and am,
>> And I won't be reconstructed, and I do not give a d—!

A federal marshal and a troop of United States Regular cavalry greeted Kirk upon his return to Redemption.

"Governor Holden?" the marshal cackled. "Why, he's to be impeached. President Grant? He'll have no more of your outrages."

The cavalry had already disarmed the bulk of Kirk's force, which had remained in town, and ordered them to leave the county and disperse. Kirk was arrested and tended to by Dr. Sam Garrett in the same cell Deke Anderson and his friends had occupied.

The Rev. Mortimer Hedgecock submitted with grace and aplomb to the shattering of Kirk's army. He saddled up and rode out with his Bible and a potpourri of niceties pilfered from the Carolina heathen—china, perfumes, tinned food, Southern bourbon—and with his redheaded girlfriend.

The Rev. Jeremiah Shanklin, meanwhile, was in no good mood. He had several dead parishioners; a drought-ridden town whose corn crop had failed, and a vandalized church defiled by the use of its sanctuary as a trysting site for drunken Federals and the sort of females not burdened by moral concerns.

The raving shrieks of local women, some of them members of his church, announced the first wagonload of bodies arriving from the battle on the muddy hill, some bluecoat, some not, some dead, some dying, some bleeding but alive.

But it is more than four years since Appomattox; how can this still happen? he wondered.

Then one of the four Redemption-area men who survived the muddy slaughter against Kirk brought word to Shanklin that Nathan Bedford Forrest had issued a sweeping verbal order to disband and terminate the Invisible Empire.

"He said the Klan has accomplished its mission, at least in Tennessee, and because of it, now Southerners have at least a shot again runnin' our own state houses and what-not," the man said. "And he said nearly as much harm as good is now being done in the name of the Klan by bad men, and even by Yankees and Union League blacks posin' as Klansmen."

Shanklin looked out a broken window of his smashed-up sanctuary at the devastation wrought upon the little town he loved, devastation that was the dividend of Radicals, fire-eaters, carpetbaggers, scalawags, and Klansmen. *How ironic that the honor, dignity, and virtue no amount of Yankee war-making could steal, has fled away from us years after "peace" came,* he reflected. He would ponder until his dying day whether there could have been something better than the original, well-intentioned Klan for the good and protection of Christian civilization in the South.

But now he must consider what should be his first step in the long agony of putting Redemption back together. He, too, had noted the departure of the Rev. Hedgecock and his red-haired friend. And the forlorn Mrs. Hedgecock and her little girls.

"Have you seen my husband?" Shanklin heard her asking as she walked among Kirk's men and townspeople alike, one little girl clutching her right hand, one the left, both of their noses running like sieves. "He is the tall, handsome young chaplain. Have you, pray tell, seen the Rev. Hedgecock? Please, have you? Have you seen my husband?"

After all the weeping, all the blood, all the drunkenness and destruction, somehow it was this sight that reduced Shanklin to sobs.

His first move was to alert the Yankee marshal to the Rev. Hedgecock's actions, and the statutory laws in North Carolina related to bigamy. His second was to invite Mrs. Hedgecock and her little girls to the modest Presbyterian manse.

The Rev. Hedgecock was caught with his redheaded hussy and jailed, then imprisoned for bigamy.

His erstwhile family remained with the Shanklins until that elderly couple who built the cabin out on the south edge of town and resided in it these past thirty-four years before being thrown out had built an addition. There Mrs. Hedgecock and her children lived until some years after the death of Mrs. Shanklin.

At that point, happily, Mrs. Hedgecock became the bride of a very different sort of pastor.

CHAPTER 73

"WHAT ARE YOU DOING, MOTHER?" LEE ASKED AS HE STEPPED ONTO the west veranda of the new president's house one bright balmy late afternoon in February 1870.

"Sewing housewives," Mary replied. "And enjoying the view of field and forest that a most thoughtful husband arranged for me to have."

He smiled as he leaned back in a wicker rocker, then said, "Housewives, eh?"

"You know, Papa," she said. "The sewing cases for the V.M.I. cadets. They still have no tailor at the Institute, and those poor boys come here from who-knows-where, without their mothers or the least idea how to keep their clothes in repair. These sewing cases are nigh as important to them as studying for their exams." Her forehead crinkled. "I must procure a new supply of pants and drawers buttons and some spools of cotton, numbers thirty, forty, and fifty, I should think."

"Ah, yes," he said, rocking, "I do believe I recollect Pendleton saying something about housewives being primarily to thank as we near the attainment of the church's building fund."

"Well, I hardly think . . ." she began. "Husband, you have something to tell me."

His furry white eyebrows vaulted upwards, then he smiled again. "I should no longer be surprised that a wife who can keep the feet of the Army of Northern Virginia warm and assure the expansion of Grace Episcopal Church can read my poor simple face."

"Are you finally to heed the counsel of your faculty, churchmen, and family alike, and travel south for some quiet and for your health, Papa?" she asked, resuming her work.

"I can no longer walk the slope from the chapel to our house, as close or closer than the college itself, without stopping to rest," he said, lowering his head, feeling the old tight aching pull inside his chest. After a moment he looked back up and over the painted landscape that was Virginia—even the Federals as of a few weeks ago no longer considered it United States Military District Number 1. "O how I long for the time when I might have a farm of my own, where I might end my days in quiet and peace, interested in the care and improvement of my own land," he said. Then, turning to her, "and where I might do better for you, with a permanent house of your own."

She reached her hand to him and said, "Robert, you and the children are my Arlington."

Tears filled his eyes. "I feel at any moment I might die."

Tenderness enveloping her face, she pushed her chair to him and took his head into the sanctuary of her arms and bosom, as he had done her so often over the course of nearly forty years.

Sheltered within her love, he remembered back to all whom he had led to their own, often horrible, deaths, and to much more as well, and said, "I wish I felt sure of my acceptance as a Christian."

"Oh, dear husband," she comforted him, stroking the white hair with pained crooked fingers. She marveled at how different was this man from the many who possessed no store of humility or awareness of their sin even as they presumed boundlessly and cavalierly on the grace of God to receive them to Himself, as if he were fortunate to do so. "All who love and trust in the Savior need not fear."

They held and hugged each other for a long moment as the sun, radiant and warm, dipped toward the Allegheny horizon.

Sitting up, heartened, he announced, "I shall go first to Warrenton Springs to visit the grave of our dear Annie, where I have always promised myself to go. I think, if I am to accomplish it, I have no time to lose. I wish to witness her quiet sleep, Mother, with her dear hands crossed over her breast, as it were in mute prayer, undisturbed by her distance from us, and to feel that her pure spirit is waiting in bliss in the land of the blessed."

She held a hand to his bearded cheek.

"I shall take Wiggie with me," he said. "She has nursed me all the winter through, even when she herself is still unwell."

She looked up at him, a glint in her eyes as of old. "Do you think travel is advisable for her while wearing that immense chignon which seems to weigh her down and absorb everything?"

"Mother!" he exclaimed, his countenance stern but his eyes merry. "I must report you to the vestry. Then I am certain they will wish to dispatch a couple of the more sober-minded among our cadre, the sort who appear to have been weaned on sour pickles, to confront you about your willfulness. And I should even fear for my own position as a vestryman; after all, Scripture says such as we are to rule well our own house."

Only Marley knew who she was—the flaxen hair and the final word she uttered confirmed her as the beautiful, untouchable daughter of the richest planter in the Upper Shenandoah county where Marley had lived for ten years before the war. The girl whom he had caught reverent, awestruck glimpses of as she grew from a little child into the elegant creature who would be Kate Chase Sprague's good friend, and one of the most desired women in all America.

Only Marley knew, and he had no intention of sharing the revelation. Now that he knew, amazement filled him that he had not divined it before. He had been so close to knowing who she was so many times, but always she was just beyond him. Always, she was just beyond him.

He wondered had he remembered her sooner, could he have saved her? He would not confront that question, at least not for a long time. Something had gone terribly wrong in her life, something, from what he remembered hearing of her father, probably long ago. Protection of her name and virtue came through the months to be more sacred to him even than had been his devotion to her while she lived.

Where the powder burns were and where they were not cleared Marley with the law. Where he was and where he was not cleared him with the public, at least the Radical leadership's version of those items.

Drink could render him no more numb than had the most horrific episode of his entire life. Other than the suicide before his eyes of his bride Rachel Anne McDowell of Valiant, Rockbridge County, Virginia, alias Anne Nelson of Washington, District of Columbia, U.S.A., no event through which he ever lived proved more bathed in irony than that Marley never again took a drink of alcohol after his beloved's death. For some months he had no desire for any. He could never claim any credit for dispensing with the pernicious habit; he simply ceased desiring it. *Or it ceased desiring me,* he thought.

Marley also began to realize the mercy of God in that he felt no keen grief over the loss for some time. Only gradually did a dull pain cobble its way into his heart. But he had no joy, and never did he smile for months.

With Anne gone he began again to attend the gospel-preaching Old School Presbyterian church whose teachings bore witness to the heritage he inherited from his spiritual mentor Stonewall Jackson. As the old, old message of Christ and Him crucified was proclaimed week by week from the pulpit; as he partook weekly of the sacramental bread and the wine at the Lord's table; as he began again to interact with humble people whose faith represented more to them than a tool for career or prestige enhancement; as he learned once more to read his Bible and pray to his God with larger intention than seeking gain for himself; as all these ancient forgotten ways met in confluence in Marley's life, he could almost feel the wounds that shone raw and ran deep, the spiritual wounds, the wounds to his very soul, most of which he had inflicted upon himself and which had been festering for years, begin to close up and heal.

Perhaps the hour is not yet too late to attempt a Bible study for the ex-soldiers like that which prospered up in Pennsylvania and which I should so long ago have begun here in Washington, he thought, hope beginning to sprout, ever so gingerly, into his heart, like the first tender buds in springtime. *I have certainly rendered myself unworthy of leading such an effort, but perhaps that new young congressman from Maryland could—he's a Democrat as I recall, and a sort of protégé to Reverdy Johnson, but he stayed with the Union, and they say he is most humble and devout.* Marley considered those last two attributes. *After all I have seen in myself and others these past years, I almost believe that had I to choose between the two, I should prefer the former to the latter.*

If not for one Wednesday prayer service, big Ben Hill's audacious rhetorical rampage the next morning would likely have affected Marley in quite a different fashion.

Hill had long posed an unsettling specter to Marley. The rangy, fair-crowned Georgian seemed to appear at the most inopportune times, such as when he happened by during Marley's set-to with Kurt Schumacher. And though Marley knew the man to have fierce convictions—and to have been the last voice in Georgia against secession and nearly the last in the South, then *the* last voice in the Confederate Congress *against* surrender—particularly as Reconstruction grew more vindictive and authoritarian in its treatment of the South, he rarely spoke in House debates. More than once, though, after Marley

728

spoke during a contentious battle, or even when another Republican did, the Pennsylvanian felt the silent gaze of Hill's intense gray eyes boring in on him. More than once Marley came close to asking the Democrat afterward, "Why do you stare at me? Why me?"

But he did not. He spoke. His fellows spoke. And they won. And Ben Hill listened and watched and gazed at Marley. And he fell ill, nearly died, and spent much time convalescing in Georgia. His fellows lost and lost again and lost some more as the years turned over bitter as castor oil going down.

Finally, on this Thursday morning, as the truth came to light about the Radical policies and Black Friday and silk-and-cravat New York barbarians who tumbled it crashing down on a nation already full of suffering and trying to find its way; as the truth emerged about Colonel Kirk and his government-sponsored war against the poverty-rent country folk of North Carolina; as Southern lands continued to be confiscated, Southern taxes raised, and Southern laws changed, all while carpetbaggers and scalawags ruled the South from the courthouse, the statehouse, the national House, and the White House; as all this and much more happened, Ben Hill lifted his six-and-a-half-foot frame with great effort from his seat and spoke. His face was pale and his voice at first low and his cadence quite slow as the gray gaze burned in on them—and on nearly the entire United States Senate, ensconced in the galleries—but no one more so than Wayne Marley.

Snickers and joke-cracking sounded forth clearly from the Radical forces.

"Tinkers may work, quacks may prescribe, and demagogues may deceive, but I declare to you that there is no remedy for us of the South," Hill said, "but in adhering to the Constitution."

From the Radicals, more snickers, and "Tinkers?" "Quacks?" "Quack, quack, indeed, you quacker!"

Hill churned forward, unaffected. "A great many Southerners flippantly say the Constitution is dead. They say your rights and hopes for the future, and the hopes of your children are dead. They say the Constitution does not apply to us. Then don't swear to support it. They say again that we are not in the Union— then why swear to support the Union of these states? What Union does that mean? When you took the oath, was it the Union of the Northern states alone that you swore to support?

"Oh, I pity the colored people who have never been taught what an oath is, or what the Constitution means. They are drawn up by a selfish conclave of traitors to inflict a death-blow on the Republic by swearing them into a false-hood. They are to begin their political life with perjury to accomplish treason," he said, his voice beginning to rise in the wake left by the disappearance of the snickers and jokes.

"They are neither legally nor morally responsible—it is you, educated, designing white men—" At this the old gray gaze bore in anew on Marley, even as outraged Radicals began to stir and murmur among themselves. "—who thus devote yourselves to the unholy work, who are the guilty parties. You prate about your loyalty. I look you in the eye and denounce you morally- and legally-perjured traitors. Ye hypocrites! Ye whited sepulchres! Ye mean in your hearts to deceive him and buy up the Negro vote for your own benefit!"

Now a roar of protest ushered forth from the Radicals on the floor—and the Senate and their supporters in the galleries—and they begin to climb to their feet and pour out of the House chamber, hurling epithets at Hill even as they evacuated, his eyes trailing them and the volume and fury of his voice growing all the while and drowning out their own.

"Go on confiscating," he boomed at their backs. "Arrest without warrant or probable cause; destroy habeas corpus; deny trial by jury; abrogate state governments; defile your own race. On, on with your work of ruin, you hell-born rioters in sacred things. But remember that for all these things the people will call you to judgment."

Now he began to pace back and forth across the front of the chamber, his bellowing voice echoing through the cavernous room as he railed at the still-diminishing section of Republicans, at those who remained, at the door through which the retreaters continued to shuttle, at the galleries he had cowed into silence.

"Ah, what an issue you have made for yourselves. Succeed, and you destroy the Constitution; fail, and you have covered the land with mourning. Succeed, and you bring ruin on yourselves and all the country; fail, and you bring infamy upon yourselves and all your followers. Succeed, and you are the perjured assassins of liberty; fail, and you are defeated, despised traitors forever."

Again he turned on Marley, in the heart of the Radical section, and whom empty desks now surrounded. "You aspire to be Radical governors and judges. I paint before you this day your destiny. You are but cowards and knaves, and the time will come when you will call upon the rocks and mountains to fall on you and the darkness to hide you from an outraged people."

He looked again up at the galleries. "And my Negro friends, they tell you they are your friends—it is false. They tell you they set you free—it is false. These vile creatures never went with the army except to steal spoons, jewelry, and gold watches. They are too low to be brave. They are dirty spawn, cast out from decent society, who go South seeking to use you to further their own base purposes. Improve yourselves; learn to read and write; be industrious; lay up your means; acquire homes; live in peace with your neighbors; drive off as you would a serpent the miserable dirty adventurers who come among you and seek to foment among you hatred of the decent portion of the white race."

He turned back to the floor, his voice reverberating from front to back, ceiling to floor. "Military occupation and authority over the Southern states led to the ultimate but complete change of all American government from the principle of consent to the rule of force and to a war of races. When Thaddeus Stevens admitted his disdain for the Constitution, he substituted the *semblance* of consent by disfranchising intelligence, by military rule, by threats and bribery. Yes, the Negro race, duped by emissaries and aided by deserters, is to give consent for the white race.

"All the guarantees of liberty wrung through the centuries from the hands of despotism are abrogated and withdrawn from ten million people of all colors, sexes, and classes, who live in ten unheard and excluded states; and that, too, by men who do not live in these states, who never think of them but to hate, never enter them but to insult."

He urged the Southern states to reenter the Union, no matter how distasteful, no matter the amount of injustice they felt, because they at least had a fighting chance with the Constitution in their hands. Delay of judicial justice, perhaps, he admitted. Danger of property confiscation, yes.

"After all, those who outlaw patriotism and intelligence would not scruple to rob." He fixed his gaze again on Marley. "The same train brings the bread to feed, the officer to oppress, the emissary to breed strife and to rob."

He thundered against the Radicals' bills that placed demands on the South not required during the war or even at surrender, then asked, "And what is the purpose of universal suffrage, of letting all the races vote—in the Southern states only I might note, not the Northern? To secure these ten states to keep the Radical party in power in the next presidential election, to retain by force and fraud the power they are losing in the detection of their treason in the North. Thus they annul the Constitution in the name of loyalty; exterminate the black race in the name of philanthropy; disfranchise the white race in the name of equality; pull down all the defenses of life and prosperity in the name of liberty; and with blasphemous hosannas to the Union, they are rushing all sections and all races into wild chaotic anarchy; and all that traitors may hold the power they desecrate and riot in the wreck of the prosperity they destroy."

Standing directly before the speaker's desk, he looked out on the chambers, but his gaze now seemed to travel beyond the battalion of empty congressional desks, above even the half-empty galleries.

"Go on and pass your qualifying acts, trample upon the Constitution you have sworn to support; abnegate the pledges of your fathers; incite raids upon our people; and multiply your infidelities until they shall be like the stars of heaven and the sands of the seashore, without number; but know this: for all your iniquities the South will never again seek a remedy in the madness of another secession. We are here. We are in the house of our fathers. Our brothers are our companions, and we are home to stay, thank God."

For the first time he fixed his gaze on the small cluster of Southern Democrats. "Still, there is not a single Southern man who advocates the acceptance of this Reconstruction scheme who was not bought and bought with a price by your enemies. And to my fellow Southerners I offer this exhortation: Never, never suffer a single native renegade who voted for the vassalage of these states and the disgrace of your children to darken your doors or to speak to any member of your family."

With this, his face glowing and fevered; he folded himself back into his seat.

Besides the Democratic minority, only a few, mostly moderate, Republicans remained in the room. Most of these joined the Democrats in a spontaneous, two-minute ovation of ear-rattling vigor.

Marley did not rise or respond in any way. But he cogitated over what he had just heard. When Colfax, smiling not at all, called a recess for lunch, Marley made his way to Hill.

"Why did you—why have you always imparted your hatred toward me?" Marley asked. "Is it because you believe me to be the worst of all my fellows?"

Hill's eyebrows climbed up his high broad perspiring forehead just a bit, and he shook his head. "Never has it been hatred for you or any of your fellows," he said, "but it has been hatred for the injustice and evil you have unleashed." His eyes narrowed a bit and he added, "And it is you at whom I have stared not because you are the worst of them all but because you are the best."

So stunned was Marley that he could say nothing, even when Hill was called away by Democratic comrades. But he knew, suddenly, what he must do. He had thought to do it for a very long time, even before she died.

I will go where I should have gone long ago, even as I championed the laws that changed their lives, he thought. *It is a land of very many ghosts for me, of deep rivers and dark memories, but I will go. I will go back to Lexington. I will go to Valiant.*

CHAPTER 74

ROBERT E. LEE AND HIS DAUGHTER AGNES SET OUT ACROSS THE South on a quest for rest and solitude.

They did not find it at first, as the carriage he had recently bought Mary passed droves of his students on their way to meet the canal boat at the wharf on the North River. Those on foot tipped their hats, as did the hundreds more who waved farewell to him at the landing.

In Richmond, Lee chanced into John Singleton Mosby, the Gray Ghost. They engaged in a warm visit, which included no reference to the war. Then Mosby brought George Pickett to Lee's hotel room.

Lee knew not what to say to this tragic figure, whose command he had sent up Cemetery Ridge and whom he had sacked after the disaster at Five Forks.

Pickett felt no more comfortable than Lee, and within minutes, after the passing of but scant conversation, Mosby mercifully ended the ordeal for all three men, rising to leave.

The two younger men, possessed of their own renown but Pickett now a broke—and broken—man and Mosby a successful lawyer, returned down the hall. "That old man," Pickett inveighed bitterly, noting as had Mosby, Lee's pale, sickly countenance, "he had my division massacred at Gettysburg."

"Well, it made you immortal," replied Mosby.

Lee and Agnes rode for the first time in a Pullman sleeping car as their train churned down into North Carolina, where less than 10 percent of the Confederacy's soldiers had done 25 percent of all their dying. When hundreds of people roared "Lee! Lee! Lee!" as the train pulled into Raleigh in the middle of the night, Lee began to wonder if his travels would prove as restful as he had planned.

Through Salisbury, Charlotte, and into South Carolina, which had lost one half its entire property value in the war and through which Sherman cut a forty-mile-wide clean swath of destruction. On into Georgia, as the crowds grew ever more enormous, the bands larger and louder, the disciplined ranks of Confederate veterans longer. Mayors and governors declared holidays and civic leaders closed stores. In one town Federal soldiers riding the train sent a basket overflowing with fruit to Lee.

In Savannah he visited with Joe Johnston; in Portsmouth, Walter Taylor; and in Columbia, Porter Alexander, whose plan at war's end to instigate guerilla carnage against the Federals Lee had quashed—and whose little daughter, born the next year, Lee gathered up into his arms and kissed.

And in Savannah, he and Agnes visited with members of the Mackay family, though Eliza and her husband and even their daughter had all passed away.

"She was very beautiful," Agnes said during one brief interlude as she and her father found themselves alone next to an old photograph of Eliza.

"Yes, she was," Lee said. He looked at Agnes and said, his eyes sparkling, "and her husband, Jack, all the way back to West Point, was one of the best friends I ever had."

Time and again the train stopped, and crowds larger than the population of the town called as one for him to make an appearance on the platform.

"Why should they care to see me?" he would ask her without jest as he rose, sometimes sleepy, sometimes his Bible in his lap, always in pain. "I am only a poor old Confederate."

After several such episodes, she marveled to herself, *He truly does not understand it.*

How happy she was when, after twenty-four straight hours on the train, they arrived in Augusta.

"Now we shall have a whole day and night to rest," Lee, his own face ashen and drawn with exhaustion, comforted her, patting a gentle hand on her back.

But Augusta would not have it.

Can this many folks live in all of Augusta? Agnes wondered as the people passed in line to shake the hand of General Lee.

It took four hours for them to pass. So many were the bouquets of japonica given him by little girls that, when they filled the room, the overflow covered a wagon, which Lee requested to deliver them to the grave markers of Confederate veterans.

Crippled soldiers on crutches, black servants, common laborers and farmers, and the sweetest little children dressed to their eyes, Agnes thought as the procession streamed past. *It is the people who have come—nothing more, nothing less.*

She started to note how many of the smallest children, little able or unable to speak, presented her father tiny cards *with their fat little hands.* A while later, she began to shuffle through the cards, a couple hundred of them. Startled, she realized, *Nearly as many of the little boys are named Robert E. Lee as all the other Christian names combined.*

One thirteen-year-old boy came unescorted to that hotel room and maneuvered his way right up to Lee.

"Hello, young man," Lee said, looking down with a respectful nod of his leonine head. The youngster could not speak a word and only stood staring with an awe he would remember but not again experience through the half-century he had yet to live.

That boy was Woodrow Wilson.

Agnes placed flowers on "Light-Horse" Harry Lee's grave on Cumberland Island, then they took a steamboat into Jacksonville.

More men and boys went for Confederate soldiers from Florida than the state had registered voters.

Agnes watched as another huge, noisy crowd—*One of the largest yet, I suspect*—flooded onto the steamer. Finally it would hold no one else, and the city leaders, several of them former high-ranking Confederate officers, urged Lee out onto the deck to see the even larger portion of the assembly that remained on shore as one of the largest bands Agnes had ever seen bellowed out "Dixie," "The Bonnie Blue Flag," and "The Girl I Left Behind Me."

Thinking, *I had best hold my ears when this group sees him appear,* Agnes was amazed when an abrupt, unorchestrated hush fell over the entire assembly. Even the band music died in midmeasure.

She saw a towering, barrel-chested man wearing an old Confederate jacket and a beard nearly to his midsection remove his hat. The men in gray and butternut on either side of him followed suit. Then so did others around and behind them. Her eyes widened as the act spread like the very rush of the sea over the sands at high tide until, beyond the reach of her sight, every man and boy who came out had removed his hat. For a full thirty seconds, Lee gazed at the crowd and they at him. Before the largest gathering of people in the history of Jacksonville, Agnes could hear the very water of the Saint John's River sloshing against the boat.

"God bless you," he said simply in a choked voice as he stepped back inside the boat.

All these scenes Agnes treasured up in her heart, because somehow she needed to see them, without even realizing she did, needed to know whether something good had been won for all the horror and loss. She felt not a participant at all during these events, but a spectator, for whom a curtain was being drawn back with tempting deliberation, that her full attention might be won before completion of the revelation.

These things she pondered even as she rode alone with her father in a friend's carriage through a tranquil forest of sun-washed cedars to a fragrant forgotten cemetery nestled in the safe spring embrace of emerald North Carolina hills.

How much of all of us she still is, Agnes realized, emotion rising in her. Nearly eight years had passed since Annie Carter Lee, the best friend she would ever have, died far from home during a war that separated her from her entire family. *Only twenty-three,* Agnes thought, tears beginning to form despite her efforts to the contrary.

They stepped out of the carriage and walked to the twelve-foot-tall granite obelisk that ladies of the area, most of them widowed and all of them poor, had sacrificed to have built for Annie in 1866. The Federals told Lee at the time he could not attend the ceremony because his parole did not then allow him to leave Virginia.

Lee had never before set foot in Annie's cemetery.

Holding his hat in his hands, he stood staring at the column as Agnes knelt and laid a wreath of white hyacinths at its foot. She stepped to him, and he wrapped an arm around her shoulder as the thoughts and the memories and the years embraced them.

After some moments he said, "She was the purest and the best of us all."

Agnes swallowed hard, thinking, *Yes, and the smartest and the sweetest and even though she lost the eye in the accident when she was little, if she would ever have let anyone take her picture, they would all know she was the most beautiful of all of us too. I have needed her so much these last many years, and I would have been so much better a person had I had either her or—just one of them, if I could just have had one of them.*

Somewhere nearby, a couple of birds sang the ancient lullabies of spring to one another, and father and daughter were alike impressed, though neither spoke of it, at how splendid a resting place it was for gentle Annie's body, until its reunion in perfected state with her glorified soul on that day of days when He returned.

A flurry of motion caught their eyes, and they saw a gray bunny hopping among nearby clover, filled with joy at everything about the fresh spring day.

"Oh, Papa," Agnes said, "do you remember when we had to—when we left for—West Point, and Annie wouldn't stop hugging and kissing the bunnies at old Arling—"

Then neither of them could bear it any longer, and they wept into one another's arms for she who was the best of them and for whom they had tried so hard to be good, she who they knew deserved more than any of them not to be the one of the family who had gone so soon, so very soon.

But somehow, minutes later while they still sobbed, without a word Agnes knew this had been a long time coming for them both. And she knew something else besides. *It* is *true,* she thought, looking up at the sky as the two birds followed each other, then at the bunny, who had scampered into a cluster of other bunnies. *It is altogether true—just as he always told me it was true, no matter how bad or mean or low or dreaded anything ever was or ever will be. Thank Thee, oh Father God, that it is all true, because Thou hast shown me in these days that nothing can kill love, no matter how long and how fiercely the storms rage. For I have seen their love; the beaten and beaten-down people have not lost their love, I have seen with my own eyes these last days!*

And even as we stand here now weeping tears of grief for ourselves—not for her, for she is free. . . . Thou wast altogether right, great Lord, to take her home first, for she most deserved Thy presence, and so kind and blessed Thou did form her that her work continues on after her more so than could have any of ours. Why it continues on even this very moment, for my dear Annie's love and my papa who holds me even now after all that has happened, their love has conquered all. And Thou Lord, are love, so I am not scared any longer—and that is what it has been these long years, not truly anger or even grief, but I have been afraid, like a little girl lost in the woods. I know now Thou cannot be defeated or destroyed, even by the greatest legions of hell or earth! Oh, thank God!

At the end both their tears ran with gratitude as having flowed through a cleansing fountain that had washed clean all the sorrow and dirt and hate of their poor, weak, untidy souls.

And it is a fountain filled with blood, she remembered, her heart swelling with thanksgiving until she feared it might burst, as she and her father read the inscription carved into the granite marker, the inscription she remembered came from one of Annie Carter Lee's favorite hymns, the one she sang to her little sister Agnes when she helped nurse her through measles, roseola, and chicken pox.

> Perfect and true are all His ways
>   Whom heaven adores and earth obeys.

CHAPTER 75

THE DAY LEE RETURNED TO LEXINGTON, HE READ A MEMORANDUM from the Washington College board. Cognizant of his growing concern for Mary's provision and care after his death, they told him the president's house would be hers, along with several thousand dollars annual income, for as long as she lived.

He bowed his head, not comprehending how they should treat so grievous a sinner as he with such generosity. He pulled out a sheet of paper and a pen, dipped it in ink, and wrote to them, "I am unwilling that my family should be a tax to the college but desire that all of its funds should be devoted to the purposes of education. I know that my wishes on the subject are equally shared by my wife."

They had never disputed Lee's wishes in any matter since his arrival in Lexington. Until now. Without pursuing the matter, they left the resolution in place.

Buoyed by the warmth of late spring and early summer, he resumed the rides with Traveller he so revered but had been unable to continue through the past winter.

"My, look how the violets and heartsease have turned out for us, good friend," he said, patting the prancing horse's neck. Soon he came across a couple of admiring ladies at a front gate who beseeched him to behold the infant son of one of them.

Feeling game as Traveller, Lee tickled the gray with his spur on the side away from the ladies, even as his gloved hands restrained the horse with the reins, so as to display his prowess with the pawing, rearing animal.

"My, my, General Lee, you still have your way with horses," one of the women cooed, much to his delight.

Doffing his hat as he rode away, the other woman called after him, "What words would you offer my son that he might grow to be a true man, General Lee?"

"Teach him he must deny himself."

As the summer of 1870 advanced, Lee journeyed to northern Virginia and Maryland to raise funds for the proposed Valley Railroad whose tracks would stretch to Lexington. He began to work toward establishment of an astronomical observation site for Virginia, hopefully near the college and in affiliation with it. He traveled northwest to the Hot Springs resort to receive water treatments, which rendered him no noticeable health benefits.

He also continued his five-year-long presidency of the Rockbridge County Bible Society. One of that organization's board members, expressing fear to Lee that his ongoing leadership posed an unmanageable burden on him with his growing responsibilities at the college and his declining health, drew the response of, "I wish to cooperate in any way I can in extending the inestimable knowledge of the Bible's priceless truths."

From Hot Springs he wrote Markie with regret at the end of August not to join him there as she wished. "It is 'late' for you to come here Markie, for I am just going away. . . . I wish that you had been with me, Markie. I should have done better."

She was frightened about the return of her nephew Edward Childe and his wife to their home in Paris, amid the Franco-Prussian War, from an American visit. "Their letters report them safe in the vicinity of Paris," he wrote. "They were at Ems when the war burst out and had to flee."

"No, I am not glad that the Prussians are succeeding in their war against France," he answered to her inquiry. He thought about what he knew was happening and what he knew too well it always meant to the people to whom it was happening.

"The Prussians are prompted by ambition and a thirst for power," he wrote. "The French are defending their homes and country. May God help the suffering and avert misery from the poor."

It was the last letter he ever wrote her.

●◇ ●◇ ●◇

Autumn returned and with it his sixth year at Washington College—and more rides with Traveller. One September afternoon he happened across the little daughters of two of his school's professors, hunched together atop the same shuffling ancient horse.

"Good day, ladies," he said, tipping his hat in respect.

Their eyes stretching wide under their sunbonnets, they said as one, "General Lee!"

Noting one of the girls had a cloth tied around her head and face, he asked what was the matter with her.

"Why, I am recovering from the mumps, sir," she said, in a voice that reminded him of his own daughters when they were little girls and sick.

His face screwed up in mock horror.

"The mumps?" he cringed. "Oh, no. I hope you won't give Traveller the mumps!"

The little girls drew back in surprise, looked at each other, back at him, then exploded in laughter.

"But," he protested, "what shall I do if Traveller gets the mumps?"

They laughed the more.

"I surmise then, the best we can do for poor Traveller in his current state of danger, is to get him away from these stifling back streets and out beyond the fairgrounds, where we might gather him some fresh air—and a good view of the Blue Ridge."

This time when the little girls looked at each other, he feared the cloth might pop off the one with mumps. They turned to him and shouted, again as one, "Oh, yes, please!"

Off the little troop went, all three chattering like magpies. And back they came an hour later, the little girls giggling and Traveller nickering and prancing. Lee deposited them at their homes, helping them to dismount but demanding a kiss from each for the service.

As he rode away, he heard the little girl with mumps exclaim, "We have heard of God, Mama, but there is General Lee!"

A gloomy pall came over him as he remembered one of the girls had lost two brothers in the war. Nearly overcome, he thought, *I fear we are destined to kill and slaughter one another for ages to come.* Then he looked back at his little friends and thought, *Perhaps, if we give ourselves to being what we should be and raising them as we should, they might do better than have we. Perhaps they will learn from our mistakes and build on our good, founded and strengthened by the love of Christ.* Feeling hope cascading over him, he drank in the fragrance that was Virginia at harvest time.

Indeed, he thought, *the march of Providence is so slow and our desires so impatient; the work of progress so immense and our means of aiding it so feeble;*

the life of humanity is so long, that of the individual so brief, that we often see only the ebb of the advancing wave and are discouraged. He pondered all this for some moments, then nodded his head as he saw Pastor Jones and his fine young son. *Just as the dominant party cannot reign forever, and truth and justice will at last prevail, in a larger way it is history that teaches us to hope.*

When he reached home, Agnes rushed out to tell him another little girl lay near death in her bed and called for him by name.

"But who is it, Wiggie?" he asked.

"It is little Grace," she said.

A chill racing down his spine, he turned Traveller without another word and cantered away. Halfway down the street he reined the horse in, turned him, and rushed back home. Saying nothing, he dismounted, hurried past Agnes into the house, and emerged a moment later, something now bulging from his coat pocket.

"She is very ill, General Lee," Susan Morrow said as she let him in the darkened house, which smelled of medicine and liniment. "She has always been so—so *feeling* a girl," she continued, her eyes filling with tears and her voice cracking. "It seems as though she has almost given up."

This mother has not slept in a long time, Lee realized in assaying her lined face and red eyes.

"Perhaps I should return at a later—" he began.

"No," she said, touching his arm then drawing back, embarrassed at having done so. "It is you for whom she has called, General. She thinks ever so highly of you, sir."

Lee blushed at this revelation.

A moment later he entered the dark chamber where lay tiny, emaciated little Grace, her usually lustrous tawny hair spread under her like a fan and dull as the eyes he had so often seen flash. When she saw him, her ashen face flickered like the orange embers of a campfire seizing on a night breeze for one final attempt at life.

"My dear lady Grace," he said, sitting on a chair at her bedside. She tried to speak, but the words just rattled around inside her throat. "That's all right," he whispered, smiling, "you needn't speak. Your eyes tell me what you are thinking." Her eyes told him she marveled at this disclosure. "Besides, I have brought someone else who knows what you think and how you feel without your speaking."

Her eyes opened in query, then glinted with joy as he produced from his coat pocket the distinguished man who was his pen wipe and placed it in her hands. She held it to her, clutching it, her eyes closed. When she opened them, tears filled them even as a smile covered her face. Again she tried to speak, until he patted her shoulder.

"Remember, I can understand your thoughts by looking in your eyes, Miss Grace," he said. "And so can Mr. Pennypacker, distinguished Englishman that he is."

Her eyes widened as she looked at the pen wipe.

"Now," he said, pulling the ancient little Bible from his pocket, laying it on the bed next to her, and reading aloud to her from the Old Testament Book of Daniel the story of how God rescued the faithful young Jewish boys Shadrach, Meshach, and Abednego from the flames of the Babylonian king's fire.

"Do you remember who was the fourth man the king saw walking in the fire?" Lee asked her.

She nodded and mouthed the word "Je-sus."

He smiled and said, "That's right, sweet Grace. And do you know that whatever fire through which God calls you to walk, if you believe in Jesus He is right there with you as well?"

He saw through the multiplied tears in her eyes the question he knew she had never asked her mother or, he believed, anyone else.

"But he *was* with your daddy, dear little Grace, through whatever fire he walked, because your daddy was a courageous Christian man who gave everything he had, even his very life, to protect those, like you, whom he loved. Your daddy left you an honorable name that will be with you all your days on earth and beyond, and which you will pass on to your children." He patted her tiny hand, which clutched Mr. Pennypacker. "Did you know that God saw fit to take my daddy home early too, darling? But how much happier they both are now because they trusted in Jesus. And did you know the Bible promises both you and me that God Himself will be the father to us who are fatherless?"

So moved was she at these words, he feared she might burst into sobs. Instead she surprised him, as she so often did, and said, with perfect clarity, a smile beaming across her face like sunrise atop the Peaks of Otter, "I am not afraid any more to die, General Lee."

Now it was he who feared he might weep.

He reached over and hugged her tiny, fevered body, feeling one of her little hands patting him. *How much more they teach us than ever we teach them,* he thought to himself.

When he reached the door of the room a moment later, she said, her voice stronger, "Pastor White at our Presbyterian church says my daddy was as brave as any man he ever knew, and he even knew Stonewall Jackson."

Lee's throat grew very tight, and he looked down at the floor, then back at Grace and said, "The brave beget the brave."

The next morning dawned damp and gray. It was September 28, 1870, the day on which began what history would call the Great Storm of the Upper Shenandoah Valley.

Mary had not slept well in her chambers. Wheeling herself out into the hall before 5 A.M., she was surprised to see Lee already dressed and about. *He has been up for quite some time,* she thought.

"Father, let me see your hands," she said as he came to her and kissed her good morning. "Don't retreat, let me see them." Examining them in the dim light emanating from the lamp in her room, she said, "Just as I suspected, Robert Lee."

Blushing, he shifted his feet.

"Oh, I've known what you were up to for a long time, husband," Mary said. Rolling herself past him, she said over her shoulder, "Whatever would all our male guests these past years think if they knew who blacked the boots they left outside their doors for our nonexistent servants?"

Elijah Sledge found few friends in Raleigh.

Conservative white Democrats were in the process of taking back control of the state government. The last sort of person they desired for that task was a black Union League Republican bluecoat sponsored by the now-impeached Governor Holden and commanded by George Kirk on his thundering trail of terror through the Old North State.

The white Republicans—carpetbaggers and scalawags alike—scrambled for their own political lives. They sought to convince white voters of their good intentions while they clung to the support of the newly franchised blacks who had voted them to office. At the same time they tried to combat efforts of the post-Forrest Klan-type groups to intimidate blacks from voting Republican. Many of those same blacks had previously intimidated others of their race who wished to vote Democratic.

These carpetbaggers and scalawags, without influence from Holden or the now-besieged Senator Pool, had no use for a man whose recent past could be emblazoned from one end of the state to the other by Democrats as a case study of why Republican rule must end.

And rather than finding a groundswell of support from fellow blacks wishing him to work for their well-being, Sledge found them either disinterested in him and his plans or outright threatened that he, in many of their eyes an opportunistic interloper, might abscond with some of their own hard-earned spoils and influence.

When word reached him a Federal warrant was out for his arrest because of his role in the Kirk rampage, he knew his dreams were finished in Raleigh.

So he now rode north into Virginia, then Rockbridge County.

I will have me part of that Valiant I helped to build even as it repaid me with the cruel sting of its lash, he thought. Noting with dismay the approach from the opposite direction of one bodacious storm, he grew bitter and dejected at the bad hands fate continued to deal the black man who tried to make something of himself.

I will have it, and I will use these pistols if necessary to get it.

Morning had come, but layer on layer of charcoal gray clouds hid the sun when Pastor Jones arrived at the Washington College president's house. He brought an esteemed, much older Southern clergyman comrade visiting him from out of town. The man was awestruck that Jones, in his early thirties, had not only been a trusted chaplain of General Lee during the war but was now a familiar friend.

Lee stood on his front porch talking with a rather shabbily dressed man and did not at first see Jones and his visitor. Jones halted some distance from the porch so as not to intrude. The slovenly man spoke, but Jones could not hear him. He could hear Lee's animated response.

"Yes, I prefer the Bible to any other book. There are many things in the old Book that I may never be able to explain, but I accept it as the infallible Word of God and receive its teachings as inspired by the Holy Ghost."

The other man nodded as Lee patted him on the shoulder. Then the man indicated a fistful of paper money and said, "Thank you, General Lee, for your kindness and generosity, sir. I will indeed put this money to good use." Only then did Lee see Jones and the other pastor.

A moment later, as Lee and the two clergymen watched the previous guest depart on foot, Jones asked who the man was.

"One of our old soldiers," Lee said.

Jones nodded, smiling to the elder clergyman, whose expression acknowledged his pleasure at seeing this latest example of the love and loyalty Jones had taught him bonded Lee and the men of the Army of Northern Virginia.

"To whose command did he belong?" Jones asked.

"Oh," said Lee, "he was one of those who fought against us. But we are all one now and must make no difference in our treatment of them."

Pastor J. William Jones would one day record this incident for the world with the many others, but just now he and his colleague experienced a rare instance when neither one of them could imagine the slightest thing to say.

Despite his surprise, the visiting pastor still supposed he had found a supportive ear when he launched into a long-suppressed tirade against the Federal government and its actions against the South, particularly those since the war for Southern independence had ended.

Lee did not respond to the outburst. Later, as he escorted the pastors to the door upon their leave-taking, he said, with gravity and respect, "Doctor, there is a good book that I read and you preach from, which says, 'Love your enemies, bless them that curse you, do good to them that hate you, and pray for them which despitefully use you and persecute you.'" He paused an instant, not wishing to sound harsh. "Do you think your remarks were quite in the spirit of that teaching?"

Lee could not ascertain whether it was horror or just plain embarrassment that covered over the face of this venerated man of God.

"How foolish I feel," the man said, staring at the floor. "I have had occasion to travel through the South somewhat since the war, and everywhere I have witnessed the suffering of the people, black and white. I have restrained my tongue from the people, not wishing to further inflame them. With you, sir, I selfishly sought to appease my own anger and bitterness."

"I fought against the people of the North because I believed they were seeking to wrest dearest rights from the South," Lee said. "But I have never cherished toward them bitter or vindictive feelings and have never seen the day when I did not pray for them."

Straightening himself, appearing the happier for the reproof, Jones thought, the elder pastor shook Lee's hand and said, "I ask your forgiveness for my poor example, sir, even as I offer to you my thanks for your own, far superior, one."

Taking the man's hand, Lee said, "No forgiveness is needed, dear pastor, certainly not from one who needs the forgiveness of God and man alike every day of his life."

Before he left his office that morning, he wrote to a friend, "I am much better. . . . My pains are less and my strength greater. In fact I suppose I am as well as I will be." For weeks, he and Traveller had walked, cantered, and galloped about the area nearly every day.

Now came the Great Storm, as the darkening blanket of clouds fell till it looked to swallow up Lexington but instead unleashed torrents of cold rain that lashed all of Rockbridge County hour after miserable hour.

Lee arrived home soaked to the bone and took his usual modest lunch. Then he retired to his favorite armchair, where the open fireplace across the room warmed him. He considered taking up the book through which he had read halfway, *Our Children in Heaven.* However, the pattering of the rain against the bay window, the melancholy view through it of the hazy mountains to the west, and Agnes's rubbing and tickling of his hands rendered him fast asleep within minutes.

Through the curtain-parted opening to the parlor, Mildred's fingers played the great German Jewish Christian Felix Mendelssohn's "Songs without Words."

Lee did not enjoy vestry meetings, and never had he relished one less than on this day. The weather still deteriorating, he rose from his chair to leave for Grace Church.

"Please stay home from this meeting, Papa," Mary urged, wheeling into sight from her room.

"It is a most important meeting, Mary," he said. "How can it not be when one item is the vestry's desire to build a new church and the other is the issue of not even being able to afford a living wage for the pastor? And I am the chairman of the church finance committee."

Her eyes searched his, then she said, retreating to a secondary line of approach, "Then do please take this umbrella, Papa."

He shook his head at that too. He had not carried or used an umbrella during the war because his men did not have them, and he could never bring himself to do so after the war.

His only concession was to don his old Confederate military cape.

Mildred still played Mendelssohn on the parlor piano, but now it was the "Funeral March."

"Life, that is a doleful piece you are playing!" he said. Then he bent down, touched her shoulder and kissed her gently on the cheek. "I wish I did not have to go and listen to all that powwow."

Outside a stiff wind blew the chill rain every which way, soaking him again long before he arrived down the hill at Grace Church, his breath coming in gusts.

The small, worn-down church, still marred by Yankee depredations during the war, could accommodate the vestrymen only in the pews of its sanctuary, cold, damp, and dim as they were. This situation launched a long, desultory discussion related to the proposed new church. Pendleton, who absented himself from the meeting because of the pending discussion on his salary, left for the vestrymen a document chronicling the "wide outpouring of the Spirit" that had led to ever-growing numbers of V.M.I. and Washington College students attending Grace Church for Pendleton's teaching and preaching.

A plain structure for the Sunday schooling and Bible instruction of the collegians, as well as the children of medium and young age, could be constructed for twelve hundred dollars, Pendleton said.

As was his way, Lee never spoke until everyone else had a chance to say their piece, and then his words were diplomatic and void of rancor, even when opinionated. He concurred in the amount the vestry would put forth for the new building and in the approval of Pendleton's request that he undertake a tour through Virginia and other states to raise the additional amount.

Then came the discussion of his old friend's salary. After all had their say, they looked at Lee. Mildred's faithful suitor, Dr. Barton—sitting near Lee's other physician, Dr. R. L. Madison—noticed that despite the plunging temperature in the sanctuary as the hour neared seven o'clock, Lee's face appeared flushed and hot, and he exhausted, though he maintained his patient demeanor.

"We are more than two hundred dollars in arrears in the payment of Dr. Pendleton's salary," Lee said. "And that salary itself, one thousand dollars annually, is, all would agree, inadequate for a man of his qualifications, abilities, and devotion, and with his responsibilities." Lee paused. "As his memorandum indicates, he offers his resignation, to take effect at the end of a year, should we believe that a younger or a different pastor could better serve us."

Beginning with Lee, every man present vouchsafed an additional monthly commitment, each man in the quietness of his own heart beseeching God to aid them in a provision, in light of their own mean circumstances, so utterly impossible through human means.

When all had spoken and done all they could do, the sum remained the significant amount of fifty-five dollars short. That figure surpassed the amount any man present had been able to commit this dark and dreary day, even for the entire year. The only sound was the rain battering the thin church roof, then draining into buckets placed all over the sanctuary under spots where the roof leaked and could not be repaired.

Lee stared around at the men. Some lowered their heads. Tears filled the eyes of others. *Good, faithful men who love their good, faithful pastor,* he thought, noticing for the first time as his throat grew tight, that it hurt. *Fifty-five dollars. How steep a hill it now is. Before the war, they could easily have . . .* Then he remembered the deep waters through which God had called William Nelson Pendleton. The loss of his brilliant and beloved son, Sandie, Stonewall Jackson's chief of staff, at age twenty-three; the loss only last month of his treasured son-in-law; the sacrifice of fully a third of the male sheep of his church flock by the war; the vandalism and damage to his church; his own jailing by those people for his defiance of their interference in Grace Church's prayers and worship; even now his wife's separation from him as she tended to their invalid daughter.

Yet he has remained faithful through it all, Lee thought, looking up at the tumbledown roof. *Never seeking greener fields, faithful, always faithful, even through his own suffering, misery, and poverty, to the sheep on this distant mountain in this remote valley with whom the Almighty has entrusted him. Always worrying about the next man's suffering, the next woman's loss.*

Even as the heart of every man in the room sank at the recognition and humiliation of not being able to pay their own beloved pastor a living wage, Lee cleared his throat.

"I will give that sum," said he.

The others sat in shock, a burst of breath escaping from one man.

"But Gen—" someone started after a few seconds.

"You cannot—"

"I believe that closes the business of this meeting," Lee said. "We are adjourned."

As he started back up the hill, shivering and hurting from the cold and rain, he remembered his own words that, *We must all be content with the bare necessities of life, if we can maintain clean hands and clear consciences.* Then he smiled to himself. *As always, God, if Thou wishes Thy poor servant to have those other forgettable items for which that fifty-five dollars was planned, Thou will find a way!*

Such a comforting thought it was that one's every need was provided for.

Minutes later he trudged up the steps, across the front porch, and through the door into the president's home. He felt flushed in the head, pained in the throat, aching tightness in the chest, cold through the rest of his body, and altogether in a daze. Water spilled off his hat and cape onto the floor as he doffed them in his spartan room. From somewhere far away, he heard Mildred's voice and laughter as she entertained a couple of courters in the parlor.

He walked by rote to the dining room.

"You have kept us waiting a long time," said Mary from the other end of the table, in a voice playful as it was stern. "Where have you been?"

He stood by his chair to say grace as he always did, but he could not think what to say, either to Mary or in thanksgiving to God. He dropped into the seat.

"You seem very tired. Let me pour you out a cup of tea," said Mary. No more levity did Agnes or Custis hear in her voice.

He moved his mouth again as to speak, but no words came. Then he straightened erect in his chair as ever had Stonewall Jackson, even as a settled look of resignation spread across his face.

"Custis Lee," Mary called out, her voice controlled with effort.

"Can I help you in any way, Papa?" Custis asked, knowing that tone in his mother's voice and at Lee's side in an instant. When Lee remained mute and did not turn to his son, Custis rushed from the room, grabbed his hat and coat, told Mildred to go to her father in the dining room, then hurried out into the storm to fetch Doctors Barton and Madison.

Mildred gasped when she saw Lee sitting with head bowed, muttering soft incoherent words. She walked to him, but knew not what to do, as an icy blade pierced her heart.

They laid him on the couch near the bay windows he so loved looking out upon his Virginia. Later Custis and the doctors moved the couch and replaced it with his bed.

"It is a venous congestion of the brain," Dr. Barton told Mary.

Physicians of a later generation would call it a blood clot lodged in the brain.

Barton turned to Mildred, her face ashen. His voice laced with compassion—and many other things like affection, desire, and love—he said, "This, in conjunction with his heart and circulatory problems, has created a state of cerebral exhaustion."

CHAPTER 76

IT RAINED FOURTEEN INCHES IN THIRTY-SIX HOURS. EVERY watercourse of any size near Lexington flooded its banks, every road washed out, all the boats and every bridge washed away. The rampaging current destroyed the new covered bridge over the North River, then it wrecked houses and barns and killed men, cattle, horses, and sheep. It stopped cold all communication from the rest of the world, whether rail, post, telegraph, horseback, stagecoach, even the canal.

In fact the stage that brought Wayne Marley up from Staunton would be the last to enter Rockbridge County for many days, and it arrived, as the apostle Paul would say, "as if by fire."

When two of the vehicle's six horses broke legs and had to be shot as the whole team—and the stagecoach—slid down the muddy, rain-hammered hill north of Lexington, Marley realized with a jolt, *I rode down this same hill when we came into Lexington in 1864.*

The days he spent on the train and stage south from Washington provided him much time to contemplate the many issues on his mind.

As the stage driver and guard put down the two maimed horses, Marley thought back to the last visitor in his office before he departed for Virginia. John Babcock caught Marley as he left the capitol building and persuaded him to return to his office to talk.

Once there, Babcock explained how he had recommended the black man Martin Robinson to find the James River crossing for Ulric Dahlgren during the long-ago Richmond raid. Marley nodded, remembering the name.

"You worked with John McEntee at the Bureau of Military Intelligence," Marley said. "You gained fame as one of Allen Pinkerton's best agents."

Babcock fidgeted at the comment. He fidgeted so long in fact that Marley opened his gold waist-pocket watch and said, "I'm doubtful you could have any new information about the Dahlgren affair that would be of interest to me at this point, Mr. Babcock, and I've a stagecoach to catch."

This spurred Babcock.

"I helped plan the entire Kilpatrick-Dahlgren raid, congressman," he said. "Though I opposed it from the start." This jolted Marley to attention. "They— the government—twisted an honorable mission into something dark and terrible and not in keeping with American or Christian virtues, or even European notions of just warfare."

"But," Marley sputtered, leaning forward, "what of Admiral Dahlgren's—"

"The semi-deranged wishfulness of a good and brave man whose most beloved child his own government sent to a brutal and needless death," Babcock snapped. "Sensible explanations exist for all his accusations. And even if they did not—"

"Yes?"

"Even if they did not, I happen to know that, over my vigorously lodged protests, our government ordered the mendacious plan the Richmond newspapers published. Their accounts were authentic, Congressman Marley."

Marley sank back in his chair. He did not know whether he was glad to finally have his answer or not.

"And . . ." he began, "just who in our government countenanced such infamy?"

"Stanton, who went belatedly last year to what I am quite certain was his just 'reward,'" Babcock said. He knew the question Marley feared to ask even though his face screamed it. "I have no evidence the president knew." Even as Marley exhaled in relief, Babcock added, "But if he did not, he should have— and he should never have had so low a creature as Stanton in so high a post, no matter his abilities." Now bitterness permeated Babcock's voice. "I know the Kilpatrick-Dahlgren raid attained for more radical elements of the Confederacy the sanction they long sought from their government to go after our own president."

Marley's eyes widened at this.

"Certain of them even traveled to Washington City itself in a failed attempt to do harm to President Lincoln," Babcock said. "Whether to kidnap or murder, I cannot say for certain—though I have my suspicions." He read the next question on Marley's face as well. "I do not believe Wilkes Booth's crimes had the sanction or even the knowledge of the Southern government."

Now it was Babcock who leaned forward, his eyes white-hot. "But this much I do believe from my own extensive investigation—it is impossible to say whether Booth would have done what he did had there been no Dahlgren raid; it is impossible as well that he would not have at least tried since there was. And now, as my West Point classmate from Texas liked to say, the horses are out of the barn."

The horses are out of the barn, Marley repeated to himself as the stage pulled into Lexington. *But how far out are they?* he wondered. He pulled out the letter, postmarked in Europe, that arrived from Kurt Schumacher earlier the same afternoon Babcock visited him.

"Even as I remain proud of much of what we accomplished, old friend—preserving the Union, protecting our industries and workers from financial ruin, in the end even ending the blight of slavery, I regret the failure of the Republican form of American government," Schumacher wrote. "I had hoped its countervailing branches of authority and its democratic participation might display for the world a new and better hope for just governance. It is to my everlasting disappointment it has not; the world will instead emulate the parliamentary form employed by the mercantilist British, embracing it as the more stable and ultimately the fairer way. This need not—indeed, it should never—have happened, but what is done is done.

"I returned to the sturdy land of my fathers in quest of a better way," he continued. "Alas, what is bad in America is yet worse in Europe. Aristocratic Prussian militarism, brute German nationalism, and nonorthodox theological innovation hold no joy for me. Thus, sober in more ways than one, I sail back to America next Tuesday for another try at contributing to 'our' becoming a good as well as a great nation. Perhaps having a wonderful wife—of sturdy Saxon stock—will enable me this time to carve out a more successful path.

"Have you convinced that breathtaking Virginia belle to marry you yet, old fellow? If she has a thimbleful of the sense I believe she does, she will say yes. Thank God my lovely and beloved Dresden is, hopefully forever, beyond the reach of armies and governments who war on women and children."

Struck by the harshness of Schumacher's last statement, Marley folded the letter as the stage's remaining horses slipped and slid until the road sludge mired them up to their hocks. At that point the driver advised him and the other passengers to collect what baggage they could carry and make for their destinations on foot.

The government had confiscated Valiant for failure to pay taxes. Marley had used his power to purchase it over the heads of several other Northerners who submitted earlier and, in at least two cases, higher bids. He planned to restore the deed to Mrs. McDowell and provide her a cash account on which to draw at a Lexington bank.

He found her working as a governess for a well-to-do Yankee merchant recently moved to Lexington. At the invitation and with the financial sponsorship of the Brazilian government, Felton had sailed to that South American land to join the growing community known as "the Confederados."

If Rachel Anne McDowell was dead, her mother was a living corpse. She barely reacted when Marley told her of her daughter's death, though he omitted any reference to suicide.

"It was that last day she went to the church," Mrs. McDowell said, staring out at the two-day-old storm. "I finally convinced her to talk with Dr. Pendleton about all that had happened to us." Now tears welled up in her eyes, but neither her expression nor her voice changed. "But just as she tried, the *Yan-kees*—" The venom in the last word sent a shiver down Marley's spine. "—shamed that cute little Culpeper boy, the one Ethan goes squirrel hunting with all the time. And then they dragged Dr. Pendleton off and threw him in jail. Then something just went snap in my baby's little head. She left that night and I never saw her again."

Mrs. McDowell looked Marley in the eye for the first time since his arrival. "Do you know when Ethan and that little Culpeper boy will be home? We've supper waiting on them, but I don't even know when Felton or Horace or my Sam will be here."

Marley caught the sad, tearful shake of the Yankee merchant's wife's head across the room. Then he folded Mrs. McDowell into his arms and hugged her. She did not move or respond then, or anymore. Back outside in the rain, he looked through the window and saw her sitting there still, staring straight ahead.

●◦ ●◦ ●◦

Lee slept for two days. For these, and the days following, as the Great Storm abated and he seemed to grow better, even able to offer one-syllable answers to questions, Mildred remained with him all day and Agnes all night. Everywhere his girls and his wife went in the room, entering it, leaving it, his brown eyes followed them. Whenever Mary rolled in, he acknowledged her presence with a tender look and a silent squeeze of her hand.

After a week Dr. Barton told Mary, "His recovery has not been as rapid as we hoped, but Dr. Madison and I do think now that he will recover."

Mary sighed with audible relief and thought, *God grant they may be right, for how anxious I still feel about him.*

Agnes could see her mother fretting herself. *Sitting in that rolling chair unable to do more than pray and stay by his side,* Agnes thought. Then she saw the silent expressions of deep, ancient love passing between her mother and father as they held hands hour after hour. She smiled and thought, *Perhaps that is enough.*

But then the brief words came fewer. And Lee started refusing medicine from his daughters; he submitted, however, upon his doctors' admonishment.

One morning, as Mildred wheeled Mary toward the dining room, a crash sounded only feet behind them, so loud the shock of it nearly knocked Mary from her rolling chair. She turned and saw that a large portrait of her husband had fallen without provocation from the wall where it hung, ruining the frame.

Were I superstitious, I would feel greatly disturbed by that, Mary thought.

More cause for superstitious concern began that evening, October 7, when Northern Lights, never seen by anyone in Lexington in their lifetime, began to rampage across the sky. The aurora continued three straight nights. Since Lexington was a town descended primarily from the Scots-Irish, the haunting strains of the elegiac old Scottish ballad flew quickly to the lips of many a local.

> All night long the northern streamers
> Shot across the trembling sky:
> Fearful lights, that never beckon
> Save when kings or heroes die.

◆ ◆ ◆

Marley stayed busy for days. As he did, he heard conflicting reports about the condition of Robert E. Lee. One day he would hear the commander was sitting up in bed, eating and conversing merrily; the next day the account would have Lee on death's door. Marley did not inquire. He remained as surreptitious as he could, only a couple of times exchanging greetings with locals who remembered him from before the war.

He rented a carriage and drove out to Valiant. Thrice he bogged down in mud; it took him all day, leaving the roads and cutting across fields to get there. When he did, he shook his head at how what he knew to have been a magnificent plantation now lay derelict, weed-infested, and deserted except for the few ex-slaves attempting to work small portions of the enormous spread.

The house itself sat locked, posted, and defaced.

He went to the bank, the town marshal, the county courthouse.

What do I do with Valiant? he wondered. His inability to restore his beloved's home to her kin was a crushing blow. He opened a cash account for Mrs. McDowell at the bank and notified the woman for whom she worked. That proved fortuitous, as the woman's merchant husband had issued orders for the former matriarch of Valiant to be gone by the end of the week.

"Her performance as governess," the woman took no pleasure in telling Marley, "has proven less than adequate."

Then he found a buyer—another Northern transplant—for the big house at Valiant, the outbuildings, and half the land. *I will place the money in Mrs. McDowell's account,* he decided. And for a fat monthly rental stipend, the Yankee merchant now welcomed Mrs. McDowell's continued presence as a boarder.

Marley continued his travels around the area. Despite the clearing of the weather, the Great Storm had so washed things out he had to walk almost everywhere he went. *There is the V.M.I.,* he thought, *where I received the education that prepared me for service in the United States military and government. . . . There is Stonewall's old place, where I learned of Christian manhood. . . . There is the Presbyterian church, where I learned of God and his Word, his justice, his mercy, and his forgiveness. . . . And there, there is the house where Robert E. Lee . . . Robert E. Lee . . .*

One day he walked up old Honeysuckle Hill where long ago he would take his rifle and pop squirrels, rabbits, and fowl. He found the very spot where he used to perch to gobble down a lunchtime sandwich; he sat looking out over the tree-laced little village.

General Robert E. Lee, he thought. He remembered the final exchange with Babcock, as that brave man rose to leave Marley's office.

"I know not whether this last will interest you, Congressman," Babcock said. "But I learned late in the war from sources of ours in Richmond that one man stood against a chorus of Confederate voices—public, press, and even to the very highest levels of their government—which demanded your execution and that of Ulric Dahlgren's other captured raiders."

"What?" Marley asked, incredulous.

Babcock opened the door to leave.

"Robert E. Lee, my friend," he said. "Jefferson Davis stopped your hanging because Robert E. Lee—alone, and savaged by some in his own government—cried out against it."

Marley sat his spot on Honeysuckle Hill for a very long time as the implications of that revelation reverberated through his head. At length he thought back to those long-ago days here, before the war.

How much of my life was in those ten years I lived among these people. It was the war, he realized. *It was the war that made me hate Tom Jackson. Then, later, even after I quit hating him, a subtle, unconscious hatred of them, of their defiant refusal to quit—to think as I thought,* he admitted in the quiet of his heart—*took hold in me. I lost my love for them and my appreciation for what all they tolerated in me and did for me, and came somehow to scorn, perhaps even to hate them, to hate them all, as I studied my Bible and taught it to others.*

"War," he uttered with loathing. "War!" he shouted down the hill. *How wrong have I been about war, about all our wars! How wrong have we all been!*

Something was in his eye now, making it hard to see the glowing rainbow of color God had splashed over these pleasant vales and meadows and forests. He tried to wipe it out with his sleeve, but it would not go away, even after he decided he would give back all he could to the veterans and the widows of the war from either army, black or white, in plots no more than forty acres each from the unsold half of Valiant, and at a nonnegotiable price of one dollar per acre.

"But, I don't under—" the Northern land agent sputtered later that day.

"And one more thing," Marley said. "No one is to know the source of the land. Some will suspect after my recent errands, but they won't know. The old Rebels would not have it if they knew, and I want them to have a chance at it too. You can tell them it was one of their old Lexington neighbors who wishes to remain anonymous. Don't worry, Mr. Lodge. Since it is priced low, I will pay you beyond the usual percentage fee of the sale."

◆◇ ◆◇ ◆◇

The morning of October 10, Lee perked up at the sound of Traveller nickering in his stall. *He senses weather coming again,* the old general thought, *or*

*perhaps he knows it is the day after the Sabbath and time for us to ride. Poor faith-
ful fellow . . .*

Dr. Madison appeared from nowhere. "How do you feel this morning?" he
asked.

"I . . . feel . . . better," Lee said.

"You must make haste and get well," Madison said. "Traveller has been
standing so long in the stable he needs exercise."

Lee shook his head and closed his eyes. Then, feeling Mildred tickling his
hand, he opened them to see rings under her red eyes and her on the verge of
tears. He pulled her hand to his mouth, kissed it, and with much love said, "Precious . . . ba-by."

She pulled his hand to her own cheek and held it for a long time.

After the afternoon brought new storms of wind and rain, thunder and lightning, clearing the Northern Lights away for good, Agnes, despite little sleep for
three days, was the first to notice the specter of pain covering her father's eyes
and face.

Then his pulse grew erratic and his breathing rushed.

As the evening wore on, Mary noticed something else. *The same look of resignation as that night at the supper table. He does not wish to remain any longer,*
she, who knew her husband in every way, alone realized.

By midnight a chill enveloped Lee, even under all his blankets, the hearth
fire blazing across the room.

"Oh, it seems as though his eyes cry out continually for us to help him, and
I do not know what to do!" Mildred exclaimed to Agnes as thunder crashed
louder than her voice, rain scourged the house, and great gusts of wind caused
the candles and lamps and even the gas mantles to flicker. Mildred looked at her
sister. "What if . . . what if Papa—" Then she burst into tears, and Agnes took
her in her arms.

What if, indeed? Agnes thought. *What if?*

In the deepest watches of the night, with Agnes and Mildred collapsed in
their beds and Custis sitting exhausted by his father's bed, another man stepped
into the dining room. He asked and received Custis's permission to spell him.

*Never was more beautifully displayed how a long and severe education of mind
and character enables the soul to pass with equal step through this supreme ordeal,*
thought the man as he watched the body so besieged by age, disease, pain, and
illness. *Never did the habits and qualities of a lifetime, solemnly gathered into a*

few last sad hours, more grandly maintain themselves amid the gloom and shadow of approaching death. The reticence, the self-contained composure, the obedience to proper authority, the magnanimity and Christian meekness that have marked all his actions, still preserve their sway, in spite of the inroads of disease and the creeping lethargy that weighs down his faculties.

Then Washington College professor and Colonel Sidney Johnston marveled, *As the old hero lies with the lamp and hearth fire casting shadows upon his calm, noble front, all the massive grandeur of his form, face, and brow remain— and death seems to lose its terrors and to borrow a grace and dignity in sublime keeping with the life that is ebbing away.*

Well-suited was Colonel Johnston to observe the trials of the valorous. For he had been sired by General Albert Sidney Johnston of Texas, commander of United States Cavalry against the Plains Indians, martyred commander of Confederate forces at the legendary Battle of Shiloh, devout Christian, and West Point comrade of Lee.

The next morning, after another all-night vigil, tears filled Agnes's eyes as her father again refused to take his medicine.

"Please, Papa, please," she pled.

He gave a slight but determined shake of his head and rasped, "It is no use."

Custis, sitting nearby, said, "But Papa, the doctors believe you will recover."

Lee looked at them, then slowly shook his head back and forth again on the pillow and lifted a hand a few inches to point at the sky.

Ever and ever those glorious dark eyes, Mildred thought as she watched this through bloodshot eyes, *speak with imploring, heartrending tones! Oh, the horror of being helpless when he needs help!*

Agnes's exhausted head dropped, long strands of dark hair hanging in her face. *I must not cry in front of him,* she told herself. *I must go be alone as I always am when I cry.*

That afternoon, as rain beat even more on the bay windows, his breathing grew louder and his pulse quieter as he descended into coma, then delirium.

Tears filled Mary's eyes as her arthritic hands held his moist still one when she heard what it was that claimed his mind and emotions in these dark colossal hours. *It is not Alexandria, not old Arlington, not us,* she grieved. Fighting back hot tears, she thought, *It is I alone who have watched, unbeknown to him, that once-happy face, defiled with sorrow unknown to words, staring out those bay windows at his beloved Virginia. It is I who have seen the lines of heartbreak still etched in his face upon his return from riding in the mountains. Oh, it is that hateful war that has taken him before his time as it has so many others!*

She prayed for a heart of charity and forgiveness, as he had.

When the names and the fights and the orders she knew too well began to pour forth from his comatose form, she thought, *He has wandered once more to those dread battlefields.*

"Tell Hill he must come up!" Lee cried out suddenly.

Oh, he never wished that fight or those battlefields, and he has never been able to come all the way home from them, she thought, bitter regret engulfing her. *Can those lost brave boys and men ever know how much he loved them?*

She leaned forward to him as his words grew unintelligible.

After a pause, he exclaimed, "Strike the tent!"

Those were his last discernible words.

Oh, how scarlet the berries in the hedge and how soft and magical the October sunshine, thought Mildred as the sun climbed radiant against an azure sky the next morning, Wednesday, October 12, 1870.

Nature seemed to grieve with convulsive throbs and now the windows of heaven are opened, thought Mary as she sat in her wheelchair next to Lee's low single bed and next to Rev. Dr. Pendleton, who in a choked voice spoke the prayers for the dying from the Protestant Episcopal Prayer Book.

"O Almighty God," the old artillery chieftain prayed for the man he had loved and revered since boyhood. "We humbly commend the soul of this thy servant, our dear brother—" Pendleton paused, composing himself. "—Robert E. Lee—into thy hands. . . . Wash it, we pray thee, in the blood of that immaculate Lamb, that was slain to take away the sins of the world."

Mildred knelt across the bed from Mary and next to the kneeling Custis, Agnes kneeling on his other side. As Pendleton prayed, she winced at Lee's hard, hurting unconscious breaths.

"That whatsoever defilements it may have contracted," Pendleton concluded, "through the lusts of the flesh or the wiles of Satan, being purged and done away, it may be presented pure and without spot before Thee; through the merits of Jesus Christ thine only Son our Lord. Amen."

Agnes, fighting back tears, moistened her father's lips and fanned his hot head. *How often have those lips kissed away my loneliness and fear,* she thought. *How often has that head spoken words of hope into my hurt and desolation.*

She passed the fan back and forth between her hands until both her arms felt as though they would drop, then she fanned yet more.

Nothing is too good for Robert Lee, she thought each time an arm began to shake.

Around nine, Mildred noticed Lee struggling. She rushed into the parlor and fetched Dr. Madison. The exhausted physician hurried to Lee, looked at him, and without saying a word turned and walked sadly from the room.

A few minutes later, it was over.

"I have never so truly felt the purity of his character as now, when I have nothing left me but its memory," Mary wrote a close friend later that day. As the fragrance of weather more lovely than she had ever seen wafted through her open window, she gazed out at the rosebushes he had taken on himself to plant for her, knowing how she loved her roses.

"God knows the best time for us to leave this world, and we must never question either His love or wisdom. This is my comfort in my great sorrow, to know that had my husband lived a thousand years he could not have died more honored and lamented even had he accomplished all we desired and hoped."

CHAPTER 77

WHEN THE DEVASTATION OF THE GREAT STORM, AND ITS LESSER sequel a few days later, prevented many of the most famous politicians, soldiers, and dignitaries, North and South, from reaching Lexington for Lee's funeral, Agnes fretted at first that God seemed intent on allowing tragic events to continue.

But the next day she looked out the window of her father's plain, white-washed little room and saw who comprised the procession that gathered in front of the Washington College president's house, then proceeded forth through the streets of the quiet mountain village at the top of the Shenandoah Valley. She nodded in remembrance of how always, "God resisteth the proud, but giveth grace unto the humble."

So, perhaps, she thought, *Dr. Dabney was right when he spoke how in the war God used His enemies to chasten His people.*

And even our own dear Rev. Pendleton, she remembered, *who told Mildred and me that one reason supreme wisdom has allowed us to be so overwhelmed may be that we must cease to be such comparative idolaters in our estimate of Virginia and our character and privileges as freemen; that we must be content to live without a country, having our hearts engrossed with that better land where no sin enters and where peace and charity prevail forever.*

"Our Savior and the apostles lived thus under foreign domination," she remembered him saying. "So lived many of the martyrs. And surely we may well follow their example in giving our affections to that better country of which, by God's grace, no earthly malice or power can despoil us."

For there they were, down from the mountains, up from the vales, out from the forests, in from the coves, the remnants of the Army of Northern Virginia, the wonder of the world, with their empty sleeves and eye patches, their scars and crutches, and their peg legs.

She watched as they marched again, once more, this time along the route that a jolly old white-bearded man rode on Christmas Day bearing gifts for all the children of Lexington. They who had been silent and respectful for yesterday's funeral and today's lying in state now began to sing as once they had sung, the song they knew he loved above all others.

And when they began to sing, the others joined them, all together, the Rev. Pendleton himself, and Stonewall's Pastor White, and the Baptist Pastor Jones and his fine young son, and young Francis Brockenbrough and young Todd Chandler, and several of those who long ago had been servants at old Arlington, including ancient "Uncle" Ephraim, who would not leave even after the Lees had and even after the Federals ordered him off.

And the boys of Washington College, and the cadets of the VMI, and Katrina and Jacob Schumacher and their eight children, including the new boy the Lord had given them just last year, and an attractive thirty-two-year-old black mother of four, who looked less than thirty and was now the most respected sewer and garment cleaner in Lexington, not to mention the most faithful attendee at her church.

And old Tom Perry the town jailer, and the lionhearts who had almost shamed themselves and their country by going through him to lynch a worthless horse thief, and Susan Morrow, and even a little girl carrying the most distinguished-looking pen wipe in Lexington, a little girl with hair once again shiny and tawny and her eyes once again flashing and her wide happy smile returned too.

And Wayne Marley and even Elijah Sledge who, finding Valiant in a shambles, and himself hungry, tired, broke, and scared, and about to rob an elderly couple in their home, had heard the singing and been moved to follow it, and then to join the procession when he learned it honored the man in whom, years ago, he had first seen the Jesus he never thought could be true for black folks.

So did these and many more lift once more through the Valley that Lee and Stonewall Jackson before him had grown to love, the old American hymn that had carried Robert Lee through war and peace.

> The soul that on Jesus hath leaned for repose
> I will not, I will not desert to his foes;
> That soul, though all hell should endeavor to shake,
> I'll never, no, never, no, never forsake!

And up on old Huckleberry Hill, where he, too, had long ago popped squirrels and rabbits and fowl, Cole Culpeper sat his Federal mount and listened, bewildered. *Where are the Yankees?* he wondered, expecting them here and expecting his final fight with them. *They musta lit out.* When he recognized the song, he knew it must be for General Lee. Then is when he heard voices calling out from the past, voices the likes of which he had not before heard and which it had taken him so very long to understand: "It was all my fault." "I'll fight for General Lee till the Yankees grind me to dust."

Despite himself, he began to weep loud and hard, trying not to, even angry with himself for doing so, even as he found himself riding down to join them.

Just after he passed the Preston place, he saw a skinny, bent woman standing out in the street, confused at the goings-on. Then she turned and when she saw him, Mrs. McDowell shouted with joy, "Little Cole Culpeper! You boys have finally made it!" And she imposed on him to climb down and to receive her hugs and her kisses.

"Come, Cole, we must go and join them," she said, breathlessly grabbing his hand and tugging him along. "I never thought I could make it, Cole. I just never thought—"

Suddenly, as they rushed down the sloppy street, she looked him in the eye, tears streaming down his face. "Oh, my dear little Cole, you've been through so much, haven't you, darling? Cole, dear—Ethan is never coming back, is he?"

Culpeper could only shake his head as sobs racked him. Then she grabbed his dirty head into her arms and held it. "Oh, it will be all right. I shall be all right—I just needed *someone* to come back to me."

Now Culpeper fell to his knees and grabbed her around her waist, wailing into her chest. "But Mrs. McDowell, none of them are coming back, ever, none of them, and the Yankees even stole our old place. It's gone forever, and they won't even let me back on it to see where Emma and me—"

"Oh, sweet Emma," she soothed him, "she is gone too. I am so sorry, Cole."

"I loved her, Mrs. McDowell. I loved her, and we sinned because none of our folks would let us marry. But she had my little boy and my little girl, and I hardly saw him, and I never even got to see her because I had to go fight the blasted Yankees!"

Waves of grief poured out of him until she thought he would collapse onto the muddy wooden sidewalk.

"Cole," she said calmly. "Look at me, dear." When he did, she said, "Did you know that your Emma joined our Grace Church after you boys left for the war? She got confirmed and read her Bible every day and became quite devout and even happy."

"And look where it got her!" he screamed. "Look where it got her—dead with my babies!"

She clutched his head as he began to sob anew. After a minute her ears perked up.

"Cole, dear boy," she said. "I believe they are coming back around to the church." She pulled him up, grabbed his hand, and began again to lead him along. "Come, we're going to the church, we both need to, to see the Rev. Pendleton."

He had not the strength to resist further, only mumbling, "I sinned way too much . . . way too long . . ." Soon they were at the steps of the little beaten-down church.

As the crowd dispersed, Pendleton happened straight for Culpeper and Mrs. McDowell. As soon as the pastor saw Culpeper, even without his beard, he remembered seeing him before, standing right where he now stood. But this time Pendleton stopped dead in his tracks. *How much he looks like our Sandie,* he thought with a shudder, *an older, sadder Sandie, even the same color hair and eyes. How could I not see it before?*

"Son," Pendleton said, clasping one of Culpeper's arms, "you come home with me for supper."

It would be Pendleton's few dollars—made possible by Lee's fifty-five-dollar pledge, but in the form of a loan only, mind you—that would secure Culpeper the forty acres of Valiant land he had once hunted with Ethan. There he would build a house first for Mrs. McDowell and then, later, one for himself not far away.

He would not again see his own mother, or Mrs. McDowell any of her children, but it might as well have been said of her, regarding Culpeper, "Woman, behold thy son!" And of Culpeper, regarding her, "Behold thy mother!"

And part of old Valiant, at least, would be a happier place than ever Valiant had been before.

Though Sandie was gone, never would the Rev. Pendleton have a more faithful young friend than Cole Culpeper, even in the labor of building the beautiful new R. E. Lee Episcopal Church in Lexington, the only Episcopal church in North America that would ever be named for a man not in the Bible.

This technicality was lost on one young Sunday school lad who years later asked Culpeper and his lovely wife prior to the boy's confirmation, "Deacon and Mrs. Culpeper, was it the Old Testament or the New that General Lee was in?"

Still, Culpeper would often think of the old days and the mighty men of valor with whom he rode and General Lee and Emma and those fields and Emma and that sun and how he had seen it shining off her golden strawberry hair one day near the spring behind the house when she took off her bonnet because a bee had gotten in it.

And half a century later, after he had seen other United States presidents deceive and maneuver the emotions of their trusting people into other bloody wars, even a world war, where always mothers grieved and widows wept and children screamed that Daddy must be coming home, he would still rock out on his porch—Mrs. Culpeper would not let him chew in the house, even though he always swallowed. And not long before it was his time to be laid under the good earth of the Valley, he would muse to himself, *I reckon I come back to a home I always had and was too fool to even know. It's a home what was good enough for Jakie and Ethan boy and Old Jack—and Emma—to give all they had for. Well, they went back to their Valley, and I have come back here too.*

I know now that the Valley ain't who runs roughshod over her or what they do to her in hate. The Valley is who she is and always has been, long before folks set their dirty boots upon her. And there's this too, that God has added a mite more to her now, what with the hearts of the people that love her with the very love she gave to them.

"Captain Sledge?" Marley asked upon stepping up to the still-blue-coated man not far from Grace Church a few minutes after the procession ended.

"Now how did you know that?" Sledge asked, suspicious. "Congressman Marley?"

Marley extended a hand and a smile to allay the surprised awkwardness. "If you know who I am, you should not be surprised that I know who you are."

Sledge's eyes darted away.

"Captain Sledge," Marley said. "I am well aware of who was at fault in the Kirk affair. And I am well aware of your capabilities."

Sledge's eyes checked to vouchsafe that no one stood within earshot before he said, "Then can you tell me how it is I got walled out like a leper in Raleigh and how it is the government has a warrant issued for my arrest?"

"Captain," Marley said, trying to calm him by taking his arm and walking him away from a nearby cluster of people. "What are your prospects, Captain Sledge?"

Sledge sighed. "Right now, all the plans I have are to find a way to get something into my belly without breaking any more laws."

Marley couldn't help a chuckle as he guided the two of them toward his hotel. "Well, I believe I can assist in that matter."

After Sledge completed a meal that well made up for better than a day without food, he shared with Marley his deflated hopes for finding a piece of old Valiant land worth working. Neither man paid heed to the anger of both the waiter and manager over the presence of a black man in the white folks' dining room, and a blue-coated black man at that.

"You don't really want to work the land, do you, Elijah?" Marley said. When no answer appeared forthcoming, he asked, "Would you consider your talents and inclinations perhaps more suited to employment on the staff of a congressman of the majority party, who is a committee vice-chairman and a sub-committee chairman?"

Marley laughed aloud. "Now don't have a stroke on me yet, Elijah, leastwise until we can get some chocolate pie into that skinny frame of yours. I warn you, though; I'm liable to be a might less popular when people around Washington figure out I've had a bit of a change of heart on a few matters."

"Change of heart?" Sledge asked.

"Well, I trust you're about as sobered as I am at this point regarding some of the idiocies of the Radical program?"

Sledge's eyes answered loudly in the affirmative.

"And you should know that my long-range plans don't involve Washington at all, unless you count the countervailing of its influence," Marley said.

"What do you mean?" Sledge asked, shoveling the chocolate pie down as rapidly as possible without embarrassing either of them.

Marley did not answer for a moment. He had as yet told no one of his long-range plans. *But this good man has suffered my examination without complaint. I, a follower of Christ, should be at least as forthcoming, should I not?*

"I've a good friend who has started a Presbyterian church out in the Indian Territory," Marley said, his one eye illumined by an excitement absent from him since the loss of—since she passed away. "He has determined it is high time white Christians set about helping rather than hurting the Indians."

Sledge thought about that as a second piece of pie arrived.

"Well," he said, "I expect I have two problems there, Congressman Marley."

"Oh?"

"Yes, sir."

"What?"

"Having to do with the words *white* and *Christian,*" Sledge said. "Last time I checked, well, I'm afraid I wasn't either one."

Marley smiled and rubbed his ivory-shocked bearded chin. "Elijah, both of those would indeed be matters of God's choosing. But in the latter case, I have noticed He has a distinct habit of utilizing His own people in the process when He gets around to unveiling whom He has chosen."

So He would again. And by the time the Indian Nations became the state of Oklahoma in 1907, many a Cherokee, Chickasaw, Choctaw, Creek, and Seminole would have long forgotten the many terrors of the blue coat for the love and sacrifice of their one-eyed, never-married pastor and the handsome former slave who taught their Christian school.

One winter day when the snow lay thick upon the ground and the flames crackled in the hearth fire, Mary saw Mildred sit at the piano for some minutes, then rise without playing a note.

"Dear Precious Life," Mary said. "How much he loved you."

"Oh, if I'd only known that was the last time I would ever hear him call me Precious Life or hear those firm footsteps, I would have thrown my arms around him and never let him go to that meeting!" Mildred blurted.

Mary paused. When she spoke, the words came slowly. "They speak of his 'untimely death.' We must not deem untimely what God ordains. He knows the best time to take us from this world; and can we question either his love or wisdom? How often are we taken from the evil to come."

Mildred's eyes flashed hot. "To me he seems a hero—and all other men small in comparison."

Her sentiments would not change. She, nor any of her sisters, would ever marry. Nor would Custis, though he would be president for twenty years of the newly named Washington and Lee University.

How many cares and sorrows are spared those who die young, Mary told herself. *Even the heathen considers such the favorites of the gods; and to the Christian what is death but a translation to eternal life? We should pray that we may all live so that death will have no terrors for us.*

She remembered this the next year, when Rooney's baby girl died. And the next, when Rob's new wife passed away.

But it was the fleeting specter of losing Agnes, who always seemed either to be sick or on the verge of sickness, that was too horrible for Mary even to countenance. *Even as Annie was dearest to Robert, so, of them all, is that kindhearted creature Aggie to me,* she thought, her eyes wet, embarrassed even to confess it to herself.

Stonewall's old Pastor White from Lexington Presbyterian Church arrived.

"Your husband told me not long ago with great emotion, his arms upraised, his eyes full of tears," White told Mary, "'If I could only know that all the young men in the college were good Christians, I should have nothing more to desire. I shall be disappointed, I shall fail in the leading object that brought me here, unless these young men become real Christians. I dread the thought of any student going away from college without becoming a sincere Christian.'"

After White left, she opened a letter from Edward Gordon, Lee's former assistant at the college.

"He is an epistle, written of God," Gordon wrote, "and designed by God to teach the people of this country that earthly success is not the criterion of merit or the measure of true greatness."

Ah, something from Markie, Mary saw next.

That cousin, single until age forty-five, had married within months of Lee's death a man who had pursued her affections for years.

In June 1873 came the long-dreamed-of day when Mary rode in a carriage up to the grounds of old Arlington itself. Her very heart felt as though a jagged stake had been plunged through it. The grand old home of babies and children, love and loss, memory and legend, lay empty and dirty. Thousands of Federal graves now covered her rose garden and lined the acres all round and right up to the very walls of the house itself. The trees were gone, cut down in every direction, except those close by the house and a few she and Lee themselves planted on the grounds.

After twelve years and traveling all the way from the southern end of the Shenandoah Valley, Mary Lee refused the urgings of the friend who drove her even to get out of the carriage.

"Turn it around and take me home," said Mary. "I wish never to see it again."

Agnes fell ill yet again. Then, thinner and weaker, she fell prey in October to an intestinal disease.

After only a couple of days, the stark realization hit Mildred that she was about to lose another whose absence she could scarcely bear to imagine.

Agnes, bedridden and pain-racked, asked her help in changing into a gown the elder sister had tucked into a hidden corner.

Mildred's eyes widened. "Why, Aggie, whatever on earth—"

"Just get it on me, sister," Agnes said in her soft way.

"Oh, heavens, Agnes, such a gown, blue and silver, and such a brocade as I have rarely seen—and certainly not since the war," Mildred marveled as she pulled it out and unfolded it. "Wherever did you get it? And when?"

Agnes said nothing. Slowly a smile began to take shape across Mildred's face. "He was Prince Charming and you were Sleeping Beauty. That is what all we younger children thought of you."

A weak smile creased Agnes's ashen face.

"Still I remember how flushed your face was and how tangled your hair after *that* carriage ride. Now don't act ignorant, Aggie; I saw it!" Mildred said, thrilled to be giggling. "Do you think you might be going somewhere?"

"Yes."

"You think he'll be there?"

"I don't know, but I expect it won't hurt to be as ready as possible in case he is," Agnes said.

Now Mildred began to cry.

"There, there you needn't fret over me, Precious Life," Agnes soothed her, cradling her head to her own breast on the bed and stroking her hair. "I'll be in a much better place than this old world."

"I'm not fretting over you," Mildred bellowed, "I'm fretting over me, being left here alone, while you and Annie are together in heaven."

"Oh, poor darling Life," her sister said, hugging her.

Agnes began to fade in and out as night came. "I never cared to live long, Mildred," she murmured, "I am weary of life."

Mildred fought back more tears.

"Please bring my Bible, Life," Agnes said, her voice weak.

Mildred returned with it a moment later, Custis behind her with a lighted lamp.

"I wish you would let Markie have it," Agnes said, holding it to her breast, her voice growing distant. "You know Orton gave it to me."

"You are—" Mildred choked, "—you are not afraid to die?"

"No," Agnes mumbled, her eyelids heavy, "because of my Savior . . . I'm going to my father . . . lay me by my father."

Then she lay still for a moment or two, her breathing heavier.

"Our Father, which art in heaven," Mildred began, misunderstanding her. "Hallowed be thy name . . ."

When she and Custis completed the line "Give us this day our daily bread," Agnes's eyes shot open and she joined her voice to theirs for "Forgive us our trespasses," then exclaimed, her face aglow, "Ah, that's the part!"

"Oh, Aggie," Mildred cried. "Whatever will Mama do?"

Mary would grieve herself to death in three weeks, her thoughts ever turned to Arlington.

Flitting sentiments touched Agnes as consciousness grew more difficult to maintain, sentiments of how everything might have been so different had only the war not come, had it not changed Orton so. *I would never have sent him away,* she thought, wanting to cry, but no tears would now come, *and then he would not have gone on that dangerous mission, and . . .*

As in the beginning, so in the end Agnes's own thoughts ran to Arlington. Always Arlington, her home. The remembrances were at once jumbled together and immortally painted across the valleys and ascents of her memory as separate, self-sufficient worlds of color and sweetness and love.

The fragrance of the juniper and jasmine drifting past the grazing sheep and up the hill from the river merged with the cameos of Annie's beautiful face—the most beautiful of all the Lee girls—yet stood strong and distinct on its own.

So did the chill that marched, sometimes when least expected, up from the river that ran along the foot of the hill and that would forever separate her and hers from all on earth that they had ever known or wanted.

Mama's renowned rose garden, with its reds, pinks, and yellows—Annie's favorite—merged and yet stood apart from the glint of Orton's steel grey eyes, his long easy gait, the sudden surprising power with which he could sweep Agnes, or the strongest thoroughbreds in northern Virginia, into his orbit.

And how dangerous could be that orbit. How unyielding and unrelenting and never letting go.

Just as the love of her father never let go. Too rarely did Arlington gaze upon his manly countenance. Yet he towered over all and any that would ever come near it.

She remembered his goodness and greatness and how he stood for all that was ever true and honest and just, all that proved pure and lovely and of good report. All that had virtue.

But the treasured pearls of one remembrance alone always came together—inseparable, indivisible, unconquerable, immortal. The day he returned home, in the year of revolution, after the long, long fight against Santa Anna in Mexico. It was the first time she had ever seen white in her father's hair. But then she had been barely five when he left for the war.

That day's reunion now constituted her final conscious thoughts at her life's end. She and gentle Annie were picking apricots when he came riding up the hill—great rows of oaks and chestnuts and elms his towering escorts right and left—ornery little flop-eared Spec the herald of his return—and dismounted his huge frame from his magnificent charger.

Orton's sister Markie, visiting from Washington upon hearing of the hero's imminent return, and Mama sat in the front downstairs foyer. Mama tended a cut on little Rob's cheek earned while fighting Santa Anna himself among the expertly formed battalions of trees crosshatching Arlington's apple orchard. When they heard the little girls' screams and Rooney's hollers, Mama looked up, and cousin Markie sprang from the bench where she sat. Their eyes met, Mama's knowing and placid, twenty-two-year-old Markie's dazzling silver reflections of the lighted chandelier above.

Without speaking, Mama remained seated, conveying her permission, and Markie rushed toward the front door, opened on cue by Nathan the butler. Mama saw her beautiful cousin's tall comely figure silhouetted in the open doorway—tense, anticipating, without breath, and looking out toward him as was forever her place, as the younger woman watched her uncle offer Sam the reins of the rented gelding.

And then he picked Annie and Agnes both up, one in each hard thick arm, and he kissed them and told them they were *his* girls. Annie giggled and Agnes's eyes closed as his two daughters clutched him. He offered silent benediction to his heavenly Father as he felt their little hearts beating against his barrel chest and as the knot grew tight and climbed up his throat.

And then all was right, Agnes thought with joy, as finally the pain, all the pain of all her years, began to leave, and the sun over old Arlington grew brighter than ever she had seen it. *And all was safe.*

Funny how when Papa died, she remembered, fading, *it was the children, the little children, all over the South, who wept most bitterly.*

His name was Robert E. Lee and he was my father.

He was our father. . . .